CHATEAUVALLON

CHATEAUVALLON

Eliane Roche

An Omnibus Edition containing
THE BERG FAMILY FORTUNE
and NEW MONEY

Translated from the French by Nicholas Courtin

GUILD PUBLISHING
LONDON

BERG
FAMILY
FORTUNE

Chapter One

The red Alfa slithered, bumped and moaned its way between high fencing. Trucks, bulldozers and mobile cranes had made the road what it was – the way into a building site.

Mozart's *Eine Kleine Nachtmusik* yielded to the work noises behind the fencing the moment the driver switched off the car's cassette player. He lit a cigarette, and aware he was playing with fire in another way, he stuck his face against a pair of fencing planks and peeked through at the masses of people swarming over the vast area. He snorted. Rather them than him.

What he saw were the foundations and steel skeletons of apartment blocks that would soon contain rabbit hutches for the simple, the meek, the downtrodden. Once again, rather them than him. Hundreds of men, many wearing hard hats in accordance with regulations and many others not wearing hard hats because they didn't care a damn about regulations, lolloped around in mud, water and gravel in the wan light of the afterdawn. They moved because the formen harassed them; and the foremen kept on at them because the site engineers kept looking at their watches and swearing; and that was because the bosses made their lives hell by phoning the site office all day.

The man with the Alfa would have liked to roam around and find out more. But there were big panels everywhere telling him *'No Admittance – Danger'*. And in case he ignored them or failed to notice them, there were men in blue tracksuits and peaked hats only too willing to escort him back onto the muddy road.

So the driver got back into the car and scribbled a few things in a notebook. He then did a five-point turn that should have been a three-point turn, and returned whence he came through a couple of fair-sized ponds. Never mind the dirty car, the firm would pay for it 'on expenses'.

He never noticed the tubby overalled man who watched his performance from start to finish from a red sentry box kind of place. When the Alfa's whine had disappeared, the watchman stopped looking where it had gone and saw a thin fellow with a toothbrush moustache coming his way. He wore a hard hat and more significantly a well-cut suit.

'I've seen him before,' said the man in the suit.

'So've I.'

'Know him?'

'Who doesn't! Paul Bossis, works for *La Dépêche*.'

'Don't care for inquisitive buggers.'

'Nobody does,' said the watchman, 'and there's plenty here that remind me.'

The pair eyed each other, both saying 'What else is new?' to themselves.

Then the man in a suit grunted: 'I'll report it.' The suit had a big plaid pattern and a red carnation in the buttonhole. Its wearer looked like a man arriving at a party afraid an empty champagne bottle would fall on him out of a tree.

Paul Bossis was just on the right side of thirty. A passive unenterprising son, he had misspent his youth doing next to nothing until his father asked Antonin Berg to take him on at *La Dépêche Republicaine*. Berg was an old friend and Berg owned the paper. What they said went, and Bossis became a reporter, not least because the two big shots were inseparable, having a common interest in the woman they had both loved passionately, a certain Gabrielle.

What Paul Bossis had yet to learn was that in falling in with the wishes of his father and 'uncle' Antonin he had signed his own death warrant.

For some time the rambling building site had intrigued Bossis, and he had frequently approached it trying to find a way in unannounced. By now he was far less unenterprising and had grown into the habit of climbing through windows when doors were shut in his face.

On his way back along the mud road he played a cassette of some Bach music, and this reminded him of Catherine. They had spent two wonderful years living under the same roof, listening to Mozart, Bach and Buxtehude, and just being in love. Life had much to offer young Bossis even if he *was* involved with that Kovalic girl, as the town's opinion-formers described her. Paul

Bossis formed his own opinions, and one of them was that nothing had made him happier than the prospect of the child Catherine was soon to bear him. His closest friend Travers was right: life was 'A1'.

He snapped out of his reverie as a lumbering ten-tonner piled high with concrete slabs overtook him, heading for a wide gate that swung open. Bossis tailed the truck as it lurched through and stuck close behind until the gate closed.

He was inside the site at last.

'Darling,' Catherine had said as they woke up over breakfast at their tiny apartment in Rue Aux Grains, 'I want to know why you have this crazy obsession about the Sablons site.'

Feigning astonishment, he told her: 'How can I put it, darling? I was born here in Chateauvallon. I grew up here and it's my town – a good old-fashioned town with plenty of monuments and old houses, shops in little squares that haven't changed since the nineteenth century. A town that's fit to live in. But now someone's adding an annexe to Chateauvallon, an extension that's going to disfigure a whole part of the country, so we shall lose our lovely paths to the woods. And in five years' time it'll be crowded; in ten years' time it will be splitting at the seams. In the end the entire town will have altered beyond hope. I'm putting it badly but I only know it makes me sick to think about it.'

'And what can you do about it?'

'Write articles. And lots of them. Warn the public, so that there's a chance of stopping the urban monster growing.'

There was a silence between them, then Catherine said: 'Are you sure there's nothing else at the back of your mind?'

Paul had blinked: 'I don't get you. What else could there be?'

There was someone else at *La Dépêche* who lived in terms of articles – and his mother's fruit tarts.

Melchior, deputy editor, forty-eight years of age and with a ballpoint between his teeth where a pencil had been clenched many years ago, knew that Bossis was on to something. His mother, who had steered him away from marriage so far, could not have wished for a kindlier son. But at *La Dépêche* he could be a martinet, especially when he was jumpy, which he was most of the time.

With one eye on the deadline, the other on the passage through the glass partitioning, he recognized the shape coming into his line of vision.

'Travers!' he barked, halting the shape in its tracks.

Travers walked with a loose stride and had a velvet eye that could flash like that of a Spanish hidalgo, which is exactly as he imagined himself in his black leather topcoat. A cultivated youth, he was never short of feminine company despite, or perhaps because of, an unkempt mane of hair that told you he had just left one bed and was heading for the next. He stopped striding and met Melchior at his office door.

'Where's Bossis? Seen him lately?

'Not since last night.'

'Hm. He was due back here after lunch with his first piece on Les Sablons. It's now five o'clock!'

'Maybe he phoned it in.'

'Wish he had.'

'Funny,' Travers mumbled, adding no further comment. As Melchior kept silent too, Travers said he was off to the Bijou-Bar for a bite to eat.

The paper's staff were the bar's best customers. As the hidalgo loped off, Melchior got to thinking that Travers was no fool, and might well know what 'special assignment' Paul Bossis had offered to cover without revealing it to a soul except his deputy editor.

Travers' bite to eat had blonde hair and laughed a lot. He had met her the previous evening at a town hall reception. He reflected that it would probably take him half an hour to find out more about her. Descending the pretentious main staircase, he gave nothing away; he never breathed a word about his conquests and might have claimed an unblemished past were it not for the boasts of his lady friends.

However, Travers was destined to see neither the Bijou-Bar nor the blonde that day. He stood for a moment looking at a group of men fixing a huge banner across the front of the building at first-floor level; it read 'LA DÉPÊCHE – 50 YEARS'. Then a car screeched to a halt behind him. He spun round to see a Renault 5 and Maryse extracting the ignition key. Maryse was one of the sub-editors. She now extracted herself from the vehicle. She wore a huge head scarf and big sun-glasses.

He chided her: 'Hey, why the disguise? There isn't a glimmer of sunshine and hasn't been for hours. Wait a minute – I know, you've shaved your head!'

10

She walked round the car to the pavement, and Travers neatly whipped off her sun-glasses. Her eyes were red and swollen.

'Bloody paper!' she snapped, glancing up at the fluttering banner. 'Give me those.'

Travers handed back the glasses with a frown. Maryse was evidently in one of her foul moods and although they were far from being close friends he knew he would hear all about it within a matter of seconds. He couldn't resist a lady in distress, and Maryse filled that category, looking up as she now was murmuring imprecations at a window on the second floor.

'What . . .' he began.

'I suppose you're going to that do tonight at La Commanderie,' she said, cutting him off.

'Well, we're launching the paper's next fifty years, after all.'

'I shan't be there. I have been given to understand that my presence will not be expected. Fifteen years I've spent on this goddam rag, and I'm being thrown out!' Her lips trembled more in anger than pain.

'Thrown out? Monsieur Antonin would never do a thing like that.'

'Grow up, chum. You know it's not the old man. That bastard Jean-Jacques put a call through, just as I was in the middle of washing my hair. Hadn't the guts to tell me himself – got his secretary to do it.'

'And she said no need to wash your hair, or iron your prettiest dress.'

'More or less. Oh, Travers, only a dirty rat would do that to me.'

'You couldn't put it better, love. And as editors go, Jean-Jacques Berg is the dirtiest of them all.'

'A public insult to mark the fiftieth anniversary.'

Travers looked skywards: 'Maryse.'

'Yes?'

'If it wasn't for the public insult, I'd say it was him walking out on you that's the real trouble.'

'Nobody likes to be cast aside like an old boot.'

'Hm, I would imagine his wife showed him how. Wives don't take too well to their husband's girlfriends. So he's dumped you. But you haven't lost your job.'

Maryse laughed shrilly. 'Sacked me? They couldn't, it would cost them a fortune in severance pay. He's not that stupid. He can

11

push me out of bed, and a fat lot I care! But if he wants me off the paper, I'll set the dogs on him.'

'After all, nobody ever died of a broken heart.'

'Nobody I know. But I could die of humiliation – the whole town will be laughing behind my back.'

Travers lit a cigarette. 'All I can say is that I can't dope his coffee with love potion, but if you like I can fix things for tonight.'

The woman's face burst into bloom. 'You mean you'd do that? Could you really?'

He grinned and gave her a pat on the shoulder. Then turned and climbed the steps two at a time. Maryse would get over it, he was thinking, and he had to admit she had it coming some day. He simply felt like doing her a good turn, an inclination he was careful to conceal.

Jean-Jacques Berg *knew* he was good-looking! But the truth was that, at thirty-six, he avoided insignificance solely through a tenuous resemblance to old Antonin, his father, and to his older brother, Armand, who put him in the shade. Jean-Jacques knew that, too, in his heart of hearts, and had the constant feeling that he had to prove himself. He affected a roguish air and sartorial elegance that fooled nobody on *La Dépêche*, where he was regarded as a nonentity carried by the thoroughly competent Melchior.

At that moment he was pacing his Louis XV office with its honey-coloured oak panelling, trying on a new suit that had been delivered the previous day. He stopped to peer out from behind the heavy curtains just long enough to see Maryse's Renault 5 parked below. Instinctively, he jerked back. He scowled at the bitter fact that he had given in to his wife, Marie-Lou.

'Darling,' she had gushed the previous evening, 'I should be so glad if I didn't have to catch sight of Mademoiselle Maryse Mongin at La Commanderie.'

It had turned his stomach, but he had managed to ask with every appearance of indifference: 'Really? Why's that, Marie-Lou?'

'If she were simply your mistress of the moment, I could let it pass. But an old acquaintance of three years' standing, well, don't you think it would be rather absurd to brag, to show her off?'

So that was that, he would not show her off, he had conveyed to her that her presence was not expected. Maryse, of course, would be humiliated but she would realize that the game was up. Besides he'd been trying to break it off for months, but each time he had backed away from the task. Thank God Marie-Lou had taken the decision for him. What's more, Maryse was too proud and moody to storm in and demand an explanation. He had arrived at the office with a load off his mind.

Or so he had thought. But now she had come in on her day off – that was definitely her car – and for all he knew she was probably charging along the passage at this very moment. He moved away from the window, hoping against hope there wouldn't be a scene.

He almost jumped out of his skin at the sound of a footstep on the pile carpet. He jerked his head round, and saw Travers in the doorway.

'Ah, it's you Travers!' Berg's voice was caught between relief and fright.

'Well, of course it's me, chief. Hope I'm not intruding. Were you expecting someone else?'

'Yes. I mean no. You . . . er . . . look pleased with yourself as usual. Come in, come in, take a seat.'

'Thanks, chief, just passing by. Wanted to let you know I'll be coming tonight. Bringing Maryse Mongin. Must have someone to dance with.'

Damn, he was trapped! Just what you'd expect from that runt Travers. No wonder he was grinning all over his silly face. Marie-Lou would go stark raving mad. He had to do something quick.

Jean-Jacques Berg's mind was groping for a way out, and all that came was a hopeless feeling that he was wrong to have put a ban on Maryse. He had lost his sense of proportion, had given a faithful employee a slap in the face, and the entire staff knew it. Marie-Lou had caught him unawares, and had ruined his position at the office. He should have seen at once that excluding her was out of the question. His father would never have tolerated it. What the hell could he say now?

Travers stared at him with an angelic smile on his fat lips.

'I . . . er . . . that is, Mademoiselle Mongin and I have had a slight difference of opinion and I was afraid, that is, I would have preferred . . .'

The man sat there laughing at him. 'You mean you're afraid she might . . .'

'Yes, that's it, there might be some embarrassment . . .'

'Aw, you don't need to worry, chief. I'll keep an eye on her.'

Travers got up slowly, flicked a military-style salute at Berg and made for the door. 'Oh by the way, any news of Bossis?'

'Bossis? What's with Bossis? Is he ill?'

The visitor was already closing the door, leaving Berg to his thoughts. His shoulders sagged, as the prospect of encountering Maryse drained the blood from his head. For pity's sake, she might try and scratch his eyes out or something. Marie-Lou could be trusted to provoke an incident. She was capable of anything!

La Commanderie was a fine building, more of a mansion than a castle. Built in the grand style, and yet not exactly stylish. Forty rooms, turrets at the corners, steep long roofs. It was neither majestic nor princely, but a confident nineteenth-century lavish bourgeois home in excellent taste.

As 5.00 p.m. came and went, clusters of cumulus clouds swept northwards overhead and the lofty walls and curves of La Commanderie were already turning salmon pink.

It was the sweetest moment of the day for Berg senior. He had owned a pile for years, but sometimes wondered whether it wasn't a little austere. He liked the evening glow at the close of a fine day, when a light breeze made patterns across the lawns and chivvied the leaves of the oaks, poplars and willows that staked out the limits of the property.

Antonin gazed out on the grounds from the esplanade and soaked in the beauty of it all. He stood almost erect, applying a little of his weight on a stick, but it was only for effect. At seventy, he had no need of support, and wielded the stick as a sceptre. Monarch of all he surveyed, he narrowed his eyes at the sight of an ugly white truck marked KOVALIC – CARRIER. Two men stripped to the waist were unloading crates from it, while a third younger man, wearing a T-shirt with some kind of badge on it, supervised operations. The men took the crates through a side entrance where a woman of some fifty summers wearing a pale blue blouse checked off the delivery in a notebook.

Old Berg noticed the youngster in the T-shirt staring at the woman. At length he jumped down from the truck and walked smartly up to her.

The fellow gave a quick glance at Antonin and jerked his head at the woman: 'You still don't trust us do you, Madame Mathilde.'

'None of your cheek, young Teddy Kovalic,' she retorted. 'I been in this here house for twenty-five years now, and I'm only doing what Monsieur Antonin ordered. So watch your step.'

'We Kovalics never let anyone down. I've got my list too, you know.'

Young Teddy had never taken to 'that old Mathilde', because of what she was, one of those toffee-nosed servants out of the Middle Ages, working for the gentry. A nice cushy job for life, whereas the Kovalics had to use their brains and guts. He would have liked to spell out the difference to the woman, but he didn't get the chance. Old Berg had crept up behind him and was thumping his stick on the ground for attention.

'What's the trouble, you two?' he demanded, in an unfriendly way.

'No trouble, Monsieur Berg, sir.'

Teddy smelt the scorn that enveloped the old bugger and could have told him a thing or two, especially as Mathilde had begun quietly smirking to herself.

Berg eyed the youth for a few seconds, and then averted his gaze, like a gladiator abandoning a victim too contemptible to fight.

'My regards to your uncle, Kovalic,' he said in a fluty voice. And to Mathilde: 'I believe there's some caviar in this batch; let the boy have a tin.'

The boy was thinking he could stuff his caviar. What he said, ashamed of his own subservience, was: 'That's very kind of you indeed, Monsieur Antonin.'

He'll get his own back on me for that one day, Berg mused. Teddy was a little gnat to Chateauvallon's richest and most powerful citizen. But the Kovalic family, the Kovalic gang as the Bergs termed them, was different. They needed watching, for they could become a menace one of these days.

He was pulled up by a junior servant arriving briskly from inside La Commanderie. He was an ill-tempered sort of brat when taken in by the Bergs as an orphan. Young Teddy didn't care much for him either – 'capitalist lackey'!

'Well how's it going, Jeannou?'

'I wanted to see what you thought, M'sieur. I think the men have done a good job.' The lad gave his employer a curt smile.

Berg strolled over to the awning, inspected it and looked around. A couple of men were checking the firmness of the trestle

15

tables before loading them with food and drink. Others were trying out some spotlights that would later illuminate the mansion in honour of *La Dépêche*. The owner judged that everything was in order.

He was interrupted by Thérèse, wife to his other son, Julien, for which he admired the boy. Frankly she was a dishy dark-haired creature whose honest sex appeal was tinged with cunning. At least that was how he saw her. It had often occurred to him that concupiscence gains in interest with a pinch of innocence. Past it he might be, but he enjoyed the way the men buzzed around her like bees at a honeypot.

She slunk over to him, and he felt obliged to remark: 'Thérèse, my child, I must point out that it is not quite the done thing to stroll around on this estate in a pair of short shorts and a see-through blouse. I am fully aware that you and Julien have advanced ideas, that you cannot help your natural comeliness, and that you would not dream of teasing your public. Nevertheless I do think you should allow for the principles and prejudices of traditional France, and wear just a wee bit more when you circulate among our staff.'

Her eyes were like saucers. 'But it's all right among the cream of Chateauvallon?' She giggled.

'You're a wicked girl. I can't help it if I was born fifty years too early!'

'I'll go and change,' she said, falsely demure. 'I only wanted to tell you someone's phoned Julien, wanting to know if Paul Bossis is here.' The old man grunted, and she went on: 'Julien thought maybe he popped over.'

'Popped over to La Commanderie? Not that I am aware of. Who wanted to know?'

'Melchior.'

The problem irritated him; he had enough to think about with the celebrations. 'Listen, my dear, as soon as the first champagne cork pops you'll see Paul appear over the horizon. Now hurry up indoors before you catch cold in that figleaf of yours.'

He chuckled fondly as she wandered off. Julien and Thérèse lived in a small house on the edge of the grounds close to the Berg sawmill, which Julien ran. Antonin's kindly visage glowed. He had to admit that the girl had won him over with her elfish ways. He hadn't cared for her as a wife for Julien, but he was growing tolerant in his old age. He could dream, couldn't he? Julien had

16

stood up to him for once, and he was right. He'd got himself a peach of a wife!

He ruminated aloud, a habit he had developed: 'Good times they were with Gabrielle. No, I didn't waste my time there!'

He realized that Jeannou had been following a yard behind all this time, and was now next to him looking down at the ground.

'Seventy years old, Jeannou. Must make the best of the last few years, eh?'

'Many happy returns,' the lad declared, and he blinked repeatedly.

Antonin laid a hand on his shoulder. 'Come on, Jeannou, let's be off to the pond to turn on those outlet valves. We want it as shallow as we can tonight. Always a bunch of idiots diving in after midnight; got the idea from Saint Tropez, they tell me. Hullo, they've turned the spotlights on.'

Once inside the building site, Paul Bossis had no difficulty merging with the landscape. There was so much coming and going that the pope himself would have gone unnoticed if he'd ridden through on a donkey.

He found his way into a tool shed and patiently waited until the site was closed for the night. The noise level gradually diminished and by 6.00 p.m. it looked as if the last of the building workers had gone off. Even so, there was a hut in some aluminium material where the night watchmen were having a meal, and he made for this, carefully walking round it and peering in. This took about ten minutes, whereupon he made a dash for the completed foundations nearby, walking down to a ladder that led to the future underground car park. It was as black as a coal cellar and smelt of gunpowder and urine. Once underground he fished out a torch and flashed it around.

He found a mass of wires in grey plastic sheathing, with just the ends poking out of some big round holes waiting to be connected to goodness knows what – maybe to one another. He examined the many-coloured cables inside the sheaths, then searched around for what he had come for: a length of scrap cable about eight or nine inches long. This he picked up, then climbed again, extinguishing the torch half way up the ladder.

Bossis approached the watchmen's hut. They hadn't moved, were arguing the toss in loud voices. Couldn't blame them for sticking inside on a chilly night like this. He must get back to the

17

car, but where the hell was it? He crept about for a good fifteen minutes, careful not to run into anything by mistake. He found it eventually, and tried to discern the gate where he had come in behind the big truck.

He recognized it. 'Shit!' he whispered aloud. It was closed. What a blithering idiot, he should have thought of that. A shiver of fear seized him in the small of his back. And then he felt himself sweating around the neck. God, he was caught! Might have to stay inside the whole damn night! He wasn't exactly scared, but his cranium was unusually hot. Bossis wiped his brow.

For a moment he toyed with the idea of crashing through the gate, but dismissed it at once. He'd need a loaded ten-ton truck to do it. 'Shit, shit, shit!' He went to the gate and tried to push through between the bars, and nearly lost an ear in the process. His only chance was to scale the gate – 20 feet high at least and with no horizontal bars to climb up with. And there were spikes at the top and a 20 foot drop if he got over without tearing his balls off. Close to panic, he surveyed the brick walls either side of the gate. No go there. He began walking round the site looking for a section with fencing instead of brick. And the further he walked the more he sweated. His throat grew parched and he started to stumble around, falling into holes, kicking his shins against rods in concrete. He was not only a prisoner but lost.

Then a searchlight began sweeping the site from a high tower. He threw himself on the ground, and a jagged edge ripped into his knee.

Gabrielle née Deverney and long dead, had given Antonin Berg four children. Florence was the eldest of them. Tall, slim and with a cascade of auburn hair – she always looked smart, though rather severe in her taste. People tended to find her on the stern side, but she might have been otherwise but for her profession, for she was a lawyer in Paris. One felt that in other circumstances she would have blossomed. However, her broken marriage cast a further veil of severity over her demeanour.

On this late afternoon she stood at the window of a room in the Relais de Chateauvallon, her forehead against the chill window pane, watching the peak-hour traffic. Once again she flicked back her sleeve to see what time it was.

At the same moment a discreet double knock caused her to

18

relax her shoulders. She was no longer 'the hatchet', as she was dubbed in the courts on account of her slick no-nonsense manner of developing her case and her skill at destroying an opponent's line of argument with a single swipe.

'Madame, it's Monsieur.'

'Send him in, please.'

The maid scuttled off, and she guffawed in amusement at the woman's startled look. Florence did not see much to laugh at these days, and it would have required a great deal more than that. She chose the least faded-looking of the armchairs in the room, and sat in it fiddling a little with her dress, checking her hands, shoes and stockings.

Quentin, Mayor of Chateauvallon, knocked and let himself in.

He was an elegant man, very much in the same mould as Florence – though certainly more inhibited than she was. He was getting on in years, his thatch of white hair told you that, but his age was hard to assess. His 'uniform', as Florence called it, was an anthracite-grey suit and a black topcoat with a fur collar. In fact, Quentin would have looked grim indeed had he not been possessed of a natural grace and a charm that few women could fail to notice. He was now paying the price of a long and harassing political career, for he was also a Member of the Assemblée Nationale and, for the past two years, Secretary of State for Defence. Monsieur Quentin was a few months past sixty, and it was useless trying to hide it.

Florence leaned forward and uncoiled herself slinkily, then stood before him. Quentin advanced with open arms and enfolded her. He arched over her as their lips made contact, and the kiss spread.

They came out of it both sighing.

'The Relais de Chateauvallon! What's the idea? Why aren't you at the studio?'

She smiled good-humouredly: 'You would have been compromising yourself as much there as here, my dear.'

He smiled in turn, shaking his head wearily: 'Had I feared compromising myself, I should not have come in any case.' He shrugged. 'At my age one starts to care less about scandal. We've been seeing each other for a hell of a long time now, and there can't be anybody left who doesn't know about it. If anybody had wanted to use it against me, they'd have done it a long time ago. I suppose . . .'

19

'. . . they thought it wasn't worth the effort.'

Quentin ignored the implied insult, and asked why she wasn't staying at La Commanderie.

'Can't you guess? Another political row with my father. He's right and I'm left, and it makes mealtimes rather tense . . . And you Georges? You seem less your old self than last time we met.'

'Last time, how long ago was it?'

'Four, perhaps five months. How time's flies!'

He spread his hands: 'It's not time that's passing, but ourselves. But I'm speaking about myself. You never change – still as lovely and appealing as ever. How do you manage it? How's business?'

'Can't complain. But tell me about your career, when do you get the Foreign Ministry? It's what you've always really wanted.'

He chuckled impishly: 'Oh, how exhausting it all is, having the nation's destiny in one's hands. I'm sure that's a line from a film.'

He nimbly produced a cigar and went about the business of lighting it. The sound of him sucking on it vied with the traffic noise from outside.

He was concealing his anxiety. Quentin knew perfectly well why Florence had imperiously phoned him to come, not an hour earlier. This was the end, and it made him infinitely sad, and weak. He knew too that it would be Florence who would strike first, but wanted so much to postpone the awful moment.

With a pretence at surprise he said: 'You say you're fighting with Antonin once more, and yet you've come for the great event tonight.'

'I've come solely to see you,' she replied curtly. 'You know it perfectly well. For a last look at you, a final rendezvous.'

His innards turned over, but he merely inclined his head, frowned at the glowing ash on the cigar, and realized with something of a shock that Florence had not even asked him to sit down. Come to that, he had not taken a seat as he normally would. So it was over, then. The superb cold statue before him was the woman he had loved to distraction, and still loved perhaps more than ever, but now would be his no longer, had already disappeared from his life in the past five seconds.

She was speaking: 'I don't blame you for not being able to get a divorce, the fact that you couldn't live with me at any stage, that you couldn't give me a child. Nor for being a stranger whom I heard about over the radio and read about in the papers. I've waited for ten years in the hope that you might be free one day. But, my dear friend, it is Glory you are wedded to for better or worse. D'you want to know something? Wicked woman that I am, I have occasionally prayed that an accident of history or a major scandal would break you. Alas, those prayers went unanswered.'

'I have always adored you, Flo,' he protested. 'I still adore you.'

'But I can no longer love you. Politics has stolen the lustre from your eyes, turned your male vigour to ice, and it has destroyed what I lived for in you.'

He let out a sigh and his shoulders bowed imperceptibly: 'I understand, I understand. But I kept hoping that soon . . .'

'Soon never came, Georges. It was overtaken by events.'

'It seems only yesterday . . .' Quentin could go no further, and at last he sat down ponderously, feeling twenty years older, weary of the constant demands that had kept him whirring like a flywheel all these years. Sad that in his personal life he had nothing to show for it. He looked up at her in supplication, beseeching her in silence to give him just one more chance to make it work out.

Through half-closed eyelids, Florence murmured: 'And this is how it ends, in a hotel room, symbol of what our love has been. In a sleazy hotel room, that's where it's ending.'

Still she stood her ground, watching him shake his head, oblivious of his cigar now extinguished and the ash spattered on his topcoat, which he didn't bother to brush off.

'So it's goodbye.'

'We shall meet up, I'm sure, in the great big world.'

A wan smile came to his lips: 'With you as the prosecuting counsel I could never hope for an aquittal.'

'Not even the benefit of the doubt,' she said softly but implacably.

He slowly got to his feet and walked to the door, where he turned with his hand on the ornate handle.

'I loved you, Flo. I love you still.

'I loved you, Quentin.'

The telephone rang, and she went over to it. By the time she had lifted the receiver and turned round, he was outside.

'Hullo,' said a woman's voice, and kept on saying it. But it meant nothing until she came to her senses to see the receiver back in its place and herself seated gaping at it like an idiot.

Her own ghost-like voice said: 'It was hard doing it, incredibly hard.'

Then she jumped up and strode over to a silver flask on the bedside table. Florence took a huge gulp, felt the whisky burn, and a mighty rush of tears welling up from deep inside her.

'Georges! Georges!' she cried, stumbling for the door.

But she halted mid-way. No, she would not do that, she was Florence Berg, the hatchet with a reputation to keep up – even in her own mind. She sat down on the bed-edge shivering in the cashmere coat she had flung round her shoulders, listening to someone trying to start a car in the street. The phone went again.

'Madame, it's for you, a local call.'

'Say I'm . . .'

Too late, the woman had put the call through.

'Florence?' said a man's voice.

'Yes.' Why can't whoever it is leave me alone? And why the devil doesn't that imbecile get his car going?

Later, when the maid hurried into the room, Madame Florence Berg was spreadeagled on the bed breathing almost inaudibly, with the grace and distinction that the gentry would never lose – at least, that was the impression of the girl who stood open-mouthed in admiration. The maid's eyes switched to the whisky flask lying on its side, she righted it and replaced the dangling receiver.

'Armand?' Florence mumbled in her sleep, 'That you Armand?'

The girl, whose name was not even Armande, looked at Madame Berg's dress, which had ridden up well above her knees, and carefully pulled it down.

Thus Angélique Deruelle acquired yet another piece of gossip she would have loved to enlarge on in the days ahead.

But Angélique would most certainly not yield to the temptation – for the simple reason that Madame Berg had slipped her a couple of hundred-franc notes, accompanied by a look that told Angélique it was more than her job was worth to remember too much.

The girl scurried off again downstairs, trying to recall anyone she knew with the name Armand.

In his narrow neat office at the Les Glycines Clinic, Armand Berg was at that hour humping on a tuxedo, watched by a rather smug-looking woman who had just come in.

Neither young nor old, neither pretty nor ugly, she was known as Jeanne when her boss was in a good mood and Fernandez at other times. Today she was definitely Fernandez, and she knew why only too well.

'Here's your vodka, Monsieur,' she declared, shaking the glass so that the ice cube tinkled, emphasising the truth of her statement.

'Thanks Fernandez.'

Armand Berg knocked back the vodka, took a deep breath and demanded to know how Doctor Sanchez was getting along. The two men had done an operation an hour ago, but they had lost the patient. Sanchez had emerged from the operating theatre ashen grey, and had fainted in the passage.

'I gave him some Tropanon, and he's sleeping like a babe,' Fernandez replied. 'Poor young fellow, just starting out and everything.'

'One never is blasé you know Fernandez. I've been a surgeon fifteen years and when I lose a patient like that I'm still churning over inside three days later. What's the time?'

'Seven.'

'Damn, can't get to the faculty to hear that thesis. Got to attend a reception.' He was slipping on his overcoat, and a sly look spread across his face: 'By the way, do you listen at keyholes?'

'No need to, Monsieur,' Fernandez replied. 'I'm sure the entire nurses' hall heard you on the phone when your brother Monsieur Jean-Jacques called just now.'

Half to himself he said: 'That idiot sticks his neck out, plays at decision-making, but he himself won't act.' In his mind he heard J-J's plaintiff whine: 'Armand, it's you she wants.'

At the door he said: 'It's a curious thing, Jeanne, I'm worried. I heard my sister answer when I called, but she seemed unable to speak. Anyhow, see you later. Don't worry if Dr Sanchez throws up when he wakes – it'll do him good.'

As Armand Berg let in the clutch he gave a glance at the clinic for the thousandth time. It used to be a notary's house but it had become shabby since 1930 when it was built, and needed a new layer of pebble-dash.

Although he could concentrate during surgery to the exclusion of all other considerations, Armand was capable at other times of handling several matters simultaneously. At this instant his brain was spinning like a gyroscope, trying to balance up his dejection over the patient who died on the operating table, irritation over

23

the price decorators were charging these days, worry about Flo, and satisfaction nevertheless at having his own clinic.

Armand was a year younger than Florence and from childhood they had enjoyed close connivance of a kind that excluded the other two to a large extent: Julien the youngest of the four, and especially Jean-Jacques, the 'streak of piss' as he called him. Besides, he and Florence looked alike, they had the same distinguished features, the same patrician bearing and the same sardonic expression worn by those who fear or respect neither men nor life itself.

As he was a Berg, he bullied his way through the traffic over the speed limit. The nearer he got to the hotel, the more uneasy he became about Florence.

It took him only ten minutes to the Relais de Chateauvallon. He ignored the cop directing the traffic and parked on the pavement – the cop ignored him because he was a Berg.

Armand threw himself through the front entrance into a chambermaid carrying a garment. She gaped over the top of it at him.

'Madame Berg, please. I'm her brother.'

'Second, second floor, Monsieur,' Angélique Deruelle stammered. 'I've just ironed her dress for her.'

'Good for you. Let me have it.'

He slung the dress over an arm and charged up the staircase. The girl shouted 'room twenty-one' and continued gazing at the magnificent hunk of manhood disappearing up the stairs in its tight trousers. She could talk about him, at least, to her friend Elisabeth!

Armand knocked, heard 'yes', and went in. Florence was in a silk peignoir packing a suitcase. She assumed a repentant air at the sight of her brother.

'What's going on? What's happened? Were you tipsy or something when I phoned?'

She looked at him speechless. Then mumbled: 'You phoned?'

'I phoned twice and there was a zombie at the other end. I assume it was you.'

She straightened up and walked over to the bedside table and began brandishing the whisky flask.

She forced a laugh: 'That's what answered you. Anyhow, glad to see you Armand, my sweet. Come and give your big sister a nice kiss, 'cos she's in a stinky mood and weepy with it.' Whereupon she planted a juicy kiss on his lips.

Boy-like, he removed the wet with the back of his hand: 'What may I ask are you doing in this grotty roadhouse?'

'Passing through, to coin a phrase. But the trip's over, and I'm off to Paris again in ten minutes.'

She had slipped off the peignoir and he let out a whistle, moving his head from left to right as he admired the curve of her long legs and thighs, the firm full breasts and bottom.

'How'm I doing?' she said, rotating. 'Let me have my dress, it'll fit me better than you.'

'I wish you were someone else's sister.'

They laughed. Armand went to the bed and threw himself on it, his hands behind his neck. He watched her working on her face – eyelashes, eyebrows, lipstick.

'Flo,' he said while she was brushing her hair, 'You're a stunning woman. What have you got to cry about?'

'I've broken off with Quentin.'

'And you paid thirty francs to do it here? Or should I say *undo* it? I suppose it was you who made the decision, socked it to him. How did he take it?'

She gave a brief frown: 'It shook him. Me too, actually.'

Florence wandered over to the bed, fixing her necklace, some pearls she had had for years.

'Hey, *fratello mio*, you asleep?'

'Sorry, I was thinking of a patient that died on the table. I've got to have the clinic painted up outside too. And now I'm here, consoling you, although I came for another reason.

She gave a little snort: 'There are days like that: you always get a puncture when you're late anyway.'

That was another side of their connivance, sharing the cynical moments, when they trod on their emotions and mocked at the things they really held dear. When their mother Gabrielle was buried when they were fourteen/thirteen years of age – they spent their time stifling giggles during the ceremony, whispering rude remarks to each other. Their lips spoke obscenities instead of the responses, and yet they were deeply shaken by their mother's death. Strange, Armand thought.

Now he was sitting up, scrutinizing the pair of hands that had been instrumental in the departure of a human being from this world. Surely he could not be losing his touch already.

'How did you know I was here?' Flo asked.

Armand hesitated: 'Jean-Jacques told me you were here – but

don't ask me how he knew. He wanted me to get in touch with you in his place; you know how brave he is about everything. I would have let it drop, but I wanted to see you Flo.'

'What was the reason, you mentioned it earlier?'

'To persuade you to come to La Commanderie tonight.'

Florence instantly adopted a huffy stance: 'To hear father ask if I'm going to Colombey-les-Deux Eglises, shrine of Gaullism, and hear his speech on 'his sure vision of France'? What's come over Jean-Jacques? He knows perfectly well that father and I simply don't get along together.'

'He told me that saddened him.'

'Huh, the peacemaker!'

'And that it looked bad in the eyes of the public.'

'That's more like it – the public! What he really means is a small circle of provincial snobs frequented by him and Marie-Lou. A fissure in the great Berg family doesn't look good, eh?'

'Flo.'

'Yes?'

'I want you to come as well. I'm sentimental if you like, but I'd love to see you for longer, and somewhere else than in this crummy joint. And besides . . .'

'Besides?'

'He's getting on, you know. Oh, I'm not suggesting a solemn sort of reconciliation, that'd be silly, especially as far as politics go. But hang it all, are politics really that important? What about ties and affections going back for years?'

'And death that changes everything, leaves the survivors wringing their hands in regret! That corpse of yours has left you mawkish, brother dear!'

Armand got up from the bed: 'I'm sorry, I see nothing funny in that.'

'I'm not laughing at that, but at Jean-Jacques wanting me at La Commanderie. If I went, it could be the end of him.'

'Of Jean-Jacques?'

'About a week ago, father wrote me a letter offering me the management of *La Dépêche*. The top job, darling. If that came out tonight, Jean-Jacques would spin round twice and collapse in the camellias.'

Armand's eyes narrowed: 'I'd love to see it – so why don't you come? After all, father has made you an offer, he has a right to hear your reply.'

Florence tossed her mane of hair and thought for a moment: 'You know, you could be right.'

The night was now as black as ink, and the Taunus slipped past the few remaining houses on the Rumilly road. Inside were the two men who had sighted Paul Bossis: the tubby chap in overalls and the man in the suit with the toothbrush moustache and a carnation. Except that the carnation had gone, withered away.

Inside, too, was Paul Bossis, on the back seat. They had pounced on him shortly after he fell on the jagged edge and while he was squeezing through a gap in the fencing.

He could have put up a fight, or done his damnedest to get away. But his curiosity had outweighed his instincts, the more so since the suit man had politely said: 'Monsieur Fournier would like a word with you.'

'Fournier? At the town hall, you mean? Why?'

'He'll tell you himself, Monsieur.'

'What if I refuse to come with you?'

'That's up to you, Monsieur.'

The exchange had dispelled his misgivings. He was intrigued now, rather than scared. When the Taunus heaved to a halt, it was a confident Paul Bossis who hauled himself out of the vehicle. Fournier would make him a proposition. At last he would have some good 'copy' to work on, he was into investigative journalism up to his neck now!

He started frowning when he saw the villa, and for an excellent reason. It had no first floor, and was one of several being built on the edge of Chateauvallon. The two others kept close behind him, and he smelt cigar smoke. Then he saw the glow of it, and finally the man pulling on it. He was not Fournier or anyone like him, but a complete stranger, sitting there calm as you please on a crate with the bright end of the cigar making his mouth shine pink.

Bossis had difficulty making out his features, the sole illumination being from a streetlamp some yards down the road, casting its light through the pane-less window frame. He wanted to run for it; oh yes, now he wanted to run, it was better on television this kind of thing, in those crime films he usually turned off after ten minutes. He should have jumped out when they were on the main road, just when the yellow Kovalic truck went past with Teddy at the wheel. It would have been easy because of the road works going on there.

27

'Fournier couldn't come,' the man said. 'He asked me to represent him.'

'OK, go ahead,' Paul said, somewhat reassured. He dare not light a cigarette, his hands were trembling, his imagination had turned the two escorts into hit-men. Bossis added: 'I've a wife and soon there'll be a kid, don't forget that.' He kicked himself, not knowing why he had said it, and in such a high-pitched voice . . .

The man stubbed out his cigar, taking time over it, gave a chuckle that would not have been out of place at a vicar's tea-party, though it had a smoker's rasp to it: 'But Monsieur Bossis, we're not playing Scarface. I'll keep you five minutes, that's all, and you'll be driven back.'

'I said OK. But what's the idea of this meeting place?'

'The fewer the walls the fewer the ears, for what we have to discuss. Now listen carefully. You are taking far too much interest in Les Sablons. I take it you are collecting material for a big piece on the project, maybe several articles. Meanwhile you have done a small story alluding to shortcomings in the basic design of the property.'

Bossis: 'We do plan a series on the project, Monsieur . . . Monsieur?'

'Skip it.'

'And I can assure you, Monsieur Skipit, that we shall if necessary refer to design faults, and any other shortcomings.'

'Your devotion to the journalist's code of conduct does you proud, Bossis, but 800 million francs is at stake in Les Sablons, and I'm sure you wouldn't wish to compromise sales by hasty unchecked reports, insinuations even.'

Bossis nodded: 'The facts have been checked all right. You can forget your buyers; they'll be told what's going on and they will be only too glad to pull out.'

The man's voice became menacing: 'Watch it, young man!'

The newsman charged ahead: 'Bad workmanship, inferior materials, inadequate joinery, absence of insulating layers – those are only the details. Two-thirds of the Chateauvallon town councillors are involved in your crooked enterprise, my friend, but I won't be grieving when they get their fingers burnt. I'm not on their payroll.'

Bossis felt the tubby guy's hand on his shoulders, and he jerked as a sharp object dug into his back. His innards turned over, the scene suddenly became unreal.

'Leave him,' the man sitting down ordered. 'Leave us both, I'd like to have a little tête-à-tête – see what we can work out.'

The others withdrew, Bossis relaxed and the man began pacing the concrete floor.

He began: 'My dear Monsieur Bossis, you share an apartment with a ravishing young lady by the name of Kovalic, who has forsaken her entire family for love of you. However, the apartment in question is modest to say the least of it, even close to being condemned by the authorities as unfit, especially as you will soon be three in that apartment. Which I knew before you told me. In any case you will certainly agree that the child ought to be brought up in better, more pleasant surroundings.'

Paul Bossis gave a little cough: 'What of it? What's your proposition, out with it?'

'You get off our backs and you'll not regret it, Bossis. How about a nice comfortable four-room apartment when the development is completed, with a beautiful BMW in the garage just waiting for you to turn on the ignition?'

'And suppose I tell you to stuff your apartment?'

'Think carefully, Bossis, before you turn it down. I want to play fair with you.' The man's voice would have won over the Venus de Milo in the Louvre. Then he rapped out: 'Over here, you two. Kindly take Monsieur Bossis back to town, he's going to sleep on it, think things over carefully.'

Bossis glanced quickly at the two as they fell in either side of him. There was no mistaking the smirks. He was trembling again now, realizing not only would the BMW never be his, but he would never need the red Alfa – still prisoner at Les Sablons – again.

The Bergs called them the Kovalic gang, but they were more widely known as the Yugoslav clan, and sometimes simply the Tribe.

The family lived on a run-down farm at the Western edge of Chateauvallon. Around the farmhouse was a large piece of land where even the weeds had a hard time growing and the ruts from the tyres could be counted by the thousand. The property was surrounded by rusty barbed wire, and the barns in the yard were stacked with crates, barrels and cans. In the containers were bottles of champagne, surplus wine, canned ham and an assortment of other food and drink that had been purchased cheap as

29

the result of bankruptcies and liquidations in and around Chateauvallon.

Teddy parked his truck close to three others in the Kovalic 'fleet', and made his way round the farmhouse looking for Uncle Albertas, the clan's chief. It was behind the house that Albertas had his territory: a bit of garden, a smaller yard for his animals, a plot where he grew vegetables.

The lad made for the light of a storm lantern and saw the older man moving about and making shadows as he fed pails of swill to his beloved pig. Nobody else was allowed to feed it and, as Teddy approached, his uncle sloshed the final pail into the trough. Teddy waited at a respectful distance, watching the fifty-year-old boss clumping around on his short legs and flat feet, his head enclosed in a mass of black curly hair. Uncle Albertas looked fatter than the pig, he thought.

At length he mumbled 'evening, uncle' and handed over the satchel with the latest takings. Albertas took it and stuffed it inside his leather windcheater. Teddy knew the old man would never check the takings, that none of them would ever dream of taking a cut for himself.

'The Bergs gave me a cheque,' he said, and Albertas took that as well, folding it into a pocket.

He frowned at the name of Berg: 'They got themselves a band too, I hear.' His way of speaking was coarse, like the croaking of an old bird.

'They've got a big do on,' he said, hearing the music borne to them on the wind from two miles away.

'Huh! One day they'll be having no more dos and they'll be issuing dud cheques. You'll see, my lad, before I'm gone.'

He eyed the tin under Teddy's arm, and the youth volunteered: 'Caviar, the old 'un gave it to me.'

'For me was it?'

'It was his idea,' Teddy said ambiguously.

Albertas put out his hand, half beckoning, and took the tin. He twisted the tag, opened the lid and threw the caviar in the pigfood. He laughed and even Teddy shivered, for he hadn't heard that sound often.

'What's good for Antonin is good enough for pigs,' Albertas announced.

'What's good for pigs is good enough for Antonin,' quipped Teddy, always keen to go along with Albertas.

But his uncle was already stumping his way to the house, the lantern swaying this way and that, and Teddy knew he had irritated the old man once again.

'Late back, boy! Stopped off for a quick one on yer way?'

'Never, uncle, I never do that.' Teddy knew he could have his pay docked thirty minutes. 'Road works on the Rumilly road, one-way traffic and then the other way, single file like. Saw Paul Bossis in a car with two blokes.' The last detail to add authenticity.

Albertas Kovalic raised his voice a little: 'That bloody rat, don't you ever mention his name again. And never forget the dirty trick he played on us.'

The clan chief was spitting with rage. If it was the last thing he did, he would wring the neck of the bastard who ran off with his daughter Catherine. Albertas slammed the door in Teddy's face, signifying there was no slivovitz at the end of this day's work, at least not for him.

Teddy went off to fetch his check-list from the truck, when Albertas reappeared: 'In a car with two men, you say? What sort of men?'

'Funny looking geezers, one of 'em dressed up like in the films. Bossis didn't look too happy.'

Albertas jerked his head to one side: 'Maybe they'll run him over for me, interfering little runt.'

Teddy watched him go back into the house, waddling up the couple of steps to the door. Silly old bugger, thought Teddy. He didn't care whether Bossis lived or died; what disgusted him was that his uncle blamed Bossis for the biggest insult in his life, asserted that Bossis virtually kidnapped Catherine, whereas it was Catherine who ran off with him, in search of a better life.

Bossis had to admit the man with the cigar was right. Their apartment was no place for bringing up a child in. There would be complaints about the baby crying, that was certain. You could hear people using the toilets all round you, could never escape the squawking kids downstairs, could tell what everyone was having for dinner. People fired off shotguns for less!

Even so, he was thinking that the apartment door was the most wonderful thing he had seen in many a year. He might have been dead by now, his head smashed in with a brick, but they had completed the journey back in silence and the Taunus had let him

31

out at the end of the road, the fat guy telling him: 'See you soon, Monsieur Bossis.'

Paul let himself in and immediately caught sight of Catherine getting ready in the bathroom. No doubt he was not supposed to see her yet, but the door was ajar. At least he had a glimpse of her curves of twenty-four summers in their satin underwear, rather than the discoloured wall tiles and the reddy-brown stains in the washbasin and bath where the taps dripped. She was humming a pop tune and her face was flushed with excitement at the evening ahead. At La Commanderie! Paul stood admiring her olive skin, her dark classical tresses, and her superb physique – as perfect as a Greek statue.

Catherine had been a wildcat when they teamed up, and he had more than once clutched his head trying to handle her outbreaks of fury, alternating with moods as black as hell. But as the months went by, he had learned to take them in his stride, had come to understand that she really did love him. Sure of his devotion in return, she had matured, and was now more vibrant and attractive than ever as she awaited her baby. People often failed to recognize her in the street, and she knew it and knew she would never slip back, never give up this chance of a lifetime with Paul.

She caught sight of him through the door and said she wouldn't be long. Paul went into the bedroom, threw off his jacket and slipped out of his shoes. He lay back on the bed. The next thing he knew was Catherine saying: 'Hey, Bossis! Are you blind or something?'

Fiddling with her black silk dress and worrying her pearl necklace, she stood waiting for the praise that failed to come. She frowned: 'Well what's wrong, how do I look?' He blinked, and she remonstrated: 'What's the matter with you, are you in trouble?'

He smiled: 'Of course not. You look terrific. I love you more than yesterday . . .'

'. . . and not as much as tomorrow.'

As they were wont to do, they recited a piece from Leo Campion: 'To think we might have been born, you in Paris and me at Vladivostok, and in another epoch!'

They hugged, and Paul avoided spoiling her lipstick.

She said: 'If we don't go soon, we'll meet them all as they're leaving.'

'I'll be three minutes flat,' Paul said, hurrying around finding things to wear.

He took nearly ten minutes, but it was worth waiting for. Bossis stood resplendent in black trousers with knife-edge pleats, and a perfectly fitting white tuxedo. They made a wonderful couple, in stark contrast to the scruffiness of the apartment. It was this as much as earlier events that made him scowl. Catherine again asked what was troubling him.

He looked hard at her: 'Tell me honestly . . .'

'Yes?'

'Just one thing. Are you happy here?'

'How ridiculous, of course I am!'

'It's not Versailles by any means, but . . .'

'I prefer it here – less housework.'

He smiled wanly: 'I mean, without aiming at a castle, you might like a better place, let's say a four-room apartment with a garage and all modern conveniences and everything, one of those they're putting up with trees, supermarket one minute away, playground for the kids and so on.'

'And who's going to finance it all, Monsieur Bossis?'

'Er . . . I'd have to make enquiries but . . .'

She took his hands: 'You know the Latin thing: where I am happy, there is my home? My translation of course.' She laughed quickly and added: 'You mustn't, even for me or the baby, mustn't be caught out with schemes we'd have to give up half way through.'

'You're an angel,' he said. After the big build-up, this so surprised her that she wanted to know more. But she knew him by now, especially that he could shut up like a clam if it concerned his job. So she spun round prettily and went back to the bathroom to add a final layer of nail varnish. She was waving her hands about to dry it when she heard him lift the receiver next to the bed.

The man with the cigar had given him a number to call. Paul at that time supposed it was a trick to reassure him, to make him go quietly. But he had got back unscathed.

'Bossis,' he said into the mouthpiece. 'I just wanted to say the answer is no. That's final.'

He replaced the receiver, then lifted it again to dial another number.

Travers grunted his way out of sleep and clutched his receiver. He was used to getting assignments at any hour of the day or night. Travers lived in a run-down studio-flat at the other end of town.

'Travers here. Paul? I'll only just make it to La Commanderie. Bijou-Bar? Can't wait? All right, see you.'

He sat on the edge of the bed, naked as the day he was born. Spreadeagled on the bed in equally simple attire was a chubby redhead still glowing from their love-making. She beamed at him from under half-closed eyelids, and stretched lasciviously while he bumped about the room groping for his clothes. He told her to make sure and shut the door when she left.

Paul's last words had been: 'Take it easy, I'm coming on foot, my car's been stolen.'

Catherine came in: 'Why are you meeting Travers at the Bijou-Bar? I heard you tell him that.'

'Something's come up. I'll be back with a taxi in thirty minutes, an hour at the most.'

'You never said the car had been stolen.'

'Don't worry, we'll get it back.'

He found his leather jacket and transferred the length of cable to his tuxedo.

'What's that for goodness sake?'

'A kind of dynamite,' he said gleefully.

'Something's going on and I demand . . .'

'Nothing to get in a flap about. Be back, gorgeous.'

She held the door open for him and he leapt down the stairs two at a time, swinging on the banisters as he went.

He was in too much of a rush to see the Taunus lurking in a shadow between two street lamps. The man in the smart suit had another carnation now. Moments before, the car phone had told him: 'The dolt has turned us down, he'll never come across. You know what's wanted, choose your own method. But don't mess it up or that'll be your last carnation.'

'How do you know I . . .'

But the car phone went dead. His fat friend still had his eyes glued to the spot he had been watching for quite long enough as far as he was concerned – Bossis's stairway. It was he who had selected the spot for the Taunus, and he had accurately forecast the journalist's reply. He knew too what the instruction would be. It was he who insisted they keep the engine running.

'There's our man. Give him fifty yards and then move off.'

Paul Bossis walked fast, on the point of breaking into a run, and the fifty yards were soon covered.

Travers looked at his watch for the umpteenth time. He felt a bit sick from his third beer at the counter. The thick mist of cigarette smoke didn't help either.

Forty minutes, and no Bossis. He could have got there at a snail's pace in that time. Travers had called their apartment fifteen or twenty minutes earlier, and Catherine told him Paul had gone off like greased lightning. Not wanting to worry her, he refrained from calling again. But he himself was growing scared, breathing in through his teeth, churning over that phrase of his: 'Can't say now, but I'm on to something, in case I can't get to you.'

'Too many late nights, M'sieur Travers?'

The question roused him. It came from a buxom blonde whom the lads jokingly termed the mistress of the house. She was throwing dice for drinks at the counter with Favrot and Edelman, a couple of young reporters on *La Dépêche*. They were as like as twins with their dry humour, though one had glasses the other not.

'Give me another fill, my little Bijou-Bar,' Travers said. 'Broke three world records getting here on time, and I'm stood up.'

'Three, love?'

'Yep. Fastest shower, fastest time putting on trousers and rollneck pullover, fastest time across town at seven minutes and only four old people knocked down. And that's not counting the poor little lady I left on the bed. Bossis'll pay for this, you can put these beers on account to him for a start.'

Edelman leaned over: 'He's in great demand today, our Bossis. Everyone's been wanting him. Melchior for example, like a cat on hot bricks.'

'Do you know why?' said Travers.

'Didn't breath a word.'

Travers slipped off his stool and phoned the paper. Melchior had left an hour ago. He tried his home, no answer – probably at La Commanderie.

Back at the counter, Maryse was waiting for him. Over her shiny dress she wore a short coat with gold threading, her make-up had been applied with a trowel and her hair was a mass of curls. If she couldn't have Jean-Jacques Berg, she could at least tell the world it didn't matter.

'So you're to be the firework display,' he chuckled.

'Well it's not likely to be you in that old pullover.'

'I can get away with anything,' he quipped, leading her to the swing doors.

A minute or so after 9.00 p.m. The Bijou-Bar had a call from Catherine. They told her no they hadn't seen Paul Bossis.

All that was most honorable and disreputable among the town's bourgeoisie, big and little, gathered that evening at La Commanderie. The reception began with a rustle of silk, satin and taffeta and ended with flying skirts and stockinged legs showing.

At various stages the wife of a powerful local tradesman used her décolleté to lure a shy tax inspector into a tumultuous *paso doble* with felonious intent; an accountant with a keener interest in profit than loss held a magistrate's wife so closely in a slow foxtrot that she felt herself blushing from her neck to her knees; a muscular young schoolmaster so swept a town councillor's wife off her feet in a tango that they returned to the sidelines hand in hand; ambitious mothers urged their daughters into frenetic rock-and-roll numbers to make sure they were not overlooked by the males young and old.

The contents of the buffet had virtually disappeared in the first hour, leaving the men with little to do but exchange handshakes that promised pecuniary reward, while the women had no choice but to show off the dresses and hair-dos that had cost them an arm and a leg.

Lending dignity to the occasion were the Prefect and Sub-Prefect with their wives, the men of law and the police, the honest stalwarts and envious rogues of the business community, the notaries public with their private fortunes – all enhancing the glitter of the reception. Without doubt this was the event of the year, possibly of the decade.

At the stroke of ten the heirs to the dynasty arrived. Jean-Jacques Berg in a Cardin tuxedo with his wife Marie-Lou straight out of a Balenciaga collection; Julien in a Mao style jacket with his wife Thérèse who had replaced her shorts with a gypsy dress; then slightly to the rear, for he was not of the direct line, Philippe Berg (also called the 'plonk merchant' owing to his business selling cheap wine) who was nephew to old Antonin and a handsome hunk of a man. Tonight Philippe sported a deep mauve alpaca suit and a coloured wife called Emilie imported from Guadeloupe, and now bringing up the rear as if she had been hired for the evening.

For a moment the dancers stopped and clapped 'the dynasty', an expression used by Travers for the benefit of Maryse, to whom he outlined the goings-on of the town's gentry and lower orders.

'That fellow's Condroyer,' he informed her, 'the long-nosed guy playing up to Madame Saviot, the notary's wife. He's always flirting to hide the fact that he's queer, which everyone knows, and in any case you can see the cool look in his eyes while he's doing it.'

'And the man in the yellow wig?'

'Saviot himself, millionaire six times over and property administrator. He could refloat a bank with his money, but can't keep an even keel with the champagne by the look of his wonky wig.'

As the dynasty went by, he declared: 'Thérèse is nice, superb in the nude and the old man dotes on her. Pity she married Julien, a pleasant enough sawmill manager, but he'll never be crowned king with Florence, Armand and Jean-Jacques in front of him. He builds theatre scenery for plays the public never sees.'

Of Marie-Lou he said: 'You know all about her, wife of your ex-lover, and crazy about money. You didn't cost her much as her husband's mistress, I'll bet.'

Maryse retorted: 'Even so, as you said earlier, it was certainly she who did not want me here.'

'Perhaps I was wrong.'

Maryse looked at Marie-Lou whose gaze passed over her. Jean-Jacques, who had waited in fear and trembling for the two to meet up, resumed breathing and for the first time in his life thought God might exist after all.

'She looks a real bitch. First time I've had a good look at her,' growled Maryse.

'No point in saying it if she can't hear,' Travers said brightly. 'Come on let's see if they've left some Moët et Chandon.'

Madame Saviot arrived with three friends as the pair emptied the last visible bottle of champagne. The ladies asked for whisky, remarking that there was nothing like a fine reception to engender goodwill.

'But I must say,' Madame Saviot declared, lowering her voice an octave, 'the evenings were quite different when poor Gabrielle ran them. I remember the last one she gave, out of this world. I was nineteen at the time. There was only one unfortunate aspect of the whole evening – it was there that I met my husband-to-be.'

A dyspeptic old lady in a fur toque intervened: 'Do you know whether those two old fogies Gilbert Bossis and Antonin still have that morbid habit of showing old films of Gabrielle? Frightfully morbid, don't you think?' she added, just in order to repeat the word, which she thought very chic.

A third woman whose chin and bosom shook as she spoke seized the occasion to remark: 'Don't you think it rather peculiar, those two old rascals living in the same house for so many years?'

'Since 1969, I believe.'

Madame Saviot burst out laughing: 'Well, they did share the same woman. Not that she showed much interest.'

They all stifled their giggles, until the fur toque suggested: 'Perhaps she had more of a liking for the other thing, our dear Gabrielle.'

In Travers's ear Maryse snapped: 'Dirty old nanny-goats!'

He returned: 'They'll be tearing Paul to bits next, come on let's get away.'

'Paul?'

'Paul Bossis is Gabrielle's son, I thought you knew that.'

'Really. Gabrielle, Antonin's wife?'

'But Gilbert was the father, or rather *is*.'

The band ripped into a noisy number. When it was over Maryse said dreamily: 'There's a thing, an old friendship between the two men based on . . .'

'. . . an impossible situation.' Travers spun his empty glass in his fingers. 'A try that was converted, as in rugger. Antonin was cuckolded by Gilbert and ought to detest the man, but Gilbert has a right to hate Antonin because he fooled him. It's a case of A pinching B's wife, but the lady is wife to A. There's no telling how their minds work but I'll bet they both loved Gabrielle sufficiently to make her their common property after she died, their joint memory. They have big enough hearts to forgive each other.'

At that instant they caught sight of Philippe Berg bearing down on them, a giant among the pigmies, confident but furtive with it.

'Let's skedaddle,' muttered Travers, 'I'm not too keen on the nephew. He's on the town council and frankly that makes him suspect in my eyes.'

'I heard he was pretty crafty.'

'No proof, but I can't stand him for some reason.'

Philippe veered off and paid court to an array of black lace and Chanel perfume spread over a rocking chair in the centre of a crowd of admirers. Marie-Lou wafted out of the chair and joined Philippe, to the annoyance of the other courtiers. The pair strolled a few paces together in silence, making for a shadowy spot, signifying ostensibly that their Highnesses wished to consult in private.

'All those buffoons around you. . .' he began.

'I wasn't listening to their nonsense, simply dreaming away.'

'At what?' They spoke in conspiratorial tones.

'The same as you, I imagine,' Marie-Lou replied laughing gaily.

'I was dreaming of an empty bank, and all the safe-deposits were open. I merely had to collect the contents.'

'And I was thinking of inheriting an immense fortune. How romantic we both are!'

'It's your kind of woman I should have married. We would have become fabulously rich together.'

Marie-Lou slipped her arm in his and laughed again, a sparkling river of delight: 'The saga isn't over yet.'

She watched Emilie for a moment, seated not far away. Philippe's wife 'the black girl', all alone in the crowd.

During this time old Antonin had fled indoors to one of the smaller lounges, to get away from the rock music – 'if you can call it music'. He picked a sofa facing a warm log fire and stared at the flames for a while. Until Gilbert Bossis joined him.

Gilbert, somewhat shorter than Antonin, had kept his dark hair and had it close-cropped. As usual he wore a tweed suit and was puffing on a pipe that kept going out. He was roughtly ten years younger than Berg. But their long cohabitation, the curious parallel existence involving Gabrielle, their comradeship in arms following earlier disputes and jealousies – all this made them almost seem like brothers. Habit and the tolerance that comes with advancing years had worked in their favour, and although they remained circumspect one with the other, they found it natural to share their daily bread and wine.

Antonin knew his step only too well and did not turn round: 'How can you bear that rabble of scroungers, I'm surprised you stayed out there so long.'

'I was looking to see if my boy had turned up, but there are so many out there.'

39

'Perhaps he hasn't got here yet. He's onto something that's keeping him busy these days.'

'What's he up to now?'

'Oh, some investigation,' old Berg said rather testily, in a hurry to get onto the subject occupying his whole mind at that instant. 'Florence has come,' he announced.

'Really?'

'Just got here with Armand. Came through the postern gate to avoid the mob. They're upstairs getting ready.'

Gilbert Bossis thought for a second: 'Well, what of it?'

'Nothing. She said "hullo papa", quite naturally, gave me a kiss, and Armand asked if we had any sticking plaster because he cut himself shaving.'

Gilbert waited once more: 'She said nothing about . . .'

'About taking over *La Dépêche*? No. Must give her time to think it over.'

'How was she, I mean, how did she seem . . .'

'Didn't seem any way in particular. You know what she's like. If she bumped into the Virgin Mary, she'd just say sorry.'

As he laboriously climbed the massive stone staircase to the first floor, Gilbert met Jeannou the young servant rushing down. He noticed the youngster's bowtie and black trousers with the silk strip down the side, finally his smart white jacket worn only on important occasions.

'Good evening, M'sieur Bossis.'

'Evening my lad. Where are you careering off to like that?'

'Important message.'

Gilbert ambled along to the third door along the passage, Florence's room when she lived there and when she came down these days. The door was ajar, and he saw she was repairing her make-up. He moved inside and she caught sight of him in the looking glass. They embraced without a word.

'It's been a long time,' said Gilbert, refreshed at the sight of her. 'Only a few months perhaps, but it's seemed like years. I miss you, you know.'

'And I miss you. You never come to see me in Paris.'

'Your father hates Paris, and he doesn't like to be left on his own.'

'The old tyrant,' she exclaimed, half in ernest. Armand came out of the bathroom with a patch of plaster on his cheek, and she

40

added: 'He's always been like that.'

'Too late to alter him now,' Armand said, pumping Gilbert's hand. 'You look great, Gilbert, younger even!'

'Thank you, Doctor. At least I can still shave without cutting myself.' He gave Armand a friendly slap on the shoulder.

'It's not a cut, I'm wearing this so people won't fail to notice me!'

Florence said: 'He scratched himself, just like he used to as a boy when something went wrong. Never was happy until he bled.'

'What's wrong this time?'

'A patient died during an operation,' she said.

'Oh come on, let's forget that,' Armand grumbled. To show that he intended to discuss it no further, he strode over to the telephone.

'Hey Florence, the receiver's off. This isn't your day for phones.'

'No! Leave it off, it's a call.'

Jeannou bustled in, followed by Travers panting heavily. He told Travers: 'You'll have to take it here, M'sieur Travers, as the other lines are busy.'

Florence explained: 'Edelman and Favrot are phoning in stories to the paper, about the reception.'

'But it's not over yet.'

'It *is* for father,' said Armand, shaking Travers by the hand.

Travers cried: 'Oh, but I didn't realize you were there.'

She spread her hands: 'Nice to see you again old chap. I see you are still a favourite with the girls, by the calls you get. Come on everyone, let's leave Don Juan to explain how he had flu and couldn't keep his date. Hurry up Armand, father's probably bitten his thumb off by now.'

They vacated the room and Travers grabbed the receiver. It was what he feared, a call from Catherine Kovalic. For a moment she was completely incoherent, and he had to wait before telling her that Paul had failed to turn up at the Bijou-Bar.

'Then where is he, for God's sake?' she sobbed. 'He was coming back for me, and that was hours ago. Travers, oh it's awful, are you sure he's not at La Commanderie? Look everywhere, he must be there!'

He took a deep breath: 'Now calm down, Catherine, there's probably a simple explanation. When I find him I'll phone you straight back, or he will.'

As he left the room, he saw Bossis senior going down, and wished him not to turn round. Gilbert moved into the small

41

lounge, and Travers crept out by the tradesmen's entrance.

'Who was it?' said Maryse as he rejoined her. The crowd seemed to be thinning out. 'Must have been important for you to leave your lady love of the evening for so long. Everybody's been making passes at me.'

Gruffly he said: 'Let's get a drink.'

'There's nothing left, I'm afraid.'

'Jeannou told me where the secret cache is for the stragglers and gentlemen. He decides who's invited.'

The place was on the far edge of the grounds, in an artificial cave hidden by rocks. Travers made straight for it, and they were delighted to find half a dozen bottles of White Horse and a few glasses, and even some caviar sandwiches in a little basket.

They sat on stools thoughtfully provided, listening to cars being started up and grinding their way out of the property. Travers sank a couple of glasses, then said they ought to be going. He still had some work to do, he said. But Maryse was not listening, she was stuck on a stool like a doll with her curls and goldeny coat, propped against a wall. He got her awake eventually, but it took all of five minutes before she was fully conscious.

They reached the main gate to the estate and found the car. Just then a taxi pulled up outside, and they saw Catherine paying it off.

She came hurtling towards Travers like a mad thing: 'Paul? Have you found him?'

'But I was coming to you. I was wondering if he'd called you.'

'No he didn't. He's here isn't he?'

Maryse said: 'Who are you talking about?'

'Paul Bossis,' he shouted. 'He's just disappeared. Catherine, oh my God, what's she doing?'

Catherine had lost all control by now and was stumbling towards La Commanderie, to the astonishment of the few stragglers braving the night air. It was about 2.00 a.m. by now. When he caught up with her, she yelled that Paul must be inside with one of 'those whores'.

'You're mad. Paul would never do a thing like that.'

She shrieked with laughter, and suddenly burst into tears. Shaking convulsively she sank into Travers' arms.

'I've been drinking,' she sobbed. 'I had to do something, all those hours and hours, phoning around and nobody answered, or else they said, oh no, they'd no idea where Paul was. Oh Lord, where *is* he?'

Travers said sharply: 'Come on, we must get back. We'll phone round again, absolutely everywhere.' He was none too sure what he meant by everywhere.

He and Maryse helped Catherine back to the house, and it was then that the incident took place. They had just gone past a small group of men and women, not paying attention, when a slurred voice hooted theatrically: 'I say, I must be seeing things. A gypsy woman? Here?'

Marie-Lou advanced towards them, pointing at Catherine: 'So we aren't content these days with stealing chickens. We come scrounging food now! Get back to your caravan where you belong, Catherine Kovalic!'

Travers put himself between Marie-Lou and Catherine: 'You shut your trap,' he bawled.

'Me shut my trap? All right clever, you tell her she needs to do more than open her legs for a young Bossis, to make her way in this world!'

Two men were with her, and they turned away hunching their shoulders. Philippe Berg's wife Emilie was in the group too.

Marie-Lou was going on: 'Huh. Your kind of people, give 'em a crust of bread and they'll bite your arm off the next day.'

Emilie moved in, grabbing Marie-Lou's arm: 'That's enough. Come on, Marie-Lou, that's enough, you've made your point.'

'Belt up, nigger!'

A blow struck Marie-Lou who shrieked, then slumped to the ground. Emilie nursed her fist: 'Get away quick, Travers. Take Catherine out of this.' She turned to Catherine: 'Forget and forgive, Catherine. The whites can't hold their drink, makes 'em wild.'

Catherine sobbed all the way to Travers' car. He put the headlights on, and they watched as the two men in dinner jackets dragged the unconscious Marie-Lou back to La Commanderie.

'She's just putting it on,' Travers growled as he turned the ignition key another notch.

Exciting shadows and highlights, with a spark from time to time, vied for interest in the great chimney at La Commanderie in the main hall. It was 4.00 a.m., but the lights remained full on.

43

Everybody had left or gone to bed, except Florence and Armand and a few servants. Brother and sister sat watching the flames, unaware of the lights blazing around them.

'He beat me down, that's all I know,' said Florence.

For three long hours they had tussled, father and daughter. The conclusion of the fight was known solely to the duellists and their seconds: Antonin and Florence, Gilbert and Armand.

Antonin's argument boiled down to this: 'When I go, I doubt strongly that Jean-Jacques is capable of succeeding me. He is an executive type, not a governor. *La Dépêche* is his private club not his venture, a feather in his hat not a reason for living. Florence, you cannot destroy my reason for living, you wouldn't do that to your father. If you refuse this, I shall know definitively that you detest me.'

She said: 'Not you, but your paper. Please don't blackmail me with loyalty.'

The old man had persisted: 'Three special editions next month, twelve districts fully covered, that's my newspaper. Influence, power!'

'But no glory.'

'You're as vain as they come, Florence. What you want is to owe me nothing.'

She fought back, but he beat her down. Florence showed the white flag, and was now regretting it bitterly.

'Oh Armand, what the hell have I got! A mouthpiece for local pensioners and bowls clubs, an in-house magazine for farmers' social clubs, right-wing *concièrges* and old soldiers still dreaming of French Algeria.'

Armand observed: 'You can do what you like with it, *La Dépêche* can change. And that's why you gave in. Although you may not realize it, you felt that deep inside you.'

Florence glared at the dying flames, her face a little drawn: 'Possibly. And, of course, it will fill a void in my life.'

'You mean . . . Quentin.'

'He's one of my voids from now on. There are others.'

'I know,' said her brother in a kindly tone.

'And it's the others that'll hurt most.'

The fire became embers and they remained grimly watching them. Each of them was surprised to see that they were holding hands, as in childhood when they consoled each other or shared a joy.

Armand said: 'You realize you have given him his last great happiness.'

'I didn't want him to think that all our misunderstandings, our antagonisms, meant I couldn't love him over the years.'

She squeezed Armand's hand. Perhaps that last reason was the true motive for her surrender. But was it so much a surrender? It could be that she was too proud to refuse, it occurred to her.

Five o'clock, and in the pre-dawn Paul Bossis's apartment was bathed in a diffused light. An advertising sign that was never switched off.

Catherine lay on the bed fully dressed with a rug over her. Drink, humiliation and terror had reduced her to a state of total exhaustion. But Travers never took his eyes off her.

He too felt he'd been awake for a couple of weeks, but he wanted to be there when she woke. Travers was fond of Catherine and saw himself as the best person to stand by her until this business was over.

They had taken Maryse home and come back to the flat, where they made a succession of phone calls. These produced either no reply or merely abuse. The duty man at the Commissariat de Police told him: 'If I were you, Monsieur Travers, I'd leave it till daylight.' He was so whacked that a snappy retort eluded him this time.

That had been the last call. And now, having removed his trousers, he lay down alongside Catherine. In a conditioned reflex his unruly member stirred, but that was the last he remembered before plunging into deep slumber.

Dawn came yellow and misty through the poplars at La Commanderie.

It was young Jeannou who gave the alert, rushing into old Berg's room without ceremony and shaking him.

There was a body in the pond, he informed him.

At that precise instant Florence was sliding between her sheets, Armand was already asleep at his place, Marie-Lou was asking Jean-Jacques for some aspirin, Thérèse and Julien were caressing each other, Philippe was ending the night in a disco somewhere, and his wife Emilie was waiting up for him in the kitchen with a cigarette.

Jeannou told Antonin Berg: 'It was my dog who woke me. Kept

45

whimpering and scratching around in my room. I went down with him and he ran off to the pond, and when I got there . . .!' He left the sentence unfinished, there was no need, he'd said it once.

'Come on,' growled Antonin tying the belt on a thick padded grey dressing gown.

A rooster's call reached them from far away as they hurried over the lawns, not bothering with the paths. The dog was back at the pond, uttering little yelps and jumping about.

Berg and Jeannou had opened the outlet valves and the water was only inches deep. Right in the middle of the pool amid crushed water-lilies was a bulky plastic shroud of the kind used to protect fur coats in stores. It was half buried in the mud on the bottom. There was no mistaking its contents.

Antonin Berg watched Jeannou advance towards the body, and the lad slashed the plastic. He tore it away at the head and revealed a face streaked with blood, the eyes looking heavenward.

It was Paul Bossis.

Chapter Two

The criminal police department were on the job within minutes of old Berg's call, parking their cars and vans any old how round the pond.

But a good distance away. They swiftly went into the routine of checking the grass, taking pictures and muttering to one another. One man was wading under the bridge and looking under the boards.

Commissaire Nicolo pronounced: 'Nothing to go on yet. He was either knocked out or killed, and then thrown in, by all appearances.'

Nicolo was rotund but agile. Middle-aged with a fair share of the world's wrinkles. He did not smile, he never did, but he was darting his eyes this way and that.

Antonin, an overcoat over his dressing gown, remarked: 'I saw the wound on the back of his neck – dreadful.'

He had ordered Paul's father to be left. The pond was about a kilometre from the house and Gilbert's room faced the other way. Probably he hadn't heard the sirens, or at least ignored them as of no concern to La Commanderie.

Inspector Germain, the man who had checked under the bridge, came over to Nicolo and Berg: 'He was struck before he was dumped, that's certain. I checked the body when we arrived, it was stiff already.'

A younger man, Pradal, said: 'I've gone over the entire area stretching thirty yards from the pond. No hope of finding anything, Monsieur Le Commissaire. It's all flattened down, tyre marks all over the place.'

Antonin gave a long sigh, reflecting on the festivities and the appalling noise that had gone on for hour after hour, during which time young Bossis had been dropped into the pond.

An ambulance came softly to a halt. Berg turned to the woman Mathilde, now sobbing into Jeannou's lapels a few yards away.

'Better get back inside, Mathilde, this isn't going to be pleasant.' Jeannou's arm enveloped her, and Berg added: 'Not a word to Monsieur Bossis, even if he's awake. I'll handle him.'

He watched as the male nurse slid the body into the vehicle. The ambulance slunk away, and he caught sight of Inspector Pradal carefully wrapping the plastic shroud inside another length of plastic.

The Commissaire said: 'You never know, might be a finger-print or two worth having.'

For a split second Antonin wondered whether he wasn't dreaming it all. But there was no mistaking the ambulance now going through the main gate. That was real enough. So was Commissaire Nicolo, who finished chatting with a subordinate and was coming over with the regulation notebook and ballpoint.

'Nasty business, Monsieur Berg. Especially for Monsieur Bossis senior.' Nicolo tended to let his words out hardly opening his mouth, as if he'd prefer to keep them to himself.

'I'm not feeling too good about it either, Commissaire,' Antonin growled.

'Of course, I was forgetting. The boy was . . . er . . . your . . .'

'My late wife's son, that's right. I don't suppose that will affect your enquiries, Commissaire. And I don't imagine you'll bother to note down that Monsieur Gilbert Bossis has been living at my place since 1969.'

Nicolo disliked jokers when he was on the job, and would gladly have hit right back at this one. Only this one was Antonin Berg, and he edged onto a safer topic.

'You were saying that the victim no longer lived at La Commanderie.'

'Hasn't for quite a while. He set up in the town with a young woman.'

'You split up?'

'No, they fell in love. What's that to do with it? Her name's Catherine Kovalic, if you must know.' It came out bitterly, so harshly he surprised himself.

'I know,' the cop said. 'Know she's expecting a kid too.' His tone matched Antonin's and to provoke Berg he added: 'A child by Paul Bossis, of course?'

'There's no need to sling mud at Mademoiselle Kovalic,'

Antonin said in a clipped voice that was a suppressed shout.

'No offence meant, I'm sure, Monsieur Berg. Sorry to upset you, but you realize naturally that the name Kovalic always brings us out in a rash.'

'That's your problem. Catherine Kovalic left her people a long time ago.'

'Because they wanted to marry her off to that Grüber fellow?'

'I don't know, and I certainly don't care. All I know is that she's broken off completely with that bunch of savages.'

Nicolo kept going: 'Could be a vengeance killing, don't you think?'

'By the Kovalics? Wouldn't surprise me.'

'Hm. Dumping the boy on your land could be some kind of ritual thing.'

Berg grabbed Nicolo's lapel, but the gesture was controlled. 'Now look here, Commissaire. Here's my theory and you can make what you like of it. That boy was not killed because he slept with Catherine Kovalic, but because he was one of my journalists!'

'That's quite a theory. How come?'

'I have no proof, no clues, and nothing I told you could ever be used. But if you're interested in the truth, Commissaire, I would suggest you take a look at Paul Bossis's assignments.'

Nicolo stiffened, making no move to note this down.

He stated drily: 'The autopsy will be tomorrow early. I'll see you are kept informed.'

Nicolo turned on his heels, leaving Antonin with the impression that he regarded him as just an old fool.

Travers woke with a start before 6.00 a.m. Catherine had not budged and nor did she now.

He got the night watchman at *La Dépêche* to let him into the library, thinking to follow up a line of investigation. A few minutes later he had a call from Antonin Berg. By the time Travers reached the estate, old Berg was slowly walking back to the house from the pond.

Travers crunched to a halt, got out and ran over to Antonin, his coat and hair in disarray.

Panting hard he blurted out: 'I should have guessed. He told me "I'm on to something, in case I can't get to you." I waited for him in the Bijou-Bar.'

'And he didn't get to you,' his employer stated coldly. 'Now pull yourself together, Travers. We must all keep our heads.'

'He was a close friend of mine, Monsieur, probably my best friend.'

'That's precisely why I phoned you at once after the police. What the devil were you doing in the library at this hour? I tried your studio place first.'

'I was working on a theory, Monsieur.'

'What was that?'

'The same as you, I've no doubt. But I found nothing in the files to back it up.'

The older man gestured to him to calm down: 'Let's not jump to conclusions, it would be unprofessional anyhow. Keep your own counsel for the time being, you understand.'

Travers nodded agreement. Berg knew plenty, more than he did, but he would volunteer nothing, biding his time.

Antonin Berg clenched his jaw, and the stubble showed white: 'But have no fear, this case won't fizzle out, I can assure you. The scoundrels who did it will pay in full, they'll pay whoever they are. Now get back to the office – I want a special edition, and I want you to do the editorial. We must be on the streets with it before noon, in the vans and the stands, everywhere, you understand! I'll phone Melchior right away.'

'Very good, Monsieur. Er . . . what angle d'you have in mind, for the editorial?'

'I leave it to you. You knew him well enough.'

Travers turned back again: 'This business is going to cause a hell of a row, I can't imagine how I'll break it to Catherine.'

'Or I to the boy's father.'

Travers was jerking his car door open, when he heard Jeannou calling his name. The youngster was racing over the grass. Commissaire Nicolo had phoned and wanted Monsieur Travers at once.

'One of our cars found Bossis's Alfa in an alley on the edge of Chateauvallon,' Nicolo said.

'When he called me and told me to be at the Bijou-Bar, he mentioned that his car had been stolen,' said Travers.

The Commissaire allowed his gaze to roam round the scruffy office, similar to so many in Commissariats the length and breadth of the country. The stale odour of several generations of cigarettes, pipes and cigars had become part of the walls and furniture. Commissaires deserved better than this, he was thinking for the thousandth time.

'The curious thing, Monsieur Travers, is that the car was as clean as a whistle, as though it had just been delivered. Or just left one of those car-washes at a garage.'

'With the blood sluiced away?'

'Not necessarily blood, but earth or dust or weeds – anything that could have given us a lead. We're waiting for the report. But that's not why I called you in.'

'Go ahead,' Travers said. He was impatient to get it over, and the cop's slow pace irritated him.

'Inspector Pradal checked the Bijou-Bar. Paul Bossis went there a lot?'

'He got thirsty like the rest of us. Had a sandwich sometimes.'

'Pradal says you waited for Paul Bossis a long time.'

'True. He called me at my place to fix up the meeting. Said it couldn't wait. Want to know his exact words?'

Nicolo gave a curt nod, and Travers vowed he would pull the head off the next person who asked him to repeat them.

'He said: "I'm on to something, in case I can't get to you".'

'Could be a lead.'

'For pity's sake, it's more than a lead, man. The fact is that Bossis knew someone was after him!'

Nicolo smiled knowingly; 'Travers, you do your job and I'll do mine, huh? We're the ones who come to the conclusions.'

'Right you are, Commissaire!' Travers jumped up, knocking his chair over as he made for the door. 'Go ahead, and I hope the conclusions come easy. Because I can assure you *La Dépêche* is putting its whole weight behind this. And we'll keep on to it, until the crime's solved.'

'Are you suggesting we need your rag to conduct our inquiries?'

'The police always conduct their inquiries,' Travers scoffed, his fingers feeling for the door knob. 'But sometimes it takes them rather a long time, that's all I'm saying.'

Nicolo raised his voice: 'Hold it a second! I'll ignore that last remark, Travers. But just one more thing: Bossis and you were close, very close. You must have some idea of any . . . er . . . stories he was on to.'

'No idea.' Old Berg had told him to keep his mouth shut, and that's exactly what he would do.

51

'Not even the tiniest little idea?'

'Nope.'

'What about the editor and the other bigwigs?'

'Bossis was a loner, and they let him get on with it. He looked for his own stories most of the time.' He turned to go.

'What about that, then?'

A loud clunk on the desk, and Travers spun round. Nicolo was now glaring at Travers over a length of electric cable lying on the desk in front of him. It was about nine inches long, greyish in colour, and showed traces of moisture. At one end Travers could see there was a red stain.

'You don't recognize it? Doesn't remind you of anything?'

'No. What is it? I mean I can see it's some cable . . .'

'Inspector Germain found it in the victim's pocket when we got him out of the pond. It has some fingerprints on it.'

'Ah!'

'Unfortunately they are your friend's. But the blood's not his. Any ideas on that?'

'I'll let you do your job, like you said . . .'

Travers charged out of the room, leaving Nicolo cursing at the length of cable. He drove off with a roar, still wondering how he could break the news to Catherine.

It was breakfast time at La Commanderie, with hundreds of birds chirping away in the eaves and trees. They had good reason to celebrate: the sun was shining in a cloudless sky.

Inside, Marie-Lou and Jean-Jacques, Thérèse and Julien, were attempting to recover. But Mathilde was not helping; she had served breakfast in tears and was now clearing away with sobs. When she was out of the room, Marie-Lou mumbled: 'Well, I only hope she's better by lunchtime.'

She and her husband had been too drunk to go home, and had slept some of it off between aspirins. They were in a foul mood, because they had hoped to be up at noon rather than dawn. The grim news imparted to them had not prevented them eating a good breakfast.

Thérèse and Julien had been at the sawmill as usual, and it was there that Jeannou told them. They hurried to the house but could stomach only black coffee. They were genuinely distraught and held hands.

Marie-Lou's remark had broken a long silence, for Antonin had gone up to wake Gilbert. The other Bergs round the table were getting worried. Not a sound had filtered down for fifteen minutes or more. Marie-Lou snorted, wondering if the tragedy had been too much for Bossis senior.

'I ought to go up perhaps,' Jean-Jacques said. But he made no move to rise.

Marie-Lou, ignoring him, said: 'Another orphan on our hands, I suppose. Poor little mite, with a Kovalic for a mother!'

'She turned up here last night. I understand,' said Jean-Jacques. 'Gave you that black eye, I'm told.'

'Well, you'd better check your sources. I fell down the stairs, if you must know.' The truth was that she remembered nothing of the scrap outside. 'Come on, we'd better go home and get this seen to at once.'

Jean-Jacques' eyes were wide with amazement: 'Don't be in such a hurry, we can't leave before we've seen Gilbert.'

They lapsed into silence again. Until Thérèse began scolding Marie-Lou for her constant attacks on Catherine. What was she to her, after all?

'You don't really expect me to strike up a friendship with a gyppo, for God's sake. Those Kovalics, you mark my words, they'll drive us out one of these days, and not only them . . .'

There followed a tirade against the Italian immigrants, the Spaniards, the Portuguese, the Turks and now, the 'Yugos'. The audience settled down to yet another of her speeches, adopting a tolerant attitude that enraged Marie-Lou still further. Her own view was that her extreme sensitivity on this and allied matters was evidence of her sound patriotism. Besides, she was affected by smell, she could never espy an Arab without fearing to be raped, or a Greek without fearing for her fortune. She had grown up that way and it was a pity a few more of the French didn't take a stand on what was, after all, the future of the nation in twenty years' time. Marie-Lou was lambasting the other three for having had 'their balls chewed off by the Third World cannibals', when Armand burst in, his face as black as night.

'Thank you so much for letting me know! It was Mathilde who phoned. Very considerate of you!'

'Keep your hair on,' Julien said. 'I knew you'd been told.'

Jean-Jacques told Armand: 'Mathilde was told to inform you. If Marie-Lou and I hadn't been here, we would probably not have been told at all. Father only seems prepared to put himself out for the great Travers.'

'Huh,' snorted Marie-Lou, 'what do you expect? We're no better than horseshit to the old man!'

'Oh, stop harping on about all that again,' Armand snapped. 'For goodness sake, this is hardly a moment for settling old scores. How's Gilbert taking it?'

'Father's upstairs with him,' Julien said. 'We've no idea how he's getting on. We're completely in the dark.'

'Why don't you go up and see, darling?' Marie-Lou scoffed. 'They need men like you up there. I'm sure you, at least, will be welcome.'

Armand addressed them at large: 'Florence, what about her?'

'Nobody's seen her,' said Jean-Jacques. 'I called the whore-house where she booked in, but she'd left without trace. Come to think of it, she probably thought the Relais de Chateauvallon failed to live up to her reputation.'

'My God, what a loving family this is,' Armand said with a snarl.

Antonin Berg stood at the end of the passage with his hands clasped behind him. Armand found him looking at the line of paintings on the wall, but felt certain his father had his mind elsewhere. The old man's patrician head stood out starkly against the claret-coloured wallpaper behind the works of art.

He jumped: 'Oh, it's you.'

'How are you, father?'

'Old, my son, older every minute.'

'Gilbert, how is he?'

'Asleep.'

'What?'

'You know how he likes to take sleeping pills even in the middle of the night. It'd take an artillery regiment to wake him at the moment.'

'But father, in the circumstances . . .'

'I'm sorry Armand, I can't bring myself to wake him. The later he knows the better. But if you want to, you can get him up. It's my duty, I know, but I simply haven't the courage.'

'That's not like you, father.'

'How I know it! We are not always master of our feelings.' Antonin sighed heavily adding: 'Florence will probably come out of this best.'

54

'Possibly, but she's not here, you know. She's left Chateauvallon.'

Old Berg was galvanized into life: 'B-but we were supposed to have a long chat today, discuss the details of *La Dépêche* and her taking it over. Surely, she hasn't changed her mind?'

Armand waved him down: 'Listen father, don't you think there's something more urgent than talking shop?'

He made for Gilbert's door and gently opened it. His father followed him inside, closing the door again with a bang.

Gilbert Bossis was sitting in a chair, stuffing tobacco into his pipe, dressed in an ancient hunting suit. The visitors gaped at Gilbert and then at each other.

'I know,' said Gilbert. 'You ordered them to keep it from me, but Mathilde told me. She wouldn't have me sleep without knowing my boy was dead.'

Antonin cleared his throat: 'I did what I thought was for the best.'

'Naturally. You have always done what you thought was best.' Gilbert regarded Antonin with studied contempt, and then asked Armand: 'There'll be an autopsy, I suppose.'

Armand nodded: 'Always are in these cases. Paul's at Saint Joseph's Hospital.'

Bossis seemed to slump in his chair: 'Will they let me see him? They'll let me, won't they?'

'Later.'

'When they've cut him into bits, is that it?' His eyes flashed. 'I demand to see him now, before they do it!'

'They couldn't stop *me* seeing him, and you can come with me. You may be sorry.'

Gilbert stared at the carpet: 'It's ages since I saw him. They can't stop me saying goodbye, seeing him for the last time. I'm his father.' Bossis's chin trembled and he had to take his pipe out of his mouth.

Armand took his hand: 'I'll fix it, but why not lie down for a bit. I'll close the shutters. Just rest a while, doctor's orders, eh?'

Bossis did as he was told, and said weakly: 'This is the worst day of my life since Gabrielle died. That was awful too, Antonin.'

Berg went to the bed and held Gilbert's head close to his chest. He said: 'This is just as bad, I feel the same as you.' These simple words of friendship released Gilbert's tears, but Berg had already changed his tone: 'I promise you this, on my word of honour:

whoever did this will pay for it ten times over.'

Old Berg shuffled out of the room, close to tears himself. He controlled himself and was glad, for Armand called out: 'How about Catherine?'

'Travers is seeing her. He's probably with her now. Poor girl. Look after Gilbert, I must go down to the paper.'

Jean-Jacques and Marie-Lou with Julien and Thérèse rose with one accord as Antonin walked into the lounge, where they had adjourned to after breakfast.

They all sat down again when he marched straight through into his study and closed the door. They heard him make three phone calls.

Shortly, they heard the Rolls scrunch to a halt outside the front door. Jeannou came in and informed the master it was ready. Antonin thereupon emerged from his study in a black overcoat.

'He knew everything from Mathilde,' he threw out as he crossed the lounge again. 'Nobody must start being sorry for him. Armand is with him.'

Jean-Jacques made a move to follow him: 'If you're going to the office, I'll come with you.'

His father retorted: "You'll find me there when you've changed your shirt and suit and had a shave. This is quite the wrong day to look as if you've just been thrown out of a nightclub!'

Marie-Lou waited for the Rolls to draw away: 'What a baboon!' And to her husband: 'What a drip you look.'

He ignored the insult, as he had so many before: 'I'll take the car, you can take a taxi.'

'With this black eye?'

But he had already gathered up his crumpled tuxedo and departed. Marie-Lou had the alternative of swearing like a trooper or bursting into tears. However, she was certainly not going to perform for the benefit of Thérèse and Julien, and did neither. They had witnessed too many jousts between her and Jean-Jacques and she slipped into the role she judged most suited to the occasion, the part most likely to win them over as allies and evoke their admiration – that of the hurt mother.

Her audience had seen the act many times already, but they were too polite to mention it, let alone deride it. With eager attention they again heard how unfeeling Jean-Jacques was as a father.

As previously she ended with: 'Poor Michel has never had a

proper father. It's never even occurred to him to let him know about Paul's death. That's for Marie-Lou to do, of course.'

She moved into the study to make the call, explaining on the way how close Michel and Paul were as friends.

While she phoned, Julien whispered: 'I didn't know that.'

Thérèse mouthed back: 'It's news to me.'

'Michel?' Marie-Lou yelled into the receiver. 'What are you doing there, you should be at school by now! A teachers' strike? What do you take me for? Get up this minute – you'll go far in life, I can see that. Just you wait till I get home. What's that, Paul Bossis is dead? I know he's dead, but that's no reason for staying out of school. I don't know what your father'll say when he finds out how you've spent your day. He'll tan the hide off you.' She smashed the phone down.

Julien and Thérèse were biting their lips when she swept in declaring: 'Such a sensitive boy. When I told him about Paul, he pleaded with me to hurry home. The poor thing. I'll call a taxi right away.'

Just then a car drew up outside, high heels tapped on the steps and the door was flung open. Florence stood there, her face crimson.

Julien went to her in the hall and asked where the dickens had she been. She wafted forwards ignoring everyone, uttering the single word 'Gilbert?' Julien pointed upstairs.

Outside Gilbert's door Florence stopped to get her breath back, then she entered without knocking and the two were in a close hug. It lasted a whole minute, after which Gilbert slumped back into his chair, and held his head in his hands.

'I heard it on the radio,' Florence said hoarsely. 'Ten o'clock news.' She gave a nod to Armand.

'They tried Le Relais, but were told you had left.'

'I went to my place in Rue de la Ferronière.' This was the small luxury apartment she bought on leaving La Commanderie.

'Thought you'd sold that,' said Bossis.

'I never got round to it, I forgot to tell you. The Relais de Chateauvallon was more suitable for saying goodbye to Quentin. The apartment was full of memories and he would have taken it badly.'

Bossis allowed himself a sly smile: 'Le Relais on the other hand was inappropriate for the new boss of *La Dépêche*!'

Florence rested a hand on the chairback: 'Oh dear, I can't focus. How can I run *La Dépêche* without Paul there, it's impossible.'

Bossis stood up and faced her: 'Then it's me you would be letting down, and Paul even more so. If you gave it up, resigned and returned to Paris you would never come back, and it would be as if you had abandoned Paul. Without you at the helm, it's perfectly plain the killers will go scot-free. You now control the only means of getting them to court, the paper!'

'That's for the police . . .'

'The police wear blinkers, and you know it. It's a certainty the killers have powerful backers, and we're going to have to be just as strong.'

She remained silent for ten seconds, her eyes shut, and then whispered: 'All right, Gilbert, don't worry, I'll do it.' Turning to Armand: 'How are they coping at the clinic without you?'

'I've got an operation in an hour's time,' he replied, glancing at his watch as if to prove it.

'Off you go then, I'll stay with Gilbert.'

Antonin Berg was giving his top people merry hell in his oak-panelled office at *La Dépêche*.

The score of them – twelve from the editorial side, some managerial staff and three print shop foremen – listened to him in respectful silence. Their eyes flitted back and forth to three historic issues of the paper on the wall: one announcing the end of World War II, another proclaiming the return of General de Gaulle to power, the third mourning the death of his successor President Georges Pompidou.

Monsieur Berg gave his orders: 'I want to make this clear: that the killing of one of my reporters will not be allowed to pass just like that. If those responsible want war then war they shall have. But let's make quite sure we know whom we are fighting and how we set about it. Now this editorial we did: either it goes too far or it funks the issue. It hints, indeed states, that Bossis was on to something big, and yet we don't say what it was. That's nonsense. It's equally fatuous, to my mind, suggesting that there might possibly be a feud going on between the Berg family and the town hall – either there's a feud or there isn't a damn feud, and anything in the conditional is pure flannel. Melchior, you must have realized this kind of stuff simply fails to come across, it doesn't stand up!'

The deputy editor made to reply as Jean-Jacques Berg joined the group. He wore a sober blue suit with waistcoat and a black tie.

Melchior coughed: 'I understand, Monsieur Berg, that you personally asked Travers to do the leader, and presumed that you'd worked out the style and content.'

Sweetly reasonable, Antonin said: 'It's not a question of understanding, Melchior. It's the job of the people to grasp the meaning of words. For example, "the town hall", what does "the town hall" mean? There's no such thing. There is, on the other hand, Monsieur Quentin, Mayor of Chateauvallon, Member of the Assemblée Nationale and Secretary of State for Defence. Well, it's his name that should have gone in, instead of us vaguely implying that the local council was involved.'

'Travers probably thought it wiser to stick to generalities, Monsieur.'

'Wiser – wiser? There's no room for wisdom when it comes to facts. They speak for themselves. First, a journalist is murdered, and there's no reason to beat about the bush with an event that is rare enough in this company and town for it to be given priority treatment. Second, I am personally in the direct line of fire, because the body was actually dumped on my property. And as far as that goes everyone at *La Dépêche* is implicated through me, indeed the entire press has had this corpse dumped on its doorstep. Another thing: I want an inset pic on the left of the splash head every day, yes every day, until the killers are in jail. Melchior!'

'Monsieur.'

'I specially asked you for that over the phone this morning.'

'I'm sorry, Monsieur, you ordered the first special issue out by 9 a.m. We made it. But we couldn't get the pic done in time for that. It'll be in the noon edition.'

The old man grunted: 'I'll accept that. Where's Travers now? I want to see him, I want to know why he's started writing with his hand up his arse.'

They all looked this way and that, and more specially at Melchior. Then Jean-Jacques revealed with evident glee that Monsieur Travers was asleep in his cubby-hole. At which Edelman and Favrot mumbled together, glancing contemptuously at Jean-Jacques.

Pleased with his speech, Berg senior roared: 'So that's it!'

Travers was indeed asleep, slouched with his collar up in his swivelling chair, his feet on the desk, hands folded like a bishop's on his belly.

Antonin Berg, observing him from the other side of the glass partition, was prepared to accept that one of his people could nod off after a gruelling assignment. But it was going too far laying a large Hermès scarf over his face to warn that he was not to be disturbed.

Maryse fell in behind the Berg party as it processed towards Travers's redoubt, and behind Maryse came others, so many that a large proportion of the staff came to a halt behind the boss.

Antonin Berg himself opened the door, grabbed Travers's feet, swept them sideways off the desk, and watched as his victim's derrière slid inexorably off the swivel chair and onto the parquet flooring.

'Shit! What blithering idiot . . . ? Oh, it's you, *boss*.'

Even old Berg failed to keep a straight face, and twitched his nose, providing a cue for the others to laugh.

'What's that?' the boss said as Travers's visage was unveiled to disclose a fairly ample strip of sticking-plaster on his brow. 'Don't say they've been having a go at you too.'

'No Monsieur, a truck braked too hard, I smashed my windscreen.' He was now standing and restoring his coat collar to the down position.

'Good,' said Antonin. 'How did Catherine Kovalic take the news?'

'As you would expect, boss.' He nodded at the special issue Berg was holding. 'Didn't care for the leader, I'm told. I didn't either. Wasn't easy, perhaps you should have taken it over under the circumstances.' He held his employer's gaze. 'Frankly I didn't have much to work on, no ammunition as you might say.'

'And you think I . . .'

'I don't know what to think, Monsieur, honestly I don't.'

Old Berg squinted slightly, none too sure how to take the remark.

Then he ordered: 'Seven o'clock tonight, at La Commanderie, I'll expect you on time.'

Antonin stepped out into an empty corridor, for the staff had lost interest after the dramatic awakening. Antonin knocked at Maryse's door and asked her if she wouldn't mind looking after 'that imbecile who puts corn plaster on his forehead'.

She raided the first aid box and was shortly ordering the patient: 'Keep still for nurse, or I'll poke your eyes out for you.'

'How kind of you. Maryse you bring out the nicest fantasies in me. What colour are you wearing today, nurse?'

He relapsed into silence as Maryse cleansed and covered the gash.

'Catherine do that?' she asked casually.

'You guessed right. Pair of scissors. She went raving mad, ran everywhere, turning over furniture, climbing on the window sill. Wanted to do away with herself, but I dragged her inside and she jabbed at me with some nail scissors. She called me everything she could think of, thinking that I had deliberately kept everything from her all last night. She was shrieking her head off and a neighbour called the police. They took her to Les Glycines, Armand Berg's clinic.'

Maryse could find nothing to say, but eventually suggested he ought to go home.

'How about going to the pictures tonight, make a change for you.'

'I'll have to be available all the time for a while,' he said wearily.

Wine exporter Philippe Berg, husband of 'the black girl' and neglected nephew of Antonin Berg, first learned about Paul Bossis' death at 2.00 p.m.

He was half-way through a business lunch with a Mr Allison from Birmingham, England, who less than an hour earlier had appended his signature to a large order for Chablis. He glanced at a newspaper lying on the next table and read: 'DEPECHE JOURNALIST MURDERED – Motive Unknown'. Paul's photo was below.

Philippe Berg suddenly felt weak, and knew he was breaking out in a sweat. It was a disaster, he must get to Condroyer at once. He told his guest he had to make a phone call, did so from the restaurant booth, then returning to say something urgent had come up, finally left the nonplussed Allison to eat his Poire Belle Hélène alone.

The town hall had told him that Condroyer, Assistant Deputy Mayor, was at Les Sablons worksite, Section Three.

Kidskin boots were not the ideal footwear, but he was stuck with them. Philippe Berg asked for directions when he reached the site, and had to manoeuvre in a hard hat through mud, breeze blocks, huge sections of reinforced concrete, winches and all the other obstacles commonly to be found on a building site.

Condroyer's sexual propensities were well known, and the men had smirked when they told him he was in the steel cabin by the yellow tower crane. But when Philippe arrived and looked in, he was relieved to see that Condroyer had no young company and was on his own, counting some bottles of red wine stacked on a bench.

'Oh, hullo,' he said as Berg entered, 'Reckon fifty will be enough don't you?'

'Couldn't say. What's the party for?' Once again Philippe was irritated over Condroyer's habit of avoiding one's eyes and seeming to look at another person further off.

'Topping-out. Need enough for thirty blokes. Glad to have you join us, my friend.'

Berg ignored the civilities. He said sharply: 'Have you seen the papers, Condroyer?'

'Fifty-two, that's two more for luck. Papers? Oh, the newspapers! Never read the things.'

'Pity, you ought to sometimes,' rapped Berg, increasingly annoyed with the other man's evasive eyes. 'If you got your nose out of your damn magazine and read today's *La Dépêche* you'd find out that Paul Bossis was killed.'

Condroyer's eyes stopped flitting for a moment: 'Paul Bossis killed? W-what . . .'

'That's exactly what I said. Murdered.'

'My God. And you were related I believe, on his mother's side or something like that. Well, that's a shock. Have they got the person who did it?'

'No.'

'Why would anyone want to do that, then?'

Condroyer was still looking at him unswervingly, and this surprised Berg. It was a look of an honest man, genuinely upset at the appalling news. Berg froze, realizing that he had no pretext for being there at all, that he had simply flown into a panic at the restaurant and rushed here to confront this pederast in rubber boots, without a shred of evidence. And why would he need evidence? Evidence of what?

'I've no idea,' he said hoarsely. Berg had come to find out something, but there was nothing to *be* found out, and even if there was he would not be told. White-faced, he realized he had made a mistake, acted on a snatch of conversation he remembered and should have ignored.

To cover his anxiety, he remarked: 'D'you think it was accidental or premeditated?'

The eyes became shifty again: 'How should I know, Berg old chap? Not our business, I'm sure.'

'You're right, but just imagine for a second that they try to pin it on us, the town council I mean.' He was thankful he had at last got it off his chest, and was now even more grateful to hear Condroyer chuckling.

The other handed him a glass: 'And who do you suppose is going to pin it on Monsieur Fournier, First Deputy Mayor if you please? And why not Monsieur Quentin himself, or me, or you Berg? And the next question is why the devil would we want to do that?'

Philippe Berg smiled and tossed his head: 'Why indeed?' He raised his glass: 'Here's health.'

Nevertheless there was no mistaking the snatch of conversation he'd heard between Fournier and a fellow he did not know with a flower in his buttonhole, and who said he thought Bossis was doing an investigation into Les Sablons. Berg had heard it in a corridor at the town hall, and more worryingly neither Fournier nor anyone else had said anything to him about it. Philippe Berg, who detested being kept out of things, instinctively felt he had to know everything that was going on in Chateauvallon.

And that was precisely why he finished his wine in one go, and was on his way to Fournier within minutes.

But in less than that time, Condroyer had been on to Fournier: 'Hullo there Fournier. Condroyer. Just had a visit from Philippe Berg, left here this instant saying he might call in on you . . . Sure it's nice of him, but he seems pretty worked up over this Bossis business in the papers.'

Fournier replied: 'He'll get over it, you know how he is. But I was just leaving so he'll miss me this time.'

And so Philippe learned on arrival at the town hall that Monsieur the First Deputy Mayor was in conference, and had to rush off to Paris immediately afterwards and that no, Monsieur Berg, he would unfortunately not be returning until Monday at the earliest.

At this Berg was more soothed than troubled. It was obvious

that he had not been told about Bossis's investigation for the
simple reason that there was nothing to worry about. He
returned to the office a happier man and took up again with Mr
Allison.

On his way there he chuckled at himself two or three times. He
must really try to take things easier, be less suspicious. He had
been a perfect idiot to imagine that the town's worthies would be
mixed up in a murder. The idea was ridiculous, especially as
Condroyer had been given an honour by Pompidou. Nobody
knew why, but he had been given an honour all the same.

Had Philippe Berg listened in on a phone conversation the following night between Fournier at his home and a fat man and a
thin man in a Toulon bar, he might have chuckled rather less.

Not that it was crystal clear by any manner of means, but it
would have been worth the hearing by the councillor who so
dreaded being out of touch.

'That you, Monsieur? Taunus wanted to give you a little call.'

'Did he get the cheque?'

'All in order, Monsieur. Carnation and me are drinking some of
it now. He's listening in.'

'Glad you're satisfied.'

'Any time, Monsieur,' said Carnation.

'Have a nice holiday, anyway. The official forms will be in the
mail today.'

The fat man took back the receiver and began to speak, but the
line was dead.

Travers, on instructions from Maryse, had meanwhile slept a
couple of hours. Having set the alarm, he checked that it was
5.00 p.m. and boiled himself a couple of eggs, just in case Antonin
Berg should forget to provide him with dinner at La Commanderie. He showered and selected his best suit, a broad check.

He preferred to keep it for big events, because it was the suit he
wore when he called on the delicious Aurore, a stone's throw
from the Place de la Madeleine. He held the post of editor at *Le
Quotidien du Matin*, a struggling Paris daily, for a shorter period
than he had hoped, for the absurd reason that the owner Watre-
pont caught him in bed one afternoon with Aurore, who happened to be his wife.

And now he decided that his pale blue shirt would be the

proper adjunct to this noble relic, along with a dark blue tie. As he completed his preparations with a palmful of hair oil rubbed into his shock of hair, he judged that he could still rate Editor any day of the week.

He was running ahead of schedule and was rather glad the phone rang as he was having a final look round the apartment.

'Favrot,' he heard. 'I've just left police headquarters. Didn't see Nicolo, but Inspector Germain called us in, Edelman and me.'

'So?'

Favrot related an uneventful tale, whose sole interest was the question as to where Travers was at the time of the murder.

'And you told him I was right there, taking it all down.'

'No, I told him you'd get in touch when he found out the time of the murder! I also said he wouldn't get to be Commissaire for a while yet.'

Ten minutes later Travers loped into Les Glycines clinic, and saw the nurse Fernandez coming out of Armand's office.

'*Buenos tardes, senora*, is the boss in?'

She jerked her head, and Travers went in. Armand rose to meet him, informing him at once that Catherine was in better shape. He had put her on a tranquillizer when she arrived, and now she was coming out of it.

'Best thing, doc. So there'll be no after-effects – the baby I mean.'

'Very unlikely. Real toughies, these Kovalics, they'll outlive us all.' Armand became confidential. 'Tell me, Travers, you get on well with my father, I believe.'

'Pretty well.'

He took Travers's arm: 'Can I ask you to make sure he doesn't overdo it on this Bossis campaign, emotionally as well as physically. He's going over the top, and it worries me.'

'Probably take years off him.'

'Possibly, but too much adrenalin at his age can play havoc with the arteries.'

Travers grinned: 'I'll watch he does an eight-hour day and no more. Unless I succumb first to the adrenalin or something else.'

Fernandez let him into Catherine's room. She was sitting up as white as the two puffed-up pillows behind her, and she had her arms slack along the outline of her body. He slunk up on her and she turned her head.

'Oh sod it, I forgot the flowers!' he said, to see if she would respond.

Still woozy, she tried a smile and waved at a large bouquet of roses in an opaque vase. 'Florence Berg sent them, she's nice.'

'Sure is. They smell nice too.'

He could think of nothing to say except how was she, but it stuck in his throat.

After a minute she said flatly: 'I feel dreadful, the way I carried on. Please forgive me. I'm ashamed, I thought you had played me along and knew all the evening.'

'A misunderstanding, forget it.'

'Sit down a bit, and give me a kiss.'

'They told me to keep it short, as you haven't pulled out of it yet, and . . .'

'I'll always pull out of it,' she said, her eyes moist, then: 'I'll never be able to get over this, never. I still can't believe it, they took his life, took him from me.'

He took her limp hand: 'We don't know who they are yet, but you can be sure they'll pay for it. We're all working on it.'

He gave her his handkerchief, and her shoulders shook: 'I'm not even a proper widow, though God knows I feel it, it's the same.'

Travers said: 'It can be arranged.'

She blinked at him: 'I didn't know that.'

'Sure it can, I promise you they can fix it.'

Suddenly she extended both arms and wailed: 'Oh Travers, thank goodness you . . .'

Catherine broke down and he took her head, kissing her brow. His own eyes were smarting, and she seemed to him like a wounded gazelle. A minute later he gently removed her arms and she lay back.

'I'll come again. Every day as long as you're here. I'll bring some flowers.' He made for the door, gave a little wave and was gone. Outside he breathed deeply.

Armand stood at the door to his office: 'How'd you find her.'

'Not much better than I feel,' he said gruffly.

Armand Berg called after him: 'You're off to La Commanderie, I believe. Father told me, he gave us a call asking how she was. If you could just make sure he doesn't drive himself too much. Try and keep him calm when he's speaking to them.'

'Them?'

'He's called a council of war.'

'Well it *is* big stuff.'

66

With this warning still in his ears, Travers was surprised to see Florence on her own. Jeannou conducted him in, and he found her with an arm on the chimney-piece staring at the flames.

She turned and he kissed her hand. Florence gave him a smile that stopped him breathing for a second or two. Antonin's daughter was a beauty in her own right, he decided.

'Catherine's coming round nicely. She was deeply touched, the flowers.'

'A few roses, it was the least one could do.' She moved over to a drinks cabinet and he admired her expensive fuchsia suit. 'A finger of whisky?'

'Five fingers would be better, thanks. My forehead, you know.'

She lifted an eyebrow: 'Father said you hit your windscreen. That's one of the truest fibs I've ever heard.'

'Cross my heart, I'll never think up a truer one.'

'The police told my brother the blood was pouring from you when they got there. Was it Catherine?'

'Only her scissors.'

She laughed gaily, and gave him a look that made him go weak.

Florence handed him his whisky: 'Not one for heroics are you Travers?'

'Never had much practice. Pity she didn't wield a hatchet, I'd have had something to say about that. But tell me, Madame, your brother said this was to be a council of war. Perhaps there's been some mistake, and I shouldn't be here.'

'Father wanted you to come, and so did I. He has something in mind for both of us. There'll be no one else. It's a committee meeting, as they say at the Assemblée.'

'An inner-cabinet meeting?'

'Exactly.' Antonin entered at that moment. 'An inner cabinet, that's right father?'

Berg nodded curtly and took Travers's hand: 'Let me introduce you to the new director of *La Dépêche*.' He indicated Florence with an open hand.

Travers gulped: 'Well, that's a master stroke! My sincerest congratulations, Madame. Your beauty will shine on us like Liberty enlightening Mankind!'

Florence put a finger to her lips: 'Not a word. It's just between us for the moment.'

'But Monsieur Jean-Jacques . . .'

'He doesn't know yet,' Antonin said, easing himself into the sofa facing the log fire. 'It's always the cuckolded who are the last to find out.' His remark was a blend of contempt, bitterness and sadness.

'Really father,' said Florence.

He shifted to indicate that they must get on with their business. Mathilde came in with a trolley loaded with caviar and liver pâté toastlets.

Berg said: 'Nicolo's given me the autopsy results.' He twirled his glass of Chablis, which he had poured after serving the others. 'Two neck vertebra crushed, the cerebellum separated from the quadrigemina on impact.'

Florence tutted, her hand hesitating as it stretched out for a caviar toast.

'He died instantly. In his pocket they found a piece of electric cable.' Travers moved forward. 'You knew that?'

'Nicolo had me in. He showed me the fingerprints and the blood on the end of the cable.'

'Yes, Paul's fingerprints, but the blood wasn't his.'

Florence said: 'That means he used the cable to fight off his attackers. What blood group is it?'

'That's their business, they have analysed it. But, you know, they can usually check a killer's blood group only when he's dead,' Travers said.

He found a salmon sandwich, and had trouble swallowing it. He sipped some Chablis and went on: 'What else did Nicolo tell you, Monsieur?'

'Paul probably saw them before they attacked him, and that was probably why they had to kill him, he said. The official theory at the moment is that this was no premeditated murder, it was meant as a warning and got out of hand. I don't believe a word of it,' Berg said.

'Did he mention that I might be the man they're looking for?'

'You!' cried Florence.

'That's ridiculous,' Berg said. 'They must be out of their minds. He never said anything about that.'

Travers guffawed: 'It was Germain's impression, they wanted to know where I was at the time of the murder.'

'Rubbish,' Florence burst out. 'They'll come up with any nonsense to make it seem that they're making progress. He should be shot.'

'Better do it from the back if you don't want to be knocked out by the *pastis* fumes.'

All three sat there shaking their heads. They chewed away for a while, waiting for the old man to resume. Antonin got up and began pacing short distances to and fro. Travers reflected that, far from 'overdoing' it, Berg was a model of calm. He'd be glad to remain as cool at seventy.

Antonin's voice dropped a little: 'Paul was here to see me a week ago. Sat where you are, Flo. He asked me what he ought to do if he unearthed serious anomalies in connection with the Sablons development scheme. He smelt a rat, nothing definite to my way of thinking or he would have come out with it. But he had a lead. What did you know about that, Travers?'

'Only that the day he died he was due to hand in a first piece on whatever it was to Melchior. I can't say what he planned to write, but I had the impression it was dynamite.'

'Paul told you nothing then?'

'I would not have kept it from you earlier, and wouldn't now, Monsieur.'

Berg leaned forward: 'Now listen Travers, I know your skills, I realize you have a nose for these things, you know what's going on in this town, you can smell it out. That's one reason I am taking you into my confidence tonight. What's more you were a close friend of Paul's. I'm telling you the little I know and I'd like to think you're prepared to reciprocate. In a word, I want you to dig like you've never dug before Travers.'

'Thank you for your trust, Monsieur.' Travers felt uncomfortable seated when his employer stood, and he hoiked himself to his feet. 'When Paul asked your advice a week ago, what did you say?'

Florence butted in: 'Yes, what *did* you say?'

'I told him to watch his step. I also warned him that I would withhold my backing if he went too far.'

Florence jumped to her feet in turn, stood with her fists on her hips, scarlet with anger: 'Well, I like that! You told him to watch his step, so you knew he could walk into a trap. And yet you refused to back him up.'

'Only if he went too far. In that event, there was no justification for us getting involved, either *La Dépêche* or myself, in any scandal he stirred up.'

'What? You left him out on a limb?' Florence chucked the rest of her whisky in the fire, a gesture calculated to show her disgust.

But Berg's retort came like a whip-crack: 'It did not arise! His

69

death has left me no choice, except one: I want the killers. From now on we're into this up to our necks, shit and everything. We're going to break this right open, d'you hear. We're going through with it!' He hesitated and added: 'Provided Madame Le Directeur consents to it.'

Travers watched the adrenalin subside and turned to Florence. 'All right, we'll go through with it,' she said quietly.

'Whatever the consequences?'

'Whatever.'

She went on to ask what gave Paul the idea of delving into Les Sablons. Her father spread his hands, he had no idea.

She turned sharply to Travers. He said: 'A couple of weeks back he asked me casually if I knew anything about two sets of accounts, the principle behind it. And about dummy invoices. I didn't take much notice, and it may not have anything to do with Les Sablons.'

The younger man had seen the next question coming up. He had expected it to be addressed to him, but it was to Florence that Antonin put it; 'In your opinion, Flo, is Quentin involved in this?'

She went white: 'Quentin? Quentin? Why Quentin? Involved in Paul's death? I never heard anything so silly. It's impossible.'

'No, I meant involved in Les Sablons. I meant, supposing that was what Paul had going. Suppose that was why he had to be rubbed out. Les Sablons is a Council project, a huge prestige programme, and it so happens that your pal is mayor of this town.'

'He's not my pal. We've broken it off.'

'I don't care a fig for your private life. I'm not talking about the man you are sleeping with or used to sleep with. I'm referring to the mayor, the member of parliament, the government minister, the man for whom Les Sablons is a veritable coronation.'

There was murder in Flo's eyes: 'You always hated him.'

'True. No special reason, just the smell of him perhaps.'

Florence fought to control her fury: 'You must be on another planet if you can imagine Quentin risking his future in shady deals.'

Antonin's eyes widened in mock-surprise: 'Did I mention anything about shady deals? I merely asked, might he be mixed up in some way?'

'His whole life would be in ruins. He would never take the risk, never consider it worthwhile.'

'My dear girl, I hardly need to remind you that his career is practically over. To put it politely, he's on the way out already. And he might think a property deal a useful way of topping up his retirement pension.'

Florence spun round in exasperation, strode a few yards off and returned with her hands spread in a final appeal for common sense. Travers again admired her impressive beauty, her womanly haunches, her long shapely legs. The skirt had ridden up on one side to reveal a smooth round knee, and he admired that too.

'You're being grotesque,' she snapped. 'How would Paul Bossis know Quentin was implicated. Travers, how would he know?'

The journalist was caught with a pâté toast entering his mouth. He pulled it back and observed that, according to rumour, Monsieur Quentin had lost favour in high places.

'Lost favour with the Elysée?' Florence demanded.

'The Elysée wouldn't say.'

'And would he be out of favour?'

Antonin cut in: 'The Presidency may know more about him than we do.' He was delighted to see Florence open-mouthed at this – Berg detested Quentin for his *affaire* with her.

'I still think it's bunk. At all events, *La Dépêche* will keep out of it. Don't count on *La Dépêche* to publish that kind of gutter talk.'

Antonin countered: 'I am still the proprietor, Florence, and I can claim my right to do an article from time to time.'

'You'd drag Quentin through the mud?'

Old Berg had a cigar between his lips: 'You wouldn't even notice it happening, Flo. Diary pieces are very useful for probing the ground, you know. We can wheel out the guillotine later.'

'Huh,' his daughter said turning to Travers. 'Nice job for you, turning over the dungheap.'

'It's not our fault, Madame, if he's not as sweet as new-mown hay.' He liked the old man's line of reasoning, but he liked his daughter's pluck, so he added: 'But we'd prefer to keep our hands clean too, that's right, isn't it, Monsieur Berg?'

Berg choked and came out of it chuckling: 'I suppose so, Travers, I suppose so.'

Two days after that, Florence dressed in black was pulling on her second glove at the apartment she had in town, when the phone rang. She cursed as she was running late already for Paul Bossis's funeral.

It was Quentin.

'I'm sorry to butt in like this. Just managed to catch you. I learned that you were back in the apartment.' He paused for a second. 'I expect you know why I'm calling.'

She grasped the nettle: 'Listen Quentin, it's not official so keep it to yourself. My father has given me the top job on *La Dépêche*, but he is holding onto the reins until further notice. Which means I am not responsible in any way for that article he wrote. I had no power to stop it before the print room.'

It was if she had not spoken: 'But what the devil's got into you? What is the meaning of those insinuations against the town hall over the Bossis case? Virtually accusations, veiled I'm sure, but as clear as daylight. What's the idea?'

Florence let out a sigh: 'I know, I know. But someone bumped off his journalist and left him in his pond. And the body was Gabrielle's boy. There's no stopping him now, he's shooting at anything that moves.'

'Nicely put, but why at me? All right, so he doesn't like me, never did. That's his problem. But that's not sufficient reason. Believe me, my town hall's under perfect control, not a paper clip unaccounted for. To suggest there's funny business going on behind my back makes me look a perfect nincompoop.'

'It's happened before,' she said softly. Then sensing he had jumped a foot in the air, she added: 'But take it easy, I believe you, I believe you.'

'You're most kind. Er . . . tell me, but you don't have to if you don't want to, wherever did your father pick up fag-ends like that?'

Florence glanced at her watch: 'Look Quentin, if they're fag-ends, what's all the fuss about?'

He was slow in answering: 'Some of the mud always sticks, and you know that. And I don't want too much of it showing right now.'

'You mean . . .'

'Nothing, nothing important . . . Flo, you still there?'

She remembered her father's theory during the inner-cabinet meeting: 'I suppose it's true, you might resign from the Ministry.' She heard him breathing hard. 'Or you could be asked to resign. Is that why you don't want any mud your way right now, Quentin? Are you in trouble with the Government?'

'Listen here, Flo,' he shouted, 'I've got trouble like everybody else, but it's nothing to do with the tittle-tattle your father's coming out with!'

In the pause that followed, she recalled her father's words, that the Presidency might know more about Quentin than they did at La Commanderie.

Florence was sorry for him, for old times' sake, but her comment was without emotion: 'I do sympathize. I do hope whatever it is will blow over quickly. And now, Quentin, I must fly. Paul's funeral. Are you attending?'

'And meet up with your father? No thank you.'

The funeral was to start from La Commanderie, and at the wheel of the car on her way there Florence was puzzled as to why she had toughened up towards Quentin at the end of the phone call. As she approached the estate she concluded that it was because he had not been frank with her. She would have responded had he opened up his heart to her, but there was no reason why he should have now. They were through, were they not? He had simply phoned her to see what he could find out.

If it were really true that he was being edged out of the Government, and after all Quentin had admitted things were not going well for him, then there might indeed be a link with Les Sablons. She realized that she was starting to believe in her father's hypothesis. The phone conversation seemed to herald a battle between two people who were now as strangers. Florence realized too that her jaw was clenched tight. The reason could be a new resolve to avenge the extinction of a young life, or the bitter aftermath of a love affair that had turned sour. It was a case of either, or, or both.

Albertas Kovalic was at the funeral too. He watched the coffin being lowered, from behind a large vertical gravestone a safe twenty yards distant.

'It was a big crowd,' he told his wife in his gravelly voice. 'The family all turned out, the place was swarming with journalists and cameras and the rest, and bigshots by the dozen. All for that dirty little squirt.'

Kovalic's acrimony went deeper than ever on learning how Catherine had been 'felled as though hit by a thunderbolt', an expression he didn't care to analyse.

From his inside pocket he pulled out the copy of *La Dépêche* he had picked up on his way back, delighted to see the fight building up between old Berg and Quentin. The rats were eating each other, it always happened in the end.

'Did you stay to the end?' his wife asked.

'Huh, to present my heartfelt sympathy? Huh!'

Marie-Lou wept like Mary Magdalene at the churchyard, and nobody failed to notice it. But they were tears of anger, and only she and Julien's wife, Thérèse, knew it.

Two days earlier they had had a colossal row when Thérèse told Antonin she couldn't possibly attend the funeral after the scrap she'd had with Catherine and Emilie on the night of the reception.

'What's that? She called Catherine a gypsy? At my reception? Right.'

And when Antonin Berg said 'right', it could only mean trouble. He had called on Marie-Lou while she was in her bath, and had marched into the steam to dictate an apology she would sign and send to Catherine Kovalic. She protested that she could not remember the incident but he ordered her to hold her tongue and get pen and paper. He stood over her at her desk as she wrote the note, shivering in the nude.

'Come on, you snotty-nosed little bitch, get this down: "My dear Catherine".'

'I can't.'

'"My Dear Catherine, I dare to hope that my presence at Paul's graveside will cause no offence to you . . ." No, start again: "My dear Catherine, I am writing to ask you to accept my humblest apologies. My behaviour was inexcusable . . ."'

'No, I can't!'

'Get it down, for God's sake: "I dare to hope that my presence at Paul's graveside will cause you no offence . . ."'

'Never, I won't do it.'

'"Your's affectionately". Now sign it. Sign it!'

As the spadefuls of earth dropped onto the coffin, she cursed everybody with witch-like fury: 'I hope he drops dead within a week, and Thérèse, and Catherine. To hell with the lot of them.'

To make matters worse, Catherine came up to her as the crowd began dispersing: 'Thanks for your letter, Marie-Lou, I was very touched.'

'Don't talk about it . . .'

'And for your tears over my poor Paul.'

Marie-Lou would have wrung her neck there and then for two pins. Instead, she took her husband's arm, urging him away. She had spent the past two days in bed, recounting the letter-writing scene with the old man over and over again. Jean-Jacques had no doubt his life would hardly be worth living for at least two weeks. She could think only of how long it would be before Catherine joined her beloved Paul six feet under the ground.

Antonin and Gilbert left the cemetery arm in arm. Florence had seen Marie-Lou turn away brusquely, and joined Catherine.

'Very impulsive, my sister-in-law.' Florence had heard every word of the exchange, and in other circumstances would have burst out laughing. Thérèse had told her everything, having learned about the letter from Antonin.

'Impulsive?' said Catherine wide-eyed. 'I thanked her for writing to me, and then . . .'

'. . . she shied off, I know. I don't think she likes being thanked. Probably embarrasses her. Generosity comes so naturally to her that she is surprised when people remind her of it.'

She clenched her teeth, to keep a straight face.

The family shook hands with everyone at the entrance to the estate, amid tears in profusion. Armand and Julien stood either side of Gilbert Bossis. Florence stayed with Catherine who was stiff and flushed.

Philippe Berg was a curious sight. His eyes were almost closed as if he were either drunk or deep in some meditation of his own devising. His wife Emilie, who wore mauve, could only surmise that he too was overcome at young Paul's death.

Then people began driving off or walking back home. Florence asked Catherine if she would care for a lift. Paul's red Alfa was still in the police yard where a pair of experts were examining every centimetre inside and out.

'Thank you so much, Madame Berg, but Travers is taking care of me.'

'I'm glad. But Catherine, I would like to see you again soon, so that we can have a little chat.'

'I'd love that.'

'I'd like us to talk over your position, you know what I mean, the legal aspects. I believe I'm right in saying you would be interested in a form of marriage *post mortem*. Awful expression, but it's the technical one that's used. It is possible.'

'That would be wonderful,' Catherine squeaked, weeping again. 'Thank you so much!'

'Promise me you'll give me a call one evening soon.'

'I certainly will, and thank you.'

Travers drove up alongside as they were saying goodbye: 'Hullo Florence. Tell me, why didn't Thérèse turn up?'

'She was unwell,' was the quiet answer.

Thérèse had in fact been scared stiff to meet Marie-Lou, and had asked Antonin if she needed to attend. The old man wouldn't have been surprised to see Marie-Lou throw Thérèse into the grave with Paul, he had told Florence.

Recalling this, Florence was seized with a fit of giggling, and sped to her own car, stifling it. Then, as suddenly, she felt weepy thinking of Quentin. A name once adored, and perhaps now signifying an enemy for life.

Her giggles stemmed from nothing but her own desperate emotions. A pall of solitude descended on her as she eased off the handbrake.

Travers and Nicolo seemed to be circling each other like a couple of Alsatian dogs.

This time it was Travers who moved first. In the car, Catherine had jumped in her seat and told him she remembered something about the piece of electric cable. When Paul took it from his leather jacket, he had quipped that it was 'dynamite', she recalled. Travers communicated this information to Nicolo. But once again he ended up slamming Nicolo's door on his way out.

And now he heard Catherine on the phone as he let himself into her place: 'Yes, that'll be perfect, I'm looking forward to it. "Bye Florence. Yes, it's urgent. Tomorrow then.'

'Florence?' he queried.

'In person.'

'You've made a hit there.' Catherine nodded eagerly. She seemed to be perking up, got some of her colour back, he thought.

'Anyhow, Nicolo played it down. There were bits of cable lying around all over the place, kids played football with them, and what kind of a clue was a bit of cable anyway! I told him the cable led to Les Sablons, and he had the cheek to say that was convenient to us because it brought in the town hall, and we wanted the mayor's guts for garters. I should read the papers, he said, especially articles by Antonin Berg.'

'So what happens next?'

'The man is a cretin. I won't bore you with the dismal details, but his main argument is that the top priority is to discover *who* killed Bossis, whereas mine is that if we find out who *ordered* the killing, the rest's a piece of cake. Either he thought I was being laughably perverse, or else he doesn't want to know.'

'Know?'

'Who's behind the murder. I'm dreadfully sorry you've got to hear all this.'

Catherine refilled his coffee cup: 'Its for Paul, and for me, and our baby. Do you think Nicolo's got something to hide as well?'

'I don't think anything, anything at all. Tell me . . .'

'Yes?'

'It's none of my business, but what's urgent about you seeing Florence Berg?'

'I had a visitor,' she replied with a quick smile. 'Lanky youth with a saxophone dangling by his side like a rifle or something.'

'Teddy Kovalic, your cousin.'

'That's him. I thought at first he was merely being curious, and he kept shifting about saying he wanted to leave home and get into a rock group. I was pretty sure he was trying to find out something. But it turns out he really does want to do a bunk like I did. Told me to be careful.'

'Why's that?'

'Grüber.'

'That monkey Albertas wanted you to marry?'

'Yes, the owner of Galeries Grüber, the furniture store. The guy with the pear-shaped bonce. He turned up at the Kovalic place, and said he was prepared to marry me and that includes the baby. My dad opened a bottle of Slivovitz for him and said he had saved the family honour. Teddy said that was all he heard. Later the two men got into a huddle in one corner.

Travers stared at the carpet: 'What's scaring you?'

'I can't say.'

'After all, they can't actually kidnap you.'

Catherine sighed and shrugged: 'I'm not sure. All this squabbling and posturing and feuding and whatnot. What's honour when all's said and done? I'm afraid of myself, that's nearer the

77

truth. I could sort of give up and become weak and poverty-stricken and finally yield to them, go back into the tribe, accepting God knows what blackmail. That is why I called Florence. She had already planned to have me for a chat about my legal position, so I thought I'd ask her about this new development right away.'

Travers got slowly to his feet: 'Sounds like sense. But I can't see you yielding to anyone, you're as hard as nails if you want to be. You do as you see fit, and after all, Florence Berg knows what she's doing. She's the expert. And as he opened the door: 'Even so, Catherine, you'd better have this door strengthened, fix stronger locks. You never know.'

Travers had orders from Antonin Berg to dig out the truth, and that is exactly what he meant to do.

He and Favrot turned up at the town hall and, in their capacity as residents of Chateauvallon, demanded to consult a document 'concerning the future plans for the town', as permitted by law.

The receptionist asked what it was, they told her it was the main specification for Les Sablons, and she practically fell off her chair. She chatted over the intercom, and told the two citizens with the manner of a dowager duchess that the specification was being worked on, that the public could request to see it nevertheless, in writing, provided the reason for the request was stated, and that a reply would be forthcoming in two weeks' time at the most.

Travers gazed upon the mouse-like face as if he had just fallen in love with the girl, and declared: 'We're in a bit of a hurry, dear. Who's working on it? I expect I know him.'

'The deputy mayor for development.'

'Ah, old Condroyer. Fourth floor, unless he's moved.'

'I was told to send you packing, but what you actually do is your own business.'

The fourth-floor usher returned from Condroyer's office to say that Monsieur Condroyer did not recall arranging an interview with the two gentlemen from *La Dépêche* and would be grateful if they would be so kind as to call back tomorrow. The usher had the air of a Vatican Guard turning away a Bulgarian waving a revolver, but Travers and Favrot growled 'sod that', pushed him aside and strode into Condroyer's office.

Whereupon Condroyer leapt to his feet shouting: 'Will you

please leave at once, you have no right in here.' Travers declared that he would leave over Condroyer's dead body.

'Why does *La Dépêche* want the spec. for Les Sablons? It has no reason . . .'

'Not *La Dépêche*, Monsieur Condroyer, I do. In the name of the law!' said Travers.

The deputy mayor suggested he might find the simplified leaflets more useful. They contained artists' impressions and photos of the site and everything. Travers said he wanted the spec., the one drawn up by the architect and approved by the town council – the one with the rubber stamp on it.

'But it'll be meaningless to you, Monsieur Travers. It's highly specialized with figures and calculations and dimensions and everything. It weighs three kilos!'

'We'll carry it between us, and with you sitting on top of it if you don't watch out,' Travers growled in his best Humphrey Bogart imitation. 'It's your baby, the spec., so I'll look after it like it was my own. Now listen Condroyer, I want that spec. and if you don't get it within sixty seconds I'll pull your head off.' Still Condroyer hesitated, and Travers added: 'I'm not asking for the address of your favourite brothel, Condroyer, which is Chez Lulu in Rue Descartes. I just want the spec.'

Condroyer went white, and ordered the usher to set up the two visitors in the library with Dossier 409.

When this was completed and they were staring at the three kilos, Favrot said: 'Condroyer looked like he was going to faint at the end.'

His colleague said: 'Because of the file or the Lulu thing. Or both. Condroyer's in love with the barman, Robert, and has his own lace knickers, bra, suspender belt and net stockings kept on the premises. Very particular whom they let in at Lulu's place. You wouldn't stand a chance, Favrot, with your bandy legs.'

Three hours, one for each kilo, they worked on the specification. It was a raw unpleasant 8.00 p.m. when they emerged from the town hall and fought their way on foot to the office through blustery wind.

Not a word was exchanged between them until they were safely in Travers's cubby-hole, where he hauled three dozen or so sheets of notes from his pocket. Favrot did likewise, and they contemplated the pile of scribbles, tables, quotations and other

79

details they had picked out.

Favrot said: 'It's as clear as mud to me.'

Travers: 'Not to worry, all this stuff means something to someone. And they'll enlighten us. But we've found out one interesting thing – you noticed the design office.'

'What about it? There was a design office mentioned.'

'Exactly, Favrot, there *was* a design office. But there ain't one now and hasn't been one for six months.'

'Why's that?'

'As Proust would say, search me. But it's a lead and I'm going to work on it. I've got a little birdie I have to see, but you go off to beddybyes dreaming of all those little noughts and crosses you've taken down from the spec. That's how Einstein worked out $E = mc$ squared, and you can't get much simpler than that.'

'He must have been a relative of yours.'

But Travers was already on his way. Favrot, whose success with the ladies could be counted on the fingers of one foot, gave a shrug. Nice guy Travers, a nice guy, but cock-happy just the same.

Favrot was wrong this time. Travers's destination was Catherine's apartment.

She was already snuggling down in bed when he rang the bell, and it was in her nightdress that she peeked through the spy-hole in the door and perceived a large wet head outside stuck on two legs in a crumpled suit.

'Travers! What's happened?'

'Battery's flat, I left my raincoat at the office. They haven't been on at you? The family, Grüber?'

Catherine turned her back and fetched a dressing gown which she slipped into. She then extracted an envelope from a pocket, removed a cheque and handed it to Travers.

'Fifty thousand francs – Antonin Berg!'

She pouted: 'Not even a card.' She mimicked Berg: 'Your boyfriend's dead, here's fifty thou' in compensation.'

'He's thinking of your baby.'

'It won't be his grandchild.'

'He's acting like it is. Trying to rival Gilbert, maybe. With a Berg, you never know what's behind it. Paul was Gabrielle's boy, so the baby's his property to his way of thinking.'

'But without even a note . . .'

Travers chuckled: 'Fifty smackers is fifty smackers. If you're so hoity-toity you can send it back. But you'd be well advised to think twice before you upset the old man. I know, I work for him!'

They sat down and Travers came to the point: 'Favrot and I have been studying some documents at the town hall. Paul referred to 'dynamite' in reference to that piece of cable. Well, there are some screwy things in the main specification for Les Sablons, and I'm going to get an expert onto it. The whole business is starting to smell distinctly fishy.'

Catherine put a hand on his: 'Why don't you let it drop.'

'But we want to get to the bottom of Paul's murder.'

'Not at any price. You could be next on the list!'

Travers said: 'Ha! It's a long list and there are plenty before me at *La Dépêche*.'

He grabbed the phone and dialled: 'Good evening, have I the honour of speaking to the star reporter Patrick Edelman?'

A slurred voice growled: 'Ah, the dreaded Travers. You have merely had the honour of waking me up, you bastard.'

Travers said: 'Seriously. I know you've got an early job at Angers, and I'll be up to my neck as well. Will you be free late on the evening after next?'

'If it's to see Condroyer doing a strip-tease, OK. But it'd better be good.'

'I see Favrot's filled you in. I want us to take a mosey round Les Sablons.'

'What's wrong with Favrot. He's the one losing sleep on those hieroglyphics?'

'No, this time I want someone with no brains and plenty of brawn.'

'You never did understand karate, old boy. You can count on me.'

Travers replaced the receiver: 'Didn't seem too keen on the idea.'

'Nor am I,' said Catherine angrily. 'You're completely mad. It's you who wants your head tested.'

There was a sharp double knock at the door. They both looked at their watches. Ten minutes to midnight. As one, they glanced at the window pane where the rain was trying to get in too.

Travers went to the door: 'Who is it?'

'Armand Berg.' Travers let him in. 'Sorry to call late like this. I'm on my way back from La Commanderie, and saw the light on.

Just wanted to see how you were, Catherine.'

'How very kind of you, Doctor. I'm quite well, thank you.'

Armand addressed Travers: 'Well nurse, is the patient taking her tablets like I ordered?'

'If you look around you'll discover she hasn't even got them from the chemist's, doc.'

'Tomorrow,' Catherine said quickly. 'I promise I'll get them.'

Armand grew serious: 'It's mainly for the baby, you must get into shape now quickly.'

The visitor declined Catherine's offer of whisky and coffee: 'I still have a call to make. My sister Florence has some people to dinner, and I promised I'd go and throw them out. Catherine, make sure you take the Sargenor and the magnesium, if nothing else.'

In silence they heard him clump down the stairs and drive off.

'*Adiós*, bedtime for me too. You wouldn't have an old brolly to lend me?'

Catherine fetched Paul's raincoat.

'Oh I couldn't . . .'

She held it out for him and gave him a friendly push towards the door.

'Armand Berg didn't look too good,' were his last words.

'He looked a bit woolly.'

They had whispered almost, and neither of them cared to analyse the reason. Or to wonder if there was more than one.

'Monsieur Fournier? It's Condroyer.'

'Condroyer! But it's the middle of the night . . .'

'I've been trying to get you for three hours.'

'I went to the pictures. What's the matter?'

'Two blokes from *La Dépêche*, one of them Travers, spent today in the library going through the file on Les Sablons. Went away loaded with notes, pocketsful!'

'Why the hell did you let 'em?'

'Calm down. There was nothing I could do. It's the law: "Any citizen . . ."'

'OK OK, don't rub it in. I knew that when your mother was in nappies. Never mind that now, I've got news for you too. Better get over here quick.'

Fournier stood waiting for Condroyer behind the wrought iron gate with its opaque glass. His was one of those old family residences that abound throughout provincial France. Neat, well-built but costly to heat. The owner opened the door immediately Condroyer slammed the garden gate and began running head down through the rain. They did not shake hands, and he led Condroyer straight into the cosy living room. Not for the first time, his visitor wondered how much this little lot would make in Paris: chairs and chests and sideboard from a century and more ago, eighteenth-century paintings. Fournier went for the real thing, a few good items in preference to a clutter of second rate stuff. He also liked gambling and women, but enjoyed them only in Paris. His wife had died five years earlier, and he cultivated an austere image in the town he had the honour to serve. Aged fifty or so, he had long legs, a short body and a narrow head. He assumed his duties with appropriate haughtiness.

'Dreadfully sorry to keep you up, Monsieur Fournier.'

'I couldn't sleep in any case. And when you hear what I have to say, you'll feel even more haggard.' He went over to the telephone, and flicked a switch. 'Listen to this call from Toulon.' He sat down, not bothering to cover his long white legs with his dressing gown.

The recorder played back: 'Monsieur Fournier, is that you? Machefer here, I have Gamel with me.'

Fournier saw Condroyer's eyebrows go up and said quickly: 'Know them?'

''Course I do, they looked after Bossis.'

The machine went on: 'You taking us for a ride or something, Monsieur Fournier? We got newspapers down here too, you know. Our little incident's making headlines in the national press. Even *Nice-Matin* is carrying articles by Antonin Berg. We never asked for this kind of free publicity in the contract. Just a five-minute job nobody'd notice, that's what it was. Looks like we could be wearing bracelets, if you don't watch out, Monsieur Fournier. Humiliating for a couple of smart professionals like us . . .'

Fournier jumped up and stopped the tape. He poured two glasses of brandy, his hand shaking.

Condroyer said: 'What's this about professional guards, what are you getting at?'

'You've forgotten already? We officially recommended them as guards at Toulon Arsenal. It's a hide-out, you might say. I told them they could go over the border into Spain with their 500,000 francs, if they got nervous. Here's what they said.'

The tape resumed: 'Bugger Spain! We could be extradited in hours, and what would you do?'

Fournier stopped it again, and swallowed his brandy. The other man had downed his in one gulp.

'They want another five hundred smackers,' Fournier said. 'And quick.'

'And if we don't cough up, it's curtains for us. What did you tell them?'

'That I understood perfectly, but they would have to wait a bit. And d'you know what he said? "Right, we'll wait, but we'll wait at Chateauvallon.'''

Condroyer jerked his glass for more brandy: 'Well?'

'We've got to head them off!'

'Head 'em off?'

'You know what I mean.'

'S-sure,' said Condroyer. But it was late, he was tired and had two brandies inside him. He was sure of nothing, and added: 'I'm sure you can handle it, dear chap.' He wasn't even sure what he meant by that.

Condroyer hated all these intrigues, especially when they went wrong. Crouched behind the wheel of his car with the rain hammering on the roof, he felt sick and lonely. It was too late even to seek consolation in Robert's arms. Besides Robert would touch him for another few hundred francs, that was certain. Lugubriously, he pictured his modest fortune draining away, five per cent at a time until he had nothing left. His mouth and nose and eyebrows puckered up a little more and he resolved to keep his money, come what may. These were hard times and he was getting on in years. He reflected no longer, he would leave it till he could think it out properly. In a gesture of defiance, he went straight through a red light on his way back to a cold bed.

Armand Berg had embroidered on the truth to Catherine. There was nobody with Florence, who was reading in bed.

She jumped on hearing the bell, then relaxed as she recognized Armand's 'code'. Something had come up, and she ran to let her brother in.

They embraced quickly and he told her. Father had been spitting blood. Mathilde had found out two days ago, but had hidden the soiled handkerchiefs and napkins, even burned some of them. He had tried to keep it quiet, but you can't get rid of blood stains that easily, Mathilde had to confess finally.

'I went to see him this evening and they were both there, he and Gilbert, watching a film on Gabrielle as usual, arguing about it as they always do. I watched the film too, right to the finish, listening to father coughing into a handkerchief, trying to pretend it was just a fit of coughing. Then Gilbert went up and we were alone. I took the handkerchief from him. I told him he needed attention, showed him the blood. He told me not to fuss, said he'd cough if he wanted to, it was normal at his age to cough a bit. Just like a kid. I said we'd discuss it properly the next day, and he threw the handkerchief into the fire.'

Armand and Florence held the whisky she had poured them, but neither of them drank.

'It wouldn't be cancer, would it?'

'I'm afraid it looks like it. It'll need some biopsies, cutting tissues and analysing them. He probably knows what he's got, but he'd never allow himself to enter the clinic. Antonin Berg does not have cancer, he'll say. And that'll be that.'

Florence took a sip at last: 'I'll have a word with him.'

Not the next night, but the night after that, two intruders scaled the fencing and jumped down into the building site.

There had been no rain for thirty-six hours, but by the light of strategically-placed lamps, large puddles shone between the concrete and steel skeletons that would one day become Les Sablons. Thirty minutes went by.

In jerkins, jeans and trackshoes the men were now stepping carefully between obstacles, back towards the fencing. Travers and Edelman paused for a moment to get their bearings.

And then a dog barked, followed by another two. Their handlers shouted.

'Rex, at'em boy. Sultan, Cosaque! Go find'em, go find'em!'

Edelman crouched, but Travers said: 'Alsatians. Gotta run for it. Don't worry about noise, they can see us already.'

The two journalists stumbled to the fencing, got over and landed flat on their faces in the mud the other side just as the dogs reached the perimeter. There were three of them. Then three shots split the air.

'Long 22s,' Edelman stated, as the dogs scratched at the

fencing, growling and yelping frantically. He and Travers crawled a few feet on all fours then got up and ran zig-zagging as two further shots rang out. One of the guards was in the roadway now, and he fired.

'Bastards, they aren't allowed . . .' Edelman could get no further.

'Save your breath. Don't lose the cable.'

They rounded a bend and were hidden behind a mound.

'The car's gone.' Edelman croaked.

'There!'

Travers lunged at the door and flung himself behind the wheel. He was in first gear by the time Edelman fell in beside him.

'Four of them,' Edelman said, looking back.

Favrot was waiting for them. He said nothing, handing them hot rum drinks.

'Gave you quite a run for it,' he said as the others scuffed their way to his armchairs, leaving little clods of mud in their wake.

Edelman threw the piece of cable on the table and they all looked at it grinning. Edelman said: 'To think we came through artillery fire for that.'

'They fired on you?' Favrot exclaimed.

'What else? Those boys don't keep their guns in a glass case,' Travers growled. 'What's the thickness, Favrot?'

He read from his notes, citing the specification: 'The nine power supply cables shall be plastic-sheathed, Castaing in type, the sheathing not less than six millimetres thick for a total length of 9.193 metres . . .'

Favrot: 'Are you kidding? This is two millimetres. Must cut the cost by half!'

Travers: 'The Castaing sheathing is costed at thirty-eight francs per metre, the spec. says.'

Favrot: 'Length about ten kilometres, let's say 400,000 francs. So they took two-hundred grand as commission! If they did that with everything, they'll soon be setting up their own bank.'

'So?'

'So there'll be sheafs of phoney invoices lying around somewhere.'

'Yep,' said Travers, stretching. 'We'll get to them later. What intrigues me right now is that, if this stuff's only two millimetres thick, it ain't Castaing sheathing. Which means somebody else made it. Who?'

Edelman: 'And guess who's going to find out?'

Travers: 'You've got three days, my friend. A good man like you will take half the time.'

Edelman: 'What I do for love . . .'

Travers swallowed a second drink: 'That's what Paul was on to. But I've got this too, Paul's, a notebook.' He handed it to Edelman: 'It's in code.'

Favrot: 'That looks like the same code Paul and I used. We left each other messages, confidential stuff we didn't want J-J Berg to know about. Leave it with me, I'll see if I can work it out. We're into this up to our necks, and frankly I reckon we're going to need help from now on. Someone in the building trade.'

Travers snapped his fingers: 'I think I've just the bloke.'

He and Edelman left. They went past Florence's block and he was surprised to see her light still on. He was tempted to call in for a whisky to wash down Favrot's gut-rot, but thought better of it. Besides Edelman was practically slumping over the wheel.

Travers would been surprised to learn that Florence's caller was Catherine Kovalic.

Travers' 'building bloke' was none other than Julien Berg. But it was not until mid-afternoon that he could get to the sawmill.

The car felt fresher than he did with its new battery, and fresher than Gilbert Bossis, who walked rather unsteadily out of a small house marked 'Office'.

Gilbert, wearing black, looked bowed, but made an effort to perk up when he saw the newsman: 'Amazing. Austrian customers for Julien. They've been hanging about for two hours, and the idiot's nowhere to be seen. I was here purely by chance, but I don't know a word of German.'

'You could have said *Guten Tag*.'

'Oh I did, but that won't book any orders.'

They shook hands at last, and Travers said: 'Er . . . the idiot, Monsieur Bossis, where would I be likely to find him?'

The old man drew himself up and pointed with an outstretched hand to a vast hangar about a hundred yards off: 'That's where he is with Shakespeare and Company. Mustn't disturb him, he says, meantime the timber business goes to rack and ruin. So sad, Monsieur Travers, a promising youngster straight out of the Ecole Centrale. Not a thing he doesn't know about public works, electronics, computers, engineering and the rest. But he's the artistic type.' Bossis raised his eyes to heaven and began stalking off.

'Monsieur Bossis, perhaps its premature, but I think the net is starting to close in on Paul's killers.'

The older man looked vaguely at Travers and said in a confidential tone: 'Much more of this and I might begin hitting out meself. Must go now, young man, got to see Catherine.'

Travers was taken aback and mumbled: 'Give her my regards.' He stood for a while wondering what he was missing.

Catherine Kovalic gave a hand to Gilbert Bossis as they squirmed their way out of the low-slung taxi that set them down at the Law Courts. Inside, they wandered about until they found the door marked 'Record Office'. Catherine took a sheet of paper from Gilbert and knocked. They went in and handed it to the clerk.

If justice is blind, its clerks are dumb, and this man glumly took them along a corridor, down an iron staircase into the court entrails and into an almost empty garage where a few neon tubes presided over the dust. A second clerk wordlessly surged forth from behind a pillar and read the sheet of paper while his colleague went back up the staircase. Number two functionary then ordered them to wait while he disappeared into the depths of the garage.

'It's like something out of an eighteenth-century *Star Wars*,' Catherine giggled. 'Relax, Monsieur Bossis, you're squeezing my arm so hard its going numb.'

Her last words were drowned by the growling of a car engine, and Bossis senior gripped harder. Paul's red Alfa appeared and his father shut his eyes tight. The man pulled up before them and got out.

'It's all there inside,' he stated, 'I mean everything that was in it.'

'In it?' Gilbert mumbled.

Catherine saw the clerk about to read out a list and hurriedly said: 'There won't be any need to . . .'

But the man was only doing his duty, and he darned well meant to do it: 'One pair of gloves, one pair of sun-glasses, six road maps, one lighter, one white scarf, one fire-extinguisher, one tennis raquet . . . Will you sign, please, the three copies, thank you that will be all.'

Catherine took the wheel, leaving the fellow wagging his head.

Funny people, didn't have much to say for themselves. Most folk are pleased to get their car back. Takes all sorts . . .

Gilbert told her he'd find his own way back, but she insisted on taking him.

A grey figure, he sat humbly in the passenger seat with a vacant expression on his face. Catherine herself was trembling as she turned the wheel that Paul had handled only a short while ago.

'I spent the night with Florence,' she said to break the silence. 'It was really too late for me to go back to my place. She has a super apartment.' The old chap could have been deaf. 'She's going to be my counsel, and won't ask a *sou* for it. Said she'd do it for Paul.'

At last he woke up: 'Counsel? Ah yes, what for?'

'It's a bit complicated, but she says the killers will have to pay damages sooner or later, and that I should waste no time bringing a civil action. Of course, we weren't actually married but that's another side of it. There are procedures for that, and it will need proof of Paul's fatherhood. That can be done, Florence said, and she mentioned a *post mortem* marriage too. Then I'll have the right to . . . to . . .' She had to stop. Gilbert had his hands over his face and was muttering *'post mortem'* repeatedly.

Florence had said many women took advantage of this during the Algerian War. She also warned her that her child would never forgive her if she failed to act now. Catherine repeated this to Gilbert.

Bossis laid his head back, and Catherine said: 'I'm sorry, Monsieur Bossis, but I wanted to find out what you thought. What should I do, Gilbert?'

He whispered: 'Exactly what Florence advises.'

They drew up outside the main gate at La Commanderie.

'Well, I'll just come in and call a taxi,' Catherine said.

'But you'll take the car, won't you? It's yours.'

'What! But it's almost new, you could get quite a lot for it.'

Bossis went crimson: 'For any fool to smash it up? I'd sooner drive it over a cliff myself.'

She kicked herself for the gaffe: 'All right, Gilbert, I'll take it.' She lowered her eyes and drove up to the steps. Gilbert got out, climbed them slowly and then turned to see she was still there in the car.

'Come on, then,' he said. 'I think we've earned a drink.'

They had coffee and biscuits, as it happened. They were in the main lounge, and kept hearing old Berg cough.

'Antonin,' said Gilbert, 'that's Antonin. Touch of bronchitis he can't throw off. A bad thing at his age.'

Berg entered, and Catherine took her leave, losing no time on the drive down to the main gate.

'Paul's car is that?'

'Yes, I let her have it.' He waited for Antonin to ask how things went at the law courts, but in vain. Gilbert knew him only too well by now, his egocentric world from which he ruled the affairs of mankind. But that was not fair, for Antonin had improved lately, had sworn to avenge Paul's death. The trouble was that mourning made one almost hate others because their sorrow did not go as deep. 'You're coughing better,' he remarked ironically.

But Antonin was examining a cheque, the very one he had sent her. She had placed it among the coffee cups.

'Huh, she's just left it. I sent it to her. Doesn't want my money then!'

'Fifty thousand, you sent her that?'

'Don't shout. You've just given her an Alfa Romeo, and she's accepted it.'

'That's not the point. I don't suppose you even spoke to her before you sent the cheque.'

'Didn't get much chance.'

Gilbert warmed to the argument. 'A Kovalic. You never could accept a Kovalic for Paul.'

'That's no reason to refuse my cheque. It was for the kid, and the kid is Gabrielle's grandchild. So it's mine too.'

'Yours? Have it your own way. I'll leave you to your senile fantasies.' He strode off.

'And I'll allow you your puerile vanities!' Antonin boomed as the door closed.

It had been another of those silly clashes that might be more serious than they seemed, Berg reflected. They had been friends for years, but they were hurting each other more and more these days. Perhaps they had been perpetuating a myth that was, in the final analysis, a convenient hypocrisy. He hoped not, the thought saddened him.

'So he left just like that, lock, stock and barrel, and checked in at the Hotel des Messageries,' Florence said angrily to her father.

90

'You had a row, I take it, with Gilbert.'

She still had her topcoat round her shoulders. It was late the same evening, and her father was lying back on his bed in the grey quilted dressing gown.

'Yes, we had words. Just words. But I had the impression they came from deep down. We quarrelled, yes.'

'But how did it start?' Florence said in a hopeless kind of voice.

'You're too young to understand,' he said. 'So you wanted to see him?'

'Yes and no. Catherine told him I was acting for her, and I wondered what he thought, that was all. She told me he was in agreement.'

Berg's eyes narrowed. 'You mean you're taking over her affairs.'

'Yes.'

'Oh well, you must explain it all some time. I'm sorry, I feel too groggy.'

She bent down and uttered 'Father' with sudden feeling.

He pushed his hand in front of her face, as if calling for silence at a board meeting.

'I know why you've come,' he said. And as Florence froze, he went on: 'Let me put you right about this. The other evening Armand rushed over to see you from here, saying I'd thrown him out, and you said "I'll go and see the old you-know-what", and that's just what I'd expect from you. You're a good daughter, Flo. But the superb speech you have prepared can stay in your handbag and I'll answer you right away: yes, I have a form of cancer, no I won't do anything about it.'

'B-but a lot of cancers . . .'

'. . . can be treated and cured, and it takes years off you. Honestly, Flo, I'm too old for that now.'

'You're only seventy!'

'Too old to be jabbed, radiated, bombarded with cobalt and stuffed up the nose with a lot of rubber and plastic pipes. Duvillers – he's the oncologist who's been here occasionally, a fellow-conspirator of mine at university – well I got him on the phone and described minutely all the symptoms, what I spat up, the pains and the rest of it. And the diagnosis? Damn serious, fatal in the short term.'

'You're making it up,' Florence cried. 'No doctor would ever say such a thing, especially on the phone.'

'You ninny, I didn't say it was me, I told him it was Gilbert Bossis.'

She stared at him. How completely cynical he was. Call it his sense of humour or his courage, he had always been indifferent to others, to himself, to life itself. It was that ungovernable vigour that had made him the detestable yet fascinating tyrant that he was. A tyrant with charm, a master of himself and others. In a flash she knew she was exactly like him, and the pity she had felt for him drained away. He would die just as she would die years later – indifferent.

There was nothing more to be said. She got up, pulling the coat closer round her: 'Goodnight father. You know where to find me.'

'I know. Thanks, Flo.'

She took his hands and kissed them. Her eyes smarted, none-theless, as she reached the door, and she turned: 'You won't die alone . . .'

'I've lived alone for long enough, *ma chérie*. So has Gilbert, the poor fellow. We've been a pair of lonely companions, but it's been a façade. Your mother Gabrielle was our one link, but she merely brought our hate together. Neither of us has ever dared to admit it, we've grown too old and too feeble too quickly. We haven't the guts to admit it. Until now, that is . . .' Florence was by his side again, his hands in hers. 'Don't say anything to a soul, this is for your ears only. Hm, I feel quite weary, I'll sleep tonight.'

'I'll stay the night, father.'

'No, I snore and cough. I don't want you to hear that all night. Go back to your place.'

'I'm your daughter.'

'Too late to worry about that,' he chuckled. 'No use crying.'

'But you are crying, my darling.'

'Tear ducts out of order, that's all. Nothing to get worked up about. Stop dramatizing, I'm not dead yet. You'll be back many times.'

Yet, even as she crept away along the passage, he broke into a fit of convulsive coughing.

Suddenly she began to run.

The morning rush hour at the Bijou-Bar was over when Travers, Favrot and Edelman met to consider their next move. They sat at the table in the corner and ordered plates of mussels; it was all that was going at 9.00 a.m. in the way of hot food.

Favrot said Commissaire Nicolo and Inspector Germain had gone to Les Sablons, but he hadn't found out why so far.

Travers said: 'I spent a whole hour in a barn that stank like a witches' cauldron, listening to Shakespeare. Some dame was stuck up on a platform thing yelling about Anthony and his horse. Wish I could remember the words, they sounded pretty good at the time.'

'What are you on about? You mean at Julien Berg's sawmill? said Favrot.

'That's the man I reckon can help us. He's from the Ecole Centrale and knows building from A to Z. I had him fill me in a bit. To be honest, nothing conclusive came out of it, but I'm less ignorant than I was. I asked him whether short measure on the electric cable might be an isolated incident, and he said these things were never isolated incidents, that in this kind of business everything was held together by something, either by force of circumstance, or complicity, more or less tacit, or else mutual suspicion.'

'You can tell he's from the Ecole Centrale!'

'He meant there was probably systematic cheating on dimensions, lowering of quality and thinner insulation for example, pressboard instead of timber as specified, plastic where steel is called for. That kind of thing. The snag is that the whole caboodle tends to get buried in concrete, and there's no way of checking then except by pulling the buildings down!'

'Dynamite, like Paul said.' Edelman put in.

'We must go carefully, I'm sure we're being watched, but we don't know by whom.'

Favrot and Edelman said in unison: 'As Proust would say, search me.'

Travers continued: 'What's needed is a check on every single firm supplying the site. Not only the official ones but the others whose names appear nowhere. For a start, who made the cable with the two millimetre sheathing?'

'Haven't traced it yet,' Favrot said.

'Well, stick at it.'

'OK boss.'

Suddenly Travers looked up. Maryse had come in, and was leaning on the counter.

'Here's my share,' Travers said, laying some coins on the table. He hunched into Paul Bossis's raincoat: 'I want to see Melchior.'

Edelman nudged Favrot: 'When she came in, I was sure he'd go up to her. I was willing to bet he'd have her before the night was out. Looks like I was wrong.'

'I wouldn't say that. She's going after him right now, look! He can see Melchior any time – and in office hours . . .'

Maryse lay rosy and nude on the bed, watching Travers getting dressed and saying it was great and her little studio was enchanting. The room was almost in darkness, with a tiny lamp with a pink shade alight next to the bed.

She said softly; 'Well now it's over, what can I do for you?'

'What are you getting at?' he said, flicking his tie into place. 'You mean you owe me something?'

Maryse couldn't help laughing at his look of pure innocence.

He added: 'You've given me everything I've ever dreamed of, my love.'

'Come on, spit it out, I wasn't born yesterday. You're not the first gentlemen who's told me he never realized quite how attractive I was. Your very words in the office this afternoon, remember?'

'How else was I to attain my wicked ends?'

'Look Travers, if you tell me it was love at first sight, I'll give you a good old-fashioned kick in the arse.'

'I haven't taken my eyes off you since that night at La Commanderie.'

'Lucky for you I was dying for a man,' she declared, slipping off the bed into a peignoir.

'So, you wanted it with the first man who came along?'

'No, with you and you alone, believe it or not.' She nestled up against him and they kissed. It might have carried more conviction if he had not then said he had to go and see Commissaire Nicolo.

'Always on the run, you're like Dillinger or someone.'

'True.'

'And what did you want to see me about?'

'You won't leave go of it, will you! Well, if you really want to do me a good turn, now I come to think of it – how about getting hold of Jean-Jacques Berg's diary for me? Last year's is the one I want. I'd like to see where he had lunch.'

'You slimey rat.'

'You'd do that little thing for me, wouldn't you, my angel?'

94

'Go and . . .'

The door slammed, her advice fell on deaf ears.

Travers poked his head round again: 'You have the most fetching eyes, Maryse.'

'You're not so bad-looking yourself.'

Nicolo glowered at Travers. 'I am not here,' he said.

'I know your not, and you have every excuse at ten in the evening,' Travers declared. 'But I also know you are a glutton for punishment when the mood takes you, and I wanted to congratulate you for your shrewdness. A Paris cop couldn't have got there in twice the time.'

Nicolo sniffed: 'I've dealt with some madcaps in my time . . . But . . . never mind, I've no time to waste. Whatever you've got on your mind, let's have it, and double quick. Huh! Shrewdness!'

Travers leaned back: 'Let me see it in operation when I've told you why I am here. And if you behave yourself, I'll tell you why Paul Bossis was done away with.'

'All right, start now and I'll give you three minutes.'

'Suppose I tell you I have some key facts, though not cast iron proof – and I'm willing to let you have them a week from now – would you be prepared to fill me in on why you went to Les Sablons? You play ball with me and . . .'

Commissaire Nicolo was in a good mood after the visit to Les Sablons. He also saw the hard-working Travers as a possible useful ally. This chat was off the record, and he was ready to play ball with a newsman spreading it around that Nicolo was a shrewd one.

'On the night of the crime,' he said, 'a filling station attendant on the Paris road served a couple of customers around 3.00 a.m. They were in a Taunus, and they sat without saying anything as he gave them a full tank. Fortunately, he noticed that one of the men was wearing a carnation, a detail that proved significant during a routine check we did on a dozen or so garages that night. Are you with me so far? Now, the Alfa Romeo used by Bossis was found spick and span inside and out, but it still had some tiny traces of a type of cement used at Les Sablons. The car had some in the tyre treads, for example, so we know it was at Les Sablons, and had been cleaned up because of that. We found something else – a carnation petal on one of the seats.'

The journalist made a show of noiseless clapping: 'Ah, if only the entire police force came up to your standard! So you went to the building site because the geezers in the Taunus were connected with it, and you checked up on the staff lists. Am I right?'

'I can say nothing more, Monsieur Travers. Now what ball have *you* got to play?'

Travers enclosed Nicolo's hands in a gesture of affection: 'We can do business, partner. *You* know who did it, and *I* know why they did it. Right?'

'Don't be too sure,' said the Commissaire evasively, taking his eyes off the visitor and gazing at the ring of dust encircling the ceiling lamp.

Chapter Three

Georges Quentin, Mayor of Chateauvallon and Secretary of State for Defence, was ousted from the Government in the week that followed. Officially, he resigned. It was put about that he was suffering from overwork.

Whatever the reason, his departure from the Government and the tension that followed were assumed to be at the root of the stormy town council meeting the following day.

An article appeared straightaway in *La Dépêche* suggesting, though without a strand of evidence, that the resignation was connected with the Mayor's handling of the community's affairs, particularly in regard to Les Sablons building site.

Thus Quentin, like Coriolanus returning to Rome, was spattered with mud. Or so he said. In the lengthy debate which followed the Socialists came out on top thanks to their pointedly ironic silence. The insinuations were flying about, but no one could agree. The media were left to conjecture whether he had left the Government in order to (i) take a holiday in the Balearics, or (ii) stand at a forthcoming by-election, or (iii) because he was involved in shady deals connected with Les Sablons project.

The Mayor said he had no statement to make personally, but in view of the innuendoes that had been made, he felt obliged to order a commission of inquiry – 'yes, gentlemen, a commission of inquiry' – which would start work the next day.

'Concerning what, Monsieur le Maire?'

'Concerning Les Sablons!'

Having satisfied the clutch of newsmen on the town hall steps, the Mayor went home on foot to work off his adrenalin, his chief regret being that he was now no longer able to seek refuge behind the net curtains Florence Berg used to draw around them in former times.

Condroyer and Fournier meanwhile sneaked past the media and went in another direction.

'My God, an inquiry, a commission of inquiry, that's all we need,' Condroyer muttered three or four times.

Until Fournier shut him up: 'Be quiet, for pity's sake. There's worse – Machefer and Gamel are in Chateauvallon. Machefer phoned me before lunch, threatening me. Five hundred thousand francs or we're for it, that's what he said.'

'They wouldn't dare. They're murderers, they'd be cutting their own . . .'

'He didn't say he'd walk right into the Commissariat, idiot! An anonymous phone call pointing to us would be enough. Huh, you wouldn't last five minutes if the police put the lamps on you.' They walked on in silence for a while, and Fournier added: 'Remember what I said the other evening, about heading them off?'

'Certainly, but how?'

'I've told Machefer he'll have his five hundred grand tonight. He told me where to rendezvous with him. Eight o'clock.'

Condroyer had to trot to keep up: 'I don't get it. You mean we're going to hand the money to them on a plate?'

'Grow up. At one o'clock Nicolo had a phone call telling him where and when he could lay his hands on Bossis's killers. He was told they would be armed and that they would certainly shoot first, because they had nothing to lose. But, knowing this, it's a dead certainty Nicolo's men will, in fact, shoot first. And even if Machefer and Gamel do fire the first shots, they won't get a second chance. We can count on Nicolo.'

'Fournier,' his companion gaped, 'it was you who phoned Nicolo.'

'You're learning fast.'

Fournier left Condroyer on the corner of Avenue Carnot and Rue Séguier, and went straight home. He thanked his lucky stars that he was a widower, and didn't have to account for himself to anybody.

He swallowed a brandy in his sitting room, and started packing.

Condroyer watched Fournier go off, and hitched up his trousers. The beginnings of a wet patch felt cold behind his zip. If Machefer didn't kill him, he would end up in jail: five years for misappropriation of public funds, embezzlement and issuing forged documents; another 25 years for incitement to murder.

He sought refuge at Chez Lulu, the love nest of the town's transvestites. There was always a welcome for him there. Robert the barman was off duty, but Lulu (dear, fat Lulu with her fancy jewellery) realized he was in a dreadful state and showed him to an empty bedroom without a word.

He wrapped the blankets round him and it was only then that it dawned on him: Robert was off duty because it was still daytime, and he had never been so foolhardy as to come there in daylight! God knows who must have seen him come in.

It didn't bear thinking about, but within minutes he was sleeping like a lamb. He was safe for the present.

Mayor Quentin's announcement of the commission of inquiry and the clashes in the council chamber reached the furthest corners of Chateauvallon before tea-time. Radio Luxemburg carried an item on it at five o'clock.

Florence was working on a case at her apartment, and hurriedly left. She reached the pavement as Armand drew up in his car. He got out, and so did a tall man in a suede jacket.

'I'm going to La Commanderie,' she said quickly.

'What's the hurry?' her brother said, amused by her haste.

'Er . . .'

'Let me introduce you to . . .'

She turned her head towards him: 'Don't tell me. I know, your picture was in *La Dépêche*, yesterday.'

'Maurice Arras,' the man said, with an engaging smile.

'Of the Institute,' Armand added. 'Just bumped into him in the street, the old rascal never told me he was here. After twenty years of undying friendship, and six years since we've seen each other!'

Florence purred: 'Armand's mentioned you – many times.' She laughed, without knowing why, and not solely out of politeness. He impressed her, his unswerving gaze and casual elegance, the thick hair going grey which put him at around fifty. 'Well, it can wait,' she said, surprising herself, and invited them in.

They left two hours later. Two exalting hours during which she had sat at the feet of the eminent and erudite Maurice Arras, soaking up the magic of his charm. That very evening he was giving a lecture on anthropology and she was amazed to discover a keen new interest in the subject, particularly the specimen now ensconced in her best armchair with his long legs crossed at the ankles. She couldn't promise, but if she could make it she would call in at the Rotary Club when she got back from La Commanderie. The side of his personality that really won her over was his refusal to take himself seriously, his little throw-away remarks that proved that he at least knew how small he was in the universe. There was no silly false modesty about him, but he accepted himself as he was, and seemed on good terms with both himself and his fellow men. It was rare to come across his kind of man.

More than once she lowered her eyes under his gaze and she told herself she was imagining things. She was sure of it when they spoke of Antonin Berg and his refusal to have treatment, for he shocked her.

'Surely we have the right to choose the way we die,' he said. 'I feel sometimes that it's the only right we possess. It is the only decision that truly depends on ourselves, don't you think?'

'That's philosophical rubbish, Monsieur Arras. None of us can tell until we are confronted . . .'

'I was confronted with it, in the case of my own mother. I did not allow her that right, and what did I give her in exchange? Three months more to live, three months of suffering.' He argued his point soothingly with moderation, giving assurance to his audience. She came out of it perplexed, wondering as she drove through the main gate at La Commanderie whether he might not be right. She would reserve her opinion.

The old man began bombarding her the moment she entered his room: 'Aha! What's the latest with your little friend? Seems they unceremoniously threw him out of the Government. I'd love to know what he's got to say about it.'

'I'm in no position to say,' Florence retorted. 'All I know is that article of yours was disgraceful. That's why I came, to tell you how indignant I feel about it.'

'That doesn't surprise me!' Smartly dressed in grey flannel suit with a bowtie, fragrant with eau de cologne, he was his old self again. She decided he could stand a counter-attack.

'Your article was totally uncalled for. No, I want you to hear me out. You heard the news, you heard the rumours, and decided to rub his nose in it. He had no alternative but to defend himself . . .'

'. . . and to set up an official inquiry. That's excellent,' he cried, slapping his thigh.

Eyes ablaze, she went on: 'It was a rotten thing to do – it made him look guilty by implication. Well, I'd better put you straight, because Quentin was not removed from the Government for any reason linked to Les Sablons. Your suggestions are disgusting.'

His tone became bantering: 'And why *was* he chucked out, my dear? Did he tell you?'

'He did.'

'So you're still seeing him!

'He told me before we split up.'

'So?'

'He was not thrown out. He asked to leave, the business of being involved in the nation's destiny, as he put it, was tiring him out. The truth is that he eased himself out.'

'He had a reason. What was it?'

'I've just told you.'

He looked down his nose, his mouth twisted: 'Fatigue, over-work, disappointment – all right, subject to verification. But Les Sablons was part of it.'

'You've got a bee in your bonnet, an uncontrollable vindic-tiveness founded on an obsession. That's serious, you know!'

He clenched his fists: 'And what else have you come to tell me?'

She held his gaze: 'That, until further notice, I refuse to run a paper that is totally lacking in dignity.'

'Huh. Until further notice? And when will that be?'

Overcome with rage and despair, she shouted: 'For God's sake, when you're dead!'

He tossed his head: 'That's exactly what was agreed. When I'm gone. No need to work yourself up, it won't be long now, and you can have a newspaper with all the dignity you want.'

She picked up her things and hurried down the great staircase. 'Hullo, that you Jean-Jacques?' she heard him bawling into the phone.

On arrival, her sole desire was to turn in at once with a sleeping pill, but there was a note from Armand in the letter-box: 'Make sure you come on to the Rotary. We'll have a bite to eat with Arras afterwards.' She wanted to cry. And went.

Miraculously she was on time, and wended her way into the crowd in the foyer. This was clearly an occasion, for the guests were virtually those that had been at the big reception thrown by

Antonin Berg. She joined Jean-Jacques and Marie-Lou. Normally she mentally shrugged off any nice things her witless sister-in-law said to her, but this time she seemed genuine enough when she gave a suppressed whistle of admiration at her turn-out. Florence accepted it in the spirit in which it was given. It was true she had surpassed herself, selecting the silver lamé dress and matching shoes, and with not a hair out of place she looked like a goddess. Nor was she in any doubt as to the purpose of all this. What she did not fully realize was how happy she looked, being more anxious than triumphant deep down.

As she stood with another couple who had called her over, Marie-Lou was prompted to say to her husband: 'Wow, your sister . . . absolutely devastating. And she was actually nice to me. D'you think she's found a new bloke?'

'I didn't notice anything. But now you mention it, she is blossoming rather. A bit *too* congenial perhaps.'

'What on earth d'you mean?'

'Tell you later, that's the bell.'

Arras had the rare knack of making difficult subjects comprehensible to the lay audience, even varying the pace and introducing little jokes and one-liners to keep the interest up. Sadly for Florence, he had to rush for the last train to Paris and their supper for three faded out with his apologetic 'terribly sorry, would have loved it, perhaps next time.'

Florence smiled wryly when Armand reported this, and she said: 'Too bad, it doesn't matter.' Her silver get-up suddenly seemed vulgar.

Armand suggested they eat together at the Del Monico, but she declined the invitation. He offered to run her home but she preferred to walk the half-kilometre.

She seized his arm: 'Look at that!' Not far from them a small group was hanging around somewhat aimlessly; it included Jean-Jacques, Marie-Lou and Quentin.

'He's putting up a brave front,' Armand whispered. 'Can't help admiring him, mingling with the very crowd out for his blood.'

She nodded. But Florence had no wish to start a discussion about Quentin at that time of night, or to encounter Marie-Lou who was gauche enough to observe that she had aged five years in ninety minutes, a fact that Florence was willing to admit but preferred to keep to herself. She gave her brother a peck on the cheek and walked off briskly. Fifty yards later her expensive shoes began pinching.

Stopping to try to ease the pain, she turned to find Quentin hurrying to join her.

Marie-Lou, who missed nothing, watched their meeting and remarked: 'Huh, so they're patching up their little quarrel.'

They were at the side of their car and Jean-Jacques ordered her to get in.

'What's the matter with you tonight?' Marie-Lou's timing was perfect, she had brought the art of nagging to a peak of refinement. 'You never told me why you find Florence "*too* congenial". That was your phrase.'

Jean-Jacques took a deep breath: 'Father's had it. Armand told me and Flo knows too. Father was in touch with Professor Duvillers, and he knows exactly what he's got and how long he has to live.'

'Oh dear, I'm so sorry.'

'So am I. Especially as it won't be me who takes over.'

'What on earth do you mean?'

'I was at the office this afternoon, and by pure chance I overheard a chat between young Jeannou, who brought in an article from father, and a pal of his. I found out that father has asked Flo to take over as boss of *La Dépêche*. That's why she's being so friendly. She's embarrassed about it. Flo's quite a bitch in her own way.'

Marie-Lou spat out: 'Don't cry yet, wait till you've lost.'

'What's to be done, then?'

'You've got to fight it, you fool. And besides it's only gossip. Florence knows nothing about journalism or running a paper, and she has a law practice that's minting money. She won't accept it.'

Jean-Jacques changed into top gear: 'Let's hope so. After all, I phoned the old man earlier and he sounded the same as always. He was quite normal with me. You're right, I'm imagining things.'

Quentin told Florence: 'I've seen your father. Got there as you were leaving. I wanted to ask him face to face why he was going for me, after showing such even-handedness, even goodwill, for so long.'

Florence said drily: 'And he told you it was nothing to do with him and that *La Dépêche* had no contract to be neutral to anyone, and the press merely reflects what's going on. Is that right?'

She was vexed over how the evening had turned out, and angry that Quentin had burst in on her sombre thoughts. She didn't bother to tell Quentin she had stood up for him.

'Yes, that's right,' the Mayor said, irritated at her tone. 'Well more or less. He simply assumes that I was pushed out of the Government, and that if there's something fishy going on over Les Sablons, I'm at the bottom of it. Not only that, he believes the commission of inquiry is a whitewash job. Oh, he didn't say so, but I got the message.' He paused and said: 'Do you think so, too?'

'No.'

'Was I forced out? Am I the town's top racketeer in your view?'

He was whining almost, excited, distraught as she had never seen him. Already he was climbing down from his pedestal, and he seemed like a drunk importuning the first person he could get hold of, in order to find a friend.

'I don't believe any of that,' she answered. 'But that's not the point. My father has made up his mind and nobody can shift him. Especially me, when the issue is Georges Quentin.'

He calmed down: 'Yes, you're right of course. He always hated us going together, I mean the fact that we were in love. And we were, Florence.'

'Suppose we were.'

He stopped walking, and she had to as well: 'Suppose!'

'I mean of course.'

But she realized that the affection remaining after the separation had gradually drained away, and that nothing was left of it now. She even wondered whether she had ever loved him at all. A vision of Maurice Arras flashed through her mind. She felt sorry for Quentin.

'You must keep your feet on the ground,' she advised. 'I'll have another go at Antonin, try to show him he's not being fair.'

To her astonishment, he became even more excited: 'I'll never let Antonin Berg walk over me. I've got plenty of ammunition and he'll rue the day he started this! Let's see how tough he is now that he knows there's a Berg mixed up in Les Sablons!'

It was Florence's turn to stop in her tracks: 'What! You can't be serious. Who?'

Quentin's mouth formed into a long line as he smiled: 'Your cousin Philippe. When I got to his room, your father was on the phone, sounded as if Jean-Jacques had phoned *him*. From your father's reaction I gathered that Philippe was in it up to his neck. You can't fool me. Good-night.'

'Good-night, *Monsieur* Quentin.'

In the flat she flung her shoes at the far wall, and dialled Philippe Berg's number. His wife Emilie answered.

'Oh, it's you Florence. I haven't seen or heard from Philippe since he went off this morning. I'm worried sick.'

Some were worried that day, some were heady with joy, and some were foaming with rage.

In the last category came Commissaire Nicolo. Despite precise instructions from anonymous callers about the location of Machefer and Gamel, the Commissaire's birds had flown when he got there.

And it was all because of the Gendarmerie Nationale. Not for the first time Nicolo predicted that the next civil war in France would be between the police and the Gendarmerie Nationale.

The target was a woodsman's hut in La Grèze forest, so obvious a blind man could have found it looking through the wrong end of a telescope. Unfortunately the Gendarmerie, who had also received a couple of anonymous calls, got there ten minutes ahead of the SRPJ with a fleet of vans and motorbikes.

Nicolo heard the siren while he was approaching the target, and when he stepped out to confront Captain Roustan he declared: 'Congratulations! All that's missing is the band of the Garde Républicaine. Don't tell me they were late too.'

Rouston apologized in a booming voice: 'Sorry Commissaire, one of my chaps pushed the siren button by mistake.'

'Well at least you needn't have turned up with headlights blazing. That's how we lost the battle of Waterloo.'

They trudged over to the hut, and Nicolo was moaning as he examined the tyre tracks and footprints.

Roustan suggested a dragnet be thrown out, and Nicolo said the target was probably half-way across the Channel on the way to Dover. Roustan threatened to take the matter higher, and Nicolo told him he'd got better things to do than argue about nothing.

But the Commissaire got little sleep that night.

Condroyer could not sleep either. He went home from Lulu's around 8.00 p.m. like a thief in the night, and paced his apartment. He knew he ought to eat and drink something, but he had no appetite. His stomach was clenched tight and his mouth was dry.

His awakening had been rude. He staggered down the stairs on hearing Robert's voice, dear Robert whose soft velvet thighs made him almost swoon. And Robert had thrown him out. Unable to believe his ears, he dived into his bag and produced his chequebook, for it was thus that he had won back his beloved so many times before.

'Clear off,' Robert said in the piping voice that contrasted so sharply with his huge chest. 'Get the hell out of here, chequebook and all. And don't poke your nose in here again. Your money stinks.'

Condroyer looked at him quizzically: 'What do you mean, Robert dear?'

'Huh, you don't know what's doing the rounds, then? There's a huge commotion about Les Sablons and the town council's going up before a commission of inquiry. That's what.' He jerked his head at the chequebook: 'Put it away, sweetie, what else did they give you for Christmas? Your account's gonna be frozen, see. And your cheques won't be worth cashing, see. And I want nothing to do with it, see.'

Condroyer spluttered: 'You're absolutely wrong. I've nothing to do with . . .'

'Oh yeah? Where's all the money come from over the past two years, where'd you get it, eh?'

The remark was unanswerable, and Condroyer hastened away.

Once in the apartment, he was relieved that Robert had refused payment. Frozen or not, his account was overdrawn. But what riled him was that Robert, whom he loved, had rejected him like some old dishcloth on the first sign of money-trouble. Condroyer was more lonely than ever, and was close to throwing things about in the deserted apartment. He had put the light on in the kitchen but nowhere else, and the dreadful starkness of it all clutched at his entrails.

He sank onto a stool, but leaped up like a shot as his doorbell rang. He emitted a little cry and went to the door like a sleepwalker. He opened it, put up his hands and said: 'I'll come quietly, gentlemen, I'll come quietly.'

Philippe Berg stood on the landing, and at the sight of Condroyer he scowled and pushed him back inside. Berg switched the lounge lights on and waved Condroyer to an armchair. He himself remained standing.

'Don't cry your heart out at me,' he said. 'I've just come from Lulu's, looked for you there. So your little cherub has given you the push-off. And stop blubbing, for God's sake! Pull yourself together!'

'Oh Lord,' the other wailed. 'Robert, and now Machefer and Gamel putting the frighteners on; they're here you know in Chateauvallon.'

'Oh yes?'

'Fournier told me. They want five-hundred smackers extra.'

'The hell they do! Where are they?'

'Lord knows. The SRPJ missed them just now.'

'How do you know that?'

'Don't listen to the news? The two of them got away just before the police arrived. We're all for it now. Fournier first, because Machefer and Gamel know he was the only one who knew their whereabouts. Then the rest of us . . .'

Philippe went into the kitchen, filled a glass and swallowed three fingers of whisky in one gulp.

'Fournier may get his lot, but not us.'

'Don't you believe it. One, two, three, four corpses. It's all the same to them,' Condroyer said.

'Hum, the net's closing in. They've already got my name, and I've spent all day walking about on the edge of town waiting for nightfall so that I could warn Fournier and you. Fournier's already gone. I went there and didn't even hear his dog – either he's killed it or taken it with him. The garage door was open, with nothing inside. Hm, with the money he's amassed, he could get away to anywhere, South America maybe. We could all finish up like Nazi war criminals in Argentina or some other godforsaken place.'

'I haven't got a sou.'

'I cleared everything out of my account today. Cashier kept eyeing me as he counted out the notes.'

Condroyer was left to his own thoughts, the first of which was that Berg had not even offered him the fare to Paris. But he was past caring now. He was finished, and for good. Even the prospect of dying failed to scare him now. He even welcomed the idea, he knew already what he would do.

But he asked one more question: 'The cops have your name, you say?'

'Not them. No not yet, but they soon will. I've still got a chance, we'll have to split up, no alternative. I won't wish you luck, that'd be asking for trouble.'

'Off you go then,' said Condroyer, closing the door on him quietly.

Philippe Berg's name had come up at *La Dépêche* that afternoon.

To begin with, Edelman disclosed that he knew the name of the cable maker: Cableco in Rouen, run by a man named Borel, who happened to be the husband of Fournier's sister.

Travers noted the information, and the two were joined by Favrot. Travers in turn revealed that he had decoded Paul Bossis's notebook.

Then Favrot said: 'But that's not all. Paul jotted down two letters, PB, and it's certain he added them afterwards wherever his code for the design office was written down. Not only did he add PB, but he also wrote down a number: 687000. I puzzled over that for hours, and it finally dawned on me. It could be a phone number. It was.'

Travers said: 'PB?'

'The very man. Philippe Berg!'

'So the design office was none other than Philippe Berg. Who naturally put the fees straight in his pocket!'

Less than a minute later Travers was informing Jean-Jacques: 'Sorry it's a Berg, but there's no doubt that this phoney design office has been hitting the jackpot. Colossal sums are involved. And for the last six months there has been no mention of the design office in the file. Councillor Philippe Berg was in Paul's sights. No wonder he spoke of "dynamite".'

'We've got to run it. Boy what a story, and what a newsman, our Paul! It's all yours Travers, but let me see it first before you send it down.'

Travers returned to his office. Jean-Jacques called his father at La Commanderie. Not that he had any pity for cousin Philippe, he would get what was coming to him. But father was still the boss.

Antonin gave two orders. The first was to find Philippe and tell him it was all up. Jean-Jacques eventually ran him to earth over the phone at a restaurant he knew Philippe sometimes patronized.

Old Berg had said: 'Tell him, and let him stew.' Which was why Philippe Berg had spent the afternoon and evening in a cold sweat.

The second instruction was that no article was to appear. But Travers was not told.

The next day Travers burst into Jean-Jacques' office with the issue of *La Dépêche*.

His head was throbbing and his mouth tasted as though it was full of putty. With Edelman, Favrot and Maryse he had celebrated the success of their perseverance rather over-enthusiastically – the more so since Maryse had learned from Jean-Jacques Berg's diary that he had twice lunched with Fournier.

'What's the big idea?' Travers threw at Jean-Jacques. 'Is this today's edition or isn't it? Or is my article in invisible ink? Or maybe I can't read all of a sudden. Or I only dreamed I sweated blood writing that article. What's the big idea – the family that prays together stays together?'

Jean-Jacques was on his feet, moving behind his chair: 'That's enough of that! It's nothing to do with me, go argue it out with my father. He's the boss.'

'Why you lousy tinpot editor, you ought to be drummed out of the profession.' Travers snarled, throwing the paper at him.

Ten minutes later, Travers scrunched to a halt outside the big house.

Jeannou tried to stop him, Mathilde pursued him protesting, but he bounded up the stairs and found Antonin Berg asleep in his pyjamas and dressing gown on top of the blankets. Or so it seemed.

Berg senior, he then noticed, was eyeing him through his eyelashes, evidently expecting him. Either he had foreseen the sequence of events, or Jean-Jacques had warned him.

'You stopped my article,' Travers blared.

'I did. My nephew Philippe may be a crook, but the thing's not ripe enough or clear enough to throw him as first victim to the lions. I'm not ready to put the noose round his neck.'

Travers steadied himself: 'And when *will* the noose be put round his neck?'

'When I tell you.'

'That's your idea of journalism?'

'It's my idea as the man in charge of *La Dépêche*.'

'Boss of the paper, or head of the clan?'

'Take your choice.'

'In that case I have no hesitation in offering you my resignation!'

He stalked out and old Berg went to the window to watch him roar off in a blind fury, two thick streams of gravel shooting into the air as he went.

Jeannou and Mathilde hurried in to apologize, gabbling that they could do nothing to stop him.

Berg shrugged: 'He's got balls, that lad.' And he chuckled in amusement.

Antonin then moved over to a small desk and wrote names on a scrap of paper: 'I want you to phone these gentlemen, I'm rather tired now. Tell them to be here at one, for lunch.'

The master of the clan eyed the three visitors from the depths of the settee in the main lounge. He wore a sober dark brown suit, white shirt and slippers. It was the first time in his life that he had worn slippers outside his bedroom.

The other three – Jean-Jacques, Julien and Armand – were standing near one of the large windows, glasses in hand. They were all looking at a painting dark with age as if they had never seen it before.

Nobody spoke, and none of them was going to be the first to do so. They waited. Then the venerable old grandfather clock struck the hour of one, and Philippe strode in, last but on time.

'Sorry to get here at the last minute,' he said. 'Emilie couldn't wake me, I'd taken too many sleeping pills.'

'I'm sure your reasons were sound,' Armand said urbanely.

'So it's a family conference, I see. Or a war council perhaps?' Philippe said tensely, glaring at them in turn. Antonin Berg had his back to him and he turned round.

'Kind of you to invite me. Not a common occurrence,' he said nervously.

'Let's begin,' the old man said.

He led the group into the dining room. Jean-Jacques tripped along on his toes like a poodle, Armand came next, followed by Philippe stiff as a ramrod, and Julien distinctly uncomfortable. Julien rather liked Philippe: they had played together as lads and later knocked about a bit in Quebec, Mexico and Mali in quest of adventure. Today this need for excitement found its outlet in his theatre and various other risky enterprises. Julien was less ready to condemn Philippe than Armand was, and declined to set himself up as his judge. He hoped it would never come to that, he reflected, taking the place his father indicated.

They had the hors-d'oeuvre and made small talk. Then Antonin carefully poured out the wine, and announced the start of hostilities.

'Romanée-Conti, '67,' he stated. 'Rather better than the stuff Philippe sells to the English and the Americans.'

'I'm sure we aren't here to study the shortcomings of my business,' his nephew said quietly.

'Of course not. How's it going, by the way? Still making a living out of it?'

Philippe tensed up and Julien thought, here we go . . .

'It's doing well enough,' he replied.

'But not enough to prevent you moving into local politics, I take it.'

'That was not for money, naturally.'

'Or to get drawn into this awful business of Les Sablons. My chaps on the paper were vaguely poking around in the muck, and my word, what should they turn up but you!'

Jean-Jacques looked smug: 'A good thing we didn't carry the article by Travers.' He observed Philippe.

'You told me it was going to the printers, but you failed to tell me it was spiked. Pretty rotten trick, letting me toss and turn all night.' Philippe spoke as a man who had drunk a chalice and a half of bitterness.

Armand crooned: 'If that's all you suffered, you're fortunate. You must have been out of your mind. If you needed money so badly, you could at least have come to the family, instead of getting us involved in a national scandal.'

Philippe hit back: 'You really think you have the right to talk of family honour?'

Jean-Jacques retorted: 'Why not, cousin?'

Philippe brought out his big guns: 'Antonin Berg, you know what I think of your supposed honour. You sent my father, your own brother, to Spain in '44. So that he'd die, which he did, through neglect. He perished alone and starving.'

His uncle snapped: 'As a collaborator with the Germans, he'd have died with a dozen bullets in his back if he'd stayed here.'

111

'You could have got him out of it, with all your money and contacts. But he had tarnished the family crest, and you threw him out like some old coat that had gone out of fashion.' He got up and threw down his napkin onto the table, turning to Armand. 'And you say I had only to ask you. What would have been the point? Nobody in this family other than Julien has shown the slightest consideration towards me. Yes, Philippe Berg, son of the collaborator you sold down the river. You are right, uncle, I have never earned a living with my wine, I have allowed myself to be drawn into a racket. But the reason must be obvious. None of you gave me a chance, none of you gave me a hand-up when I needed it. So much for the Berg millions!'

He was panting with rage, and suddenly stopped, sinking onto his chair.

For a good thirty seconds, he stared before him into the void, as did the others.

At last Julien said: 'You could have asked me.'

'I couldn't have taken your money, that kind of thing breaks up friendships, and I valued our friendship.'

'Shall I bring in the roast, Monsieur?' Mathilde whispered. Nobody answered her and she crept out as stealthily as she had come in. There was another long silence, during which Antonin coughed quietly into his handkerchief. Armand watched him anxiously.

Then the old man said: 'We have strayed off the point.'

'All right,' Philippe said levelly, 'Let's get back to it. I raise my glass to the solutions you have decided.' He swallowed the rest of his Romanée-Conti.

Antonin Berg leaned back: 'First, you must disappear before the whole business blows sky-high, go far away and quickly. You can count on us, whatever you may think, and we'll do all we can to make sure you survive this one. I'm not saying *La Dépêche* will defend you, only that it will suggest mitigating circumstances.'

'And secondly?'

'You will come clean. You are known to be naïve, without defences so to speak, easily influenced. Much will be forgiven you, and nobody will believe you are a crook at heart. At worst, a poor imitation of one.'

'Father!' cried Julien. 'That's nasty.'

Philippe got out of his chair for the last time: 'I'm going. Goodbye, cousins. Whatever else I decide to do, obviously I can't possibly be here to attend your funeral, uncle.'

Nicolo read through the typescript of Travers's unused article without comment. He re-folded it and stuffed it in his inside pocket.

'In view of the way I've been treated,' Travers told him, 'and since I consider this as a deliberate bid to pervert the course of justice, and because Paul Bossis was my close friend, I feel free of any moral obligation to my employer. The more so as he no longer is my employer, and has no morals himself.'

The Commissaire shook his head in renewed disbelief: 'Philippe Berg, who would have imagined it?' He looked up as Pradel came in and said: 'Let's take a peek at Philippe Berg. That makes two.'

'Two? said Travers.

'One of the town hall bunch did away with himself. An admission of guilt, if ever there was one. Condroyer was fished out of the Loire this morning, his lungs full of water – so it wasn't murder.'

Travers left the office, but Nicolo called after him: 'Fournier is a third. His gardener chap found his dog with its throat cut. I went along assuming we'd find Fournier's body too. No such luck. He's cleared off with his toothbrush and his new car.'

Travers mooched around Chateauvallon. He had a drink in a bistro, swallowed a plateful of sauerkraut in another, made sure he ran into no one he knew, saw half the film showing at Le Trianon cinema, and let himself into Maryse's apartment with the key she had let him have.

He lay down on the bed and studied the bumps in the ceiling, reflecting on his new status as an unemployed journalist. It was funny that he should come to this, but he had little inclination to laugh. Perhaps he would later. It was Emilie he felt sorry for, as she sat aghast while Nicolo grilled her husband Philippe. They had two children, and a picture rose before him of the two kids at the door watching their father taken away in handcuffs. What the hell, he had it coming to him: what was that beside the murder of Paul? What an unholy mess it all was.

Travers made an attempt to catch up on some sleep, but it proved hopeless. When Maryse bustled in at seven o'clock bearing ravioli and a bottle of chianti, he was on his feet preparing to leave.

'I'm going for a stroll,' he said. 'I'll be back, but can't say exactly when.'

'They told me you handed in your resignation.'

113

'I showed my story to Nicolo. It seemed the right thing to do, but maybe it wasn't. Be seeing you, angel.'

Maryse let it drop, merely saying limply that she'd got a fresh pineapple.

His stroll took him three kilometres away to Emilie's fashion and shoe shop. He took his time, reluctant as he was to face her. He found her fixing price tags on a rack of coats, and heard the children babbling away in the next room. The black girl had gone a shade paler, but she was still pretty. A bird from the isles who had faded a little.

'Have they taken him away?' he managed to say. 'I suppose Nicolo flashed my article around.'

'Nicolo, I don't understand? How could Nicolo have an article that never appeared? He didn't say anything about that, but Philippe mentioned it, and I believe he heard about it today at La Commanderie.' She took a few steps and went on: 'Nicolo just turned up, said he wanted to ask a few questions about the rumours going the rounds. Your article had nothing to do with his visit. Or perhaps it did . . .'

'Oh no,' he said vaguely. Travers was relieved that Emilie did not see him as an informer, which he in fact was, despite his legitimate motives. 'I'm still sorry I wrote it.'

'It's done now,' she said neutrally. 'Philippe came back as if he'd seen a ghost, not so much because of that article, but because the family have dropped him. Anyhow . . .'

The tears were welling up and Travers said: 'Yes?'

'He's gone, left me some money, packed a suitcase and rushed off in the BMW. Never even kissed the children goodbye.'

'But Nicolo?'

'He turned up afterwards. I told him Philippe had gone on a trip and I didn't know where.'

'But you do know.'

'I don't.' She forced a little laugh. 'Nicolo was in a state!'

The pinched look returned as she described how two cops searched the house from top to bottom, as if they were looking for a dangerous robber. 'You must think he is a robber, Monsieur Travers, don't you?' She seized his arm.

'I can't say,' he replied, avoiding her eyes. 'I just do my job, which is to keep the public informed. What I came to tell you was that, now I think of it, I'm not too proud about the article, or happy generally.'

114

Travers returned to Maryse's place the worse for drink at 2.00 a.m., and woke after noon, recalling only that he had lolled around for hours in some kind of disco where Teddy Kovalic played the saxophone.

He must have asked Teddy about Catherine, because he remembered he said she was fattening up, and that old Bossis was nice to her, and to him as well for that matter. Travers grew sentimental about that, and he made a mental note to see them both.

Still reluctant to move too fast, he remembered too how he had phoned Florence at about 9.00 p.m., and was told by the cleaning woman that Madame was handling a case in Paris and would not be back for a few days.

Travers got his watch in focus and switched the bedside transistor radio on, waiting for the news. He was not disappointed: Deputy Major Fournier had cut his dog's throat and fled; Councillor Condroyer had drowned himself; Councillor Berg had also disappeared just before a police raid on his home. The newsreader added: 'Naturally we shall keep listeners informed as events develop in this case, which is the number one talking point in Chateauvallon and for miles around. Ah, a new item has just come in this moment: Monsieur Perugino has been appointed as the examining magistrate . . .'

Travers guffawed, eased himself off the bed and found a note from Maryse: 'When you warm up the ravioli, make sure you add a little water to stop the saucepan burning.'

Ignoring the instruction, he slowly drank most of the bottle of chianti which Maryse had hardly touched. After which he sank back into sleep, and into the River Loire where he struggled side by side with Condroyer against a flood tide of chianti that kept throwing them on the bank at the feet of Commissaire Nicolo, standing in his underpants with a fat grin on his face.

Judge Perugino, a surprisingly youthful-looking man with a black suit and white skin, a pear-shaped head and a lantern jaw, called Nicolo into the office provided for him at the Chateauvallon law courts.

'We're getting nowhere fast it seems, Monsieur le Commissaire,' he stated somewhat obviously. 'Either through incompetence or deliberate obstruction, we seem to be stumbling from one fiasco to the next: Fournier vanished into thin air,

115

Condroyer drowned, Berg as slippery as an eel. Not to mention Machefer and Gamel. The media haven't got onto this pretty pair yet, no doubt because they don't even know they exist, but it won't be long now. And when they do turn them up, how will you look then? You're already beginning to look like a . . .'

'A what?'

'Do not force me to be rude.'

'These sudden and unforeseeable mishaps cannot be blamed on me, Monsieur le Juge, and . . . er . . . believe me . . .'

'All right, I believe you. And there's something else I believe: from now on you've got to pull your finger out.'

'My view exactly, Monsieur le Juge.'

The magistrate leaned forward, making Nicolo jump: 'I want the lot of them and Berg first of all. He's still in this country, that's for sure. Why Berg? Because that's the big name in this case, a chap from one of the nation's top families among the accused – the public will love it, Nicolo. It shows everyone that the Judiciary can't be bought off. If you're worried about a little mud flying about – it won't stick to us. So get going, Commissaire, and get some results!'

Nicolo rose politely: 'Very good, Monsieur le Juge.'

'The border posts? Ports, airports?'

'All covered.'

'I don't want a chink anywhere,' barked the magistrate, who liked to combine a military style with the exhortations of a business tycoon. 'Don't forget: Berg, Berg, Berg . . .'

Which left Nicolo wondering precisely who was going to get anything out of this: the nation, or just the powers-that-be somewhere else wanting the guts of the powers-that-be right here.

Fournier might well disappear for months, Condroyer was dead, and as for Quentin – there'd been neither sight nor sound of him. Maybe they were keeping him for later.

Nicolo entered the Commissariat to tear a strip off his men.

He had regained his composure by the following morning and strode nonchalantly into the building to find Emilie Berg waiting for him.

'Is it me you wanted to see?' he asked.

She had installed herself in the waiting room as the cleaner was still sweeping up cigarette butts, cursing the entire police force for not bothering to use the ashtrays provided. Why anybody wanted to smoke anyway was beyond her – dirty, smelly habit.

Nicolo led Emilie into his office, but before speaking to her interrogated Pradal over the intercom: 'Bring in that telex.' This was done and the Commissaire nodded his satisfaction.

When Pradal had gone, he said: 'Right, Madame Berg, what's bothering you?'

'Last night about nine o'clock,' Emilie began, 'I was still at the shop doing some accounts, and I couldn't face going home to an empty house. The children were in the back room good as gold, and then I heard some little taps on the shutter on the street side, because of course I'd locked up. Well, I immediately thought it must be Philippe coming back quietly, if you see what I mean. So I naturally opened up again right away, and there in front of me, Monsieur, were two men in stocking masks, and they pushed me back into the shop.'

'Go on.'

'They wanted Philippe. Said they knew he wasn't at the house because they'd been there. And I told them he'd gone, and couldn't imagine when he'd be back. I was that scared, Monsieur it was awful. They went on about Philippe running out on them, and started shouting and bawling. He ran out on them like everyone else did, that's what they said.'

'Go on, Madame Berg.'

'After that, one of them went to the till and emptied it, and the other one got a knife out and slashed some dresses, about twenty they slashed. I couldn't move, I was terrified they'd get to the children – you can imagine. Anyway, the man at the till said: "Don't take much these days, do you?" I kept quiet and he said: "We'll let you know where to send the next lot. Keep your mouth shut too, think of the kids".'

'Then?'

'Then they went off.'

'Can you remember any physical details about them? Clothes, shoes, height and so on?'

Emilie did her best, and saw the Commissaire starting to smile. She remembered some more, and the interview ended with Nicolo taking her hands in his and thanking her surprisingly warmly. He told her he would send a man to guard her and the children: 'He'll stay with you as long as necessary, but I don't think that will be long.'

Evidently, she concluded as she was shown out, the Commissaire reckoned he knew the men. But he had gestured at the last moment as if he wanted to add something, then apparently had thought better of it. Still, he had been smiling, looked at her almost tenderly.

Inspector Germain arrived for work as she left the building. He made for his superior's office.

'Found Berg?' He jerked his head at the departing Emilie.

'Got him last night on the Swiss border.' He flicked his hand at the telex. 'We'll have him back within hours. But she doesn't know, and I didn't want to tell her. Nice girl. She'll have to know soon enough. She . . . er . . . was here about something else.' He brought Germain up to date, and Germain agreed a fat man and a thin man could only be Machefer and Gamel.

Nicolo extracted his holster and gun from a locked drawer: 'Her description was as clear as day. They smelt funny, she said.' He checked the clip on the pistol. 'They smelt of earth, like in the woods, she said. A vaguely mushroomy smell . . . I'll bet you anything they're in those old mushroom tunnels in Grèze Forest – less than a kilometre from this goddam office! We'll both go, and get Virel and Castagnier. This time we'll do without the Gendarmerie Nationale . . .'

When you've been asleep fifteen hours and it seems more like three days, and you open just one eye and notice that there's someone in Maryse's bed next to you who isn't Maryse, and it slowly dawns on you that the someone sitting there is a man and he looks the spitting image of Antonin Berg – you naturally vow never to touch another drop of chianti in your entire life.

Travers woke to the noise of Antonin coughing and mumbled: 'What's this – the last rites? Am I that bad?'

'I've been searching for you high and low,' his employer said. 'But Maryse spilled the beans and gave me the key.'

Travers rose unsteadily and got into Maryse's peignoir – its short sleeves embroidered with white swans reached half-way down his biceps and the hem an inch below his crotch: 'If daddy could see me now!'

Berg told him: 'Your piece was in today's issue.'

'What about my resignation?'

'Stick it up your peignoir, there's no reason for it now.'

'How come? You told me it was too early to go for Philippe.'

'AFP put out a story. My nephew was caught at the Swiss

118

border a few hours ago.'

Traver's face became grim: 'I'm sorry it turned out that way, and I mean that. I was only acting according to my principles, Monsieur Berg, but I'll say this – he looks like the fall guy in all this, to my way of thinking. Running away was a bad move.'

Old Berg shook his head: 'I'm partly to blame, because I told him he should either clear out or give himself up. I said that if he chose to run he could count on us.'

Travers lifted an eyebrow: 'And now they're bringing him back, and you'll have to let him fight it out for himself.'

The older man said nothing. Travers took a shower and returned bright as a button, resplendent in a looser garment of pink silk with crimson inlays and a flock of parrots staring impertinently through strategically-placed branches.

Antonin took no notice: 'I was too hard on him, but it was my instinctive first reaction. I was wrong. What I'd like, Travers, is for the paper to give him a break. If we could somehow avoid taking his defence, while reducing his role in this affair to its just proportions.'

'But I'm not Mr Big at *La Dépêche*, Monsieur, there *are* others.'

'I know. But I'm asking you to follow this thing through to the end now. The article with your byline today gives you the right to pull no punches . . .'

'. . . even if I do later.'

Antonin said: 'I am only asking you, not telling you, only asking you. After all, you yourself suggest he's been used, and that's my belief too.'

'I don't *want* to be awkward, Monsieur,' Travers said quietly.

They shook hands firmly, aware of sealing a bond, and Berg drove off in the Rolls, Jeannou at the wheel.

He eased himself against the seat, pleased with his performance. By going down on his knees he had flattered the man's vanity. While he could not depend a hundred per cent on Travers, he was certain he would entice him over to his camp before long. It simply had to work out. Nobody in the Berg clan was going to escape the fall-out from Philippe's escapade. A Berg nabbed at the frontier was one of the stories of the year. But Travers had skill enough to defuse what old Berg was now mentally referring to as 'the stink bomb'.

Especially as his code of professional conduct would be suscep- tible to a hefty pay rise, in the wake of Antonin's flattery. That

119

was how Antonin saw it, as he tapped the letter in his inside jacket pocket. He decided that Travers should get it in three days' time.

What the local press magnate, with his contempt for adversaries, did not know was that Travers had decided to pull his punches over Philippe for quite another reason. His own personal code of ethics had been called upon when he realized just what this scandal would mean for Emilie and the kids.

Nicolo had called her a nice girl. Had he known, Travers might have shaken hands with the Commissaire on that.

Chapter Four

A forlorn group of press people and onlookers stood in the drizzle outside the Law Courts the next day, swapping rumours and speculating on what would happen. The newsmen were local correspondents from the nationals, the radio stations, news agencies and the FR3 regional TV network. The story was still only at the news stage and the commentators were biding their time.

Philippe Berg had arrived handcuffed, that was the one solid piece of 'copy' so far. But there was some confusion about another exploit carried out by Nicolo and his side-kicks, namely the arrest of a certain Machefer, believed to be one of Paul Bossis's killers. It was said that Machefer put up a fight and was badly wounded in the head, or according to another version in the liver. Another snippet, given by a male nurse to a reporter, related that Machefer declared in the ambulance that 'the big shots had better watch out from now on'.

Machefer's accomplice, called Gamel or Trunel or something, made a getaway. A reporter told Nicolo: 'You'd have had the other bloke if you'd brought the gendarmes in with the dogs.' Nicolo winced at this and said they wouldn't even have got one of them if the gendarmes had been in on the act.

Travers was there, and when Philippe Berg emerged from the building he caught sight of Florence, leggy and smart in a shiny mac, but lost her again in the crowd surging around the steps. Berg was no longer in handcuffs but was flanked by a locally-known lawyer, Maître Blanchet, and his wife Emilie.

Florence strained forward in an attempt to hear what Philippe said in a brief statement, but gave up, noting only that although pale, he appeared confident. Blanchet and Emilie bundled him into a car amid a barrage of flashlights.

She wended her way to Travers: 'What did he say?' To her chagrin he seemed annoyed, and merely glanced at the overnight case she was holding. 'I've just got here from Paris. What's the score?'

Travers quoted: 'I am at liberty, I am innocent. As to those who are after me, I wouldn't sleep too soundly if I were in their shoes.'

Florence said: 'He means you, I suppose. I read your article.'

'Can't be sure, but I don't think so. He was getting at someone else. I've got to find out who, because, Madame, I'm assigned to cover the whole case from now on. Your dad's idea.'

She laughed: 'Fancy putting the prosecution onto it. Does that mean father's out to get him?'

'The prosecutor is now transferred to the defence. That is, he's got to roll back his campaign, put his kid gloves on. For the moment, at any rate.'

Florence half-sneered: 'Must pay more, I take it.' She scowled at him contemptuously.

'It'll be offered before long, but don't worry, I'll turn it down. I'll be wearing the kid gloves but my fingers will still be free to move.' He gave his pseudo-military salute and left.

She turned to see Quentin waiting for her and raising his hat: 'Threats like that from a man on a conditional discharge can't do him any good. You look superb, Florence.'

She beamed at him: 'As always. It must be the Paris air.' In fact it was the two delightful hours she had spent with Maurice Arras in a smart *salon de thé*.

As if he was thinking on similar lines, Quentin said he wished to apologize for his remarks after Arras's lecture at the Rotary Club. He was sad for Philippe, and upset for Antonin Berg.

Mocking him, Florence said: 'So your indulgence and courtesy have returned to you. That's nice. The commission of inquiry cleared you absolutely, I understand.'

'Completely. It was found that I could not possibly have known that Fournier, Condroyer and . . . hrumph . . . Berg were messing about behind my back. But tell me, how do you know that already?'

'I was in the same compartment as your wife, and she told me.'

Quentin's jaw dropped: 'You mean you talked about it?'

'Yes, quietly and politely, with no malice aforethought, as befits ladies who have shared the same man and do so no longer.'

'I'm relieved,' he said, thinking that that put paid to any hopes he might still have entertained with regard to Florence. He found he still desired her, and he carried her small case as they strolled along. He escorted her to the block where she lived, where they had spent such happy times. He wanted to tell her something about himself, for example that his stand-in at the Assemblée had stepped down, so that he, Quentin, could resume his seat now that he was no longer a Minister. But he sensed that it was the wrong moment.

He handed her the case and said: 'Well . . .'

She said brightly: 'Oh, do you know Maurice Arras?'

'No, why?'

'I wondered, that was all.'

'Well, I'll bump into you again before long. Goodbye Florence.'

Who the devil was Maurice Arras?

Florence felt weary and was looking forward to a nap.

She unlocked her letter-box and had to lean against the wall. There was a scribbled note from Mathilde. Her father had tried to do away with himself!

Mathilde was waiting for her on the steps. Immediately, she assured Florence that Monsieur was alive, and uninjured.

They rushed up to his room, and Florence saw at once the large calibre pistol on the bedside table. Mathilde pointed at the ceiling and she saw a hole in it.

'Jeannou and me heard it go off, Madame, and when we got here he was just there holding the gun. He was running one of those films of Madame Gabrielle. Oh, we *was* frightened. Thank the Lord he's all right. Do you think he'll try it again?'

'Where is he?'

'Afraid I don't know, Madame. He told Jeannou to drive him off in the Rolls, and that was hours ago.'

'I'll wait.'

'Yes, Madame.'

Gilbert Bossis and Catherine were nearing the end of lunch at the Hotel des Messageries, when Antonin Berg stormed in.

Or rather, hobbled in. He was wearing a jet black overcoat that seemed too long for him and had a thick white muffler round his neck. He used a stick, and leaned heavily on it. His voice rattled when he asked if he could join them.

'I'm lunching with my daughter,' Bossis said, emphasizing the relationship. 'If my daughter has no objection . . .' Berg sat down with an effort. 'Well how are things? We came to see your nephew in handcuffs, did we? You can't deny it – Catherine saw you in the Rolls outside the courts. She wanted to look into the eyes of one of my Paul's killers.'

'He's my Paul too,' Berg croaked, trying not to bring on another coughing fit.

'Not yours!'

'Have it your way! But I loved the boy.'

'You don't expect me to swallow that on the pretext that one of your hacks attacked Philippe Berg.'

Catherine sensed the other tables listening, and ordered: 'Keep your voices down.'

'My hack will go through with this,' Berg puffed. 'Catherine, you know Travers after all.'

'He's straight, I like him. He'll go through with it. I know how fond he was of Paul. What I don't know is why you want *him* to handle it.'

Bossis chortled: 'But of course you know why. It's to save himself, save the family honour. Besides, going through with it is a joke, since Philippe is the scapegoat anyway.'

'That's precisely what I am resolved to prevent,' Antonin said. 'He's a crass idiot, but I'd like to get him off the hook. He'll pay, if there's anything to pay. I'm not saying anyone, neither myself nor the family. None of us has besmirched ourselves, other than Philippe, but we shall all get dragged through the mud. That's what I want to avoid, that'll be Travers's task. He'll go right through to the end with it.' He was thumping on the table and glaring at Catherine. Some people turned in their direction. He added: 'So much the better if Travers manages to prove him innocent while he's at it.'

Berg got up, took three paces and then came back, standing over Bossis: 'Gilbert, I can't look at Gabrielle's films alone, I'm too old. That's all I came to tell you, and the rest was a charade. I'd really like you to come back to La Commanderie,' he said in a loud voice, so that the other tables turned to watch him slouch his way out.

Gilbert said: 'He's like some old tragedian, but he can still bring tears to my eyes. I can't but like him, Catherine.'

Florence looked up and saw him enter his room.

She blinked and frowned. She was not to know that Jeannou had dropped him at the main gate, and he had walked up to the house. His daughter was deep in thought and realized he was there only when she heard him wheezing. In silence he unwound his white muffler and wriggled out of his coat, throwing his stick on the bed.

Antonin stared at the gun in Florence's hands. He took it from her and she made no attempt to keep hold of it.

He examined the magazine and said: 'You've removed the bullets, but I still have a whole box.'

'Unfortunately I couldn't find them.' She went to him and kissed him on both cheeks, no longer wanting to scold him. The old man was grey and thin and unsteady on his feet.

She said: 'So you wanted me to become manager of *La Dépêche* earlier than planned?'

'And for it to become respectable, like you said, as quickly as possible? Perhaps.' He gave a chuckle. 'No, don't worry, nobody shot himself yet by firing up at the ceiling! I suppose it was Mathilde who told you about the incident.' He sank onto the bed.

'Incident!'

'D'you prefer the term exercise? I wanted to make sure the gun still worked properly, that's all.'

'Why?'

'Why what?'

'Oh skip it,' she snapped. 'Nobody ever has the last word with you.'

'Oh yes they do. Yes, they certainly do.' He tapped his chest to convey his approaching demise.

'Oh, stop playing about,' Florence shouted.

Suddenly he grew serious, pleading almost: 'Tell me you'll take over, Flo. Tell me you'll keep your promise and the whole thing won't collapse after I've gone. Or I'll finish it here and now, d'you hear?'

'Blackmailer! You have my promise. If you want me to swear I'll swear it. But in return, promise me you'll stop the shooting practice.'

He looked at her out of the corner of his eye, and she realized he'd have his own way in the end. She expected him to laugh out loud, and was alarmed when he didn't. He looked so worn out, and she was astonished to hear him murmur that he'd asked Gilbert to come back. He had done it in public, humiliated himself, he said.

'No you didn't humiliate yourself, you sought peace. And

there's nothing dishonourable in that.'

'Don't you believe it, my girl. I'm afraid to be alone. I can't stand all these ghosts, all these threatening events.'

'What ghosts, what threats?'

'Your mother,' he said waving at the big screen. 'Your mother and Paul Bossis. The spectre I have become. As to the threats, well Philippe was detained . . .'

'And freed.'

'For how long? *There's* a crack in the wall that surrounds me. Jean-Jacques's another. Keep in to yourself, but Jean-Jacques is hand in glove with Fournier, with Fournier who's on the run with his money. And close to Condroyer too, the drowned rat, drowned because of Fournier. Travers told me the dates your brother and he lunched together.'

'That doesn't prove . . .'

'Who knows? I'm uneasy about it. And I'll confess something to you: I intend to bribe Travers.'

'I know, I was with him, he said quite a lot.'

'Well?'

'I'm thinking what you're thinking: you haven't bought him, he'll do what *he* thinks.'

Antonin grew excited: 'Precisely. I realized my mistake too late. He'll see it through all right, but I can see now that he'll find us at the end of it. He'll learn about Jean-Jacques for a start, which is just about enough to do for us all, kill off *La Dépêche* and have us run out of Chateauvallon.'

'Does that mean Travers has to be bumped off too?' Florence laughed, but it came out closer to a giggle.

He chuckled as well, and again she detected that perfidious and dangerous scowl of his. He shook his head in a senile way and replied: 'No point, he's too smart. Even from his grave he'd report who killed him!'

They both laughed, this time whole-heartedly. Florence hurried on to say that, when she had Travers under her thumb, she'd show him just how far he could go. She knew this was the kind of gutsy language her father liked, and she so wanted to please him, to draw him out of his melancholy. She would not have many more opportunities.

After a silence Antonin rasped: 'I'm counting on you. You're like me.'

'Not entirely, thank God.'

126

She put her coat on. It seemed a good moment to leave, with the old devil perking up.

'I'll call in on Gilbert and tell him to come back.'

'Thanks, Flo.'

She smiled in a kindly way at his heavy humour, another hint that he may be moving into a new phase. Then he told her to take the box of bullets from his little desk. 'Take them away,' he muttered.

Old Berg stared unblinking as the car moved down to the gate. Then he turned and looked at the pistol still lying on the bed. Finally he shuffled across to a cupboard and extracted a shoebox. Inside was a wooden carton full of bullets.

Three days after his release, Philippe Berg was summoned by the examining magistrate. Maître Blanchet picked him up in his car, and Florence went with them to give moral support to her cousin, as Emilie could find nobody to stay in with the children. This last fact took some of the wind out of Philippe, who realized he and his family already appeared to be outcasts. Everyone was avoiding them.

In view of this, it was easy for Berg to become certain in his own mind that he would be charged formally before the day was out.

Blanchet kept telling him: 'Don't be silly, Monsieur Berg, there is no reason to suppose that he'll charge you. And remember, a charge is not a conviction, far from it. If you're charged, it will enable me to have access to all the relevant documents. I can defend you much better at that stage.'

'I'm grateful to you, but it's me they'll be sending to jail.'

Florence broke in: 'I've been finding out a few things about Perugino. He seems to be one of those exalted kind of judges, the new generation. And it's my feeling he doesn't want to get at you at all, but is aiming much higher.'

'Meaning?'

'Higher, just that.'

'A bigshot? Someone at the top? Quentin perhaps?'

'I wouldn't know.'

'He'd be an excellent target,' Philippe said with a little laugh that could be taken several ways.

They had to wait about an hour in the passage outside the judge's office. Philippe and his lawyer went in, and Florence used the time to run over some papers she wanted Catherine to

127

sign later that day. She would certainly be late, she imagined, for despite her remarks to Philippe she was not optimistic and expected to be in the passage for some time.

She was wrong. The discussion was harsh but brief. Maître Blanchet led off, his main point being that his client had no connection whatsoever with the Bossis affair. He was brought up sharp with the reminder that the Prosecutor's Office would decide that, and that this was merely the stage of the initial inquiries.

'Prosecutor? He'll throw it out too, Monsieur le Juge! This inquiry in no way adversely affects my client's position, unless, if I may say so, you decide to combine the two questions.'

Perugino looked at him contemptuously: 'I must ask you, Maître, to let *me* decide how I proceed.'

'Even so, Monsieur Le Juge, I make bold to suggest that it will prove difficult to show that my client has any complicity in the murder, bearing in mind that he was a relation to the victim.'

'We shall see, Maître. Now, Monsieur Berg, I understand you were in charge of verifying the town council's tenders and contracts: also that your design office, which was deleted from the main specification, did work on Les Sablons. You will realize, I dare say, that the investigation Bossis was carrying out mentioned you very directly?'

'That doesn't prove that . . .'

'That you recruited the killers?'

'Certainly not. I consistently refused to get mixed up in this business.'

Maître Blanchet closed his eyes and rounded his shoulders.

'Aha!' cried Perugino, 'so there was indeed a connection! In order to refuse something, something must be proposed. Monsieur Berg here was, therefore, aware of the plan. He must have known that Fournier was going to get rid of Bossis, his relation! Berg, did I say that you yourself committed the crime? I did not. Nevertheless, you allowed it to be committed.'

'An absolutely simplistic deduction!' Blanchet cried in protest, loud enough for Florence to hear it on the other side of the door. She knew what that meant. She jumped up and started pacing about. A clerk came out and got two gendarmes to sign a paper, after which they went into the judge's room. The rest she could recite by heart.

'That will be all for today, Maître. You are now detained, Monsieur Berg, conditional detention pending further inquiries.'

128

Philippe sat up as stiff as a poker. One of the gendarmes produced handcuffs and clapped them on Berg's wrists. The judge informed him that this was required by law, and looked pleased. The door swung open and Florence heard Philippe cry out: 'You're using me to get at Quentin.'

The judge gave a practised chuckle: 'Quentin? Why on earth Quentin? You must be imagining things, Monsieur Berg.'

Blanchet joined Florence: 'But Perugino's not imagining things.' They watched Philippe walk down the passage, a gendarme on either side, his back hunched.

At length Florence said: 'Article 137 of the Penal Code. The choice of the means of constraint is the sole prerogative of the examining magistrate, dear colleague.'

'We'll see what the Public Prosecutor's Office says about it,' growled Blanchet. He looked like a fox that has had its tail pecked off by a chicken.

The wall clock told them it was just before 6.00 p.m. The radio was softly playing background music.

On the kitchen table Catherine was signing the papers as Florence looked on.

She told Florence: 'I hope this helps. Poor Florence, it's awful for you. Philippe actually in prison, it's hardly credible. Please God he's not guilty of anything. On the head of my child I wish it, I swear I do Florence.'

Florence feigned indifference: 'It's a lot to hope for. Judge Perugino confirmed he could be an accessory to murder, according to Blanchet. He couldn't have been, you must believe that Catherine.'

The girl looked at her gravely and nodded. With her tummy quite big now, she possessed a certain dignity.

'If you say so, I believe you,' the girl said.

'Thank you. Oh dear, it was dreadful having to tell Emilie, can you imagine it! I'm spending the night with her, it's the least I can do.'

She had not bothered to contact the family. They all knew. The news of a Berg in jail had spread over the town and was on every editorial desk in the country by now.

In point of fact the clan took the news with every appearance of calm. From *La Dépêche* Jean-Jacques phoned his father, and Antonin simply said it was to be expected, that he had not

129

imagined Philippe would turn up for afternoon tea. Jean-Jacques thought that was funny, and so did Marie-Lou when he told her.

Florence knew that Julien would feel bad about it. She felt whacked out herself, more concerned about Emilie and the children than for Philippe.

Catherine was chattering on again, telling her she preferred not to know the result of the scan: 'I don't mind which it is. Girl or boy, it's Paul's baby and that's all I care.'

'That's exactly how I felt when I was expecting. I hoped it wouldn't be an idiot. I had a girl.'

The girl smiled: 'Paul told me once. Alexandra, seventeen years old.'

'Well, you are well informed! Yes, Alexandra, seventeen. She's in the United States with her father. At first I kept her with me in Paris, and then when she was thirteen she wanted to go to America on holiday, to Florida. I suppose it was too wonderful and in the end she stayed. We aren't enemies, of course, but I gave in to her father. A father is so appealing, so reassuring, so fascinating. Especially when he's a well-known writer, rolling in money with hundreds of friends.'

'Oh, I am sorry,' Catherine said softly.

'What the hell!'

Florence prepared to leave, collecting the documents and her things. Then she froze, waved a finger at the radio, and Catherine put up the volume. Quentin was speaking in the solemn yet rather facetious style often adopted towards the press by public figures. She had heard it often.

Unfortunately, his remarks were almost over, and all the two women heard was: 'Out of personal ambition? Personal interest? No, gentlemen. If I am going before the electorate, it is to give them the opportunity of telling me from the bottom of their hearts what they think of me. My only ambition today is to become an ordinary member of parliament once more . . .'

Florence cut him off. Catherine could not resist giving a nervous laugh: 'I thought you were friends.'

Florence glanced at her out of the corner of her eye: 'We used to be.'

She went back to her own apartment to fetch a few essentials for the night. But before leaving for Emilie's house, she dialled a number.

'Quentin,' said Quentin.

'It's me. I just wanted to tell you something. I am sick and tired of public figures who seek office *because they have no personal interest or ambition.*'

'But you don't . . .'

But Florence had replaced the receiver.

Quentin went back to the chair at the other end of the living room and resumed reading the book he had laid down on the pedestal table.

'Florence Berg,' his wife said, 'Know her voice anywhere.'

She was seated before the empty grate on a settee whose back faced the room. Quentin saw only her ash blonde hair.

'What a pest she is!'

Madame Quentin said calmly: 'A pest who would have liked you for herself, rather like me.'

'For God's sake, she doesn't understand . . . Neither of you understands that if I don't stand for election everyone will draw the obvious conclusion. Huh, they'll say, Quentin not standing? Well of course, it's because he's mixed up in that business about Les Sablons! It's been a close shave, and I'm never going to let that happen now. D'you hear me, never!'

She remonstrated, indicating to him by her manner that he should keep his cool – but he ranted on about his just anger, his humiliation, how women were impossible and incapable of understanding these things . . .

'But we understand only too well when it comes to being left on our own.'

Quentin strode to the door: 'I'm going for a walk.'

'Take a scarf, *chéri*, and don't forget to tell Florence I entirely agree with her.'

His true motive for calling on Florence was still cloudy in his mind. Even so, he was prepared to admit that he wanted her assurance that he had to stand. In one way it seemed a pretty weak kind of façade he was putting up. It might render him a more obvious target, one that was easier to hit.

However, as he left home Florence was ringing Catherine's doorbell again. She had called Florence over the phone.

'You scared me when you came on the phone, I was convinced the baby was on its way. What's all the excitement?'

'Excitement's right. My dad's been here, yes the Great Albertas

Kovalic, I didn't want to let him in but then I realized he'd just break the door down. I'll skip the details . . . he was so awful . . .'

'What did he want?'

'He wants the baby to be a Kovalic and not a Bossis.'

'He's a bit late for that!'

'I didn't mention the legal arrangements you are doing for me, because he'd have thumped me. But he was screaming bloody murder anyway, so I think he guessed what was going on. He could see after a while that I had my own ideas, and he said I'd be sorry one day.'

Florence gave a little sniff: 'What's that supposed to mean?'

'Can't say. He finally said that choosing the name Bossis or Berg was asking for trouble. One day they'd be elbowing each other aside to lick the Kovalics' boots, he said.'

'Huh. Did he say he'd be back?'

'No, he said I'd come round on my own.' Catherine paused and bit her lip. 'Do you think I could possibly ask Travers to c-come and s-sleep here? I could fix up a camp bed in the small room.'

'I can't think of a better idea! It would be good if Travers were here. I'll ask him if you like.'

'Oh no, we are close enough friends. I'll do it, but I wanted your opinion. I mean, it might be embarrassing in some way.'

'Afraid of gossip?'

'Rather.'

Florence put an arm round Catherine: 'My dear girl, better to be a wee bit afraid of gossip than terrified of the heavy mob. Get Travers over as quick as possible, he could be your survival kit for the next three weeks.'

Catherine turned round, they exchanged a little hug. 'Thanks, Florence,' she said.

Machefer's partner Gamel was holed up on the Eastern edge of the town. With Machefer in clink he decided to lie low at a hundred francs a day, in a tumble-down terrace house occupied by an ex-street girl called Adolphine who served him food no respectable pig would touch. It was a lot of money for nothing, but she asked no questions, not even his name.

It occurred to him that nothing would be easier than to slit her throat, but some neighbour would be round likely as not in less than a day to ask if she was all right.

He was out of money, and eventually decided to risk a visit to

132

Philippe Berg's wife Emilie. He left the hovel one evening and tried to look inconspicuous, which was far from easy with no one in the streets and the whole town glued to their television-sets.

As he approached the Berg villa a police car came out of the next turning and he froze in a gateway. The patrol slowly disappeared, and he investigated further. After a while he concluded that there was no guard on the house. But he also decided he wouldn't do it that night. The slut would have to wait for her money.

On the following evening he put in a phone call to Emilie Berg from a callbox. Emilie phoned Florence at once.

She phoned Emilie literally trembling from head to foot. She had all the ground floor lights on, and carried a big black kitchen knife in her right hand as she opened the front door with her left.

'They phoned here,' she blurted out, 'the men who messed up the shop, they phoned.'

Florence led her to a chair: 'Take it easy, Machefer's detained.'

'Yes, I mean the other one. He said he's coming here tonight, and I've got to wait here all night with the money. I'll have to let him have it, he said if I told the police a friend of his would snatch one of the children and that would be the last of the kid.' Emilie sat panting on the edge of the chair, her knees clamped tight. She might have been somewhat less wound-up had she known that Gamel was as scared as she was, and that he hadn't a friend in the world except Machefer.

She was still holding the knife, and now put it down on a coffee table. Florence knew that its only function had been to give her an ounce or two of courage – she could never have defended herself with it against a determined killer. Florence kept quiet; if you can't think of anything useful to say, don't say anything, she thought to herself.

Emilie was wringing her hands and she wished she could work something out for her.

The phone bell split the silence. 'It's him again!' Emilie screamed.

'Florence?' the man said.

'Travers!'

'Catherine said you were there. How's Emilie?'

'Come right over at once. And Travers, give some kind of signal, a whistle or something.'

'I'll whistle "Keep the home fires burning".'

As he had said, Gamel let the front door knocker drop lightly. He too was trembling. He had come into the town as naturally as he could, but had been forced to freeze several times. Now he was sick with fear, but prepared to hit out if the Berg black girl had prepared a reception committee.

But it was Travers who received him, with his head in Gamel's solar plexus. Less than a minute later he was on a tiled floor with his hands bound behind his back and Emilie's knife at his Adam's apple.

'Name?' Travers said. 'The name of your pal? Where's he now? Hurry up. One, two, three and it goes in. Right? One . . . two . . . three.' Travers dug the knife in and Gamel gasped. 'Four . . . Five.' The knife went in further and Gamel bled.

When Nicolo charged in ahead of Germain and Pradal, Gamel was unconscious, and there was a large sticking plaster on his neck.

Gamel had spilled everything, that is, he admitted he had no accomplice waiting to kill the children. Nicolo had him taken away in the ambulance Travers had told him to bring.

And now the Commissaire said to Travers: 'I'll give him another going over, but I don't reckon we'll get any more. Machefer is the only partner he ever had. In any case, nobody would risk a kidnap or killing like that, just to get a few banknotes for a day or two.'

He turned to Emilie, recovering with a large glass of Scotch; 'We've met up quicker than I expected, Madame Berg, but I've some more good news for you. Machefer has formally declared that your husband had nothing to do with Bossis's murder. He told us Fournier and Condroyer told him about it, but that Monsieur Berg didn't believe they would go that far. Our friend Gamel will confirm that, or my name's not Nicolo.'

Emilie sobbed with joy and seized the Commissaire's hands: 'He'll be released now, right away, won't he?'

'That depends on the examining magistrate.'

Germain and Pradal were watching the ambulance go off, Nicolo went out to join them and Travers followed him. They shook hands: 'Good work Travers, I'll recommend you for promotion.'

'Not at all, Commissaire. It was you who grabbed him, I only called you in.'

Nicolo gave him a hefty thump on the arm and got in his car.

The tyres sang 'Keep the home fires burning' as Pradal flung the vehicle in the direction of the Commissariat.

Judge Perugino sat in the office lent to him the next afternoon scowling at Maître Blanchet.

The lawyer had requested an immediate audience, and had now revealed to him that Commissaire Nicolo obtained a formal statement from Machefer and Gamel to the effect that Philippe Berg was in no way involved in the murder of Paul Bossis.

'Since when,' Perugino said looking down his nose, 'has an office of the criminal police provided confidential information to defence counsel? Most improper. But we'll let it pass. Monsieur Berg is innocent, you say? I think we should take another look at the proceedings of the first audience.'

Blanchet said: 'As you wish, Monsieur le Juge, but I don't think we shall find anything connecting my client with murder.'

Perugino resumed his supercilious air: 'If you don't mind, I too have an excellent memory, Maître. Your client *refused* to become involved, those were his very words. But he was aware of the intention to kill Bossis. Did he tell Bossis? Did he alert the police? He did not, Maître. He made no such move. I am justified – and I shall no doubt do so – in charging him with failure to assist a person in danger. And that, my dear Maître, is tantamount to tacit complicity in a murder.'

Blanchet's eyes narrowed, but he smiled. Such vindictiveness on the part of young Perugino was close to persecution. He bit his tongue and decided to appeal to the natural connivance that exists among young men of law, just as members in the Assemblée join each other for a glass of Chablis after attacking each other in debate.

'Between ourselves, dear friend,' he said, 'I can't believe you are really out to get Berg. What's the point? I can only suppose, knowing your intelligence and artfulness, that you are aiming at something quite different.'

Perugino fell for this tactic. He had no doubt of his own intelligence, but he wondered whether he was *that* artful. To be honest, he wished he was, and he found it rather delightful that Blanchet saw him as a modern Machiavelli.

With the suavity of a Richelieu, or so he hoped, the judge said: 'Since we are discussing intuitions, dear friend, mine is that your client is trying to cover someone more highly placed than himself, in fact far bigger.'

'An intuition founded on . . . ?'

'My intuition!'

Well I asked for that, Blanchet told himself – either he's making a monkey out of me or he's a perfect humbug.

The defence counsel quickly ran through several names in his memory and threw out: 'Quentin.'

He was careful to show that he intended to state rather than ask, thus hoping to force Perugino against the wall while risking nothing by pronouncing Quentin's name in a neutral tone of voice. He had uttered the name much as he might have advanced a pawn in a game of chess. Perugino was no fool in fact, and Blanchet thought it more than likely that the judge had actually sought to extract if from him. On the other hand, he had to show Perugino that he was not some clod of a lawyer whose client kept secrets from him. Consequently, he repeated with a mysterious undertone: 'Quentin. Hm, why not?'

'Indeed, why not Quentin?'

'Yes, why not!' Blanchet by now was unsure who was fooling whom.

Perugino walked him to the door, and Blanchet now felt that his client's position might not be as bad as all that. First, because the judge had come with him to the door; secondly, because Perugino had calmly added: 'It's very simple, my friend. If Berg decides to make a clean breast of it, he will find the prison gate opening of its own accord.'

Which Blanchet duly repeated to his client within the hour.

Philippe Berg said: 'A clean breast? About what?' And then turned his back on Blanchet.

A plea for conditional release went in after that, and was rejected a few days later.

Chapter Five

While Philippe languished in captivity, Chateauvallon society had further developments to chew on, and the rest of the Berg family went about its business feeling it was quite able to do so without him.

And, although Gamel denied that he and Machefer were responsible for Paul Bossis's death, Chateauvallon was glad he was under lock and key. Meanwhile, its citizens continued to demand action against petty theft and break-ins.

Gilbert Bossis went back to the big house. He was bored with the repetitive menus at the Hotel des Messageries, sat glumly for hours in the foyer or his room, and remembered tenderly the walks he used to take along the lanes and in the woods gathering mushrooms. Also, he had adopted the role of protector and escort to Catherine and was irritated in the extreme now that Travers had moved in with her. In any case he yearned for his old routine, and his return to La Commanderie would show her his dispproval in an obvious manner. She had not even attempted to dissuade him, however.

Soon after Antonin's eruption in the hotel, he told her: 'I've a mind to go back home after all.'

To which she replied: 'You'll be so much happier there, it's true.'

Antonin spotted him as he was returning from Julien's little theatre in the barn. Gilbert was emerging from a taxi with his suitcase.

'Well, old chap, what brings you to La Commanderie?' Berg enquired, displaying neither joy nor surprise.

'I'm told you're declining rather fast these days.'

'You don't look too good yourself, come to that.'

'No one could survive the diet I've been on. I need a change.'

They entered the house arm in arm, and began once more to watch the Gabrielle films in Berg's room.

Berg would say something like: 'She still has the same effect on me as the day she played *Intermezzo* at the Workshop in '45.'

And Bossis would retort: 'Except that it was in '38 when she played *Intermezzo*, and it was at the Athenée, my dear Antonin.'

As before they had their rows, but they were shorter, ending in a bout of coughing from Antonin as often as not.

Besides Bossis was keener to know how the Machefer-Gamel saga was proceeding. He wanted to know the date of the trial, and all the details about the guillotine. Antonin veered away from the subject, worrying in a confused way about the extent of the fall-out they could expect. His chief concern was to 'be gone' as he termed it before the flak started flying from the court. He had seen some of Travers's articles and gently suggested he could soften his line a little; and Travers had done so – his true reason being remorse over his role in Philippe Berg's downfall. The old man thanked him for his cooperation, never suspecting that Travers had decided he'd had enough of Chateauvallon, and had been in touch with a former colleague who was now editor of *France-Matin* in Lorieux.

The venerable pair began to take strolls through the La Grèze woods with shotguns slung from their shoulders, each watching the other to see if he would tire of stumbling around aimlessly, and each returning to the house satisfied that the other was bearing up less well. Often they took a rest on the benches in the theatre and watched a wild-haired Julien and curvaceous Thérèse holding rehearsals for the Shakespeare play.

The evening of the première, when the cream of Chateauvallon sat squirming on the benches, was a success in its own way, since the actors were sufficiently quiet for the audience to engage in its favourite sport of relaying gossip. Wasn't it surprising that Catherine Kovalic was shacked up with that Travers, you know the journalist? How awful that they'd transferred that poor Philippe to another prison. As to the play, well it could have been a lot better as entertainment, but Madame Moribeaux was really quite impressive with her bit about Anthony and the horse.

Afterwards, everyone made sure they congratulated Antonin for producing such a talented son, and for looking so sprightly. And how was dear Monsieur Bossis? Hadn't he come for the play? Antonin said he preferred the cinema.

The reason Bossis stayed away was that he could not bear seeing Catherine and Travers together. He was completely unaware that Catherine at that very moment was at the clinic suffering from labour pains. He was told around midnight as he returned from a muddy walk round the walls of the property. The audience had dispersed at the theatre, Julien was smiling at his success and Antonin was in a deep sleep.

Jeannou turned out with the Rolls and drove Gilbert into the town.

The baby was a long time coming. Travers had arrived at the apartment to find the pains starting, and had got her to the clinic at once. For hours he paced the corridor, trying to resist chain-smoking.

At length a nurse appeared from nowhere, scurried over to him and announced: '*Bravo Monsieur, un beau petit garçon, trois kilos cinq cents!*' She waved him in and he edged up to Catherine who was still panting, leaning heavily on her side. The woman who had delivered the baby showed him the infant 'He looks like you,' she declared, beaming on the wrinkled thing in a transparent cot.

Travers went to Catherine: 'Are you all right Catherine, *ma chérie*?'

She mumbled: 'Is that you, Paul? It's a boy. Isn't it wonderful!'

Travers tiptoed out, explaining to the women that he was a friend and that the father was dead. He phoned Gilbert Bossis, and sat in a tubular chair with a canvas seat and backrest. After a minute he bowed his head and grief welled up from somewhere round his heart.

Bossis found him like it, and feared the worst: 'Something gone wrong, Travers?'

'A boy, three kilos and a half.'

'But you're crying!'

'Paul, Paul . . .'

Travers got up and Gilbert took him in his arms: 'You're a good lad, Travers, a good lad.'

And off he scampered, bearing a couple of dozen flowers he had pinched from vases at La Commanderie. They directed him to the room where Catherine had been wheeled off to, and Travers left on foot.

There was no question of going back to Catherine's place. He had no place there, she had no need of him. Travers felt curiously on his own again, useless. Suddenly, a whole mass of confused thoughts welded themselves into a single conclusion. And this was that the real reason he had contacted *France-Matin* was so that he would not have to see Catherine again, or the baby. Though strangely, he almost believed it was his.

He had bucked up by the time he reached Maryse's apartment, where he found the occupier with Favrot, who was occupying her bed.

'Dreadfully sorry, you chaps,' he said, raising an imaginary hat. 'I fear I am in the wrong apartment.'

Maryse looked up at him repentantly from the pillow: 'I'm sorry too, but you disappeared – didn't even see you at the office as you've been out on jobs so much.'

'I've been doing cleaning jobs of an evening.'

She sat on the edge of the bed: 'Well, what happens now?'

'Ah now, there'll be baby's bottles. It's a boy, you guys, and it weighs three and a half kilos!'

'It!' said Maryse in disgust.

Favrot broke in: 'Sorry Travers, I'll push off if . . .'

'Oh no you won't,' Maryse cried.

Travers raised a hand: 'You stay right where you are, old boy. Sweet dreams.'

Whether they dreamed or did something else, he was past caring when he eased himself down on the camp bed in Catherine's apartment.

Two evenings after that he was on his way out of the clinic when he bumped into Florence.

'*Salut* Travers, how is she, and the baby?'

'She's just beautiful, but the kid's a bit cool. Won't even look at my rattle.'

She laughed, and he immediately asked: 'Any news about Philippe?'

'You know as much as I do. I hear you're off to *France-Matin*.' He gawped and she hurried on: 'I've just got here from Paris.'

He quickly changed the subject: 'Either you're just arriving or just going. Lorieux's an old friend of mine, and I still see him quite often. It's true, I want to leave Chateauvallon.' But she had not let up and he had more or less been forced to expand on the *France-Matin* business.

140

'Why are you going?'

'Several reasons.'

He glanced down and then looked up again. He was again struck by the intensity of her gaze. In other circumstances . . .

'You're a dirty louse, Travers,' she said, her eyes boring into him. 'You can't do that to me, I need you on *La Dépêche*.'

He gawped at her again: 'You?'

'Me. And sooner than you think!'

The formal transfer of power took place three days later.

Antonin Berg summoned the entire staff and the ceremony was held in the editorial room, where the outgoing boss kept his fur-collared coat on.

Florence, who had returned to her old room at La Commanderie, brought him in in the Rolls. She took him up to the first floor where the personnel had been waiting an hour. He leaned on her arm as he entered the room, but declined the offer of a chair.

Old Berg scanned the assembly, and told them his health no longer allowed him to run the paper. He thanked them for their loyal service and added: 'It's a tough business dying, my friends, at least it is for me. I console myself with the thought that my departure will not be a disappointment to everyone!' A few chuckles, and he flicked his gleeful eyes from Favrot to Travers to Edelman, Melchior, Armand Berg and Julien Berg, finally to Jean-Jacques and Marie-Lou who stood unmoved. 'Those who have sometimes disliked what they took to be my old-fashioned views will be relieved to learn that they have been proved right at last. As Florence is my oldest child, I hereby hand over the succession to her.'

Without thinking, almost the entire company turned to look at Jean-Jacques. He was pale and kept his eyes on Florence, who looked elsewhere. With something of a show, he bowed towards her, for the simple reason that there was little else he could do. She wondered for a moment whether he had still hoped for the job up until the last minute.

Neither Armand nor Julien nor Thérèse indicated that they had known since the previous evening. Certainly, they were sad for J-J, but they were glad Florence would be at the helm. Not for the first time Armand reflected on the simple fact that could not be gainsaid: people liked Florence.

141

The inimitable Marie-Lou was responsible for the only hitch at the ceremony. Travers recounted it when he popped in to see Catherine at the clinic.

He said: 'The old chap was already on his way out, shaking a few hands on the way, and it was really rather moving. And then Michel, you know Marie-Lou's boy, yelled out: "I say, mother, has dad been booted out?" '

Catherine exclaimed: 'Good Lord, what ever age is he?'

'Seventeen, but seventeen or not, Marie-Lou gave him a swipe that would have felled an ox. Old Berg was already in the corridor, and asked what was going on. Anyway it's over now – the king is dead, long live the queen!'

Her majesty accompanied her father back to La Commanderie in the Rolls. Neither of them spoke until he suddenly asked: 'My goodness, what's *La Dépêche* going to do about your Quentin fellow, I mean for his election campaign?'

'Father!' she chided. 'He's not my Quentin anymore, I've told you a thousand times.'

He patted her hand: 'You know Florence what I am going to die of? Relief!'

Antonin Berg died that same evening.

He was sitting in an armchair watching one of the films, but he was unable to focus on it. Gabrielle was on the screen in all the beauty and grace of her twenty years, listening in an evening gown to the silent avowals of her partner Tino Miranda. As they used to in the old pictures, she looked in front of her demurely with downcast eyes. Then, her eyes looked out of the screen to the staring eyes of her husband, who had at last joined her in another place.

Florence came in just before midnight to see how he was. The only sound was the low hum of the projector, the room cosy with the dim light from the screen casting weird shadows on the curtains and the walls. She saw her mother's hand kissed by the once-fabulous Tino Miranda. And then saw her father. He had faded out. Around his neck was a pearl necklace that had belonged to his wife. On his lap was a note in his handwriting: 'Necklace for Catherine. I wish her to be considered as *part of the family*.' He had underlined the final phrase, and she found this rather wonderful, pathetic too.

Florence roused Gilbert Bossis. He followed her into the room

142

in his pyjamas. Gabrielle filled the whole screen as he entered, and his initial thought was that she belonged to him alone from now on. But he immediately realized that, without Antonin, she was no longer alive for him. He began sobbing.

Florence went out and told Mathilde. Then she phoned her brothers.

Laid out in a new suit and surrounded with candles, Antonin Berg seemed ill rather than dead. Mathilde was kneeling at the foot of the bed praying.

Marie-Lou was in the main living room compiling a list of people to invite to the funeral, and Julien and Thérèse, who had stayed with their father all night, had gone back to their place to get some rest.

'And who's keeping the vigil tonight, it's already eight o'clock?' said Marie-Lou.

'Florence and myself,' said Armand, now on his fourth brandy in the window seat. He was glaring at Michel who was playing with Julien's kids. Michel looked angry, and for a good reason; since his mother had clouted him in public, he wanted to get his own back in some way. He had learned that Marie-Lou was a stupid name, the sort of name used by whores.

Armand was pouring her a brandy, and she said: 'Not much for me please. Keeping vigil over a corpse, what a thing, especially this one.'

'Kindly keep your thoughts to yourself, in that case. I happen to be his son, and so is your husband.'

'Oh yes, sorry,' she said, adding: 'I've got a hundred and fifty-seven so far.' She sucked on her ballpoint.

'What?'

'Guests.'

'Not many. Try inviting some of your enemies.'

'Hey, you've drunk half the bottle.'

Armand wished he had detested his father less often over the years, but consoled himself with the thought that he had loved him deeply at moments. In the centre of the large room the youngsters were playing, squabbling, laughing. Death was one floor up for them, and the old man couldn't have meant much to them: too distant, too gruff. He always said they made too much noise.

Jean-Jacques arrived from *La Dépêche*; 'Couldn't get away, it's been a heavy day.'

143

Marie-Lou could not resist the jibe: 'How're you getting along with the new boss.'

'Oh, she received the condolences of everyone we knew,' her husband replied, ignoring her and addressing Armand. 'And then she brought out her new broom. D'you know what she kept saying? "Thank you everybody, but the paper goes on". Anyone would think it was some kind of circus. Then old ma Frochot, the chief accountant, asked if she'd like to see the guvnor's office, and she said no, she wanted somewhere else. The office would remain shut until further notice . . . After that? Well, she had all the editorial side into the main office, and sat at Melchior's desk. She picked up the front page on father's death reading ANTONIN BERG DEAD – ADIEU PATRON.'

Jean-Jacques warmed to his theme. ' "What's this drippy line? It's over the top," she said. I told her it wasn't pathetic stuff for the concièrges, but the style of *La Dépêche*, exactly what our readers would expect. And she said: "Whose idea is this? Is that what they want?" I told her there were certain traditions to be adhered to, and she said if they were bad traditions and out-dated they ought to be done away with. She said: "Messieurs, are we journalists or professional wailers?" I said I took responsibility for the issue, and she just said: "Right, the meeting's over, I want another front page!" Melchior said the first edition was already on the machines and she said to scrap it. And that was that. No further discussion. Melchior came up later with what he called the new look on old paper, the one Flo wanted. The world news was bumped up and the local news played down. No pictures of father, but a twenty-line box headed LA DEPECHE MOURNS. She said it was perfect, and Melchior said the setters were furious because they didn't like being messed around. And d'you know what she said: "I'm not just being whimsical, Melchior, let's keep things in perspective. Tomorrow I'll send round a note: every news item to be treated according to news worthiness." Melchior asked her if she expected to sell any copies on the Champs-Elysées, and she said why not, we wouldn't be the first regional paper with a national audience.'

Jean-Jacques concluded: 'Melchior said, well if that was what she wanted. And she quoted William of Orange: "You don't need to hope in order to try, or to succeed in order to persevere." Melchior gave up after that.'

It was generally agreed throughout the building that she was

144

too heavy-handed. The majority considered she could have paid rather more respect to existing methods and style, but a fair number of people seemed to be quite excited at the idea of the changes.

That was the report Travers gave her one evening in her new office.

He came in at her express request, and said: 'You want to know what they think of you after the heat and battle of the day?'

She laughed in a brittle way: 'Exactly. I feel a little tired and the excitement's over for a bit. I'm wondering if I haven't overdone it.'

Travers went over and served himself a cup of coffee from a machine: 'You really want to know?'

'Yes, go ahead.'

Travers looked her straight in the face: 'Go on as you are, and a week from now you'll have an all-out strike on your hands. Print workers have their own principles and susceptibilities, and they don't like being told they're behaving like a bunch of nincompoops. A paper with a print run of 350,000 is not produced by imbeciles.'

'I never suggested it was.'

'It's implied. A lot of men see it that way.'

'Jean-Jacques exasperated me with all this guff about customs and traditions and whatever.'

'The trouble is everyone's taken it pretty personally. Oh, they don't think too much of Jean-Jacques, but they feel he's on their side. They don't like you scrapping your dad's paper without a by-your-leave.'

Florence said nothing for a while, and then: 'I'll try and take it more slowly, then.' Another pause. 'What do you think?'

'Me?'

'Yes. Are you for or against me?' She seemed irritable and he remained silent, preferring to move over to the window.

Travers turned and said: 'Lorieux asked me to lunch today.'

She failed to grasp what he was saying, but then she flushed: 'Ah yes, Lorieux! Very well, Monsieur Travers, no need to spell it out – you're leaving the ship, is that it? Lorieux means big money, the Boulard Group, the rat merchants! How much are they offering you? Plenty of scope for you there; twelve dailies, seven mags. I'm not in the same class with my puny paper.'

She was standing, and he could see her shaking with fury. Perhaps with disappointment too.

'He told me . . .'

'I don't care a damn what he told you,' she rasped, making as if to storm out of the room. 'Go and join the Boulard empire, but I'm warning you, you won't be doing journalism there but scribbling hack stuff for illiterates. You will be rich, but you'll have sold out.'

Travers knew his women, and he knew that it wouldn't take much for this one to burst into tears.

He said quietly: 'Lorieux asked me if *La Dépêche* would sell out. He also said that you would soon be in need of capital. He also reckoned that *La Dépêche* would fit in very well into the Boulard group. Finally, he suggested I phone him at regular intervals to fill him in on what was happening here.'

'Well?'

'Well, we were eating spaghetti with tomato sauce at the time, and I chucked the whole bloody lot over his head.'

She closed her eyes tight, not sure whether to laugh or cry: 'Y-you-you're with me? Oh, Travers!'

Travers nodded: 'On one condition. That you never, ever again take me to be the bastard you think you've been looking at for the past five minutes.'

They fell into each other's arms. Florence's eyes were wet and shining: 'Oh God, Trav, thanks, thanks for everything. For crying out loud I've *got* to have you with me!'

Their lips were close, but they both pulled back in time, and they were left holding hands.

'Cheers,' he said, giving her his absurd military salute. 'I'd better go and see Catherine.'

'Oh dear, with all that's been going on, I never thought to ask you about her.'

'She's fine, the baby too. Catherine has some kidney trouble, nothing serious, but they're keeping her in for a bit.'

'Give her a big kiss for me.'

'Sure, a big kiss from you.'

She blinked and noticed he seemed sad. What did he mean, or was she imagining things? Goodness, he couldn't be falling for Catherine!

A tiny pang of jealousy brought her up sharp, or was she imagining that too? The feeling remained until she reached La Commanderie, and only then did it go away. Her thoughts switched automatically to Maurice Arras, and suddenly she was happier.

The children's voices no longer echoed through the grounds. Michel took them back to Julien and Thérèse at the sawmill, and then quarrelled with his mother when she wanted him to play Scrabble with her and he refused. He then went home on his own.

Florence found Armand having a nap on the settee in the main living room.

'He's getting ready for the vigil,' Marie-Lou told her. 'Sank practically a whole bottle of brandy.'

'And what did *you* drink?' Florence asked.

But her sister-in-law did not hear the remark, for she plunged into the matter uppermost in her mind: 'Huh! So you threw out Jean-Jacques. Who the hell do you think you are, chucking your weight about? You've no right!'

'Keep your voice down, there's a dead person in the house.'

'Don't worry, he won't hear me.'

Florence remained rooted to the spot as Marie-Lou strode about: 'I did not dismiss Jean-Jacques and, as you say, I've no right to. However, as I left *La Dépêche* fifteen minutes ago, Melchior told me J-J was announcing his resignation to all and sundry. Looks like he's upset about something.'

Marie-Lou surged forward: 'All right smartypants. But you humiliated him in public. He told us all about it.'

'Where is he?'

'He came, had a drink and went.'

'Him too!' said Florence. 'Why's everyone so thirsty all of a sudden? What's new apart from all that? Don't tell me father's risen from the dead. If he had I suppose I'd have found you in tears.'

Marie-Lou swept her guest lists from the table, and the phone rang: 'That must be the twenty thousandth time. How people loved him, our Antonin!'

It was Travers, to say that Catherine had had a visit that afternoon from Gilbert Bossis. He brought Gabrielle's necklace and the written wishes of Antonin. She was overcome.

Florence commented: 'What a shame they took so long to get to know each other – that was always happening with my father.'

As she hung up, Gilbert came in.

Marie-Lou shrugged and said pointedly: 'Florence was asking what the latest news was.'

'Your father gave me a letter some months back, to be opened after his death. Here it is. No flowers, no speeches, quietly – and cremation.'

'All that work for nothing,' Marie-Lou whined, looking at the papers on the floor.

'Pick them up,' Gilbert said, 'they might still come in useful. For a birth, marriage, first communion, or someone else's death.'

'Jean-Jacques, for example,' Marie-Lou snapped. 'Given how drunk he was, it wouldn't surprise me. It'll be your fault, Florence!'

Florence merely said: 'I'm going up to father.'

There was a vigil in progress at the Kovalics' place that midnight. Four people in a big room, saying nothing.

Those present included old Gregor, who was so thin and dry you could have snapped him over your knee. He had been the 'godfather' of the family before handing over to Albertas. His wife was next to him, like a mummy. Two widowed daughters-in-law completed the group, Zoë and also Marfa who was Teddy's mother. Gregor was as stiff as a poker in front of the fireplace, but moved his head from time to time looking at the wall clock above the glass door to the kitchen. The two young women knitted baby clothes, and had no trouble keeping their mouths shut; they had done it for most of their adult lives. But they exchanged glances furtively now and again, such was the abiding power of the old man over them.

They all heard the van slosh its way into the yard, and still nobody spoke. Nor did they move. It was young Teddy who burst in first, pulling off the gauntlets he wore for driving in order to keep his hands smooth for the saxophone. Teddy had told Catherine he was leaving the clan, but he had funked it so far. Now he walked cockily into his bedroom and closed the door behind him. He knew that no one would have asked him questions – certainly not the women because Gregor would have shut them up, nor Gregor himself because information was Albertas's prerogative. That was the kind of sacred rite they had in the family, and his cousin Catherine called it their 'tribal structure'.

They asked nothing when Albertas came in, another of the customs being that the newcomer should speak first. Albertas had gone out hours ago dressed like a toff, but returned with his waistcoat open, his tie loosened and without his hat. He was also stiff in his movements, a final confirmation that he had been drinking and drinking a lot. His 'diplomatic mission' had evidently failed, Gregor said to himself as Albertas lurched into the next room without so much as a belch of recognition.

148

The big room was in bright colours and as clean as a municipal nursery. It even had a cradle garnished with silk and lace. All that was missing was the baby.

'So she sent you about your business, did she my son? She won't come home and have the women take turns with the baby?'

'What else d'yer think?' Not only had she told him to keep away, she had forbidden him to touch the baby, hugging it close to her. 'Paul, she's calling it Paul.'

Albertas still had her words hammering at his eardrums.

'No,' she had said, 'he's not a Kovalic, he's a Bossis! And I'll bring him up on my own, thank you. And his father's friends'll give me a hand.'

Albertas had waved a bundle of banknotes at her: 'Here's 100,000 francs, is that all right for a dowry? Built up day by day since you was born. With this you can leave Chateauvallon.'

'In return for what?'

'In return for the baby!'

The door opened behind them and two nurses came in wondering what all the shouting was about. Behind them was her lover, the one they called Travers. And he had shoved him out again, and he could thank his lucky stars he didn't break his neck on the stairs.

And now the two widows' needles clicked faster as they heard the rest of the account. Secretly, they admired Catherine but kept their eyes down, glancing at each other only when Albertas shouted: 'You know what that toffee-nosed bitch said to me? She said she'd never be one of the Kovalic women who have to keep their tongues and open their legs every couple of nights. Treated us like we was savages, she did!'

Marfa, the younger of the two, whispered quickly: 'If only they could see themselves.' Nevertheless it was Zoë who received the Parthian shot: 'She's gone over to the other camp, that's your doing, bringing her like you did. The baby'll be a Bossis, and old Gilbert the grandfather. 'Cos that's something else too – that Florence Berg's fiddled it so we couldn't have the kid.'

Gregor intervened: 'You've had too many. What's all this about fiddling, first I heard of it? Fiddling or no fiddling, you're as much the grandfather as old Bossis. Don't you worry, we'll get even with them before long, mark my words.'

The Kovalics' desire for the baby came from deep down in their guts; it was a matter of pride, of honour. But there was more to it

149

than that. When they arrived in Chateauvallon in '45 they were cold, miserable and universally rejected. And they never forgot it. One day Gregor had gone to the Berg residence asking for work – he was prepared to shovel shit if necessary – and the guvnor had told him to come back when he'd learnt something other than 'pidgin'. The guvnor was Antonin Berg, and they never forgot it. Later they had bettered themselves – but they remained cut to the quick deep down in their hearts.

Little Paul was a way of hitting back, and they would have their revenge not only on the Bergs but on Bossis and Travers. It was a pity that Antonin Berg had died too soon . . .

Julien walked into La Commanderie around 11 p.m., going straight up to Antonin's room where Florence had snuffed out the candles and put the light on.

'I couldn't sleep,' Julien said. 'I've never been an orphan, feel strange about it. When mother died I was too young to notice. Why all this light?'

'It's more cheerful.'

He could find nothing to answer, and said: 'Marie-Lou gone home?'

'She was in a blind rage, Jean-Jacques left before I arrived, drunk as a lord, it seems. If he killed himself on the motorway it'd be my fault. My fault too if he went off with another woman.'

Julien said: 'I can't laugh, with father there.' He looked at the old man, and thought he seemed older than when he died, and wondered whether his sister had the same impression.

Florence mumbled after a while: 'Armand's downstairs sleeping off the brandy. Not like him to . . .'

'Evade his duty? Perhaps he is sorry he did nothing to help him.'

'Possibly. He's a frustrated doctor as well as a bereaved son.'

The phone rang downstairs, and Florence started to go out when it stopped.

'Wrong number, I suppose,' she sighed. The silence was eerie now.

Julien yawned then said: 'Hey, what about Alexandra?'

'I phoned her from the office,' his sister said, stubbing out a cigarette that she had just lit. 'But don't imagine she'll get the first plane over. She won't be coming.'

'But I think she was fond of her grandfather.'

150

'You think so? Perhaps you're right. But it's been too long.'

'I should have thought she'd make the effort, all the same.'

'I'm not surprised. You know, last Christmas I asked her if she'd like to come over and see us. I was a bit depressed at the time, and I even begged her. She didn't say no, or yes either. The fact is she didn't come.'

Julien commiserated: 'It may not mean she doesn't care. Perhaps she suspected you were trying to see if you still had a hold over her. And I'm not making that up, that's what she wrote to me.'

'Lucky you, you're the only one she's ever written to. You're her godfather, but I'm her mother. I must have gone wrong somewhere, and I expect she told you where.'

Julien glanced quickly at her and replied: 'I think she never forgave you for keeping her from her father all that time.'

'Fair enough, but bygones can be bygones, surely! Oh Julien, if you only knew how I loved that girl, we seemed to be so close. I wanted her over because I wanted her, I was feeling lonely. It's all so silly. One day I'll simply grab her by the scruff of her neck like a mother cat!'

Julien laughed: 'Just you try! I'd guess she's as strong-willed as you are.'

Something went bump in the passage. It was Armand, hair awry, face puffy. 'Travers just phoned,' he said.

'Something's happened to Catherine . . .'

'Yes, I mean no. She-er-had a visit from Albertas who wiped the floor with her, and her temperature went up. But that's not why he called. He dropped in at the office and found out that Jean-Jacques has misbehaved himself.'

'Oh Lord, what's going to happen next?'

'Caught for speeding, drunk-in-charge, punch-up with a pair of cops, injured one of them. Our little brother is at this very moment drying out as guest of the République.'

'Sweet Jesus,' said Mathilde from the doorway. 'In jail! Let's hope he's out for the funeral!'

She snivelled and placed a pile of sandwiches on the bedside table.

Jean-Jacques would be free within a matter of hours, Florence heard from the prosecutor Jean Midoux, an old acquaintance, when she called on him.

She had phoned him at once and he had phoned the Gendarmerie where the Captain said one of the men was prepared to forget the whole thing, but not the other as he was missing two teeth.

Midoux told Florence the case would go forward and there was nothing he could do about it.

She went from there to the office and phoned Armand at the clinic.

'There is one possible way out,' she told him. 'We could get a high-up to head the case off. Midoux suggested it, and it's likely he was referring to Quentin.'

'What are you waiting for, then?'

'Armand, I can't ask Quentin any favours now.'

'Marie-Lou could. For once her generous attributes might serve some purpose. I'm sure Quentin's been eyeing her for years.'

Florence sighed: 'I called in on her, and found her in bed dying of shame with an ice-pack on her forehead. She told me to do my own dirty work, as it was me who had got him into the mess.'

Armand eyed the ceiling: 'So you want me to do it instead.'

Florence pouted: 'Could you, please? You're on good terms with Quentin, aren't you?'

'I'm not actually. Apart from that, I have had a ghastly day: two hernias, one appendicitis and a prostate. Travers might be better, he knows Quentin and has the gift of the gab.'

His sister looked puzzled: 'My God you're jumpy, Armand! You're not cracking up or something. You were peculiar last night too.'

She heard the phone slammed down. He called her back within seconds: 'OK, old girl. But ask Travers first. If he sends you packing, I'll put my oar in.'

Florence got short shrift from Travers too. She had him paged throughout the offices, and then got on to the clinic again. No, they told her, Travers had taken the lady home.

Catherine screamed her delight when they entered the apartment. Not only was it spick and span, but there was a new carpet and an even newer cradle with lots of lace in the bedroom, and a thing that did six bottles simultaneously. The baby was equally impressed and yelled for an hour on arrival.

'Aren't you just the most wonderful man, Travers!' she shouted over the noise of the baby. 'You did all this?'

'No, Gilbert did most of it. But the bottle sterilizer's mine.

152

What a row he's making.'

'He's hungry, quick where's the milk?'

'In the fridge. Have to get a new one soon.'

'I've got to economize from now on.'

'I'll ask around, see if I can get you a job.'

Catherine went out and showed the baby to the woman across the landing. While she did so, Travers sat down and knitted his brows. It was then that Florence rang.

'She's fine, thank you, and so is the newcomer.'

'Well, you don't seem very pleased about it. Are you down in the dumps too?'

Travers replied roughly: 'D'you think she ought to be here at all, with her kidney trouble, and Albertas calling at the clinic . . . Ah, you know about it. Her temperature went to 39.5 but they still kicked her out, and I reckon she put the thermometer in cold water. She was longing to get home, said she felt safer here with the baby. Frankly I'm scared, she's not at all safe, to my way of thinking.'

'But Travers . . . she had to leave sometime anyway.'

'I suppose you're right.'

There was a silence, and Florence said: 'Travers?'

'Yes Florence.'

'Perhaps she wanted to come home because you're there, and she feels safe with you.' He said nothing, and she asked him what he was so afraid about.

The reply was a long time coming: 'She's young . . . a man in the same apartment, close, too close geographically, as you might say . . . For pity's sake, we've both got real blood in our veins!'

When Florence called Armand again, it was to say that Travers had refused to see Quentin. Travers could not ask a favour of someone on whom he might have to compile a case, if she saw what he meant. Not only did she see, but something inside her quivered with satisfaction. But Travers did not know that.

'All right, then, I'll do what I can for the spoilt brat,' he told Florence.

Florence Berg apologized to the staff for her abrupt and authoritarian manner. They were gathered in the editorial room, and she raised a laugh when she said: 'People are already calling me William of Orange, and even just The Orange.'

She went on to explain that she had always taken her own

decisions and would continue to do so, but she had no wish to dictate to people. From now on things would be kicked around more in little meetings like this, and everybody would have their say as far as possible.

The parley was to prove a wise move, for the staff began to like this woman who had enough savvy to crack a joke against herself, especially when she was still in mourning.

Evidence that she was gaining ground came in the form of Marcel Legault, the print shop foreman, who produced a modernization plan out of the blue. He told her several of the men had worked on it, and the basic idea was to switch to colour stereo printing. Florence put the idea to Madame Frochot the chief accountant, who produced a cost estimate in a surprisingly quick time. She told her and Legault she would put the scheme to the next board meeting.

Others at the meeting raised topics dear to their hearts but nothing was decided.

She had to break off at one point for a few seconds in the middle of speaking, having caught sight of Jean-Jacques on his way into the room. He looked uptight, and she lost track of what she was saying. She was not to know that Marie-Lou had screamed at him when he got home: 'She's made you her subordinate, and now you're in her debt for wangling you out of jail.' As he showered and shaved, he reflected that Florence had acted on his behalf solely to demonstrate her power over him. He had a hang-dog look as he entered the meeting at *La Dépêche* and noticed that everyone was studiously ignoring him as if there had been no incident at all. Florence, on her side, was entitled to a quick smile from Jean-Jacques, and she surmised that there could be only one reason why he had turned up: to put a spoke in her wheel.

Gamely she pressed on, telling them they had to decide how *La Dépêche* would handle the upcoming by-election at Chateauvallon.

Jean-Jacques immediately moved in with his spoke: 'In plain terms, I take it this means we have to decide what our political angle is going to be.'

Florence retorted: 'I must have been plain enough, since you have understood the position perfectly.' General mirth broke out at this, and she continued: 'Is it your view that we do not need to reach a decision on that?'

'My view is that we have to be careful about upsetting people.

154

We are a moderate paper whose readers range from far right to far left. We've got to exercise tact.'

Florence was not going to let him get away with that: 'I've seen some of that tact in print: "On the one hand this, one the other that, and it remains to be seen and so on and so on and so on . . ." Is that what you mean? I'm sorry, from now on *La Dépêche* will have an opinion of its own, and it will give it.'

Madame Frochot spoke up amid an uneasy murmuring among the staff. Whatever the change in tone, style or approach, they could lose readership and the accounts would start to show it in a matter of weeks.

'We'll lose some readers and win some others,' Florence declared.

'It's risky,' Jean-Jacques cried, rising to his feet. 'We're not here to play roulette. Do you realize how dangerous this sort of thing is?' He looked around him soliciting support, and a spasm of anger seized Florence.

'Less dangerous than driving a car. I get the impression you like driving dangerously at night!'

'Let's leave my private affairs out of this,' he snapped. 'If this idea of yours goes wrong, it won't be you out of a job when the print run starts sliding, as Madame Frochot has so rightly pointed out. You're taking a risk with staff numbers.'

'We'll talk about that later. If jobs are under threat we'll deal with it,' Florence exclaimed. 'The issue I'm putting to each and every one of you right now is this: are we in business to sell sheets of paper?'

'We are providing news – and background,' Jean-Jacques shouted.

And Florence shouted back: 'News without comment? Unbiased sludge that everyone can take any way they like? News devoid of responsibility and offering no guidance as to the future? I call that disinformation and it's not worthy of us!'

The meeting got out of hand after that, with arguments and jibes flying between groups and the two main protagonists. But after a minute the confusion settled down, and Travers, who had arrived unnoticed, stuck up his hand. Florence pointed to him.

'Take it easy fellers,' he boomed, 'we're not going to take over from *L'Humanité* or *Minute*, for God's sake! As we're discussing the question of a political stance, may I point out that this is indeed a moderate paper and we carry opinions broad enough to please just about everyone, and I don't see why we can't give backing to a moderate candidate. That's a political line that shouldn't lose any readers, surely!'

The name 'Quentin' started buzzing around the editorial floor, and Florence saw fit to drop a bombshell: 'We are certainly not going to champion Quentin. *La Dépêche* wouldn't do that! I find it hard to believe that Monsieur Travers is being serious calling on us to support such a candidate.'

'It was just an idea.' Travers held her gaze.

She refused to waver: 'I can see that the idea has sympathizers. I suppose because there's no risk in it. I'm sorry, but I feel I should remind you that Quentin's handling of affairs in Chateauvallon is under keen scrutiny at the present time. Certain revelations will be forthcoming in due course, and I have no hesitation in saying that decency and caution ought normally to have prompted Quentin to keep out of this election completely.'

She had thrown out a challenge and the audience took it up, chanting: 'Who then? Who, who, who? Let's have the names!' The uproar continued for a good twenty seconds and Florence finally declared that she had yet to make her choice.

Jean-Jacques thrust himself forward: 'If we are going to be led into the wilderness, can we at least have some idea where we're aiming for? We're like a bunch of camels going round in circles.'

Young Edelman quietly asked what would happen if Florence called upon them to back political views they found distasteful. It was the question everyone had at the back of their minds, and it was neatly put.

And Florence neatly parried it: 'The eventuality is covered under the industry's labour agreement, Monsieur Edelman. You are free to evoke the conscience clause at any time.'

The remark brought the meeting to a close, and the staff dispersed, some already mentally running through their contacts elsewhere, others deciding they would stick it out whatever the line adopted by *La Dépêche*.

Armand dropped by around 7.00 p.m. Florence summarized the discussion and concluded with the quip: 'Camels or no camels, it's going to be a bumpy ride.'

He laughed, and then said: 'It's all fixed for J-J. The action is being withdrawn.'

'Did Quentin play ball?'

'Pretty well, or as well as a man can without knowing what you have in store for him. You wouldn't have a drop of Scotch handy, I suppose?'

'In that small cupboard there.'

'Shall I give Jean-Jacques the good news?'

'Leave it till tomorrow. He won't come to any harm worrying a bit. It'll pay him back for worrying me this afternoon.'

She watched him knock back a large Scotch, and then another immediately afterwards.

'Armand!' she said in disbelief.

But he was already on his way out: 'See you tomorrow at the ceremony.'

As elsewhere, the crematorium was the grimmest edifice in the whole town, and the cremation ceremony the most boring of all events. Those attending were ushered into a pseudo-chapel affair and they all sat in lines listening to an endless Bach chorale on tape as the uniformed attendant kept looking at his watch to make sure they weren't running behind schedule on that day's list. The full complement of Chateauvallon's high society turned out, despite the deceased's wishes, and they all jabbered away oblivious of the 'ceremony'. Speculation developed between the rows of chairs as to who would inherit what, but all in mouse-like whispers to avoid the comments reaching the ears of the family in the front row.

The will was read the next day at the offices of Monsieur Saviot, the notary. Julien got the sawmill, land and woods; Armand had his Les Glycines clinic and the share portfolio; Florence acquired the majority shareholding in *La Dépêche*, along with the position of company president; Jean-Jacques found he was the owner of three apartment blocks in Paris and five other buildings in Chateauvallon. The old man left a tidy sum to Mathilde and Jeannou with thanks for their devoted service. As to Gilbert, he got nothing, apart from the right to spend the rest of his life at La Commanderie 'because his retirement pension is enough for a man of his age, bearing in mind that he will be housed and lodged'. Through the mouth of Maître Saviot, the family heard Antonin Berg's voice speaking from somewhere in the big house. Saviot read out: 'It was here that you were born, my children. This house is a symbol of our family and I want it to remain a bond among you. Consequently, I am not proposing to split the property. We shall always be together, because it is under its trees that I wish my ashes to be strewn.'

And it was Gilbert Bossis who did the strewing. Gilbert stayed away from the cremation ceremony, because through Florence he already knew what his share would be. He told her: 'In death as in life – a rotten bastard.' It was assumed by those at the ceremony that he was too distraught to appear in public. Another absentee was Quentin, who was in fact putting the finishing touch to his black tie when a spy of his at *La Dépêche* phoned to report Florence's remarks about his candidacy. He promptly changed back and told his wife he would not be going after all. 'Like father, like daughter – a rotten bastard,' he said.

In the crematorium basement people at last began weeping when an official trundled a trolley past them bearing a cigar box containing the ashes. Mathilde had to be helped away. The ashes were taken on the back seat of the Rolls to La Commanderie, and the other cars followed.

In their car, Marie-Lou told Jean-Jacques; 'Anyone who feels they have been done can always contest the will.'

Her husband said: 'I'm hard done by morally, but in any case it's difficult to argue it out in practice.'

'Unless you can show that your father was not in his right mind.'

Young Michel chipped in: 'Pity they don't burn the dead with all their goods and assets. You wouldn't seem so disgusting.'

'Box his ears, Jean-Jacques!'

But Jean-Jacques remained unmoved, himself reflecting that she could have waited a day or two before mentioning the will.

Their car overtook the one with Armand and Florence and Jean-Jacques wound the window down and stuck his head half-way out: 'By the way, thanks for seeing Quentin on my behalf.'

Later, Marie-Lou was in a hurry to get away, as she had a fitting at a dressmaker's who did perfect copies of Chanel fashions.

Flo and Armand watched them drive off, and they stood in silence.

'Sad?' she said.

'Rather. You too?'

'Surprisingly so, it's impossible to say how one will react. Armand, you said yesterday there was something worrying you. Let's have it, I want to know.'

They were on their own in the big living room. Julien and Thérèse had gone, so had Melchior, Maryse, Travers and Catherine.

They heard Gilbert Bossis bumping his way down the stairs, and they exchanged worried glances. He came in wearing a morning suit he had picked out for the first time in twenty years, and smart shoes to match.

Florence said: 'Dear Gilbert, he asked you to . . .'

'I wanted to make him wait a moment,' said Bossis, heading for the front door. Brother and sister followed him out to the Rolls where the ashes awaited him. He stood thinking for a minute or more and then opened the car door.

'Come on then,' he said, talking to the cigar box. 'It's a fine evening. How do you feel about it all now, old chum? Pleased with yourself? Vanity vindicated? I'm glad to do this, you know.'

And he walked awkwardly off with the box tucked under his left shoulder.

He went on: 'You didn't want people to turn up, but they did. Even the Kovalics, Albertas and Gregor, according to Mathilde. They shook hands with the family, including Catherine. You had a lot of friends after all, dear chap. After all, Albertas is little Paul's grandfather the same as I am . . .'

The last light engulfed him on his way to the pond. The two watchers went in again.

The lights were ablaze in the living room, and Florence said: 'But Armand, there must be a treatment for it.'

'Of course there is,' he laughed bitterly, 'but it never succeeds. I've got acute precocious rheumatoid arthritis in the right hand. It's turning in like a chicken's claw. It's the end of me as a surgeon.'

Florence blew out her breath: 'Oh God. I haven't been able to think of anything else since you told me.'

'Two deaths in a single day at the clinic.'

'Stop that! It's a grave challenge, but there are a hundred other reasons for living.'

'Tell me some of the best!'

'Idiot.'

She let him pour out the brandies, and they sat waiting for Gilbert to return to the house.

The wind was getting up and Gilbert released the ashes so that they wafted away two or three yards: 'One for Paul, one for Catherine, one for Gabrielle . . .'

His cheeks were wet when he plodded up the steps into the house.

It was only a tiny rumour at first, but is spread steadily in the couple of weeks that followed. Dr Armand Berg was going to stand in the election. Nobody took it seriously, as it was unthinkable that this known and admired surgeon would give up his career to throw himself into the hazardous political maelstrom. Besides, it was said, he had never shown the slightest interest in politics.

Then Dr Berg arrived at the Prefecture to register as a candidate for election as the Member for Chateauvallon. The media were on to it at once, and a camera team of two appeared from FR3. Armand confirmed his candidacy when they met him coming out.

'What stung you into action?' said a girl from *L'Eveil de la Loire*.

'Mademoiselle,' he replied, 'I don't need to be stung. Like Jules Romains' hero Le Trouhadec who was suddenly drawn into a life of debauchery, I suddenly want to do something for our town of Chateauvallon. That's the only reason why I am moving into politics.'

The man from FR3 needed an exclusive statement and asked if his campaign might be centred on the business of Les Sablons.

Armand replied: 'Court proceedings are in hand, and we must await the outcome. However, I do feel that this business indicates that something has gone astray in the administration of our town, and I want to cure the patient, if I might put it that way as a doctor.'

'What are your feelings about Monsieur Quentin?'

'I shall no doubt have something to say about him in due course,' he said levelly, and jumped into his car.

He smiled to himself behind the wheel. It was true he wanted to serve the community, but he had indeed been stung into it when he felt the full impact of his disability. The idea of becoming a useless passenger appalled him. But Florence had grilled him for the whole two weeks since that evening at La Commanderie when she had come up with the idea of a political career.

'The Assemblée!' he had cried. 'You must be mad, I'd hate it!'

'It's better than neurasthenia. You must face up to it.' Another time she had reasoned: 'Look Armand, I'm in search of a candidate the paper can back. You're a gift from heaven. Just think, you are a leading figure in Chateauvallon, one of the best known and esteemed. Why there's no reason why we can't pull it off. It'll be wonderful.'

Florence had kept on at him day after day, listing his qualifications for the job, dismissing the lack of political instinct, and then finally she had produced the analogy of curing the patient, and he had capitulated. Today he had crossed the Rubicon.

As for Quentin, his jaw dropped a couple of inches when he saw Armand on the Regional FR3 news. He was looking in as he regularly did, with his stand-in Adrien Jerome, often referred to as his grey eminence.

Jerome commented: 'A slick move, nicely done.'

'That's Florence, typical of her, I'd recognize her style anywhere. She could have found someone with more weight to block my way.'

His colleague chuckled to see Quentin so put out: 'Don't under-estimate him. He's not in politics, and neither is Florence. But two bold amateurs can do a lot of damage, especially when they've got La Dépêche. Another thing: as Mayor, you have a good many adversaries in your path. There could be a second round in this election.'

'I'll get through in the first round.'

'There's no reason why you should get through without a fight every time.'

They discussed it for a while longer, and Jerome said Armand Berg had a weak point 'and that's what we'll go for'.

'What are you thinking of?' Quentin said guardedly.

'His name. Armand Berg's not so very different from Philippe Berg in the ears of the voters, and Philippe Berg happens to be in prison. That's something they can stir in with their coffee before they go to the polls.'

Quentin sighed, and then jerked up his head: 'No, we must be careful. No question of bringing that into it. It wouldn't be right.'

'Right or wrong, it would be effective. Since when has your career been as white as driven snow?'

He half expected Quentin to silence him with a crushing affirmation of his rectitude, but in fact he merely sighed: 'What a life it is, always having to fight, trading blow for blow. I'm weary of political life, I can't deny it.'

'I know.'

'You know what?'

'I know you've been getting flabby, starting to look your age and more. That's Florence too!'

'Forget that, and don't mention it again.'

161

Jerome shrugged: 'As you wish. She's given you the brush-off, and now she's going to stab you in the back. Nice work.'

'Oh, clear off.'

Exactly at that moment the Parliamentary Private Secretary at the Interior Ministry in Paris, a stone's throw from the Elysée Palace, was reading a telex that had just come in. He crumpled his copy and turned to his aide: 'Tell me, Charleville, their Prefect down there, is he asleep or simply a fool?'

Between the PPS and Cornedieu, Prefect of Chateauvallon, there existed a long-standing antagonism, due partly to a row over a woman.

Since the Prefect had won the joust, Charleville thought it prudent to declare: 'He is both asleep and a fool, Monsieur.'

'It's absolutely incredible,' the PPS cried in delight. 'Telling us at the very last minute before the campaign starts that a man named Berg is to fight Quentin.'

'Well, Monsieur, Berg registered by the skin of his teeth.' Charleville thought it wise to put a word in for the Prefect who, when all was said, had a certain influence, an influence that could increase at some time in the future. He further deemed it useful to add: 'But Monsieur, would you say that this little doctor .... I mean, does he stand for anything but himself?'

The PPS removed his glasses and rubbed his eyes with a fist: 'His name's Berg, dear fellow, which is a name that moves mountains in Chateauvallon. They've got *La Dépêche*. Cornedieu is a nitwit, and I want to see him in forty-eight hours.'

While Armand was performing a hernia operation at the clinic, he was being discussed that night in the Bordello at a hamlet called La Clairière. The word was hardly appropriate but it was used to describe an abandoned hut adopted by the youth of Chateauvallon, Michel Berg being one of the leading lights, along with Teddy.

Young Kovalic's saxophone inveigled a classless audience who retreated to the place as a bastion of liberty where they could hide from the town's strait-laced citizenry. Hashish was available, though not obligatory as a vice.

On the night in question, a few of the youngsters were dancing close-up to the saxophone, others were chatting or petting in the shadows away from the oil lamps hanging on the crumbling walls. There must have been a dozen people there that evening enjoying themselves in a grim, rebellious way.

Then the name Berg came up. Michel, Marie-Lou's boy, was in a sullen mood because Anne, a pretty seventeen-year-old carbon copy of a current film heroine, had spent the entire evening so far undulating with a certain Roland to the honeyed strains of Teddy's golden instrument. The difficulty arose from a simple but common anomaly: Michel yearned for Anne, whereas Anne had eyes only for Roland, and Roland was sneering at Michel. Eventually the loser in this triangle of love saw her mouth squashed against the lips of his rival, and he moved in.

'No need to make a meal of it,' he muttered, making as if to take over.

'Keep your hands to yourself,' she retaliated, pushing him away. 'Just because your uncle's on telly.'

'Clear off,' said Roland with confident brevity.

It was Roland who received the clout really intended for the tantalizing Anne. Teddy stopped playing and a large blonde girl with frizzy hair yelled: 'Gosh, you're not going to scrap over that Doctor bloke, for chrissakes!'

'I think he's rather nice . . .' another girl began, but the reason was drowned by a yelp from Michel as Roland jabbed a knee into his crotch.

Eager hands pulled them apart, and Roland snarled: 'Nice? He's just like the others. The only thing they're interested in is making money. You won't get a free abortion from *him*, darling.'

Teddy chipped in: 'Berg!' Michel swung at him shouting: 'I'm not having my family dragged through the mud by scum like you. Scum, that's what my uncle Armand thinks of your lot!'

He slouched off towards the door and was already outside when Anne whined: 'What do you want to go and upset him for? It's true, the doc's nice, even if he is his uncle.'

Thus, even before the election campaign was launched, Armand Berg became the object of bitter controversy and passionate antagonism.

Armand was able to judge the full extent of his fame the following day when a wizened old man in pyjamas stopped him in the corridor outside his office and declared he would vote for him.

'Well thank you, Monsieur Clément, I need all the . . .'

'And d'yer know why, doc? I was all bunged up before you operated, and now I'm pissing like an old horse.'

In politics as in life, what counted were results, Armand pondered. At least he had succeeded with another prostate job. As he drove to 45 Rue de la République where Florence had summoned him, he recalled the old man's parting remark: 'What's more, you know your cousin Philippe being in jail, well that don't matter to nobody, does it?'

Many voters might think not, but many would. One thing was certain: none of them would fail to take account of the fact.

Jean-Jacques bounded into Florence's office with a typescript. She took one look at the headline and said: 'Ah, that's a piece I asked Favrot to do, a profile on Armand.'

Her brother seemed visibly to inflate himself: 'I warn you, I'm not having this on the front page. I stopped it. I may not be your favourite brother, but I'm the editor, and it's the editor who hands out the assignments.'

'And I'm the managing-editor among other things, so stop flapping about. You don't like us backing Armand?'

'Exactly,' he said leaning his fists on her desk. 'I've been away for four days, and I just happen to find out by chance when I get back.'

'You were away, that's all.'

'So I was away! The fact that he's a candidate is his affair, but I consider it underhand that you made your own decision to back him in *La Dépêche*. This is pure folly, and it's a new and worrying factor for the paper. It concerns us all.' Florence leaned back as he put his points. 'There's too much about the Bergs, Chateauvallon's fed up to the back teeth with the Bergs, and I should think our family's been quite prominent enough as it is, with the stories on Philippe splashed all over the front page.'

Florence began sharpening a proof-checking pencil: 'Luckily he's the only one in jail, but you missed it by a hair's breadth, brother dear. Quite honestly I find it amazing that you cannot see your way to giving Armand support. Especially as he got you out of detention.'

There was no answer to that, and he snapped: 'Oh, go to hell!' The room shook as he slammed the door.

45 Rue de la République was a small shop with a big window. And when Armand first saw the window he froze in his car seat. It was covered with posters reading: ARMAND BERG. A NEW MAN. A NEW CHANCE.

Nervously, he slid out from behind the wheel and quietly closed and locked the door. Inside he was met by a tweed-suited sporty type, about forty years of age, who bore down upon him with an outstretched hand. 'Marc Chambonnas, publicity. Engaged by Madame Florence Berg.'

There followed, within seconds, a summary of the strategy to be pursued. Armand Berg would not be launched like a washing powder, but the objective would be to ensure a favourable image. The candidate would avoid smiling too much in front of the cameras, he would hit home with short phrases, points that hit home without giving the rival candidate time to reply. If our candidate had to reply, he must do so by guiding the argument along different lines.

'You need to develop a more open laugh, Monsieur Berg. And, of course, you must wear light blue shirts for TV.'

'Is that all, Chambonnas?'

'Far from it. We need an unwavering line on Les Sablons, and on your cousin.'

Armand's hands went up: 'Not again! That's all I hear these days – my cousin, my cousin, my cousin.'

The publicist paused all of two seconds and ran on: 'If you intend to avoid attacking Quentin on the personal level, you will be making a huge mistake. The other candidates will drag you through the mud. You yourself can keep your nose to the ground and keep it clean if you like, but you'll finish up with a flat nose and nothing else! It will still be dirty.'

He changed the subject: 'Aside from Quentin you have the far right candidate with three per cent, the Communist ten per cent . . .'

'. . . The Socialist eighteen per cent and me twenty per cent.'

Chambonnas raised a stern finger: 'If you don't mind, I would reverse those: yourself eighteen and the Socialist twenty. I know he would normally get eighteen, but the Socialists are on an upward swing everywhere and it will be reflected in this vote. That is the fly in the ointment, Monsieur Berg. Your only chance of getting to the second round with Quentin is to overtake the Socialist.'

'Logical.'

'Which means – pardon the expression – your case must be built on solid foundations. Even if you are nice to Quentin, he'll be using your cousin Philippe to pull the rug from under you and you'll be left out in the cold.'

Armand winced, trying to keep up with this dynamo of a strategist, as he went on: 'We'll have to live with him, but we'll be hitting back. Now, your market is roughly the centre left and the right-wing pinks. And they don't like monkeying about, believe me.'

'You mean my cousin must be eliminated from the reckoning?'

'I mean you must fight back with everything you have. No holds barred, Monsieur Berg, no holds barred.'

So it was him or them, Armand mused as he drove off. Kill or be killed, and no fraternizing with the enemy before you shoot. Ah well, so be it.

He would be back tomorrow for his second lesson.

One of their first forays, he and Chambonnas, took them for a walk round the covered market one sunny morning. Travers and a photographer were there to underline the importance for the voters of this significant event, and to get material for the paper.

Armand shook hands by the dozen, spoke to a chubby blonde fishwife about the operation he performed on her two years earlier, and commiserated with a junk dealer about the ruinous taxes imposed by the present administration. From time to time the candidate gave a quick glance at Chambonnas to make sure he wasn't doing anything wrong, and then moved on to the butcher or the florist or whoever else seemed vital to the campaign. Finally, Armand chatted for a while with an assortment of women who had done their shopping but thought they'd just hang on a bit in case anything happened.

It did. Quentin was striding into the market just as Berg was emerging. One up to Berg – the first one in was the winner, or so he hoped on this occasion. However Quentin was accompanied not only by his deputy Jerome, but also by a whole retinue of ladies-in-waiting and a TV crew. Quentin was smiling as if he was about to buy up the entire covered market and everything in it. The two candidates met and shook hands, chatting for fifty or sixty seconds. The camera whirred but as there was no sound engineer their remarks were lost to posterity.

'Doing your shopping, Monsieur Berg?'

'Taking a day off, Monsieur le Maire?'

One up to Armand. They both laughed irrelevantly but with immense gusto.

Armand, rightly or wrongly, saw fit to thank Quentin for his intervention on behalf of Jean-Jacques, and Quentin effected a princely wave of the hand and declared that it was no trouble, no trouble at all.

But he added: 'Rather brave on your part to stand at Chateauvallon, I must say. You have a somewhat embarrassing cousin.'

One up to Quentin. Berg replied: 'We are related but there is nothing in common between us.'

'Ah, but you have to prove that to the voters, Monsieur Berg.'

'I shall, Monsieur le Maire. The voters will certainly recall that my cousin was one of your guiding lights at the town hall.'

'And what might you be implying by that, Monsieur Berg?'

'Only this, Monsieur le Maire, that we have our families thrust upon us but we choose our colleagues.'

Quentin assumed a self-righteous air: 'I believe you said on television the other day that you were not in favour of personal slanging matches.'

'Ah, but it was you who lobbed the first grenade, Monsieur le Maire.'

'I have plenty more ammunition where that came from,' cried his adversary with an exaggerated laugh.

Maître Blanchet was waiting for Armand when he walked into the campaign rooms.

'Last night Judge Perugino added another charge, accessory to murder,' he said at once.

'You could have told me earlier.'

'Couldn't get to you. I was at a case in Diviers this morning.'

The previous morning, Gamel stated under interrogation that Philippe Berg introduced him to Fournier, now on the run. He said he regarded Berg as one of the chief officials responsible for Les Sablons. Machefer confirmed Gamel's allegations.

'That's a lie!' Philippe replied.

Perugino broke in: 'You can't deny that you knew Gamel before everyone else did. He served under you in Algeria.'

'That is possible. I commanded several different units.'

Fournier was looking for a killer, and it was you who put him in touch with Gamel, a specialist in the summary execution of prisoners.'

Armand asked Blanchet: 'Does my sister know about this?'

'She does.'

Blanchet and Chambonnas watched Armand walk stiffly out of

167

the campaign HQ, then hurl himself into the car and drive off at breakneck speed. The two men looked at each other as if they had just lost someone dear to them.

'What does Philippe Berg say about it, Maître?'

'More than a week ago I urged him, pleaded with him to tell me everything, to confide in me. He remained tightlipped.'

'Maybe he's scared someone will do away with him in jail.'

'Who can say?' Blanchet stared at the back of the posters in the window. 'There's one thing he knows only too well. He is a pain in the arse for everyone, Quentin as much as Armand. He realizes he can expect help from no one now. Did you see how Armand went off? His cousin is nothing but an empty old tin can clattering along behind him. Or to be more precise, a grenade with the pin removed.'

'I can't see what Perugino's aim is,' Florence said. 'I'm even wondering if he has one at all, or whether he simply wants to see some heads roll. It's his job, after all. Emilie visited Philippe about an hour after the new charge was made, and Philippe swore to her that his hands were clean that he would never be on trial for murder.'

Armand said: 'It's enough to be an accessory, and that'll put paid to my election, that's for certain.'

His sister smiled at him as he lowered his gaze: 'You're like a little puppy, Armand. You didn't want the bone, now it's being whipped away, and you start yelping.'

'Poor Philippe. But you see . . . Oh, this ghastly feeling that I'm being stabbed in the back through Philippe. Why's Perugino out to get me?'

Keep your sense of proportion, darling. It's my opinion he's just forging ahead for the sake of his career. On the other hand, I do know that the Interior Ministry is wheeling out its artillery. Cornedieu, our beloved Prefect, was summoned to Paris as soon as it was known you were standing. He's a sick man and it wasn't until the beginning of this week that he got there and was torn off a strip. You're the son of a top man here, and father always backed the right, yet you've gone over to the opposition. They're afraid it's something that'll spread.'

'What happened, then?'

'The PPS was crystal clear. He said: "Quentin may no longer be a minister, but he's one of us and he's got to get through, whatever

168

the cost. I want Berg eased out. Any ideas, Cornedieu?" And Cornedieu, who would have handed over his wife on a plate to make up for pinching the PPS's girl that time, suggested using our little rival here. He said: "As you know we have two papers, *La Dépêche* and *L'Eveil*." Anyhow they decided to bump up *L'Eveil*, giving it exclusive stories and stacks of advertising, drawing as much revenue as possible from us. In other words . . .'

'Slashing our jugular vein,' said Armand.

'Quite. Even so, the PPS wanted to know how *L'Eveil* stood politically and Cornedieu told him: "Its stance will be whatever you wish, Monsieur".'

Armand quipped: 'And I suppose you were under the table listening to all this.'

'I wasn't, but the First Secretary Charleville was. It so happens that a long time ago, I . . . er . . . yielded to his advances, shall we say, and like an upstanding gentlemen he phoned me and warned me. Pretty decent, that was.'

Armand wagged his head: 'So what are your plans?'

'I'm going to head them off at the pass,' Florence declared, adding a smile that made Armand catch his breath – it was exactly like the one their father adopted when he went in for the kill.

To be honest, Armand derived a measure of comfort from his sister's quiet confidence. But he was disheartened by the advent of so many items of bad news one after the other, and did not ask for further explanations. He knew Florence preferred in any case to keep her tactics to herself. She had always been like that.

He returned to the clinic in the mood of a poor bloody infantry-man obeying orders and hoping the minefield had been properly cleared. He sat in his office for a moment, and then went along to the woman he had operated on that morning, a hysterectomy. It might well be the last surgery he would perform.

For Armand had made the most important decision in his life by far. If he failed to get elected, he would do away with himself. He wouldn't suffer, he knew the means, but he would show the white flag and to hell with the minefield.

Travers eventually quit Catherine's apartment and returned to his own place. Neither of them made a fuss about it. Travers gabbled some reasons, and Catherine understood what was behind them, as if she too wanted to leave it vague. He had done what he could and she was eternally grateful, but there was no point in trying to stay together. There was nothing between them but a deep friendship and it was best that they part. By unspoken agreement, they would not see each other for a while.

But a week later he was taking a short cut through La Maladrerie Park and he spotted her some distance away strolling along with Gilbert Bossis who was pushing the pram. He wanted to about-turn, but feared he'd been seen – he had no choice but to go up to them.

'Thank God you've turned up,' Gilbert said with forced gaiety. 'If you've got a joke ready, now's the time to tell it. I can't make her cheer up, she looks like she's just lost all the housekeeping money!'

Travers wanted to give her a warm hug, but because of Gilbert he simply gave Catherine a tap on the cheek. It turned into a few strokes.

'What's the trouble, love?'

'He's started his nonsense again,' she said with a pout and a shrug.

'Her father,' Gilbert explained as they walked along. 'He's phoning her every night. Wants the baby, and sounds like he's prepared to use force.'

Catherine decided to get it off her chest: 'I don't think he'll go that far but he keeps saying he can get a court order because I'm without money and can't provide for the baby. Says he'll reverse the proceedings. Oh, if only I could get that *post mortem* marriage thing, it would solve everything. I could change my name and my father would lose all rights over me and the baby.'

They strolled along a few yards and Gilbert said: 'I can't do much in the way of money, I'm afraid. I get some royalties from an invention I patented years ago. She can have some of it, but she's so pig-headed . . .'

She moved over and started pushing the pram herself: 'What do you think of him after all this time?'

Travers said: 'Huh, it's less than a couple of weeks. He looks super. Tell me, does Florence know about this business?'

'Oh, I wouldn't bother her now, with the election and everything.'

They got to the park gate and she said: 'Pop round and have a decent meal one evening.'

'There's something I'd never turn down. I'll give you a call.'

Gilbert Bossis said: 'Yes, all three of us.'

'Yes, why not?' said Travers with a cough.

Florence called Travers in about Emilie. He had asked if she had a moment.

'What's the trouble?' she asked.

'I'll tell you in a minute. But first I'd just like your opinion about Catherine.'

He told her the latest developments, and she said: 'Albertas would never use force. It would be asking for trouble, and he knows it. His lawyer will have told him. On the other hand, I don't like this angle about being unable to provide for the baby, that's dangerous. She's got to find work, anything to start with.'

'That's what I was hoping you'd say.'

'What can she do?'

'Type, shorthand, accounts perhaps? She's got brains and I don't suppose she'd be reluctant to take a job.'

Florence laughed: 'Anyone would think she's your daughter.'

'Well she could hardly be anything else.' Florence lifted an eyebrow but said nothing, and he went on. 'Let's forget that. But is there anything you can offer her here?'

'Not just now. But Armand might need help at the campaign headquarters. I'll talk to him tomorrow. Now, what's this about Emilie?'

Travers changed his tone to one of urgency: 'I haven't actually seen her, but I went past the house. Awful! Can we go together?'

Florence jumped to her feet and rushed across the room for her coat: 'Whatever *are* you talking about?'

'You'll see!'

They found Emilie in the kitchen, propped up against a cupboard. When they entered she recoiled and her eyes showed terror. Florence squatted down and took her in her arms.

'Oh Florence! What have I got to do with it? What have I ever done to anyone?' She sobbed so violently that they could only just understand what she was saying.

'We're here now, don't worry my sweet, we're here.' Emilie stumbled to her feet and the two women hugged each other, Florence rubbing her neck and fondling her hair and giving her little kisses.

On their way in they had seen the fanlight over the front door with the holes where the stones had smashed through. They had read the graffiti; BERG – RACKETEER – MURDERER.

'It's the same at the shop. I d-daren't g-go out . . . the children at school . . . getting at them . . .'

Florence said firmly: 'Listen Emilie, whatever Philippe's done it's not your fault and not the children's. People are nasty when this kind of thing happens, they love to hurt others, take it out on them. But I promise you they won't do this again. Travers, we'll put an end to their little game.'

'Right on!'

Travers drove them fast back to *La Dépêche*. Neither spoke.

At last Travers growled: 'Everyday shit, thrown by everyday people. Sickening.'

'We'll rub their damn noses in it, Trav.'

She turned towards him and glared furiously.

'I know about shit,' he muttered.

Florence couldn't help laughing.

It was not until they were back in Florence's office that she said vehemently 'And what the hell are you doing about the rest of this goddam business?'

'The rest? Oh, Les Sablons. Well, I've got stacks of facts. Figures, names, sums involved, details of where the money went. I'm working on the idea of how and why property has become part of the crime wave. We can get about ten articles out of that, starting with a recap on the main property scandals in the past decade. I could get going whenever you like.'

She tapped a ballpoint on her teeth: 'Mustn't let it all out at once. I suspect it would be better to wait for the opposition to make a few mistakes first. Let's see how the first round goes in the voting. If it looks bad for our man, we can open fire. How does that seem to you?'

'Just perfect, *mongénéral*!'

He moved towards her and took her by the forearms.

'I think you're great, Florence. I respect you, I'm fond of you, and I'm damn well going to kiss you – for Catherine!'

'Lucky Catherine!'

Travers drew her to him, she offered no resistance.

Lowering his voice, he said: 'There's nothing more than this between Catherine and me.'

He gave her a long kiss.

Florence said: 'Not *bad*!'

'Nectar,' he rejoined with a grin.

172

She pulled slowly away: 'Now clear off, Don Juan.'

He went to the door and she added: 'That should not be regarded as a precedent, I reserve my options, Monsieur le Juge.'

'Let's have lunch tomorrow,' Travers said quickly.

'Sorry, family get-together. Another day certainly.'

'We'll be older.'

'But more mature.'

The Bergs and Gilbert Bossis were seated round the oval table at La Commanderie. They were all ill at ease, except Maître Saviot who was the neutral party at the gathering. The subject was the death duties.

Armand arrived last, with a preoccupied look on his face which they all failed to notice except Florence, who knew the reason: the latest issue of La Dépêche, a copy of which was poking out of his jacket pocket.

He sat down without a word and waited for Saviot to begin. He told them that duties would total between sixteen and twenty million francs. Saviot went on to tell them that he believed it was possible to agree with the tax people on the market value of the woodland and property.

Marie-Lou cut in: 'You mean for the shares of Jean-Jacques, Armand and Julien. My information is that we shall be asked very soon to pay part of the total duties. This means that my husband will have to sell some property, and Julien some of his woodland. What about Florence, though?'

Florence said: 'I was waiting for that.'

Saviot watched Marie-Lou's pencil darting about among her notes as if it had a life of its own: 'Madame, for the tax authorities a newspaper is a goldmine, and for the proprietor it's a bottomless pit. These are two approaches that are particularly hard to reconcile, although I shall be working on the problem.'

'Which will take an awful lot of time,' Jean-Jacques said.

His wife took him up: 'Yes time, a hell of a time. Contrasting with the speed with which we shall have to stump up our money. Why is she allowed longer?'

'Because I haven't been evaluated yet,' her sister-in-law said with irritation.

'Meanwhile, I don't see why you can't sell some shares in La Dépêche. To Jean-Jacques, for example.'

'Madame!' the notary said with some force, angered that the

proceedings were being thrown out of gear.

Florence said 'no' quietly as Saviot spoke. She would not sell any shares to Jean-Jacques.

'Why not to someone else?' Jean-Jacques declared blandly.

'So that the paper slips through our fingers, so that the Bergs lose the majority?'

Marie-Lou guffawed: 'It's your business.'

Julien countered: 'It's a matter for all of us.'

Marie-Lou played her next and final card. She announced that she was considering refusal of the inheritance, that she intended to claim a court ruling under which the Berg fortune would no longer be of benefit to one member of the family, while all the others lost out. This seemed so outrageous a charge that, amid the general vituperation that followed, even Jean-Jacques had to offer a disclaiming shrug.

'Your father was gaga, otherwise he'd have made an equitable will,' Marie-Lou screeched. She rummaged about in her notes and repeated: 'Equitable! equitable!'

Her husband told her to pipe down, furious himself at the idea of being the son of an imbecile. As for Marie-Lou, she pursed her lips and her eyes smouldered at the thought of the plot devised against her. She got up determined to go home to bed and rest with an ice-pack on her careworn brow, while she worked out how to get her revenge on Florence.

Her departure caused no comment, except from Jean-Jacques who croaked: 'You wait till she gets me home.' He left as well, followed by the others except for Florence and Armand.

'We ought to have given Maître Saviot at least a cup of coffee,' Florence said after a while.

'He got more than he bargained for anyway,' Armand quipped. Simultaneously, he slid the copy of the newspaper across the table at her.

She said huffily: 'I've read Travers's article, thank you very much. No recriminations, please, we've had enough already.'

Armand gaped at her incredulously: 'Florence, do you really believe it's any help in my campaign to insult people, call them fascists and scoundrels, charge them with skulduggery?'

'And you think we should keep quiet about Emilie's windows being smashed, her walls daubed, her children terrorized?'

'Listen, from the very beginning of this campaign Philippe has been thrown in my face again and again. By falling in behind his

174

wife Emilie with such vehemence you are simply putting yourself in the same category as him. You're backing all the Bergs without distinction, and the paper's support for me is valueless.'

Florence prepared to discuss it calmly: 'Not all the Bergs. I'm backing you, and Emilie. Not Emilie as a Berg but as a wife and mother, a person who has been persecuted in a cowardly way. Armand, try to understand. I know what I'm doing. And after all your programme calls for more justice, tolerance, respect for people's dignity. Surely you agree that Travers's piece is along those lines, giving a hand to the weak when they need it. Don't worry darling, that's how the public will see it. They never make a mistake when it's a matter of the heart, and believe me you'll benefit from that.'

Her brother looked hard at her and said: 'Hm, someone said much the same thing at the campaign offices. She said it was great news that *La Dépêche* had thrown all political caution to the wind and was promoting me as the honest and fair-minded candidate.'

'What was that?'

'Catherine Kovalic. Travers was with her.'

'Cheeky devil Travers, he got in first. I was supposed to explain to you about her, but he's spoiled my surprise. Are you going to take her on?'

'Travers told me you wanted it, and I suppose that's correct.'

'It was *he* who wanted a job for *her*. But I always give in to him anyway.'

Armand blinked in amazement, and she laughed. It was a ripple of light-hearted merriment at his facial expression, but also a subtle and delicious dare – subtly telling him that she alone could understand him.

At the notary's meeting, nobody noticed Gilbert Bossis slip out.

He went casually away from the house, looking back surreptitiously to make sure he was not followed, and then when he was off the estate he strode along at the double. His destination was the Kovalic farm.

Gregor caught sight of him approaching. He was in the pigeon loft, and scampered down the rickety ladder. He rushed into the house.

'You sure he's coming here?' Albertas barked.

'Where else?'

'Well, we'd better see what he wants,' Albertas said somewhat stupidly, getting into a jacket.

He was standing four-square on the threshold of the farmhouse when Gilbert ploughed his way through hens and ducks, marching up to Catherine's overbearing father. Gregor had beaten a retreat into the kitchen but intended to miss nothing of what followed. The women Marfa and Zoë were out of sight.

Bossis and Kovalic looked at each other for a long time, each fearing that a wave or a polite greeting would lose him some strategic advantage. At length Albertas gave a slight nod and went in, followed by Bossis. They crossed the main room and came to a halt in Albertas's office, the small room with the low ceiling.

'And to what do we owe this honour?'

'I've come to advise you that it would be best if you let Catherine go her own way. I know she's your daughter. But it's useless going on about it, I know your opinion by heart.'

Albertas's face was inscrutable. He was impressed with the quiet conviction in Bossis's voice. He had expected a stand-up argument whereas they were, in fact, already sitting down. Albertas was soon assuring the visitor that he had never threatened a living soul, but that obviously he wanted his girl to come home – that was natural.

'You want your daughter, Monsieur Albertas? I wonder. What you really want is the baby, and your natural inclination is to go and take him, to kidnap him. But, Monsieur Albertas, you are a man of experience, you are capable of reasoning these things out, and you wouldn't make such a grave mistake.'

Albertas inclined his head at this tribute to his sagacity and intelligence, but he still could not see where Bossis was leading the conversation. Consequently, he took the initiative himself and asserted roundly that the baby was his by right. A claim that old Gregor indicated his approval of by vigorously nodding his head.

'But you have the baby!' Bossis cried. 'You have him because he's a Kovalic. Kovalic like you and Bossis like me.'

In Albertas's eyes this took them no further, and he asked innocently: 'What does all this boil down to, Monsieur Bossis?'

'He is grandson to both of us. My dear fellow, obviously you don't want to lose him, but nor do I after all's said and done. On the other hand, if you have any ideas about snatching him away, I shall prevent it.' Gilbert's voice had risen sharply towards the end, and this made Albertas sit up.

He said: 'Me take the babe from you? But it's you who took him from me! And it's me who's got the right to say I'll prevent it.'

On the other side of the door, Gregor mumbled further approval, unaware that Bossis was smiling and that Albertas could think of no way to counter the other's diplomatic overture.

'You're a worthwhile sort of fellow, Albertas.'

'Hm, that's as may be. And if I leave young Catherine alone, what's in it for me?'

They moved out of the office and Bossis said: 'For you? Not the baby, that's for certain. But you have my friendship. Grandads are meant to be friends, don't you agree? You'll see later how this lad, Paul Kovalic, will be so happy to have a couple of grandfathers to play with him in the park.'

'And in this yard here. We can play football!'

That virtually ended the exchange, and Bossis went trundling off, watched all the way by his newfound colleague. Albertas reflected that old Bossis had got one over on him, but he somehow didn't feel too bad about it, even felt pretty noble when he came to think about it. At last he took his eyes off Gilbert's receding form and saw his own father staring at him.

'Well, what's up with you?' he demanded. 'What are you looking at for the love of God?'

'I never said anything.'

'Huh! Well, I'm telling you I reckon he's a decent old stick that Bossis. I told him we must be friends, and we made some deals.'

That same evening around eleven Armand Berg sat with a final brandy at a table for four which the waiter at Les Messageries had cleared.

Florence came bustling in. She had vaguely hoped to run into Travers. He was not at the paper or at the campaign offices, which were closed. No doubt in the arms of some girl.

'I thought you might turn up,' Armand said as she took a seat opposite him. 'How about a nightcap?'

'No thanks. How did it go?'

Armand had dined with his publicity man Chambonnas and a certain Peyrol, who was the Socialist candidate and a high ranker in the Party. It had been Peyrol's invitation, his purpose being to persuade Armand to withdraw, leaving him sure to beat Quentin as the left vote would be behind the one man. It had been an eventful discussion, and Armand gave his sister a quick run-down.

'And the conclusion?'

'We ended up committed opponents.'

'And all he had to offer you was his gratitude?' Florence's eyes bored into him.

'I suppose I was meant to infer that I would receive a cushy number of some kind with a fee to match. Well Flo, it's been nerve-racking and tiring – I'd like to call in at Les Glycines, while I'm still the boss.' He looked at her quizzically: 'You don't seem your usual bright self either.'

She wrinkled her nose: 'You aren't the only critic we've had over the article on Philippe. Gilbert's mad. I was off to La Commanderie when he came back from a walk, looking like a two-year-old. But he changed when he saw me, told me that in defending Emilie I was siding with his son's murderer. I objected strongly, told him his logic was screwy and that Philippe's innocence would be proved in due course. He wouldn't listen. Told me Philippe was on a charge and that's all he knew and that was that. Slammed the car door in my face.'

'Who'd run a newspaper!' said Armand with a yawn. 'I'm off now, coming?'

'I'll see if they can find me something to eat.'

It was a double brandy she had. The quarrel with old Bossis had thrown her off-balance. And there was Travers too – she'd been looking for him everywhere. So much for the old-pro Florence who'd been around. Suddenly, she hated Travers for being so important to her, for undermining her self-confidence.

She paid and called the clinic. She wanted to tell Armand she'd join him, had lost her bearings, was uneasy being on her own.

'Sorry, Madame, there's an emergency, would you care to phone in an hour?'

The patient, an adolescent girl, was being resuscitated with the breathing apparatus, eyes closed, deathly pale. Fernandez watched her boss who had his eyes glued to the screen showing the patient's heartbeat.

At length, he returned to the girl's side and opened her eyelids.

'Can't be older than sixteen,' he muttered.

'Seventeen, Monsieur. Name's Anne Vernier.'

He studied her for a moment. She was a pretty, rather common-looking brunette, sexy probably. This was the girl Michel had been scrapping over at La Clairière a few nights before. Michel was waiting in the passage.

Armand told Fernandez to keep an eye on the girl, and went out to Michel. His nephew stood staring stupidly at nothing and was almost as white as the patient. Armand's hand smacked the boy across the cheek – Michel staggered back in fright.

'Bloody fool. Heroin! If she doesn't pull through, you're in big trouble. You idiot!'

'She's not going to *die*, uncle Armand?'

'It's what you deserve.'

The boy moaned: 'It wasn't me, honestly. I don't know who it was brought the drugs. Roland probably.'

'Was he the short blond kid who brought her in and went straight off?'

'Yes, he kept giving her drinks, but I didn't know . . . She's not going to die, is she?'

Armand thundered: 'I want the names of all the people there, understand? I won't have drugs in this town. We're lucky not to have any to speak of. Come on, names!'

Michel looked hard at him, half in defiance but half ashamed: 'Give them my name.'

'So, Monsieur wants to take full responsibility. All right, but if she does give up the ghost, you'll be held responsible in law. You fool!'

Armand Berg went back inside the room.

Anne Vernier pulled through, but only just. In the early hours Armand sat down at his desk, a broken man. He was tired, terrified of his own infirmity and of so much suffering and death, convinced that he had made the mistake of a lifetime by going in for politics, disgusted with the constant hopeless fight to go on, the struggle without reward.

With a rattle in his throat he told Fernandez: 'I've had enough. And as for the battle to reach the Elysée, I think I'll leave it to someone else . . .'

The next day Philippe escaped from the magistrate's room, and added to the long list of woes afflicting the Berg family.

The gendarme who had brought him in removed his handcuffs in accordance with standard practice, and Philippe grabbed the

179

man's pistol. He lined the gendarme, magistrate and defence counsel up against the wall. He then locked the door from the inside, opened the window and jumped onto a car roof from the first floor.

He grabbed a motorbike from a waiting Prefecture messenger and roared off as several gendarmes rushed out of the building.

Impotent, one of them phoned the alert from inside while the others stood sheepishly looking down at the caved-in car roof.

Chapter Six

That evening in Les Messageries, Travers and Florence had their meal together, the one they postponed for a more mature moment.

Two hours earlier they had learned of Philippe's sensational getaway, which the police had kept quiet for as long as they could.

'They won't take long to catch up with him,' Travers said.

Commissaire Nicolo and Inspector Germain found the motorbike abandoned on a patch of waste-land. Since the road barriers were in place only fifteen minutes after the alert, the fugitive must still be in Chateauvallon, Nicolo concluded.

Florence was looking grim, and Travers felt obliged to remark: 'Florence, this worrying will be the death of you. You've spent the whole meal brooding on your editorial – it's all there in that pretty head of yours, from the opening sentence to the final exclamation mark.'

She gave a wan smile: 'No, only the general angle. Let's go back and write it together. You think it's strange?'

'No. I was wondering what it's like to be a woman. Perhaps you do too.'

She laughed: 'Oh don't worry, I'm every inch a woman, but I like a fight too. This Philippe business has started the adrenalin going again, I was getting flabby.' She put a hand on his. 'I'm all right, ready for action.'

They got up and he held her coat for her: 'Need a shoulder to lean on?'

'A bit. Maybe because you kissed me that time.'

'There's always another time.'

'OK, but not tonight, we've got work to do.'

'Right-ho, Monsieur.'

181

Armand joined them in Florence's office in the early hours.

He was exhausted. There'd been a cardiac arrest and it had taken three hours to save the patient – Anne Vernier. But he had no need to reveal a professional confidence.

He threw a glance at the heavily-corrected typescript on his sister's desk: 'Jumping in with both feet?'

'We've just finished it, see what you think,' Florence said. 'Unless you're not interested.'

'Oh I am, immensely. But I have neither arms nor legs nor eyes. So read it to your little brother.'

Her basic view was that the safest and most effective technique this time was to put a key question to the 350,000 readers; this would force them to square up to the moral challenge.

She read out: 'A man in full possession of his senses, a former paratrooper, boldly chooses to jump eleven metres at the risk of killing himself or being shot. Is he *necessarily* guilty? To flee is to admit the crime, and it cannot be ruled out that he is guilty and wished to avoid punishment. But let us examine the matter from a different angle: the standpoint of a desperate man who, though innocent, has been made a scapegoat by the real criminals. If this were so, he would feel hamstrung by devious intrigues, while at the same time the Judiciary is itself caught in the same web of lies. He commits an incredible mistake, he makes a getaway. But this escape can only signify a pathetic cry for help, backed by the hope of arousing public opinion and making the public ask further questions.'

Armand was pacing the room slowly, and Florence broke off to say: 'Well?'

'Well put, but it's not going to get Philippe out of his mess, if I'm not mistaken.'

Florence countered: 'That's not the intention, although it may be a side-effect. What we have to do is stand back, to keep our distance. We are merely advancing a possible interpretation for his leap from the window.'

Travers added: 'The readers will get the impression that we are being honest and objective – capable of being disinterested over Philippe. But, they will also get the idea that we know who the real culprits are.'

'It's getting to sound better,' Armand chuckled. 'Who are they?'

'For now, that's between Travers and me,' his sister said.

'We've a stack of ammunition, but we're not sure where best to target it.'

Armand left them to it.

Travers said: 'Aren't you going out on a limb? We don't know *that* much, our net is full of holes.'

Florence laid a hand on his arm: 'My concern right now is to inject a little more confidence into that brother of mine. He's whacked out, always dealing with emergencies.'

There was a short silence and Travers said: 'Well, work is over, here's your coat. May I kiss you now, Madame?'

'Gladly, Monsieur.'

He acted the fool a bit: 'On second thoughts, in view of the herring I ate . . .' Florence threw a coat hanger and he dodged it.

She said: 'You might end up interesting me if . . .'

'If?'

'If you weren't an employee, Monsieur Travers.' She stalked out, delighted at having had the last word, though annoyed about the herring.

Twenty minutes later she drove through the main gate into La Commanderie, and failed to notice a dark car parked between two large bushes.

Nicolo and two side-kicks were inside. They believed Philippe Berg may well have gone to ground at the big house, and they were crouched, cold and aching in their seats, waiting for the sun to rise at 6.40 a.m., give or take a second or two.

Only then, by law, could they enter and search the premises.

It was a search that Nicolo was to remember all his life. Or so he told himself after Gilbert Bossis let him in clad in a dressing gown and swearing profusely.

'You must be out of your mind, Nicolo. Me harbour a man charged with murdering my own son? Pshaw!'

'Take it easy,' Florence chided, hurrying to meet the police. 'Do your job, Commissaire. Mathilde, do show these gentlemen all the rooms, and don't forget the cellars. If you find an iron mask, we've been looking for it for decades!'

Nicolo, even more averse than usual to wisecracks, said with gravelly menace: 'What does that remark signify, Madame?'

'Oh, just my little pre-breakfast fun.'

The procession got under way: Mathilde, Nicolo and the two side-kicks.

183

Gilbert whispered: 'If your father was alive, they would never have been allowed to search this place. Did you send for them?'

'It can only be the examining magistrate, nobody else has the right. Someone may have got at Nicolo or the magistrate, someone worried about our political activities.'

'Quentin?'

'Possibly. But there's Peyrol too, and he asked Armand to step down. He is a socialist, and so is Judge Perugino.'

Gilbert stammered: 'Imagine their supposing that I'd shield Philippe . . .'

'You, me, the whole clan. They'd love to catch us red-handed, whoever *they* are,' Florence murmured, her head buzzing with names.

She made some coffee in the kitchen, and found Mathilde chuckling away with Gilbert when she brought it in.

'They went in the bedrooms on tiptoe,' she chortled. 'Didn't even look under the beds, never opened a cupboard, that's a fact. I reckon they're more disturbed than we are.'

Gilbert said: 'Julien's going to be upset when they find him. He wanted to lie in.'

'Julien? What do you mean,' Florence said.

'As they took the children back to school yesterday, I had them here last night. Said they could sleep here if they liked.'

Mathilde interrupted: 'But Monsieur, they went back to the sawmill early, before the police arrived. I heard them.'

'Funny, must have changed their minds, ' the old man said.

Nicolo and his men came in as if they had been scribbling on the walls. 'Sorry to have troubled you, Madame, Monsieur.'

When Florence returned after seeing them off, Gilbert had disappeared. She slid behind the wheel of her car thirty minutes later, hoping to get the issue when it came off the presses. She was keen to see what the editorial on Philippe Berg looked like in print.

At about the same time Thérèse, looking like some Hollywood cowgirl in her jeans, was making some tea in the sawmill office. She spilled the hot water on the desk as Gilbert Bossis erupted into the room bearing a double-barrelled shotgun under his arm.

'Gilbert, nice to see you! What a surprise . . .'

'Not the first. How about your nocturnal visitor?'

'Huh?' exclaimed Julien from the doorway. 'What are you raving on about?'

'I'll show you.' Gilbert surged towards a door on the other side of the office, and kicked it open.

Lying on a camp bed, struggling to get out of a blanket, was Philippe Berg.

Gilbert pointed the shotgun at his chest.

'Gilbert!' cried Thérèse. 'Julien!'

'Keep your hands off me,' Gilbert snarled, positioning himself against a side wall and jerking his head. 'Over there.'

The couple moved so that Gilbert had all three covered.

'So that's why you crept out. Couldn't leave an old chum on his own. Especially Paul's killer.'

Julien moved in front of his wife: 'Put that thing down, Gilbert. Put it down. Philippe never hurt a fly in his life.'

Philippe edged his way to the front: 'I swear to you, Monsieur Bossis, that's true. I know everything looks stacked against me, I know I'm mixed up in things, but I never killed Paul.' Gilbert remained silent, the gun held steady. 'All right, go ahead and fire, but you'll regret it, I've got something to tell you.'

Philippe thereupon deliberately turned round, offering his back. Gilbert knew he could not fire, and so did the others.

'Call the police, Julien. Nicolo's not so daft, he could smell him. Call them, man! I could turn this idiot into a colander, but the guillotine's better.'

Julien spread his hands: 'Wait a second! He said he had something to tell you.'

'That's a bad joke, Philippe Berg.'

'So you won't listen. You're thirsting for blood, for vengeance, and you don't want me to be innocent. Is that it?'

Suddenly Gilbert gave up, slamming the gun onto the desk: 'Well you've got guts, Monsieur Philippe Berg. Out with it!'

Philippe came forward again: 'They're trying to pin Paul's death on me, and the charge of accessory to murder is only a start. I would be eliminated with the guillotine blade or by accident in my cell, that's the idea. And it's because of that that I escaped, it's my only chance.'

'I'm still listening.'

'Well get this. There is a letter, written proof that the killers are being protected by a top politician. It's an official letter with the Ministry's name at the top, and signed by the Minister himself.'

'Let's see it then.'

Julien shifted: 'It's for sale.'

185

'For sale!'

Philippe Berg moved forward: 'You've got to understand, Monsieur Bossis, I have no choice. I'm not safe here and I don't want to put Thérèse and Julien at risk in any way. I have to disappear – for Florence and Armand and Jean-Jacques. But escaping is an expensive business, and I need 100,000 francs. That's the sale price.'

Gilbert rubbed his chin: 'Whose signature is at the bottom?'

'Quentin's.'

Gilbert did not get the 100,000 francs.

Florence said Philippe was a crook, and was bluffing. He wanted 100,000 francs and that was all. Anyone who had spent three years in a town hall could fix it; a letterhead and a forgery as the signature. Child's play, she scoffed.

Armand backed her. Gilbert had not even seen the letter, but he believed Philippe because he was desperate to get Paul's murderers. As for himself, even if the letter existed, he would refuse to use it in the campaign.

With Gilbert on his way down the steps at *La Dépêche*, Armand said: 'It's pathetic, he'll move heaven and earth to get that money together.'

Florence remarked: 'He told me that he'd buy the letter, even if there was one chance in a hundred that it was the real thing. If it was, he'd get Quentin, he said. Failing that he'd get Philippe.'

'Poor devil, he's living for vengeance now,' said Armand. 'By the way, our nurse Fernandez likes your editorial. Says she admires the way *La Dépêche* is sticking its neck out but not going over the top.'

Travers entered: 'That's what several people told me, they seem to be with us on the whole. Too early to reach any conclusions yet.'

On his way out, Travers asked Armand how Catherine was coming along at the campaign office.

'She's doing a great job, old chap.'

'She thinks you're great too. Oh, by the way, I saw Gilbert Bossis going out, looked like he'd eaten a trayful of fourteen-point type. Never even said good morning.'

'A slight difference of opinion between him and us,' said Armand.

Armand drove back to the clinic, from where Florence had summoned him urgently to see Bossis.

It had been an awkward moment. Anne Vernier had decided to

186

make a dash for freedom, and he had caught her on the stairs. She had pummelled his chest and promptly fainted. Hypoglycaemia, he diagnosed, and ordered blood tests. The results were worrying.

The opinion polls looked bad too, with Quentin seemingly heading for victory. His number two, Jerome, said these polls were out of date as soon as they were published, but Quentin said the voters saw him as a tower of strength, a guarantee that things would be in safe hands. With Armand Berg's platform shot full of holes, the socialist Peyrol was his only real contender, along with the man from Paris.

'Ignore Berg at your peril,' Jerome warned. 'He's from Chateauvallon, and he's got his sister at *La Dépêche*.'

'Ha! Everything in his favour, but he has no programme. "Open administration"! What's that supposed to mean? Forget all that: the polls, *La Dépêche*, Berg's programme. Phooey! It's cousin Philippe and the search at La Commanderie that's going to start them thinking. Seen Florence's whistling in the dark in the latest issue?'

'She's floundering. She can write what she likes, but the voters still see Philippe Berg as a killer. We have to show them they are right.'

Mayor Quentin had misgivings about using Philippe Berg as a campaign factor – but he was the only sword of Damocles they had to brandish over the heads of the Bergs.

That evening Florence was late getting home. She was still wound up when she drove through the gate at La Commanderie, having racked her brains on new punchier posters for Armand, fought with advertisers demanding lower rates for space or else they would pull out, and finally clashed with Jean-Jacques – all before arguing for two hours with an intractable tax inspector called Chambard.

Added to that she had the uneasy feeling as she walked to the taxman's office that she was being followed. She was right in this, but she could not know that the man's name was Sorlin and that he had been on her tail for several days on orders from Jerome.

'Make sure you check on her private life, Sorlin,' Jerome had ordered.

'See if there's anything fishy, Monsieur Jerome?'

187

'Exactly, and it would be convenient if something was, understand?'

Ditto concerning Armand Berg, especially for Armand Berg. And not a word to Monsieur Quentin, because Jerome knew his boss would turn a blind eye to *any* method, provided he knew nothing about it.

Florence's elegant legs were like cotton wool, and Gilbert Bossis was in no better shape when he got in an hour after she did, to find her curled up asleep on the big settee in the main living room.

She surfaced from her nap and saw that Gilbert was in his best suit, but made no comment in view of their row over the mysterious letter and the 100,000 francs. Florence watched him pour himself a brandy, a sure sign he was in no mood to be trifled with. Then he asked if she would like one.

'No thanks,' she said, clearing her throat.

'Well, here's health, mine anyhow. What a day! I tried the bank with my patent as collateral, but they wouldn't hear of giving me a loan.'

She said: 'I'm very sorry Gilbert, but I can't. Don't hold it against me.' He gave a shrug. 'Not only am I against throwing money down the drain, but the tax people are coming down on me like a ton of bricks, and I've the least-negotiable asset of anyone. Sixty million at least, that's the valuation put forward by that pig Chambard for *La Dépêche*. Sixty! When I think that Saviot reckoned he could get a compromise figure. When I told Chambard we always made a loss and that the only people who would be interested would be a political party or a major group wanting to influence public opinion, do you know what he said? "The Boulard Group". He said that the Boulard Group was proposing a price to buy me out, and that Monsieur Boulard's figure would be his figure. Which means Chambard knows Boulard wants *La Dépêche* and that he even knows how much he's prepared to invest. I couldn't help asking the damn vulture what percentage he was getting out of it.'

Gilbert said: 'A dangerous move.'

'I just couldn't contain myself anymore.'

'You should always at least pretend that the tax people are just state employees.' He poured a brandy for her, and this time she took it.

'And Jean-Jacques, true to form, didn't let me down. I'd just got back to the office and he rushed in, wanting to know how I'd made out. I told him.'

'And he told you it was your problem?'

'How did you guess? He also said he was the natural heir to the paper, and that, having done him out of his inheritance, it was quite right I should pay the price instead of him.'

Gilbert took a swig and suggested: 'Why not refuse the inheritance? Or else you can sell. Sell part of it to me. You know, Florence, I want to see you all right. We'd work well together.'

She started to speak but it changed to a mumble. After a moment, Gilbert asked her what she had said.

'I said I'd think it over. I always say that when I'm in a fix. But one thing's certain, I don't want Jean-Jacques – even as just editor he gets on my nerves.'

'You mean professionally speaking.'

'No, as a person.'

'But he's still your own brother.'

'With a dagger, called Marie-Lou, permanently at the ready.'

They poured out another brandy each, but neither of them drank it.

In her room she got into something casual and sat down to write to Maurice Arras. Three bad starts found their way into the waste paper basket, and she funked a fourth. Perhaps it was a good idea to unload her cares onto the great brain, but on the other hand he might give her a polite brush-off. In fact, the whole thing was starting to look ridiculous, and she got into bed. As she cleaned her face for the night, she began thinking out a long letter to Travers, and was only half-way through it, when she dropped off to sleep.

It was splendid weather for the first round of voting, but few in Chateauvallon voted early.

They enjoyed their moment of power. Not so the candidates. Florence said later she bit her nails to the quick and smoked at least two packets of cigarettes. Armand Berg was a model of calm. When Travers reached the campaign offices around 11.00 a.m. and said the abstentions were 'colossal', the candidate said the radio was forecasting rain for midday.

Travers was pop-eyed and went over to Catherine: 'He doesn't care a damn, your bloke.'

She tilted her head: 'Seems like it. He told me that when he sees the posters saying VOTE BERG he thinks it's someone else.'

At the voting centre at Saint Charles school, Gilbert ran into Albertas Kovalic. He also deposited a dollop of spittle on a poster of Georges Quentin, to the amusement of the citizens doing their duty as voters. Albertas deemed this was not the moment to mention that his wife was knitting something for little Paul.

Chambonnas, the publicity man, went for a stroll with his candidate and lost him. He finished up at the Bijou-Bar, where Travers rolled in while he was downing his third glass of beer.

'I've lost my general, so the battle is over,' he growled.

'He only looks indifferent,' Travers said, accepting a drink. Personally, he was feeling pretty good. As he had left the campaign rooms Florence had said he looked worried.

'I feel it, how about you.'

'I never feel that bad when you're around, Trav.'

The said Trav was even perkier by 2.00 p.m. He was wet inside and it was wet outside, for the weather had turned and a blanket of dark grey cloud was thickening fast. The voters would come in from their picnics and vote. At about the same time, Jerome made a similar observation to Quentin, who was chewing at his cigar just as Florence was burning up cigarettes elsewhere.

At four the heavens opened and there was a rush for the polling booths. Everybody saw it as a good sign, but for whom? Meanwhile, each party saw itself as benefiting from this sudden upsurge in interest.

Armand was the last to learn the results, having gone to the clinic to see Anne Vernier.

She greeted him with a protest: 'If you're a real doctor, see if you can do something with this bloody transistor. There's supposed to be a rock concert on Europe One, and all I get is politics. Bloody liberty, that's what it is. Oh sorry, doc, didn't want to offend you.'

He chuckled: 'Seems you're the one who's shocked.'

'Me shocked! That'd take some doing. You wouldn't imagine what shocks me. The generation gap they call it.'

He grabbed a chair, twisted it round and sat with his arms on the back: 'Fascinating. Tell me more.'

'What's fascinating?'

'Everything. Your natural form of expression, your gift for summing up a situation. So there's a generation gap? Where did you get that idea?'

'Of course, you think I'm daft.'

'Shooting off like that could prove something.'

Anne Vernier tossed her head: 'So we're into morals now. And your lot with their double whiskies and whatnot, is that any better?'

'It's a slower death than your way. And for pity's sake don't jigger about like that, you'll start your heart racing.'

'What do I care? So I'll die quicker, and who's to say I don't want to? At least I won't finish up an old hag.'

'I'll lay some chrysanthemums on your grave, with a card reading: "Here lies Anne Vernier, who threw a wonderful future away with her childish obstinacy".'

She eyed him: 'You're a sadist, you're.'

'That's my line, yours is vanity. In fact, you don't count at all, you're pig-headed and stuck up, in revolt against goodness knows what, perhaps against yourself and your nihilism.'

Suddenly she pouted and he wondered what was coming next. He *was* fascinated, she was like a creature from another planet and she startled him. Now she was smiling and he became guarded.

'You make me laugh with your sermons, like some priest. Say, when you mess about with me does it turn you on?'

He preferred not to react to that. But in fact he was reacting, with anger that he could not get through to her. He got up and at the door he turned and cracked: 'Keep laughing, my beauty. Laugh as much as you can while you still have time.'

She grew pale: 'You mean I really am ill?'

'If you weren't I wouldn't have kept you a minute longer than necessary. You have trouble with your platelets, it's the blood . . . how can I explain . . .'

'Don't bother. Your old cow of a nurse told me. But it's because she detests me.'

'How absurd . . . Well it's true, she does detest you.'

'Why?'

'Because you are detestable.' It came out as a mixture of rage and dismay.

'Do you detest me too ?'

He came back and took her hand: 'No, Anne. I couldn't detest you. I hate you so little I want to save you, get you out of this.'

He felt her sharp nails dig into his wrist as she whispered: 'Doctor, it's not much fun living, but I'm real scared of dying.'

'You won't die, believe me. I'll come back and see you later on.'

191

At 9.00 p.m. the definitive results of two *cantons* in Chateauvallon constituency were issued:

Votes cast: 3,162

Peyrol, Parti Socialiste	703
Lambert, Parti Communiste	251
Berg, Centre Gauche	645
Quentin, Majorités Diverses	1,563

Later a TV commentator said: 'We have only half the polling stations, and it's not possible at this stage to say whether Monsieur Quentin, well in the lead, will win an outright majority. It could be he'll get through on the first round. If there's a second round, he'll probably be fighting the socialist Peyrol, who is slightly ahead of the other non-communist candidate of the left, Dr Armand Berg.'

At the campaign office Florence said: 'It's not over yet. The outskirts are going for the PS, but Peyrol will do less well in the town. The old districts don't like outsiders.'

Meanwhile, Jerome at the town hall: 'Good, it's all up for Berg. He's got as many as he can hope for.'

The transistor in Anne Vernier's room at Les Glycines, 10.00 p.m.: 'Three new polling stations, with Quentin just in the lead. Peyrol still ahead of Berg, whose chances now look hopeless.'

At 10.20 p.m. there was a phone call for Armand at the campaign offices: 'This is Anne Vernier, I've just heard it on the radio. I'm so sad you never made it. I'd wanted you to win.'

'What happened to the rock concert?'

'Aw nuts!'

Far from the tumult, the phone rang too at the sawmill.

'Julien? Gilbert here, give me . . .'

'Here he is.'

'Listen, I'm still trying to get the jackpot. I mean, it doesn't look very hopeful, about the . . . er . . . document, I mean.'

'Gilbert . . .'

'Yes?'

'No fooling, you know his word of honour is the only thing left. On the head of my children and Emilie – I swear my document is authentic.'

'I'd like so much to believe it. Give me a bit longer.'

'If you trust me, you won't regret it. But if you can't cough up within forty-eight hours, three days at most, I'm leaving, and we'll have to hope for the best. I have to think of the people I'm with, they don't deserve to suffer on account of me.'

Gilbert said: 'With words like that, your honour remains intact. You're a scoundrel, but you're not a bastard. I've got an idea that may yet work.'

'Move fast, Gilbert, move fast!'

'All right. But remember this, if you pull a fast one on me, you're a dead duck anywhere in this world.'

'Anywhere. I know.'

It was close to midnight when Armand Berg walked into Les Glycines clinic once more. He had promised he would, and he kept that promise. As if waiting for him, Michel his nephew stumbled up to him as he went through the main door. He was carrying a huge bouquet of flowers on his way out.

'What are you doing here at this time of night?' Armand demanded. 'How come they let you in?'

'The radio,' he spluttered. 'They're all listening to the damn radio. Even Anne is. Bloody politics! Wasn't even interested in my roses, just about chucked me out, Uncle Armand.'

'You know better than I do what a ghastly character she has!'

'I'm going to get drunk,' the rejected swain declared.

Armand stood for a moment looking at the roses Michel had thrown into the gutter. He sympathized, unable to conceive of a more vexatious sign of defeat than to have one's roses rejected. He went inside and along the passage, unaware of a man concealed in the shadows. Armand was carrying Michel's roses.

Anne Vernier's eyes doubled in size as he went in: 'For me?'

'For you. A small gesture, but as you don't care for roses . . .'

'That's true.'

'All right then,' Armand said firmly, heading for the window. 'I'll dispose of them, unless you prefer to do it yourself . . .'

'Put them in the vase over there, please.'

'They are to say thank you for your thoughtful call in my hour of defeat.'

She laughed: 'You *are* funny, I must say.' It was a kindly laugh and she contemplated the roses with an air of wistful interest as Berg clumsily arranged them.

'I've never had roses before.'

'What of Michel's?'

'They'd smell of nappies.'

Fernandez came in at that point with the girl's father. Anne Vernier's expression changed completely, and she seemed afraid. This was curious, Armand thought, as her father appeared to be a quiet, unassuming man as he shuffled over to the bed and planted a timid kiss on her forehead.

'My girl, what's happened then?' he said. 'Is it serious, Doctor? I had no idea. They told me she was here when I got home this evening. I'm on the trains, always away from home.'

Armand warmed to him: 'Nothing to worry about, Monsieur Vernier. Anne passed out in the street quite near here, and we're looking after her. Nothing to worry about, she simply needs rest. We'll have her up and about in no time.'

'But what's she got?'

'Too much coffee, too many cigarettes. Sent her heartbeat up a bit. She'll be on her feet in a week.' He exchanged glances with the girl, who was visibly relieved. He was too busy with her father to notice her gaze soften in gratitude at this first 'good turn' anyone had ever done her in her life.

'Ah, those cigarettes, always got one dangling out of her mouth, Monsieur. Mind you do what the Doctor says, naughty girl.'

'Sure I will, papa.'

Father and daughter kissed each other on the cheek, and the man crept out, giving a weak wave. Not for the first time Armand felt a wave of . . . of what? Pity? Sorrow? They were so vulnerable, both of them, and he was supposed to be God Almighty at that moment. He felt a thickness in the throat.

Returning, he found the patient eagerly waiting to speak to him: 'You didn't tell him, did you?'

'Professional ethics forbade me, at least for the moment.'

She scowled at him: 'I'm under age, you ought to tell him really. You didn't want to upset him, was that it?'

'More or less.'

They smiled at each other. Anne waited, and at length he drew nearer the bed, and for an instant she wanted to tell him her heart was racing again. He placed his hand on her brow, and she seized it swiftly, transferring it to her cheek. It felt soft and warm. She had difficulty raising her eyes.

'I was really sad about you being beaten,' she declared. I turned the radio off as soon as I knew. Funny, I wanted to cry. That Peyrol, bleedin' sod!'

194

Her loyalty affected him: 'If you'd been more faithful as a listener you'd have found out I beat the sod 20.3 to 20 per cent.'

Her face lit up: 'You're making it up!'

'Cross my heart. I'm all set for the second round, so I'm a good guy after all, still heading for victory!'

She blushed: 'I *thought* I heard old Fernandez say congratulations. I thought it was because you were chatting me up. She was shocked, I thought.'

'You think too much.'

At that moment Fernandez entered with a rustle of starch, telling Armand he was terribly late and they had called from Les Messageries.

'Got to go and eat,' he explained to Anne Vernier, as he pulled his coat on.

'With a woman?'

'No actually, with my sister.'

Fernandez was back again three minutes later, and frowned at the patient. Vernier was asleep already, and smiling in her sleep. Well, that was one good thing at least.

The following day's *France-Soir* contained a small diary-piece by the Chateauvallon stringer Richot.

It read: 'Loud applause greeted Armand Berg from friends and supporters, when he arrived late at Les Messageries restaurant in Chateauvallon from his duties at his clinic, after topping the socialist Peyrol's vote as centre-right candidate by a hair's breadth. General opinion locally is that Berg's chances will increase rapidly in the next few days, and that the abstainers could come in from the cold to give him support. Amid heady optimism, champagne flowed like water . . .'

Richot phoned in his story ahead of a clash between poster teams one hour later, in which three people were hurt, one seriously. Travers found out within minutes that one of the attackers in this incident was a certain Rouquin, head of Armand Berg's poster team.

The news caused consternation at the restaurant, but Armand swore he did not know the man, had never seen him in his life. Travers suggested it was Quentin up to his tricks, or more likely Jerome. Florence cut in and said they would make enquiries later.

She'd intervened sharply, and for an excellent reason. Armand had just told her quietly that he didn't care a damn for the

195

campaign or the abstainers he was supposed to rustle up for the second round. He told her he'd fallen in love.

'Oh Lord,' she said. 'What next? Pull yourself together, for pity's sake, this is serious.'

'And love's not serious?'

'Not between two rounds of an election you could win.'

'Politics isn't everything.'

'It is for those who are in it, and you're right in the thick of it.'

'It was you who dragged me into it in the first place.'

'To get you out of your blind alley. Oh Armand, please be sensible. I did nothing wrong.'

'It's not your fault. I'm in love, that's all.'

'You just think you are.'

'Flo, I adore you, but you're not running my whole existence. I have my own feelings, my own life.'

His sister glared at him: 'Who is she?'

'Nobody you know.'

'All right, you love a nobody, and that's incompatible with politics.'

'What's incompatible is politics and me. That's what I've been trying to hammer into you for the past fifteen minutes.'

A new bunch of supporters tumbled in and cheered Armand. Florence made a bid to swing her brother back into the mainstream of the evening and raised her glass to his victory next Sunday. Just then the brass band of Les Joyeux Drilles du Quartier Saint-Paul burst in and struck up with a cheery march. Armand ploughed his way to the bar and drank four fingers of Scotch in sixty seconds.

Shortly afterwards Florence unburdened herself to Travers who quipped: 'Doctor heal thyself.'

She could not sleep that night, nor could Travers.

Gilbert Bossis took a walk in the grounds that Monday, stalking along with his stick and occasionally taking a swipe at a flower or an overhanging twig.

He had seen Florence rushing off on goodness knows what errand. If she had problems, so had he.

Bossis had been on the move for about thirty minutes when he spotted Albertas Kovalic stumping past the main gate heading for the house. His first reaction was to hurry indoors, but he relented after a few paces. Albertas was special, they had a treaty, he was his honoured guest almost.

Albertas said cheerily: 'Hullo there, Grandad. I expect you're pleased for Monsieur Armand.' They shook hands.

'Hold on, anything can happen, the fight's not over yet. Quentin got 48 per cent, and you'll see him get through, the skunk. If only I could think of a way of eliminating him! I would, wouldn't you?'

'Like a shot, Monsieur Gilbert!'

'And to think I've got it all planned out, only I can't carry it through.'

Albertas looked askance at him: 'That's double talk, Monsieur Gilbert.'

'I need 100,000 francs and I can't lay my hands on that much.'

He fell silent, aware that he had said too much. He asked Albertas what he had under his arm, and Albertas said it was a set of baby clothes.

'My women knitted it, you see, but we thought to ourselves seeing how Catherine wouldn't take it coming from us – we said to ourselves, perhaps you might be able to let her have it. No need to say where it comes from. That way the little mite'll have something from our side of the family, as you might say.'

'Yes, I'll let her have it. That's very kind of you. You must thank the ladies. Don't worry, you can count on me.'

Albertas drew himself up and went on: 'That ain't everything. There's this here doll, it's arms and legs move about like. And it can wear all kinds of things like uniforms, soldier, sailor, what you like. Young Paul will be able to play with it later on. You can get them in Paris, but this one's from America, so it's special.'

'From America!'

'I wrote to Bernard and told him to find something for us out of the ordinary, and he sent this.'

Gilbert cocked his head to one side: 'Bernard? Who would that be now.'

'My nephew, o' course. Been there these three years. Place called Harvard.'

'Harvard! Well that's a turn-up, I must say. I had no idea.'

'Going to be a big shot. A real manager, like they say.'

'I sincerely hope so. My warmest congratulations.'

To Gilbert it was becoming clear that Albertas had not finished yet. Kovalic said: 'About the christening. Wednesday, ain't it? I was wondering if we couldn't have the reception at our place. It's a kind of tradition.'

197

'You think Catherine would agree to that?'

'Might do if you put in a word.'

Bossis shook his head sadly. He didn't believe he should go that far, it was up to Catherine.

Albertas jerked up his chiselled face: '100,000 you said?'

Gilbert nodded curtly.

'Well,' said Albertas, 'If grandads can't help each other out, we're not up to much. You have a word with Catherine and I'll see if I can find the money for you. Think about it.'

He left forthwith, striding off while Gilbert gazed at him in disbelief.

Gregor was giving his view: 'That means to say that the Bergs are short of 100,000 francs. So he came to us, that's right, ain't it?'

They sat in the big room and old Gregor emphasized the point: 'That's the position then?'

'It looks like it. He must have gone to the others first, and got no results. Maybe it's because of the election expenses, or the death duties. That'll cost 'em a packet.'

'That's their business,' the oldster said with a chuckle.

Albertas dug deeper: 'Bossis's problem is Quentin, he wants to rub him out.'

'Well, what's to stop the Bergs helping him? It's in their interest after all.'

Albertas tried to work it out: 'Either they don't have 100,000 or they don't want to give it to him. I don't know the ins and outs of it, why should I, but it looks to me like there's a pretty big bust-up on the way, and everyone's going to be in on it, including the Bergs.'

Another pause and Gregor said: 'Bernard then?'

'What about Bernard?'

Gregor heaved himself out of his chair and reached for the phone: 'You'd better do it. Phone him up at Harvard and tell him to get back here quick.'

Albertas took the receiver and started to dial: 'Well said, dad. What we need is a manager.'

Armand Berg rushed to *La Dépêche* from the municipal hospital, and ran into Maryse in the corridor, who pointed to Florence's office.

'Put your crash helmet on, she's climbing up the wall.'

When he entered her office, she confronted him with eyes ablaze: 'Ah, here he is. So it was you who took on that thug Rouquin. Chambonnas has just told me.' The publicity agent was trying to shrink into his chair.

He said: 'I'm sorry Armand, it wasn't me as your sister suspected, but you!'

'What are you going on about? I don't deal with that kind of thing. I've never set eyes on this Rouquin fellow, and you know perfectly well I would never recruit gangsters like that. This is Jerome's doing, it's just like him to bribe one of our people.'

Florence softened her tone: 'Quite so. But meanwhile we're sitting here with egg on our faces.'

'All part of the game. I've just been to the hospital, and the chap he beat up is called Gustave Renan. Broken wrist, face like a lump of putty. Luckily no skull fractures or neck trouble.'

Armand added that he was already suffering the consequences. The duty doctor asked him whether he'd come to see his toughies' handiwork, and someone in the street called him a killer. 'News spreads fast in Chateauvallon.'

Chambonnas got up: 'I'd better take a walk, put about some better news.'

Florence pursed her lips and glared at her brother: 'You seem in better shape today. What came over you last night? You frightened me.'

'And now?'

'You're back to normal, unless I'm very much mistaken?'

'Let's say that my bout of lucidity is over. Or, if you prefer, I am once more aware of my obligations to your good self. I must be off, Florence. Nicolo's called me in.'

'Nicolo!'

'This Rouquin chap was part of our mob.'

As he left Florence's office, he found Chambonnas in the corridor chatting with Melchior.

Chambonnas told him: 'I forgot to mention it. FR3 wants a TV debate between you and Quentin. Antenne 2 is going to take it from them.'

'Me and Quentin! Don't be absurd, I wouldn't last sixty seconds.'

'Your sister has said we'll play along.'

'Ah well, I suppose that settles it.'

'Be at the Rue Dancourt studio at five for the screen test.'

199

Armand left the building in a daze. Evidently Flo had taken no notice whatsoever of his outburst the previous evening. 'Tomorrow's woman today!' he muttered, devising his own advertising slogan.

Armand had not even placed his buttocks on the chair when Nicolo moved in on him.

'Very considerate of you, Monsieur Berg, to call in on the injured man. I appreciate your remark, too, about being the first to take his attacker to court.'

Berg's eyes narrowed: 'Nice of you, too. Now get to the point.'

The Commissaire stuffed his pipe slowly and lit it with as much fuss as he could muster: 'Frankly, my first impression is that this is a frame-up; it was all round the town before the papers came out and before the early morning news on the radio. A whispering campaign that spread everywhere with lightning speed, no doubt because it was professionally mounted.'

'Who mounted it?'

'I think I know who, but I'd rather not take my inquiries that far.'

'Why on earth not?'

'Because I can't prove a thing.' Armand stiffened in anger and Nicolo lifted a hand. 'Five people were involved and only Rouquin was identified. More accurately, recognized but not formally identified. The details he gave your campaign office were false: name, first name, address. He is unknown to the police and he has disappeared without trace. Furthermore, Monsieur Berg, we can't be sure it was he who hit out in this brutal way.' Nicolo pointed his pipe stem at Berg. 'Let it drop, Monsieur Berg, that's my sincere advice. If you build this up into a big issue, it'll go against you. No smoke without fire, the voters'll say. Berg wouldn't kick up such a fuss if his hands were clean, they'll say. As you are well aware, this town is a town of petit bourgeois people and working folk, who like nothing better than to have a go at the rich. And the Bergs are rich. Think it over, Monsieur, in your own interest.'

Armand was in two minds as he left Nicolo. The Commissaire chose to turn a blind eye on the business, as if he was trying to stamp out the beginnings of a plot against him. At the same time, he was trying to spike his guns if he had any ideas about fighting the threat to his good name.

He summarized this to Florence in a call from a phonebox. She advised him to wait and see, which was just about all he could do anyway. Finally she told him he would be late for the studio test. He said he had to call in at the clinic for a couple of minutes.

Without so much as a respectful knock, Jerome barged into Quentin's office at the town hall, a bulky file against his left hip.

Quentin was ending a phone conversation and replaced the receiver, glaring at his number two.

Jerome stared back, intrigued at his superior's silence. He said at length: 'Here's the stuff for the TV debate. It's all there, lots of little traps he can't get out of. It'll be a walk-over for you, believe me.'

Quentin ignored the file as Jerome placed it on his desk: 'That was the hospital, and the lad's as well as can be expected, they say. Hardly your fault, I suppose . . . Own up, Jerome, this was your scheme, own up!'

Jerome placed a hand on his heart: 'I find it tough luck, but how can you imagine . . . ?'

'I don't imagine, I *know*. Tough luck? Really shitty would be a better term.'

'Some of these incidents can be effective,' the other said as if he were pronouncing an eternal truth that was nothing to do with him. He held Quentin's gaze, and the Mayor eventually lowered his eyes, looking at the file but not opening it.

'A walk-over, you say? One of these days you'll be walking over me.'

'What a curious thing to say,' Jerome protested innocently, a pose he was good at. It fooled everyone, except Quentin, who now prayed that Jerome had nothing else up his sleeve. He also knew he needed Jerome.

But Jerome was already well into another scheme, involving Armand Berg's reputation. If Sorlin played this one right, the blow should prove fatal.

Anne found Armand surly. He told her he was out of his depth in politics, and that to tell the truth he felt as confident about the second round as a baby in a rugger scrum. 'I've disappointed you, Anne,' he said with an attempt at humour.

'If you have, I prefer you that way . . . vulnerable.'

'You can say that again!'

She went on confidentally: 'You know, I didn't care too much for the big boss style. You were arrogant.'

'But you were pleased I jostled my way to the front in the first round.'

She took his hands and brushed them with her lips. Neither of them was aware of a curtain being moved a few inches to one side in a house opposite the room.

'Yes, I liked that,' Anne said. 'But it was really because you were so pleased with yourself. After all, perhaps I like you anyhow. But I still go for the little boy who wants a sweetie from his little Anne.'

A new expression came into his eyes: 'Little boy's right, wanting a sweetie's right too, and so is I love you.'

He took her gently and bestowed a fervent kiss on her mouth. She responded, flinging her arms around his neck. The embrace lasted an eternity, but Sorlin with his zoom lens got in four good pictures long before that.

Superficially, Armand looked pretty seedy when he got to the studio for the test, Florence thought. But she saw the other signs too, and assumed he'd been with 'nobody' again. It suited him, she realized.

The engineers showed extracts from TV newsreels of Quentin during the previous campaign. Chambonnas said the idea was to analyse Quentin's technique, his planning during debates, his easy style as he gabbled away about nothing, answered questions that were never put to him and ignored key points where he was open to attack. It was vital, Chambonnas said, to counter these skills.

'Look at this, Armand,' he said. 'It's Mayor Quentin at his best.' The video recorder showed him saying: 'No, my friends, I'm not speaking as a Minister in Paris, nor as the Mayor of one of France's large towns, but simply as an ordinary man who speaks as his heart dictates . . .'

Chambonnas cut it there: 'At that point you move in.'

'That's all very well, but how?'

'How you like,' said Florence. 'You could start chuckling, while you think of something.'

Chambonnas said: 'You can ask him to whom he's referring. Think of him as a big yellow balloon you're going to stick a pin into.'

They got the recorder going again; 'When I say an ordinary man, I mean a citizen first of all, the ordinary everyday citizen with his guts, his sense of fair play . . .'

'Attack!' yelled Florence.

And Chambonnas played Armand's role: 'Are you suggesting, Monsieur Quentin, that there is something incompatible between being a Minister and a courageous and decent citizen of Chateauvallon?'

They all roared with laughter. Other extracts followed, and after a while Armand tried his hand, storing up standard quips and interruptions, pitching in all-purpose questions.

At the end of the two hour session Chambonnas said: 'Not bad for a beginner, not bad at all. The main thing is to keep your voice firm, don't gabble, keep the interest up.'

In the car Florence added her advice: 'Don't let him get away with a thing. You're too kind. Quentin's basically a loyal, competent kind of chap, though sometimes rather weak. I know him. But when he's out to win, he pulls no punches, and neither should you.'

A planning conference took place at Les Messageries in the banqueting room around a huge table strewn with camera scripts, notepads and other documents. Destrez was to produce the programme, and he had two assistants. The staffs of Berg and Quentin were mingling.

Also present was a certain Bonvent, a bailiff who solemnly recorded the two sides' agreement as to the time allowance for each candidate, the number of close-ups each, the other shots and the general views. These points as well as the venue for the debate caused not the slightest friction. Then Quentin put up his hand for silence.

'I have a feeling,' he said turning to Florence with an enormous smile, 'that Madame Berg has an alternative idea for the venue.'

'Yes,' she said, smiling to match him. 'I was thinking of *La Dépêche*, in my father's old office. It would be a tribute to his memory.'

Had Florence suggested he should remove his trousers outside the Prisunic supermarket, Jerome could not have been more aghast. 'Is that suitable for all the equipment?' he said, realizing at once that it undoubtedly was.

Destrez said: 'I know the room, it'll be just fine. Is Monsieur le Maire agreeable to that?'

203

'Of *course* he was, Quentin beamed. They could have a genuine battle of ideas on the very spot where Antonin Berg had given the best of himself. It was a brilliant idea.

'That will be a wonderful way to give tribute,' he said under the irate gaze of Jerome, 'to a great man who enjoyed universal respect, and whom we all wish could still be among us today.'

He then went over to shake Armand's hand and wish him luck.

'Kind of you, Quentin, and good luck to you.' Berg had difficulty imagining Quentin as the man who pulled no punches. An image of the fight between the poster teams leapt into his mind, but he forced it out again.

Back at the town hall, Quentin was surprised to see Jerome no longer shooting daggers at him. He was actually whistling to himself, and he instantly concluded that his number two had pulled off some further strategem. But what if he had? It was nothing to do with him.

Jerome was whistling, but he was thinking fast too. Sorlin had come up with a superb set of photos – Berg was compromised beyond redemption. The big question was when to release them. Not before the TV debate, better wait until the last minute, the eve of the voting when Berg would have no time to launch a counter-attack.

It was pitch black and Florence drove fast, as she always did. She had collected Armand from Les Glycines clinic, and was certain she had now located 'nobody'. But for the moment it was Catherine who was uppermost in her mind.

'Well,' he said, 'aren't you delighted to be Paul's godmother?'

'Yes, but I'm not so delighted that Gilbert suggested to her the christening could be at the Kovalic dump. What's so funny, what have I said?'

'I'm tickled at what's waiting for us at La Commanderie.'

'I've never been impatiently waited for in my life, that's for sure.'

'Your suggestion is absolutely outrageous,' Armand said, still chuckling. 'But I admire your cheek.'

That afternoon Catherine had rejected Gilbert's idea outright, and Florence had immediately proposed La Commanderie. Not least because of the perverse pleasure she had at provoking her sister-in-law Marie-Lou. That she had achieved her purpose soon became clear.

In the living room she found young Michel whose mind was

evidently elsewhere, Gilbert Bossis who had had 100,000 francs whipped from under his nose because of Catherine's refusal, and Julien who said he couldn't stop long as Thérèse had gone off to see a friend who was ill in bed.

Jean-Jacques and Marie-Lou entered regally a few moments after Florence and Armand. They had been staying at the house for three days, not out of respect for Antonin's wish that they all be together under one roof, but because their own house was being repainted and paint always set off Marie-Lou's migraine.

Marie-Lou bounded across to Florence: 'Tell me, it isn't true!'

'You know perfectly well it's true, because your husband was there when I saw Catherine and he told you at once.'

'Which I had a perfect right to do,' Jean-Jacques said grandly.

His wife cut in: 'And the christening here? With the whole of the Kovalic tribe? Great! But I'm against it, I'm against it, absolutely against it! You knew that Julien.'

'I know now and it doesn't make a scrap of difference to me.'

Florence said suavely: 'But my dear, I knew you'd find it wonderful and that you'd be against it. You always are against anything wonderful.'

'We weren't even consulted about it,' Marie-Lou growled.

'You wouldn't be being racist, by any chance.'

'Everyone is. The Arabs are, so are the blacks. Only their racism is all right and mine's not I suppose. Julien, what does your wife think?'

'Nothing at all, she doesn't know. But she's bound to have no objection.'

Marie-Lou's blazing eyes darted from one to the other: 'But you're all raving mad. They are nothing but clowns, those two!'

Armand, in a peacemaking mood after his friendly encounter with Quentin said: 'Marie-Lou, don't you feel you're making a mighty fuss about nothing?'

'Nothing! So you're agreeing to it. I had hoped that at least you . . .'

'Your hopes are, as from now, dashed.'

'Very well,' she said. 'Let them come, but mark my words. It's the same as the blacks, the browns, the yellows and the rest. Give your hand to the Kovalics and they'll bite it off.'

She made as if to continue, but her son Michel spoke up, reminding her that this was Gilbert's home too and that he too was Paul's grandfather.

Marie-Lou lowered her voice and said it was not down in writing that the Bergs had to provide a home for all the infants that had chanced to be born as the result of their grandfathers' escapades.

This was too much for Florence who demanded that Marie-Lou retract at once. Wild-eyed, Marie-Lou pivoted on her high heels and was clearly preparing to snub Florence, but Gilbert came back at her.

'I accept your apologies,' he said amiably. 'And to cap it all, I have pleasure in announcing that my grandson's christening will take place at the Hotel Des Messageries. I'm afraid, Marie-Lou, there'll be a slight whiff of Yugoslavia, but if anybody is afraid they'll be overcome, they had better stay away.'

Thereupon he stalked out, head held high. His only problem now was to convince Albertas. Kovalics might be willing to have the ceremony at La Commanderie, but a hotel was against everything they believed in.

A silence fell upon the others, broken by Marie-Lou: 'I like that better. Well, when's it to be?'

'Tomorrow,' Florence said. 'Catherine chose the date. Not that you really care. You're simply wondering what to wear, that's all.'

'Huh! Are you out of your mind? You don't imagine I'm going?'

She went nonetheless. With Marie-Lou, curiosity was stronger than prejudice. She was dying to see how the almighty Florence and the almost as stuck-up Armand would cope publicly with confronting a gang of gyppos. Why, they'd probably turn up in a dustcart or something . . .

Already she was accepting a Scotch from Armand with a big smile. With a straight face he raised his glass to toast 'this outstanding family occasion'.

Julien had slipped out and joined Gilbert as he was ending a phone conversation.

'Philippe's about to give up, Gilbert. He's wetting his pants, he's so scared. For himself and Emilie and the kids. That's where Thérèse has gone.'

Gilbert frowned: 'Dangerous, with all the cops about.'

'I'm glad she takes that kind of risk.'

The old man laid an arm on Julien's shoulder: 'I've just been on to Albertas. He agrees to Les Messageries, on one condition, that he pays the entire bill. So that tallies with their traditions or whatever. Anyhow, you go back home now and tell Philippe he'll get his money tomorrow. As for Quentin, we're going to roast him alive!'

Albertas Kovalic was true to his word. He slipped an envelope containing 100,000 francs into Gilbert Bossis's jacket pocket as the combined families posed for the photographers under a cloudless sky outside the Orthodox church in Rue Dom-Perignon.

Gilbert was unable to get it to the sawmill until evening, because Albertas said it was another of their traditions for the two grandfathers to take wine together at the farm, when the banquet at Les Messageries was over.

This meal proceeded without incident. Catherine found herself at a safe distance from her family betweeen Florence and Travers. Marie-Lou wore a beige suit, copied from Chanel by Emerence Dupont. More than once she looked down her nose at what she revelled in calling 'this ridiculous business', but she joined in the songs from Montenegro. She even remarked to her neighbour that the Kovalics didn't eat with their fingers after all. How amusing it was, fascinating even, to rub shoulders with 'the other half'.

The luncheon ended earlier than it might normally have, as all the Bergs said they had engagements that afternoon and were late already.

Thus it was that Gilbert went home with the Kovalics, and the sun was low in the sky by the time he reached the sawmill. Solemnly he handed over the money as Philippe gave him the letter.

As was natural, Mathilde and Jeannou were at the christening and banquet, so Julien had no trouble borrowing the Rolls and leaving a note to say he had. At 11.00 p.m. that night Philippe curled up in the boot and Julien took the wheel, with Thérèse next to him. She intended to take a turn or two at the wheel during the long journey ahead. Although they knew the area for a hundred miles around Chateauvallon like the back of their hands, they zigzagged through the country lanes afraid of meeting a roadblock at every turn, or even just a couple of motorbike cops. It needed just one policeman to signal them to a halt, and three Bergs would be in jail that night.

Philippe had said at the last minute: 'No. No, I can't let you take a risk, there's no reason for you to. I can find my way.'

'It's a long way on foot to the Swiss border,' Thérèse had said.

And Gilbert, who was standing by, said: 'Give me a call when . . . I mean, when you're all right.' He watched the car move off without lights, and supposed they would put them on in a minute. Marie-Lou had called Julien and Thérèse 'clowns', and she was right.

He then hastened to the big house, and read several times over the letter that would eliminate Quentin. The house was deathly quiet. Mathilde and Jeannou were probably asleep. The others were not back from the TV debate yet – no doubt they had decided to have a drink somewhere afterwards.

Gilbert listened to the silence, and wondered where the safest place would be for the letter.

Everybody except Gilbert, Julien and Thérèse must have watched the debate between the newcomer Armand Berg and the old trouper Georges Quentin. They had circled each other hesitantly at first, then relaxed when they had got the measure of each other, and finally traded verbal shafts.

It was Berg who got down to business first, declaring: 'Monsieur Quentin, you have just called me your dear friend. I feel obliged to remark that I cannot possibly be regarded as your dear friend in view of what I know about Les Sablons.'

Quentin put in a thrust: 'That's a calumny! The commission of inquiry exonerated me.'

Berg: 'After which, the Government promptly dispensed with your services. Correct me if I am wrong, but I gather that the Government asked you to step down.'

After that exchange, it was Berg all the way and Quentin used up his time in empty tirades. He was left grimacing, smirking and raising his arms to heaven as Berg described him as a political climber, loaded with honours as the result of his scheming, but ending up as a mere functionary disgraced by his deep implication in a series of shady deals.

Grandly, Armand Berg concluded: 'Your time is up, Quentin. You have become a fossil!'

The studio gong sounded and Armand felt like General de Gaulle.

Florence judged the debate a draw, an opinion shared by Chambonnas. Jerome believed Berg had overdone his winding-up and thought Quentin could pick up some votes as the underdog.

208

It was indeed a draw, if the polls the day after were anything to go by. The candidates came out neck and neck.

It was after the poll results came through that Jerome opened his desk drawer and extracted Sorlin's photos.

Then he put in a call to the newspaper *L'Eveil*.

L'Eveil came out with a special edition at 4.00 p.m.

The front page banner headline read: CH'VALLON CANDI-DATE IN SEX SCANDAL. Adjacent was a photo clearly showing Dr Armand Berg lying on top of another human being, apparently a woman, probably young, but whose face was hard to identify.

The entire edition was snapped up within the hour and the population spent the rest of the day being shocked, angry, sceptical or credulous according to taste.

At *La Dépêche* Travers charged into Florence's office, having ploughed his way through groups of colleagues in the corridor. He found her red-faced and scowling at a copy of *L'Eveil*.

'Where's Armand now?' he demanded.

'Disappeared.'

'That I can understand.'

'Not because of this,' she snapped, throwing the paper aside. 'He disappeared during the night, *before* this. I kept calling, but no answer. At the clinic it's like a madhouse, with poor Fernandez holding the fort as best she can. She told me: 'The doctor stopped by last night after the television thing, Madame. And when he knew he rushed off.'

'When he knew what?' said Travers.

'That Anne Vernier had cleared off. That's who "nobody" is.'

Travers rapped: 'Where does she live?'

'That's the trouble. She had no admission card, no documents at all at Les Glycines. No address.'

'And a drug addict too.' said Travers, who knew the story in *L'Eveil* by heart. 'Some sex scandal. Oh, Christ!'

The rival paper had had this as its comment: 'Far be it for us to meddle in Dr Berg's private affairs, but the photo we publish cannot be passed over. Firstly because it was taken in the eminent surgeon's clinic. Secondly, because the young women in question is understood to be a minor and addicted to drugs.'

Quentin saw the paper almost as soon as Florence did. He was red-faced too, though for different reasons.

209

'It's blackmail,' he shouted at Jerome. 'That's not strategy, it's blackmail.'

'But I only asked Sorlin to get me a few pictures of Berg. How was I to know that he . . .'

'You knew perfectly well, and it was you who gave the photo to *L'Eveil*. I want no part of this, it's disgusting. Get out of my sight, get out!'

'I'll get out,' said Jerome levelly. 'But don't forget the polls. Without me, it's all up with you!'

Later Madame Quentin told her husband: 'You've thrown him out. Fine. But he'll come back through the window. I know him, and I know you too.'

Armand Berg knew nothing of the uproar. He was asleep at the time.

All the previous night, he had driven round and round Chateauvallon, frantically barging into bars and discos. Around dawn he went to Anne's father, who fortunately was taking some days off owing to him.

Monsieur Vernier was as grey as the first light of day.

'Something wrong, Doctor?'

'She's run away from the clinic. I stopped by to ask her what she thought of the TV debate, and . . .'

'Sit down a bit, Doctor, you look all in. How about a drop of *Calva*?'

He downed a *Calva*, and another and another and another. Saying nothing but missing nothing of the place where Anne Vernier was brought up. He felt curiously in tune with the modest dwelling and its tasteless wallpaper and simple furniture. He did not see the kitchen, but sat in the main room watching Monsieur Vernier get his stuff together; he was off to Dijon, he said, and would not be back until Thursday. Armand marvelled at this way of life.

The candidate hoping to reach the Assemblée Nationale was close to tears when Vernier said: 'Y'know, Doctor, my daughter and me, we don't hit it off. Since her mother died, we've hardly said two words to each other. There don't really seem much to say. Sad really. So I can't tell you why she cleared off from your clinic. I don't suppose she's turned up here.'

Armand had a fifth glass and slumped onto the table. Vernier got him going and took him up to Anne's bedroom. And that is where he passed the day, in Anne's bed in the little house on the outskirts of Chateauvallon, while the tale of his exploits with her went the rounds of the town.

When he surfaced from sleep, he found he had all his clothes on and felt like the bottom of a hotel dustbin.

To be precise he woke at 3.00 p.m. and took ten minutes to reach the top of the stairs. He then thumped down them, hearing them creak. He saw the empty bottle on the kitchen table.

Someone was scrabbling in a cupboard, and turned round as he shuffled in. It was Anne!

They looked at each other. Eventually she spoke, but in angry tones: 'Oh, it's you. What are you doing here?' Her face seemed sort of screwed up.

Armand went across to her, seizing her arm: 'And where the devil have you been? What happened? Why? I'd like to know.'

'Take your hands off me. You're hurting.'

'Where have you come from?'

'You wouldn't know him. Roland. Friend o' mine.'

Armand nodded his head slowly: 'The little runt who got you the drugs, and brought you to the clinic. Don't tell me you're sleeping with *him!*'

She played the little madam: 'I am sleeping with him, and it's not the first time, if you must know.' She got away from him and began rubbing her arm, glaring at him with that animal look of their first encounter.

'I . . . er . . . thought you . . . loved me,' he said pathetically. 'I must have imagined it. What's all this linen and stuff?'

'*My* linen and stuff. I'm moving in with Roland.'

He slapped her and she took it without flinching.

'Now get out, Doctor!'

He said: 'I didn't mean to do that. I'm sorry. But tell me – what's gone wrong between us?'

'Nothing . . . everything. It's my fault.'

Suddenly she began weeping. In buckets, saying in broken phrases that she couldn't stand seeing him on the telly.

'You left just afterwards. Tell me about it.'

'I was ashamed.'

'I don't follow you.'

'I felt awful about myself. Hearing you speak so la-di-da, I knew you were going to be a big shot, and I was, well, a nobody. I

211

said to myself I was, well, being nuts. You'd forget all about me after the voting and all that.'

He smiled through his stubble: 'Anne. I love you.'

'Huh. In the Assemblée? Don't make me laugh, you couldn't ever drag me around with you. People would talk.'

He took her shoulders: 'Let me look after my future.'

She stayed in his grasp but turned her head: 'Forget it, Armand, you're very decent, but it wouldn't work out with me.'

She freed herself and he tried to catch her. She pushed him off: 'Sleep in my bed if you like.'

Anne Vernier left with her things, unaware of the photo in the paper. At least, he shared that with her.

The evening meal could not have been more miserable. An air of gloom hung over La Commanderie. Florence reflected that some days were definitely not worth getting up for.

The assembled company comprised Florence, Jean-Jacques, Marie-Lou, Michel, Gilbert Bossis and Armand. Gilbert had told them Julien and Thérèse were on a trip somewhere. He failed to mention that he might jump up from the table at any time when the phone rang.

Florence was thinking of the three million francs her taxman had given her as a round figure that afternoon. Where did he think she would find three million? Saviot said he could get a loan for her.

It was at that point that Armand strode in late: 'Have you seen my windscreen? I haven't even got a windscreen any more!'

A pillar of the community among the town's citizens had heaved a cobble-stone through it. It was the perfect end to a god-awful day. When Anne had gone, Armand had returned to her bed. Later he had driven to his own place, showered, shaved, drunk two Scotches and had another nap, not really caring if he never woke up again. As far as he was concerned, the world could end there and then.

Around 7.00 p.m. Florence had phoned and told him to join them for dinner.

'Angry with me?' he had asked.

'Not angry, sad. Sad for you and for that little lady called "nobody".'

'Huh, "nobody" has become "nobody no more", you'll be interested to hear. I'm too good for her, it seems. But she hadn't seen the story when she said it. Nor had I, so I couldn't tell her I'd been toppled from the throne.'

The dinner ground on its weary way until the dessert. Gilbert was called to the phone, and came back muttering something about the border. Nobody seemed interested.

'I want to show you something afterwards,' he told Florence.

She said she'd go up with him. But her real concern was whether Anne Vernier would want to return to him if she knew what a state he was in. She had nothing against the girl, and Anne had a mind of her own. Armand claimed he loved her, but then that was nothing new in his case. Armand must have drunk the equivalent of a bottle of Burgundy during the meal, and she ordered: 'That's enough now, give me the decanter.'

'I'm launching myself into the void,' he declared solemnly.

Michel sprang to his feet: 'That's not funny, uncle. Stop it please. I used to respect you, but after what you've done with Anne I'll never speak to you again.'

Even Marie-Lou and Jean-Jacques were so impressed that they took Michel off to see a film.

Armand looked at Florence idiotically: 'What's the matter with him all of a sudden?'

'He happened to love her, that's all,' she said. They sat there twirling their empty glasses.

Gilbert breezed in with his letter: 'Good, the others have gone. Philippe's got across the border. He hid in the sawmill, and Julien and Thérèse got him out. I paid 100,000 francs so that he could go – I bought this.'

Florence took the letter, and read it carefully twice.

She said: 'It's his signature, that's certain. But we must have it authenticated. My God. Quentin. I can't believe it.'

It turned out to be one of the big political stories of the year for the French media, who picked it up from *La Dépêche*. It was almost a side issue that Armand Berg got in at Chateauvallon. The second round percentages were: Armand Berg 54 per cent, Georges Quentin 46 per cent.

Florence's paper published the letter on the Friday, with certification by two experts.

It read:

Monsieur Le Directeur, Arsenal de Toulon
Monsieur Le Directeur,

I should consider it a favour on your part if, for the two positions of guard which you have created, you would kindly consider the applications from Messieurs Gamel and Machefer who will be providing you with their career details, which I vouch for.

Georges Quentin

'It's a real bombshell,' Travers said. 'Quentin pushing Paul Bossis's killers!'

Armand was reluctant for it to be published, it frightened him from the moral point of view. Jean-Jacques was firmly against using it, now that it promised victory for Armand.

Florence decided to go ahead. Travers confirmed her view that the bombshell would knock Quentin out for good. Bossis said: 'You are holding my revenge in your hands, Flo.' One of Florence's motives was that this would pay Quentin back for not putting her before everything else. Bitterly, but with a wicked delight, she realized it was the end of the man who had shared her bed, the memory of happy times, the author of perhaps the cruellest moment in her life.

As to Quentin, when he entered his lounge bearing a copy of *La Dépêche*, his wife asked him point-blank whether he had really appended his signature to the letter.

'Yes I did,' he confessed, looking years older now than before he had picked up the paper. 'Don't ask me when or how it came about. I was told to sign it, you understand, just as I signed hundreds of letters placed in front of me. I was trapped, it's as simple as that.'

'What are you going to do?'

'Nothing. It's too late, the campaign finishes officially at midnight. In any case, what's the use? Berg's won.'

'It's his sister who's won. She cocked her gun a long time ago.'

'Probably. But I never would have imagined she'd go that far.'

The Berg scandal's career died before it quite began, and the Mayor's collusion with the killers became the big talking point. The two affairs could hardly be compared, it was judged, and Armand undoubtedly gained more friends than he imagined as the result of his escapade. All the world loves a lover, and that went for Chateauvallon too. Not only that – it emerged that a good many people regarded Quentin's team as sinning more grievously than Armand Berg in that it used underhand tactics. As elsewhere in France, people were deemed to have a right to a

214

private life, without 'them' poking their noses in.

On the night of the election Jerome walked into the grandiose banqueting room at the town hall and was confronted with an enormous buffet shining disgustingly under the chandeliers. The *maître d'hôtel* stood with his waiters in front of caviar, salmon, pâté de foie gras, exotic fruit, legs of lamb, red wine, white wine – including champagne – and bouquets of flowers.

'Ah, Monsieur Jerome,' the boss said. 'What are your instructions?'

Jerome took a glass, poured himself a large Scotch, downed it in a go and a half, then threw the glass on the floor.

'Eat it,' he said.

As luck would have it, Jerome's path took him past Berg's campaign office, but he changed to the opposite pavement fifty yards before he got there.

The rooms were crammed with young and old of both sexes, hugging, laughing, screaming, flirting and rolling merrily around from room to room. Armand himself had taken refuge in his office after a while and he watched a strange kind of ballet dance through the cubby-hole's window as Chambonnas, Travers, Maryse, Catherine, Jean-Jacques and others moved this way and that and twisted and turned to the muffled roar of the talk. Suddenly Florence opened the door and the noise rushed in with her.

'Playing wet blanket, darling?' she said, looking radiant he thought, for the first time for days.

He tilted his head but could think of no reply. Before him on the desk was *L'Eveil* with its scandal story: 'It's over now. Thanks, Flo, you got me in.'

'So did Quentin.' She wiped the beginnings of a tear from one eye with a finger.

'Poor fellow.'

His sister said with a harsh note in her voice: 'I don't think I regret it. You know, Armand, we had some good times but he also did some beastly things to me?'

Chambonnas burst in: 'Television in twenty minutes, Armand. I'll take you.'

Florence too was watching the ballet next door now. Then Armand left her and began slapping people on the arms and generally horsing around, as befitted the occasion. For the ump-teenth time, someone thrust a glass of bubbly in his hand and he was toasted. Then Florence saw Chambonnas and Travers take him off.

Someone else saw him hustled into the Rolls from the big house and driven off. Anne Vernier. She had been standing in a doorway a few yards down the road on the opposite side. Anne was happy, proud of him, but feeling desperately small. When the Rolls disappeared round a corner, she began weeping silently.

She would probably never speak to him again, probably never even seen him again until the next election except maybe on the telly. He had forgotten all about her.

Chapter Seven

Quentin was found dead early on the morning after the election by two kids on their way to school along a path in La Gravelle woods, not far from La Gentilhommière, a country style *auberge* used by bigwigs from a wide radius round Chateauvallon.

His head lolled out of the open window of his car, and the children cried out when they saw the sticky red stuff filling the hole in his skull. The heavy body was hunched foetus-like against the door.

The news reached La Commanderie over the radio some time later. Julien and Thérèse heard it while they were having breakfast. Marie-Lou obviously heard it simultaneously, for she soon bustled in wearing a pale pink silk peignoir.

'Good Lord, you look frightened,' she said. 'It's a bit of a shock. Who the hell could have predicted that *this* would happen!'

Florence came in fully dressed, prepared to grab a quick coffee and piece of toast before hurtling off to *La Dépêche* for a heavy day. She was smiling, but suddenly halted with her mouth open: 'What's happened? World War III or something?'

'Quentin's dead. Just came over the radio,' Julien said.

Florence shook her head slowly, gulped and waited for more. Julien added: 'Near La Gentilhommière. Suicide I assume.'

'That's not possible. It can't be true!'

She spun round and hurried up the stairs. The others heard her door slam.

Marie-Lou said: 'Not possible? On the contrary, completely logical.' She poured herself coffee. '*La Dépêche* killed him off with that awful letter business. Naturally, he had to do away with himself. That's what Jean-Jacques says.' He came in at that moment. '*Cheri*, I was saying . . .'

'I heard. I was against the wretched thing being published. Still it's too late now, and in any case there's no proof why he did it.' Marie-Lou glanced quickly at him, surprised at his assertive tone. He added: 'It's Florence I'm sorry for.'

He was selecting a croissant when Gilbert Bossis lurched in from the grounds wearing rubber boots and a shooting jacket: 'Jeannou's told me. How did Florence take it? I suppose she knows.'

'Having a little weep upstairs, I imagine. She went up when we told her,' Marie-Lou said.

Bossis snorted: 'Won't catch me crying over it, though I won't stop anyone else. He shot himself? Very well then, that's his admission of guilt. If I might venture a suggestion . . .'

'Go on then,' said Julien.

'I'd suggest he did it to spite Florence.'

'That's where they used to go, La Gentilhommière. Ten years they were together,' Marie-Lou said. 'Suicides are always to spite someone.'

Gilbert guffawed again: 'Why not to spite himself? He had reason enough.'

He left the room mumbling. He wanted to tell Florence he was with her in spite of everything.

But Florence had sneaked out by a back door.

She walked for hours in woods and along country lanes, trying to tire herself out and force her nerves to calm down.

She succeeded at last and slumped against a farmhouse wall with wire netting fixed on top. A couple of dogs were barking at her a few yards behind it. Florence turned her back on them and rubbed her forehead. Then she heard a woman telling the dogs to be quiet. The woman came out into the roadway and Florence looked up. The two women stared at each other in disbelief.

'Madame Berg!'

'Madame Kovalic!' She blinked and looked about her, and repeated: 'Madame Kovalic.'

'You don't look very well, Madame Berg. Come in and have a coffee.'

'Thank you, Madame, I think I will.'

She followed Zoë inside and allowed herself to be served. Florence hestitantly explained that it was so long since she'd come this way that she hadn't recognized the farm. In answer to

Zoë's probing, she said she was simply out walking. Madame Kovalic repeatedly glanced at her rather slyly. Did she know something? Florence realized she probably intimidated this quiet woman who kept herself to herself and would certainly not allow herself to ask anything personal. Zoë started saying she was on her own with Marfa, just the two of them without the men – 'peace and quiet it is, Madame Berg, without them going on at us all the time'.

'Of course,' Florence responded, not quite knowing what to say. 'So they're away.'

'Gone up to Paris, they have. Albertas, Gregor and Teddy. Roissy airport, they've gone.'

'I see.' She pulled herself together and showed interest.

'Gone to fetch Bernard flown over from America. Bernard's my boy.'

She was genuinely attentive now: 'I didn't know. That's funny, I have a daughter and she lives in the United States too. Well I must be on my way, Madame Berg. You've been most kind, the coffee did me a world of good.'

As she waved and went off, Florence suspected Madame Kovalic thought she was slightly dotty. In fact, she was more than surprised herself that the news of Quentin's suicide had made her lose grip on herself to that extent. She had told Armand that it was hard to forget the past, and it was true. Now the harm she had done to Quentin would remain with her for the rest of her life.

She found the building humming away, routine there being more powerful than any single day's events.

Melchior, Jean-Jacques and Travers followed her into her office, asking her to approve the pictures their photographers had taken before the police reached Quentin's car. Nobody made any comment about her late arrival or the way she looked, and she quickly said she'd leave it to them.

'I'll handle it,' said Jean-Jacques. 'Three pix, OK?'

Melchior said Travers had bashed out a good story, but she didn't want to see it. She simply asked what Nicolo said.

'Well,' said Melchior, 'That he killed himself. With his own gun, of course.'

Florence was aware that they all seemed to be behaving towards her in a curious way, as if they were afraid she would

219

disintegrate and leave a pile of dust on the carpet. She bucked up: 'What have we got going for the editorial?'

'We'll need a piece on Quentin's death,' said Jean-Jacques. 'Do you want to do it?'

She shook her head, and told him to do it. He brightened at this, feeling his importance, and secretly hoping his sister would go on approaching things in this way.

'What shall I say?'

'Do it your way.'

'Hey, hold on. You've been firing your big guns at him all through the election campaign. If I've got to provide him with a panegyric I need an angle.'

Through clenched teeth she hissed: 'I've no ideas. Half-mourning perhaps?'

Melchior suggested: 'The risks of high office, something along those lines, that ought to do it.'

'Good man. Doesn't commit us in any way, just observing, not judging the man. It's not for us to judge Quentin.' J-J stared hard at his sister.

Melchior coughed: 'The readers will want to know why Quentin killed himself.'

'We don't have to guess,' Travers cut in, seeing Florence go a shade paler. 'And that's all anyone can do at this stage, guess.'

'We'll cover that letter,' Florence decreed, getting up. 'I'm sure our adversaries are thinking up their visions right now. Put some of those forward as well, if you like.' She spoke offhandedly and went over to get her coat.

'I'll give you the draft editorial within the hour,' Jean-Jacques said.

'Don't do that, Jean-Jacques, I'll leave it up to you.'

She left and the three men looked at each other, each wondering where she was going.

Travers said: 'It's knocked her sideways.'

Jean-Jacques sniffed: 'She'll get over it.' He left in turn muttering 'risks of high office, risks of high office . . .' Melchior followed him.

Travers went over to the window, pushing a curtain to one side. He saw Florence cross the street and watched her walk along the pavement.

Maryse came in and he said: 'She's genuinely shaken. Could be she's still in love with him.'

220

'And you?' Maryse said with a cheeky look. 'Surely you're not jealous of a dead man.'

The Minister was beside himself: 'First we're standing here with a bloody nose after the election. And now we've got an ex-Minister's suicide on our hands!'

He had just finished on the phone and now turned to his PPS: 'That was from Chateauvallon. I can see the headlines tomorrow in the opposition press: MAJORITY IN TROUBLE. GOVERNMENT STAINED BY EX-MINISTER'S BLOOD. PUBLIC DEMANDS EXPLANATION. Some damned thing like that. Well, man, what do we do now?'

'I wouldn't know, Monsieur le Ministre.'

'We do nothing at all. What is there to do? Send them a demand for right of reply? What do you think?'

'A sound idea, Monsieur le Ministre!'

'No, that's ridiculous. Better say nothing, showing our contempt, proving we are above the mêlée.'

'Which we are, of course.'

'Of course we are. But with that idiot doing away with himself, God knows what the other side will put forward – they'll probably suggest that it was we who did away with him.'

His underling ventured to observe: 'Luckily the radio people are playing it down. One commentator said it wasn't the politician who killed himself, but the man.'

The Minister reflected for a moment: 'A nice distinction. By the way, what about the Prefect down there?'

'Told me that, although some journalists are resurrecting that awful Les Sablons business, he personally was convinced of Quentin's integrity.'

'But, as we know, the Prefect's a fool. What's he say about the fellow's death?'

'Nothing yet. But he does suggest that any political implications concerning this unfortunate incident might be overlooked, if it were found there was some business to do with a woman.'

The Minister's face lit up: 'Huh, not such a fool after all.'

'However, there's a snag, Monsieur le Ministre. If we dig into Quentin's love life, we shall come up with Florence Berg, I'm afraid.'

'Bah!' cried the Minister. 'So she's a firebrand is she? Did she sleep with Quentin?'

'Used to, Monsieur.'

'Of course. Poor Quentin!'

'I meant to say that they had been . . . er . . . estranged for some time, I understand.'

'That's a good reason for giving it a go, isn't it? Even if it's not proven, a few rumours should do the trick.'

The PPS tried to head him off: 'She won't like her private life being laid bare. Let's not forget that it's her paper that forms their opinions in Chateauvallon, that her brother is now in the Assemblée, and that Madame Berg has sharp claws.'

'What an absolute idiot he was, that Quentin. Clearing off like that without saying why, without so much as a by-your-leave.'

'Absolutely, Monsieur le Ministre.'

'He had a reason, the fool. Well, never mind, let's just keep Florence Berg in reserve. But we won't provoke her unnecessarily. Those claws might be sharper than we think.'

Florence sat in the corridor at Les Glycines, listening to Armand handing over various files for Dr Bonnot, who would be replacing him during his absence.

'I can't say how long it will be,' he was saying, 'but the parliamentary session ends two months from now, and I'll be rushing to catch up with things. I'll be back for weekends, of course. Be out and about in the constituency.'

He came out, chuckling to himself: 'Florence!'

He showed her into his office and she said: 'I had to see you, I'm so . . .'

'Groggy? Take a seat. And feeling guilty? Is that what you want to tell me?' She said nothing. 'Nobody's guilty. Quentin did away with himself because he lost his seat, that's all.'

'The letter . . .' she stammered.

'I was against using it, remember? Everyone was, but you went ahead, as if it were your duty. You got more than you bargained for, but it doesn't make you responsible for what's happened.'

She forced her lips together: 'And just suppose he simply signed it among a pile of letters put in front of him? It happens all the time.'

'When you're a Minister, you check everything.'

'And supposing it was a forgery, which I thought it was at the start?'

'Then you should have gone on thinking it. It's too late now.'

Florence stared glumly at the desk edge: 'You're hard on me. It was mainly for you that I decided to use it. The experts said it was his signature, and he deserved to pay for that kind of chicanery. And because I wanted you to beat him, and that was what really decided it for me.'

Armand lifted an eyebrow: 'Nothing else?'

'Oh, I don't know,' she said, waving a hand. 'Old hurts, old bruises perhaps.'

Her brother leaned forward: 'Listen Florence. If I had really wanted to lay the law down that day, if I had absolutely forbidden you to carry the story, you might have thrown the letter in the waste-basket. But I let you do it. I was the one who would gain from publication. If you really want to find the culprit, I am the one who's guilty of Quentin's death.'

'I don't want a culprit. I'm only thrashing about, trying to sort it out in my own mind. It's awful . . .'

'Let's share the burden. "A worry shared . . ."'

They got up and fondly embraced.

'The train leaves in an hour,' he said.

'Goodbye, Doctor. Thanks for your soothing words. I'm never fonder of you more than when you play the good Samaritan.'

'Who knows, I might even be an apostle one day,' he laughed.

From the outside La Gentilhommière remained the original hunting lodge in the Norman style. Except that the high black gates with their lancet features, the faultless lawns and tennis courts were a clear sign that the establishment was reserved for the well-heeled rather than the common run of mankind.

It was more specially a house of assignation, and the well-to-do performed within its mahogany-panelled rooms amid marble and mirrors those exercises which lesser mortals tended to restrict to back alleys and haylofts.

Consequently, it was understandable that the proprietor Emile Tronchet should mutter a despairing 'what now?' to himself when Nicolo, Germain and Pradal pulled up outside and got out with a purposeful banging of doors.

As he moved forward to greet them, a tall youngish man in a suede lumberjacket and flannel trousers went by carrying a small crocodile suitcase, informing Tronchet that he'd left the money on the counter. The policemen turned and watched him go out through the gate ignoring their presence.

'Some of your customers get a good lie-in, I see,' Nicolo said amiably.

'They sleep when they like, but at midday they pay again,' Tronchet muttered.

'And who might that swell be?'

'Sure I don't know.'

Tronchet seemed in such a dejected mood that the Commissaire felt constrained to tell him they weren't raiding the place, only passing by.

Even this failed to cheer the proprietor, who said from the depths of his gloom: 'However long you stay, it's bound to make the guests uncomfortable.'

'I don't suppose you've got even a single guest right now.'

'Fortunately.'

Nicolo maintained his casual tone: 'After all, it's not our fault if Quentin decided to spend his last night here.'

Tronchet turned and conducted them inside: 'How do you know that, then?'

It was Madame Quentin herself who had told him, but Nicolo kept it to himself.

'Let's go into my office,' Tronchet said.

But Nicolo brought the little group to a halt: 'If you don't mind, we'd like to speak to the staff.'

'All I've got at this time of day are the backroom people. They never see the guests.'

'Possibly, but it's amazing what they do notice when they're not supposed to.' Germain went off and the Commissaire snapped: 'Quentin, which room?'

'Seventeen.'

'Pradal number seventeen.'

Tronchet led Nicolo into his office: 'You won't find anything there. How about a quick one?'

'Never on duty. Did Quentin come often?'

'Sometimes.'

'On his own?'

'Yes.'

'And before that?'

'With someone.'

Nicolo gave a quick smile to show there was no hard feeling: 'No need to tell me who it was. We both know. He arrived at what time for his last night?'

'About nine.'

'How did he look? At that time he knew already he was beaten in the election. The early results were indicating as much.'

Tronchet said he could not say. It was his busy time and he couldn't worry about such things. In answer to further questioning, he also said nobody saw him leave and he must have sneaked out during the night. There was no-one specially on duty at night.

Pradal returned: 'Seventeen's been cleaned.'

Nicolo jerked his head at Tronchet, who volunteered: 'I was not to know you didn't want it done out. And in any case, it hasn't been done out, because the bed wasn't touched. As a matter of fact I wondered about that.'

'You're not the only one. Well, thanks all the same, Tronchet.'

Nicolo and Pradal returned to the car and waited for Germain who was at a side door with a young woman wearing a blue overall.

'Her name's Sofia Leriche,' he said getting into the car. 'She deals with the wines. Unusual. There's also an old gardener who's on his last legs and a cleaning woman who must have left school about the age of eight. They don't know who Quentin is.'

'Does that worry you?'

'No, but Sofia Leriche does. I think you ought to have a word with her, chief, she looks fishy to me, as if she knows something. Just an impression, of course.'

The Commissaire was back in the car fifteen minutes later. He said nothing at first, and then: 'She spilled the beans, but it's not worth a thing. Just ideas, no hard facts to work on.'

Germain and Pradal swapped glances via the rear-view mirror, both certain the chief was holding out on them. Germain still thought she looked queer.

Then Nicolo spoke: 'Know who else was there last night? The swell we saw coming out. And d'you know who it is? His name's Kovalic, Bernard Kovalic from the United States of America. He tried to get Sofia Leriche into bed with him.'

He shook his head slowly: 'Stone the crows! A Kovalic at La Gentilhommière! What is the world coming to?'

He looked like a million dollars to Zoë when she first saw him.

'Lord save us,' she rasped, 'it's him, Bernard my boy!'

They hugged and Zoë called Marfa who ran up with a pigeon

she forgot to put down. She had just that minute wrung its neck.

They all embraced and kissed and talked all at once. Eventually Marfa's mouth opened wide: 'The others, where are the others?'

The young man said: 'I expect they're still at Roissy, waiting for me. I caught the plane yesterday and got here early.'

The two women stood back, horror on the faces. They were thinking there would be ructions when the others realized what had happened. The lad went on explaining, but they didn't hear him.

'It may seem crazy,' he was saying, 'but I wanted to find my way here on my own, unescorted. Didn't want to be looked after right away, just thought I'd get the feel of things first. Maybe it *was* crazy. And another thing: perhaps I wanted to kiss you first, before . . .'

'Before what?' said Zoë slowly, lost in amongst his explanations.

'Before I found out why they called me over,' he said scowling.

'It's because we all missed you.'

He found this an unconvincing answer, but said: 'OK, so you missed me. Why did you miss me?'

'They'll explain it all,' Marfa declared at length. 'It's men's business, all that. You must be hungry, Bernard.'

'No, I've eaten.'

'You must be tired. Did you stay the night in Paris?'

'No.' He chuckled, amused to see the women's faces. 'I spent the night here in Chateauvallon, at a place I dreamed of going inside when I was a kid. I used to go past it when I was looking for mushrooms, and it was full of swish cars and couples eating caviar – it was marked up at the gate on the menu. No hope of me getting inside then. But that's where I spent last night, La Gentilhommière, and I've come straight from there. It cost a fortune, but it was worth every cent – sorry, centime!'

Marfa exclaimed: 'But that's where . . . I mean, it has an awful reputation. Whatever did you go there for?'

Bernard roared his head off: 'To eat caviar, what else?'

'The Godfathers are putting the screws on me,' Bernard Kovalic wrote jovially a few days later in a letter to his girlfriend Phyllis Bianchetti, an Italian girl who was working at Bloomingdale's at the time to get some money together for her last year as a sociology student.

'They were real mad at wasting money on the trip to Paris Airport. I never realized how dirty the farm was. Not dirty so much as small. They do transportation and delivery of all kinds of merchandise, and it seems like they are rolling in money. Soon after I arrived they killed the fatted calf for me, the prodigal son. They managed to reproduce the atmosphere of back home, complete with folksongs. The old folk had a lot of fun, but the younger ones stared at me like I was something out of a zoo.

'It was good to see my cousin Teddy again, because we used to play cowboys and Indians as kids. He wants to run away and be a rock star in Paris. He plays the sax pretty good.

'You may remember I often spoke of the local gentry, the Berg family. My folks see them as the symbol of French oppression of immigrants. They are wealthy people who ought to be cut down to size, brought down a peg or two one of these days. This is the main subject of conversation here at the farm, although the Kovalics have shaken some of the mud off their boots over the years. It worries them, gnaws into them, a sort of hatred that gives them an identity in their own eyes.

'Things got real bad when my sister Catherine went off with a member of the Berg Clan called Paul Bossis. He was murdered but Catherine was pregnant and now has his child. At the christening the two clans got together and the Kovalics did a "great favour" for Gilbert Bossis, Paul's dad – but I still don't know what it was. Anyway, it was on the surface, because the Kovalics are still out to get them. Which is why they called me over, at least not me but my Harvard know-how, the rich yank who knows a few mafia tricks, the guy who's going to get things sorted out!

'They want to give the Bergs the *coup de grâce*, the knock-out blow, because they are in financial trouble it appears. I can't say any more at this stage, it needs analysing.

'You're not going to believe this, but my dad has handed over to me his spoils of war so far, consisting of all the gold ingots he has accumulated over thirty years. I told him to keep them until I needed them.

'As an hors-d'oeuvre, I've been to a funeral – to get my hand in. They were burying a fellow called Quentin, one of the town's fat cats, and I went along discreetly to see who's who in Chateauvallon these days. Teddy picked them out for me, including one of our main targets, a dame called Florence Berg,

227

whose the Godmother of their family. So, it's going to be me or her.

' 'Bye now, honey. Love and smoochees – Bernard.'

Apart from Bernard and Teddy, nobody at the funeral saw Florence standing discreetly behind a tall stone cross.

When it was over, she rejoined Travers in her car, and told him to drive off at once. But just then she saw Madame Quentin bearing down on her. Travers saw her too, and they both said 'uh-oh' simultaneously.

Travers quickly added: 'She's making a gesture, you'll have to respond.'

She slid out of the passenger seat again, and the two women met a few yards away. Travers wound down the window and prepared to listen.

'You are running away from me, Madame,' Madame Quentin said with a smile.

Florence responded politely: 'I feared you might feel my presence here was unseemly. I wanted to express my sympathy, but didn't dare do it in public.'

'Well, you've done so now. I was sure you would attend the ceremony. After all . . .'

'Yes, after all . . .' Both women smiled wanly.

Madame Quentin went on: 'No doubt you imagine I hate you.'

'That's something I find hard to think about.'

Quentin's widow said: 'You may be surprised to know that I never hated you, ever. At least I supposed I did to start with, but then I told myself there was no point in . . . After all, as it was you, the *affaire* did him credit . . .'

'And you soon realized I wouldn't steal him from you, I've no doubt.' Florence was trying desperately to lose the brittleness in her voice. She wanted to be so calm.

'Did you try?'

'Never,' Florence lied, telling herself it was the decent thing to do. 'Besides, he had two wives, you and his career in politics.'

Madame Quentin tilted her head to one side: 'Politics, and then me. It wasn't easy for me.'

Florence patted her hair and assumed they were about to part, but the other woman's expression became serious, almost confidential.

'You know, he didn't kill himself because of the election defeat.

In fact, to be honest I believe he was rather glad about that. For some time he'd been talking about giving up political life. To hell with the career, he said more than once. It was you who caused his collapse.'

'Are you really suggesting . . .'

'That he killed himself for you? Not at all. I expect you're disappointed.'

'Of course not, on the contrary . . . But why?'

'Who can say? Only *he* could. Even the letter business . . .'

'I'm so very sorry about that. I sincerely regret it.'

'It's of no importance, that wasn't the reason either. He knew the score. He could easily have countered that, and his career would have gone on, I'm sure.'

Florence gaped: 'I'm sorry, Madame, I don't follow you. I thought he would feel dishonoured, and I've been regretting . . .'

'Dishonoured? Come now, Madame Berg. The dishonour is all yours.'

After which, Madame Quentin went quickly to her car.

Back with Travers, Florence said: 'I think she was trying to tell me I was insignificant. Very well, if that's how it is, we must make hay while the sun shines. Let the dead bury the dead, etcetera. Taking me out to dinner this evening, Monsieur Travers?'

Travers looked at her regretfully: 'I'm awfully sorry, I've promised Catherine tonight.'

'Too bad.'

Travers coughed: 'I'd like to ask you something. I'm worried about her – money, if you see what I mean. She did a good job during the election campaign, I think you'll agree. You couldn't take her on at *La Dépêche* then, but I understand old Pérégrin is retiring soon. I was wondering if you might take Catherine for the library.'

'But, Monsieur Travers, I thought you were in love with me.'

'But I am indeed, Madame Berg.'

'And with Catherine too, of course.'

'Er . . . I must have notice of that question!'

Florence said nothing in response to that, and Travers kept glancing surreptitiously out of the corner of his eye at her, as they drove in silence to the office.

They pulled up outside *La Dépêche* and she grinned at him: 'Tell Catherine it's all right, we'll take her on.'

A few days after that, the examining magistrate told the assembled press that, subsequent to an exhaustive investigation, the final report of Commissaire Nicolo clearly established that the late Mayor of Chateauvallon did, with his own revolver, take his own life by means of a 9 mm bullet, probably whilst in a state of depression induced by overwork.

And on the day after that, two eminent members of the French ruling coalition, Messrs Marceau and Bessac, assessed the consequences of Quentin's departure with Jerome in the late Mayor's office.

To these persons and some others, Quentin's death would normally have been regarded as a tragedy. However, Quentin was not only a confounded political liability towards the end of his life, but he had made himself even more of an irritation by losing an election. At the same time, Jerome accepted, without an insincere display of grief, the burdens of office that automatically fell to him, as the government coalition continued to hold a majority on the town council. In a word, Jerome donned the mayoral sash until the next local election – long enough, as Jerome observed, 'to allow the wretched Les Sablons business to die the death'.

'It's already dead,' Marceau and Bessac said in unison.

'But it may come back to haunt us,' Jerome declared sagely, adding that he had 'major plans that will divert the public's attention'. He meant a sports stadium, day-nurseries, expansion of the industrial development zone, and concerted efforts to boost jobs in the constituency. Marceau and Bessac assured him that the subsidies needed would be forthcoming. But there was some fuss about a special allocation for *L'Eveil*, the paper that published the compromising photo of Armand Berg. Bessac said the photo business was an error that proved disastrous in the end, so there was no justification for funds. On the other hand, said Jerome, the paper might be bought up by the opposition. To avoid such an eventuality, the two men admitted that the paper warranted a modicum of financial support.

In the wake of this polite exchange, Bessac erupted: 'That nincompoop Quentin! Let Florence Berg escape from his bed, not only losing *her* but losing *La Dépêche* for our people.' It was universally agreed that 'another solution' would have to be worked out to deal with this woman who had become 'public enemy number one'.

Florence Berg's 'public enemy number one' was the taxman, now demanding a 'first payment' of three million francs within nine days.

As Jean-Jacques remarked to his wife that evening in the restaurant Le Thélème: 'Florence has her back to the wall. Whether she likes it or not she will be forced to sell some of her shares.'

'To you, I suppose,' Marie-Lou said.

'Naturally, I'm her brother, and I happen to have the money available.'

'The Boulard Group has it too, and they'll be bidding. If you tell Florence that she can kiss goodbye to the paper unless she gets a helping hand from you – you know what she'll do? She'll sell out to Boulard to avoid being rescued by you.'

Jean-Jacques guffawed: 'She hates Boulard, calls him a wastepaper salesman.'

'Ah, but she hates him less than she despises you. Now you listen to me. I can pull this off if you promise me that, for a little while at least, you will refrain from making jibes at her and will be nice to her.'

'Is that all?'

'I know that brotherly love is wearing a bit thin in your case, but for God's sake try to be nice.' Her husband blinked in disbelief. 'You, we, have to demonstrate that we are not interested in rescuing her out of self-interest but because we want to save her from falling into Boulard's hands, save the great *Dépêche* from a fate worse than death.'

'And you think she'll fall for it?'

'It's worth trying, you've got nothing to lose. And your first move is to tell her with your hand on your heart that we no longer intend to renounce the inheritance.'

Jean-Jacques was overcome: 'Marie-Lou, *ma chérie*, I am beginning to think you may be heaven-sent.'

'That's as may be,' his wife said primly. 'But hold your fire for a bit. Let her start running around in circles first.'

They nodded agreement, and dug into their dessert.

But Florence had a trump card up her sleeve, one she hated to play, but a card that would keep her in the game. She would sell her interest in the law business plus her apartments in Paris and Chateauvallon.

It was one evening when she was phoning an associate in Paris from La Commanderie to find out how much her share in the practice would fetch, that Mathilde whispered to her that a Monsieur Vernier was below and would like a word with her. He told her that Armand and Anne were 'going off' together.

'I've been away for a week,' Vernier said, 'and when I got in an hour ago I found Anne doing her packing. She said she'd reached a decision, that she loved your brother, and was going off with him to Paris.'

Florence said: 'Really? I didn't know he was back in Chateauvallon!'

Anne's father gazed at Florence from the depths of his melancholy: 'Madame, I think it ought to be stopped. Anne is seventeen and your brother is about forty, if I'm not mistaken. They are from completely different backgrounds, and I can see trouble looming. I'm sure you'll agree with me.'

'I do indeed, Monsieur Vernier. But will anything we say do any good? My brother does sometimes listen to what I say, but love, I fear, is deaf to all warnings.'

Vernier threw his arms up: 'I'm worried about my daughter, you see. She is still a minor. It's true she goes her own sweet way, but I am still her father and I have the duty and right to make her think twice. To be honest, I can't see myself doing it without your help, Madame Berg.'

'My help?'

'Well, I was thinking, you have plenty of influence, you know people, and if you can get me transferred to somewhere hundreds of kilometres away, on the other side of the country, my daughter will have to come with me.'

Florence drew a deep breath: 'I'm not too sure I can manage that, Monsieur Vernier. I'll try and do what I can . . .'

'You promise you will? It's for the good of them both, you realize that.'

'I promise,' Florence said with a hint of irritation, and she walked him to the front door, indicating that the interview was at a close.

For the good of them both, she reflected after seeing him out. But they wouldn't like it. It was hard to deny Vernier's concern, but she hated his forcing her hand, expecting her to do the dirty work – it was underhand, distasteful. Armand might never forgive her, and after all love was such a rare and precious thing now that everyone was so much on the make all the time. The fact remained, however, that the girl was under age and that promised a whole new chapter of calamities for her brother. This new development was all she needed to make it a perfect week.

To crown it all, she encountered Gilbert in the dining room, mulling over the magistrate's announcement, not believing a word of it. Mercifully, he refrained from going over the whole business again, no doubt because she had promised the previous evening that she would do a piece for *La Dépêche* on the decision. He was chomping at a sandwich and half-heartedly doing a crossword puzzle. When she came in he glared at her.

'Peckish?' she trilled, to head him off, and made for the whisky bottle.

'Not really. I haven't had dinner, I've just got in from looking after Catherine's baby. She was out for dinner with Travers.'

'Again!'

'I'm not too keen about it either.'

'Travers is her only real friend, I suppose,' Florence said coolly, to convince herself as much as Gilbert that that was in fact the reason. 'Apart from you, of course. But you must excuse me, I have an urgent call to make to Paris.'

Bossis, annoyed that his recriminations had been cut short, said: 'You don't look too bright.'

'Sorry, but that's how I am looking these days. I'll say good-night, then.'

'Hold on! You can't share it without a partner – eight letters starting with S.'

'Solitude.'

The phone was ringing when she reached her room.

'Madame Berg?'

'Who's that?'

'I have some information that might interest you.'

'Call the paper, if you don't mind, there's always someone to take copy.'

'Ah, Madame Berg, this concerns you personally. It's about Quentin – he didn't commit suicide, he was executed.'

'Then the phone went dead,' she told Travers.

'A hoaxer. Millions of them about. Think nothing of it, you may get more calls.'

'He was so calm, choosing his words.'

233

'They always choose their words, sometimes take hours thinking them up.'

'But again at three o'clock in the morning? Naturally I had to come at once,'she moaned.

Travers could not have been calmer, as he pottered about putting his place in order: 'My dear Florence, when Quentin died you got it into your head that you were partly to blame, so you listen to any rubbish that might take the weight off your mind. But that's no excuse for you to run about Chateauvallon at three in the morning.'

She got up from the chair: 'Of course, I see. The phone calls have thrown me off-balance. I could have spoilt a pleasant tête-à-tête for you. I must be going.'

He seized her hand: 'Tête-à-tête?'

'It's your business, Monsieur Travers. Your private affairs are nothing to do with me.'

He spun her round and drew her to him: 'Madame Berg, I have two suggestions for you. Either you go back home and take a sleeping pill and forget the phone calls. Or . . . are you listening?' She nodded. 'Or you stay here and we wait for the dawn, by which time your nerves should have composed themselves again.'

Physically, they were close as he said it. The room was small and for the first time she had a full whiff of his male smell. Not only did she feel weak, her pulse was faster, hammering at her ribcage. Her vision seemed to be narrowing and things were happening inside her. Oh no, surely she hadn't come for *that*. Quickly she thought of Catherine and took a step back.

'Thanks, Travers,' she said noncommittally, 'I think I will take the first bit of advice.'

'If I were a wolf. I'd say you were wrong.'

'But you *are* a . . .'

He assented and enfolded her, his palms holding her waist close to him then running over her back. She gave in and when they kissed their past encounters seemed as nothing. They took their pleasure hungrily, neither admitting it but clinging anxiously not wanting it to end. Travers was in a tatty old dressing gown and for a moment she was tempted, but pulled away.

'Oh Trav, that was lovely, I mean it,' she sighed. 'But it's late as it is!'

The moment had passed, and she made for the door.

'Very good, Madame Berg,' he said, opening the door for her. 'So sorry your programme is always so full.'

'Good-night, sleep well.'

'I will, I hope. Florence, seriously, if that guy calls again, I'm here. Don't forget that, I'm always here.'

'Perhaps he will,' she whispered.

As luck would have it, her shortened night's rest was followed by yet another new challenge.

Through Maryse, acting as spokeswoman, the works committee made a formal request for an extraordinary general meeting, as was its right under Article 27 of the Company Statutes when the employees held at least ten per cent of the capital. There was no alternative but to agree a date. The subject was: job security.

This and other events meant that she saw Travers but was unable to speak to him.

He himself was in a hurry to get home. All he wanted was his bed. After Florence had left the night before, he hadn't managed to get a wink of sleep. There are few things more frustrating than receiving a visit from a beautiful woman in the middle of the night who, after falling into your arms, suddenly takes herself off again.

Preoccupied with these thoughts, Travers failed to notice the Kovalic truck nearby as he opened his car door.

Inside the van Teddy said to Bernard: 'Quite a dump, Chateauvallon, don't you think? Boring, just boring.'

'We'll stay right here just the same,' Bernard said.

'We've been here half an hour already. What's *La Dépêche* to you except a building.'

'Catherine works here, and I want to see her.'

'Could have left already, seeing what time it is.'

'You may be right. OK, let's go. That geezer who just came out, know him?'

'Travers. One of the journalists. What about him?'

'Nothing.'

Travers's day was not over yet. A big car with headlights ablaze pulled across his path as he was leaving. He waited a few seconds and, as the driver showed no signs of moving, he got out angrily and walked briskly over. He found a man at the wheel alone, soft hat pulled down and a scarf hiding the lower part of his face.

The man said: 'You're not doing your job, old man. Start digging again.'

Travers hated strangers who called him old man, especially those dressed like Al Capone. 'What the hell are you on about?'

'Quentin.'

'What about Quentin?'

'Think about it, old man. That pistol, what hand was he holding it with?'

'Aw, get out of it,' Travers growled, starting for his own car. But suddenly he did begin thinking, wondering about the phone calls Florence had.

He returned to the big car: 'The right hand.'

'Ten out of ten. Now think some more.'

The man gunned his vehicle into movement, and went off fast. Within minutes Travers was back inside *La Dépêche*.

'And you think he could be the same man who phoned me?'

'There's only one. There can't be more than one person in this town playing the mystery man, otherwise people would notice.'

'And when you told him it was the right hand?'

'He told me to think some more.'

Florence delved into a drawer, extracting a photo of Quentin's hand holding the gun.

They both looked intently at the photo for a while, side by side behind the desk.

Suddenly Florence said: 'Of *course*. Travers, we're losing our grip.'

'Oh, no we're not. I got there just as you did. This needs checking.'

The same photo lay on Commissaire Nicolo's desk at 10.00 a.m. the following morning. Nicolo and Travers were looking at it.

Nicolo said: 'All right, citizen, what's screwy about the picture. A hand holding a 9 mm pistol, so what?'

'The hand is the right hand.'

'Go on.'

'Quentin was left-handed.'

Nicolo beamed upon Travers like a schoolteacher who has discovered the only bright pupil that year: 'Monsieur Travers, will you please lay your right forefinger on the desk. I want to show you something.'

Travers frowned: 'The right forefinger?'

'Precisely.'

Nicolo's visitor did as he was told, and regretted it instantly. The Commissaire raised his paperweight and banged it down on the aforesaid forefinger, apparently with great relish. The finger, which had turned a bright red, shot to Traver's mouth.

'What the hell . . .' Travers said but fell silent when he discovered he was looking into the wrong end of a gun barrel.

'Now try holding that with your right hand,' the cop ordered. 'Don't bother, you can't do it. Now Travers, I want you to take this photocopy of a report by our police doctor to Madame Berg. It will explain everything.'

Travers took the sheaf of papers: 'What about my finger? You ought to be locked up.'

'You should lodge a complaint at the nearest police station.'

Later, Travers watched Florence's elegant finger as it traced a path across the police doctor's report. It read: 'The index finger of the left hand was very badly bruised and under the nail a deposit of blood had collected. A few hours prior to death, the victim's finger was squashed, possibly in a car door. From this it is highly probable that the victim was unable to use his left hand.'

Florence slipped the photocopy into her drawer: 'It could be an explanation.'

'A convenient explanation that settles the whole business, no matter what Al Capone says.'

'Travers, did you tell Nicolo about . . .'

'No. Neither the phone calls you had nor the fellow who blocked my path when I left here. It wouldn't have done any good. Nicolo has the whole thing sewn up, that's clear.'

Florence smiled in a kindly way: 'Let's keep those parts of the story to ourselves. Now, I want to see your finger.'

He started unwinding the bandage, and she helped him. In a gesture of gratitude she deposited a long kiss on the swollen black finger, looking into his eyes.

'It was worth it,' he grinned, making a melodramatic gesture with his free hand.

There was a knock at the door, and Travers passed Marie-Lou on his way out. Florence caught sight of Armand in the passage.

'Come in Armand, don't stand out there.'

'I want to see you privately,' her brother said.

Marie-Lou slammed the door to: 'That makes two of us, and I'm first.'

She went on to explain that she knew that the tax people were on to her, and that she and J-J were prepared to sell one of their apartment blocks to help her out.

Florence said: 'And in return I take it you want some shares in *La Dépêche*.' She grinned at Marie-Lou, hoping it would end the encounter. Not only did she know perfectly well what answer she would give her sister-in-law, but she was impatient to see Armand. He ought to have been in Paris at that moment.

Florence told Marie-Lou she appreciated their gesture, but that she would manage on her own.

'You know, Florence, we really want to help. Think it over.'

'I will,' was all that Florence replied.

When Armand was alone with her, he said simply: 'Anne.'

'Yes, Anne. She's shacked up with you in Paris.'

Armand said gruffly: 'Stop fooling, Florence. She ought to be with me in Paris, but she never got there. So I came back, and I went to her home. I suppose you know the rest.'

'No, I don't.'

'Stop that! All I found there was a piece of board saying HOUSE TO LET. And now I want to know what you've been up to. I want it straight, Florence. The whole move took place within two-days, as I found out from the neighbours. That's lightning speed, even for French Railways. Someone intervened at the very top. Who?'

'Since you know so much, why ask me?'

Armand threw himself forward so that his fists reached her side of the desk: 'Why? Why did you do it?'

'Vernier wanted the transfer. I backed his application.'

'You had no right.'

'I certainly did have the right. The right to spare his daughter Lord knows what problems, and to stop you making a first class idiot of yourself. You can't be trusted, Armand.'

Armand sneered at her: 'Hooray for bourgeois morality. The satyr and the seamstress, is that how you saw us?'

'More or less. I'm sorry.'

'Well, I don't care a damn about your views.'

'That's up to you. But you have no right to behave this way.'

'That's up to me, too.' He made for the door. 'I don't suppose you'd have the decency to tell me where she's gone.'

'You're right. I promised not to.'

'I'll find her.'

'There's probably a railway station close by. Besides, if she loves you as you claim . . .'

'She does, and I believe her. She loves me, that's what rankles. You're jealous, out of love yourself, and you are simply trying to sabotage the love between two other people. You're frustrated, that's what you are. Uptight with your own damn chastity. You want revenge!'

Florence remained unmoved as her brother thumped on the desk: 'As I was saying, if she loves you, she will find a way. Make sure your trains don't cross.'

Armand flung open the door; 'I'll get her! And I'll come back and get you too.'

He slammed the door to, and she ran out from behind the desk: 'Armand, Armand! It's because I love you, because I . . .'

The extraordinary general meeting took place in the boardroom the following afternoon.

There were a score of shareholders present. They were not deliberately hostile, it seemed, but neither were they helpful. It became clear that the object of the meeting was to force her into a minority position. Jean-Jacques and Julien were there along with Maryse Mongin, and a small fellow called Monsieur Leveuf who said he represented Armand Berg. So that was how Armand planned to hit back at her.

Florence began by asking quietly why this special meeting was necessary. Leveuf asked Maryse to 'give the figures'. She did so: sales of the paper down four per cent in two months, three hundred subscriptions cancelled, a large number of advertisers pulling out. Florence said it was a manoeuvre in 'high places' designed to counter the vigorous new policy of *La Dépêche*. Leveuf retorted that it was precisely this new policy that had caused the readers to give up the paper.

'And what does the public want?' she demanded.

'A more moderate tone,' Leveuf said.

'You are acting for my brother?'

'I am carrying out my instructions, Madame.'

Jean-Jacques warned that the paper was heading for disaster. After which Leveuf said his client, Monsieur Armand Berg, was proposing the setting up of a supervisory committee, whose task would be to ensure that the newspaper maintained its role as a general news daily.

'Wonderful!' exclaimed Florence. 'We get him elected, and now he's in the Assemblée, back we go to DOG BITES MAN! Not while I'm in charge!'

Leveuf fought back: 'I must point out to you, Madame, that you have an interest of only forty per cent.'

Julien blurted out: 'And I must point out, Monsieur Leveuf, that *La Dépêche* is a family concern and that I have fifteen per cent.'

There was a silence and Florence said: 'Thank you Julien, at least I have *one* brother. Very well, if this resolution is passed, I shall step down. Those in favour?'

Leveuf, Jean-Jacques and two union officials raised their hands. Everyone else hesitated.

'Those against?'

Other hands were raised. The minutes recorded that forty-five per cent were for, fifty-five per cent against.

Travers met her in the passage and grinned at her.

'So you know the result?' she said.

'Maryse wants to skin you alive, I suppose.'

'Only because she can't have your skin, I suppose. I'm a sacrificial victim for you. Come on, let's have a drink.'

The phone rang as they went into Florence's office. She picked up the receiver, frowned and signed to Travers that he should listen in on the extra earpiece. It was the same voice as on the other occasions.

The voice said: 'You are making a mistake, Madame. You should trust me. Quentin was murdered. Very well, then. I shall expect to meet you tonight at midnight in the car park under the Grande Place.'

'Which level?'

'I shall find you, and I shall have proof with me.'

There was a click, and Travers and Florence looked at each other.

'Look,' Florence said, 'if there's one chance in a thousand . . .'

'Right you are. I'll be there. You know what happens to women in those underground car parks!'

It was not until 2.00 a.m. that Travers phoned her. She was biting her nails at La Commanderie.

'He didn't turn up,' Travers said.

She let out a sigh: 'Perhaps he's tired of the game.'

'Maybe, maybe not.' He paused. 'I suppose you want to go to sleep now.'

'Now it's you who's joking. I couldn't sleep to save my life. Quite apart from the weirdo, there's Armand and his idyll and Leveuf and the tax people. I think I can sell off my interest in the Paris practice and sell my apartment. I've already got three names. But that will meet only the first payment. For the rest I'll have to see Saviot. Anyhow, you get some kip Trav, and thanks.'

Travers coughed: 'I'm sorry, but there's something else you must add to your list. When we met in the passage after the special meeting I forgot to tell you something. Jean-Jacques and Maryse left the room ahead of you, and as I told you she was spitting with fury. She joined Jean-Jacques and they had their heads together, but I heard Jean-Jacques tell her they had lost 'only the first round'. They both cheered up at that, and swaggered off together. Just a small point, but it may mean . . .'

Florence said wearily; 'We'll just have to steel ourselves for the next round, that's all. After all, perhaps they simply went off to bed together. They've done it often enough before.'

What Maryse said to Jean-Jacques in the wake of their defeat was: 'I must talk to you for a couple of minutes, I must.'

And Jean-Jacques replied: 'My dear Maryse, it's not the end of the world, it's only the first round of the battle.'

'You listen to me. Whatever happened in there, I can see a head-on clash between you and your sister. Naturally, I'm on your side, as I'm against her methods and her policy. Not only that – they're trying to set me up over Catherine Kovalic, I can feel it.'

'I guessed as much myself.'

Maryse did a little wriggle: 'Well, *chéri*, remember me when you finally have the whip hand.'

'*Chéri*, you said? Sounds like old times,' Jean-Jacques said with a malign twist to his mouth.

'Why not?' she crooned.

Catherine Kovalic was becoming a pain in the neck, to put it mildly. This little madam, so clean she almost squeaked, was set to replace her as editorial secretary, as evidenced by the walkabout she had been given with detailed explanations of what went where and the rest of it – including page layout work. And who had taken her round? Maryse herself. Then, that morning while they were working together at their separate jobs in the secretaries' office, Catherine had a visitor, a presentable young man she didn't introduce to Maryse. She had marched over to him and pushed him out into the corridor saying: 'I'll be back, Maryse.' So this was the 'widow's' man of the moment . . .

The man was in fact Bernard Kovalic, Catherine's cousin, and while Maryse was smirking to herself as she plotted her downfall, the cousins were merely going over past history, with Catherine wanting to know all about the United States and Bernard extracting from her the reasons why she had abandoned the Kovalic homestead.

'You're not going against me, Bernard, you understand I had to?'

'Sure I do. So you're working here in the library.'

'Until they've got something better. I'd like editorial secretary, I'd jump at it if it came my way. You interested in old cuttings, that's what we call the library?'

'My girlfriend Phyllis back in the States once had to do research on a political scandal that occurred in the 1940s, and I helped her go through stacks of cuttings. Fascinating it was. I got to like research.'

Catherine bubbled: 'You'd like to see the cuttings here, I'm sure.'

'Well, if it can be arranged, but if not it doesn't really matter.'

'Of course it's possible. What subject?'

'Oh, just Chateauvallon. It's my birthplace, and I was here until three years ago. Be nice to know how the old place has been turning over since I left. Things like shops opened and streets coming down and whatnot.'

All-agog, his cousin cried: 'I'll get out the issues over the past three years.'

'You're a good kid,' Bernard declared, giving her a peck on the cheek. 'But then you always were.' He started to move off and then turned round: 'I never told you how sorry I was about what happened. That's really what I came for, to ask if I couldn't take a peek at little Paul one of these days.'

'Whenever you like,' Catherine said joyously, giving him a peck too.

She watched him walk away, swinging his shoulders yankee-style, and found herself melting. He was so unlike his uncle and his grandfather.

Mathilde and the cook were in a foul mood. The meal was being done at Maison Dutrieux et Charlot, even though it was only a family luncheon. Those fancy waiters in tailcoats laying the table

242

were doing her job. Still it was no business of hers now; she had told Madame Florence she was most put out and was prepared to leave her position if Madame so desired. And Madame Berg had said it was up to Monsieur Armand.

It was indeed Armand who had sent out the neat invitation to all the Bergs reading: 'Armand Berg requests the pleasure of your company at a special luncheon at 12.30 p.m. on . . . at La Commanderie – an exclusive family celebration with a surprise for everyone.'

Florence was the only one in the family who knew he had returned the previous evening from Paris. She knew what the surprise was to be too. Julien and Thérèse were in the dark, as was Jean-Jacques who had got back that morning from a weekend in Deauville. Everyone besieged Florence, and she had simply replied that perhaps Armand was going to announce that he was joining the Government. Jean-Jacques supposed the luncheon was one of Armand's bizarre pranks, while Marie-Lou said the whole thing was a disgraceful waste of money.

'Incidentally, where *is* Armand?' Marie-Lou said.

'Upstairs,' Florence said, 'In the baby's room, but it's only for a time. He has transferred his clinic to Dr Bonnot and let his apartment go. Taxes again!'

And the conversation turned to taxes while Jean-Jacques poured out the aperitifs. The caterers' staff were excused this duty so that the family would be able to speak freely. None of the others doubted that Florence knew exactly why the event was taking place.

Julien mentioned that he was selling an asset known as the Neuville Ponds, and Jean-Jacques said: 'What we didn't get up to there!'

'Too bad,' Julien shrugged. 'I made a single lot out of it all, and my neighbour had it for a song, knowing I was up against things money-wise. I'll just about make the sum I need.'

'You shouldn't have given in like that,' Jean-Jacques said. 'Of course, when I saw what the banks were asking for a loan, I told them they could keep their money. I would find it elsewhere.'

Marie-Lou exploded: 'Which means my father. It's my father who's getting you out of this jam. And you, Florence? Still in a mess?

'Not anymore, dearest. I've pulled out of my law practice and sold my apartments. It's enough.'

'For the first payment, but what about the rest?'

Florence smiled caustically: 'I am still considering your generous offer, of course.'

'She's not forgotten it.'

'I've only got one sister,' Jean-Jacques said blandly, turning to Florence. She smiled back sweetly, and went off to fetch a glass for Gilbert Bossis, who came in at that moment.

'Still yapping about money, I see,' he chortled. 'You'll be pleased to hear I've sold my patent. I can pay back Albertas. What a relief, I must say.'

This drew no comment from the others, who were huddled together next to a window.

Then Armand bounced in, putting on an act of his own invention. He made for Florence: 'How now, little sister? Still angry about Monsieur Leveuf, or am I forgiven?'

'I've already told you, I forget such childish nonsense.'

'So do I,' Armand cried. 'Family! I no longer hate you, I think I even love you all. So glad you could all come to my party. Ah no, I don't see Emilie.'

Thérèse answered: 'She's gone. She called me yesterday, told me she was joining Philippe with the kids, wherever he is.' She gave a tiny cough.

'She's out of her mind.' said Marie-Lou. 'The cops'll follow her. Now come on, Armand, what's this great surprise we're supposed to be getting?'

There was a silence, Armand braced himself and theatrically declared: 'There!'

Anne Vernier stood in the doorway, looking as if she might well take fright and run away. She was pale and gulped twice.

'I present to you – Anne! Anne Vernier, a name you have perhaps heard, and here she is in person. Strasbourg turned out to be within my reach.' He led Anne in by the hand as he was speaking.

Florence told Anne: 'When I saw you last night I was too stunned to say much. Anyhow, welcome among us after all.'

'I like the "among us" but not the "after all",' Armand said, striving to be amicable.

'I take it back then.'

'Oh, don't do that, Madame,' Anne said gritting her teeth. 'Thank you for your welcome, after all.' Her fingers were tight round Armand's biceps.

244

He said: 'They won't bite you – yet. Just say hullo and I'm sure they'll answer.'

'Hullo,' Anne said looking at the floor.

'Hullo,' they said in chorus.

The introductions were made and the company took their places at table. In the hour that followed, Anne was shown kindness by Thérèse and Julien, light-hearted condescension from Jean-Jacques, angry disbelief from Marie-Lou and indifference by Gilbert Bossis. None of these feelings were openly expressed, but for the newcomer the meal was an ordeal. She stuck it out, knowing that she would never have to go through it again. Her other thoughts she kept strictly to herself.

Florence found her pretty, but alas common. She still found the whole business harrowing. Fortunately, she was able to leave before the Norwegian omelette, pleading an appointment with Saviot the notary.

'There's a new procedure,' said Maître Saviot in his braying voice. 'By law, one is henceforth allowed to avoid part of one's estate duties by donating to the State certain works of art in the possession of the heirs.'

Florence gave only half her mind to him. On her way there, something else had cropped up, and the first thing she did when Saviot led her in was to ask to use the phone. She ordered Travers to wait for her without fail at the office.

'This should present no problem for you whatsoever. Your father was a man of sound taste: one Monet, a Gericault, the two Corots.'

'The Watteau, a Ruydsdael. So these can be handed over to the State.'

'Exactly.'

'There's a snag, however. They were jointly inherited. So suppose one of my brothers suddenly finds he has a new interest in works of art?'

'Deals can be arranged, as you will see Madame Berg. Don't worry, everyone will agree to this procedure, for the simple reason that they all stand to gain by it.'

'I hope to God they can be persuaded.'

'Meanwhile I'll stand in for Him, if you wish. You can leave it to me.'

'If you can persuade them, Maître, I'll recommend you for promotion when you reach the gates of heaven.'

Travers was waiting in her office.

'Saviot must have fitted you up with a pair of wings. What's the panic?'

'Do you know apparently there's some new law . . .'

'Yes, instead of paying tax, you can . . .'

'Oh Christ, Travers, you know that too. But seriously, do you know what's happened? Armand showed off the Vernier bit of fluff at La Commanderie in front of us all, and we've been celebrating it. Should I laugh or cry?'

'I adore you when you laugh. It's like a silvery . . .'

'And when I cry?'

'Ah, then I love you even more. Not much chance of that, though.'

'There's something else. I pulled up at a garage on the way, and went into that sort of shop thing they have, and when I got in the car again a man spoke behind me in the back seat. It was the mystery man, Travers. He told me not to turn round, and I just glimpsed his arm when he moved the rear-view mirror so that I couldn't see him. He said I was wrong to send you to the underground car park instead of going myself. Here's what he said, if I can remember it accurately: "Travers and you, Madame, it's all the same. You should stick to what I say. It would be wise because, you see, I'm taking a bigger risk than you are in this business. Now listen carefully. The police claim Quentin killed himself with his own revolver. That's a lie. It was a crime done up as suicide, a good job it was too, except for one detail – the killers couldn't get Quentin's own gun. That's where it all falls down." We were driving along by now and he said: "Now that you know the facts, see what you can do about it". Then after that he told me to stop the car, and he got out in Rue Gambetta and disappeared in the crowd before I could get a look at him.'

Florence ended her account and looked steadily at Travers.

'Those were his words, you say: "I'm taking a bigger risk than you in this business"?'

'Those were his words.'

'Curious.'

'What are we to do, Travers?'

'Not we – you.'

Within the hour Florence was in the Quentin living room, telling the late mayor's widow that, despite police assertions, a mysterious source had informed her that Quentin did not die by his own hand.

Madame Quentin said: 'Let me show you the gun, Madame Berg.' They went into the study and she pulled a desk drawer open. 'That is the permit to carry a weapon, and that's the gunsmith's invoice.'

'The same number,' Florence stated. 'Would you be prepared to lend me these two documents?'

'You as a journalist?'

'Strictly as a journalist.'

Madame Quentin held her back as she was preparing to leave. She extracted a bundle of letters from another drawer: 'Your letters, Madame. He kept them in a secret compartment, little knowing that I knew about it.'

'You've read them?'

'Of course. You write well, Madame, and not like a journalist, but as a woman! Take them please, they are yours now.'

Nicolo was in a bad temper. He was looking forward to seeing a film when the arrival of Madame Berg and Travers was announced. They stated their business and he went off for fifteen minutes while they waited in his office.

Now he was back with a jute bag from which he pulled out a gun with a label on it.

Nicolo said: 'You say the permit was for a PA 50?'

Florence glanced at the permit Madame Quentin had given her. She said that was so.

Nicolo placed the gun on his desk: 'That's your PA 50.'

Travers took it and checked the number: 59302. He repeated the number to Nicolo.

'Well?'

'The permit is for serial number 52507.'

The Commissaire checked and re-checked, he gaped at them both in turn and said: 'Bloody hell.'

Florence was more explicit: 'This permit is for the pistol Madame Quentin has just shown me in a drawer at her house.'

'So Quentin was not killed with his own gun,' Travers said.

Nicolo gave a cough: 'All right. I didn't have this information. Even so, I am not so sure as you are that the discrepancy is that important.'

'But it's still further information, Monsieur Nicolo,' Florence said with an encouraging smile. 'Something that was, how shall we say, overlooked.'

'Are you telling me we ignored it?'

'No.'

'Oh yes, Madame, that is what you are implying. But I'm telling you that it was not overlooked, but it is always possible in the course of an investigation that an oversight may occur.'

Florence and Travers stifled their amusement, as Nicolo drummed his fingers on the desk and said that he would initiate further action in the light of the new information.

'Especially as the magistrate closed the file, Monsieur Nicolo,' Travers said. 'The matter of the oversight, as you call it, may well lead him to reopen the file, even if there are no other . . . er . . . oversights.'

'Other? What do you mean by that?'

'Nothing special,' Florence said.

'So that's it. The police version of the facts is not enough for you, you want your own facts.'

'Neither yours nor ours, Commissaire. Just the facts.'

Nicolo was trembling with rage: 'All this fuss about nothing. Could be a simple mistake by a clerk somewhere. Makes no difference to the truth of the matter. Quentin killed himself with a PA 50, and that's all there is to it. And as for your activities, not only did you push Quentin into killing himself with all your so-called revelations, but you're keeping on with it to excite those readers of yours when your circulation is falling. That's what you're after, Madame Berg!'

The Commissaire stood behind his desk breathing heavily like a bull.

Travers said: 'I'm beginning to understand why the police and we newsmen don't always see eye to eye.'

Florence and Travers got up to leave. Madame Berg was roused at last, and remarked to her employee: 'Luckily we're interested in facts, Monsieur Travers, the real ones.'

Left to himself, Nicolo collapsed onto his chair and rocked back and forth. Then he slowly extended his hand to a button on one side of his desk: 'I want all you layabouts in here double quick. Jump to it!'

He then decided to watch his two visitors going out through the yard of the Commissariat. This he did from behind a pair of lace curtains that should have been replaced about six years earlier.

248

Travers was saying to Florence: 'So we've come up with a new fact, but the reopened inquiry will end no differently. There's no need to kid ourselves.'

'I tend to agree, to be honest. It might just be that a clerk put the wrong number down. It's too risky to give it any play in *La Dépêche*. Let's keep our feet on the ground. The only real line we have on this is our mystery man, and what's that worth in print?' She put a friendly hand on his arm. 'I don't like pussy-footing around either, Trav, but I don't like the smell of this.'

'We go to press at midnight. That gives you five hours to make up your mind.'

Meanwhile, behind the lace curtains, Germain and Pradal were going through the mill, ostensibly because they were fatheads, but in fact because Monsieur le Commissaire had missed his Stanley Kubrick film. Not for the first time he wondered why the hell anyone wanted to be a cop.

Young Teddy Kovalic was griping too, and he regaled the other Kovalics in plain terms.

'I've been doing nothing for days 'cept drive Bernard around in the van. We've seen everything, but that's not enough. All round the outskirts, building sites, bits of waste land. And I still got to do my deliveries as well. Haven't touched my saxophone for days, I haven't. While Mr Bernard Kovalic spends his time filling a notebook. Anyone'd think he was writing a book or something!'

Bernard said calmly: 'Anything else?'

Albertas grunted: 'That's enough for him. Now let me have my say. And look at me when I'm speaking to you.'

Gregor took Bernard's shoulder: 'Look at him when he tells you.'

Bernard did look at him, but only to take his leave. He strolled slowly over to the door, crushed his cigarette on the wall and said quietly: 'I'll use taxis.'

'At the price they are?' Gregor screeched. 'Albertas, tell him what's on your mind. Speak to him now!'

Albertas pulled himself up: 'What's on my mind is that you're costing us a fortune, young Bernard. Using gallons of petrol for nothing at all. Teddy's right, you're just pissing around, that's all you've done since you got here. You don't reckon I got you over here for that?'

'I never asked to come over. If it doesn't suit you, I'll pack my

249

bags and git as soon as you like.'

Never in the history of the Kovalic family had a junior member spoken that way to the older men.

'You're nothing but a pair of old fossils,' Bernard said with a toss of the head.

The two women in a room above made hasty gestures in what was supposed to be the sign of the cross. The crisis blew over, and Albertas even forgot to mention Bernard's call on Catherine at the newspaper, something he had nursed since Teddy had inadvertently let it out. There was another reason why the storm subsided: Albertas suddenly noticed just how pale and steady Bernard's eyes were – he had the gaze of a killer, it seemed to him. He had to admit that here was a man who could stand up to the Bergs. And that brought new hope to his bitter heart. Teddy concluded much the same, as Bernard returned to the group. It seemed to Teddy as he received a sharp look from Bernard that the Harvard man was not only brainy but dangerous too. Nobody could scare Bernard, that was certain, and it was best to be on Bernard's side in any argument.

So it was that Teddy said: 'Forget it, Bernard. Forget me blowing my top. I just got worked up.' He realized what nobody would ever say outright, that Bernard was over here to do a serious job of work, that the family needed him, and that the two older men had avoided giving him a lesson for the simple reason that Bernard scared the pants off them.

'Right ho, then,' Albertas said. 'We'll keep on with the van Teddy. All I was trying to say, Bernard, is that you're going slowly and I can't see what you're up to.'

Bernard consented to be appeased: 'I'm not slow, just careful. I'm taking it step by step, and it's not simple. Nothing would be easier than to blast this town off the face of the earth but that's not what we want. We want the town for ourselves.'

Albertas and Gregor exchanged a quick glance, and Albertas said: 'You're right, of course you're right. D'you need any money while we're about it?'

'That won't be necessary, but I need time.'

'You've got it. But I'd be obliged if you wouldn't stub out them cigarettes of yours on the wall.'

'I'll agree to that,' Bernard said, 'since you asked me nicely.'

Albertas's nephew eyed them all one by one. He moved across to the big cupboard and took out a bottle of brandy distilled when

he was only a boy. He poured himself a glass, raised it and said:
'To the Bergs!'

Bernard then drank it, on his own and in silence.

It was silent in Florence's room also. She stood looking down on
the counterpane at her letters to Quentin. She had spread them
out but lacked the courage to read through them. There was no
point, the past was the past.

She shivered in her peignoir and moved over to the fire blazing
in the small grate. Mathilde had got it going before she retired for
the night, and now it was midnight, or as near as made no odds.

Florence was wondering whether to add a log to the fire, when
the phone rang.

'Hullo,' she said weakly.

'Florence!' Travers said. 'Anything up? You sounded like you
were calling for help.'

'Perhaps I was. I'm alone, it's deathly quiet, Armand and Anne
have just left for Paris, and all I'm left with are my own thoughts.'

Before leaving they had come to her room, dressed and ready
to go. Armand had told Anne to say *au revoir* nicely to her future
sister-in-law.

Artlessly Anne had retorted: 'Why wouldn't I say it nicely?
She's always been nice to me. What she did was meant for my
own good.' And she had planted two big juicy kisses one on each
of Florence's cheeks. Florence had wanted to cry afterwards.

Travers was saying: 'What's your decision, then?'

'We'll forget about the damn gun. Let the dead rest in peace.'

In the background she could hear the rotaries whirring away at
La Dépêche, and voices yelling instructions.

'I agree with you, Florence,' Travers said. 'Sleep tight then.'

In a dream she replaced her receiver, gathered up the letters
and threw the lot on the fire. They gave forth a light that made her
wince, but after a while she chivvied them about until the last of
them was aflame. Then watched until there were only ashes
subsiding onto the embers.

Chapter Eight

One morning, while in the last deep phase of sleep, she was wakened with a message from the mystery man that had her on her feet within seconds.

Florence immediately called Jean-Jacques and told him to be at the office in thirty minutes without fail. She then skipped her shower, splashed her face and flung on some make-up, before scrambling into the same things as yesterday and running down the stairs.

She found Jean-Jacques and Travers chatting in her office. Jean-Jacques took her coat which she threw at him, and she sat down decisively behind her desk. The two men stood to attention as she got her breath back.

'Messieurs,' she said, 'I have just been described as an imbecile for telling Nicolo about the discrepancy over the guns. And why? Because, my mysterious caller told me, Commissaire Nicolo's sole part in the Quentin affair is to *stifle* it. I was further informed that this was no suicide, but a murder planned, contracted and carried out at the very topmost level. Nicolo was ordered to pronounce it a suicide, and he had no choice but to obey. What do you think of that?'

'Perfect!' Jean-Jacques said with his nose in the air. 'I take it you would like my opinion?'

'I've just asked for it.'

'Perfect again! I'm the other imbecile who's told nothing. The spare wheel that's never used. But when things get hot I am turfed out of bed at the crack of dawn, because Travers is no longer enough.'

'Don't be an ass, J-J, I want clear thinking from both of you. This is serious.'

Jean-Jacques paused and then said: 'All right. My view is that this stuff is so ridiculous it could only have come from some nut-case.'

Travers muttered: 'There are some nut-cases who know what they're talking about. This one's proved well-informed so far.'

'So far. I was unaware that I was being let in at the end of an ongoing saga.'

'Do be sensible, Jean-Jacques,' Florence said. 'Start being nice to your darling sister and let's for once work together for the paper. I value your opinion, and I mean that.'

'I've just given it. What's yours Travers?'

'Same as yours, I find it incredible. But we can be sure that, darling or not, your sister is already working on her own hunch. You've been mulling things over pretty thoroughly, haven't you Madame Berg?'

'You're right. We're going ahead with this.'

'So the dead can't be left in peace?'

'They've got eternity ahead of them. We have only a few hours.'

She outlined her plan: *La Dépêche* would come out with a piece that skipped any reference to Government complicity, yet mentioned the existence of the two guns. But indirectly, asking might there not be two guns. 'Let's have it cunningly put in the conditional . . .'

'It's an amusing approach,' Travers said coolly.

'I can't go along with that,' Jean-Jacques said. 'We're attacking the Government. And you can be bloody sure they'll make you pay for it. They simply won't be able to ignore it. Even in the conditional!'

'Travers?'

'Even in the conditional.'

'I go along with you two,' said Florence, bursting out laughing. 'See how we always manage to agree in the end?'

Armand Berg stood shaving with nothing but a towel round his waist in the apartment he had rented two weeks earlier in Rue Astorg, Paris.

He frowned as the phone rang, and left Anne to answer it. Who the devil could be calling at 9.00 a.m.?

'For you,' came the sleep-laden voice of his beloved. 'A woman.'

He grunted his name into the mouthpiece, and then said: 'You

253

Florence? No, I'm up and about, but I've got a committee thing in less than an hour. What's up?'

Anne snaked her fingers round his neck: 'I adore you,' she whispered into his ear.'

'Stop it, you're tickling. Yes Florence, I'm still here, state your business, sister dear.' Then later. 'The conditional's all right, but it'll fool no one of course.'

Anne now had him on his back and was climbing onto him. She moved the receiver away with her hand and lay full length on him, her lips playing with his. With one foot she expertly cut off the call.

Back in Chateauvallon, Florence heard the click and raised her eyes heavenwards.

'Armand agrees,' she told the two men. 'He's in a hurry but I got the message.'

The story hit the streets early the next day, and the expected chain reaction got under way.

The fall-out reached the PPS at the Interior Ministry in the form of his superior, who charged out of his office and into the PPS's. On the latter's desk lay a copy of *La Dépêche* with a short piece bang in the middle of the front page. The Minister grabbed a red crayon and ringed it. He then looked fiercely at his subordinate.

'Two revolvers! And the other media picking it up. Now the whole damn country knows there was something suspicious about Quentin's death. I won't have it. The President won't have it.'

'Nor will I, Monsieur le Ministre.'

'I take it you've demanded an explanation from our idiot Prefect in Chateauvallon?'

'I was about to . . .'

'About to! Well get cracking at once, or there'll be another killing – right here!'

The Prefect of Chateauvallon was whiter than the Minister was red, as he took the call.

'I want to know,' the PPS said, 'how *La Dépêche* comes to be raking over the muck. In particular, why they come out with material that has no official foundation. The President and the Prime Minister are shouting blue murder – I mean they need a full report within the hour . . . I don't care whether you're shocked or not shocked, Prefect. That a newspaper can suggest that a former

Minister has been murdered calls for a little more than shock on your part. Your career is at stake, Prefect. Now get to it.'

The shock waves went as far as Commissaire Nicolo.

He heard the Prefect over the phone: 'Understand this, Nicolo, police officers have had their careers ruined for far less than this business.'

And so the reprimand went down the hierarchy. Pradal had the misfortune to enter Nicolo's office just as he was ending the conversation with the Prefect.

'Pradal, you will be pleased to know that I am recommending you for the Agricultural Medal of Merit and for early retirement. That means you can grow artichokes in dignity for the rest of your natural.'

Anne Vernier knew nothing of all this commotion, as she settled voluptuously into her new life in the eighth *arrondissement* of Paris. Already the thing was starting to become a drag.

On the evening following the bombshell in *La Dépêche*, Armand was prompted to ask her: 'You look a little jaded, my little one. Anything wrong?'

'No, nothing.'

'But you're in a peignoir already!'

'Well, I've only myself to look at in the mirror,' she pouted. 'You just go from committee to committee. We make love twice a day, once in the morning and once in the evening. And that's my riotous living!'

'But you must take things easy. Simply imagine to yourself how wonderful I am, and I'll reappear, you'll see.' He grinned impishly.

She gave him a playful slap on one arm: 'Yes, you're wonderful, but you're a pig just the same. Unfortunately I love you, especially just now.' She gave a little wriggle.

'Ah, now that's fortunate, because I've spent the day sitting on hard old chairs thinking how soft your arms are going to be.'

'No wonder the nation's in such a state,' Anne gurgled, naughtily opening her peignoir and going into a striptease. Armand was catching up fast and his expensive suit and shirt were in a heap on the floor within seconds.

Armand was snoring gently around 3.00 a.m. when she put the light on on her side of the bed. Carefully she hoisted herself up on one elbow and looked down on this full-grown male she was finding so hard to get accustomed to. She recalled the tiff – it was only a teeny-weeny one, but it wasn't the first. Mentally she shrugged, as her thoughts switched easily to the way they had made love, thrashing about on the bed, falling onto the carpet and carrying on there. Besides, he had given her a couple of Mozart records and a book by Tolstoy – which made her frown at the way her father and Florence had referred to the 'intellectual gulf' between Armand and herself. What did that matter when you were made for each other, when you were physically so well matched? Anne realized she again felt the first tingle of desire even then, but she would not wake Armand. She had done this only once and he practically threw her out of the bed.

Even so, she decided as she gently lay back and switched the light off, he *was* a bit of a pig, expected her to loll around all day in a kind of four-star prison cell. Her last thought was of La Grange back in Chateauvallon.

Interim Mayor Adrien Jerome called a press conference at the town hall to refute the big story.

Several local officials flanked him as he faced a score of reporters and correspondents, including two people from Paris, at least half a dozen photographers, two TV crews and naturally the trio from *La Dépêche* – Florence, Jean-Jacques and Travers.

'I am speaking to you,' Jerome said in a clear rehearsed voice, 'not as the first citizen of Chateauvallon, but as the close friend and colleague of Georges Quentin. I speak with the authority that comes of twenty years' friendship, twenty years' working together.'

He settled into his discourse, even allowing himself a passing smile: 'I knew Georges Quentin as intimately as any person can outside his own family. Oh, he had worries enough, and don't I know it. But they were unrelated to his physical security, because Georges Quentin had political adversaries, but not an enemy in the world. Which is why I have asked you to come along so that I can refute categorically the infamous fabrication that he was assassinated. If he *did have* enemies, I can only propose that you seek them out as the source of these rumours. These are the people who indirectly link the existence of two revolvers to the idea that he was murdered. As if it were not evident that a man who has decided to take his life will use the first weapon he can lay his hands on!'

All eyes turned to the group from *La Dépêche*, and Jerome deftly stepped down from the dais, only to be headed off by Florence, who raised a finger and elbowed her way towards him.

'Just one question, Monsieur le Maire,' she said firmly.

'I have answered them all,' he barked, moving steadily for the exit.

Florence pursued him: 'Since the Mayor will not reply, I ask the friend and colleague whether he believes Monsieur Quentin was in good health just before he died.'

'In perfect health, Madame.'

'But weighed down with worries?'

Jerome could not decently dodge the question in the presence of the press corps: 'Worries that went with his office.'

'So, he would not have killed himself in a fit of depression?'

'That is my belief, absolutely!'

Florence tilted her head in formal thanks: 'That is all I wanted to know, Monsieur le Maire.'

Back at the office Jean-Jacques weighed into her: 'You have declared all-out war. You are dragging us into a conflict of the utmost danger.'

Maryse backed him up: 'You are involving us all in this, and it's hardly fair, even though we might share your general impression of events.'

'You were there?' Florence said.

'At the back.'

'And you think I went too far with just one question?'

Maryse retorted: 'It wasn't a question, it was a boomerang. If Quentin was not depressed at the time, people will infer that he killed himself because of you, because you published that letter.'

'I am unlikely to forget that it was because of me, as you say,' Florence retorted.

Jean-Jacques waved his hands at her: 'As for the murder theory, the two guns don't amount to a shred of evidence.'

'Have it your way,' Travers interjected. 'But the two guns exist, and there's a reason. Now I'd like to make a suggestion. Our story's caused havoc, it's a major topic at the Assemblée this very moment. We know that through Armand. We need a follow-up or the thing will fizzle out. We need new ammunition.'

Jean-Jacques said: 'That's all very well, but if you invent your ammunition it comes out as rumours, defamation, libel.'

Florence demanded: 'What's your suggestion, Travers, please?'

'We must identify the man who's been phoning in. Find him if we can. I strongly suspect he is leading us by the nose, and we have to know where he's leading us.'

'Words, words, Monsieur Travers,' Jean-Jacques scoffed.

'I have the exact words we require,' Florence said, taking a sheet of paper from her top drawer. 'Here's what we publish: FOUND TUESDAY DWARF POODLE, SAINT-JEAN DISTRICT. APPLY LA DEPECHE.'

'Have you gone mad, playing at small ads?'

'It's code. The man himself told us to put it in the small ads if we wanted to get in touch with him. Well, since there's no other way, we insert it.'

The ad appeared in the 5.00 p.m. edition and the mystery man phoned the paper late that evening. The call was switched at once to Travers, who noted the rendezvous point: a hamlet called Vieilles Carrières. He informed Florence at once, adding that the encounter was to be at 11.00 p.m. the next day.

Vielles Carrières was some distance from the town, a craggy remote spot with great puddles that never seemed to drain away. It had some ruins of workings that were never completed, and a scattering of old refrigerators, sopping mattresses, buckets and a hundred and one other objects dumped from miles around.

Travers told Florence he would go there with Favrot and Edelman.

On the morning in question two men in rubber boots could be seen, if anyone cared to glance that way, slopping around on this very stretch of desolate countryside. They kept turning and stopping and then starting again, going this way and that as if they were looking for something.

'The fact is,' Maître Saviot told Bernard Kovalic, 'that all this dates from the next but one mayor before Quentin. Lejonchoy he was called, but I don't suppose you remember him.'

'No.'

'It was a gigantic project. See that concrete over there? Well, the idea was to build a dam and control the River Loire so that they could form a huge lake, the biggest in Europe it was said, with sailing boats, beaches and so on. The Government was prepared to give vast subsidies for it, but the voting in Chateauvallon went

258

the wrong way and it was goodbye to the big scheme. By the time Quentin became mayor, it was thought the thing could be resurrected, but it wasn't his project and he pushed it to the bottom of the pile. Now look at it.'

Bernard Kovalic made no comment. Not for the first time that day, Saviot wondered whatever he had in mind, calling him out here to look at Vieilles Carrières.

'Of course,' Saviot said, as much as anything to cover his own embarrassment, 'anyone could get it for practically nothing, but who wants a giant rubbish tip?'

Bernard said offhandedly: 'Nobody, although . . .'

'Who then?'

'I mean that, for a small outlay, you could make a white elephant pay. Turn it into petfood, say.'

'Ha ha, white elephant is right!'

'But it's still an elephant.'

Saviot glanced quickly sideways at Kovalic, then raised his eyes to heaven.

At three o'clock, four hours after the rendezvous time, the cigarette ends in Florence's ashtray were starting to overflow on the table by her bed.

Travers had said he would phone, and finally she could stand it no longer. She dialled his number. Three more times she dialled pointlessly, and then fell into a fitful sleep before dawn.

Florence was trembling when she parked outside *La Dépêche* a couple of minutes after 9.00 a.m. Her jaw dropped at the sight of Travers locking his own car door.

'What happened?' she said, her eyes blazing, when he came over. 'I didn't sleep a wink, of course. You were supposed to phone me, for pity's sake. There was no reply at your place.'

'Come up and I'll tell you,' he answered quietly.

In her office he told her: 'It was a flop, he got away. We heard him running at one stage, but that was all. We got there and waited, then started meandering around with flashlights, and then Favrot fell in a puddle. Incidentally, he's cocked up his ankle or his knee or something. We took him home and that's where he is now. We were whacked out, so we didn't fetch you.'

'I was worried stiff, you should have phoned at least.'

'To tell you nothing happened?'

'Are you all right?'

'Suit's in a mess, so's my pride. The awful thing is that we were within an ace of grabbing him. He was trying to look invisible next to some dam foundations, and we could see his outline perfectly. When Favrot fell down, Edelman and I put our torches on, and he did a bunk. I told him over the phone that I'd be on my own. Sorry, a fiasco.'

'He'll get in touch again.' Her intercom buzzed. 'Yes? Right, send it up.' To Travers: 'The lab's got hold of something.'

Travers growled; 'He may not get in touch, that's the worst of it'. We've probably scared him for good.'

Catherine came in, placed some photos on the desk, Florence and Travers exchanged surprised looks.

'Did you see,' said Travers. 'Her eyes are red. Looks as though she's been crying.'

'Maryse probably, it's happened several times.'

'Really?'

'Yes, really, Monsieur Travers. You jumped into bed with Maryse, and now Maryse assumes you're jumping into bed with Catherine. That's why.'

Travers displayed mock-disgust: 'For pity's sake, you can't even have a little fun these days without someone flying into jealous rage. I'd never sleep with Catherine, cross my heart Florence.'

She countered with mock-surprise, her eyes wide: 'But I believe you, Monsieur Travers. From now on, I gather, *my* heart is where you build your fire.'

'One of these days I really must give you a straight answer.'

'Meanwhile,' she said. 'Take a peek at these.' As she said this her personal teleprinter began buzzing away and she went over to it. The colour had faded from her cheeks when she returned to the desk, but Travers was too busy studying the pictures. They showed Quentin's head after he died.

'Amazing!' he gasped.

'Certainly is,' she said turning her face away so that he would notice nothing in her appearance.

'He's been prettied up. The big bruise on the forehead has gone. The holes have been plugged!'

'Any ideas who did it?' she said quietly, still overcome by the teleprinter message.

'Possibly the funeral people, after all. They try to make it easier for the relatives.'

'That's all very well, but suppose he was knocked out first and then killed at leisure. Suppose he was prettied up so that people would overlook the bruises on the forehead.'

Travers drew back: 'Hold on a second. You're forgetting the police pictures were taken right away. They showed nothing suspicious. The police doctor said nothing about them either, just that Quentin's head hit the car door.'

Florence had recovered somewhat: 'If Nicolo was told to sweep the affair under the carpet, he would start by having a go at the police doctor's scruples.'

'You're still left with an 'if'. Which is all our mystery man has ever offered us, an affirmation without proof.'

Florence took a deep breath and let it out again: 'So it's a blind alley.'

'Afraid so.'

Two days later Nicolo held his own press conference in the Commissariat designed to 'put the record straight as regards the two revolvers mentioned in this affair'. He declared that both guns belonged to Mayor Quentin. The PA 50 he used to kill himself came from his young brother Pierre Quentin, a lieutenant who lost his life in the Algerian war. The late mayor had kept it as a souvenir and had forgotten to register it, which was of course a minor offence. Nicolo went on to express his disapproval of a newspaper that had built the question of the two guns into a major issue.

Travers suddenly threw in a question: 'Monsieur le Commissaire, this gun from the young brother, did Quentin keep it as a souvenir in the glovebox of his car?'

Nicolo thrust his chest out; 'That seems to be the case, Monsieur Travers, and we have evidence from ten people about it.'

That ended the press conference, and Florence looked so dejected that Travers insisted she have a pick-me-up in the Bijou-Bar. They perched on their bar stools, thinking their separate thoughts, and Travers noticed two tiny tears rolling down her cheeks.

'Oh Florence,' he said. 'I could have gone on, but it would have looked bad. Nicolo worsted us on the guns, but there's more than one way of skinning a rabbit. It's not the end.'

'It is the end for someone I know. Two days ago, and I can't stop crying.'

'Who?' he said quickly. 'Who's died?'

Florence squeezed his hand: 'Tomorrow. I must go. No, you stay. I'll tell you tomorrow.'

Travers watched her tugging at the heavy door and slipping out before it closed on her. Now he too felt like going.

Armand found Anne asleep when he got back that evening.

'Hey, wake up! It's only seven!'

'I'm sleeping off the boredom,' she said, obviously in a foul mood.

He promptly ordered a table at Bagration's, the restaurant celebrated for its wines, its film stars and its prices. On the way in the taxi she was bright enough, but once they had been shown to their table her bright eyes seemed to lose their lustre and she suddenly felt like a waif among the capital's upper crust. Even her dress, one of the nicest Armand had bought for her, seemed cheap. They spoke in monosyllables during the hors-d'oeuvre, but Anne had to admit she was really proud to be in the company of a man whom several people had waved discreetly to already from the other tables. Nevertheless, she picked at her food.

'Something wrong with the caviar?' Armand asked at length.

'Yes, it's got a fishy taste.'

Armand smothered his face with his napkin and shook with laughter. Twice he tried to explain where caviar came from, but he had to give up. His convulsions made her feel worse, and she took a sip of champagne, It tasted awful! From then on, she began scowling at the ranks of waiters ready to attend to her every need, for they annoyed her too – watching her with their beady eyes all the time. They ploughed on through the duck course with Armand making suave remarks about everything and nothing, striving to impress his audience. He knew, and she knew, and probably some of the other tables knew too.

Eventually she said: 'When are we going?'

'But I've ordered the desserts,' he protested.

Armand took an urbane view of her discomfort. She would learn, she would even come to enjoy the good things in life in due course.

'All right then,' she rasped. 'But no more champagne.'

'Of course not, I've ordered profiteroles, and they need a sweet wine.'

Anne gazed at him doll-like and declared sarcastically: 'I'm learning something every minute.'

Armand himself was starting to be put out. Why the hell couldn't she just adapt to the spirit of the evening, for God's sake? He gave no hint of this, and lifted a finger. The head waiter bowed over the table and Armand asked for the wine waiter. The latter appeared with the profiteroles. Or at least Armand thought it was him, but it turned out to be a rather tubby sixty-year-old senator who bowed in Anne's direction and said to Armand: 'Good evening, dear friend.'

'Oh good evening, Senator.' He made the introductions: 'Senator Trimaud – my wife.'

'Delighted to meet you, Madame.'

Anne just managed a smile as their palms met. She felt like crawling under the pile carpet. How dare Armand show her off like some call girl! She would be the talk of the Senate the next day. Anne pushed the dessert away from her, and stalked off to the ladies' room.

When she came back Trimaud had pulled up a chair and was congratulating Armand for a 'remarkable' speech he gave at the committee meeting that afternoon; 'Ah Madame, Your husband quite won us over. I could not help thinking of our dear friend Quentin. Such a sad . . .'

'He's not my husband,' she blurted out. 'I'm his mistress, and if you don't want to ruin my evening, please talk of something else but politics and Quentin.'

'Anne – Anne,' Armand whispered desperately. 'Do excuse her, Senator. Anne, are you feeling all right?'

'Sure I'm all right. I've just been to the toilet and it cost me ten francs. That's daylight robbery, Monsieur Le Senateur.'

The Senator chuckled for all he was worth. Oh, he must tell that one, he was thinking. He bid them farewell and trundled off, still chuckling.

Armand looked as if he could kill her.

'What's wrong, *chéri*? He had a good laugh didn't he?'

'You don't realize that stories will go the round now about me.'

'They'll say you're sleeping with someone you picked out of the gutter.'

Armand quickly settled the bill, and then realized that a tall, pretty brunette was tripping towards their table. The wine waiter!

'I'm so sorry, we shall have to leave,' he said tensely. 'My wife doesn't feel well.'

Anne was already half-way out, and Armand scurried after her with as much dignity as he could manage. He was just aware of the head waiter calling out: 'Table five, Sofia, please.'

Travers, still at *La Dépêche*, called Florence at La Commanderie.
He said: 'Sofia. Sofia Leriche. Heard the name?'
'No. Why?'
'There's a new development. I'm coming out.'
Ten minutes later Travers arrived and Florence was waiting for him half-way down the stairs.
He said: 'They told me you weren't coming into the office today. Not feeling well?'
'None too good. But what's the new development? I still can't recall the name Sofia Leriche.'
He led her outside and they sat in the car: 'You used to go to La Gentilhommière occasionally, that's right isn't it?'
'With Quentin. Ages ago, of course.'
In reply he took a cassette and slipped it into the player between them. A voice came out and Florence froze. It was the mystery man.
The cassette said: 'Well Travers, so you wanted to kidnap me! Imagine three of you turning up. Tell the boss she had better not play with fire, and tell her I've got far more on her than she has on me. But I'm of a kindly disposition, and I've got something else for you. She's called Sofia Leriche, age about thirty, used to work at La Gentilhommière. She kept her eyes open on the night of the drama. Saw some fascinating things, Travers. You have to find her.'
Travers switched it off: 'I've just been there, and it's shut down for the annual holiday. But I found an old bloke doing some hoeing, and he told me this Sofia Leriche looked after the wines there. What's more she disappeared, he said, exactly two days after Quentin died. Said he thought she was working in Paris.'
They sat there in silence for a moment, and Florence said: 'A woman wine waiter's a rarity. Funny, I didn't notice her. That could mean she wasn't there during the period I went to La Gentilhommière.'
'That may well be so.'
'If she left when your bloke said she did, and if she saw some "fascinating things", it means she got scared.'
'I'm there ahead of you. But scared of whom?'

264

'I'd give a lot to know.'

'How much?' Travers said with a laugh. 'If your price is right I might be able to find out. Hey Florence, what's the matter with you. Did you hear what I said?'

Florence gaped at him as if he'd pinched her bottom: 'I'm sorry, Trav, I had a sort of blackout. What were you saying?'

'I was saying I know why you were crying yesterday in the Bijou-Bar, and why you're in a bad way this morning. Catherine showed me the message off the teleprinter, you left it on your desk: "Death of the celebrated writer Ernest Wilson at Hartford, Connecticut . . ." Florence, I didn't know he was your husband. I'm so sorry.'

She stared ahead: 'A drunkard, a lousy drunkard I knew in Montparnasse. But I loved him at first sight. He was my only big success story, Trav. I got him off the drink, got him going, the layabout, got him away from the hangers-on. For years he jabbered on about the great novel he was going to write one day. And in the end he wrote it. Yes, he wrote it in the end.'

'*The Way the Veteran Ended*. Pulitzer Prize.'

'Yes. And he wrote ten others. They were my books too, Trav, and I'm so proud of him. Then one day he went back to the United States and stayed. France was too small for him after they discovered him over there. But it was no use, I tried to make a go of it with him there, but finally I had to ask for a divorce.'

He left her to her thoughts for a while, and then said: 'Your daughter, Alexandra isn't it? Catherine told me . . .'

'She's gone too.' Florence gave a hard laugh and Travers looked sharply at her. 'She went too and never came back. She found her father and the States more congenial than I was. That too was a sort of victory, I suppose. Travers, I'm telling you things I've kept to myself all this time.'

'Now that Wilson's dead, she'll be coming back.'

'We are so very far apart, the two of us.'

In the further silence that followed, he looked with her into the reopened wound. Travers yearned to take her in his arms and tell her he loved her deeply – loved her when she was unhappy, fighting fit, triumphant. Loved her for herself.

What he said was: 'Florence, never forget, I'll always be here – with you.'

She turned with infinite sadness, and buried her head in his chest.

Then, plucky as ever, she came out of it. She smiled through the tears and said: 'I wonder if you'll ever get around to asking me to marry you. Unless I do it first!' She gave a friendly gurgle and he knew everything was back to normal between them again.

'So that's your price for finding Sofia Leriche!' he said with a grin. 'OK, you're on.'

His tone was bantering, but after that he held her hands in his for a long while.

He found her two days later.

But he could not find Florence when he turned up at *La Dépêche* later on the third afternoon. He called La Commanderie, and Jeannou knew nothing of her whereabouts, except that she was 'at a meeting with the family'.

The meeting was in fact at Maître Saviot's office. Armand had made the trip, even though he arrived late. He seemed to be in a bad mood and did not open his mouth for the first half-hour.

Saviot told them the assessors had come up with a total figure for the paintings that coincided roughly with that worked out by the Ministry of Culture. The Ruysdael was to be excluded, as it proved to be a forgery. The total value, twenty-five million francs approximately. This meant the rest of the estate duty was covered.

'All's well that ends well,' Saviot beamed.

'Except for me. I'm the big loser in this,' Jean-Jacques expostulated.

Maître Saviot carefully explained how he would benefit from the scheme like everyone else.

Marie-Lou chirruped: 'My husband means that he gains less than the others. Without *La Dépêche*, which Florence has got, my husband would have had no difficulty paying the death duties. *La Dépêche* is forcing him to give up inestimable treasures.'

'But they *have* been estimated,' Saviot retorted, his mouth twitching. 'But to reply to your point, I have as it so happens prepared an arrangement which I think your co-heirs would subscribe to readily. I propose that you all cede to Jean-Jacques Berg four per cent of your stake in the paper, which will give him thirty-two per cent in all. Madame Florence and Monsieur Julien have already signified assent, with Madame Florence retaining thirty-six per cent, which we call a blocking minority. It means nothing can be done without her consent.'

'In other words you still have the final say,' Jean-Jacques said scornfully. 'But we haven't heard Armand yet. What's your pitch, Armand?'

'Whatever you want,' he said gloomily.

Florence cadged a lift from Armand after the Saviot gathering: 'All right, little brother, spill the beans. Anne's run out on you, is that it? I expect it's my fault again.' She was in a good mood, Maître Saviot – Almighty God – having snatched her from the gates of Hell.

Armand was driving like a man possessed, at twice the speed limit and up a one-way-street the wrong way, as he narrated the saga at Bagration's.

'After all, ten francs *is* rather overdoing it, I must say,' his sister commented. 'Mind you, it wasn't me who told her to check the rates in the ladies' room.'

'Ah,' said her brother. 'But if she behaved like a witch at high mass, it's because she felt inferior to the people around her. And that's your doing, Florence.'

'I deny it! It was her father. Armand, if you don't mind, a hundred kilometres an hour is asking for trouble. Calm down, for goodness sake.'

He ignored her: 'The next day I got back from the Assemblée and she'd gone. At least I thought so, but she rolled in about midnight. Naturally I demanded an explanation and she said she'd had enough of spending the day cooped up and so on and so on . . .'

'Can't say I blame her.'

'After which I fancied I heard your very words: "I shall never fit in with your circle, I lack the culture, I don't even know the difference between fish knives and meat knives".'

'Not guilty. I would never say a thing like that.'

Armand swung the car into the last bend: 'Then yesterday I had to go to Rennes for the day. When I got back she had gone again. But without taking her things. So naturally I waited, and I waited all damn night. Finally that morning I at last opened my letter box, which I had forgotten to do the night before, thinking she was in the flat naturally. And I found her goodbye note. Here it is. Read it, read it out loud.'

'Stop the car then.' He obeyed her and she read: '"Armand. I have thought it over, and I don't think it is going to work out for us. Your sister is right when she says it can't work between people as different as we are in age, in situation, in their life style . . ."'

Armand asked Florence: 'When did you tell her that?'

'I didn't. Of course, to be frank, it's what I think, but I would never say such a thing except to you or her father.'

Armand grabbed her arm and she gave a squeal: 'You phoned her while I was in Rennes! You never could accept the idea that I might at last find happiness. You're evil, Florence, but you've done it this time. It's finished between us!'

'I don't care what you think, you fool!' Florence shouted, struggling with the door catch. She stumbled out, going down on one knee, then stood back to watch Armand in a blind fury swing the car round and drive off madly back to Chateauvallon.

She buried her face in her hands, and then when it was quiet she looked around her. Wherever she was, it was nowhere near La Commanderie! She had been sure they were at the final bend before the main gate. It couldn't be true, she was in the middle of nowhere. Close to panic, she tried to recognize the road, the fields, the hedgerows, the trees. Then at last she saw that she was at Vieilles Carrières.

There was nothing for it but to find her way home on foot. She started out, reflecting grimly that there was only one person in the whole bloody world she could trust now – Travers, her Trav.

Florence had gone about a hundred yards when she saw one of the Kovalic vans on the roadside. She approached it cautiously, and found there was no one in it or apparently nearby. There was just the van.

Whatever could they be delivering there?

But Bernard and Albertas had seen her, and they wondered whatever was she doing roaming around the country on her own.

They were standing just outside a roadman's hut, and now began stumbling over the rough ground, among the rocks and refuse.

'Well, where are we going?' Albertas said.

'This is it,' Bernard said, bringing them to a halt.

His uncle uttered a contemptuous laugh: 'Here? What are you getting at?'

'It's for sale. We can get it for a song.'

Albertas looked at him, then scanned the area, then looked at him again: 'Is this what you mean? This pile of rubbish? You expect me to buy this? I wouldn't have it if it was given me. Is that what they taught you at Harvard?'

Bernard waited and said: 'I've seen the development office, and they see nothing against it. I'm going to see the town architect tomorrow.'

'Mantelet? That guttersnipe?'

'Sure, that guttersnipe. He said he'll give me the complete drawings, the whole of the plans.'

'What's your idea, then?'

Bernard said: 'All I'll say at this stage is this: You still want to get back at the Bergs. Well, this is where it starts, and you'd better begin fishing those gold ingots out, because you're going to need them soon.'

'OK, yankee.'

They trudged slowly towards the van, watching the silhouette of Florence Berg on her way back into town. Neither of them spoke but they were both studying the woman whose downfall they now planned.

As the van drew up alongside, Albertas politely asked her if they could give her a lift. She said that was very kind of them, and she *was* feeling rather tired.

The three of them were squashed up in the cab and Florence asked if this 'fine young man' was the same Bernard Kovalic she had known as a lad. And Albertas said it was the very same boy, and he was at Harvard now. That was absolutely marvellous, congratulations Monsieur Kovalic, she said.

She clambered down awkwardly outside *La Dépêche* and thanked them profusely with a cheery smile.

The two men were smiling too as they watched her mounting the steps. They admired her legs for a moment and then drove off.

Feeling more dead than alive, she ambled into her office to find Jean-Jacques there with Melchior, Maryse, Edelman, Favrot and Travers.

'Oh, hullo,' she said, dispirited. 'What's going on?'

'Travers has found the young woman, Sofia Leriche,' Jean-Jacques told her dully. 'We're handing her to you on a plate.'

For an instant, Florence could not have cared less if he'd found the Queen of Sheba. She only knew that she was glad to see

269

Travers again, more thankful than she had ever been throughout this whole nightmare series of events.

She smiled weakly and said: 'How did you manage it?'

'It took about thirty phone calls,' he said. 'I hoped the hoeing bloke was right, so I aimed for Paris thinking that only the posh restaurants and hotels actually had wine waiters. So I went through the lists and ticked them off. Then I started phoning. Eventually, after about thirty calls, I got to Bagration's where they said she was employed. I told them I was from Gault-Millau.'

'Brilliant,' Florence exclaimed.

'I must say I agree with you. Anyhow they got Sofia Leriche on the line and I said I was doing an inquiry into wine waiters. I took the next train up and collected here after work. I took her to some bar where she said she usually had a herb tea of all things, to help her sleep. I kept on about the inquiry and she wanted to know how she had been chosen. I said I chose her myself because she had once served me at La Gentilhommière in Chateauvallon. Needless to say, that wiped the smile off her face, and she said I was from the police. I had to grab her wrist to stop her running out there and then. I got her to sit down quietly again and explained who I was and mentioned the paper, told her I wanted to help her but said that she must explain why she had left the place in a hurry and what she saw at La Gentilhommière on the night of Quentin's death.'

Travers moved over and perched himself on the front edge of Florence's desk: 'She denied everything, wondered what I was talking about. All of which I had expected. I told her what she already knew: that she was frightened out of her wits, which was why she couldn't sleep. Anyhow, I extracted the whole story. Well, after midnight that night, there were a few stragglers when she ended her shift. She paid a visit to the cellar because there was a new boiler and she wanted to check the temperature. Sofia Leriche was coming up the stairs again and had turned out the light when there was a sudden flash of light through a small cellar window. The light went out and then came on again about three seconds later. Sofia went back down again and crept over to the small window. She got onto a stepladder and looked out, to see a car's headlights flashing on and off. Then a man went past the window heading for the car, and he bent down to talk to the driver. After that the man went over to his own car. Sofia recognized him; it was Quentin. Then, she said, the two cars drove off.'

Everyone in the office shifted position and Travers added: 'That was to be Quentin's last journey. Sofia told me she felt she had to get away, and that nothing would have made her stay after that.'

Jean-Jacques said: 'Whom was she afraid of?'

'Everybody, but most of all the police.'

Maryse interjected: 'The police! Why them?'

Travers nodded knowingly: 'Simply because when the police called at La Gentilhommière Nicolo questioned her.'

'And she told him nothing,' Florence suggested.

'On the contrary, she told him everything I've just told you. I repeat, everything! But Nicolo just looked at her, 'in a funny way' she said, and didn't follow it up. Now just imagine what went on in her mind. She obviously concluded that she had said too much, and that after Quentin it might be her turn . . .'

Travers looked straight at Florence: 'Mademoiselle Leriche has authorized us to tell her story in full.'

Florence's face lit up: 'Tomorrow. The whole lot. This'll be some front page! You realize what this means? Either Nicolo's whole argument collapses because he has ignored a key witness, or else he's for it because he's tried to hush the whole thing up.'

Jean-Jacques sprang into life: 'I object! If this appears I quit *La Dépêche* forthwith. This Leriche woman has invented the entire story, and even if it's true nobody is going to take it seriously, if only because there's no way of proving that it was Quentin she really saw that night.'

'She says that it was Quentin, and who can prove the opposite?' Florence cried. 'Whatever way you look at it, Nicolo's conduct looks highly suspicious to say the least. Even the most unlikely witness must be taken into account, that's the law.'

Jean-Jacques moved over to the door and turned the handle: 'I hereby tender my resignation.'

'Using the profession's conscience clause?' his sister demanded. 'It's your conscience against the facts.'

But Jean-Jacques was already in the corridor, and Maryse threw back at her: 'I'm using that clause too, Madame. Facts you say? You are using a suspect witness as a weapon for your own purposes, in order to satisfy a personal grudge and clear yourself of responsibility for Quentin's death.'

Florence replied: '*Ma chéri*, if Nicolo's hands are clean, let him prove it.' But Maryse too was already out of the office. The door slammed to.

She surveyed Travers, Melchior, Edelman and Favrot. Travers

would back her, but what of the others?

'Melchior?' she said. 'I wouldn't hold it against you.'

He gave a shy smile: 'But I would hold it against you if you gave up now. So would Monsieur Antonin your father.'

During this exchange Favrot and Edelman had mumbled something between them, and it was Edelman who said: 'Madame, Favrot and your humble servant have questioned their consciences and discover to their horror that they don't have any. We're with you.'

They took the opportunity to make their exit, and she heard them chattering outside: 'This may be the craziest thing yet, but we're even crazier.'

It was quiet then, and Travers went to her. Gratefully she sank into his arms. 'This time it's double or quits,' she said.

Travers fondled her hair: 'Let's face it, Florence, we've neither of us been so shit-scared in our lives.' When they drew apart he added: 'Boss, if we have any adrenalin left when this lot's over, I think we'll end up loving each other for ever.'

'Exactly, Monsieur Travers. And if you would kindly lock me in your arms again I can honestly say my happiness is complete.'

'Honestly? I believe there's one thing missing. Your daughter should be here with us.'

She sighed: 'We can't have everything, I suppose. Oh Trav, why did you mention it? Why now?'

'I had no choice,' he said, grinning broadly. 'She was on the phone just before you walked in here.'

'Alexandra?'

He nodded: 'She's coming over, she's flying over, she's due here Friday. In person, yankee accent and all.'

Florence pursed her lips: Alexandra! Alexandra!' She was laughing through misty eyes.

Travers said: 'There's another new development. I have a story that's been hanging around far too long, and I'd like to go ahead – with your permission, of course, Madame Berg. It's about this handsome newshound falling in love with his boss, who's a sort of Valkyrie and . . .'

Florence put a finger on his lips and with her other arm scooped up her coat from across the desk: 'You can go ahead, Monsieur Travers, provided . . .'

'Provided?'

'Provided you're giving me an exclusive!'

NEW MONEY

Chapter One

In the absence of the Editor, it was Florence Berg herself who gave the nod.

The old rotary at *La Dépêche*—variously known as the Machine, the Grid Iron or the Bloodstained Whore of a Bitch depending on who was actually addressing it—whispered, then hummed, then throbbed and howled into the bigger than usual print run. Few people in Chateauvallon and a wide area around would have had it otherwise, least of all the smaller rival *L'Eveil* which was also picking up useful circulation in the battle between two daily papers.

La Dépêche Republicaine was Chateauvallon's food for thought, the springboard for its activities, perhaps even its heart and soul. It was as important to the adult population as the school where they had learned to read and write, as the Prefecture, the high street, their job, possibly their wife or husband.

Founded more than half a century earlier by the late Antonin Berg, the town's most powerful citizen, the paper had gained a new lease of life under his daughter Florence. It was a livelier paper, carried more punch, was altogether more dauntless in its handling of news and analysis.

When from the depths of his bed at La Commanderie the old man had ranted and pleaded for her to take over from him, she had hesitated. And in the end she had insulted him to his face and given in, sacrificing her thriving law business out of loyalty and according him his last great joy and satisfaction. She also accepted because she was a winner by nature, liked the cut and thrust of opinion-forming, was hungry for the power that comes with proprietorship of a provincial daily possessing more than average clout.

Florence was tall, well put together and had a good head of chestnut hair. She also revealed the kind of tenacity needed to guide the paper through a difficult period that began with the murder of one of its own reporters, Paul Bossis, and had been followed by the death in mysterious circumstances of Mayor Georges Quentin, formerly Secretary of State for Defence. Both occurrences were good for sales but bad for Florence: Bossis happened to be related to Florence and had shacked up with a Kovalic girl, and Quentin happened to be her own ex-lover.

In the maelstrom of decision-making that befell her between these events, Florence Berg discovered that the only person she could really lean on was Travers, a reporter with a built-in stabilizer who had been on the paper for ten years. There existed between them a firm liking and mutual respect. In the heat of battle they had kissed and hugged more than once, but they had taken it no further and neither of them knew exactly why. Their relationship remained complex and ambiguous.

On this particular night as the machine began converting newsprint into a new issue with a life of its own, Florence reflected on the noisy editorial conference that evening. She had decided to go ahead with Travers's exposure of slapdash police work on the Quentin case. His bylined report pointed strongly to murder rather than the suicide conclusion the SRPJ criminal police had opted for somewhat hastily.

The Editor, Florence's younger brother Jean-Jacques, had fought her all the way. A good scoop was all very well, so was investigative journalism, but Travers had unsheathed a two-edged sword and was risking the paper's future quite unnecessarily. Florence held firm and Jean-Jacques resigned there and then, along with his secretary Maryse. The animosity between brother and sister had come to a head when old Antonin ordered her to step into his shoes; Jean-Jacques was a career journalist and held that he was the natural choice for successor. As to Maryse, she had been Travers's girlfriend for a while and now seethed over his complicity with the high and mighty *patronne*. When the defectors stepped out into the corridor, Florence Berg found herself with just four men on the editorial side whom she could count on: Deputy Editor Melchior, Travers the paper's linchpin, and two other runabouts called Favrot and Edelman.

The five of them watched the first closely staggered copies inch out along the output conveyor. A man in blue overalls crumpled up the first five or so copies and then let Travers pick out two of the good ones. Together they scowled at the banner headline SUICIDE OR MURDER? and the sub-head POLICE HIDE FACTS, WITNESS CLAIMS. Nobody spoke and Florence took a deep breath. She turned to Melchior, still wondering whether he had sided with her out of loyalty to her father, herself, the paper or what. She noticed that Melchior's face was the colour of putty and now realized he was opening and closing his mouth like an old carp's.

'Well all right, Melchior,' she said. 'We're out on a limb but there's no need to . . .'

She got no further. Melchior seemed to inflate, his head fell back and he began toppling backwards. Travers caught him.

'Get a chair,' he yelled above the thrum of the press, now moving at full speed.

Favrot shoved an ink-stained wooden chair under the seat of Melchior's pants and held it there: 'Don't worry, Madame, he always jerks like that, it's one of his turns. Had one last year and got over it right as rain.'

Florence ordered: 'Get an ambulance all the same. Lay him flat.' She carried the weight of his head while Favrot and Edelman eased him down onto the print room's concrete floor.

'They'll be here at once,' Travers cried, returning from the phone. 'You don't look too well yourself, Madame. Been overdoing things maybe.'

'Could be.'

'Look, the run's started, let me take you home.'

'But what about . . .?'

'He'll pull through,' Edelman said tossing his head.

'Coming round already by the look of him.'

Travers took Florence's wrist and led her out. Weakly she attempted to shake him off: 'I must stay.'

'No Florence. I'm giving the orders this time!'

For weeks they had been performing a nuptial dance around each other, eyeing their every meaning, enduring their physical attraction. They knew full well that they were poised for the stage beyond the jokey professional partnership they had worked up since Florence had taken the paper in hand.

But they held back. After all, she was his boss and paid him wages, and in any case she was not sure she wanted to join the list of his conquests. There was Catherine Kovalic too, the girl from the immigrant clan that hated the Bergs' guts; she had lived with the slain newsman Paul Bossis whose baby she had had in 'widowhood'. Travers, Bossis's closest friend, had more or less taken Catherine in charge, taking her out for a meal quite often whereas Florence would have preferred this to be not quite so often.

Florence Berg made no objection or observation when he stopped the car outside his own apartment block, led her inside and up to his bachelor pad. She could not have raised the energy to argue it out in her own mind. The tension of the past weeks had been too much for both of them, and they knew that their moment had arrived. Travers had the situation sized up perfectly, even if *she* felt lost. He stood her next to his bed and peeled off her clothes reverently. Expertly too, and she was glad of that, sighing when he kissed her hand and slowly lowered the ultimate flared satin garment past her thighs and knees, helping her to step out of it. He laid her between his sheets and joined her within seconds. Languidly she consented to his caresses; watched him through her eyelashes when he kissed and bit her nipples so that they jutted out and she felt the initial spasm of desire; allowed him to part and bend her legs; finally moaned ethereally when he entered her and brought her to a diffused climax, taking his pleasure at the very instant her teeth cut into his shoulder.

She released a soft groan that came from the beginning of time and said: 'Oh Trav, the exquisite *relief*! You're absolutely wonderful. I've lived like a nun since Quentin and I broke up. I needed you, in exactly that way and no other.'

He lay down beside her, smiling fondly, and she crawled over him, smothering him with kisses and giggling. They slept in that position.

Though not for long. At 2.00 a.m. she stirred, jerked herself alert and declared: 'Good, I'm going home now.'

'That's what you think! You know, if I were a susceptible fellow I'd . . .'

She grabbed his ears and gave him a long kiss with lips still swollen from arousal: 'No you wouldn't, not to me. I'm sorry Trav. I want you to sleep well and set the alarm for 6 a.m., you're off to Paris first thing.'

'Orders is orders,' he said gruffly, resentful at her shrugging off what was after all a moment when the world had changed for both of them. Or might have.

'I want you to find out everything that happened to Quentin during his last year as Minister of Defence.'

'You mean you don't know?'

'We split up before he resigned.'

'Not an easy assignment, stirring up your lover's private life.'

'That's about it. See what you can dig out.'

Travers squinted at her: 'Could be embarrassing for you, and risky for me.'

'We're tough enough to take the risk, both of us,' she said fixing her skirt. She scooped up her overcoat and kissed him again.

Travers caught hold of the hem: 'I may sound naïve, but I'd just like to know whether my delectable *patronne* is quite sure she should have gone ahead with that piece I wrote.'

She held his gaze: 'I was never sure at any instant.'

'Then why the devil? Where's the logic?'

She chuckled: 'And sleeping with you, is that logical?

279

Who said I was logical? Bye-bye handsome, have a good trip.'

And she skipped out leaving him in the nude, contemplating the shrivelled remnant of his brief passion.

Before leaving for Paris, Travers looked in at the close of a town council meeting, which Favrot had been covering. His colleague filled him in, and stressed that Bernard Kovalic had been formally invited to attend the meeting.

The Kovalic clan, tribe or gang (according to sentiment) had arrived at the end of World War II and set up at an old farm on the edge of Chateauvallon. They came from Yugoslavia, were Orthodox in their religion but unorthodox in the way they had risen from sheer poverty to a wealth that was starting to rival that of the Bergs. The influence their money commanded bore no similarity to the abject cringing they had to go through in the early days, doing any work they could get hold of, mostly jobs few Frenchmen would deign to look at. It was said that when old man Gregor Kovalic asked Antonin Berg if he would like him to sweep up the leaves in the drive at La Commanderie, Antonin told him: 'Your smell is too overpowering, Gregor, I couldn't enjoy my roses any more.'

The story served to illustrate their immigrant status, but they stuck it out and bought a garbage truck which they operated on a new estate on the town's edge under contract to the council. Several trucks later they were emptying the dustbins for the whole of Chateauvallon, a concession the Kovalics enjoy to this day. They diversified into furniture removals and other haulage, using Yugoslav drivers, yet still living in the old farm which they bought cheap due to its tumbledown condition. It was their base today, and it was correctly assumed that, despite the muck and the crates and the rubbish and the poultry, they had stacked a tidy sum away over the past three decades or so. The Kovalics kept to themselves, disclosed nothing, had extensive business interests and kept their women virtually as slaves.

Hence the significance of Bernard Kovalic's presence at

the meeting. And what he had to say was lifting the tops off the heads of the councillors. His young steely eyes flashed from one listener to another as he outlined a building project of colossal proportions for Chateauvallon. And he did it in impeccable French with a slight American accent, for Bernard had been called back from Harvard by the clan. That was some months previously.

Bernard had been discreet so far and people really knew very little about him. Through Catherine, who had broken off with the family when she started living with Paul Bossis, Travers was one of the few in the town to know that he was nephew to Albertas, Catherine's father and *de facto* head of the clan.

'What's he pitching for?' Travers whispered.

Favrot told him: 'He wants to reactivate that old scheme for damming the Loire. He's already bought the land, and is proposing to clear it using Albertas's trucks. Then he'll build on it. He's got the financing buttoned up, and Jerome's eating out of his hand. Now that he's taken over from Quentin as mayor, he hopes the big project will get him re-elected.'

'Bernard's going to make us all rich, starting with Jerome and the Kovalics, I see.'

'They've got a name for it already: the Aqua Viva Project.'

'Let's hope we don't drown first. Your turn for a front page splash this time, old boy. Be seeing you.'

Travers turned to leave the press bench, and saw Maryse two yards away: '*Salut* Maryse, how are you making out? Plenty of free-lance work?'

She poked her nose in the air: 'Huh, I wouldn't ask you for any.' She relented. 'I could change my mind though. I hear they're going to make you the Editor.'

'Until Melchior's back in harness, that's all. He's in better shape already.'

'That must break your heart. *Salut!*'

Nasty with it, Travers said to himself, shrugging her off and giving Favrot a wink. Then he caught sight of Lorieux, whom he'd worked with years ago in Paris. Lorieux was one of Boulard's men and Boulard the press magnate was hoping for a quick killing as Florence got into financial difficulty with *La Dépêche*. Travers felt the enemies closing in on him, former colleagues who had become his adversaries because they were Florence's foes. What was Lorieux doing in Chateauvallon? Travers hurried out, avoiding combat.

Now he was in the main hall watching Jerome's hand under Bernard Kovalic's elbow as they emerged all smiles. On the steps outside the two men pumped hands as only those can who have pulled off a big deal.

Those next to them heard the mayor say: 'You'll have to excuse me, Kovalic, I should have liked lunch, but I've been invited by Madame Quentin, and I can't possibly let her down after that dreadful article in *La Dépêche* this morning. They must have gone mad. Wicked, absolutely wicked!'

Bernard nodded agreement, but made no comment. The Bergs had been the number one target for the Kovalics for too long, and the clan had its own ideas on what was or was not wicked.

'Another time then, *Monsieur Le Maire*,' he said with a polite tilt of his head.

It was Jerome who had invited himself for lunch with Maud Quentin, after he had read the Berg 'rag' and in the wake of a phone call from Paris. The good lady had managed to produce sweetbread of veal, which she had cooked herself time and again over the years because her husband had loved it, praising her on every occasion that it appeared on the table. Georges was sparing with his compliments and this was one way she could collect a few.

Madame Quentin had much to be sad about. It was not so much Quentin's ten-year liaison with Florence that had made her existence a misery, but his passion for political advancement. Their marriage had held together but only just, and she had accepted the situation, supposed that it would never change. Maud had not held it against Florence, as it was in the nature of things for husbands to wander, although they could hardly be called friends. On seeing *La Dépêche* that day Madame Quentin's reaction had been prudent; she believed she knew how Florence's mind worked, and suspected there might be something in the murder theory.

'You see, Maud,' Jerome was saying, 'Kovalic's project means jobs for people, and for the future it means visitors, holidaymakers. Georges would have gone along with it, I'm sure . . .'

'Gone along?' she said in a dream.

'Kovalic's plan!'

Maud smiled wanly: 'Oh do forgive me, I was thinking about something.'

Jerome tapped her hand: 'I do understand, dear friend, it's as awful for you as ever, naturally.'

'Oh it's not Quentin being gone, it's that article that worries me.'

The mayor sat upright and declaimed: 'How right you are. That woman is merciless. Led Georges a dog's life, and now produces this rubbish . . .'

'Are you so sure it's rubbish? I read it closely, and the questions are good ones. They're the kind I keep asking myself. Florence knew Georges as well as I did, let's face it, and she can't see Georges doing away with himself. Nor can I, to be frank. I cannot bring myself to believe he committed suicide!'

Jerome threw his head back: 'Oh come now, you can't really subscribe to that nonsense. You'll simply add to your own torment, Maud.'

'I'm not subscribing to either theory. It is a matter of conviction, I'm haunted by the idea that my husband was murdered.'

'You have no right!'

'Well thank you!' He had kindled her ire.

'Florence is flying a kite! Her conjectures are false, utterly wrong! You'll see, I will prove it to you in due course, and I'll show *La Dépêche* what it means to pander to the public's basest instincts. Trust me. Maud!'

Madame Quentin delicately scooped up a forkful: 'As

you wish, Adrien. I'd rather not go on about it.'

When it came to trust, Jerome had never given her much assurance, even when he was Quentin's chief aide, working for him with what she had to admit was a conscientious loyalty. It was an intuitive feeling and she saw no reason to change her belief now.

As to Jerome, he felt he had succeeded in convincing her, at least for the moment. Adrien Jerome was wily and intelligent. But psychology was not his strong point.

It was otherwise with Boulard, who had built up his empire without illusions as to the public and the people he dealt with or against. It was his view that everyone, man or woman, could be relied on to tick with the same basic mechanisms: glory, vanity, jealousy, rarely love. His own motivations were money and power, that was clear to himself and everyone else. But his deepest satisfaction stemmed from the way he made his puppets jump, obliged them to perform exactly as he intended from the moment he began attaching the strings to them.

His chief victim at this time was Florence Berg, but she was refusing to go through the motions he wanted. He was sure he had her within his grasp when the tax people moved in on her with the estate duty after old Berg's death. He had never imagined she would sacrifice all she had, selling out her law business and the rest to keep control of the Berg paper. He hated her for that, for making a fool of him, and he had decided on a fresh approach, meaning to wear her down. He had sent Lorieux in to get the facts he needed and promptly told Jerome to see Madame Quentin, knowing that it was more than his life was worth for Jerome to disobey.

'Jerome then shook hands with Kovalic and went off for lunch at the widow's,' Lorieux was informing Boulard back in Paris. 'I didn't find out what they said.'

Boulard rapped: 'You couldn't be expected to. But I know. He did exactly the opposite of what I asked. But Jerome's a valuable man. He's on the spot, he's the mayor and he's got the morals of a tom cat. The trouble is he's a

284

political animal, with an electorate he wants to hold on to, and unfortunately he wants to be loved like the rest of his kind. I instructed him to convince the widow her old man was murdered. You can see why of course.'

Lorieux gave a smirk: 'Of course, Monsieur, I think I get your point.'

'Huh, well I'll bet my boots he did exactly the contrary, couldn't bear to see the effect on her, simply had to console her and win her gratitude. Mind you, Lorieux, he may have played into my hands without realizing it.'

His underling twitched his head.

Boulard went on: 'Also working for me is the meathead to beat all meatheads, Jean-Jacques Berg. I phoned him at the crack of dawn and he came running, along with his wife who rejoices in the name of Marie-Lou and controls him at the top of her voice. She's delighted she got him to accept my proposition and since 2.00 p.m. precisely today he is the Managing Editor of *L'Eveil de la Loire*. Mind you Lorieux, he detests that sister of his and prays every night against her I'm sure, but he does have a sense of family— blood's thicker than water and all that codswallop. He may let us down in the end, but meanwhile he can be trusted to make life hell for Florence Berg.'

The press baron sat musing like an old warthog, and Lorieux dared to suggest: 'There's this Kovalic fellow I told you about, Monsieur.'

Boulard sniffed: 'Too young, my friend, too young. Kovalic, Kovalic? I know that name. Wasn't there some skulduggery about them a few years back? Tinpot waste merchants, aren't they?'

'That's right but the case was dismissed.'

'So we've got nothing on Bernard Kovalic and the rest of them. You'd better hurry back to Chateauvallon chop-chop. See the old man and the lad. See what they're really made of. You'd be surprised how useful the unlikeliest people can prove to be.'

Lorieux was back in Chateauvallon that same evening at Les Messageries hotel.

*

285

Travers was in Paris, starting his spadework at the Defence Ministry itself. Quentin had resigned well before his death and his personal documents must have been shifted ages ago by himself or his successor. But Travers argued that you had to start somewhere, an approach that usually produced at least one good lead.

At mid-morning he put in a call to Florence: 'That you *patronne*? It's me, anyone with you? Good. I'm on to someone, Quentin's secretary who's still there, and I wish you were here.'

She laughed: 'You didn't get far with *her*! Am I right?'

'So right. I tried my inimitable charm and found her impregnable. I even mentioned your name to see the reaction. Doesn't even know you.'

'You must be getting old.'

'Stop that, and listen. The secretary has her own secretary, and this one's about a metre tall and as cute as a mouse. On my way out she followed me, and told me she had some information I might be interested in.'

'Aha!'

'Well this little mouse had a special kind of job with Quentin. She used to invent official meetings for him while he got up to his tricks, as she called them.'

'Get on with it darling. What tricks?'

'She'll tell all for five thousand francs, otherwise the mouse stays in the cheese, or vice versa.'

Florence said levelly: 'I told you, money's no object, don't be a fool.'

'All right, all right! You coming up tomorrow?'

'I wouldn't dream of not meeting my own daughter!'

Travers stared into the middle distance, looking out from the phone-box. Florence had last seen Alexandra five years previously, and this was to be a great moment in Florence's life. At the age of thirteen Alexandra had chosen to live with her father in the United States, and her mother had never got over it. It had given her the wistful look that added an element of fragility to an otherwise intrepid demeanour.

'Don't you want to see me a wee bit too? A fellow gets

lonely in the big city.'

'Of course, you idiot. I love you and I'm mellowing as the minutes go by. I can't wait to see what you've got from the mouse too.'

The call saddened Travers. Sure, she had said she loved him, but her daughter and the Quentin mystery took precedence. He snorted and thought a moment about role-reversal; was this how women became possessive in the days before feminism? One thing was certain, falling in love with Florence Berg was no bed of roses.

He strode over to the bar close by, and rejoined the slightly built girl he had described to Florence. She even had mousey hair, he saw.

'It's fixed; five thousand,' he told her. 'I'm listening.'

They chose a remote table and ordered two more coffees.

'His last mistress was called Arlette,' she said. 'Spent a lot of time with her, she had a studio in the rebuilt district around Rue de Flandre. They were together for eight months, give or take a day or two, until he died. He was genuinely fond of her and trusted her. I know this by the way he used to come back looking years younger. He used to take a file with him sometimes when he went to her.' Travers lifted an eyebrow. 'Yes, a file, and I'm sure that if you want to find out anything, Arlette's your next call. I'll give you the address, but be smart, don't say a word about me or the ministry. She'd only clamp up.'

'My middle name's discretion,' he assured her.

And hers was jealousy, he fancied.

In the Concorde beginning its approach procedure to Roissy-Charles De Gaulle Airport, Alexandra Wilson had her eyes shut and was taking deep breaths.

Attractive she certainly was at eighteen years of age, and had been well able to take care of herself since her father's death. But at this forbidding moment as she prepared to meet her mother she was quivering, and might well have snapped the head off the first person who addressed her. She was sorry she had decided to fly supersonic, for three

287

and a half hours was far too short a time between the glittering universe she had known with her father and the tense world of her mother. Her innards would have adapted better on a slower flight instead of bubbling as they were now.

She had loved her father to distraction. He was a heavy drinker and harebrained in many ways, but he had always been patient and devoted to her. Several times he had said that his would be a short life but a gay one, and it had hurt her every time. She believed everything he said, and knew he was not kidding. She had been forced to fend for herself before time, and it was still proving too much for her. Her confident air had a *tremolo* to it, and when her mother sent the telegram reading 'If you are lonely, don't forget me' she was surprised to find how relieved she felt and had answered at once.

Ever since she had decided to stay in the States at the end of her second summer there, they had regularly written to each other. They were bright, kind letters but devoid of sentiment. Clearly Florence had played it offhandedly from the outset, forcing the humour no doubt, although she could not be sure. Alexandra had matched her style, as much as anything to dissimulate the guilt that kept nagging at her. Now she had taken the plunge and was grateful to Florence for wanting her over in France. Even so, mothers came in all versions and Alexandra was frankly more apprehensive as the minutes passed. What kind of woman was she, would she let bygones be bygones, would she pounce on her like some dotty old hen?

The truth was that she had deliberately fled the overbearing influence of her Berg family five years earlier, more specially the ubiquitous patriarchal weight of Antonin Berg. If anyone had told Florence that she had been over-strict with Alexandra while yielding to the old man's authority on every occasion, she would have protested vehemently. But that is exactly how Alexandra saw things at the time, and she yearned for the easygoing way of life her dad had slipped into. Indeed, he had more than once confided to her that it was the Berg side of Florence's character that had ultimately been the cause of the divorce.

And now, as she feigned sleep, the girl knew she wanted to see her mother, to fling herself wet-eyed into her arms. Yet at the same time her jaw firmed with the resolve that she would never, ever, buckle under to the Bergs. Old Antonin was dead, and she would never again have to submit terrified to his coldness and sudden flights of temper. She had received the invitation to the funeral too late and was glad; even in his coffin he would have poisoned the atmosphere for her. Jean-Jacques's son Michel, her cousin, had written to her often with a kind of ongoing story of the Bergs' existence, and as far as she could gather the air at Chateauvallon was still full of toxins. People had been killed, the mayor had shot himself through the head, the air was rank with conspiracy. Then again, her uncle Armand had been elected to the Assemblée Nationale, beating mayor Quentin. Her mother had taken over the paper and was stirring up all manner of scandal. Alexandra hoped to God she had not taken over grandfather Antonin's bloody-minded character too. The girl would have loved to clear that up in a heart-to-heart talk over the next few days. But would it be possible? Maybe they would just hate each other! She tried hopelessly to imagine what she would be like, standing there waiting with a big smile and a baggage trolley.

But Florence was not there waiting. Alexandra collected her luggage from the rubber conveyor belt and had to find her own trolley. As she emerged from Customs she knew at once that her mother had not come. The disappointment formed a huge lump somewhere inside her, and she erected an instant shield of armour around herself. Grimfaced and on the brink of tears she began wheeling the trolley and looking at the direction signs.

Then a man came up to her: 'Good afternoon. Alexandra Wilson?'

'That's right,' she said in French.

'My name's Travers, I work at *La Dépêche*. We spoke over the phone when you called the office the other day.'

'Glad to meet you.'

'Your mother is extremely sorry, she's on her way, but something held her up. Fortunately I was in Paris on a job and she was able to contact me. Asked me to collect you.'

'Collect me! Really, Monsieur Travers?'

'I'll take you into Paris with your things, we can have a drink, and hey presto your mother will meet us.'

'Don't bother. I'm not a kid any more, I don't need my mother to work out my schedule thanks!'

Travers did not flinch, but made to take over her trolley: 'Um, she's reserved rooms, a suite, in a comfortable hotel and there'll be just the two of you. She'd be terribly disappointed.'

'Well why don't you take her out and show her the bright lights—Gay Paree and all that!'

Travers smiled broadly: 'Oh come now, you don't really mean . . .'

'All this is a lot of fuss about nothing. Your compassion for me is swirling around like—like some cheap after-shave lotion. And I'd be grateful if you'd inform my mother!'

'B-but where will you go?'

'Oh don't worry about that. I'll see her at Chateauvallon in a day or two. Tell her not to put herself out too much!'

Alexandra grabbed the trolley and charged off with it to a car hire booth. Travers left her to it.

An hour later Travers sat perched on a stool in the Hotel Intercontinental playing with a concoction five fingers high with a slice of lemon stuck on the rim of the glass. He felt like an old uncle who had lost a child in his charge.

He was instantly alert when Florence swung through the door he was watching and bore down upon him.

'Alexandra! Something's happened to her! She wasn't on the plane! She's had an accident!'

He waved her down: 'She was on the plane and she's all right.'

'Well—where is she?'

'My dearest Florence, my love. Sit down, tell the man what you're drinking and calm down. You make me nervous.'

She plumped down on a stool he pulled up for her, white-faced and pinched.

'Everything's all *right*,' he said blandly. 'She arrived on time but was kind of tense, and decided she'd prefer to hire a car, which is even now, at this very moment in time, almost certainly half-way to Chateauvallon.'

'She was mad I wasn't there, that's it.'

'On the contrary, she looked pretty cool to me. A lovely girl, you can be proud of her. She simply wanted to do it her way and I gathered she doesn't go too much for the big embrace, that's all.'

Florence took a gulp at the drink the barman had just put down: 'You mean she's gone off on her own to Chateau-vallon!'

'That's as I understand it.'

'I'm going after her right away.' She thrust the glass back on the counter.

'Thank you *patronne*.' She tossed her head at him and he added: 'You could say hullo if you've got the time.'

Florence relented: 'I'm sorry Trav. I'm like a wasp in a jam-jar. If you only knew what's been going on today. At La Commanderie they've been doing everything wrong. I had the blue room done out ready for her, and Gilbert and Mathilde decided she'd be better, more on her own, in the rooms Jean-Jacques and Marie-Lou had last year.'

'You should have had a vote on it.'

'Please darling. Mathilde has taken over since father died, thinks she's got some sort of mission in life, tries to tell everyone where they get off.'

Travers tilted his head: 'Why not let her have her own way, or wait till Alexandra makes her own decision?'

'Those rooms are dirty, and I don't want my daughter to feel we're poking her into something out of the Middle Ages.'

'So you cleaned it out and that's why you were late.'

Florence took her glass again: 'What *is* this anyhow?'

'Whisky, you ordered it.'

She giggled and squeezed his hand: 'It wasn't that, but something else. Armand turned up as I was leaving. He's got over his mood and has come up with something really big. Came specially to tell me, by train of all things. I pleaded with him to come back to Paris with me, and said we could talk in the car. But he said he couldn't cope with my tantrums. The cheek! He said he realized I was in a hurry to get to Alexandra, but that what he had to tell me was more important and concerned the whole future of *La Dépêche*. So I gave in and I was right. Oh Lord, I'll never forgive myself for not meeting her. I still feel dreadful. Why ever did she just clear off like that? Alexandra!'

'She said she'll see you in a couple of days at Chateauvallon. Keep calm, let it work itself out, it's the only way, believe me. Now what's this about Armand?'

Florence swallowed: 'It's about your article.'

'Is Armand for or against?'

'Neither, he says, although he says I'm wallowing in Quentin's death. Not his problem, he says, I'm a free agent and so on and so on.'

'Florence, sweetest, if you don't spill it quick I'm going to the men's room.'

'Well, he had dinner with some people yesterday and learned that some highly placed government chap has absolute proof on a private basis that Quentin really did shoot himself.'

'Did he convince you?'

'No. I said that kind of proof would have come out long ago. But according to Armand our lords and masters hoped the Opposition would go along with the murder theory, and would later have egg on its face when the official denial was issued. That's why it was held back, in reserve.'

Travers took a sip at his drink: 'But the Opposition didn't budge.'

'That's what my brother said, and he was delighted to see me out on my own with no backing of any kind.'

'Charming. And he believes it himself, the suicide proof?'

'Bluff. An attempt to make me climb down and agree it was suicide.'

'I think you're right, and I'll tell you why, even though Madame Florence Berg seems to have forgotten she gave me an assignment.'

Her face lit up: 'But of course. What have you found out?'

'The lady's called Arlette, and she was his bed-mate for the last eight months before he died. He left her a damn great envelope full of documents, which she has consigned to a safe place. Arlette is wetting her panties she's so scared, and convinced her studio's been given the once over. She wants to sell those documents, and to you only. She's in a hurry and suggests you meet up tonight or tomorrow morning. A phone call and she'll come running. You've reserved a suite, why not use it to good purpose?'

Florence became coy: 'To spend the night with you?'

'I'd be delighted,' Travers said urbanely. 'Business with pleasure, the key to happiness.'

La Commanderie seemed smaller than she remembered it, but Alexandra was impressed.

The car crunched to a halt outside the main door, and she waited a bit. There was no sign of life and she was curious, though not annoyed. From the letters she had received from her mother and Michel she knew that Florence and Gilbert Bossis were in permanent residence, that Julien the youngest of the Berg sons called in often with his family from the cottage and sawmill he ran on the edge of the grounds, that Jean-Jacques and Marie-Lou had gone back to their redecorated house and turned up occasionally, finally that Mathilde continued to serve the family as she had done for donkey's years.

Alexandra entered the ground floor and wandered about. She ran into the cook who said everyone was upstairs. On her way up she met Mathilde who raised her arms to heaven and cried: 'But you were not supposed to come today, what's happened, where is your mother?'

The girl told her and Mathilde went on: 'Well, Alexandra, you haven't changed a bit. As wild as ever.'

Old Gilbert Bossis joined them, wearing an old shooting outfit and a cap that was back to front. Trickles of sweat slid down into his eyes, but he was a picture of joy.

'Mathilde, you old fool, of course she's changed, it's

been five years! My word, but you're a beauty. I'm speechless.'

'Then don't say anything,' Alexandra cried with a laugh. 'Or rather, tell me why you're dressed up as a tramp.'

It was Mathilde who answered: 'Because we're cleaning the walls of your rooms. You've got here too soon. We thought you'd like your own little corner, and your mother said to clean it up, and we haven't got any men . . .'

'What a slave-driver you are, Mathilde, or were you always like that?' the girl exclaimed.

'She gets worse every year,' Gilbert chuckled. 'She should be wearing thigh boots and wielding a whip. We're all roped in: me, Julien and his wife. She phoned Michel to come but his mother wouldn't let him. She gave him another of her famous clouts around the ears.'

Alexandra was flabbergasted: 'You mean she hits him? They still beat up seventeen-year-old boys over here?'

'Marie-Lou does,' snorted Julien, arriving on the scene with his wife Thérèse.

Alexandra flung herself into her uncle's arms. He had always been one of her favourites, because he was the least Berg of the Bergs.

They drew apart and he whistled: 'What a peach you've become. I was worried about how you'd turn out, but you were worth waiting for!'

Thérèse hugged her tenderly, and told her: 'Don't worry about the Lamentations of Mathilde, darling. There's a room all ready for you, the blue one which your mother got ready herself. Jeannou will take your things up. Remember Jeannou, the lad who was here before you left? He's a kind boy.'

Alexandra rejoined: 'I'm sure he's very kind, but don't let him touch my bags. I want to spend tonight in a hotel.'

Mathilde tossed her head: 'Well there's a thing!'

'I've always wanted to stay at least one night in Les Messageries, ever since I was a little girl. It's a sort of dream thing.'

Everyone went quiet and eventually Gilbert said: 'You

294

know your mother was so upset at missing you.'

'She shouldn't have been.' The girl looked round at them. 'You *are* funny, all of you, so sentimental, so formal it's not true. Well so long, I'll get some kip.'

She danced out, blowing them kisses. The group stood nonplussed, convinced that she was really off only when the car was twenty yards down the drive.

Mathilde was the first to speak: 'What a strange girl! Do you think something's the matter with her? Perhaps she's angry with her mother.'

She turned to Julien who said: 'I don't know, really. I couldn't say.'

Late that evening Arlette arrived at the Intercontinental by taxi. She was a comely woman of about thirty with a mass of hair, fleshy lips and legs that commanded attention. She wore a suit with a neat fur collar and carried a large sling bag. Arlette was youthful, appetizing but lacking in distinction, Florence decided with bitter satisfaction. At sixty, Quentin would have enjoyed such a woman.

Florence offered her a seat and a drink.

'No thank you, Madame, you're very kind, I . . .' She left the sentence in mid-air indicating that she was too flustered to eat or drink.

'As you wish. We'd like to be on our own, thank you Travers.'

When he had closed the door to the suite, Arlette said: 'Thank you, Madame, it's best on our own. I didn't tell your journalist everything, because . . .'

'Yes?'

'There are some things only you should hear.'

'I quite understand,' Florence beamed, not quite able to keep the irritation out of her voice. 'This might take ages at this rate!'

Arlette took a deep breath: 'These papers. Well, Georges asked me to hand them over to you.'

'How funny. Couldn't he have done that himself?'

'I mean to say, I was to give them to you if anything happened to him, if you see what I mean.'

'Oh, so he thought something might happen to him then?'

Arlette was already lost: 'I don't know really. Men can be so peculiar, though he wasn't of course.'

Florence looked at Arlette and Arlette looked at Florence, who for the life of her could not imagine what she was supposed to say or think.

Suddenly Arlette blurted out: 'He did not do away with himself, Madame. I think the same as you do, it wasn't possible, not him. It couldn't be true!'

Florence frowned: 'You're saying that as if you were being asked it. Would you be prepared to say it to others?'

'Yes, yes I would, Madame.'

Florence got up and paced the room, then faced her visitor: 'I can't understand why you didn't let me have these papers right away.' Her tone had a hardness to it. Arlette buried her face in her hands. 'Why was that?'

The younger woman removed her hands and there were tears on her cheeks: 'When he died I was left without a sou and I . . .'

'In plain terms you wanted to make some money out of this stuff.'

'Yes,' she whispered.

'Have you opened the envelope?'

'Er—yes. I didn't tell your journalist that either.'

'I believe you said they were data sheets. That means information about people, is that it?'

'Yes.'

'Important people?'

'Yes.'

'Serious matters, compromising facts?'

'I don't know much about it, but that's what it seems like. They scare me, honest they do. They're hot, if you see what . . .'

'I'm sure they are. But is there a letter for me among them? An explanation perhaps?'

'No.'

'All right, I'll take your word for it. So these sheets are for me, since you said so. But I'll pay you, as you're rather short.'

Arlette grew indignant: 'You don't understand at all. I don't want money, I just want to get rid of the things, hand them over to you and forget all about them. Here they are, take them and I'll clear off.'

'But, since I'm willing to pay . . .'

Arlette remained silent, extracting the envelope from her bag. The seals were broken. She gave them to Florence, her eyes still moist.

The woman semed to wheeze: 'I haven't done many good turns in my life, but now's the chance . . .'

'But why ever?'

'For my own satisfaction, so that I can look myself in the face. And for him too. He was so . . .'

Florence cut her off. She was touched, but sickened too. This weeping figure had been Quentin's mistress, just as she had, and she found the link distasteful.

'Yes,' she intercepted levelly. 'But I also run a newspaper, and quite apart from money a newspaper can help people . . .'

'Help me!' Arlette said virulently, almost with hate. 'Help *me*? I'm just a call girl and I don't care a damn for your help. I can't see how you won't understand.'

'I understand, I'm sorry, I should not have mentioned it.' She accepted the envelope.

Arlette rose and buttoned her jacket, heading for the door: 'I'll find my own way out, no need to come down.'

Florence had no intention of doing so, and they parted company. Left on her own, she spread a few of the sheets out on the table. As she scanned them her expression changed from interest to astonishment, and finally to wonder. Hurriedly she put the documents back in the envelope, glanced at her watch and on an impulse flung on her topcoat. Florence then stuffed the envelope in her bag and quit the apartment in haste.

She drove to Armand's flat. When her brother had declined her offer of a lift back that morning he had said he would return by the last train. He had in fact entered the flat a mere thirty seconds before she rang the bell, and still had his coat on when he opened the door. Florence thrust the envelope into his hands at once.

'Read them,' she ordered peremptorily.

Armand pulled out a sheet, then two more, by which time his eyes had doubled in size.

'My God,' he breathed, 'you've got a goldmine here. Deliver this little lot to the Elysée and you'll come out with a fortune.' He snatched at some more and scanned them, wriggling out of his coat.

'See how everything ties up, people working hand in glove,' Florence chattered away.

'It's a best seller any day of the week. I never would have thought it of Quentin, never imagined he fished about in the sewers to this extent. They should have made him Minister for Public Conveniences!'

'That's enough of that.'

'But he couldn't have got all this together with nobody knowing. He could have been assassinated, one false step would have been enough. Are you absolutely sure this is his writing?'

'I was with him for ten years, it's his writing.'

Armand nodded in agreement: 'You should know, but if this was typewritten I'd say it was a forgery.'

'Of course, but it wasn't and it's not. I'm as shaken as you are.'

'Anyhow, it's a bombshell, and it's up to you whether you throw it about.'

'I haven't decided yet what I'll do. I'm thinking of your informant last evening at the dinner. I still think he was bluffing about the suicide, trying to intimidate me.'

'And I think exactly the opposite, even after reading this set of data sheets. Or rather, I might be a little less certain. Think this through properly, Florence. Your Arlette woman said this envelope was for you, but there's nothing written down to say it was.'

Florence's head went this way and that: 'I'm in—in . . .'

'The shit?'

He took her gently into his arms, like old times, and she began chuckling quietly.

'Well, you haven't been much help,' she said, 'but you found the right word!'

She repeated the word to Travers back at the Hotel Intercontinental where she found him grim-faced.

'Only a superior intelligence such as your dear brother possesses could have reached a conclusion of that complexity,' he growled with heavy sarcasm. 'You were right to rush to him first. A valuable man is our Armand.'

'Darling, please don't sulk. He *is* my brother.'

'You could have told me where you'd gone.'

Florence adopted a schoolgirl attitude, hands in front and twirling left and right: 'Sorry darling.'

'And don't call me darling. I'm just the poor birdbrain who stayed in here worrying where the hell you were and whether I should call the police.' He got up and moved towards the room intended for Alexandra.

'Travers!!!' Florence screamed.

'Goodnight *patronne*, pleasant dreams.'

The door slammed behind him and Florence collapsed sobbing on the settee.

She was still there curled up when he eased open his door three hours later. Travers stood expressionless, studying the streaks in her make-up and a run of mascara. Then a slow smile took over and he bent down on one knee and kissed her brow. She groaned her way out of sleep, looked around in a daze and put a hand out.

'André, kiss me.'

'What happened to Trav?' he grinned. She had never used his first name, nor did anyone else. Curiously he felt his own eyes smarting.

'Sorry I shot my mouth off, love.'

'Sorry I went off like that.' She gave a big smile. 'Isn't it marvellous, we had a lovers' quarrel—our first!'

They hugged each other, kissed wetly and long, their teeth hitting once or twice.

She added: 'It's a new day, and it's going to be wonderful and rub out yesterday which was . . '

'Don't tell me, I know just the word.'

Florence squirmed out of his grasp: 'We'll leave at once, I never want to come back here again.'

'Pity, it's a good hotel.' A pity too, he was thinking, that there was no follow-up. Right there—on the settee!

It was Florence who drove them to Chateauvallon, while Travers scrutinized the Quentin documents in the wan first light of the new day.

The previous day had been horrid for Florence, but Lorieux slept the sleep of the just. Everything had gone like clockwork. He had called on Albertas Kovalic and spoken about the trial years ago to get him nicely dangling, then he had soft-soaped him, affirming that he had been the only journlist at the time to have backed him up.

'You remember, Monsieur Kovalic? I wrote that your success story had cast a shadow over the big families in and around Chateauvallon, and that they wanted to get their own back.'

'Big families, you mean the Bergs?' Albertas had rasped.

'Naturally. And when the case was dismissed, you thanked me personally. Don't you recall that?'

Albertas made an effort and then said: 'I might have done, can't say. Anyway, what are you after this time? Want something from me? His tone was gruff and his eyes black with suspicion.

'Not at all,' Lorieux chuckled. 'Just passing through, thought I'd look you up.'

'Well you've seen me now. Let's have a little drink while you're here.'

The next day in Paris Boulard demanded: 'Then what happened?'

Lorieux continued: 'We drank some of his Yugo firewater and passed the time of day. He rambled on about his nephew Bernard and his projects, about the dam on the Loire. I saw the old chap too, Gregor, who spat on the ground every time the name Berg came up. Gregor hates their guts but Albertas envies them, and they both want the Kovalics to elbow them aside. Bernard's their secret weapon, as it were. A smart kiddie with plenty of class.

His triumph will be theirs, that's how they see it.'

Boulard nodded a couple of times: 'It squares. You've done a good job. Apart from me, the Kovalics are the Bergs' bitterest enemies, and you're in with them. Good lad. There's no stronger force in this world than hate coupled with envy. Believe me, I *know*! Thanks to you and your Yugos, Chateauvallon is ripe for the picking.'

'Nice of you to say so, Monsieur. Madame Berg won't know what hit her!'

'Don't count your chickens, Lorieux. She's got plenty of cards up her knickers yet. Now, put me a call in for young Kovalic. And fix a table at Lasserre's for tonight. Nine o'clock.'

For a moment Lorieux thought he was to be the boss's guest, but Boulard was soon telling Bernard: 'I'm having your mayor Adrien Jerome for dinner tonight at Lasserre's. I'd like you to join us. There'll be just the three of us. Can you make it?'

'Yes, Monsieur,' Lorieux heard Bernard reply like a shot.

He then told his employer: 'It'll be your usual table, Monsieur.'

'That'll be all for today, Lorieux, thank you. We'll leave Lady Berg in peace for today. Let her stew a bit, this needs handling right.'

Travers sat waiting for Florence in the car outside Les Messageries.

She came tumbling out: 'Alexandra's gone, twenty minutes ago with her cousin Michel. I'll drive, shift over. The car's gone but her things are still there. We've got to find her!'

'Are you sure she slept there?'

'Yes, she arrived direct from La Commanderie, and the time tallies with what Mathilde told us. She did not have dinner, but ate a huge breakfast: eggs and bacon, a whole basketful of croissants and half a jar of strawberry jam!'

'What was Michel doing there?'

'He arrived while she was eating. He kissed her on the

neck from behind and she practically socked him one. Didn't recognize him. Anyhow, that's what Solange told me; she was on duty. She realized then that the girl was my daughter, said she saw it just looking at her, and said she was as pretty as a picture. For pity's sake, I'm the only one who hasn't damn well seen her yet! At this rate I'll have to wait till next year.' Travers glanced cautiously at her as she added: 'If she wants to play hide and seek with me, that little madam, she's got it coming to her.' Travers let her go on. 'I'm fed up with her, that's what. Fed up to the back teeth with my goddam yankee daughter. Sick and tired, d'you hear!'

Her passenger held on for dear life as she hurled the car round a town bus. He was roaring with laughter.

'You know who you remind me of right now?'

'My father, I know. What do I care?'

'But he never really scared anyone.'

'That's what you think. Now pack it up, two lovers' quarrels within hours of each other is too much. Trav, André, I really do love you, and I'd show you if I had the time.'

He laughed again: 'That's your father all over—the stick and the carrot!'

'I'm not fooling,' she said throwing him a ravishing smile. 'I can't wait. First the office and then . . '

He raised an eyebrow and pulled out a sheet from the Quentin envelope.

'I don't want to nag, André, but you've been looking at those wretched things ever since we left Paris. You must know them by heart. What's your frank opinion? Be honest.'

'I'd feel better if we were on to something from another source too. His wife perhaps?'

'I doubt if she could corroborate anything.'

'There's someone else, someone closer to him than any woman, for our purposes.'

'Jerome, you mean. I'll call him from the office at once. Good idea.'

'Are you going to show him the envelope?'

'I don't think so, I can't say. I must find a pretext for meeting him.'

'Try your charm on him.'

'Stop picking on me.'

'Yes, *patronne*.'

'And stop calling me *patronne* when we're on our own.'

'No darling. I mean yes.'

They laughed, and Travers played the fool, pulling lots of funny faces.

Her call from the office produced the news that *Monsieur Le Maire* would not be back from Paris until tomorrow.

Replacing the receiver, Florence told Travers: 'Destiny has stepped in. Perhaps I ought to see Maud Quentin after all. We have another day in which to prepare for Jerome, and to decide what we think of Arlette's bombshell; she told me I was free to fire it off.'

Jerome was sitting with Arlette at a cafeteria table in the big round terminal building No. 1 at Roissy Airport.

'And she asked you to give evidence if necessary, and you said yes?'

'That is so, Monsieur.'

Adrien Jerome gave her his political smile: 'You did right, she was certainly delighted at that. But in fact this business won't get that far, and even if you are called to give evidence you won't be available of course.' He leaned back satisfied. 'I've never been to Caracas, they say it's a fine city. I'm sure you'll be very happy there. Imagine starting a whole new life, I envy you. Arlette, you're a highly attractive woman, so make sure you hook a really wealthy oil magnate.'

'God willing!'

'Check again to see if you've got your passport, and your ticket. Don't forget, the Sudameris bank, an account has been opened there for you. Good luck.'

'Thank you for everything, Monsieur.'

They rose, and Jerome congratulated her on her smart dress and coat. She looked sad and Jerome said he'd go as far as the boarding gate.

'I can find my way. You must have plenty to do.'

'Not at all, not at all. Gives me quite a lift to be seen with an elegant young woman, Mademoiselle.'

He made sure the Boeing lifted off the runway before he quit the airport. You could never be too sure, and he checked that he had seen the right plane take off.

Then he hurried to his car. If the traffic was not too bad, he would just about make it to Lasserre's by nine.

Chapter Two

Jerome was up early the next morning. Too many key facts had emerged at Lasserre's for him to be away from the town hall another day. Things were certainly hotting up now.

He took the appointment of a new managing-editor at *L'Eveil* with a fair degree of aplomb, even though it was Jean-Jacques Berg. Old Antonin Berg must be turning in his grave!

Jean-Jacques thought the same, with immense pleasure. He was getting his own back on the old sod and on his toffee-nosed sister.

He needed such high-flying thoughts to give him a boost when he called a staff meeting. The personnel consisted basically of four sad-eyed journalists who had little to look forward to but their retirement pension. They were working their time out and were glad of *L'Eveil* as a haven of peace and quiet until the day when they could put their feet up. They matched the paper, a run-down affair with about one-twentieth of the circulation *La Dépêche* commanded. True, between the two rounds in the last parliamentary by-election, the paper had run a hard-hitting story against Armand Berg. But he had beaten Quentin and the public's interest had been short-lived.

Never mind, Jean-Jacques was the boss now, with the title of managing-editor instead of just editor as he had been at *La Dépêche*. So Boulard was behind him. Jean-Jacques had at Boulard's request sold some of his shares in *La Dépêche* to a mysterious 'finance house', but that was none of the four journalists' business. His wife Marie-Lou had advised him to do what Boulard told him, the story went.

'Messieurs,' J-J Berg declared bouncily. 'I'm delighted to make your acquaintance, and I know we'll give the old paper a new look from now on. The first leader in a paper under new management is all-important, sets the tone for the future. So I propose to write it myself and deal with the ethics of the profession. As you are only too aware, for the last four issues *La Dépêche* has been running a campaign against the police, which means the government, asserting that they have been hiding facts about Georges Quentin's death. Obviously this can hardly be called ethical, simply coming out with serious allegations without bothering to back them up.'

'Quite right, *patron*,' one of the men interjected, and Jean-Jacques gave him a quick smile.

'That's my starting point. I'll demand to see the evidence, the real evidence behind the allegations. Naturally, and I'm sure you'll understand, I won't give it my byline but will just sign it *L'Eveil*. Unless you have any objection, because when all's said and done *L'Eveil* means all of us.'

'No objection,' the same man said. 'It'll be nice to have things clear-cut.' The other three murmured agreement.

'Well, let's leave it there for now. I'm sure we'll work splendidly together. Thank you.'

The four men sloped off, J-J Berg took his jacket off and hung it up, then planted himself in front of a typewriter. He inserted a sheet of clean white paper with a backing sheet and rubbed his hands together. He looked ceilingwards for about thirty seconds and began thumping away.

He failed to notice Maryse until she appeared over the top of the machine in a neat chocolate brown coat. Politely she waited for him to finish his sentence.

'Hullo,' she said.

J-J Berg scowled at her: 'You could have knocked. I'm very busy you know.'

'You must excuse me, but it's urgent. I'm out of a job, old chap, and it's because I backed you up against your sister. First, I deserve some consideration for that, and secondly I've just seen your star reporters nearly falling asleep at their desks. I think you need me to shake them up a bit, don't you?'

'In other words, I've got to take you on, or else? That's called blackmail, sweetie.'

'You had me cheap enough in bed for eight years. I'm due for a good turn.'

Berg shrugged. He was calculating how many weeks of nagging he would have to go through from Marie-Lou if he recruited Maryse. Thinking too that if it wasn't that it would be something else. In any case Maryse was a competent secretary.

'All right,' he said sounding almost friendly. 'You can use that locker over there.'

He resumed typing the leader.

At *La Dépêche*, Florence was going through the hoop. Favrot said he was worried: a paper could lose readers by teasing them for four days and then failing to produce a hard follow-up.

'People might say there's nothing in it, or that we've lost the courage of our convictions,' he said.

Florence said quietly: 'I've got your follow-up, Favrot. I have come into the possession of certain highly intriguing documents. But I need a little more time to analyse them. Just one more day, will that suit you?'

'In that case we can say that in the next issue . . .'

'We'll say nothing of the kind,' she retorted, leaving the editorial conference with heels clicking.

Edelman asked Travers: 'Is that right, Travers? What documents?'

'How should I know?'

'Liar!'

'She said to say nothing, so we say nothing. What sort of an army do you think this is?'

Acting editor or no, Travers was uncomfortable. It was Florence's pigeon and in any case he wasn't sure he liked the look of it after going through the data sheets once more. Six of the sheets named ministers who had taken bribes, 'it is alleged' (he noted mentally). The details were precise and damning, but he had urged Florence to let justice take its course. Hand them over to the authorities, he had told her. She had said that in law she was not obliged to do so, that the Quentin case had been disposed of officially. Florence had further objected that she wanted to be free to use the documents as she wished, in the interests of the paper.

Their relationship was as mixed up as ever, he reflected. She was due to spend that night with him at his place, but they were clashing professionally.

'Right,' he said. 'Let's look at the entertainments. Have we got enough for a whole page this time?'

Like Travers, Florence was thankful they made good lovers, were physically at ease and liked each other. Romance was all very well, but friendship and esteem were good too.

Work was not so good, however. She was as anxious as Travers, if not more so, hoping the decision would come like some message from heaven. But fast!

On her way back to her office, one of the secretaries ran up: 'There's a young lady to see you, Madame. I tried to keep her out and she refused to give her name.'

Florence looked in the direction the girl was pointing, and gaped.

'Alexandra! So *there* you are!'

In seconds, Florence had taken in the height, width and quality of her very own daughter, seen her legs, her bosom, her hair—everything, including the glow and the freshness of her beauty, complete with American accent! Within seconds, too, they were clasping each other, rubbing their cheeks and necks and hair together.

Florence squeezed her lips tight. No, she mustn't cry. Oh God, she had a daughter and she was here—like an oasis in the desert!

'At last, darling, we've met!' Florence cried, laughing through the mist. 'You are the only person in the whole wide world I want to see now.'

Alexandra gave a confident chuckle: 'Don't you like

anyone else?'

'I just want them to go away for a few hours. You'd never imagine the rush and the noise and everything.' They smiled at each other. 'You've made my day. Let's get out of here, it's a madhouse. I know, we'll go for a ride and let our hair down.'

'A great idea.'

As she inserted the ignition key, Florence said: 'You're not going to believe this, but I was just about to creep away to the cemetery.'

'What!'

'Yes. I go there when I want to be on my own. I stand next to the family tomb and talk to your grandfather. He's not there, he was cremated of course.'

'Well let's go there then. At least it'll be quiet!'

'Not if he answers back! To tell you the truth I was hardly suited to take over the paper, and I get out of my depth quite often. I need his inspiration. Goodness knows we quarrelled enough when he was alive, but now I think I understand him better.' She turned the key and the car moved forward. 'A lot of people, and I was one of them, thought he was a pig-headed old tyrant. But now I realize we were all wrong, he was really quite shy in his own way.'

'Shy!'

Florence modified her description: 'Not shy exactly, but retiring. Yes, I mean it. He was reserved, afraid to show how kind he really was, because he was so tender and vulnerable deep down.'

Alexandra was unconvinced: 'Huh! It must have been a hell of a way down!'

'And I failed to see it. We argued all the time, and when I think how often I must have hurt him without realizing, I go hot all over. I couldn't find the key into him, so to speak, not *his* key.'

The girl frowned, trying to understand: 'That happens, happens all the time I suppose.'

'I really grasped his character after I took over from him.'

'Became him, you mean?'

309

'In a way. Anyhow, you're here now and I'm me and you're you. I couldn't possibly become your grandfather!'

They laughed: 'Oh yes you could, darling *maman*. I ought to call you Antonine. Hey, that's not a bad idea!'

'Now you're laughing at me. I hope it's in good fun.'

'Well stop talking about yourself.'

'Me talking about myself?'

'You haven't stopped, but you don't even notice it. Exactly like grandfather.'

'Alexandra . . .'Florence began and broke off. She was on the point of telling her daughter that she mustn't jump to conclusions, that she mustn't talk to her mother like that. She bit her tongue.

'What a funny way of looking at me,' she murmured. 'I like your free thinking, the way you come right out with it.'

'It's a freedom I'm holding on to, *maman*.'

Phew, thought Florence. It's like an obstacle race.

They drew up outside the cemetery and walked as far as the family tomb, a pretentious edifice erected by Antonin's own grandfather when his wife died. It was planned for several generations.

Alexandra said: 'So you hear grandfather giving you advice even though he's not here. Strange. But that's cemeteries for you, they're all the same, make you think of the dead. My daddy's not here either but all the same . . .'

Florence held her daughter by the shoulders: 'Perhaps we ought not to have come after all.'

'Why not?'

'It makes it all come back for you. Are you still upset?'

'Terribly. He was real nice to me, there was a lot of affection between us.'

'I was upset too when I heard. Couldn't help thinking back to how he was, how he might have been, how we sort of imposed our limitations on you.'

They went back to the car, a small Renault 5 Florence was running at the time. She inserted the ignition key, but Alexandra laid a hand on her arm.

She said: '*Maman*, before we go back I'd like to ask you something. I want to tell you about a thing I found among his papers, in his desk. You may not like what I'm going to say, but I have to come out with it. It's a statement you made to the court some time before you got the divorce. When I was small and we were there all three of us in the States.'

Florence faced her: 'I know what it is: the inquiry into Mary Hatfield's death.'

'Yes, that's it. I know your statement by heart.'

'And you want to recite it to me.' Florence strove to remain natural, almost indifferent. A look of immense distress had contorted her daughter's face.

Alexandra said: 'I don't need to recite it. You know what I mean. But I can't stop hearing it in my mind's eye, it's kind of engraved there. The first question they asked you was: "Do you think this was a shooting accident? Your husband says he slipped when he aimed the gun". And you said: "It may possibly be that he staggered or something like that". And the second question was: "On that weekend did your husband want to go alone to your house in Maine?" You said: "Yes, but in any case I didn't want to go with him". Third question: "Did you know he was going there with Mary Hatfield?" You answered: "I didn't know it would be Mary, just that there was another woman going. It happened to be Mary but there were five of them and they all stood about equal with him". Fourth question: "Is it true that his drinking bouts became increasingly frequent?" You said: "Not exactly. For two years they had been so bad they could hardly get worse".'

Florence stared at her own hands on the steering wheel while Alexandra was talking. Her daughter added: 'Last question: "During these bouts did you ever fear for your life?"'

Her mother broke in with the answer: 'Yes, frequently.'

Alexandra said: 'So you know it by heart too.'

'It was true and it was the only reply, that's why I remember it. We'll go over it again if you like some day. Why don't you pop in at La Commanderie or at the office? Just make a call to Mathilde and she'll lay an extra place at

311

the table. I'm sorry, but I have an important meeting fixed at the paper.'

'Is it very urgent?'

'Yes darling. Believe me I love you, and I'm so thrilled you've come back to Chateauvallon. But we'll have to hurry now, my chap won't wait. Where shall I drop you?'

'At the hotel. Michel will be there.'

'You seem to get on well.'

'Pretty well. We laugh a lot, and talk a lot. We go over the whole family, saying what we think. And d'you know what he says? He says there are only two clean Bergs.' Florence waited. 'Julien and you.'

'And what's your opinion? You don't have to answer.'

'I agree about Julien. He's great. But as for you, I'll have to see. I'm being honest, *maman*.'

One in the eye for you, Florence was still thinking as she walked down the corridor to her office. Even so, she felt relaxed after her first encounter with Alexandra. She was even excited at the prospect of getting to know her better.

The man she was to meet was waiting in her office. He was a stout bald man, a handwriting expert. She excused herself for being late and asked him to take a seat.

'Well?' she said, subsiding into her own chair.

'I've been working all day on the document and the letter you gave me. I had them looked over by the best experts there are, and it seems certain to me that the writing is the same.'

Florence said: 'The letter was from someone very close to me, you obviously realize. The fact that I myself didn't doubt they were written by the same person—that must have been a factor.'

'Indeed, Madame, emotional reactions are all very well, but I have to be extremely careful. I start out with the idea that a forger may be involved. I don't say there might be one or that I suppose that there is one in this case, I say outright that this is a forgery and I try to prove it.'

Florence got up, circled the desk and came to rest in front of the graphologist: 'And have you proved it?'

'No.'

'And that is your professional conclusion? You're absolutely certain?'

'I never say absolutely. I just say I am almost certain.'

'Almost!'

'There's a one per cent chance I'm wrong, two per cent at the most. That's a good figure.'

'Let me have it in writing. A report saying you are ninety-eight per cent certain.'

The man squinted in irritation, then drew an envelope from his briefcase: 'Here are your documents, Madame, together with the report.'

'That's very satisfactory, Monsieur. Do collect your fee from the accounts. I've told them to settle at once.'

She wanted to kiss his bald head for him, but thought it wiser simply to escort him as far as the lift.

Then she returned to her office and told Mathilde to expect Alexandra that evening, the next, or on some other evening.

Albertas Kovalic was feeding his pigs. It was the best moment of the day for him. Confident in his hidden wealth, he still liked to fatten up his pigs and his poultry. It was his favourite time for thinking about things, planning future moves, ruminating. The dough-like mixture he fed the pigs inspired him as he kneaded it with his rough hands.

And that evening he was wondering about Bernard, thinking that he might have let a scorpion loose by bringing him over from Harvard. He had done more for him than for anyone else. For his daughter Catherine he had paid for a course at the Pigier secretarial college; she was brainy but he had left it at that. It was quite enough for a daughter, especially when he reflected that the little bitch had run out on the family just as soon as she got her diploma for shorthand-typing!

He would never recover from that. Nor would he get over the deaths when the Kovalics did mine-clearance work, and when the Asian flu struck, killing off his wife

313

and his two brothers. Now all he had was his old father, his sisters-in-law and their sons Teddy and Bernard.

Teddy had turned out to have the brains of a gnat. The only thing that interested him was the damn saxophone, but he did the delivery work with the van all right in Chateauvallon, and Albertas had to admit he was a willing sort of lad.

Bernard was something else. Right from elementary school they had picked him out, the teachers had. Bernard had a fine brain, an amazing memory and a 'sense of logic', as they said. So they got him on, and old Gregor had gladly paid for his education, so that he could go off to America, become a gent, make his way in the world. Now he had come back to Chateauvallon. Albertas chuckled to himself: 'Operation Bernard' which was the same thing as 'Operation Anti-Berg'. The boy had caught on quick, understood everything that was expected of him. Knew just how to get results, Bernard did, and looking no more like a Kovalic than if he'd been born in a castle. That was really the trouble. Albertas suspected that Bernard had lost the family spirit, was no longer willing to go along with the Yugoslav traditions and respect for the head of the family. He had a hard look about him, even when he was with his own people. Why, he hadn't been back more than a day or two when he started his independent ways, pleased himself what orders he took. Albertas and his father Gregor had discussed it at length, but they had accepted his cocky ways. You had to take the rough with the smooth, they concluded. After all, the boy had done what was expected of him over in America.

They had given in all the way, getting him a swanky car, a studio in town, a set of clothes that had cost a small fortune. They had gone along with his big ideas, dipping into their reserves to start the big scheme he had thought up. Wasn't their aim to frighten them into submission, those Bergs, with their financial success? Gregor had often said: 'Before I leave this world I want to see a Berg begging me for a *sou.*' Anything beyond that was of no interest to him; all he wanted was that dramatic event. He used to

314

think about it many times, smiling to himself.

Bernard didn't say much, kept himself to himself, just smiling and saying 'I understand perfectly'. Maybe he did understand, but he didn't really *feel* the need to crush the Bergs like the others did. Naturally he wanted to get rich and be famous and get all he could out of life, but it went no further than that. Bernard wanted to be *like the Bergs* but he wasn't *against the Bergs*.

'That's just not right, not right at all,' Albertas told his pigs.

Michel and Alexandra met up at Les Messageries and immediately went out again, looking at shop windows.

They went in one shop and bought identical pullovers and giggled about it. Then Alexandra said she'd like to find some magazines and books in English. Could you get them in Chateauvallon? Michel shrugged and said there was only Le Grande Librairie bookshop, and there was no certainty it had any. She tugged at him and they went there; it was where she had bought her comics when she was a small girl. While they browsed and picked up and put down books and papers and magazines she suddenly heard a male voice behind her.

'They don't have them in stock, Mademoiselle, but they'll order them if you want,' the voice said.

She spun round and saw a lantern-jawed man, fairly young, with a thatch of black hair. She squinted at him trying to remember where she had seen him before. In any case she could not recall his name.

He introduced himself: 'I'm Bernard Kovalic. You're Alexandra Berg, if I'm not mistaken.'

'No, Alexandra Wilson.'

'Of course, how stupid of me. I offer you my condolences, Mademoiselle. It must have been tough for you, and what a loss for the world of letters! I've read all your father's books. He was a truly great writer.'

'That's nice of you. You're American?'

'Born here, but I've just spent three years at Harvard. Came over four months ago.'

'I don't believe it!'

'It's true none the less. I even had a buddy who was crazy about Alexandra Wilson. Had fantasies about her, couldn't stop yapping about her day and night. I imagine you know who it was.'

'Burt Hickok,' she grinned.

'Good old Burty.'

'That's funny us both knowing him.'

'Alexandra,' Michel intervened. He was as white as a ghost, visibly jealous and grim with it. 'If I were you, Alexandra, I'd find out from him what this Burty gink looks like.'

Bernard gave a chuckle: 'Oh, I could talk about Burty all day long. He looks like an inverted question mark and his most becoming feature is a beauty spot right between his eyebrows. Same guy?'

'That's him. How extraordinary! If you knew Burty, Michel, as well as I do, you'd never stop laughing. You've got him exactly, Bernard. Delighted to know you.'

They slipped into English: 'Hope to see you again before long.'

'Me too, Bernard, so long.'

Alexandra wriggled her arm into Michel's and they left the bookshop. She noted that her cousin was huffy and could not understand why.

'What's with you?' she said. 'Can't I have a chat and a laugh with another boy? You know you're my favourite cousin.'

'Apart from a few kids there aren't any others! Now listen to me and stop being so smart. Bernard Kovalic followed us from the moment we left the hotel, I was keeping my eye on him. He drove along behind us in a big Renault car like some KGB agent. That was fishy enough, but a Kovalic in a swanky car like that is even fishier.'

Alexandra pouted: 'Perhaps it was me he was following. Maybe he thought I was attractive.'

'You're pretty all right, but it wasn't *any* girl he was following. Bernard Kovalic was interested in the Berg girl.'

She looked at him as if he had gone out of his mind: 'How did he know I was a Berg girl, as you say? What's that to him? I've only been here two days.'

Michel brought them to a halt. He spread his hands: 'I turned up yesterday morning at the hotel, and that's proof that news travels fast in this town, especially if you do nothing to hide your presence. What a mad idea to take a room at Les Messageries too! We have a highly efficient grapevine here, and within the hour everyone knew that Florence Berg's daughter had come back and that she was staying at the hotel—at least, everyone who was interested in knowing.'

Alexandra was genuinely confused: 'But why should Bernard Kovalic be interested in that? I'm trying to understand.'

'Because he's a Kovalic, and that's a good enough reason,' Michel said with a hint of anger. 'How can I explain it? It's like the Middle Ages, with the Kovalics and the Bergs fighting for power. Surely you can't be the only person in Chateauvallon who fails to see that!'

'Old-fashioned rubbish, that's all it is.'

'If you like, but you just see after you've been here a while.'

'Hm. Well anyway, I've got a proposition for you. I want you to be my guest for dinner at La Commanderie.'

'What!'

'Yes, I saw *maman*, and she said I was sort of permanently invited. A phone call was enough, she said.'

Bernard watched them from inside the bookshop, and saw them go into the nearby tearoom. For a split second he toyed with the idea of going in after them and continuing the conversation with the girl. But he lacked the courage to maintain a cheerful line of chat in the presence of the other fellow. Who the hell was he in any case? Some childhood friend of hers no doubt, a spoilt brat whose only merit was that his parents had had him! A bourgeois idiot, that was sure.

He thought about the boy with Alexandra for some

time. He found it strange that, although he had kept his ears and eyes open constantly over the past few months, he failed to place him. Strange, but it was of no consequence. He'd get to Alexandra Berg—or rather, Wilson—in due course. Nobody could stop him: that boy, her mother Florence, Albertas. Thinking of Albertas made Bernard reflect on the Kovalic-Berg conflict, which seemed pretty ridiculous in the final analysis. Were they going to do a replay of Shakespeare's *Romeo and Juliet*, for pity's sake? Bernard thought some more, this time about Boulard and Jerome; his dinner with them had made it very clear that they too were against the Berg family. This might well suit him eventually, since he could use the Boulard press to drum up backing for his money-making schemes, and Jerome was the mayor after all was said and done. They seemed to be anti-Florence rather than anti-Berg. However that may be, Bernard decided he had better play things their way, would be wise to go along with them. Which meant that he would be one of the conspirators plotting her downfall. So be it.

Even so, when it came to Alexandra he would play it *his* way. The big question was: what sort of a game would Alexandra play?

It had been agreed between them that Travers would collect Florence around 9.00 p.m.

He was on time, and she was ready. He pulled up outside the main steps at the big house fully expecting to wait a quarter of an hour while she messed about. To his astonishment she heaved open the front door as he was applying the handbrake, waved goodbye to the people inside, and ran down the steps like some teenager going off on her first date. With his customary observant eye he noted her careful make-up and grinned at the bloom on her cheeks.

'Hullo bright eyes,' he said gaily, pushing the other car door open for her.

'Guess who came to dinner,' she bubbled, as he took the car round and made for the main gate.

'The President of the Republic?'

'Better than that—Alexandra! And tomorrow she's going to move in, she'll be in the blue room. Isn't it wonderful! We had a heart-to-heart natter this afternoon, and I said she could come whenever she wanted, and she's coming tomorrow. I was delighted when she turned up for dinner tonight. We're making progress.'

'I'm glad for you, Flo. Let's celebrate it, I've got a bottle of champagne on ice. Thanks for keeping our date.'

He groaned within as she said: 'We'll drink it later, but we have to call in at the office first.'

'The office! They can do without you, the paper's gone to press. They don't need you, I do.'

'They're holding the front page, I phoned them.'

'Huh. The Quentin papers, eh?'

'I mulled it over all day, and I could feel myself deciding to go ahead with publishing them. I took the plunge when I was having my bath before dinner.'

'Had Alexandra already arrived for dinner?'

'Yes. Why do you ask?'

'Because this morning you were decidedly hesitant, and I can't see that there's any new factor since then.'

Florence glared at the road ahead: 'I don't need factors, I've decided, that's all.'

Travers accelerated: 'So it's to be Watergate, French style! Curious, but the *Washington Post* is run by a woman too.'

'Whatever does that mean?'

'It means you mustn't revamp the front page just to impress your daughter.'

'Are you off your head, Travers? Alexandra has nothing to do with it.'

'I never said she had, I was just putting forward a hypothesis.'

'Well you can keep your suppositions to yourself!'

She turned to face him, giving him a black look. She looked ahead and then gave him another, saying she would first call Madame Quentin. Travers told her it was she who had lost her head. They left it at that.

319

As they parted company in the corridor at *La Dépêche*, she told him to get on with doing the new front page story while she phoned Madame Quentin.

Five minutes later he joined her in her office to tell her: 'Sorry Flo, I can't even get the lead down. I don't feel the story. Did she give us anything useful, something we could work up into an angle?'

'I didn't phone her for that, just out of courtesy. I told her we had the data sheets.'

'And I don't suppose she cared a damn. All she's concerned about is that she's lost her husband.'

'You're being ridiculous.'

'And you're stark raving mad.'

Her eyes blazed: 'We're not going to argue about it. Just get on with the story. That's what I pay you for!'

An hour later he was back, admitting defeat, saying that this was his fourth attempt.

She ran her eyes quickly down the typescript: 'No, it doesn't hold up. You're writing a thumbsucker, and what I want is a big worldshaker.'

'You haven't read it right through.'

'I don't need to, it's all screwed up somehow.'

Travers gave a sigh of exasperation: 'Maybe I should take a bath and get some inspiration. Why don't you do the bloody thing yourself! Give yourself a byline too!'

Florence was close to panic, the minutes were passing: 'Please Trav!'

'I'll take a walk outside, it's the only way. I'll be back.'

Travers strolled over to the Bijou-Bar and was not surprised to find it almost empty at this late hour. But he was amazed to see Catherine Kovalic sitting on her own at a table in the shadows contemplating an empty coffee cup, the picture of hopelessness. He ordered a whisky.

'Tomorrow will be a better day,' he said quietly, slipping onto the chair facing her. She looked up and blinked. 'Come on, get rid of it to uncle Travers.'

She attempted a smile: 'I'm really alone now. There won't be a *post mortem* marriage after all, because there's no irrefutable proof Paul intended to marry me. Which is

320

true, because we never even discussed it. We didn't see the necessity for it, like lots of other couples. Well, that's that.'

'Have you told Florence?'

'Not yet. She's got plenty to think about already.'

Travers cleared his throat: 'Things are not exactly running on tramlines at the moment. Give her a couple of days. She's been advising you on it, and you never know, there may be some way of lodging an appeal or something.'

Catherine's shoulders quivered: 'No, there's no appeal. The baby will be called Paul Kovalic, not Bossis. I shan't even be a real widow. My father will be delighted.'

Travers said: 'Facts are stronger than notions. You know he's Paul's boy, so you are a widow.'

'And alone.'

'Nonsense. We're all with you like a family: Paul's dad Gilbert, Florence, me . . .'

'Florence has got you, and you can't deny it.'

'Huh, if you could see her at this very moment cursing and moaning over a story I've just written. We had words about it and that's why I'm here.'

Catherine had successfully fought back the tears: 'It's your life, the two of you. I'm deeply fond of you both.'

'And vice versa,' he said with a kind smile, taking her hands firmly in his. He turned pensive himself, regretting that there was no more convincing form of physical contact at that moment to convey his tender feelings, notwithstanding his urgent passion for Florence.

He gulped down the rest of his whisky, and said gently: 'I know you have the strength to bear it, Catherine. I wish I could stay a while, but this story's too big, and proving a pain in the proverbial. I'll have to go. We'll have another chat about it.'

Travers embraced her quickly on both cheeks and left, carefully avoiding too abrupt a departure.

He found Florence with her hair straggling over her face and visibly excited. Her eyes shone like two beacons.

'Ah there you are. Your pussy-footing has rendered me a service, darling. Of *course* you couldn't get it on paper. It's I who had to do it. And I've done it!'

321

Travers relaxed: 'So you're going ahead with it.'

'They're setting it now. I took it down like a big girl. I'm proud of it too.' She struck a pose and declaimed: 'I've stopped bobbing and weaving, I've landed my punch!'

'You could have let me take a look at it first.'

She continued play-acting, imagining herself as Florence the Great, back in her role at court.

'I accuse,' she cried, pointing a pregnant finger at Travers. 'I accuse six members of the government of being accessories to murder. I accuse six ministers of plotting and organizing the slaying of their colleague Georges Quentin, in the hope of eliminating, through his death, the evidence he accumulated of their financial iniquities. I accuse the judiciary of professional incompetence in that it inadequately verified the hypothesis of suicide!' She broke off: 'What do you think?'

Travers was grinning broadly: 'It's clear cut, that's the least one can say. If that's what you really want . . .'

'Actually, although I didn't see it in print, I had the whole thing worked out in the bath. You did right to tell me. I wrote the bloody thing myself, I had the feel of it from the outset.'

'And now you're exhausted.'

'Not at all. I want champagne, I want kisses, I want love!'

'It's all waiting for us at my place.'

'Where else? Tonight we storm the Bastille!'

They disregarded the lift and scrambled down the stairs hand in hand, giggling like a pair of schoolkids after the bell has gone.

The nationals and the agencies picked up the story, and it became a major item throughout the country from the moment the radio and TV news bulletins carried it, making it their lead.

The Cabinet got together within hours and the Opposition latched onto it. Within twenty-four hours the original 'I accuse' had exploded into a firework display of counter-truths, half-truths, comment, shock, drama—the whole bag of tricks. It was chortled over in the bistros, trembled over in high places and shrugged over by concierges leaning on their brooms.

From Paris, from far and wide in France and from abroad calls by the hundred were put in to *La Dépêche* and La Commanderie. And the callers got the same answer each time from the paper's staff and the servants at the big house: 'Madame Berg is out, no I don't know, she didn't say.' Had they contacted Catherine Kovalic, they would have been hot on the trail, but the few who reached her stopped there.

Florence and Travers savoured her triumph in his bed, where she made it more than plain that this was her greatest day since she took over the paper. In the early hours he threw some clothes on and went out for some croissants and copies of *La Dépêche* and *L'Eveil*. Both issues had gone to press around the same time. J-J Berg's was headed PROVE IT!, Florence Berg's read SIX REASONS FOR A MURDER.

He burst into the room laughing like a drain.

'Doesn't it look great!' Florence screamed. 'I did pretty well for a beginner!'

'Your poor brother. His first issue, and you knackered him!!!'

They lunged at each other and tumbled around joyously, getting tied up in the sheets.

At the same instant, J-J Berg sat like a deflated football bladder behind his desk, scowling at the typewriter on which he had produced his masterpiece, and at Maryse.

'I don't believe it, it's not possible they could have known,' he moaned. His gaunt face contrasted with the impeccable suit he was wearing. The shouting headlines on the two papers before him mocked his expensive tie and the white handkerchief in his top pocket.

At home the maid had brought the two papers with breakfast into him and Marie-Lou. The subsequent tirade on his incompetence had gone on for so long that he had fled the house on an empty stomach and sought refuge at the office, only to suffer the derision of Maryse in unspoken form. At least, that is how he felt her presence as they contemplated the evidence of his very own journalistic calamity.

'It happens sometimes,' she said, relenting, and went on to cite cases where the media had been caught out through bad luck. 'You've lost a battle but not the war. That's the newspaper business for you.'

Jean-Jacques threw up his arms: 'Please, Maryse, we can do without that. It's a disaster and we'll never live it down. What the hell can I answer to that?' He buried his face in his hands.

'Take a look at this first,' she ordered, handing him a sealed envelope. 'It's Boulard's counter-attack, which Bernard Kovalic sent in.'

'Boulard? Kovalic? What the devil are you talking about?'

'*L'Eveil* is Boulard's, unless I've been dreaming.'

'Yes, but I'm the man in charge here. What's Kovalic got to do with it anyhow?'

She said slowly: 'He's going to work here from now on. He'll be here at eleven o'clock, but don't get any illusions, he's an early riser and he delivered that personally to my apartment at the crack of dawn. Your name's on the envelope.'

'Good grief, a Kovalic working here! This is the end.'

He felt the envelope as if it might explode. He was some time making up his mind to slit it open.

Bernard was indeed an early riser, it was native to him, in the Central European tradition. The world belongs to those who are on their feet by 7.00 a.m., he believed.

After handing the envelope to Maryse, a missive entrusted to him by Boulard himself some thirty-six hours earlier, Bernard phoned Les Messageries, where Alexandra paddled her way out of sleep and said: "Lo, who, oh it's you.' She then sat up and a broad smile brought life to her face.

'Burty told me something else about you,' he informed

her. 'You are an accomplished horsewoman, and I'd be delighted to join you in a canter this very morning.'

'Today? Now?'

'There's no better time. It's not raining, the country has never looked better, and I know where we can find the finest mounts for kilometres around.'

Humming as she rushed through getting up, Alexandra told herself she was beginning to like Chateauvallon. Yesterday La Commanderie had started to feel like a real home, probably because her grandfather was no longer there. She continued to live with the memory of her father, and she realized it would not be easy adapting to the new circumstances, but she was slowly gaining a new enthusiasm for living and Bernard Kovalic's evident intentions towards her were part of this new appetite. Feeling peckish she grabbed a couple of croissants from a basket downstairs and prepared to be wooed.

Twenty minutes he had allowed her, and he turned up as she nipped into the nearest ladies' room to check her boots, her jeans and the pullover she had bought with Michel. She glanced at her watch and supposed that he must have arrived, but decided to keep him waiting five minutes. She re-tied the ribbon holding her hair swept back to make her look older.

A long time later she dismounted, gloriously warm and flushed. 'You were right,' she laughed, 'it was marvellous.'

They had ended with a splendid gallop through ground mist that glowed in the sun's early rays.

'I know La Gravelle woods like the back of my hand,' she said. 'Used to ride here often when I was little, but they were such broken-down old nags I asked mother if I could stop it. Oof!'

Getting her breath back, she pumped out tiny clouds from her parted lips and twisted her head about as she undid her hair. It fell into place in loose blonde curls about her shoulders, and she inhaled the smell of the earth and the horses and the stables.

'You ride very well,' Bernard said, handing over the bridles.

'I started when I was only three. My father bought me my first pony on my third birthday. I've no excuse for bad technique.'

Bernard laughed: 'All I got on my third birthday was a good hiding. In fact I got one every day. My father was a hard man, and frankly he was a tyrant with me. I regret to say I never missed him when he died.'

They turned and strolled towards Bernard's Renault, and Alexandra slipped her arm in his.

They were silent for a moment, then Bernard said: 'Have you read *La Dépêche*?'

'Solange tried to show me while I was going through the hall, but I didn't have time to look.'

Bernard jerked his head knowingly: 'You'll get a surprise when you read it. It's your mother's day of glory.'

'Really?'

'Chap on the radio said: "If Florence Berg's aim is to destabilize the government, she is certainly succeeding". She's upset the whole apple cart.'

Alexandra adopted a snooty air: 'She presumably thought she had to do it.'

'Read the paper first. She's taking enormous risks, you know.'

'And no doubt she calculated them in advance. She knows what she's doing, I can vouch for that. She's a brave woman, my mother.'

Bernard waited an instant and said: 'When I talk of risks, I mean in Chateauvallon.'

Alexandra retorted: 'I understood you the first time.' She withdrew her arm from his, and Bernard pretended not to notice.

'Shall I run you back to the hotel? Or would you prefer somewhere else?'

'La Commanderie, please.'

'Back to the family seat.'

'Yes, and for good.'

'Naturally, at turning points in life, the family counts. Solidarity with your mother, of course.'

'Not at all,' she said.

Bernard opened the passenger door for her and ceremoniously bowed her in. He took his seat behind the wheel.

He made no move to start the car: 'My grandad Gregor says—and he has a stack of tales like it—that your grandfather refused to give him a hand up when he and his wife and three boys were short of food. Neither of us was born then, Alexandra, but our path through life was decided then, according to him, on the steps of the town hall.'

The girl shrugged: 'I can't see my destiny in this place.'

'Nor can I. I've been thinking. Suppose that the big break for the Bergs and the Kovalics happened to be us, you and me. Suppose their chance to stop this ridiculous feud was Alexandra and Bernard. It's been going on long enough.'

'Romeo and Juliet, you mean?'

He grinned: 'I thought of it first. We only need two or three rehearsals.'

With that he slipped his arm round her neck and began kissing her curls, then lifted her hair and kissed her neck. She remained motionless, apparently willing, and then suddenly froze.

'That's enough; stop it please.'

His hand was on her arm now, having crept round her back. She calmly lifted it and gave it back to him.

'Something wrong?' he said, beginning to look sheepish, and added sharply: 'Because you're a Berg and I'm a Kovalic, because of social distinction? You're reverting to type?'

She waited before replying, and then said quietly: 'I couldn't care a fig about you being a Kovalic. No, it's something else. We don't gel, Bernard, I'm sorry. It's just one of those things; it's nobody's fault.'

There was no answer to that, and Kovalic gunned the car into life, released the clutch and raced off like a rally driver. The girl strove to retain her dignity, reflecting as they bounced around in their seats that she must write to Burt Hickok, ask him what he thought of Bernard Kovalic.

They were politeness itself when they said goodbye

outside La Commanderie. Then Bernard drove to *L'Eveil*.

Ten minutes before Bernard got there, Jean-Jacques opened the Boulard envelope. He read through the sheet of paper several times, whistled his amazement, deflated further and looked up at Maryse.

'You know what it is?'

'Roughly,' she said with a smirk.

'But I can't run that!'

'Of course you can.'

'It's impossible. Surely they don't imagine . . .'

Maryse covered his mouth with a hand, as a mother would stop her boy talking nonsense.

'But they do imagine, old chap,' she said. 'And they're dead right.'

'But Maryse, I can't print that without Flo knowing first. She's my sister, for pity's sake. She's certainly made me look a fool plenty of times, but that's no reason why I shouldn't warn her.'

'Think carefully before you do.'

Jean-Jacques squirmed with his inner conflict, and at last he stood up and held on to the desk.

'I've thought it over, and I have to go. She must know that this—this abomination is not my idea.'

'So what? What would she say?'

'Certainly not thank you!'

'You can't get out of running it.'

'That's not the point.'

'Oh yes it is, the only point. Sit down and listen to me. Whether she likes it or not, this article will appear tomorrow.'

'I suppose so.'

'Then what difference does it make?'

'She'll realize I had good intentions.'

'Phooey! She'll realize you're salving your conscience and cheap at the price.'

They looked at each other, feeling like spare parts. Their instinct was right, for Bernard Kovalic appeared at that moment in the open doorway resplendent in his riding gear. He took the bit firmly from J-J Berg's gaping mouth.

'My dear Berg,' he gushed. 'As you see I'm already in harness!' He enveloped the other man's hands. 'Wonderful piece of yours—punchy, short and sharp sentences. Just what's wanted. We're going to make a hard-hitting team, I know it.'

Jean-Jacques wore the expression of a huntsman whose horse has bolted through a forest glade and left him clinging perilously to an overhanging branch.

Florence resurfaced in the afternoon, leaving Travers to look after things at *La Dépêche*, while she went home to La Commanderie. Jeannou had fetched Alexandra's belongings from the hotel after lunch, and her daughter was settling into the blue room.

'I've upset Mathilde and Gilbert,' she told her mother. 'They wanted me to have the apartment.'

'Who cares,' Florence said breezily.

'Gilbert's adorable. He got Julien and Thérèse to come because he knows I like them so much. But they spent lunch teasing me all the time.' The girl held up a couple of T-shirts.

'I'll let you carry on,' Florence said. She herself was more than pleased that Mathilde had been taken down a peg. 'I've some correspondence to catch up on. Let's have dinner in town tonight, just the two of us. I promise I won't tease you.'

When they met later they saw that they had both dressed as if for a wedding. They chuckled over it and walked to the car arm in arm.

'Sorry to take you back to Les Messageries, but I've fixed up to see Travers there when we get to the coffee.'

'Oh I'll like it. I've only actually had one dinner there,' Alexandra said.

'How nice to be together, after the confusion when you first got here. Well, what have you been up to all day?'

'Except for arriving here, nothing really, just messing about.'

The girl was reluctant to mention Bernard Kovalic, and

329

was too inhibited to ask her mother about her day. They said little on the way, and it was not until they were chewing on their smoked salmon that they began talking in earnest. They had asked for a side table, were both keenly aware that the other diners were discussing them in whispers; they could tell by the constant glances. They were the press heroine and the daughter back from the States.

'You've created a sensation, *maman*. How you had the courage to do it beats me.'

'I have never believed that Quentin killed himself.'

'I still don't understand, to be honest. Perhaps he found out too much and it was decided to get rid of him. Even so, what was the purpose of all his digging around: concern for public morality, or simply material he could use in a jam?'

They were almost whispering. Florence said: 'Possibly both, I can't say.'

'But you knew him well.'

'Thanks for reminding me,' Florence said with a twisted smile.

'Oh dear, I didn't mean to criticize, I promise you. I've no right to reproach you for anything, honestly *maman*. I'm simply curious to know the ins and outs. Georges Quentin was either an upstanding public man or a lone crook of some kind, and I imagine we shall never know now. And there's the Gang of Six on the other hand.'

Florence's face brightened: 'Oh that's good, darling. May I use that some time—the Gang of Six?'

'You can buy the rights! But what about you? What a tremendous risk you've taken, actually naming the six ministers.'

'To be frank about it, I did consider another strategy, coming out with the data sheets one by one, as it were, and building the thing up gradually. I could have kept my best cards up my sleeve, but in the end I thought it would be unworthy of *La Dépêche*, it would have been a sort of continuous blackmail. I opted for the frontal attack.'

Alexandra wagged her head left and right to show her

admiration: 'I absolutely agree, and I think you've been honest and brave.'

They were chatting gaily when Travers loped in. He gave little bows to both of them, and they told him to pull up a chair, which a waiter did for him.

'Nice to see you Monsieur Travers. We didn't really get to know each other at the airport. It was entirely my fault, I was so het up about everything.'

'Couldn't wait to get down here. I understand.'

'Yes,' she said and gave a little giggle.

Travers casually slipped a small sheet of paper to Florence, containing some figures, as he continued addressing her daughter: 'So you're still mad about our marvellous town?'

'I love it. So exciting! I certainly turned up at the right moment.'

Travers acted blasé: 'It really hums here all the time, you'll see. We were just waiting for you to arrive before we set the fireworks off.'

Florence was frowning, and interrupted them: 'This really is 350,000? I mean you're not having me on?'

'That's it, *patronne*. We're up to 350,000 as against 329,000 a week ago.'

'That's superb, although our immediate aim has nothing to do with circulation. But it's nice to have. Do you think we can keep it up?'

He raised his hands: 'We've got no choice. We also have exactly six new libel fights on our hands.'

'We can pay, then, with the extra sales.'

'Your logic is simplicity itself, I love you *patronne*.'

'Likewise,' she said gaily. 'Oh, here's the opposition.'

They saw a group being conducted to a table for three.

'Quick, *maman*, who are they?'

'The woman is Maryse Mongin, a defector from *La Dépêche* along with Jean-Jacques. I don't know the others, possibly staff from *L'Eveil*.'

Maryse said as she went past: 'Good evening, Madame Berg.' Her tone was mocking.

It was Travers who replied: 'Good evening.'

'I was not talking to you. No need to wish you good evening or goodnight, I suppose.'

Alexandra blinked and interrogated her mother with her eyes. Florence simply beamed at her, holding her gaze. Alexandra turned to Travers, but discovered he was already half-way towards the competition.

'Now listen here,' he snapped.

'*Do* excuse me, I have guests,' hissed Maryse.

Travers wagged a finger at her: 'Another crack like that and you'll be in trouble. I don't have to take that from you or anyone else.'

'Of course, darling Trav,' Maryse sneered. 'You'd better watch your step, big boy. Wait and see the letter.'

'You've sent me a letter?'

'You and some others. But with *your* intelligence I'm sure you'll get the hidden message—from me personally.'

Chapter Three

The population of Chateauvallon were offered music while they sipped their coffee next morning. Their eardrums were assailed from 7.00 a.m. onwards by a roving van from *L'Eveil* blaring out military marches interspersed with the message: 'Make sure you see *L'Eveil* this morning. Get a copy now and see the sensational proof that Quentin killed himself. It's all there in a letter in *L'Eveil*. Get a copy of *L'Eveil* now!' Then it moved on to another pitch.

The racket reached the ears of Florence and Travers, and Travers obediently climbed into his trousers and got the sensational proof that Quentin killed himself. On his return to the studio he found Florence pacing the room like a lioness. She had his dressing gown over her shoulders, and she had made no attempt to make coffee. Travers had forgotten the croissants this time.

Together they ran through the story. Travers had bought two copies.

'Armand told me about this, and I can see what he meant now,' Florence said with gloom in her voice.

The letter read as follows:

My Dear Minister, but first My Very Dear Michel,

As the customary formula has it, when you read this letter I shall have brought my life to an end.

My action will be interpreted in various ways, I am sure, and I want one person at least—you, my good friend for always—to know the true motive.

I am killing myself because of the property scandal that has left a stain on my town's affairs. I have nothing to do with this.

I wish to stress that I did not decide to do away with myself because I lost the election. I expected that.

I am doing it solely for the reason you know about. I was mistaken, I failed, I intend to pay for it.

Fraternally yours until the last second.

Georges Quentin

'Get into some clothes,' Florence ordered, doing so herself. 'We must get to the office quick.'

Virtually the entire staff was there before them, heavy eyed, the journalists unshaven, their shirts and ties not necessarily right for their trousers and jackets.

As the pair reached the editorial floor, Favrot was addressing the others. Florence took Travers's jacket sleeve and held him back. He turned and saw she was surprisingly well turned out, make-up perfect, nothing askew. He fingered the stubble on his chin and noted her air of authority. She put a finger to her lips and they avoided being seen.

'Let's consider this fact,' Favrot was saying, also displaying uncharacteristic authority. 'Curiously, the Minister of Justice had this letter the day after Quentin's death, or the day after that at the latest, we can be sure.'

'Yep,' said a young fellow with a show of efficiency. He had joined the paper as a trainee a short time previously.

Favrot went on: 'Now, there was an official inquiry, and it seems astonishing that the Minister said nothing, never even told the examining magistrate not to waste his time. No, he simply let the police waste their time. And later on we raised the question of the two guns that were found, and still the Minister made no move. Subsequently we ran the story citing Sofia as a witness, and he still kept his mouth shut. Viciously, this guy deliberately allowed *La Dépêche* to run its stories and get out on a limb.'

'Why us?' Edelman barked.

'A good point, but there's another: why give the letter to *L'Eveil*? Why release it to a tinpot paper with a circulation of less than 50,000?'

Florence strode in: 'Nicely put, Favrot. I appreciate it. But I still wonder whether you too aren't wasting your time. It might be better if we all kept our own counsel for the moment. I mean that.'

Favrot surged forward like some demonstrator: 'But *patronne*, we can't just do nothing!'

'Fine, and if you have any ideas what I can do, it's bingo for you. I'm in my office, and you can come right in whenever you like.' She gave them all a fleeting smile and left for her sanctuary. They watched her tap-tapping her way along the corridor, and listened for her door to close.

'It's amazing how she keeps going,' Edelman said.

'Amazing,' Travers rejoined, 'but just one more setback and she'll fall over. So give her a break, you fellows. She'll be her old self again within no time at all.'

'With you as her doctor?' Edelman quipped.

At that moment the deputy editor Melchior came in, pale from his attack but the same Melchior with the bald head and loyalty lines on his face. He had been with the paper nearly a quarter of a century.

'Hey, you're supposed to be in hospital!' Favrot cried.

'I was until half an hour ago. But I rose again in the hour of need!' Melchior joked. The lads came round him, taking his hand, patting him on the back.

Travers discreetly escaped to find Florence in her office. She gave no reply when he tapped on the door, and she said she hadn't heard. Travers brought her a cup of coffee from the machine, and she gave a little jump of surprise on seeing it.

'Thanks,' she rasped, and covered her face.

'Drink it hot,' he ordered.

'I couldn't get it down.'

'Try. Who's in charge here anyway?' he said, trying to shake her out of the mood.

'Certainly not you or I. They've taken over.'

'Who's they?'

'We'll know some day, I suppose,' Florence replied. 'They must be slippery customers. For example, having that letter printed in facsimile form means that nobody even imagines it might be a forgery, pure invention. Smart move, that.'

'I'm no handwriting expert, but for me the data sheets and the letter are the same person.'

She became alert again: 'D'you know what the graphologist told me? That he sets out with the idea that the thing's a forgery. And it so happens that I do too in this case. There's a forger in there somewhere, Trav, I'm certain.'

'Which, the letter or the data sheets?'

'One or the other. One of them is forged because they contradict each other. There's another point, and you hinted at it the other day: each one of these sheets is a defensive weapon. Well, if a man takes the trouble to assemble an arsenal *that* complicated, he is highly unlikely to shoot himself in the head afterwards. Common sense.'

'Ah, but suppose something else occurred and he changed his mind?'

Florence had recovered already, scenting blood, the adversary's: 'Just let's run over it again. Either the data sheets are genuine, so he was murdered. Or the letter is genuine, the sheets are forgeries, and he committed suicide.' She swallowed the coffee noisily, and hurled the plastic cup in her waste basket.

'Right,' Travers concurred. 'Which means that someone's been leading us by the nose from the start, from the time when that mystery voice began phoning in and putting us on the track of the murder theory.'

They were both pacing the room, and Florence said: 'Then the mystery man faded out, never phoned again. He left us out on a limb, Trav. What does that signify?'

She added a hiss of irritation, and at that moment the phone rang.

'Yes,' she rapped, easing a haunch onto the desk edge: 'Oh, it's you Armand, no I'm not busy. Go ahead and bawl me out, it'll do you good, and won't harm me.' She handed the extension to Travers.

They heard: 'I warned you Florence, I'm not in the Assemblée for nothing, I hear things. You should have heeded my warning.'

'Anyone can make a mistake, and it was my turn this time. We're fighting a guerrilla war, and nobody knows better than the Assemblée how hard *that* is!'

'So you asked for what you're getting. But, sister dear, my name's Berg too and a lot of people here are throwing custard pies at me. I'll be the court jester before long if I don't watch out. I am losing all credibility!'

'Big words.'

'I use the words that suit the occasion. You don't seem to realize that things are at fever pitch in Paris, with the Right doubled up with mirth. Yesterday the Opposition was accused of shoving you from behind, today you're flat on your back. Thank you Florence; in one hour from now I've a meeting of the parliamentary group, and the only idea I can think up is to tell them you're not my real sister but an impostor.'

'Hold on Armand. Talking of that, suppose the letter is a forgery?'

'Oh no, don't try that line in your rag, for Christ's sake. The entire country will be laughing. It's your goddamn data sheets that are forged. You've been taken for a ride, and you'd better be quiet about it now.'

'All right, then! Cheers.'

She replaced the receiver, and Travers put down the extension.

'I have to admit the letter looks authentic,' Travers said. 'But note that Quentin said he was shooting himself "for the reason you know about". The Minister can invent what he likes to explain that phrase.'

'Then let him. Even so, I am convinced that letter is a forgery. Imagine that, a Minister of Justice guilty of fabricating false documents and making use of them! That ought to go down in the history books!'

Travers looked at her quizzically, and she continued: 'Let's stick to what's happening here. The mystery man's voice came from here, didn't it? And the publication of the letter was here too.'

'But not the data sheets.'

'Are you sure? If the letter is genuine, the sheets are not,

337

and nor is the voice. So someone fed us the voice and the sheets. Why? To sink *La Dépêche*.'

'Slowly but surely,' Travers said.

She stared hard at him, making little beckoning signs, telling him to come right out with it.

'My God,' he said.

'You've got it.'

'Boulard! You mean Boulard!'

'Exactly. Boulard wants to take us over precisely at the moment when the paper's not worth a *sou* to any buyer. He might even get *La Dépêche* for a nominal sum, when he's asked to kindly step in and save the paper! And that, my dear Travers, is why *we* are going to save it. OK, I've behaved like an idiot, I'll admit it. But from that point, now that we are starting to comprehend what's happening, we can forget our pride and counterattack.'

'Easier said than done.'

Florence licked her lips. When they had run up the stairs and come across the newsmen discussing the crisis, she had returned for a moment to the state of infancy. She was the little girl who had done a naughty thing and would surely be punished. Now she smelled blood, and it had to be Boulard's.

'I propose to reveal the whole campaign against us, from A to Z. And we'll say clearly who's behind it.'

'Wow!'

'We have our backs to the wall, and that gives us strength. The readers love skulduggery involving politics and money. We'll blow up a big portrait of the valiant orphan girl—that's me!—being preyed on by the big bad wolf. My God, Trav, the pages will be wet with the tears of our loyal readers.'

Travers took her right hand, bestowed a courtier's kiss on the back of it. 'And what can I do for the orphan girl?'

'You, kind sir, will pack your toothbrush and find me the forger.' He gave an ironic whistle. 'Find him and the battle's half won, the rest is easy.'

He gave some little nods: 'I'm beginning to believe in this. I do love simple straightforward orders.'

338

'It won't be that hard if you keep at it eighteen hours a day. You've got a good lead in Quentin's sexy piece.'

'Arlette?'

'All you have to do is build a fire in her heart, quicken her pulse, offer her the prospect of heaven here below—and she'll lead you to the forger. A piece of cake!'

They both laughed hugely, and Travers drew her to him. They exchanged a businesslike kiss.

He told her: 'I'm proud to know you. I don't know about heaven, but if I have to I'll walk through hell to get that forger.'

'Then jump to it. Keep phoning in, either here or to La Commanderie.'

'I promise.'

From the window she watched him run down the main steps and make for his car. Then she drew some paper from a drawer and began roughing out some ideas; they came fast, tumbled over one another, and she made few corrections. At one point she phoned for sandwiches and another packet of cigarettes.

Later she called in Edelman and Favrot. They worked out the dates and details of the mystery man's phone calls, and got all that down on paper from the moment when he contacted Florence at La Commanderie and told her Quentin had been murdered. It had been a line she was all too ready to pursue, for the simple reason that she found it impossible to believe he had done away with himself. The caller had suggested evidence she could follow up. Subsequently Travers, Edelman and Favrot had tried to grab the man after Florence agreed to meet him, but there had been a mess-up. Shortly afterwards Travers had received an anonymous cassette which pointed to Sofia Leriche; she had the unusual job of woman wine waiter, and had provided evidence which *La Dépêche* had printed in its first clear accusation of slapdash work by the police.

'Thanks boys,' she told them. 'I'm going to look this over again, get it sorted out in my own mind. I want to listen to that cassette once more. You've been a great help. I'll be back this evening.'

For the third time, the cassette ended in silence. It had told her nothing and, more importantly, she still could not place the voice, or even imagine what the man might be like, his age, his merits and weak points. It occurred to her that there was a market for a voice expert, just as there were handwriting experts. Maybe they existed. She must ask Travers when he phoned in.

The family gathered for the 8.00 p.m. TV news and Florence joined them. The others were Julien, Thérèse, Alexandra, Michel, Gilbert and Mathilde.

'No comments please,' Florence ordered, knowing the Chateauvallon affair would be included. 'Let's hear the news first.' She was not entirely surprised to see the Minister of Justice being interviewed as part of the newscast.

Asked why he had not produced the letter earlier, he said coolly that there was no reason for divulging its contents: 'I had no reason for keeping silent or for saying anything. I was simply in possession of a letter whose private, even intimate nature is perfectly obvious. If you read it again you will realize that Georges Quentin clearly had no wish for it to be made public.'

'On account of the words "for the reason you know about"?' the interviewer asked.

The Minister dodged the question: 'I finally decided to release the letter after a lot of insinuations, which became a flood and were of course most distasteful. After all, he was a friend of mine and I simply had to protect his reputation. It was not an easy decision to reach, very painful.'

'Knowing that you would be asked about "the reason you know about"?'

'I knew it, yes,' the Minister snapped. 'Knew it and resolved not to answer. The Prime Minister is the only person qualified to give the go-ahead, and I shouldn't think he will. Obviously, as Secretary of State for Defence, Georges Quentin had responsibility for difficult and delicate matters.'

'Arms sales, you mean?'

'Don't put words into my mouth. In fact he was called

upon to handle a number of projects one of which, to be honest, was hardly a success.'

'The Latin American affair?'

'Latin America and elsewhere. It fell down and Quentin was deeply upset about it,' the Minister declared with vigour. It was put about that the government wanted to ease him out, but I can affirm that that is untrue. He offered his resignation, and it was with *immense regret*—and no minister will gainsay it—that we reluctantly accepted it. Georges Quentin left the government at his own request and honourably, just as he chose what he saw as an honourable way of departing this life. That's what the public must know.' He glared out of the screen at each and every one of the French voters looking at him. 'I never imagined I would one day be obliged to set the facts to right personally, but the behaviour of certain biased media has left me no choice in the matter.'

Florence got up and switched off: 'He spoke well.' She was absorbed in thoughts of the man she had known so well for ten years. Nobody else spoke and they all looked at the empty screen.

Then she added: 'I can't flush out of my mind the notion that he still ought to have released the letter earlier. But basically, he's right. I liked his "very painful decision" bit. Well he's a pain in the neck to me!'

Nobody sought to deny that, and eventually Mathilde said dinner was served.

'You'll have to excuse me Mathilde, I shan't be dining. I have to go back to the paper.'

'Huh, the paper. Might be better if you kept away from it until this blows over,' Mathilde retorted.

'Come now,' Julien chided her. 'Please.'

To everyone's surprise she spun round on Julien and released a torrent of recrimination: 'Please? Please indeed! When the paper's on its last legs, when everything's falling around us! Can't you recognize a slap in the face when you hear it, or are you that thick-skinned? I'll tell you this, I felt the slap, and in Monsieur Antonin's time nobody would have dared refer to *La Dépêche* as "certain biased media" and complain about its "behaviour". Do you really think the Berg family can show its face in Chateauvallon now? 'I'm not going in, I'd be ashamed. I know I've only the right to keep quiet, to sulk in my own little corner, but that's the last straw, and nobody can stop me speaking my mind. When I think of Monsieur Antonin, I feel I have the *right* to upset Madame.'

At these last words, Mathilde planted herself squarely in front of Antonin Berg's daughter.

Florence said quietly: 'You've always stood on your rights, and there's no need to make all this song and dance about it.' She left the room and went upstairs.

Alexandra said: 'Come on Michel, let's go.'

'You too,' Mathilde wailed.

'We're having a pizza with some friends.'

Mathilde scowled at the others: 'Anyone else while we're about it, before I bring in the soup?' If she had brought it in and thrown it at them they could scarcely have been more amazed.

'We're all staying,' Gilbert mumbled in an attempt to calm her down.

It was a quick, silent meal.

André Travers was silent too, and Florence waited in vain for his news.

He had some news, but preferred to keep it to himself. He had started his investigation with a call on Arlette, finding the bird flown. The concierge was emphatic; Mademoiselle had gone off with all her things and she didn't know where.

That was all in a day's work, but unfortunately it had only just begun. He rang dozens of numbers committed over the years to a now-floppy, dog-eared notebook that never left him. He also ploughed through the library copies of more than one national paper. Which brought him to 5.00 p.m. and a serious lead. At 7.00 p.m. he walked into a gymnasium bearing its more up-to-date title of body building club (in English), used by women of all ages who worked all day and spent part of the evening repairing the damage, while still hoping they could get a film or night club in before their minimum five hours' sleep. For this they paid good money to a forty-year-old man growing quite tubby from the takings, who shouted and swore at them; the ladies loved it.

At first he took no notice of Travers, and then suddenly recognized him: 'Well look what's turned up, and to what do I owe the pleasure of your intrusion?' He jerked his head at the clients: 'They're not for sale, if that's what you're interested in.' He raised his voice: 'Come along there, pick 'em up, I want to see little piles of fat on the floor by the time you leave.' He grinned at Travers: 'So you found me; that worries me. I went out of my way to hide up behind bars for two years, then I ran two bars of another sort in the provinces, and finished up here doing an honest job of work—at least, they do the work and I put the elastic bands round the cheques. Ha ha ha!'

'Looks like you're doing all right.'

The instructor pointed to his charges: 'When I've finished with them, they'll all receive a free T-shirt reading "Venus de Milo". Ha ha ha! But that's enough of that. What's your problem?'

'I want your advice.'

'I hope it's not Lorieux who sent you, like eight years ago. He was the one who got me in the clink: gave me the job and when it got too hot for him he sent the blue meanies to see me. Nice chap, I don't think.'

Travers attempted to match his jargon: 'You still in the art business?' He meant forgery.

'I'm a reformed character.' As if to prove it he went over to the customers, patted a couple of bottoms thinly clad in boxer-style briefs, and came back.

'Now about this advice,' Travers said. 'This has nothing whatever to do with Lorieux, but he's involved remotely with a problem I'm dealing with at the moment.'

The other man told him: 'Same kind of thing as eight years ago?'

Travers ran over the story of the data sheets, and asked who was likely to do that class of job.

343

'There's only two ginks I reckon'd do that. One's living rent free at the taxpayer's expense, if you see what I mean, and the other comes right off the top deck—a real genius.'

'With what's at stake, it can only be the genius. What's his moniker?'

'Are you kidding? I don't give away names like that. You take me for some kind of crook?'

'Only asking you to sell it to me. An honest straightforward transaction.'

The other thought for a while: 'You say Lorieux is losing you sleep?'

'I get less and less these days.'

The man went over to correct a woman's posture, and returned: 'Forget the buying and selling. You can have it as a little present, on one condition: you give Lorieux my regards when you kick his teeth in. Give me a bit of paper.'

Travers handed him this and a ballpoint. The instructor jotted down a name and address.

Outside, Travers memorized the details and threw the paper down a drain. He decided against phoning Florence; better to produce some results first.

Alexandra and Michel had invented the friends, and they chewed their way through their pizzas on their own. The girl hardly opened her mouth except to push another forkful into a doughy mass that was already making her jaw ache. It was a slow kind of fast food, she quipped. Mathilde's little speech had impressed her, and she wondered about this big setback for her mother so soon after her arrival from the States.

Michel sent discreet little glances in her direction and finally said: 'Let's go for a run round.'

'All right,' she mumbled. 'If we go back to La Commanderie, we might as well enter a monastery.'

'I've got an idea.'

He took her to La Grange, a disused hut converted by the town's youth into a makeshift disco. It held some sad memories for Michel, especially the night Anne Vernier had thrown him over, only to shack up with his uncle

344

Armand, whom she had also walked out on after he became a member of parliament. Michel still disliked Armand but he had forgotten his unrequited love sufficiently to put in an appearance, even at the risk of bumping into Anne Vernier again. He told Alexandra it would be better if he walked in first, and when he did he was struck by the scruffiness of the place, the patches on the walls between the curling posters, the crates used as seats and the smoky oil lamps. Alexandra gave a laugh when she saw it.

'Huh, if you wanted to surprise me you've succeeded. Must be the crummiest joint west of the Champs-Élysées.'

'It's all we've got for anyone under twenty-one.'

'No wonder there's hardly anyone here.'

'Sometimes it warms up later.'

'It's hard to imagine.'

'I believe it does. Had some good times here last year.'

They stood watching a guitar player and a drummer rocking this way and that without conviction, observed morosely by perhaps a dozen boys and girls sipping Coke.

Michel explained: 'It was the one place I could be sure no Berg would set foot in. It was better than nothing.'

'Can't they get any better players?'

'They put discs on sometimes. There's a sax player who's not too bad.' As the two found a crate to sit on, the musicians put a little more enthusiasm into their efforts. This was because the selfsame sax player came in at that juncture.

'Great, it's Teddy,' yowled a trio of girls, who ran over and kissed him on his cheeks. He responded cheerfully, for all the world like a pop star embracing a crowd of fans. An electric current zipped from Alexandra's neck to her knees, when she caught sight of the dazzling smile that contrasted with Teddy's thatch of curly black hair.

'The cock of the walk,' she exclaimed, half to herself.

His retinue of girls accompanied him to the plinth, and Teddy threw an arm round the prettiest girl's shoulders: 'OK, spin it fellers.' This in English. The girl put the disc on and the three musicians began splicing-in with the playback. Michel eyed Alexandra cautiously, and saw her preparing to like the noise. Then she suddenly moved quickly to the turntable and stopped the disc.

'You don't need that,' she cried.

'What's the big idea?' the guitar player bawled.

Teddy's face flashed in the direction of the interloper, accepting the challenge: 'We're on our own boys, let's take it from the beginning, and make it jump!'

He tapped out the tempo, shoved the mouthpiece between his lips and the saxophone wailed out a complaint.

Alexandra gave the musicians a big smile to encourage them, and told Michel: 'They lack courage, that's all. They're better without the playback.'

'Why, you're dead right.'

'I wouldn't get up early to hear it, but I've come across far worse.'

'I don't want to be romantic, but I'd say he was playing just for you.'

'That's because I put in a request. What's his other name, Teddy what?'

'Teddy Kovalic.'

'Another one!'

'Bernard's cousin, you know the Harvard gentleman.'

'Oh him! I could go for Teddy though!'

Les Messageries was a far superior 'joint', especially that night with its restaurant lights blazing and a large table set out in the centre, loaded with flowers and with a dozen bottles of champagne lolling in their ice-filled silver buckets.

From a distance and growing louder came the chant: 'We're the best, we're the best—*L'Eveil, L'Eveil*, get your copy now!!!'

A gallimaufry of journalists and others from the paper rolled this way and that, followed some yards behind by Jean-Jacques Berg, his wife Marie-Lou and Maryse. Marie-Lou, whose philosophy of life could fairly be summed up as 'If they're dirty, burn them', hung back closer to the next group consisting of Mayor Adrien Jerome and some other local worthies. Bringing up the rear was the solitary figure of Bernard Kovalic.

There was an onlooker too, Catherine Kovalic who was on her way home and slowed down until the mayor's group had passed by. She failed to notice Bernard, who scared the life out of her as he emerged from the shadows. He on the other hand made no attempt to avoid her, and she found herself quaking in his arms.

'Ah, cousin Kate,' he said in a voice of cast iron. 'Come and join us, be my guest.'

'Who's "us",' she squeaked with mouse-like fury.

'*L'Eveil*, of course, we're celebrating our reorganization.'

'Oh yes?'

'And partly our little victory this morning. A good start, you can't deny it.'

'Yes, we really appreciated it at *La Dépêche*!'

'As a fellow pressman, I appreciate the compliment.'

'What ever are you talking about?'

Bernard said airily: 'By pure chance, during a casual conversation, I got the offer of a job: a salvage job on *L'Eveil*, or rather supervising the salvage job. Exactly what I've been looking for for ages.'

'Tell me more.'

'There's no secret. I'm interested in anything that fits in with my—er—career plans. Now, how about joining us in a bottle of bubbly?'

Catherine shook her head, saying nothing.

'But Catherine,' he urged. 'We're friends, surely. You were pleased to see me call on the baby and find out how you both were.'

'Your little victory this morning is not something I care to celebrate.'

Maryse came out of the restaurant again, saw Bernard and said: 'Ah, there you are, Monsieur Kovalic, we thought we'd lost you.'

He and Catherine were not far from the entrance by now, and Maryse came down the steps carrying a full

347

glass: 'Why, it's Catherine. How are you dear?'

'Quite well, thank you.'

Maryse waved the glass about: 'Settling into journalism? I must say I was surprised to see you taken on with so few qualifications, but you're lucky at *La Dépêche*, Madame Berg knows less about it than even I do!'

Bernard said firmly: 'Kindly leave us, Mademoiselle Mongin. Tell them I shan't be a moment.' He faced his cousin. 'Still in archives, haven't they promoted you yet?'

'They will soon.'

'We've got a place waiting for you at *L'Eveil*, if you're interested.'

'Why should I be?'

'More money, with your baby and the future to think of.'

'No other reasons?'

'Plenty,' he said. 'As you've noticed over the past two or three days, the storm clouds are gathering. I'd feel better if my cousin sought shelter where it's safest.'

'Anything else?' She gave a suggestion of a smile, and Bernard responded.

'Yes, you're a Kovalic. If that's what you want me to say, I'll come right out with it. The Kovalics stick together.'

She feigned coyness: 'That's a lot of reasons, too many perhaps.'

'Hard to say. But think about it. So it's no to the bubbly?'

'Yes, it's no. I think better without the fizz.'

Travers had a good meal to set him up again when he left the gymnasium. He slept well and was up at dawn. The man he had to see lived in a large provincial town, and his informant had described the rambling old house on the edge of the town.

He took a couple of deep breaths and rang the bell. A man of sixty or so opened up and glared at him with alert eyes that sparkled. He had the look of a successful trades-man, an impression confirmed when he led Travers into a sitting room looked down on by a Vermeer and other fine works. The room was cluttered with chests of drawers and statues. They chatted a while about these and the man asked how he could help him.

'I, how can I put it, I'm looking for a person who does copying.' The man's affable manner had disarmed Travers, and he doubted that he would bring himself to threaten him if it came to that. He was glad when the man launched into a short lecture, it gave him time to recover.

'I wonder,' his host said, 'whether you have the right term. There are copiers and forgers. A copier does ordinary work, but a forger has to be brilliant. I, for example, am a Mozart among forgers. I was an infant prodigy, and already produced my Bac certificate as a boy before I even sat for the exam! People make much of the joy of creating, but there is nothing, nothing I say Monsieur, to compare with the heady wine of a successful forgery. When I think of Leonardo da Vinci I can well understand the frustration he suffered!'

As he spoke he gave Travers a tour of his achievements: engravings in glass frames, a papal bull dating from the fifteenth century and much besides.

Travers stopped the flow of words: 'And writing, do you handle writing?'

'Naturally, it's the ABC of the business. Now, my friend, let's get to the point. Would you be wanting some letters done so that you can break off with a tiresome mistress?'

Politely Travers put him right: 'Actually I haven't come to place an order, but to ask you if you'd kindly look at these two documents.' He handed him two of the data sheets attributed to Quentin. 'Take your time.'

'Care is the first virtue of the good forger,' the man said, scanning the sheets. 'Now the eye, you need a perfect eye. This one, now let me think, this one's mine. Yes, definitely my work. Not as perfect as I would have liked but the client was in a devil of a hurry. I did about twenty, probably took twenty thousand francs off him for that.'

Travers was flabbergasted to see the old chap move over to a desk, pull out an order book and turn over the pages. He said: 'You mean you put it all in a book! My God, you

349

have a funny way of keeping things quiet!'

The man drew himself up: 'Monsieur, I never make promises to keep my mouth shut. The client approaches me, I give him my price, I do the job, he pays and that's that. Everything goes in the book, including VAT, and I pay my taxes in full as an official independent worker. These sheets, for example, I did them six weeks ago, that's right, six weeks that would be.'

'I wonder if I could ask you the client's name.'

'Of course, here it is: Madame Marcel Proust. I remember her, but to be honest I think it was probably a false name!'

'To be equally honest, I'd say you were telling the truth!'

They laughed and Travers clutched the man's hands, then hurried out. The Mozart of the counterfeiters watched him roar off with a squeal of tyres.

The routine at *La Dépêche* was proceeding like clockwork when he pulled up outside, this time with a squeal of brakes. He charged up the steps, and bowled along to Florence's office, where he barged in without knocking.

'I've got everything!' he cried, suddenly stopping sharp. The room was empty. He did an about turn and headed for the editorial room. On his way, Catherine called out to him, and he reluctantly skidded to a halt.

'Travers,' she said, 'I've got some important things to tell you. Last night I ran into my cousin Bernard, who was on his way to a banquet being run by *L'Eveil*, and . . .'

'Speed it up, Catherine.'

'Well, if you're not interested . . .'

'I am but I'm in a hell of a hurry.'

They stalked down the passage together and she continued her account: 'I was given to understand that the plot against Florence was set up right here in Chateauvallon. Of course he never said it outright but it was clear enough to me. The things going on in Paris are secondary. The whole affair began here, and it will continue here.'

'If it continues at all!'

'Whatever you think, something more is brewing in Chateauvallon.'

'You're undoubtedly right. Have you told Florence all this?'

'She hasn't been in yet, I called La Commanderie as I thought this was urgent, but they said she wasn't there.'

Travers felt the sweat under his armpits: 'Where is she then? What the hell's she up to?'

'I thought she was with you.'

'Not at all. By the way, did you find out what Bernard's links are with *L'Eveil*?'

'In charge of reorganizing it.'

'Fine. And he's got a job for you in the new set-up?' He stopped just inside the main editorial room.

'How did you guess?'

'The Kovalics stick together. He doesn't want a Kovalic on the enemy's side, is that it?'

'I suppose so.'

'Well, my sweet, the storm clouds have been gathering for long enough now, and it won't be long before you hear the clash of steel. Wars have broken out for less, and history's not over yet!'

He had a hand on Catherine's shoulder. Favrot, Edelman and the others stared at him as if he were drunk.

'Where's the boss?' he demanded.

'We were waiting for her to turn up. If *you* don't know, how do you expect *us* to?' Edelman said.

'It's not possible,' Travers said, raising his arms. 'Aw shit, it's the one day she ought to be here. Bloody hell, I've got hold of a piece of evidence that sticks out like a monkey's arse. The data sheets were forged!!!'

'Aw shit, as you so delicately put it,' Favrot moaned. 'What happens next?'

Edelman brightened: 'We'll do a leader and head it: "We're a bunch of idiots, but we don't half have fun!" And we'll sign it Suckers To The End.'

'Shut your trap,' Travers snarled. 'I've found the bloke who did the counterfeiting.'

'He told you, just like that?'

'He did. Spilled everything.'

Edelman waved his arms about, play-acting: 'That's Travers for you, boys. A real father confessor: "Forgive me father for I have sinned, made a fortune telling lies, but I won't do it again—ever".'

'That's exactly where you're wrong. He's real proud of his work, ridiculous as it seems. You can go and inspect his books whenever you like, it's only fifty kilometres from this room. Quite apart from anything else, there's a fantastic story there just waiting to be told.'

'Well go ahead.'

'Not without the go-ahead from our esteemed *patronne*. But between ourselves I'm getting worried. Someone had better call La Commanderie again.'

Everyone looked at Béatrice Bonnenfant, a trainee reporter. She said: 'I'm sorry, Monsieur Travers, I've tried about six times and Mathilde's fed up with me. Madame Berg left at 8.30 last night and nobody can trace her.'

'Incredible. Anything might have happened to her!'

'Not so incredible. Can't she spend the night in someone else's bed if she wants to?' said Edelman, being clever.

'Cut that out,' was all Travers could find to say. He feared the worst, but was incapable of producing a picture of it.

Unaware of the disasters trooping through Travers's mind, Alexandra and Michel were back at La Grange disco that same evening.

'So you like it here?' Michel said, more than ever boyish.

'It's not bad. Nice for tourists! I'm just glad to be away from La Commanderie. You should see their faces, and the phone keeps going every ten minutes. Gave me the creeps.'

'Don't worry, Aunt Florence has travelled up to Paris for something, and she just forgot to tell anyone.'

Alexandra wanted to discuss something else, anything but that, and she said irritably: 'It's not like her to forget. Anyhow it's *her* life.'

'Maybe she's gone to meet a lover.'

'How should I know? It's her business, she's a free agent.'

Michel had noticed that Alexandra was hard to get inside, she seemed offhand, sort of wriggly. He shrugged and supposed some girls were like that. Wily.

'How about a dance?' he said.

'Later perhaps. I just want to look on. But I like it, better than yesterday, I'm getting used to the place.'

The disco had filled up well tonight, and things seemed to be humming more. There were fewer wallflowers and the floor was bouncing up and down as couples stamped out rock and roll, now making a big comeback. The band was pretty terrific and Alexandra swayed excitedly on her crate. At a sign from Teddy, the others reduced their volume and he moved into a solo break, striving to get the most out of the only means he had to express his skill, his art, his emotions, his very soul. Young Kovalic's memories and aspirations, his hesitations and frustrations plunged and soared on a roller-coaster heading for another world. A world that few adults would comprehend, but the youngsters of Chateauvallon absorbed it as a sacrament. He was playing better, far better than he did last night, Alexandar realized. Perhaps because he had more to say this time. She caught his eye and threw him a smile, remembering her little scene when she switched off the disc. He smiled back through his eyes while his mouth curled over the smooth black mouthpiece. The instrument writhed and he could only follow it.

'Like it?' Michel said, breaking into her thoughts.

She signed for him to keep quiet, and gave herself up to the sensual delights of Teddy's magic snake.

Then it was over, and she struggled to emerge from the dream. Teddy acknowledged the applause, then chucked the sax at the drummer, jumping down from the plinth.

He reached Alexandra and said simply: 'Coming?'

She blinked, took his hand and got up. They went outside, neither of them uttering a word. Michel came to his senses and elbowed his way to the door just in time to see Alexandar's skirt fluttering from the pillion of Kovalic's new Honda bike.

Travers sweated out the best part of the day, suffering the slings and arrows of his colleagues, until even they lost interest in the game. He was assailed by the growing conviction that if he did not act nobody else would. And that went for the Berg family too.

Soon after 7.00 p.m. he made his decision and within minutes was facing Commissaire Nicolo across his desk.

Nicolo regarded him with a jaundiced eye, having received what he eloquently referred to as a gutful from *La Dépêche*. Try as he might he could not find it in him to forgive the Lady Berg for her frontal assault on his professional competence. He felt strong when Travers disclosed the reason for his call, strong enough to play the kind uncle.

'The first thing I'll tell you, Travers, is that I'm prepared to overlook what's happened in the past. You played tough over this Quentin imbroglio and you lost. Now we can be friends again. I understand your position and I can make allowances.'

Travers remained cool: 'Be that as it may, I'm not here to play footsie with you, but to find Florence Berg. She's been missing twenty-four hours now.'

'I know, you already said so. And I've already said it's no business of mine.'

'Still got a lump in your fat belly, eh Nicolo?'

The said belly spread over the desk edge as the commissaire leaned forward eyeball to eyeball: 'Now you listen to me. If I say it's none of my business it has nothing to do with that little madam making a monkey out of me. People have tried it before and burned their fingers. The reason is that what you are asking me to do is—and I'll cite the official requirement—"an inquiry in the interests of the family". And I've had no request from the family. But hold on.' He addressed one of his inspectors handling some files three yards away: 'Germain, did the Berg family phone in while I was out?'

'Not to my knowledge.'

Nicolo spread his hands at Travers: 'However, if you can show a connection with the family, a secret marriage for example, that changes things.'

'That's good, Nicolo, we're getting somewhere. It may not stand up for long, but a secret marriage is just the excuse you need. How about it?'

'It's not an excuse, it's the fruit of my experience. You know, nine times out of ten, we find that the good lady in these cases has run off with a nicer guy, and if your bird's done that, you'd better not be seen crying your eyes out on my shoulder. You'd look silly.'

Travers gave some little nods: 'And the fact that she's right bang in the middle of a national scandal doesn't worry you either.'

Nicolo leaned back and a thick layer of fat dropped down under his chin: 'She's a woman, Travers, and they're no different than they used to be. They're like musical instruments and sometimes they go quack.'

'Don't try out-phallocrating me, Nicolo. Suppose she's decided to end it all, is that none of your business too? Maybe something went snap.'

'You don't scare me, my friend, I know all about suicides, remember?' He emitted a laugh designed to put Travers at ease.

Travers muttered: 'Even so, Commissaire, if I were in your place I'd start thinking pretty fast what my first move would be. This could rebound on you.'

'And of course, as a journalist on *La Dépêche*, you know all about rebounds. But we don't sell headlines, Travers, we do an honest day's work, that's all.'

Adrien Jerome learned of Florence Berg's disappearance from Inspector Germain, subsequent to the Nicolo-Travers tussle. Germain was an ally of Jerome's and did a few odd jobs for him for a modest fee and the assurance of a cushy little job at the town hall some time in the future.

The mayor was the last to leave work that evening and the town hall lights began switching off as he went down the steps. Germain caught him off-guard, he was tired and pasty-faced, his lips in a set sneer, but he recovered and said: 'Oh it's you Germain.'

'Sorry to catch you like this, but I couldn't tell you over the phone.'

'Get in with me,' Jerome said, heading for the rear door of a black Citroën CX his chauffeur was holding open for him. 'I've had a dreadful day and I want to get home.'

'But your driver'll hear us.'

At that, Jerome took a deep breath and led Germain away a few paces.

'Florence Berg has been missing for twenty-four hours.'

'Wanted a change, I expect. Even a duchess likes a little romance now and again, you should know that.'

'That may be so, but Travers came in and reported it to Nicolo. I heard it all. If Travers is in a tizzy about it, there's every reason I should be too, if you see what I mean.'

'Why, what's giving you cold feet?'

'Travers reckons she's bumped herself off.'

Jerome struggled to retain his calm: 'Highly unlikely, but if she has I can well understand it. The irrefutable evidence in *L'Eveil* could make anyone die of shame. The blame would be put on *L'Eveil*, so what's the problem?'

Germain's hands were whirling: 'The problem is the build-up to it. If Nicolo gives Travers a grilling, Travers will come out with the whole sequence: the anonymous calls, the voice, the cassette. He or Madame Berg still has the cassette, that's for sure.'

'You're beyond suspicion, Germain. You're one of the finest mimics I've ever heard. That's why I asked you to perform that little service for me.'

The inspector took a step nearer: 'Neither Travers nor Florence Berg had the slightest idea whose voice it was. But Nicolo's another matter; we've worked together for years, and he knows my voice, knows I do imitations at police gala nights. He'll know well enough whose voice it is on tape, and he'll come right out with it. I like working for you, *Monsieur Le Maire*, but I've taken more than my share of risks. I won't take the rap, I warn you, no sir!'

Jerome fought to stay calm: 'Has your *patron* started inquiries?'

'Not yet, he has to have a proper request from the family.'

'Got any ideas then?'

'Now it's ideas you want. I'm in this thick enough.'

'Take it easy, you'll think of something, you're not a cop for nothing. Keep your eyes peeled and play it by ear.' He ended with a gay chuckle and shook hands with Germain.

Jerome sank into the rear seat of the car and felt the blessed cool of the leather under him. He released an immense sigh and hissed through his teeth.

'Trouble, *Monsieur Le Maire*?'

'No no, nothing serious. But if you're not in too much of ₊ a hurry, I'd like to make a last call before I turn in.'

The tiredness had left him. He knew in a flash what had to be done.

Travers went to La Commanderie and found Gilbert Bossis with Julien and his wife Thérèse. They looked miserable, and Thérèse said did he have any news. She poured out a coffee and gave him a brandy without asking him.

He ran over his chat with Nicolo and concluded: 'So it's obvious I've done as much as I can, and it's you who have to trigger off the search.'

Gilbert said: 'Naturally we're thinking along the same lines; I mean, that we ought to do something. But we don't want Florence bawling us out for making a fuss about nothing. To be truthful, I don't know what to do, and I simply keep running over the possibilities in my mind.'

'So do the rest of us,' Julien said.

Travers was thinking they could sit on a fence long enough for it to collapse under them. He realized just how intimidated they all were by Florence. And that went for him too.

The phone rang, and Thérèse grabbed it: 'Oh it's you, Armand.'

'Well, any news?'

'Nothing. Travers has just rolled in, that's all. He's got nothing either.'

357

'I want to talk to him,' Armand rapped. And when Travers took over: 'Listen Travers, listen carefully. You probably know something the rest of us don't, simply because you're so close to her. For example, nobody knows better than you do how she really took that story in *L'Eveil* yesterday. Was it just another setback, a challenge, the end of the world or what?'

'I'd say she reacted pretty well, and she certainly didn't go all wet and weepy. Ah, hold on Armand.' Travers was aware of the others running to the window to see a car arriving. They signed to him that it was not Florence's. Travers went on: 'Just a car, but not hers. Carry on.'

Armand said: 'You didn't have a row or anything like that?'

'No.'

'She never at any moment gave the impression of someone at the end of her tether, likely to do something stupid?'

'On the contrary, she'd only been in the office five minutes so to speak when she'd already mapped out a new campaign. Even gave me an assignment.'

'To do with those data sheets?'

'Yes.'

'But that's great news. Why didn't you say? She wanted the proof that they were forged, is that it?'

'Quite. I have the proof, but she disappeared before I could give it to her. Ah well, I'm afraid I'll have to phone you back. Sorry.'

Travers left Armand holding a dead handset. And for a good reason. Mathilde had brought Jerome into the lounge. It was his car that they had heard, and Mathilde had welcomed him like the Angel Gabriel. She was in a foul mood, disgusted with the family, even Gilbert, Julien and Thérèse. That little hussy Alexandra was the last straw, using the place as a hotel and going off to eat outside and spend half the night lord knows where without so much as a by-your-leave. Mathilde would undoubtedly have had one of her turns had she known that the girl was at that moment pinned in a state of ecstasy under Teddy Kovalic on a roadside verge fifteen kilometres out of Chateauvallon. She assured Jerome that he was not putting them out at all, they were deeply touched that he had taken the trouble to call on them.

'I learned that you were extremely concerned,' he told them, shaking hands with them all in turn. 'As I was going past, I saw the lights and wondered whether you had any news.'

'None, worse luck,' said Gilbert. 'Nice of you to pop in.'

The mayor said smoothly: 'Of course you're out of your wits with worry, I so understand. But there's probably a simple explanation. I'm surprised the police don't act, although I know why. But Nicolo's a stickler for the rules. They have to be careful, as usually it's a family thing. On the other hand the families are naturally reluctant to make a fuss. It's hard to know what to do.'

Gilbert gestured to him to take a seat, which he did, declining a brandy. Travers eyed him carefully.

Jerome continued: 'Rules are all very well, but as mayor I ought to order the police to start looking at once. I'd like your opinion first, though.' Julien mumbled noncommittally. 'I'll go ahead if you like, unofficially. But if you are absolutely against it, then of course . . .'

Julien said: 'I'm not absolutely opposed . . .'

'Then in that case I'll tell them. Mathilde, I'd love a really strong coffee. May I use the phone?'

Jerome called the commissariat, the duty man at the town hall, some council staff, and concluded: 'You coming with me, Travers?'

'Naturally, *Monsieur Le Maire.*'

Within an hour of the mayor's Citroën CX leaving the Berg residence, the town hall sprang to life again as the co-ordination centre for Operation Florence Berg.

Police cars and vans were patrolling in and around the town, several town hall secretaries manned phones at a long table, and the mayor had ordered sandwiches, beer and orange juice from a bar that was still open.

Jerome and Travers cleared a path through the victuals to spread a large-scale map of the region on the table. Plain clothes policemen consulted with them every so often. The ashtrays quickly grew messy and the room filled with haze.

At length one of the girls yelled across: 'Monsieur Travers, they've found a Renault 5.' He jerked his chin for details. 'Renault 5 turbo, colour black with red lines, in a country lane off the Orleans road. Car empty containing only maps and one packet of Peter Stuyvesant with five cigarettes.'

'Nothing else?'

'No occupants, no luggage. Licence plate number . . .'

'That's it! Tell 'em I'm on my way!' He checked the position on the map.

When he arrived the police had touched nothing, and the driver's door was still open. Men were scouring the immediate area.

Chapter Four

Alexandra and Teddy fell in love with volcanic lust, and they needed few words to get it on record. That it really was love neither of them doubted when they split up at the main gate of La Commanderie, each privately saddened as well as sated for the while.

'See you tomorrow, I mean today,' Alexandra said like millions of kids before her. Teddy was more practical and told her where.

Walking centimetres in the air, Alexandra approached the big house and was astonished to see most of the lights on. That could be either of two things: her mother was back, or she was not. Perhaps she was dead or injured. Alexandra gulped and came down to earth.

Nobody bothered to ask where she had been. But they all told her at once that her mother's car had been found. Travers gave her the details.

Then Gilbert said: 'I gather that the door was open because she ran away to escape some attacker.'

'Don't jump to conclusions,' Travers said. 'The door was open, that's all we know.'

'Someone could have forced it open from the outside,' the old man went on.

Alexandra cried out: 'We're not playing hunt-the-thimble. When you don't know, there's no point in making things up, it only makes everyone edgy.'

Travers defended him: 'He's only trying to understand, Mademoiselle. Like the rest of us.' The girl irritated him; what had she against Gilbert Bossis, and in any case what was she doing rolling in at this hour?

Julien asked if anyone had checked the petrol tank.

'Full,' said Travers. 'She may have planned a long trip.

On the other hand she may not have.'

Mathilde volunteered: 'I've checked her room, and she's taken a biggish suitcase.'

'At last a useful clue,' Alexandra declared.

'She took her toilet bag, her broken-check suit, and as far as I can make out one or two dresses.'

Alexandra concluded: 'When a woman goes away with those things she means to show herself, not disappear.'

'Now *you're* making things up,' Gilbert said. 'What do you mean by that?'

'A short trip, for example.'

'Just for the fun of it,' Gilbert scoffed.

'Why not? When everything's going wrong, you need a change.'

Travers tut-tutted: 'Not her style, Alexandra.'

'That's only your opinion.'

'I'm only saying . . .'

The phone went. As he happened to be the nearest he answered, listened, then handed the receiver to Julien: 'Your brother Jean-Jacques. Wants someone from the family.'

Julien put the receiver down on the directory: 'Not me, then!'

'Nor me,' Gilbert added.

Mathilde moved over: 'I'll take it. Yes? Julien won't answer nor will Gilbert or anyone else, Monsieur Jean-Jacques. Not surprising after what you've done to your sister.'

Jean-Jacques hollered: 'But I'm worried too.'

'About time too,' said the worthy woman. 'You should have thought of that before. If you want to know my opinion, your father always knew you were the oddball of the family, but this time you've outclassed yourself. Brought shame on the whole Berg family!'

Whereupon she slammed the receiver down. By now Alexandra was fiddling with the olive-shaped switch on a table lamp, switching it on and off.

'Stop that, for God's sake,' Julien rapped. 'What have you got against your mother?'

362

'What's that got to do with it?'

'Nothing. I'm just imagining your face if the worst happens.'

'The worst? You make me sick all of you. Anyone'd think she was two years old. I know *maman*, she's tough as houses. What's your opinion, Monsieur Travers? Has she done anything indicating any dramatic outcome?'

'No.'

'No row between you yesterday?'

'I was on a reporting job.'

'And before that?'

'She worked out a riposte against *L'Eveil*. I agreed fully with her plans.'

Alexandra, eyes blazing, said: 'I didn't mean the paper. What about your personal relations? Unless that's indiscreet.'

The others observed the joust between them. Travers raised his voice: 'The answer is no in both cases. No you are not being nosey and no there was no clash. What about you, did you have words yesterday?'

'Neither yesterday nor the day before. Our trouble began much earlier than that. Goodnight, Monsieur Travers, goodnight everybody, I'm going to bed.'

She pranced out, skirt a-swaying, and Mathilde mumbled: 'Perhaps we all ought to.'

Jean-Jacques Berg stood staring at his telephone after Mathilde hung up on him. His mouth was pinched tight, his face without colour.

His wife Marie-Lou scoffed: 'You were always daddy's little boy, and now you're nurse's little boy. I don't suppose you'll ever grow up now.' She shrugged her contempt and went up to bed.

Jean-Jacques waited a good half-hour before going up, and was immensely relieved to find her asleep. He slid in beside her and lay there awake until dawn.

He phoned La Commanderie again, and Mathilde told him there was no new development. He found Marie-Lou and young Michel bowed over their breakfast.

'No news about Florence,' he told them, taking his seat.

'Huh, she's certainly got you on the hop,' his wife said, dunking her *baguette* in her coffee, and flicking back the sleeve of her peignoir.

'Why me specially? I'm not directly concerned, of course.' Jean-Jacques poured some coffee. 'If people cleared off every time they were caught out printing rubbish, there wouldn't be anyone left to run the press! No, you can be sure, this has nothing to do with me.'

'Unfortunately, that's what everyone will be thinking.'

'Let them. My answer is that journalism is a serious business, and you can't run a paper like playing dollies. I did a professional job of work, that's all.'

He scowled at Michel who was stifling the beginnings of a laugh. He avoided eye contact with the boy, spread butter on his bread, placed it on his plate and went on: 'I'm no cub reporter, and everyone knows that too. If you want my opinion, I would guess she's planning some dramatic jiggery-pokery against us. I can feel it. This looks like a put-up job to me.'

'Huh, you've no proof of that. Florence boobed badly with this business, and as she'll never admit she's wrong, she is trying to make everyone feel sorry for her. "Oh how dreadful it all is," she's saying, "Everyone's on to me, and I can't stand it any longer". She's right: everyone's worried sick, moaning and groaning, crying their eyes out.'

Jean-Jacques brought the bread to his mouth, then lowered it again.

'Can't get it down?' Michel said.

His father ignored him and said quietly: 'Even if the worst happens, and she's gone and . . .' He failed to finish.

'Why call it the worst?' his wife said. 'Would it be the worst—for you?'

'Certainly! From the moral point of view I can imagine nothing worse.'

'Don't overdo it, your morals will settle down again, don't worry. But materially speaking?'

He protested: 'Really, Marie-Lou, do you realize what you are saying?'

'Yes,' she smiled, 'Only . . .'

'Only what? Since you think of everything in terms of money, don't hold it back, let it all hang out!'

She remained composed: 'Let's say that, if the worst came to the worst, some would say you were damn wrong to move from *La Dépêche* to *L'Eveil*.'

Michel interjected: 'Especially to sell your stake in *La Dépêche*. You'd look a proper turkey!'

His father snapped: 'I didn't sell my stake, but yours. Because I was morally obliged to.'

'Morals again?'

'Yes, Monsieur. You don't suppose I could go along with what your aunt's been doing with your grandfather's paper!'

Michel told an imaginary guest: 'Admirable. I never realized I had such a moral father!'

J-J Berg raised a fist, and lowered it at the sight of Marie-Lou's flashing eyes.

In the heart of France close by a village called Saint-Paul-sur-Loire at a hamlet named La Jouterie there is an enchanting unpretentious manor house in white with a slate roof nestling in grounds noted for their herbs.

This is the home of Artus Balestra, an eminent biologist of some fifty summers, tall, elegant and well-proportioned. Sporting a superb head of silver hair, Balestra appears with regularity on television when comment is needed on his particular branch of science.

While Jean-Jacques was staring at the ceiling alongside his sleeping spouse, Balestra spent an uneasy night. The previous evening his gardener had seen, on his way back from Saint-Paul, the figure of what he described as a youngish woman walking along the road uncertainly. She seemed incapable of keeping her balance and when he reached her she stumbled and collapsed onto the grass by the road. The gardener had lifted her up and laid her in the back of his van. Balestra had got her to bed and watched over her, taking her pulse regularly and listening to her breathing. At length he retired to his own bed and wondered what to do about this attractive lady dressed in such good clothes, youngish indeed and appealing to the eye.

When his housekeeper turned up for duty he handed the unexpected guest over to her, and went through his pre-breakfast routine thoughtfully.

'How did she get here?' the housekeeper said.

'She collapsed not far from the gate. I can tell you no more than that.'

'What should I do for her, Monsieur?'

'Simply watch over her for the moment. She's obviously in a state of complete exhaustion, but there doesn't seem to be anything medically wrong with her. She's not in a coma, if that's what you're thinking. So let's wait until she wakes up. It could take hours, and when she does wake, just tell her there's nothing to worry about, and fetch me.'

Balestra had put the woman in one of two beds in the room, and he left his housekeeper to it. Just then he heard his gardener calling, and hurried downstairs, tying his bathrobe.

'We've found this in the ditch on the other side of the wall,' the man said, lifting up a fair-sized Vuitton suitcase. 'Must be hers.'

'Obviously. Lucky you happened to come along when you did.'

'What's wrong with her?' the gardener said in his forthright way.

'Nothing, as far as I can see. But if she'd spent the night on the grass, she'd have developed pneumonia for sure in last night's mist.'

'Well, thank the Lord for that. I was that scared! When I saw her bowl over, I thought she'd pegged out.'

Taking the suitcase, Balestra said: 'I'll keep this, and see you later on, Victor.'

Artus Balestra turned to go, but Victor said: 'If I might make a suggestion, Monsieur.' His employer waited. 'I know she's in good hands where you're concerned, but to cover yourself you ought really to call a doctor. I mean we don't even know where she's from or anything.' He ended lamely.

Balestra thought for a moment: 'You may be right about the doctor. But I have a suspicion I know where she's from.'

He then climbed the stairs two at a time to get dressed.

Albertas Kovalic sat in his office like a man possessed. This time his rage was directed not at Teddy or at one of his sisters-in-law but at a flashy Mediterranean youngster who was protesting vehemently.

'I keep telling you,' he declared urgently, 'that's what they told me to tell you.'

'So you're telling me!' Albertas shouted. 'But if your people in Trieste want to bellyache they'll have to tell me face to face. Whatever you say goes in one ear and out the other, d'you hear! I don't like hearing things indirectly. I deserve more respect than that, d'you hear!'

The young man's jaw took on a firmer aspect, but he said nothing.

'All right,' Albertas went on. 'You've got that in your noddle. How are they there? Your wife and kids?'

'They're fine, like usual.'

'Good. And Marko's cancer?'

'Getting worse,' said the youth, lighting a cigarette.

'That's life.' The phone went and the older man answered: 'Hullo, Albertas Kovalic. Madame Desvignes? Good day to you, Madame, can I help you?'

Albertas could never be obsequious, but he was polite with customers. He listened patiently at a yapping noise from the receiver.

As her tale developed, a change came over his countenance and his mouth moved forward and back as the tension rose in his mind: 'I don't understand it, Madame Desvignes. It's marked here plain enough: delivery Desvignes 10.30. I underlined it, and young Teddy's usually on time. He's been held up, that's the explanation. But I'll get on to it right away, *Madame*. It'll be there as soon as I can locate Teddy. Sorry about that, my regards, Madame Desvignes.'

He replaced the receiver, and growled: 'All right, skedaddle, you.'

'What'll I tell 'em then? It's understandable, raising it from ten to fifteen per cent, they don't like it.'

'Listen laddie, I had brains when your mother was in nappies. I can work it out for myself.'

'Twelve would be better'n fifteen.'

'Fifteen it is. Now clear off!'

Old Kovalic watched him slip out through the yard and drive off in a blue Italian-registered BMW.

Albertas picked up the phone: 'Maison Lanjouinais? Oh this is Kovalic, sorry to interrupt you, but my young nephew had something for you at ten o'clock. Did he deliver? Ah, very good. Sorry, I know you're busy, but Teddy's got behind today. I'll find him. Thanks very much.'

He stormed out of his office slamming the door and waddled over to his Citroën 'Deux Chevaux'. Teddy was somewhere between Lanjouinais and Madame Desvignes. 'May have broken down, but if that little bugger's run out of petrol, he'll pay for it. No one should run out of petrol,' Kovalic muttered.

He found the van, parked on a stretch of road between warehouses and a piece of grass. It stood there as resplendent as it could in its straw yellow paint with the letter K on each door and its grey tarpaulin. Albertas stopped the car some distance before he reached it and walked carefully along the edge of the grass. The cab was empty and he went round the back and raised one of the flaps ever so slightly. His eyes popped. Teddy was lying on a plaid blanket in a space among the crates and cartons, with a girl sitting next to him doing up an expensive-looking scarf. Albertas noted a box marked with the name of Chateauvallon's priciest women's shop.

'Oh you shouldn't have done it,' the girl said, bending over to kiss him.

As she neared his lips, she saw Teddy's eyes fill with terror.

'Out!' his uncle shouted. 'Out of there this minute!'

'Yes uncle,' Teddy gulped, struggling to his feet. He walked gingerly to the back of the van. Albertas grasped him with both hands, threw him onto the road and began kicking him in the ribs.

'Get up!' Albertas yelled. 'Up! I'll show you—fornicating instead of doing your work. I'll show you, yer little devil!' Spittle formed on his lips as he pulled off his trouser belt and whipped the boy mercilessly. Twice the belt struck Teddy's privates and he yelped.

Alexandra jumped down from the van: 'Hey, have you gone mad or something? Stop hitting him. Teddy, defend yourself!' She elbowed her way between the two and faced Teddy's uncle. The belt struck her in the face from one eye to the chin.

'Get away!' Teddy screamed at her. To his uncle: 'Leave her alone, leave her alone!'

'Who is she? Who's this little bitch?' Albertas stopped thrashing.

'Alexandra Berg,' she said swiftly. 'I think you know my people.'

For a moment Albertas remained motionless, heaving to get his breath back: 'If they ask you who did that to you, make sure you tell them it was me.' He spat a practised gob in her direction, and drove Teddy up into the driving seat with his belt. 'Now get back to work. And don't forget, I'm following you.'

Alexandra watched the two vehicles go off, and put the scarf over her head. Albertas Kovalic's fury did not entirely surprise her, but what galled her was Teddy's failure to fight back. She set out to walk back into Chateauvallon, heading in the direction of the cathedral.

As she entered the editorial room at *La Dépêche*, heads rose to look at her one by one, including those of Favrot, Edelman, Melchior and Travers. She went up to Travers.

'Anyone would think I was a ghost,' she said. 'Didn't Mathilde phone to say I'd be in?'

'She did,' Travers said. 'But not looking like that.'

'It's nothing serious. What's the latest news, then?'

'Still nothing on your mother. But listen, how did you get that weal across your face?' He studied her black eye, split lip and gash on the forehead. 'Bump into a door, or something?'

'Fell off a horse.'

'Right onto your riding crop?'

'Exactly. So we still don't know mother's whereabouts?'

Favrot butted in: 'Only one false trail about an hour ago.'

Travers told her: 'Nicolo's still holding back. Everything's been done so far by the municipal police, but Nicolo's bunch won't move without a formal request from the family. He's even more pig-headed after the municipal police found the car. He's like a brick wall, and I'm sick of bashing my head against it! I've had as much as I can take, and I'm going ahead myself.'

'*La Dépêche*?'

'Looks like our best bet, we've got 300,000 circulation and there must be one or two readers with a clue or an idea.'

'I can't fault that,' Melchior remarked.

'And I'll take full responsibility whatever happens,' Travers added. 'I'm still Acting Editor until the *patronne* decides otherwise. Now you, Melchior, ought to be in bed, you naughty boy!'

'All right!' Melchior said with a chuckle.

Travers went on: 'I'll be sticking my neck out, and well out. We'll have to splash this, making it clear that Florence Berg disappeared immediately after the story in *L'Eveil*.'

'Very good,' said Alexandra.

'I didn't ask your opinion.'

'But you can't stop me giving it.'

The girl calmly strolled into an empty office and plonked the phone down in front of her, flipping through an address book. Some of the staff went back to work.

'Hullo,' they heard her say into the mouthpiece. 'I'd like Bernard Kovalic please. Not at the office? Never mind, I'll call back.'

Watched by a dozen pairs of eyes, she returned and stood in front of Travers: 'You couldn't care less about what I think, but it would be best if you could say you have my approval as her daughter. You have it. I want her back too.'

Edelman said drily: 'She'd better not come back too fast. If she sees her daughter's face in that state . . .'

He ground to halt. Nobody thought it funny.

Florence slept sixteen hours, motionless in one of the two beds in Balestra's guest room.

She was awake when he came in that time, and as on the previous occasions he touched her shoulder lightly. 'Hullo,' he said and smiled.

Florence opened her eyes, and shut them tight again. The sun was streaming in. Then she opened them again and squinted at him, her arms stretched out on the bedcover.

Then she looked down at the pyjamas: 'These aren't mine.'

'That is correct,' he laughed. 'I see you have a keen sense of who owns what. They're mine. When you arrived you had no luggage, but we found your case. Here it is. That at least is yours.'

She tried to hoist herself up, and fell back: 'How did it get here? How did I get here, for that matter?'

'We shall know within a matter of minutes. You've been playing truant, it seems to me.'

Florence sat up for good: 'I asked you what I was doing here?'

Artus Balestra cocked his head: 'Only you can answer that. All I know is how you arrived—on foot and whacked out. You dropped your case ten yards from the spot where you flaked out next to my gate.

'This is crazy. Why did I come here?'

'As I said, only you can answer that. But there's no hurry.'

'Where am I?'

'Ah, the classic question. In my house which is called La

371

Jouterie, and it's in the *commune* of Saint-Paul-sur-Loire.'

'But it's twenty kilometres from Chateauvallon!'

'Twenty-three to be exact, Madame Berg.'

'You know who I am?'

'You have just mentioned Chateauvallon, and your initials are on your bag. I'd have recognized you in any case. You're quite a celebrity; every time I've eaten out at Chateauvallon, your name has cropped up with the dessert.'

'I'd prefer to be less of a celebrity at the moment.'

'No doubt, but I find your company charming.' He smiled in a kindly way.

'That's nice of you, Monsieur—Monsieur?'

'Artus Balestra.'

'Of course!' she cried, at ease suddenly. 'I should have recognized you. Your photos are everywhere. Artus Balestra!'

He spread his hands: 'Artus indeed, and alas. I went to some trouble to discover how that preposterous un-Italian name found its way into my dear mother's brain, but I found out that she insisted on it. She was from Milan, of course. I've got used to it.'

Florence laughed unrestrainedly. The situation was really quite comical, and her host was nice. He submitted to a lengthy scrutiny on her part. She was thinking there was something about him that reminded her of Maurice Arras, on whom she once had a crush. They must be about the same age; he was a scientist too, and with the same amused half-cynical attitude that was strangely soothing in its effect. She decided she was happy, but the feeling only lasted for a few seconds.

'The paper!' she cried. 'You've told them at the office?'

'Not yet,' he said, sitting down on the other end. 'Perhaps I should have, but I sensed this was some kind of adventure and I took the liberty of doing nothing. It's your decision.'

'Decision!' she wailed. 'If you only knew, if *I* only knew.'

'Let it ride for a while. You're unsure what preceded

372

your arrival here and you're just coming out of a long bout of fatigue, because you've slept sixteen hours non-stop, and almost certainly because you're starving.'

'Ah,' was all she said, shaking her head confusedly.

He left her and came back in five minutes. 'It's the crack of noon, and not too late for breakfast. Your eggs are ready, *Madame*.' He laid a tray on her lap, and she gave him a huge smile.

He told her: 'You now have a crucial decision to make. Either you look at the eggs, or you throw yourself upon them. But I warn you, I don't propose to eat them for you.'

It proved to be the oddest day she had ever experienced in her whole life, possibly the most delightful—certainly since she had taken over *La Dépêche*.

Having devoured a vast quantity of food, she set about appraising her situation. Her name was Florence Berg, she owned a newspaper printed and published at Chateau-vallon. Some person, she could not identify him or her, had assaulted her verbally and she had escaped in her car, believing that a ride in the country would soothe her nerves. That was the extent of her awareness concerning the immediate past. And now, many hours later, she was in the home of a noted scientist with her suitcase but without her car. Her memory had gone into limbo and it didn't worry her a bit. She felt happy, her surroundings were quiet and fragrant, and she was prepared to wait calmly for what followed.

Already, she had realized that her host Artus Balestra had contributed to her peaceful awakening. He was hand-some, amusing to listen to, alert and caustic, yet imperturb-able and reassuring. Whatever worries she had seemed to be those of another person. The crucial instant had been when she told him she had no clear view on whether the paper should be informed. It was not until dinner that they raised the subject again, kicked it around and at last reached a decision.

Meanwhile they spent a blissful afternoon strolling through the woods in and out of the sunlight, chatting

373

about everything and nothing, a little about themselves, demystifying their place in the universe, mocking past, present and future.

During this walk Artus explained something of the transient amnesia (that was his term) that had occurred to her: 'I don't want to hurt your pride but this has happened to many many others, Florence Berg. I've probably read through about a dozen clinical descriptions including the likely causes. Or to be quite honest I've skimmed through them, because it's not in my precinct.'

'What were the causes?'

'That, I can't remember,' he laughed. 'I'll confess I'm a dreadful pupil, but please don't let on about it, I'm so ashamed.'

'You don't sound like it.'

'That's because I'm a champion when it comes to self-satisfaction. My shortcomings worry me. I am smug about myself.'

A tiny worm of doubt wriggled into Florence's mind. Was he just playing the fool, or was he serious? She found him good company in any case, and slipped her arm in his. In a caressing voice she murmured: 'Your shortcomings don't look too bad at all, in your precinct.' She waved her hand at the surroundings.

'I'll tell you something else. I'm crafty, because I don't have a precinct, do not specialize. My work covers biology as a whole. When you're bottom of the class you should never get caught with a definite question. I've a finger in every pie and am willing to try anything. Sometimes it produces a valid discovery, but there's a lot of luck to it.'

Florence brought them to a halt: 'Come now, you very nearly got the Nobel Prize, if I'm not mistaken.'

'That was the product of media hype. They thought I photographed well.'

'And you don't any longer?' she said in a girlish squeak.

Balestra ignored the question and Florence failed to notice. He said: 'The fact is that my rival at the time, whose name was Wurtz-something-or-other, had a face as long as a fiddle, poor chap, whereas I was *being seen* with an up and coming actress. Lived with her, actually.'

'I remember.'

'The *paparazzi* were over the moon. Just think—beauty and the brain! They were clicking at us all over the place: Rome, Paris, Maxim's. And all the time I was trembling with fear that they'd find me out. Thank God, the Wurtz-bloke got it.'

Florence, who had given up trying to sort the truth from the quips, laughed easily. Again she held him back.

'Tired?'

'Not at all,' she said brightly. 'Curious isn't it?'

'Not really. When I examined you last night it was obvious you were in perfect health.'

'You examined me!'

'Of course. Then I got you into my pyjamas. I was certain that the organic causes boiled down to immense physical fatigue, and I thought and still do that we can forget all about it after your long snooze. You've taken a packet lately.'

'It's never stopped, one thing after another,' she said, her real thoughts trying to imagine him handling her. She was bewildered to find that the idea did not vex her.

'What I think happened,' he was saying, 'is that you decided you'd had enough and would shut up shop for a while, to put it in common parlance.'

'I'm sure you're right,' she whispered, as they resumed their walk.

The shadows lengthened. The two speeded up, heading for the house as the delicate diffused sunrays showed signs of turning into a chilly mist. They had said no more about her leaving. Artus kept up his chatter, aiming to fascinate her, for he saw himself as a charmer, a magician with words and ideas performing for a wide-eyed audience. Even an audience of one stimulated him.

But reluctantly at dinner she mentioned that she had a family, who were certainly starting to worry about her. The table sparkled, the porcelain, silver and crystal flickering in the light of the candles and a cosy log fire a couple of yards from them. Artus wore a velvet smoking jacket and Florence had picked the more flattering of her two dresses.

They clinked champagne-filled glasses and she said sadly: 'Now it's my turn to worry, about the family. I should have thought of it before.'

'You are still rather bemused over events. It has been too much of an effort for you so far,' he said kindly.

'It's the country air, I've had a lovely day, Artus,' she said, giving him a ravishing smile. It was his move now!

But he went on: 'I knew what your treatment ought to be, and as you've put yourself in my care, I'm ordering you to have another twelve hours' convalescence. I once decided to disappear from the face of the earth.'

'I didn't decide, it happened.'

'So it was with me, to be honest. It was running away or else running into trouble and I couldn't square up to it.'

'Your shortcomings would be unveiled?'

'You could put it that way. Let's say my pride was heading for a fall, and no one likes that. But let's not talk about it. Another time. Because there'll be other times.'

She laid a hand on his arm: 'I do hope so. I feel completely at home here, so much so that I'm overcome with guilt.'

He gave a sort of cackle: 'I'd like . . . I mean, one word from you and I'll run you back to La Commanderie. But I've a better idea, Florence.'

'Yes?'

'It's to do with your turning up again. You'll have to in the end, but if you go back now or tomorrow morning before your twelve hours' convalescence are up, you won't be any further forward, you won't have gained anything.'

'I don't want to gain anything.'

'You see, you're not cured yet, otherwise you wouldn't talk like that. You're a winner, Florence, you have to win this hand!'

'How do I do that?' she cried.

'You must reappear in all your glory, showing clearly that you *decided* to disappear. You'll be saying: "I had you scared out of your wits, my friends, but you haven't seen the last of me yet. You just wait!"'

'What then?'

'Oh, we'll work out something. You'll turn up like General de Gaulle when he went to see General Massu at Baden Baden in May '68. Only you'll look far more attractive than he did!'

'So do you if it comes to that,' she laughed gaily.

'Thank you, my dear Florence,' Artus declared, kissing her fingers. 'But we need someone to organize the show. I'm thinking of your brother Armand. He's in the Assemblée, after all.'

'Shall I ring him?' she said excitedly.

'Let them all stew for a while, we'll launch this thing tomorrow morning after we've seen the papers. We must sleep on it.'

'Right, *patron!*'

They went upstairs and, as they prepared to leave each other's company, Artus said: 'What struck me most about your wandering along is that you clung on to your case for hours and hours. How possessive you must be, it's frightful!'

'Frightful,' she grinned, allowing him to kiss her hand.

Inside her room, she immediately checked her appearance in the mirror. She was positively radiant! Florence looked inside the case, and saw her nightdress.

She stood for a while thinking of Artus. Neither her husband nor Georges Quentin had made her feel so *allied* to them as she did to Artus Balestra. She liked his looks, his style, even his defects. He could be a liar, a bluffer or full of his own importance for all she cared. The fact was that he fascinated her.

Florence shut the suitcase, put on Balestra's pyjamas and slid gracefully between the cool sheets.

Alexandra believed, wanted with all her might to believe, that her mother was invulnerable. The girl admitted to herself that she was in a spin, but she was certainly not worried.

377

She thought about Teddy as well. He won her admiration in a flash, because of his eyes and his energy, and because he could do something well—play the saxophone and make it sing. Then it occurred to her that she would probably not have thrown herself at him so quickly, had she not been so agitated over the events surrounding her mother since she came over from the States.

Albertas Kovalic's thrashing of Teddy, and the bestial way in which he had lashed at herself, gave her plenty to mull over. The weal and the gash and the black eye had been expertly attended to by Mathilde, who mercifully had made no reproach, not scolded 'her baby'. Mathilde had even drawn her to her bosom afterwards and rocked her like she used to years ago.

Her inner wounds she resolved to cure in her own way. From La Commanderie she put in a call to Bernard Kovalic.

Bernard was unsure how he felt about the incident, when Albertas gave his embroidered account of it. At first he was astonished, but the shock swiftly turned to jealousy at the thought that Teddy had 'got in' where he had failed. In the end he decided she had what she deserved. But Bernard Kovalic had not been to Harvard for nothing; he was a planner and he realized instinctively that he was likely to need the Berg girl. She was a card he could play more than once, he suspected.

'Albertas acted as head of the family,' he told her, 'but I'm sorry you got some of the punishment. You can't deny you were partly to blame, but I'm very sorry it turned out like that.'

Alexandra exclaimed: 'I didn't phone you to hear your apologies, Bernard. I want to see Teddy. I want to know what your uncle's done to him.'

'Huh, you're that interested in Teddy? Looks like you're getting along fine.'

'Well yes. Does that worry you?'

Bernard positively crooned: 'Oh I don't really know. Anyhow, I'll tell you where Teddy is. He's locked up in one of the barns at the farm. The shutters are closed, the door's padlocked and the window handle's been removed. Not much light or air in there. Every now and then his mother takes him some bread and water, and empties his slop pail.'

As he enumerated the grim details, a smile spread over his face. He imagined Alexandra's face, the blood draining from it, and laid on the description with a trowel.

In a trembling voice, Alexandra shouted: 'You mean he puts up with that? Why?'

'It's the law of the Kovalics,' he pronounced gruffly.

'And do you get thrashed that way?'

'Not any more.'

'Huh, and why would that be?'

'Because I've left the cave,' he said, laughing uproariously.

'Congratulations,' the girl said with heavy sarcasm. 'But I still want to see Teddy. Someone must get him out of there.'

'I'll think it over,' Bernard replied, in the manner of discussing a deal.

His caller banged down the phone. Her mother was intriguing her, and now Teddy was in a fix. But it was Teddy she bothered about more.

Florence never left Travers's thoughts. He pined desperately for her, added to which he had to make a professional decision that affected both her and the paper.

While Artus and Florence were making friends by the log fire and planning her big comeback, Travers called on Jean-Jacques Berg. One look at him made it plain that the man was in a dreadful state, something akin to terror. Several times he had phoned *L'Eveil* and been told that *Monsieur Le Directeur* was ill in bed and would be at the office very late, and possibly not until tomorrow.

'Oh, good evening, Travers,' Marie-Lou said, letting him in. 'Any news?'

'Nothing. I'd like to see your husband.'

'I'll find out if he's in. He was hoping to get to the editorial conference . . .'

'You can tell 'em better than that, Marie-Lou,' Travers

snapped. 'He's not there, and you know it. He's not going because he's hiding up. I'll wait.'

Marie-Lou's eyes doubled in size as he moved towards a bench affair in the hall.

Jean-Jacques's voice rang out: 'I'm not hiding, whatever gave you that idea, Travers! Maryse?'

'She said you'd got migraine, so I assumed you'd decided to sit it out in the comfort of your own bed!'

'I *have* got migraine, and it's no joke.'

'It's all in the mind, old boy.'

Marie-Lou came back and squawked: 'It's none of your business. What right have you to come in here . . .'

Traverse played his Humphrey Bogart act: 'You, swee-tie, if it's not too much trouble, get lost. I'm here on business that concerns me, your husband and his con-science if he's got any left. It's not for your ears.'

'My conscience is *my* business,' J-J Berg declared pontifi-cally. He approached the others.

'I'm sure it is. But I've noticed that every time anyone behaves like a shit, he says it's his conscience. I should know, I've done it myself. I'm a shit, but a successful one!'

'Oh,' said Marie-Lou, with her mouth to match.

'Not for your ears, I said. And as you're a lady, I can only advise you to go knit yourself some earmuffs.'

Marie-Lou clamped her mouth firmly shut and stalked out. Jean-Jacques let out a sigh of relief: 'Come into the office, Travers, take a seat.'

Jean-Jacques led him to his study, but Travers remained standing: 'What's it like at the Kovalics' place?'

'What!' exclaimed the other. 'What are you on about now?'

'You're in their camp now, and that's the simple truth. I could add that, as a Berg, you'd make a very good Kovalic. You're a slimy rat, Jean-Jacques, but that's just a personal tribute. Let's get to the facts.'

J-J Berg decided to hit back: 'All right, you want the facts. There's only one, my friend. I left one paper and joined another. Satisfied? People do it all the time.'

Travers's eyes narrowed: 'Oh no. You didn't just move

from one paper to another. You quit the Berg family and went running to the Kovalic tribe.'

'You're out of your mind! You're obsessed, that's your trouble.'

'The trouble came when you sold those shares in *La Dépêche*. That's another fact for you.'

'What of it?'

'To the Kovalics.'

'To a group,' Jean-Jacques countered.

'The Boulard Group.'

'No.'

'One of their front companies.'

'No.'

The to-and-fro came to a halt. Travers let out a laugh, and Jean-Jacques frowned: 'What's so funny? All I know is that when you're out on your ear you don't ask for an identity card from the guy who gives you a job. I would remind you that that was my position. Thanks to my sister, I was out in the street looking for work. That's a fact too.'

'I'm crying my eyes out, Berg. But I'm going to take another bite at your conscience. You don't know it, but I do and I'm not the only one, that *L'Eveil de la Loire* is Bernard Kovalic, acting under instructions from Edmond Boulard.'

Jean-Jacques turned away and began pacing: 'You're being ridiculous, Travers. Wherever did you get that idea?'

'From Lorieux. Know him?'

'By name. But I know enough about him to tell you you're lying. It's an old trick: telling a lie to get at the truth.'

Travers snapped: 'You're so right, and I've got it. If the lie was a lie, you'd have said so, protested, invoked your honour and conscience. But you didn't, Jean-Jacques, you merely quibbled. Good night to you, I have what I came for.'

As Travers made to leave, Jean-Jacques said: 'You're easily pleased.'

'When I don't like the smell of a place, I cut it short,' his visitor cracked, banging the study door to.

With this exit line, Florence rushed back into his mind. Not only was he sick with anxiety about her, but she wasn't there to give him the nod, now that his article was clicking into place. He would not be cutting that short when the time came.

He sought the warmth of friendlier faces in the Bijou-Bar close by the office. He could have drunk a whole bottle of whisky without turning a hair. What he needed was the familiar scene like old times, before the paper was plunged into a maelstrom that had threatened to drown them all, day after day after day. Favrot and Edelman were there engaged in their favourite sport of 'making' a girl as a joint operation. The victim this time was cute enough, a girl recently appointed as the paper's correspondent in Paris. Travers fitted a bar stool under himself and watched them compete for a night out with her, each denigrating the other and selling himself. One of them would win, that was sure, as the girl giggled enough to wet her panties. As he stared intently at her, she said why couldn't they give him a drink, and at that Travers joined them. He tried to match their wisecracks, but his heart wasn't in it.

Favrot won, he went off with the girl, and Travers and Edelman remained to argue who paid for the drinks.

After lengthy consideration, Bernard Kovalic decided it was time they let Teddy out. He foresaw no difficulty as he had the whip hand over his uncle, and had virtually taken over as head of the clan.

He sloshed into the yard in his up-market Renault, clad in a fur-lined coat he had had made for him in Paris. Albertas let out a whistle with his teeth when Bernard entered the house as he was topping off his meal with a little glass of slivovitz.

'Glad to see yer, boy,' he grated. 'Don't come around much these days.'

His nephew looked at him without batting an eyelid. Albertas had come to fear those steely eyes: 'I'm here to tell you I want Teddy out.'

'Tell me, tell me? What kind of talk is that? I decide that.'

The Harvard man vouchsafed a smile: 'That goes without saying, uncle. But I'm thinking of the family's interests. He ought to be seen about by now.'

'So he can find his alley-cat with my blessing?'

'When it's a Berg girl, a Kovalic will lose interest after a week, don't worry about that.'

'A week or a lifetime, it's all the same. I don't want our people mixed up with them.'

'And Catherine?'

'Couldn't do nothing about it. Stuck in my throat, it is, that whole business. Lucky the babe'll be called Kovalic. He'll be back later with us. Paul Kovalic, nice name.'

Bernard humped off his coat, got a glass from the dresser and joined the old man. He said 'All right if I join you?' He did not wait for an answer. 'See here uncle, look at it this way. If Teddy puts the Berg girl in the family way, that won't hurt us. It'll hit them, and that's just what you want.'

The argument fell on waste ground, for Albertas shouted: 'No it ain't. I don't care how high and mighty they are, I want to see the Bergs brought down right enough, but I don't want the girl to be ashamed. When your name's Berg you have to have principles. Let her keep herself clean.'

Bernard endeavoured to follow his mind: 'For God's sake. Suppose she just loves Teddy, suppose the miracle of love swept them off their feet.'

'Miracle or no miracle, it's got to stop.'

'Why ever? Might cause a laugh or two.'

'It's no laughing matter.'

'Nor crying either. We'll make sure it works out all right.'

Albertas wagged his head, finished his drink and laboriously got to his feet: 'You got no morals left, Bernard, and that's a fact.'

His nephew grinned broadly: 'Morals have changed, uncle.'

The older man walked around the table, caressing the ornate varnished chairs. He sighed: 'It's a funny world. If there ain't no morals any more, we'll be living like pigs. What about that? What about that, eh?' Albertas threw up his hands and returned heavily to his chair.

Bernard poured him another nip: 'Don't take on so. I just wanted to give you my version. Teddy's an adult now. Why not let him stay in there for another night, and then decide what you want?'

Albertas acceded to that, and threw the slivovitz down his throat. They sat silent for a while.

Bernard said casually: 'By the way, I saw a BMW pull in here this morning.' He swirled his drink round.

'A BMW?'

'A blue one, with a Trieste numberplate. Who was that?'

Albertas leaned back, equally casual: 'Just a friend of my old cousin Marko. On his way to Paris. Stopped by to have a look at us. It doesn't look good for Marko. I don't reckon we'll see him alive again.'

'He came to tell you that?'

'It's a good enough reason.'

Bernard muttered: 'If that's all he came for. This isn't the moment to let things slide.'

Albertas jerked up his chin: 'I've never let things slide. I'm not going into mourning yet, my lad.'

'I'm very glad to hear it, uncle,' said Bernard, giving him a friendly smile.

As Bernard spun the wheel of his car the headlights swept the barn. It was divided into sections by means of timber partitions, and in one of the sections was Teddy.

The boy listened until the hum of the car engine merged with that of the town, and he squatted down again in the pitch dark. He knew the family was usually in bed by ten, but he waited, fingering a torch his mother had sneaked in to him with the evening meal—consisting of soup and bread instead of bread and water!

At length he moved over to a corner and, with the lamp, located a length of fencing wire which had been buried in the hard dirt floor for a long time. Albertas had a habit of locking up his nephews here and they had hidden the wire. He used it now to open the heavy lock on the door.

In the course of that day, Albertas had brought Teddy some bread and water and had then gone further along the barn to mess about with something. Teddy meant to find out what. Through the lock he had seen very little, but his keen musical ear told him his uncle was manipulating some paper. He also mumbled some numbers, after which he seemed to wrap everything up amid a crackling of straw and hay. Finally his uncle's silhouette had gone back past the keyhole.

And now, shielding the torch carefully, he crept out of his prison and saw the familiar table outside with a folded jute bag on it. On the wall opposite that he saw a mound of hay, the same one he had heard Albertas moving about in. Teddy now chivvied the hay about and found a long leather bag with a strap and a closed padlock. There was a gap in the leather closure and he pushed his bit of wire through this and stirred it about inside the bag. It was paper, as he had guessed. He fiddled around and extracted a piece of paper. A split second after pulling it through the gap he recognized it as a hundred-franc note. He quickly lifted up the bag and judged its weight, allowing for the bag itself. There was a fortune in it if the rest was in hundred-franc notes!

Quivering with excitement, he stuffed the note in his pocket, put everything back as it was and went back to his place.

Travers duly printed a story about Florence's disappearance in the next morning's issue.

But the result was a disappointment. The public snatched it up in the street, and the topic remained in people's mind for a while. Nobody came forward or phoned in.

Nicolo did though, yelling at him for making the SRPJ criminal police look ridiculous again. He then set out to make Travers feel a perfect idiot.

'Your kidnap idea was logical,' Nicolo told him. 'So much so that I even thought of it myself.'

'And?'

'And Pradal and I had a mosey round her jalopy, or at least where it was. If she was kidnapped, she struggled. If she struggled, there'd be traces.'

'Did you find any?'

'Not a trace of a trace. There weren't any traces and there never were.'

'Get stuffed,' Travers growled.

'Lucky we're bosom pals, Travers, or I'd rope you in for abusive language to a police officer in the course of his duty—if I was carrying out a duty.'

Travers got through the rest of the day with routine jobs. The show must go on. This culminated in the daily editorial conference, at which he took little part. Shortly after that, at 7.30 p.m., Alexandra and her uncle Julien put in an appearance. The girl's face still looked nasty, but she was smiling. So was Julien, and Travers regarded them both peevishly.

'We've come to look at the television, is that all right?' said Alexandra.

'Has yours broken down at La Commanderie, Mademoiselle?' Edelman asked.

'The rest of the family are looking at it. But Julien and I thought we'd like to watch it here with the staff.' She glanced at her watch. 'Not much time to wait.'

Travers realized instantly that she was referring to the main news at 8.00 p.m. He said quickly: 'There's some news?'

Julien beamed: 'No comment! It's a surprise, it'll be on Antenne 2 channel.'

They all stared wide-eyed at the pair.

It was the first item. The anchor man said, building up to it slowly: 'All's well that ends well. *La Dépêche Republicaine* in the Loire Region reported in its issue today that it had no news of the owner Madame Florence Berg who had been missing for four days. Suicide or kidnapping were feared. Rumours spread throughout the day in the press and political circles.' (Travers snorted; why did they have to tell it backwards?) 'Rumours stemming from revelations by the paper that were widely regarded as unfounded. Then late today, the mystery was cleared up. Madame Berg called in at Agence France-Presse. We were there when she left the building.'

The screen showed Florence emerging from the agency building, impeccably dressed and in Travers's view looking insufferably pleased with herself.

She said: 'I've nothing to say, I have handed in a statement and you'll be getting it.'

'Have you been under pressure from anyone?' a reporter said.

'Have you been in hiding?' another asked.

Florence raised a hand as more questions came: 'Read the statement, I've nothing to add.'

Back on the screen, the newsreader said: 'Here's the statement: "In the past few days the public has been able to appreciate the fury deployed by a certain press empire in its efforts to appropriate my newspaper. Not only do such methods reflect on those responsible, but they can only fly back in their faces. *La Dépêche* is taking up the gauntlet." Unquote. Pakistan. Convergent sources say . . .'

Alexandra cried gleefully: 'Not bad for a beginner, was she!'

'Looked fine,' Favrot said.

'A bit terse for a statement, but that's all to the good,' Edelman commented.

'What do you think, Travers?' Julien wanted to know.

'Terse and effective. But tell me, did you know your sister was going to do that? Who else knew?'

'I did,' Alexandra said. 'Armand called Julien this morning. *Maman* had phoned him, telling him among other things to let us know, Julien and me and nobody else. We didn't tell Gilbert and Mathilde until just now when we left the house.'

'When she phoned Armand, where was she?'

'I don't know, he didn't say. Perhaps he didn't know either.'

'What else did she ask him to do?'

'How should I know? Probably told him to warn AFP and the TV people.'

Travers turned to Julien: 'No doubt. A well-organized news item. Good little speech too.'

The group broke up. Travers felt a bitter taste rising from his solar plexus and entering his throat.

Florence had dinner in Paris with Armand. He drove her back to Chateauvallon, and she said she wanted to pop into *La Dépêche* for two minutes.

'I'd like to see if anyone is waiting up for me,' she said.

'Travers is for certain.'

Travers was. He was on his own in the main editorial room, with a couple of desk lamps on. The rest was in darkness. He jumped out of a doze when she switched the other lights on.

'What are you doing here?' she said as he uncurled himself from one of the chairs.

'An obvious question,' he said derisively.

'Did anyone tell you I would stop by?'

'No, why should they? I've been waiting four days and three nights, getting accustomed to my new grey hair.'

She twittered: 'Oh you shouldn't have done. I'm so sorry. You don't look very cheerful.'

With a herculean effort Travers produced a smile: 'Where were you?'

'Oh somewhere. I don't have to account for it to you.'

'That's nice.'

She put a hand on his neck: 'To be honest about it, I did think of giving you a call this morning.'

'Good idea.'

'But you probably noticed, I didn't.'

'Now why would that be?'

'I'm not sure yet. When I am I'll tell you. Promise.'

She walked off and gave him a wave from the door.

'Armand's waiting for me outside with the car,' she stated, in a matter-of-fact sort of way.

Chapter Five

Alexandra woke early, her eyes opening like a doll's when she sat up. She thought of Teddy, as she did every day when she took her first few conscious breaths.

Then she remembered. Her mother must be back now! She would surprise her, she decided, and hurried out in her pyjamas. Her mother was not in her room but she found her at her desk, phoning. She was dressed, made-up, stunningly smart and radiant.

'I'm sorry, *Madame*, I didn't realize,' she was saying. 'What's that, 22.24.24? Oh I see, that's his apartment. Thank you, *Madame*.'

Alexandra broke in: 'Telephoning Bernard Kovalic at 7.30?'

'How do you know?'

'That's his studio. The Aqua Viva office is 22.00.00.'

'Well you *are* informed!'

Florence said it softly. She was not sure how to approach her daughter, who had been in bed when she finally returned home and immediately started discussing what had happened in her absence with Armand, Gilbert and Mathilde. She learned of the vicious swipe Albertas Kovalic had given Alexandra, and decided not to wake her. She also received the news that Boulard, Bernard Kovalic and Jean-Jacques were in collusion; Gilbert said Travers had told him.

She was unsure which of the items shocked her most. She had scarcely slept, and linked the two. It was as she had feared, things moved fast against her as soon as her back was turned.

But now she continued in her quiet tone: 'Are you friendly with Bernard Kovalic?'

'Certainly not. He tried. Took me to the stables and tried to jump me in his car on the way back.' As her mother said nothing she went on: 'Nothing happened, I pushed him off. But he left me the two phone numbers.'

Keeping it low key, Florence said: 'Mind if I call right away?' She got no reply from Bernard's studio, and put the receiver down.

Neither of them spoke, and then Alexandra said: 'Why don't you say something about my face, *maman*?'

'Perhaps I wanted you to mention if first. I'm dumfounded. Did Albertas really do that to you, my sweet?' She ran her hand over the girl's golden curls, then touched the marks with a finger.

'Don't go all soft about it, I don't want that. Yes, it was Albertas. He was proud of it, came here and boasted about it, like a terrorist.'

'He caught you with . . .?'

'Not Bernard, Teddy.'

'What did Teddy do?'

'He got more lashes than I did.'

'And he let his uncle do *that* to him?'

'They're not like we are. They have their own code of honour.'

'They're savages,' Florence hissed.

'It's not as simple as that, *maman*.'

'Whatever do you mean? As if I didn't know the Kovalics inside out. When I was your age they were tramps, already savages!' She moved away from her daughter.

'Please, *maman*!'

Florence reached the window and stood looking at the well-kept grounds: 'They would never have dared hit me, I can tell you. Perhaps I'm . . .'

'Because you wouldn't have got yourself into a position to be hit, is that what you mean?' Alexandra was close to tears, but they were tears of anger and her mother knew it.

'I don't mean to be harsh, sweet. I simply don't like to see you hurt. Do you love him—Teddy? What do you like about him, is he tender? You get on well together, is that

390

right?' Alexandra shook her head. 'You'd rather not talk about it?'

'Not like that, not now.'

'How and when you like. I'm always here.'

'You're here *now!*' her daughter cried, running pink-faced from the room.

Florence lit a cigarette, rewrote Bernard's two numbers and rang them both. Still no reply from either. Then she thought of *L'Eveil* and made a third call. Maryse answered.

'You're on the job early at *L'Eveil.* I'd like Bernard Kovalic. This is Florence Berg.'

'I recognized your voice,' Maryse said, 'but I don't know if . . .'

'Get him please!!!'

Maryse covered the mouthpiece and said: 'I can tell her you haven't got in yet.'

But Bernard took the call: 'Good morning, Madame Berg. To what do I owe the honour?'

Florence went straight to the point: 'I'd like you to come to the house and have a talk. Can you be here in half an hour?'

'Certainly, Madame Berg, I'll be right there.'

When he finished Maryse said: 'Are you mad? It's not for you to go there. You're not under her orders!'

He smiled amusedly: 'First, she is a lady and I am always polite to ladies. Secondly, I'd like to see the enemy territory. Thirdly, I want to see what she looks like after we've given her a pasting.'

To herself, when he had gone, Maryse muttered: 'And fourthly, we're printing 13,000 and she's gone over 300,000, and I'd personally like to know how she manages it!'

As top dog at *L'Eveil*, all Bernard Kovalic had done so far was to bring a camp bed into his office, and sleep on it occasionally. He had been told that Antonin Berg did that on important occasions.

Were there an official chronicler of Chateauvallon, he (or perhaps she) would have described the Florence Berg/

Bernard Kovalic encounter as historic.

An official communiqué would have said that 'the two leaders had a frank and businesslike discussion ranging over a wide spectrum of current affairs and outstanding matters; the talks were held in a friendly atmosphere'.

The truth of the matter was that Florence chainsmoked for the half-hour or so as she waited for the Harvard lad in her office. He was now to learn what they didn't teach you at Harvard, she vowed, pacing the floor. Better to be nervous before than during, she opined. And when the young man who was supposed to know it all arrived in his chariot of fire, she removed the ashtray, checked her hair—a man would have done as much, she assured herself—and sat like the Empress of all the Russias behind her desk.

'Good morning again, Monsieur Kovalic,' she said, rising and taking a few paces to meet him. She smiled grandly.

Bernard gave her a courtly bow and lifted her hand to his mouth. She reflected that he should have brought his lips to within one centimetre of her hand without lifting it at all, but let it pass. He wore a grey flannel suit and a tie that she supposed was American. He fitted rather well into the room.

'I won't take up too much of your time,' she said, without asking him to take a seat. 'I asked you to come so that I could tell you that our circulation has jumped even higher today, thanks to you.'

'I am happy for you, Madame.'

'How charming. But that seems to indicate that you have entered this contest with a blunt sword.'

'I assure you I am not to blame for that.'

'On the contrary, you are deeply involved. But with what object, to make me swoon away like some weak damsel of old? To bury me in scandal perhaps? However that may be, your aim is to discredit our paper. You're new to this business, but I can assure you the French press has seen this many times over, and the public is used to it. There's nothing so old as yesterday's news, Kovalic, and the public disregards it.'

Not to be outdone, Bernard countered: 'Nevertheless, Madame, you were hooked . . .'

Florence cut him off: 'Nobody hooks me. I don't bite, that is *your* game.' She gave a rehearsed sigh. 'You know, Kovalic, none of this is of any real importance. You can tell Boulard I imagined him rather more skilled than he has shown himself to us. His approach is more than crude. We are not in the school playground.'

'Monsieur Boulard knows what he is doing, I imagine, in view of what he has achieved,' Bernard said levelly.

'But are *you* in control when you allow one of your people to rough up my daughter?'

'As regards that, I assure you—and I mean that—I had nothing to do with it.'

'You have nothing to do with anything, it seems. How do you fill out your day?'

'My uncle has his own ways, in conformity with the customs of another epoch. Please accept my apologies in the name of our family.'

'I do. But kindly make sure that this sort of thing does not occur again.'

'You can count on me, Madame.'

Bernard was fuming, but concealed it well. He knew she was treating him like some *domestique*. She was deliberately conveying to him that his expensive suit, his prestigious tie and the Kovalic gold was of no account beside the eminence of the Berg dynasty. He hesitated, preparing to end the discussion, but she stopped him.

'I'm counting on you more specially since you are in a sense part of us, if I am not mistaken.'

'I'm sorry I don't understand.'

'My brother transferred some of our paper's shares to you.'

'Very few.'

'I know, but enough to annoy. Boulard knows what he is doing, isn't that so? None the less you are one of us and you will enjoy our board meetings I am sure.'

'I don't plan to . . .'

She laughed gaily: 'I was only imagining what you

393

would be like as a son-in-law. All mothers do that.'

Bernard was in a quandary, wondering if Florence Berg was deliberately provoking him, or whether she really imagined she was bringing him to order. His conjectures were spared him, as Alexandra appeared in the doorway. He noted her severe dress, her flaming scrutiny, her imperial bearing. He held her gaze.

'Bernard,' she demanded, 'I saw your car outside. What are you doing here? I asked you to have Teddy freed.'

'Your wish is my command, Mademoiselle, and I have done the necessary. Teddy is waiting in the car.'

'Well, why didn't you say so?' She darted out and the top-level discussion continued.

'What about Teddy as a son-in-law?' Bernard said with a smile that was almost a grin.

'I am trying to imagine it, as a mother.'

'I should have guessed.'

They went over to the window.

'They seem to be arguing,' Florence said.

'Your daughter has a mind of her own. So has Teddy. They are tense after their separation.'

'It begins to look like it,' she said, opening the window slightly.

'Get out, you blithering idiot,' Alexandra was shouting. 'I want to talk to you.'

'No I won't,' Teddy brayed. 'I'm not setting foot in your castle. It gives me the creeps.'

'We'll see about that!' The girl stalked round the car bonnet and sat in the driving seat. Florence and Bernard gaped as the car sped off.

'Ah, she's kidnapped him,' Florence said. 'Have no fear, Monsieur Kovalic, she will not demand a high ransom. Jeannou will drive you back into town.'

'Please don't go to the trouble. I'll call a taxi.'

'As you wish, Monsieur Kovalic.' She called the taxi company herself.

Bernard stood on the steps of La Commanderie in the drizzling rain waiting for the taxi, observed by Gilbert,

Mathilde, Julien and Thérèse and their two children. Florence was there too.

She told them: 'It's his own fault, he insisted on waiting outside. I wasn't going to keep him by force.'

'You did right, I don't like his face,' Julien's daughter said.

'Julie, don't be impolite,' Thérèse scolded.

Gilbert intervened: 'Why do you drink your coffee standing, Florence? Drinking like that on an empty stomach can't do your health any good.'

She gave him a peck on the nose: 'I missed you, Gilbert, you and your rules of hygiene!'

'Where did you go, Auntie?' Julie said.

'You won't get an answer to that,' Mathilde remarked. 'She took us all for a ride, but we'll never find out where.'

'I was with friends. Charming friends.'

'So charming they didn't care about the rest of us biting our fingers. Never even thought to give us a ring.'

'I thought you were dead,' Julie squeaked.

'Then you were silly. I'm here right as rain. I'll tell you all about it some day. Now I must fly.'

She gave them all a huge hug and left.

The *patronne* was back with them, and it was to be a normal day like any other. But the staff were curious, some irritated, others thankful and sincerely glad it was over.

When she drew up outside *La Dépêche*, the doorman buzzed up and there must have been about thirty people waiting for her outside the lift when it arrived on the editorial floor.

The trainee Beatrice Bonnenfant surged towards her with an enormous bunch of flowers: 'Oh *Madame*, we were so frightened!'

'That's sweet of you, but there was no need. I went off and I'm back, that's all. Back to the treadmill,' Florence laughed.

She put her arm round Beatrice and they all moved into the main room. She sat down and Melchior and the others waited, ready for battle.

Melchior said: 'We can skip the questions, *patronne*. All we want are the answers.'

'All right,' she said decidedly, leaning back with her hands crossed behind her mass of hair. 'The position is this: I did not believe that Quentin killed himself, and I wrote as much. We were told there are these signed documents. But we know what a minister's statement is worth. A minister signs a hundred or more items a day, and with a rubber stamp. Yet finally I had to give ground, it's done with.'

Favrot whispered something to Edelman, the others muttered, and Travers kept his own counsel.

'And this business about the forgery?' Melchior proffered.

'When you can't prove anything, forgeries are authentic. That's life.'

Travers spoke at last: 'So we admit we were caught with our pants down?'

'Admit or no, the doubt will always remain. It's called suspense in the business. Meanwhile our readers are sticking to us and the readership is on the up and up. That's true, anyhow!'

'And we have to keep it up,' Melchior growled.

Florence scratched her head: 'We'll think of something in the next two or three days. In short, you obviously realize there were people behind this campaign. I wanted to find out who and it took a day or two. I now know. Guess who?'

'Boulard,' Melchior stated.

'The very man, but this time we've got him over a barrel. We're going to give him the full works.'

'And how do we explain your disappearance?' Travers said.

'I spoke of suspense, and sometimes you have to create it. Someone greater than I understood that, and he didn't even bother to explain afterwards.' Travers and Melchior swapped glances. 'And now I want us to get at that bunch of idiots at *L'Eveil*.'

'But your brother!' Melchior exclaimed.

'He should have stayed with us. But I'm not after him

396

particularly, it's the other one. I've been working on him already. So get to work all of you.'

She spent the day at La Commanderie but was back for the evening editorial conference.

As it drew to an end, Travers got her alone and asked if she was deliberately avoiding him.

'Perhaps, perhaps not,' she said.

'You can do better than that, Florence,' he said earnestly. 'I spent four days in agony, and you know it. But it's over now. For the future, between us, I think I have a right to know where I stand. Let's not dramatize this; I'd like us to have a quiet drink at my place and talk it over.'

She tossed her head: 'But that's a wonderful idea. How about right away?'

Travers was unsure how to take her, and simply helped her on with her coat. They must have exchanged a dozen words in the car, and Travers's face was a mask. He drove fast, purposefully, and Florence smiled noncommittally.

Once in Travers's studio, she said: 'It's nice to be back, I'm glad we came.'

'Fine,' he said, which meant nothing. He flung off his trenchcoat, got out the whisky and glasses and tipped out some ice cubes. Florence kept her coat on and stood in the middle of the room as if she were seeing it for the first time.

Standing, they clinked glasses and he said: 'You'll understand, I'm sure. I find you ambiguous somehow.'

'Ambiguous?' she repeated.

'Not clear cut, if you prefer.'

'Not clear cut? What does that mean?'

He was breathing deeply: 'It means we haven't grasped the situation.'

'So you want to examine the situation.'

'Why not take your coat off for a start?'

'No, I'll keep it on. What's up Travers? Are you building up to a scene?'

'I haven't had a scene with a woman for at least ten years. I'd like you to take your coat off.'

She shook her head, and Travers shrugged then sank into his favourite armchair, stretching his legs out.

Florence smiled, and Travers smiled. She was flushed, he was white-faced.

At last she said: 'I—er—I've met someone.'

'Go on,' he said, 'it's still a bit vague.'

Whether she had prepared the account, Travers never knew. But it came out falteringly in little rushes, rather incoherently: 'I felt completely alone, I thought they were going to kill me, I really did . . . I kept thinking what my father would have done in my place.' She removed her coat and sat down. 'I had never felt the need of him so much . . . Antonin Berg . . . And then I met this man . . . It was quite by chance . . . Yes I want to explain it, I *need* to tell it, and you are the only person I can tell it to . . .'

Travers frowned: 'Is it that difficult?' He had come to believe he had something really big going with Florence, and what she was saying made him feel like some school chum. He attempted a smile at her as she held her still-full glass of whisky and went on as if she were in a dream.

'It's hard. I'm not used to it, you see.'

'Used to what?'

'Being pampered, being taken over . . . safe . . . in the warm. You see what I'm getting at?'

'What sort of fellow is he?'

'How can I say? He's a scientist, about fifty, attentive, with ideas. Agence France-Presse was his idea. I let him take over . . . I was in a daze, you know.'

She gave a giggle, seemed to come down from the clouds and took a gulp of whisky.

'You're great, Travers.'

'Great?' he said, blinking fast.

'You listen to my rambling on like this. I don't imagine . . .'

'So you're going to see him again, this chap?'

'I don't know, it was left rather in abeyance.'

'In abeyance! Well, there's a thing.' He rose and hoisted his glass. 'Here's health to Monsieur in Abeyance!'

Florence said: 'Don't laugh at me, please.'

'I'm not, I can assure you of that, I'm not laughing.'

Travers knocked back his whisky, and poured himself another.

'Stop drinking like that,' Florence said.

'"Stop drinking like that"! That's just the kind of thing I need. And what else can the great Travers do in the service of *Madame*?'

She giggled again: 'What an ass you are, Travers. I was looking at you at the office today . . .'

'Ladies should never look at gentlemen in the morning.'

'Stop acting the fool. I was thinking what the devil you were doing in this town.'

'Thank you. What's the matter with this town?'

She began walking in small circles: 'I believe you are worth far more than Chateauvallon, and you know it.'

'Tell me more.'

'If you wanted to, you could easily find a job in Paris. You only need to . . .'

Travers banged down his glass and joined her: 'Now listen, Florence, don't push me too hard. "You're great Travers", "stop drinking Travers", "you're worth more Travers". What *is* all this, come out with it straight!'

'What's got into you?'

'Maybe I actually like it here, working in a one-eyed town on a one-eyed paper!'

'Huh, thanks for the one-eyed paper. But honestly I thought . . .'

Travers was delivering his words faster now: 'You should stop saying what you think, if you're capable of it. You are treating me like some kind of teddy bear, and you do the same with your own daughter. You run your paper like it was some bowling alley. It can't last, Florence. "We know what a minister's statement is worth", "sometimes you have to create suspense". Did you really say that without laughing? You kept on about goddamn suspense. I went hot for you!'

'The others didn't.'

'How do you know? You disappeared and didn't hear their remarks. And when you get back you produce ten minutes of pep talk that hasn't a leg to stand on, and it's goodbye to yesterday. Is that journalism *à la Berg*? Your father must be doing a foxtrot in his grave, old girl!'

'Old girl!!! What the hell am I doing here?'

Florence put her glass carefully on the table, grabbed at her coat and took a step towards the door.

'I'm starting to wonder too,' he said.

'Well you won't have to wonder much longer!'

'Good night, Madame Berg!'

Florence lunged at the door, heaving it to on her way out. The whole place seemed to shake.

Travers turned the key in the lock with a despairing gesture, then returned to his armchair. He put his feet on the table, clasped his hands behind his head and looked at the ceiling.

'Shit,' he said after about a minute, and switched his vacant stare to the wall opposite.

La Commanderie was in complete darkness, and Florence Berg let herself in with her key.

She was furious at taking that glass of whisky at Travers's place; it refused to go down and was stuck somewhere just under her heart. She had not eaten, but was past it. Even so there might be some soup or equally soothing food that would keep her going until morning, while helping the whisky on its way. She took her shoes off in the hall and crept through the dining room, switching on just the wall lights. She let out a tiny yelp when a man's back came into her line of vision. She recognized Gilbert a split second later. He was bowed over the table with a bottle of wine to keep him company.

'What are you doing?' she cried.

'Thinking,' he replied, turning to face her.

'In the dark?'

'It became dark without me noticing it. I ate alone tonight, and felt lonely. Julien and Thérèse can't always dine with me, I realize that. It's not much fun for Thérèse, darling girl that she is.'

'What about Alexandra?'

'Hasn't turned up for dinner for about a week. Eats

400

pizzas in town with Michel, she says.'

As he spoke, Gilbert grew increasingly lugubrious. She forgot her own troubles at the thought of how hard it must be for him. His boy killed, watching time go by, playing tricks to ward off solitude and boredom. It wasn't always fun for him either.

She fetched a glass and poured herself some wine: 'What's the trouble Gilbert?'

'Oh nothing,' he said and gave a shrug. 'Just old age, Flo. I'm an encumbrance to the youngsters, to the older ones and to myself.'

'There's something else, isn't there?'

'Your damn paper's an encumbrance too.'

Florence drank her wine and poured out another glassful: 'Well, so that's your opinion too!'

Gilbert jerked his head up: 'Hey, steady on, that's a Calon-Ségur '62 and there are only three more left.'

'Stingy,' she said trying to lighten the atmosphere. 'What's up with *La Dépêche* now?'

'It's getting on people's nerves,' he said vaguely. 'Trying to ape the Parisian papers, you are, and that's ridiculous here. Ask Mathilde, she says the same. She's fond of you, you know, whatever she may have said the other night. But the paper's not the same for her, and she's not the only one.'

'Sales are staying up.'

'Perhaps, but people in our town won't stay loyal if you don't give them what they want.'

'Anyone would think you were born in Chateauvallon!'

Gilbert looked at her with greater interest: 'That title "People in our Town" was a feature your father started up. Every week he used to write up some family, and it lasted two or three issues until the next family. Told all about them, what they did, what they thought and how they lived. There were photos showing dad at his work, the children playing, mum giving the baby its bottle. Remember it?'

'I do indeed,' Florence said reflectively, 'although I was in America at the time. Father had copies sent to me. But tell me, weren't there some court cases?'

'There were,' Gilbert agreed. 'But the thing was a huge success, and people used to clamour to be written up. Sometimes they took *La Dépêche* to court, but most of the people we covered put the articles up on the wall, had them framed! I bet there are some still in the old houses.'

'Funny you should bring that up.'

Gilbert conceded: 'Just rambling.'

A silence fell between them and at length Florence said: 'I'm off to bed. Night-night Gilbert.'

He pointed at her glass, still half-full: 'Drink up first, don't mind me, you're in your own home.'

She did as he said, musing: 'Yes I'm in my own home. I was born in Chateauvallon!'

Outside in the grounds, Alexandra watched until her mother's light went out.

'Come on,' she told Teddy, 'we can go in.'

'I'm not putting a foot in that house,' he growled, not for the first time that day.

'It's my home, Teddy. You've got to sleep with me in it, otherwise I'll know you don't care for me, and I'll never speak to you again.'

Teddy remained sitting on the lawn: 'Hm, talking rubbish, it's not possible.'

Alexandra strode off, her arms making her skirt dance before his eyes. Teddy's jaw dropped and he was on his feet in an instant.

'Wait,' he said in a loud whisper, and then awkwardly: 'I love you too much.'

Alexandra grinned at him: 'Take your shoes off, we'll go in the tradesman's entrance, and it's tiles there.'

'Then you'll tie me to the kitchen table, like a good dog.'
'Silly!'

Inside, she pushed him against a wall and herself against him all the way down, giving him a mouth-kiss.

'Come on,' she said afterwards, 'I'll show you something.'

She took him up to the top of the house and into a room

where Antonin and Gilbert used to run old films of her grandmother Gabrielle. After old Berg died, Gilbert refused to enter the room, but Mathilde had it kept dusted and cleaned as of old. The curtains were kept drawn. Alexandra put the light on and told Teddy to sit down. Then she selected a reel of film and got the projector going. A young woman in 1930s style appeared on the screen; she wore a low-waisted muslin dress and a hat with a broad brim.

'Who's that?'

'My grandmother.'

'Cor, you should see mine!'

'Don't be daft, that was forty years ago! She was a great actress, you must have heard of her.'

'I never went to the silent pictures.'

'It's not a silent picture, I just haven't put the sound on, don't want to wake anyone.'

Teddy glowered at the actress making theatrical gestures, and the slick-haired toff kissing her hand. Then the man covered her arm and face with kisses after she took her big hat off. He stared incredulously at her crinkled hair.

'Must have been nuts, making films like that,' he said. 'But she's like you, or the other way round. I like that.'

'That's a lovely thing to say.'

'Yeah, she's dressed like a tart, but she must have been a beautiful woman.'

Alexandra smiled at him: 'She was a great actress, a top star.'

'What's a star? She gave her Pekinese caviar?!'

'Oh Teddy, it's you who's nuts. A star, well it's like Elizabeth Taylor, Borg, Charlie Parker. You're a star in Chateauvallon, maybe later a world star.'

'Maybe,' he said without conviction. 'A star in Chateauvallon won't get me far. What a dump!'

Alexandra stopped the projector but there was still some light from the screen. She went over and kneeled down in front of him, clasping his knees as he slouched in his armchair.

'I believe in you, I believe you'll be a star,' she breathed.

'Not a hope,' he said. 'Your grandmother was a star, but in films, and that's easy beside show business. It's full of sharks and you have to have spikes instead of teeth to get anywhere at all in show business. Blokes like me blowing an instrument, there must be thousands all over the country.'

'But if you're the best?'

'Got to practise six hours a day, and how am I gonna do that? And you have to team up with other good players, otherwise you don't get any better.'

'Well?' Alexandra whispered, stroking his hand.

Teddy withdrew it: 'Well nothing. I'll be the star in Chateauvallon, that's all.'

'That's awful,' she wailed. 'Can't we try?'

'Yeah, you can try and get a good tape going, but you need a sixteen-track console and they don't come easy, and you want blokes who can work it right. If you can fix up all that, it's only the start.'

She said: 'What's all that cost in money?'

They had been over it several times, and Teddy said it again: 'A proper set-up, well it'd put you back at least forty thousand.'

'And your family?'

'Uncle Albertas, you mean? You'd never guess how many times he's thrown my sax on the dung heap.'

'How did you buy it?'

'Rescued it from a shop what went up in flames two years ago in Tours.'

'Rescued?'

'Sort of.'

Alexandra took his hand once more and kissed it hard. Then she curled a hand round his neck: 'This little girl wants to go to bed with her Teddy Bear.'

They switched everything off and crept with infinite care down to the blue room.

That morning Florence woke up briskly. The affronts and nonsense from Travers and Gilbert had receded into her unconscious and she could only focus on one idea. She was sure it would work.

She bustled into work, and the staff wondered what was coming next. She was evidently in one of her dynamic moods.

'Where's Travers?' she demanded.

It was Catherine Kovalic who replied: 'In Orleans.'

'What's he up to there?'

Melchior explained that the correspondent at Gougé died yesterday of a heart attack. He was a good man and there was a constant fight there between the communist council and the catholic college. It wasn't all that interesting but a lot of local readers got excited about it, he said.

'Have we a replacement?'

Favrot said: 'I doubt it, nobody wants to hole up there. The correspondent's house goes back to the owner too.'

Florence said: 'Would Travers be all right on his own at Gougé?'

Favrot and Edelman looked at each other, and let their jaws plummet in disbelief.

'We'll see about it. Anything else?' she added.

'We've a newsprint problem,' Catherine said. 'Truck drivers' strike, and we've enough for three days. I think there's a way out, and I'm working on it.'

'Keep behind it and keep me informed. Any ideas for the front page?'

Melchior looked quickly at her and coughed: 'We've got Helmut Schmidt at the Chinon nuclear plant, or the hostages at BNP Montluçon, and there's the picture of Miss Indre-et-Loire . . .'

'Sounds good, what else?'

Melchior's teeth bit into his top lip, then his bottom lip, and he licked both lips: 'Well there's the follow-up to—er—the affair.'

'Let it drop,' Florence rapped.

Melchior pleaded: 'But Florence, we can't do that. Travers has done a great job, and was only waiting for your OK when you got back. It's sensational, the readers will go for it.'

'I don't think they will,' his employer said coolly. 'Don't have any illusions about that. In any case, I'm not interested in it any more.'

'Travers will go bonkers.'

'Don't dramatize things, Melchior. He'll get his expenses.'

Melchior gawped an instant and said: 'Well, you're the boss.'

'And don't you forget it. What else?'

'Artus Balestra is in the running for the Nobel, official.'

Florence cooed: 'Now *that's* interesting. Let's do a page feature on him, his bio, his achievements. It's actually official?'

'Stockholm contacted him, and they're doing the usual enquiries. But the prize isn't for five months. Perhaps a bit early for a page on him.'

'Not at all, he lives near here. Good for the town's prestige and all that. Next?'

'Two pages sport, and the rest.'

'Perfect,' Florence cried joyously. 'Now I want to put something to you. I've no doubt you remember the regular feature my father started called "People in our town".'

Silence. Favrot and Edelman again swapped glances, and the reply was left to Melchior.

'Of course.'

'Huh, you're not exactly glad to recall it, I see. didn't you like it?'

'It's not that . . .'

'Well what?'

'Your father stopped it. The court cases.'

'But people loved it!'

'The readers did. So did the families, until they saw it in black and white. Mind you, some went along with it, but others we covered thought we let too much out, or not enough, or that it wasn't quite right. Well, in the end it was starting to become very awkward.'

'Surely my father didn't give it up because of a few court cases.'

'Your brother Jean-Jacques was against it.'

'Strange. I like the idea. We'll start it up again.'

Melchior eyed her carefully: 'Are you certain . . .'

'Absolutely. You'll announce that we're resuming it shortly. And you can start digging on the first family—the Kovalics.'

A confused hum developed in the room. Several people looked at Catherine, who looked as if someone had thwacked her between the shoulder blades.

Melchior wheedled: 'May I ask where you expect this to lead us?'

'It'll give us an all-round boost. In any case the Kovalics like to keep in the shadows, and we're going to put the spotlight on them. Albertas will go mad, and that suits me. What's the matter, Catherine?'

'Oh nothing, I was just listening.'

'But darling, you're on our side, and you have been for ages.'

'Of course, *Madame.*'

Florence went on: 'I want this to be done ethically, but thoroughly. I want their origins, how many they are, who's died, how they got where they are, their situation now. Should be quite a sizzler.'

Catherine sidled out of the room. Florence pretended not to notice, and continued: 'Everything must go in, but without snide comment. We can punch up the admiration due to them: they're one of our families, stalwarts of the town, a big success story. I think you've got the general idea.'

Melchior blew his cheeks out: 'Yes, *Madame*, I think we have.'

Albertas Kovalic felt successful. He had bought a Mercedes, a light coloured overcoat, several smart ties. He felt so successful that when Teddy came back after his night out he never said a word, kept his sarcasm to himself and his belt round his waist.

The womenfolk asked no questions, simply breathed a little easier hoping it would last. Zöe nearly fell through the floor when she received a sparkling ring for her sixtieth birthday, a golden snake with emeralds for its eyes and with a circle of half-carat diamonds.

Albertas had gone with Bernard to choose it, and decided on the priciest ring in the shop. The tag said 96,000 francs, he tried to haggle, got nowhere and finally paid for it with 500-franc notes which he drew from his pocket. Or to be more accurate he counted out nineteen bundles of ten notes held together with paper clips and laid them on the counter, hoping the girl would accept the sum, then he frowned and added two more notes. The money he thereupon returned to his pocket was twice as much, and Bernard's eyes were like saucers. The girl handed him his wrapped box with a greedy smile, thinking of her commission, and they left.

'Do you always carry that amount of money on you?' his nephew said, nodding at the remainder in Albertas's pocket.

'Sometimes, not always, depends what I'm buying. I like to have the notes on me. Of course I'm obliged to have a bank account, but I prefer to feel the money.'

Bernard twitched his head: 'But uncle, nobody can be a really big man in business without using the banks. I'd like to take a look at your accounts.'

'Don't trust me, eh? I've just spent a small fortune on your mother, and tomorrow we'll be downing champagne by the bucketful. What do you want to spoil it all for? For once in my life I act the playboy and all you can do is ask to see my accounts.' Albertas ended mimicking Bernard's voice.

Bernard played him along: 'Of course, you're right. But one of these days we'll have to go into the books. The Aqua Viva accounts have got to be snow white.'

'One of these days then,' the old man said. 'Now off you go, I've got a date. Make sure you're there tomorrow; the old girl ain't sixty every day.'

They parted, but Bernard followed close behind him with a stern look in his eye. Albertas unlocked the Mercedes and shoved his barrel-like torso onto the seat, sighing voluptuously.

408

The brain of the family watched him drive off heaving the steering wheel round like a forty-ton truck's. He wondered how long it would be before the first wing was crumpled.

Bernard had put him out, to be sure, with his pettifogging ways. There were times when he regretted financing the boy's costly studies at Harvard. Bernard had turned out insolent, rebellious and nosy.

But the mood lasted only a minute, and Albertas wriggled his bottom on the fresh-smelling leather upholstery. He cackled as he thought of his sister-in-law and the ring; he could see it all, how he would summon her and she would come all a-trembling, and he would hand her the package and then he would tell her to go on and open it, and she would be all fingers and thumbs and then practically faint when she saw what it was!

The engine purred deliciously and he took the Merc round by the airfield. There was no Air-Inter service to Chateauvallon but the airfield always had some businessman arriving or taking off in a small private plane. An old crate took people up for a spin, there was a small flying club with some planes as well as the gliders. There was Didi too, a diminutive redhead who served at the bar.

Albertas took in the whole of the small room when he entered the bar. At a corner table sat a man of about thirty in a leather bomber jacket and sunglasses, drinking a pastis. He was well-built and looked cocky. Didi was swapping gibes with him from the counter.

'*Salut* Aldo,' Albertas cried, joining him. 'I'm a bit late but that won't worry you. Had a bit of shopping to do and it's not always easy to find what you want.'

He called out to Didi for an espresso coffee, waited until she served it and said low key: 'Well lad, everything go off right?'

'Smooth as a baby's bum, Monsieur Kovalic. Got mixed up in a military corridor because the traffic controller got it wrong, but I saw what had happened and the radars didn't pick me up. Otherwise it went fine.'

'Are you sure of that?'

'Ninety-nine point nine per cent.'

'And at Villacoublay?'

'Nothing to worry about, as sure as I'm sitting here.'

Albertas observed him darkly, and the other observed him right back. The older man said: 'Cost a pretty packet all that, eh?' He slid a bulky envelope from his inside pocket. It found its way deftly into Aldo's jacket, and Albertas became sorrowful as he drank his coffee. He never liked to see money leave his hands.

He had taken a small sip when his attention turned to a scene outside. A young woman was out there with two children talking with a pilot who held his scarf and helmet in one hand. The man was shaking his head vigorously and showing his watch to the woman. Then the man walked away.

'Don't look round, Aldo, see in the mirror. That woman with the kids.'

'What about them?'

'That's one of the Berg women. Julien's wife, him that runs that sawmill.'

'Nice-looking piece.'

Albertas said in his gravelly voice: 'Looks like that other bloke didn't want to give 'em a ride. She's upset and the kids are angry. My God, she might bring them in here. Now quick, do me a favour, I can't explain, but I'd really be obliged to you.'

'You want me to do overtime?' the other grinned.

'After what you've taken off me, it's not much. Just a quarter of an hour, that's all.'

Aldo retained his smirk as he looked at the woman explaining to the children, and then back at Albertas: 'All right. Then what?'

'Tell you later. You know how to look after a lady, I know. Get me?'

'I'm not so sure, but I'll stick my head out for you, Monsieur Kovalic.'

Albertas said: 'Just chat her up nicely, and I'll be in touch in two weeks. *Salut.*' He pulled the brim of his large felt hat over his eyes and slipped out.

Aldo moved to a better table with his glass and waited as the woman came in with her children. The three sat on bar stools and the argument went on, the children saying it was her fault and whining about it. Poor Thérèse went into a tizzy, telling them to behave themselves and they would try another day. Aldo's lips parted; he liked women in distress, they turned him on.

'Two packets of Rothmans, Didi,' he said, going up to the counter. 'Add it to the drinks.' He put down a 200-franc note so that Didi had to fiddle about with change, and took his sunglasses off, smiling at the little boy who was edging towards him.

'Hullo,' he said in a friendly tone.

'Hullo.' The boy was curious but shy. 'Are you a pilot?'

'That's it.'

'Have you piloted a Mirage?'

'Of course, but I'm not today.'

'What have you been in today?'

Aldo swung round and pointed discreetly: 'See that little red plane out there? That's mine.' He placed a hand on the boy's shoulder, and the boy gaped at a Cherokee quite near the building.

Thérèse said: 'Jean-Claude, don't annoy the gentleman.' She gave the gentleman a diffident smile.

Aldo chuckled: 'Don't worry, Madame, I know children.'

'Have you got any?' Thérèse enquired.

'No, but I've seen some!' he quipped.

'They're so disappointed. I said they could go up in a plane, but we got here too late.'

Aldo twitched his head as if he had just thought of something: 'I'm not so sure. If you like I could give you a short run round, all three of you.'

Thérèse gleamed like a light bulb: 'You don't mean it!'

Aldo ordered Didi: 'Take for everything.' Didi made a face, and counted it up again. The four left the premises.

From behind the wheel of his Merc, Albertas saw them go up to the Cherokee, then Aldo handing them up, then

411

Aldo getting in. Kovalic saw the airscrew begin rotating, then the plane bumping to the end of the runway, then the plane taking off and disappearing behind a low hill.

Finally Albertas turned his ignition key.

For the two kids, the trip was the greatest event in their lives so far.

They squealed delightedly when La Commanderie came into view and they buzzed the house and the grounds. They saw their own house and the timber yard and gave a cheer. Throughout their spin they argued about which house was which, and where they were.

Their mother sat beaming, occasionally laughing at them. Some of the smiles went in Aldo's direction, and occasionally he turned round and met them.

What Aldo could not have known was that Thérèse had felt miserable for months. Oh, she wasn't heading for a breakdown, far from it. But she had been fidgety since she and Julien had helped a cousin, Philippe, get away from the police. He was later caught. That had been a moment of excitement, and she had been more than a little bored since then. It was nothing to do with Julien, she told herself, he was the nicest and the best of the Bergs in every way and she was grateful. The trouble was that nothing ever happened to him, and therefore to her. She had become a kind of wallflower at La Commanderie; Florence was in permanent residence and her masterful ways affected everyone, Mathilde tended to throw her weight about although she was still a servant, Gilbert was grumpy all the time, and Alexandra was unstable and demanding. It was rather refreshing to soar into the air and look down on La Commanderie as on a doll's house; soothing to get away from her fastidious routine with just the children and this polite, smart, jokey *new man* who was giving her another kind of lift with his bedroom eyes.

Thérèse had a flush to her cheeks when they disembarked, and the pilot said: 'Come on, let's have another drink.' The children ran off to the refreshment room,

412

thrilled at the flight and knowing they would be later to bed that evening.

'Fine kids,' Aldo declared in a tough voice.

'Are you sure you haven't got any?'

'Never had the time. I'm married to a squaw, the plane's a Cherokee.'

She laughed: 'That's clever. It must be wonderful to be a pilot. Oh, I quite forgot, how much do I owe you?'

Aldo jerked his head up: 'Now it's you who's annoying me. It goes on expenses.'

'That's nice of you.' A pause and she said: 'You know, you really look like a pilot. Up there in the sky I wanted you to kiss me.' She gave a giggle at that.

They came to a halt and he took her hand: 'And now you're back to earth?'

'How did you guess?' she said gaily, taking her hand back.

'What are you doing this evening?'

'Why? Are you free?'

'No, I'll be in Switzerland within the hour.'

'So it doesn't matter what I'm doing,' she said.

'I just asked,' he returned lamely.

Thérèse said gloomily: 'In Switzerland within the hour. You're lucky, I yearn to do some skiing but I can't stand night trains.'

'I can fix that too.'

Thérèse looked into his eyes: 'I have a husband.'

'Well, doesn't he like skiing?'

'Yes, but he doesn't like flying.'

She burst into laughter, took his arm and propelled him towards the bar.

The children were already sucking Coco-Cola through a straw and telling Didi their house was no bigger than the bar from up in the air.

The Kovalic women fed the fowls as usual the next morning. Then Albertas said they had the rest of the day off. Teddy would do the midday meal.

More precisely, it was one of Albertas's business part-

413

ners, a local caterer who provided the meal, which Teddy unloaded from one of the vans. The dishes included a magnificent sturgeon, a huge ham flavoured in the local style, paté, taboulé, caviar of aubergine and much more besides.

By the time the two women had donned their finery, the victuals were spread out in the main room and the first guests had arrived. The Kovalics were all there along with their allies in Chateauvallon. When they were nearing the end of the feast, Albertas presented Zöe with her fabulous ring and the younger Kovalic men popped the champagne corks to the strains of an accordion brought to life by a cousin who could play Yugoslav folk songs for two hours without repeating himself. Before an hour had gone by they were singing and dancing. Then Albertas called on Teddy to give them a tune on his saxophone, which surprised Teddy and delighted the company. Candles burned before icons in the room and the women clustered round Zöe admiring her ring, and sending glances towards Albertas, who felt more successful than ever. So much so that he more than once gave Bernard a hearty slap on the back, pleased to see that the lad was fitting in at last.

The sole disappointment, though nobody mentioned it, was the absence of Albertas's very own daughter, Catherine. She said she had to work, and Albertas silently absorbed the insult, not wishing to spoil this of all Sundays. There was another reason why he cast it out of his mind. She might be as pig-headed as he was, but one day she would come around and they would make their peace.

It was a quite different Albertas who read through the first article in the new series 'People in our Town' two weeks later.

As usual he had *La Dépêche* propped up in front of him at breakfast and was thinking to himself there was nothing in the paper these days now that old Antonin's girl was in charge of it, when he found himself staring at the name Kovalic. He returned to the heading and read it again: 'A Clan Succeeds'. Hurriedly he absorbed the first few para-

414

graphs, a slice of bread growing soppy in his mug, his face deepening in colour.

He let out a loud 'Aaarrh' and threw the paper on the floor.

'What is it Albertas?' his wife said.

'Medicine,' he rasped. 'Get my medicine!!!'

Zöe rushed to get water and pills: 'Whatever is it?'

'Look at that!' he commanded, gesturing at the crumpled newsprint. He swallowed some pills.

'You know I can't read,' his sister-in-law said.

'Well just look at the pictures. Look!!!'

He stormed out of the room, and Zöe picked up the paper, looked through it and jumped when she saw the photos. She rushed into Teddy's room, where the boy was shaving. He wiped the rest of the soap off his face with a towel.

'Read me that,' Zöe told him. 'It must be dreadful, your uncle nearly choked himself.'

'Let's look at it, and stop worrying. It can't be that bad.'

As he read, Teddy too started licking his lips in agitation. His own picture was there with Bernard's, and the caption said 'The younger generation'.

'Read it out, boy!' Zöe cried.

'Well, the headline says "People in our Town" and this here says "A Clan Succeeds".'

'Clan, that's us? Hurry up, for goodness sakes. Your uncle choked about the middle of it.'

Teddy read out: 'Nobody has failed to see the yellow trucks marked with a big K plying their way through Chateauvallon during the past 15 years. K for Kovalic, a name so familiar to the townspeople, almost a symbol, but the sign of a speciality. Everything you throw away, have cleaned, have carried, removed—the Kovalics handle it. From old clothes to hospital linen, from worn tyres and tarpaulins to the waste paper from our own daily is dealt with by the Kovalics. These are no rag-and-bone merchants, however, because they have expanded over the 15 years. Who owns 40 per cent of the Hotel des Messageries? The Kovalics. Who are the owners of the Banque Française

Unie to the tune of 30 per cent? The Kovalics. Who are the landlords of the two superb apartment blocks just completed in Rue Colbert? The Kovalics. Who manages the big municipal waste tip at Les Sablons? The Kovalics. And why not say it, for it's a secret to nobody: a fleet of 30 vans, 15 trucks including six 40-tonners, innumerable delivery mopeds and the repair shops to go with them—the Kovalics again! And it is rumoured that all this is merely the tip of the iceberg . . .'

Teddy came to a halt and raised his eyes to meet Zöe's. But she had her head buried in her arms, outstretched on the table. Her whole body was shaking.

'Aw shit,' he said. 'It can't be true.'

The woman let out a wail: 'How should I know! They tell such rubbish in the papers. All I know is that your uncle just about collapsed!'

Teddy croaked: 'I reckon I'm going to collapse too. And to think what a rotten old sax I've got.'

Zöe recovered, took the water jug and pills and swayed her way out: 'I must see how he is. Don't go away, I might need you.'

That same afternoon a still-irate Albertas got into his old 'Deux Chevaux' and drove as far as the town hall. He walked the rest of the way to *La Dépêche*.

The doorman tried to stop him, but Albertas elbowed him aside and said he had an appointment. He charged past, fingering his belt, preferred not to use the lift and bounded up the staircase like a savage dog.

'Where is she, that there Florence, where is she?' he barked.

The clan leader stalked through the editorial room looking left and right, kicked some desks and chairs. The desks jerked out of position, the chairs tumbled over and a couple of typewriters crashed to the ground. He swept papers off the desktops and found his way into the setting room. There some of the print workers moved towards him and he pushed them off. People started opening doors in the passages, and Florence was one of them.

Her face developed a broad grin and she turned round

to Artus Balestra, who had called in again subsequent to the flattering article *La Dépêche* had printed about him.

'I think I know what the trouble is,' she said. 'Actually I didn't expect him so soon. I'll have to confront him.'

Balestra said: 'I'll go with you.'

Together they headed for the loudest noise, and ended up in the print shop. Fortunately Kovalic had chosen a moment when the machine was idle, and he could only glare at the beast and clench his fists impotently by his side. Two big fellows, taller than him and stouter, advanced towards him carrying iron bars.

'Kovalic!!!' Florence yelled. 'Why don't you grow up?'

Bull-like, the Yugoslav spun round, looked at her for a long moment and said slowly: 'Madame Berg, you have pushed me in the muck.'

Balestra advanced: 'Pack it up now.'

'She rubbed my nose in the muck,' Albertas said.

'On the contrary,' Balestra said smoothly. 'You've got it all wrong. I'm surprised at you. It's not worthy of you.'

It was the best thing he could have said. Artus saw Albertas drop his chin slightly, and knew it was over. He took him by the shoulder and led a docile Kovalic out of the print shop, to the astonishment of virtually the entire personnel.

Florence was rooted to the spot, feeling that there was something uncanny about Artus and Albertas. There was a connivance between them, a sort of understanding, a dependency perhaps. She herself was fascinated by Artus Balestra and it might be that he had old Kovalic in his power too.

It was curious, but the two men had never met, as far she knew.

Chapter Six

Albertas had reacted with animal fury. Bernard consulted a lawyer.

The lawyer phoned *La Dépêche* almost as soon as the paper hit the streets. Melchior answered and turned on an amplifier so that others could hear. The Kovalic article, the caller said, infringed Articles 905 and 907 of the Civil Code, which laid down that the private life of any individual citizen may be publicly disclosed solely with the written consent of that person. Consequently the publication was liable to seizure.

Florence was listening to the amplified voice, and when Melchior replaced the receiver and interrogated her with a glance, she said she had anticipated such a move. Meanwhile she had done what she set out to do; shaken the Kovalics.

'Naturally,' she added, 'we shall have to forgo the second article about them. The readers won't like it, but we'll tell them why.'

Travers pointed out: 'That's against the law too. We can't attack a person who seeks to safeguard his privacy.'

Florence looked daggers at him: 'Not at all. We shall name no names. We can say that the readers thought they were reading a free and independent newspaper, but the law forces us to stop publication of one of the favourite features, and we can't even say why.'

'It must be short,' Melchior said gruffly.

Florence said: 'Travers can do it. He knows what to write, don't you Travers?' Travers merely nodded.

Catherine broke in: 'You know that we lost a half-page on the ad side today?'

'What?'

'All the Kovalic budget. Domingo's ready-to-wear, Durand Modern Homes, Gedeon Taxis—the lot. About one-tenth of the revenue.'

Florence scoffed: 'They've broken their contracts, and they'll pay damages.'

She stormed out, and Travers muttered to himself: 'I'll believe it when I see it.'

The atmosphere was tense at *L'Eveil*, where Bernard had marched in full of himself after instructing his lawyer. Jean-Jacques Berg and Maryse patted him on the back when he told them, and when Edmond Boulard in person phoned him from Paris, he too turned up the amplifier so that they could join in his moment of triumph.

Boulard, however, was circumspect. He was by no means certain that the threat of confiscation was the best tactic in this case. Boulard said he simply wanted to warn him, telling him to be careful.

This put the damper on Bernard's mood, but J-J Berg could already see Kovalic switching his ads to *L'Eveil*.

'Wise up, Jean-Jacques,' Bernard said. 'My uncle won't insert ads in a paper with no circulation. Anyway, I'm off for a bit. See you later.'

On the pavement he bumped into Teddy, looking as if someone had tied a knot in his saxophone.

'I was going by,' Teddy said. 'Thought I'd say how-do.'

'How-do then.'

'Well, I wanted to ask if you'd do me a favour.'

'Another one! This is hardly the best day. Besides I've got about two francs on me.'

'Couldn't you just change this?' Teddy said, drawing a hundred-dollar bill from his pocket.

Bernard glared at him: 'Where d'you get that?'

'I earned it. Played the sax for some people and they gave me that.'

'Who are you kidding? All right this time, but it's the last.' Bernard produced 600 francs.

'The dollar's at 660.'

'You reckon banks work for nothing?'

Teddy sighed: 'So that's how the Kovalics made their fortune. You know, that article revolted me. I've got nothing.'

Bernard smiled, not unkindly: 'It's the lot of the artist, Teddy.'

'I've got less than you have. But it's me poking Alexandra!'

Bernard wagged his head and went off. Teddy fingered the 600 francs, thinking it must be enough for a dinner for two at Les Messageries, a slap-up dinner too, for Alexandra and himself.

Teddy was young, Teddy had a lot to learn, but he was well-intentioned. Between Alexandra and the boy, the body fluids had mingled regularly in the two weeks since Zöe got her ring. Albertas had made no fuss and Florence had accepted his presence at La Commanderie most nights without a murmur. Now the lad wanted to take it further, to make a gesture that signified it was for keeps between them.

But the row over the Kovalic feature in *La Dépêche* had cast a cloud over their romance, and now Teddy sought to get the dinner in before outright war broke out between the families. At Les Messageries they would be known to everyone, and some would be surprised, others shocked, some might say good for them. Teddy had thought it all out, and he simply wanted them to be seen together, as if they were getting engaged. Yes, he vowed to take her there, whatever ensued. He put the idea to her, and she flung her arms round his neck. She thought quicker than Teddy and within seconds she was describing what both of them would wear, fixing a time early enough for them to make the most of a long evening.

Solange the waitress stiffened when she saw them come in hand in hand, and she guided them deftly to a side table, out of the way. Teddy, had he been been ten years older, might have insisted on a more prominent table, but he was unsure of the etiquette, and merely sat silent for a while with the uncomfortable suspicion that it wasn't going quite as it should.

Suddenly Alexandra grabbed his hand: 'Guess who's just walked in? My aunt Marie-Lou, the family rattlesnake. Guess who's with her? Your cousin Bernard.'

Teddy was wise enough to look at the newcomers out of the corner of one eye. He knew that, at least, it was wrong to stare. He saw Jean-Jacques and his son Michel follow the other two into the restaurant.

'The centre table as usual?' Solange said obsequiously. Jean-Jacques nodded. They all seemed preoccupied, except Michel. The group went through the inevitable routine of studying the menu, hesitating, changing their minds and thanking Solange for their aperitifs, finally placing their orders.

Marie-Lou said in a low voice: 'I still can't believe it. You've got the best lawyer, and she . . .'

Bernard hushed her: 'Listen. My lawyer, we, can stop her publishing more, but we can't make a case against her. There's no libel.'

Jean-Jacques added: 'Florence is a fully-fledged lawyer, in case you've forgotten. She knows what she's up to.'

'But there must be a weak point.'

'If she continues, yes. But she won't of course.'

'And you can't do anything in L'Eveil?'

'Nobody reads it,' Michel contributed.

Marie-Lou made as if to reprimand her son, but Bernard said: 'Leave him, he's right. My uncle wouldn't like that anyhow.'

'So you're capitulating.'

'Anyone would think it was you being attacked.'

'I'm Jean-Jacques's wife,' she said irrelevantly. Michel grinned and she said: 'What's so funny?'

Michel jerked his head to indicate Teddy and Alexandra. The others had not noticed them, and Michel said: 'Look over there and you'll laugh too.'

The youngsters were already having their dessert. They were dipping into each other's plates, and Teddy's spoon slipped, throwing whipped cream onto Alexandra's face. To put matters right, Teddy then proceeded to lick the cream from her face.

'Incredible!' Marie-Lou declared. 'Jean-Jacques, Bernard, do something!'

'Do what?' her husband said, at last seeing the couple. 'Who is it?'

Bernard said quietly: 'My cousin Teddy with your niece. Don't you recognize them?'

'No, as a matter of fact. How did they meet, have they known each other long?'

The lovebirds realized they were being watched, and went on just the same. Marie-Lou was reduced to opening and shutting her mouth in despair. The young diners took Teddy's banana from the banana-split dish and started chewing from opposite ends. Then Alexandra's half-peach dropped onto her blouse and Teddy went after it with his teeth.

Jean-Jacques turned back to the table of four: 'Does Florence know about this?'

Marie-Lou said: 'You ought to tell them to behave themselves. It's your cousin, Bernard!'

Exactly at that moment, who should come in but Florence and Artus Balestra.

Alexandra said quickly: 'Stop it now Teddy, here's my mother.'

Teddy had two fingers in Alexandra's cleavage, extracted the dripping half-peach and ate it with over-played greed. He was enjoying his performance.

'Ask for the bill,' Alexandra said, wiping herself clean.

'Already?' Teddy was genuinely dismayed.

'Everyone's seen us, we've had a good meal and upset Jean-Jacques and Marie-Lou. What else do you want? Let's go home and celebrate in bed.'

'All right,' Teddy grinned. He called Solange over.

The waitress, who had seen everything, just as she always did, gave Florence and Artus a table on the other side of the room from the youngsters, well away from the centre table.

Curiously Florence had noticed nothing, it seemed to Solange as she took the money from Teddy. She was shocked to see Teddy and Alexandra brazenly approaching Madame Berg, hand in hand. Both the young people's hair was in a fair mess, and their lips bright and swollen.

'Good evening, Florence,' Alexandra said.

'Artus, this is my daughter Alexandra and her friend Teddy Kovalic. May I introduce you to Artus Balestra, whom you've heard about. So you've had dinner here? Off already?'

'Yes, we're going,' Alexandra said, with a touch of bravado, which only her mother could detect. They left politely.

Artus turned to Florence: 'You're not her mother, I don't believe it, you're making it up.'

'She's eighteen, Artus.'

He wagged his head and observed: 'A pleasant young man. Like a faun, a rustic deity with horns! Charming.'

'Yes, I suppose so.'

In Balestra's company, Florence agreed with everything. It was a habit since the day at La Jouterie. Subdued in his presence she consulted the menu and said what she wanted. Then looked up to see Marie-Lou towering over her.

Her sister-in-law began: 'I know it's none of my business but . . .'

Florence made the introductions. Balestra rose and shook hands with Marie-Lou: '*Enchanté, Madame.*'

'You were saying?'

'Your daughter had dinner here, and behaved atrociously. I feel it my duty to inform you. She was indecent. And with a Kovalic of all people, with all of Chateauvallon looking on!'

Florence looked hard at her: 'If I'm not mistaken, you too are dining with a Kovalic, with Chateauvallon looking on.'

'It's not the same thing at all.'

'You don't sleep with yours, though. Perhaps you are not his type.'

Marie-Lou went white, opened her mouth and shut it again. She whirled round and went back to her table.

Balestra studied the menu, and Florence said: 'I mentioned her and my brother Jean-Jacques to you. That's a sample. Anyhow, to change the subject, what's the news from Stockholm?'

'They're coming tomorrow.'

'To check your morals?'

'Yes. Suppose I've committed bigamy, or slept with my kid sister!'

'Or you were a homosexual,' she laughed.

'Yes indeed.'

'You're not going to tell me there hasn't been one among the Nobel Prizewinners!'

'He would have slipped through, been married with children.'

She kept on giggling: 'But seriously, you *are* a bachelor, and there's no telling.'

Artus gave a chuckle, took her hand and kissed her fingers.

A few yards away, Marie-Lou said: 'I think we ought to leave before they start throwing the soup at each other!'

Thérèse had never been more restless, and at length told Julien she had a yen to spend a few days in Switzerland with their friends the Mattons.

The implication was that this would be a trip for both of them. Not unexpectedly for Thérèse, her husband said it wasn't a good moment for him and that in any case he was not mad about snow. She said it was too bad he could not get away but she knew he could look after himself and a few days on his own wouldn't kill him.

All this was said in a light-hearted style, and Julien admitted that the upheavals at La Commanderie and *La Dépêche* had taken their toll on both of them. A break would do them both good. That is what he said, but secretly he was intrigued, wondering whether this signalled a new phase in their life as a couple.

They were what old Antonin used to call 'a modern couple', by which he meant extravagant and even slightly dissolute. Julien and Thérèse Berg were indeed purposefully non-comforming, violently hating the idea that they could be assimilated to the bourgeois family Julien had sprung from with their out-of-date, make-believe hypocritical ways, concerned only with return on capital and playing to rules that were fast disappearing in France, Europe and worldwide. They strove to be 'natural', intellectual and ecologically-minded as far as possible. Julien's private theatre at the sawmill was one of the results. Another had been the earlier stretch of several months when they had lived on a sailing boat.

Yes, Julien was intrigued, but showed nothing. Respect for the other's liberty was part of their ethos. When he later came to reflect on it, he realized that what really seemed curious was her approach. Until the last moment she had acted the part of the wife in chains who was determined to break free. This led Julien to be specially kind while he feigned indifference and normality.

'Off darling?' he said, looking up from a board game with his daughter, as Thérèse clumped into the living room with a large bulging travel bag. She was wearing a leather jacket and a bonnet that covered her ears.

Julie the daughter quickly took four pieces on the board and he said: 'Just because I was busy; I'll get my own back!'

Thérèse took a hesitant step towards them, lost somehow and said quietly: 'Well, here I go.'

'Hope the snow's right for you,' said Julien, attacking his daughter's game.

'Aren't you going to kiss *maman*?' Thérèse asked.

'You can see I'm playing with *papa*!'

Julien remarked: 'Sure you wouldn't like me to drive you to the station?' His voice lacked any conviction.

'Absolutely sure,' his wife said more buoyantly. 'Have fun.'

The players stared at the board, then Julien suddenly led Julie to the window to wave goodbye, but it was too late and Julien was not even certain that Thérèse saw them waving as she drove off fast.

For a few seconds Julien thought about taking the other car and catching her up and kissing her goodbye on the station platform. But Julie said: 'Let's get on with it.'

Thérèse had no intention of going to the station. She had a map on the passenger seat and kept stopping to check her way. Eventually she emerged from a wood and saw an uncultivated field before her: the dusty road stopped there and she contemplated the empty field that resembled a vast lawn. There was a hut close by and she drove in first gear, stopping a few yards from it. She then extracted a key from her jacket and undid the padlock on the hut door. Having got the car inside, she locked up again and squatted on a piece of tree trunk with her travel bag.

Only the twitter of a few birds could be heard for a while, and she scanned the sky, wondering where the plane would come in. After what must have been five minutes she heard an engine, and she took a while to realize that the engine was that of a motorbike coming up behind her. She spun round and saw a man pulling up, with a bag across the petrol tank. The man kept his helmet visor down.

The sight of him made her catch her breath. Suddenly she didn't want to be there, a shamelessly easy woman setting off with a man she hardly knew. From some conversation years ago she recalled in a flash: 'It's the woman who's always to blame.' How could she turn back now? Who was the man on the motorbike anyhow?

As he dismounted, another engine purred and spluttered somewhere in the field and she saw the Cherokee taxiing towards them.

Aldo jumped out of the plane, ran towards her and led her with her bag to the cabin: 'Clever you, to have found the place. I half expected you to lose your way. Thought you might not come at all.'

'Of course I did,' she hastily replied.

As Aldo held her hand to help her aboard, Thérèse turned to see the motorbike chap run into the field, deposit the bag—it was a long like a golf bag—and then go back to the motorbike. He then roared off leaving the bag some distance from the plane.

'Funny,' said Thérèse.

'Don't worry about him, get in.'

She took the seat he pointed to and Aldo went for the long bag, placing it carefully in a compartment near the tail. He then made sure her door was closed and fixed the seatbelt round her.

As he revved up, she shouted: 'Killing two birds with one stone?'

'Can't hear you!'

'What's in the bag?'

'What bag?'

She already had her suspicions, ranging from gold ingots to a Soviet kalashnikov rifle.

Thérèse cried louder: 'I get it, there's no bag.'

He grinned at her and nodded cheekily.

Albertas was hoping Bernard had forgotten the business about checking the accounts, and he was not going to remind him.

One morning Bernard arrived at the farm with a bulky file held against his hip.

'*Salut*, boy,' the old man said. 'Come to tell me about another of your lawyer's great ideas?'

'Forget him. I'm here to discuss money.'

'You short?'

'No,' Bernard said curtly. Albertas noticed he had that steel-eyed look about him, and he heard his nephew go on: 'I've checked over all the bank accounts, and I'm worried. There are no debits, and Aqua Viva is costing money already.'

His uncle said cautiously: 'Aqua Viva's your business.'

'And it's started up. I've done the main schedule, taken on staff, booked contractors and labourers. There are some contracts already signed.'

Albertas looked even more distant: 'That's how it was supposed to be. You sign, I pay. Somebody want their money, then?'

'No.'

'What are you on about?'

'You pay in cash. Where do you get it?'

'If anyone asks, boy, you can tell them . . .'

Bernard's eyes became slits: 'I don't work that way, Albertas. Otherwise I'd have stayed in America.'

Albertas jerked his head up truculently: 'And who paid for that—America?'

'If you want your money back, you can have it. But it won't be in cash, I warn you.'

His uncle winced: 'What have you got against ready money?'

'Nothing. I just like to know where it comes from.'

'Your old father, may God bless him, always said the ways of Providence are impenetrable.'

'But the bank entries aren't!'

Albertas winced again to indicate he was a misunderstood man: 'Why do you say such things to me? I'm all square. You looking for trouble?'

'I want to avoid trouble. And if you don't come across quick, I'm pulling out.'

'Ha,' said Albertas, laying his rugged hands across his chest. 'Hoity-toity. You forget who you're speaking to.'

'No I don't, and you keep your belt on with me.'

'You won't get out of it that easy.'

'Nor will you, have no illusions about that!'

Like a pair of fighting cocks, they circled each other. The older man said: 'You've no sense of family, that's your trouble.'

'One word from you, and I'm off,' Bernard said levelly.

They were still glaring at each other, neither daring to blink, when Zöe burst in, followed by a woman neighbour who brandished a copy of *La Dépêche*.

Zöe cried: 'Albertas, she's started it again. Clara's read it out. She's started, that Berg. Says we're stopping her printing her paper. I told you nothing good would come of this. You had it coming to you!'

Immediately the two men crouched over the paper shoulder to shoulder. The editorial on the front page had been written by Travers, but they were not to know. They assumed it was 'that Berg'.

Clara cackled: 'That woman's after you, I always said so.'

428

Bernard reached the end ahead of his uncle and said: 'You're wrong.'

'That's what you think,' Albertas shouted, throwing the paper across the table.

'She's unable to publish her articles, and is defending herself as best she can.'

'Dead crafty, that woman,' Albertas said with emphasis. 'She throws muck at us, writing everything about our family, we stopped her and now she's attacking the Kovalics another way. You know what they call that? Racism. And the people here will love it, that's all they're looking for—scapegoats! He's a fool, your lawyer. Should have let her go on as she was, then we'd have been the victims. Now it's too late, she's going to make it ten times worse.'

Bernard threw up his hands: 'She's got her back to the wall, I tell you.'

Albertas ignored him: 'Zöe, you get all the family together. We'll defend ourselves in our way, without lawyers. Just the family like we've always done. Aha Bernard, *now* you can see what ready cash means!'

Bernard shrugged his jacket on, and strode out to his car. Albertas followed him. From the doorway he shouted: 'Unless you've gone over to them!!!'

Travers could not remember when he had felt so downhearted. That evening he was miserable, an old man, worn out. He strolled the streets trying to decide whether to chat up a girl in the Bijou-Bar, drive out somewhere twenty minutes away and treat himself to a good meal, or go home and pull the blankets over his head.

He had had as much of Chateauvallon and *La Dépêche* as he could stand. And of Florence. Not only that, Edelman and Favrot weren't funny any more, didn't make him laugh. Journalism was a dirty game, all women were bitches, even the damn pavements were full of dogshit, and he was a poor bloody bastard incapable of making up his mind.

A few yards ahead of him he caught sight of a Coca-Cola can, took a little run at it and kicked it for all his might far down the empty street. The raucous clatter gave him an instant of satisfaction and he wondered with a sniff whether he could find another. Maybe he would just kick this one round and round Chateauvallon! He stepped into the gutter to carry this out, when he realized the block of flats there looked familiar. Catherine Kovalic! She lived up there, and there was a light on. If he went up, she'd probably slam the door in his face. They had not said much to each other lately. It was worth a try. If he just said he was sorry and offered to make it up a bit with her, it would cheer him up, he supposed.

When she opened the door, he could hardly recognize her. Under her apron she had on a swish satiny dress and he could see the table laid for several people.

'Excuse me, Catherine. I was just passing by. I'll come back some other time as you've got company.'

'No, come in Travers.'

She was being polite, and he demurred. She went into the kitchen and he had little choice but to follow her. She opened the oven and a leg of lamb crackled. Catherine basted it and shut the door again.

'Looks good.'

'If there's anyone to eat it! What do I care!'

Catherine's eyes filled with tears. He had seen her cry many times after Paul was killed, he had stayed on a camp bed to keep her company, and he had stood by her when Albertas had threatened her.

'What's the trouble, sweet?' he said gently.

'Everyone—everyone—j-just uses me,' she cried, sinking onto a chair.

'Don't worry, they'll turn up.'

'They won't turn up,' she wept. 'They're already here!'

Travers blinked. From the bathroom came sounds of giggling, water splashing, shouts and sighs.

'That's what happens. You invite people to a nice dinner and they start by having it off in the bath!' she wailed.

Travers stifled a laugh: 'Haven't they got a bath of their own?'

'Huh. They've locked the door, and when I told them

the meal was ready they just laughed.'

'Oh my poor girl,' Travers said, hanging his mac up next to a crash helmet. Catherine pouted gloomily as she mixed something for the salad. Travers took the spoon from her.

'Wipe your eyes, and I'll do it. I'm expert at this. Who is it, your cousin Teddy?'

She blew her nose on a hankie from her apron and nodded.

'Not much sense to him. Who's he with?'

'Guess.'

'Florence's girl?'

She nodded again: 'How come you're wandering about?'

'No special reason. Thought I'd call in and have a look at you.'

'Well, that makes a change. Thanks for coming.'

Travers stopped stirring, turned off the leg of lamb, brushed Catherine's curl from her brow and marched towards the bathroom.

He yelled through the door: 'Come out of there this minute or I'll knock your heads together!'

Travers waited all of three seconds and then hurled himself at the door, which yielded. The water babies gaped at him in disbelief. He took a big towel and threw it at them.

'Get out and get dressed!'

When he returned to the kitchen, he found Catherine staring miserably at the still-bubbling leg of lamb.

'It's burned to a frazzle.'

He grinned at her: 'That's just where you're wrong. It's only the gravy that's been burning. No need to have that, it blocks up the arteries. Where's the board?'

He was into his stride now and got the lamb onto the board. He began slicing it carefully: 'Your son around?'

'Why?'

'Just wanted to see him, that's all.'

Catherine screwed up her face and studied him: 'You seem queer somehow, Travers.'

'Got a headache.'

'I ache everywhere.'

'When do we get married?'

Catherine attempted a smile but began crying again: 'You've gone soft in the head.'

Teddy said from the door: 'Smells like you poured petrol over it.'

Travers said to Catherine: 'Are you sure we need them for dinner?' He was desperately trying to get some kind of repartee going among them all, anything but this grim seriousness.

'We can't throw them out.'

'If we're in the way . . .' Teddy said.

Alexandra shoved Teddy aside and declared: 'Well, I think I'll leave you.' Teddy took her hand and she withdrew it.

'We're both invited,' he cried. 'You can't go now.'

'Oh yes I can. Have a lovely evening—family!'

Alexandra gave Teddy a quick peck on the nose, waved to the others and pranced out.

'Cor,' said Teddy.

Catherine and Travers shrieked with amusement.

'Teddy old chap,' Travers said, 'it's time you found out. There's more to women than blowing bubbles at them!'

Shortly before dawn the next morning one of the van drivers delivering *La Dépêche* was hurrying to make up for lost time. He was running nearly half an hour late, and was darting faster than usual from the van to the dropping-off points and back.

His routine was smooth. He would pull up sharply, jump out and open the back door, then scurry bent-over with the pile of papers to the doorway, up the alley or wherever it was, then close the door and get back into the driving seat. Usually the whole sequence took less than a minute.

He was delivering at a paper shop in Rue Jean-Jaures, when a man with a woollen ski bonnet rushed over to the van, undid the fuel cap, set light to a pre-shaped wad of cotton rag on the end of a stick and stuffed it into the fuel tank. He then ran off.

The van went whoosh and was engulfed in flames, as the driver hurried back.

All he could yell was 'Help, fire!' and lights came on in the flats around. Someone called the fire service and they arrived within minutes. The men did their best but it was hopeless. The van was a smouldering wreck fifteen minutes later. Around 5.00 a.m. a breakdown truck took the remains back to the loading bank at *La Dépêche*.

Commissaire Nicolo, alerted by Inspector Pradal who had been called automatically at the police station, stood looking at the useless vehicle. He was not surprised to find the stick close to the scene, which merely confirmed what he had already concluded as he put on his trousers. It was a case of arson, and no argument. He had then gone to *La Dépêche* and asked to see the driver.

'Can't explain it, *Monsieur Le Commissaire*, no I can't,' the driver stuttered. 'I was bowled over, and when I ran to the van there it was all alight and the papers on fire.'

Nicolo said: 'You didn't see anyone before you arrived?'

'No. No one, specially at that hour of the night.'

'Must have been someone. That stick didn't get there on its own.'

'I was inside the yard, Monsieur Nicolo. Never saw a thing.'

Nicolo thought and then asked: 'Been doing this job for long?'

Melchior, pale and unshaven answered for him: 'About fifteen years. Very conscientious.'

'How many copies?'

'Seven or eight thousand.'

'Eight thousand! They're no friends of yours, I see.'

'Me?'

'Not you personally. The paper. Has Madame Berg been told?'

'Not yet,' Melchior said. 'I'm always called first if there's any trouble.'

Nicolo took a deep breath: 'Another blow for her. Mind you, I'm not surprised, but you don't have to repeat that to her.' Nicolo drew Melchior aside. 'What you can tell her is

433

to keep an eye on the drivers. Just a piece of friendly advice.'

'Watch them or give them protection?'

'Both.'

In the wake of the fire Bernard Kovalic, Jean-Jacques Berg and Maryse gathered at *L'Eveil* as the clocks neared 8.00 a.m. They were drawn together at such times like puppets jerked into action by yet another of life's daily dramas. That was the role of the press, and they all felt it.

'Anyone would think there was a fire!' Marie-Lou had moaned from her pillow as Jean-Jacques clumped about looking for trousers, shoes, tie and the rest of his bold front against the world.

'There is,' he muttered. 'A van from *La Dépêche* completely gutted.'

'And you're rushing to get your orders, as usual,' his wife said in a voice of vitriol-coated barbed wire.

J-J Berg knew it but wasn't going to admit it. He was starting to perceive his move to *L'Eveil* as the worst day's work in his life. But on arrival at the office he was relieved to see that Bernard Kovalic was as perplexed as he was, awaiting orders too. And when the phone rang in Bernard's office all three of them jumped.

Bernard replied with an automatic smile on his lips. Within ten seconds it had faded: 'But Monsieur Boulard, what an idea!'

Jean-Jacques turned up the amplifier and they heard Boulard say: 'It's only an idea, someone could have forced your hand.'

'Who? You're the only person . . .'

'I never gave you that kind of instruction.'

'And I would never have carried it out. I like vans!' Bernard said with a suspicion of a snarl.

'So it's a row between drivers?' Boulard demanded sharply.

'No idea, Monsieur.'

'I understand they have three Kovalics among the drivers at *La Dépêche*.'

Bernard's jaw was clamped, his back teeth together: 'What am I to understand by that?'

'Nothing, but you may have remote cousins you don't even know about. They may . . .'

'And it'll get back to me—the blame?'

Boulard said: 'No, it reflects on me. And I'm the one who's paying you. I don't like this business, Kovalic, and I want to know what's at the bottom of it. In *L'Eveil* you'll play the story down. We must keep our noses clean.' He rang off.

Bernard neatly replaced the receiver, and saw the rabbit eyes of the other two.

Berg said: 'There are times when one would like to change one's name.'

'If your sister hadn't done that feature on the Kovalics . . .'

'I never liked her way of running *La Dépêche*, that's why I left.'

'That's a great help,' Bernard said with unforced irony, fetching a sports bag from a cupboard and leaving in a hurry.

Maryse looked heavenwards: 'Thank God for jogging. If he didn't have that, he'd go mad. It won't change his name but it calms him down.'

However that may be, Bernard had further cause for anger when he prepared to get into his BMW after an hour's running. Quite by chance Travers, Edelman and Favrot went by in a car, apparently having done much the same thing, for they were in tracksuits. Bernard waved them down and asked them about the van fire, adopting a supercilious attitude; but this to no avail, for the others gave gibe for gibe and he ended up feeling more of a slave to the almighty Boulard than a Kovalic worthy of the name. He got inside the BMW, a recent acquisition replacing the Renault, and felt the affluence pervade his body and spirit. He began breathing easier.

When Florence reached the office she was told Melchior was at the loading bank.

435

She found him in deep discussion with an arm-waving fellow wearing a flamboyant but crumpled suit, with dishevelled hair and a fruity voice. At a glance she deduced that this was the man supplying the 'guards' they had ordered for the van drivers. Florence retreated behind a pile of unsold copies and listened.

'But how many men can you let us have?' Melchior was saying.

'During elections we can produce about one hundred men in this region, perhaps more. Depends on how many they let out on bail.'

Melchior started: 'I'm sorry I don't understand.'

The others explained: 'Well, they're not choirboys, you know. Done a term, many of 'em. How many was you thinking of having?'

'Do they carry guns?'

'That's up to you. Some of them have got licences, and some have lost them, as you might say. 'Course with guns it's a bigger fee.' Melchior jerked his head in interrogation. 'Let's see, I can let you have either sort for four hundred francs if you take ten or more, and we'll overlook the VAT, social security and all that stuff.'

Florence showed herself: 'That's a lot for sitting in a van at night in a quiet town, just driving around.'

'That's the job, Madame. And vans catch fire. Of course they have to eat like everyone else. I tell you what, let's say three hundred francs and food supplied.'

She was out of her depth, but gave a nod to Melchior. 'All right,' he said.

The man smiled through wonky teeth: 'You won't regret it, Monsieur. They're real professionals.'

Florence and Melchior went in together. She said: 'This sort of thing brings me out in spots.'

'Me too. The drivers don't like it either. But what choice have we? Someone's declared war on us, and we are obliged to act. If ever anybody was killed . . . '

'You're right,' she said with a snort of anger.

Julien Berg was strolling this way and that in the car park at

Chateauvallon station. To break the monotony he made for the bar opposite the station and got some money out for a packet of cigarettes.

At the door, he came face to face with Marie-Lou, a carton of Peter Stuyvesant under her arm and pushing her purse back in her bag.

'Hullo stranger,' she said.

'Meeting Thérèse,' he volunteered. 'And you?'

'Dentist upstairs. Thérèse been on a trip?'

'Went skiing.'

'In summer!'

'Oh, you can find snow high up. We've some friends, the Mattons, and they have a chalet in Switzerland. They've been asking us to go for two years now, and Thérèse thought . . .'

Marie-Lou changed her tone: 'I'd like you for dinner one of these days. I'll give you a call. Give Thérèse my love, I'm in a bit of a hurry.'

Thérèse appeared to be in less of a hurry. The separation had unsteadied Julien and he smoked four Gitanes in a row before he heard the train draw in. He waited on the pavement as the first passengers streamed out, then went inside as the bulk of them came through from the platform into the ticket office. Two minutes later he had to admit: his wife was not on the train!

Still frowning, he emerged into the harsh sunlight and heard a car horn beeping several times. He squinted and at last realized it was Thérèse sitting calmly behind the wheel.

'Want a lift?' she said, her white teeth sparkling at him. His heart gave a jump, he was glad to see her, he had had his doubts.

'B-but I didn't see you come out.'

'Naturally, I wasn't on the train. Drive, please Julien, I'm exhausted.'

He went round and got in, as she slid over to the passenger seat: 'What happened?'

'Well,' she said chattily, 'I missed the train when I went but managed to catch it up at Amboise, which was quite an

437

achievement. That meant I had to get off at Amboise coming back, to collect the car.'

Julien had to concentrate on driving for a second, then he asked: 'Why did you drive to the station instead of the house?'

Laying a hand on his thigh she said: 'I thought my darling husband would be meeting me at the station, and I was right.' She gave him a kiss on the cheek, leaving a dark red blob.

'Nice holiday?'

'Rather bitty. We flew mostly, because there wasn't really enough snow. Yes, we went flying. In a plane.'

'I imagine so. Nice of the Mattons, I take it they paid.'

'Not at all. They have a friend who has a plane. A pilot.'

'Presumably. With sunglasses and everything?'

'Everything!' she said in a teasy voice, hoping he would relax and talk about something else.

He did: 'Just after you went, Julie had a nosebleed. It went on for a while, but I didn't call the doctor.'

The traffic was unusually snarled up. Julien sniffed and muttered at the idiot in front.

'You could have given me a ring,' his wife said.

'I phoned about four times, *chérie*, but couldn't get a reply. You must have been out each time.'

He let in the clutch, the car surged forward about two lengths and he braked hard.

'Ouch,' Thérèse said.

'Sorry,' he replied curtly, rubbing at the lipstick blob.

Chapter Seven

Florence Berg was brushing her magnificent mane of hair, making huge strokes and leaning her head this way and that, when Alexandra came into her bedroom in a bathrobe. Florence wore a satin bra, flared knickers and a slip over them.

They looked at each other for a moment via the mirror, sizing each other up. They still hadn't quite jelled, as Alexandra would have put it. It was she who broke the silence, pointing to a wad of banknotes in her mother's bag.

'Could I have some, *maman*?'

Florence counted out a few notes: 'Enough?' The girl nodded and Florence added: 'If you have a minute I'd like to ask you something. Who's Barnes?'

'Why do you want to know? Did he phone?'

'At 3.00 a.m. When you talk to him, you could point out the time difference across the Atlantic.' She dug into a jar of cream.

'He's one of dad's agents.'

'So I gathered. He was on about a manuscript. What was he getting at?'

'Dad's diary.'

'Yes?'

'Barnes must be mad, I've got the only copy with me.'

'Really!'

'I ought to have mentioned it to you, I suppose.'

Florence stopped making up and turned to face Alexandra: 'Manuscripts are valuable, you know. You're not up to something?'

Reluctantly her daughter said: 'The publisher paid a big advance on it.'

'I can well imagine it. How much?'

'Eighty thousand dollars.'

Florence gave a little whistle: 'That doesn't worry you?'

'Yes, but that's not the problem.'

The forced smile left Florence's face: 'You've lost it!!!'

'Oh no,' the girl said in a matter-of-fact tone, moving across to the window, thrusting her hands in her trouser pockets. 'I'll explain it. The secretary did the whole typed copy, then did it up and sealed it, and asked me to take it to Barnes because there was a mail strike on. I said I would but I stopped by the house first. I kept looking at the file for hours, and then I undid it and read it all.'

'Uhuh.'

'Well then I went back to the office, and it was at night and empty and everything. I found the drafts and copies and put it all in the incinerator. That was the night before I flew here. I brought the manuscript and never went to see Barnes. So now you know!'

She stood squarely facing her mother.

Florence's eyes were larger than usual: 'Why ever did you do that?'

'I didn't want the publisher to see it like it was.'

'You didn't care for it?'

'Yes, but . . .'

'What period does it cover, the diary?'

'When you were married. You want to read it?'

Florence replied: 'No, because you won't show it to me anyway.' She was shaking with fury, and to hide it she slipped her dress on and put a pair of tinkly bracelets on, biting her top lip just the same. She added coldly: 'Is there anything else you want from me?'

Alexandra eyed her slyly: 'You could help do the cuts.'

'You mean you'd dare to make cuts to your father's personal diary?'

'He may have wanted that,' the girl retorted, staring boldly into her mother's eyes.

Florence's hand flew to the girl's left cheek, and Alexandra let out an 'Ayeee!' She snuffled and began shaking.

'I'm sorry, I couldn't help that. Forgive me.' Florence

took her daughter tenderly and ran her hand over her hair.

Alexandra drew away sharply and shrieked: 'Why do I get on everyone's nerves?! Haven't you had enough of me?' She went out stiffly.

Florence returned to her make-up, her lips compressed. The tears flowed, she seized some cottonwool and wiped her face. Then when the tears stopped, she started making up again.

Albertas Kovalic sat opposite his accountant's desk, a man named Caprioli whom he'd known for years and called on almost daily in the grim file-lined office in the old part of the town.

'I wondered if my nephew Bernard's been in to see you?'

'Er-yes. Twice as a matter of fact. Spent several hours here, asked to see everything, the bank statements for all your accounts. But don't worry I didn't show him the blue file.'

'You did right, Caprioli. We'll have to let him see it one day, as he's my nephew. But only after everything's finished.'

'Finished?' Caprioli said servilely. He was around fifty, had thinning pepper-and-salt hair, darting eyes and a suit he apparently wore in bed.

Albertas leaned forward: 'I'm going to stop it, it's getting too big a thing, and I want to keep out of jail at my age. If you want to know, I've got diabetes and I don't trust those doctors. Got to think of the young ones too.'

Caprioli swallowed: 'But your cousins in Trieste?'

'They can sort it out. And nobody can tell relatives just by looking at them. I'm stopping it, I say. Just one more delivery, because it's too late to stop it now. But that's the last of it.'

'They'll be hopping mad.'

'Let 'em hop. They'll understand or they won't, we'll have to see.' Albertas eyed the accountant. 'What's come over you then? Money? There's plenty of it about, we always found a way before. But don't worry about your pension, we'll be in retirement together.'

The head of the Kovalics rose, letting out a big breath and puffing out his cheeks. He went over to a small mirror, viewed the set of his wide-brimmed hat, then lit a cigar.

He went back to the desk and the two men faced each other. He said: 'About Bernard. Don't tell him anything yet. When I say, you can show him the blue file, but don't explain its contents. He'll need at least a year to work it out, and he'll give up before then. Bernard's a bit weak, not a true Kovalic.'

It was a Kovalic driving the second van that was set fire to. With him were two of the guards *La Dépêche* was paying for.

Even before they had left shortly after midnight, there was trouble when the driver claimed that the two men were there to keep a check on him. The fleet manager sorted it out, as much by his bulk as his authority, and the Kovalic driver grumbled his acceptance.

One of the escorts carried a gun. He was a tall, honest-looking fellow called Robert who chatted with the driver, asking him about his job, its good points and bad. Kovalic had sworn he wouldn't open his mouth, but he relented. By 1.00 a.m. or so he suggested that Robert give him a hand with the carrying, as it would speed it up for them all.

The other escort, Jacky, was unarmed. Curiously, this short blond man kept niggling Kovalic, almost as if he were deliberately provoking him like some little insect. Robert made several attempts to intervene, and Kovalic sat and fumed although he crashed the gears more than once. He reckoned this Jacky had a sly cunning about him, the sort of man who liked picking a fight.

The paper van met Teddy and Alexandra coming the other way. The two Kovalics hailed each other.

'A mate of yours?' Jacky demanded through a lump of sandwich soaked with beer he was swigging from a bottle.

'My cousin.'

Robert was having a snack too, and to make things more comfortable he had unbuckled his belt and parked the

442

gun in a compartment near the steering wheel.

'How many cousins you got?' Jacky said.

Kovalic, heartily resentful of this whole escort business, remained silent.

'Stacks of Kovalics, ain't there?'

Silence.

'I got a pal says when he can't sleep he counts Kovalics.' Jacky nearly choked over his sandwich, he was laughing so much.

The Kovalic driver pulled the van up sharply: 'Just take your bottle of beer and clear off.'

Jacky's face switched to the angelic: 'Here, what's a matter with you, all of a sudden?'

Robert butted in: 'Take it easy, we're on a job and that's all there is to it.'

Nothing was said for a while, but the cab was filled with hate. It oozed out of Kovalic and Jacky, swirling round the long-suffering Robert between stops. But for a couple of hours the job progressed, with Kovalic and Robert taking the piles and placing them at the pre-arranged points, and Jacky knocking back the beer and taking it easy.

The van came to a halt and Kovalic said: 'This one and one more, then we knock off.'

The driver and Robert jumped out once more, taking four bundles. They were in the working-class district with only council flats to be seen. A few lights were on in the flats, but there was nobody about, not even a dog sniffing at one of the trees planted some three years earlier. The men dumped the bundles behind a paper shop in an alley and emerged rubbing their hands where the string had cut.

'Christ!' said Kovalic. 'Where's the bleedin' van gone?'

'There she is,' Robert pointed. 'Jacky's idea of a bit of fun. He's got it in for you. Forget it, it's not worth kicking up a din.'

They ran towards the van, now parked in the middle of the road. As they approached, they saw Jacky holding several screwed-up copies of *La Dépêche*, and setting light to the tapered end. He then pushed the flaming torch into the fuel tank. The vehicle was quickly ablaze. Then to their horror, the two saw that Jacky had taken Robert's gun and was pointing it at them.

'Stay where you are,' he said. 'Stay right where you are!'

Kovalic ignored him and ran to the cab where he planned to grab the regulation fire extinguisher.

Meanwhile Robert told Jacky: 'Come off it, don't be a cunt. You've got no licence.' Jacky kept the gun trained on him. 'You must have gone daft or something, let's have that thing.'

Kovalic now ran back with the extinguisher, Jacky spun round and aimed at Kovalic, Robert hurled himself at Jacky to get the gun and it was Robert who received the bullet, right through the heart. Immediately Jacky jerked the gun round at Kovalic now already lying flat behind the flaming van, and the second shot reached its mark too.

Jacky then threw the gun into the flames and ran off, only to come back and kneel down beside Robert's body, sobbing loudly.

Some thirty minutes later, Nicolo and his men were marking out the bodies with chalk before taking them off, looking for bullet cases, noting details and banging off pictures.

Jacky was in a police van, having offered his wrists to the handcuffs without a murmur. The commissaire was as cheerful as a lark; this time he had the killer.

Florence Berg was roused by a call from the public prosecutor.

In an immediate reaction she phoned her brother Armand in Paris.

'Sorry Armand,' she said as he growled his way out of sleep. 'They've got another of my vans, and this time there are two dead. One of them's a Kovalic, my driver, been with us for two years, nothing to do with the farm lot, a decent fellow. But he's a Kovalic and that's bad for us. You've got to come and help me, Armand. After all, this is your constituency!'

She then called Melchior, and was put through to him at

444

the loading bank. He was trying to produce a measure of consensus between the drivers and the guards, helped by the fleet manager and the guards' recruiter.

'I might as well tell you they're almost at each other's throats, Florence. The guards want to leave and their boss won't let them, saying they're yellow.'

'But it was a guard who fired.'

'They claim he was shooting in self-defence.'

'Against whom for pity's sake?'

Melchior grew confidential: 'Listen, Florence, for the moment they are being held back, but they want paying at once, in cash. I don't think you need to worry too much, but anything could spark off a fight. Don't forget some of them are armed!'

'In cash, now? How much does it come to?'

'Around nineteen thousand. We haven't got that here in the office.'

Florence hesitated for an instant, and said: 'Right, I'll get onto that. I'm coming, you can tell them.'

Melchior replaced the receiver on the wall phone, wiped his bald head with his handkerchief, forgetting the sweat pouring down his face, then took a deep breath.

He told the guards' recruiter: 'In twenty minutes you'll have your money. And after that, you can clear off.'

Melchior told the fleet manager to get all their names. He thought it might help in the follow-up enquiries.

Florence woke her bank manager up, got the money and handed it over to Melchior.

She then sat back in her office chair and tried to recover from this latest turn of events, only to be roused by the deputy public prosecutor coming through the door.

'You see, I have called simply to inform you that your evidence will certainly be needed.'

Florence replied dully: 'That's very kind of you, coming just to tell me that. But at 8.00 a.m.? Anyhow, since you're here, perhaps we could talk about something else. Two of my vans have gone up in smoke. They cost a lot of money . . .'

'Two men's lives are costly too.'

'Too true. But tell me, Monsieur, do you want all this to go on?'

The deputy took a pause and said: 'I must reveal that the people in Paris dislike what's going on in Chateauvallon.'

'As if we liked it! The simple answer surely is to make sure I'm protected. I suppose you'll say you are short of personnel, is that it?'

'You have enemies, Madame Berg. But it does seem that it was you who opened Pandora's box.'

Florence let out a big sigh: 'It's our business to open up boxes. But that's by the way. Tell me why an official of your standing needs to come in here at breakfast time and inform me that I may have to give evidence.'

'I am doing this unofficially,' the man said.

'In that case I'm asking you, kind sir, to do something official for me: find a way of giving protection to our people in Chateauvallon. Is there anything else you'd like to tell me?'

'Yes,' he said, 'Good luck to you, Madame Berg.'

Following this inconclusive exchange, Florence went back to La Commanderie and lay down fully clothed on her bed for a while.

Mathilde came in with some tea and toast, but the mistress of the house said she was not hungry.

'Dear Mathilde,' she said. 'I'm once again all-in. Please be a sweetie and take my shoes off.'

Mathilde did so: 'What are they saying in the town?'

'I've heard nothing of course, but it's not hard to imagine. Where's Alexandra?'

'In her room. D'you want to see her?'

'Yes please.'

The woman went off, and Florence slipped off her skirt and blouse and crawled between the sheets. She yearned for a week in bed, best of all in some place like the Gobi Desert. Two minutes later Alexandra was standing at the door rubbing her eyes.

'D'you realize what time it is?' the girl said.

'Yes, I'm just going to bed again. Is your chap here?'

'Yes.' The girl was clothed in a T-shirt and from Florence's horizontal position it was obvious she had nothing else on. It seemed unsuitable for what she had to say.

'One of his cousins has been murdered. His van was set on fire.'

'You want me to tell him?'

'Not yet.'

'Then why did you wake me up?'

'I wanted a little chat with you. Come in with me.' Florence moved over, but Alexandra refused the overture, causing another little stab at her mother's heart.

From a seated position on the carpet she demanded: 'What the devil's going on in this dump?'

'It's your dump darling, you were born here, and I'm slowly going mad and need you.'

Alexandra half rose and put her elbows on the bed: 'Haven't you got anyone else?'

'Your father would have helped. At this moment I could do with him to lean on. But . . .'

'Then it must be serious. What's with that van thing?'

'It was the firm's.'

'Papa hated vans and trucks. Newspapers too. *Maman* I'm going back to the States.'

Florence took the blow on the chin: 'I was expecting you to tell me so.'

'Don't you mind?'

'Do you think I deserve it?'

Alexandra could find no answer to that.

'Alexandra,' her mother said lifting the girl's chin, 'what's worrying you about that manuscript?'

'Didn't you find anything? Under the bed where I put it last night?' Alexandra scrabbled under the bed, pulled out a sheet of paper and squatted on her heels.

'One morning,' she read, 'I woke up saying who was this woman, who was this child, what was this town? I said what was I doing here? It was as if everything had been taken from me during the night. Thus I left without warning. They were with me but behind a pane of glass. At that

447

point I was afraid. Between chagrin and fear I chose chagrin. Florence too, I suppose. The little one had plenty of time ahead of her, and we could sacrifice her for a bit. Her mother had no scruples, nor had I. And then I returned, somewhere else, liking the idea that I had lost them, for it meant I would find them again . . .'

After a moment Florence said: 'He didn't find *me* again.'

Alexandra cried: 'You can see why I didn't want Barnes to have that. He never stopped talking about you.'

Florence extracted herself from the bed and went towards the bathroom: 'It wasn't easy for me either. I was only slightly older than you are now at the time, you know.'

Her daughter followed her, the sheet of paper held weakly in her hand: 'That scared me what you said just now. They're killing people here now?'

'Everyone's gone mad.'

'Isn't it your fault a little?'

'Nonsense.'

'You know I really think I'll go back to the States.'

'Perhaps you're right, they don't kill people much over there.'

Their eyes met and they both laughed.

Pradal asked Jacky more urgently: 'So you were asleep, is that what you said?'

Nicolo and he had been going at the man for thirty minutes already, running over the same questions again and again. That was how the SRPJ Criminal Police did it, and they supposed it was the same the world over.

'I told you I was tired out.'

'Where were you in the van?'

'In front.'

'And you woke up and found the back was on fire and you were all on your own on the cab seat?'

'That's right. I heard someone shout, and it was my mate pegging out.'

'How did you know?' Pradal snapped.

'Well, I got out of the van and saw him lying on the ground.'

448

'Where, how far away?'

'Where you found me, I think.'

'Kovalic let you get out?'

'He couldn't see me, it was thick with smoke.'

The two cops kept up the pressure: 'Where was Kovalic?'

'In the van or on one side of it, I can't remember.'

'What did you do?'

'I yelled at him "get out for Christ's sake". Then he fired, and I went into the fire.'

'Brave man. You're not afraid of fire.'

'Why d'you say that?'

'No reason, tell us more. You went back into the flames, and then?'

'I overpowered him and got the gun off him, he tried to snatch it back, I can't remember. Anyway the gun went off.'

'All inside the flames?'

'Right next to it. I was on my knees outside of it. He was inside in the flames.'

'So you were acting in self-defence. Is that what you're trying to sell us?' Nicolo snarled.

'What else could it be but self-defence?'

'It could be a bloody great lie, Jacky, and you know it.'

A uniformed policeman came and whispered to Nicolo that the Kovalic family was outside and wanted a hearing. The Commissaire said he would get to them later, but he glanced through the window to see Albertas in his Mercedes with the two women, also Teddy, and Bernard in his BMW. Albertas got out of his car and started yelling: 'It's incredible. I'm a citizen of this town like any other, I've a right to see the police!'

Bernard called him back: 'It's not the right moment, Albertas. Later.'

'They're giving him the once over, that bloke,' Teddy added. 'They can't see us now.'

'I'd give him the once over! I'm going to organize the family. We'll get him when he comes out!'

Teddy cried: 'No uncle, we'll all end up inside!'

'Fathead!' Albertas threw at Bernard. But Bernard failed to hear him, the mobile phone was bleeping in his car.

Albertas went on: 'I want to know who paid that rascal to kill one of our boys.'

'Another man was killed, one of the escorts,' Teddy protested.

'They've got plenty more. He fired the second time to hide the first shot. Oldest trick in the business.'

Bernard hastened back from his car: 'Let's scarper, the lot of us. The guards are on their way.'

Albertas drew himself up: 'Let 'em come.'

'Twenty of them, with guns?'

'We'll take 'em on.'

His two nephews bundled him somehow into the Mercedes, and Teddy took the wheel. The two cars backed and circled their way out of the yard just as the guards arrived on motorbikes.

Nicolo saw them and flung at Jacky: 'Here are your mates. Want to have a little chat with you, I shouldn't wonder.'

Jacky stammered: 'I want a lawyer. And it's up to you to protect me.'

Nicolo grinned: 'Not against your friends. I expect they'll take you off shoulder-high, carry you in triumph for avenging one of their pals.'

'No!!!' Jacky shrieked. 'They're trigger happy those guys!'

'All right, we'll keep you here,' Nicolo said. 'Now where were we? There was this smoke, you say, and you got out of the van . . .'

'Oh my gawd,' Jacky moaned.

Early that afternoon the usual editorial conference was in progress at *La Dépêche*.

'It's my belief we'll never get to the bottom of it,' Melchior was saying.

'I won't accept that,' Florence rapped. 'Where do you think this is, Chile or somewhere?'

Travers said: 'Let's keep calm and think it through. We

450

all agree it was a planned job . . .'

'Who planned it?' Catherine Kovalic said.

'There's a Kovalic dead,' Florence said, pacing the room and lighting a cigarette. 'Which means they're not suspects. In any case they wouldn't go that far.'

'Your view on that?' Travers asked Catherine.

The girl did not answer at once. She bit her lower lip and said at length: 'They are capable of it, capable of anything. I don't like admitting it, but I have to.'

'Boulard?' Melchior suggested.

It was Edelman who replied: 'He stabs but doesn't shoot. Not his style.'

Florence said half to herself: 'Would Boulard burn our vans, kill my drivers?'

Painstakingly Melchior set out to recapitulate, but a young woman journalist burst in: 'That's the end! Les Glycines Clinic has been raided now!'

Florence cried: 'My brother's clinic? Well come on, out with it!'

'Someone broke into the safe, *Madame*. Two wealthy women patients had jewels in it, they live alone and handed over the valuables during their stay. Gold necklaces, a magnificent river of pearls apparently, and some rings. Worth a fortune. I've got the women's names if you want them.'

'Later. So it really is a planned attack, planned from start to finish. But when's the finish? Whoever they are they want the Bergs. We'll get them. Edelman, you cover the clinic, and above all get the staff talking. Get to it right away!'

At that moment, the fleet manager came in, to announce that the drivers were preparing a one-hour work stoppage in memory of the Kovalic who died. He also told Florence they wanted an end to the escorts, and he agreed with them. He was expanding on the theme when Travers broke in.

'Radios,' he barked.

'Exactly, Monsieur Travers,' the man said.

Florence blinked uncomprehendingly, and Travers

451

went on to explain that the vans all had radio-telephones years ago, but that they had been taken out because of the chatter between drivers that slowed up delivery.

'I understand,' Florence said. 'But that's the answer now that we're fighting a war. Let's have the radios back. I'll tell them myself. Come down with me, all of you.'

Albertas was arranging the funeral of the Kovalic driver, taking suggestions from the two women, Bernard and Teddy.

He sat at the big table in the farmhouse with eyes like buttons, telling them this had to be the finest funeral Chateauvallon had seen for many a long year, with the best coffin, the smartest hearse and all the trimmings. No expense spared, and he would finance the whole thing. The Kovalics would show them, the bourgeois of Chateauvallon! Be showing the entire far-flung Kovalic family too that the centre of the Kovalic clan was here, where obedience and respect were due.

Bernard left at length with orders to fix up the invitations, he made his way to *L'Eveil*, where Jean-Jacques Berg had drafted an editorial comment, and had pasted up some dummy pages headed BLOOD FLOWS IN CH'VALLON.

'Can't you do better than that?' Bernard shouted. 'It's as daft as your usual headlines. You've got to implicate your sister?'

Maryse cried: 'Whatever for?'

'It's *La Dépêche* that came out of it worst,' Bernard roared.

Jean-Jacques was visibly trembling and breathing heavily. 'So we're waving the battle-axe again,' Maryse remarked.

'We never buried the hatchet,' Bernard said, going over to the dummy. He found a red felt pen and wrote the new headline: LA DEPECHE SPATTERED! 'That's it, and no other will do,' he announced.

He then stomped out, slamming the door, leaving the other two staring at each other.

452

When Florence had put up her apartments and her stake in her law business for sale, to settle the first batch of estate duties, she had failed to find a buyer for her studio in Chateauvallon. She decided at length to hold onto it, seeing it as a symbol of her independence, a refuge for any unforeseen event to come. Occasionally friends had used it, and once she let it to an American who was doing research for a book on life in the French provinces. It had been her love nest for years with Georges Quentin, and around the time that she met Artus Balestra she set about doing it up again.

Now a woman came in regularly to keep it clean, she had herself brought in linen and a few clothes, and she even used it on some nights when the presence of young Teddy Kovalic in the blue room at La Commanderie depressed her.

On the night following the double murder, she planned to meet Armand very late at the office and told herself she might as well spend the night in the studio. In the early evening she told the office she was going there and would be back later to see her brother.

She wanted nothing so much as a relaxing bath and time to think things over, and had run the bath and undressed when the doorbell went. Florence let out a curse and immediately supposed that Armand had turned up sooner than he intended. She put on her slip and briefs and flung open the studio door, not bothering about a bra.

On the doormat stood Artus Balestra looking like death warmed up in a crumpled beige suit and fingering his tie. She gave him a huge smile.

'Good evening, my name is Balestra, I'd like to see Florence Berg,' he said politely.

'A moment, sir, she is on the telephone, will you come in?'

She danced into the middle of the room, leading him by the hand and making a joke of it. She was thrilled to have him in her very own studio, and evidently in need of her. She then realized that he was using his tie as a bandage, and discovered a scratch on the back of his hand.

'Let me see this little pimple or whatever,' she said gaily.

453

'It's not a pimple and it hurts.' She kept smiling, ignoring his curious attitude, as he went on: 'Tell me I can turn round and go again.'

'You're tired, so you'd better sit down for a while to start with.'

Balestra drew a hand across his brow and said dramatically: 'Oh Florence, my life has become a nightmare, a Swedish nightmare!'

'Really, are they still nosing around?'

'They won't give me a moment's peace. They want to know absolutely everything, all about what I've been doing for the past few decades, all about my ancestors. My father didn't show up too well during the war, actually, and . . .'

'Could that compromise you?' Florence said going into the bathroom in search of some ointment.

When she began tending his scratch, he said: 'And now you're hurting me too!'

'Don't be a cry-baby, Artus.' They had touched before, and she had put her arm in his, but there was something more intimate about playing the nurse.

'Of course I'm a cry-baby. You ought to know also that I am finicky and obstinate. Anyhow, I understand you're being hounded again.'

'Somebody's trying to make me lose my temper, but now that I know what the game is, I can cope with it. A woman can be obstinate, or weak, at will. I'm sure you know that. Yes, my dear Artus, I have two corpses on my hands now.'

She so wanted to forget about them too, but she couldn't be rude. Especially as her mood was euphoric. She glanced at the water in the bath, with its steamy wisps above the surface. Artus was going on and on about widows and orphans and insurance, and she would have just loved to take a bath with Artus, so that they could be really silly together.

To her astonishment, she heard him say: 'Oh, I see you have a bath ready. May I steal it from you?'

'Go ahead, I must have known you were coming.'

Florence was even more startled when he promptly took

454

everything off except his underpants, and jumped in the bath.

'Do you always bath in your pants?'

'Er, no, I'm sorry.' Balestra took them off under the water. 'Is your readership falling?'

'I don't think so,' she said, 'and it may be rising. People love blood. Even so I feel exposed.'

Artus quipped: 'So do I. D'you think you could let me play with my plastic duck all alone for a couple of minutes?'

This was another surprise, but she made nothing of it as she closed the door behind her and stood in the room containing the bed. For ten seconds she listened to Balestra splashing about. Then it dawned on her that *this could be it!* What an idiot she had been not to realize it at once. Florence took her two flimsy garments off, the slip and the briefs, then got into something even flimsier designed to reveal more than it concealed, then dabbed some of her sultriest perfume behind her knees, on her bottom and arms—the whole at lightning speed. After that she switched off the ceiling light, and skidded between the sheets, listening to Artus singing some opera thing and telling herself that a man singing in his bath must be one of the wonders of the world.

Florence had to admit she had been building up steam from the moment he came in, and now she lay with her eyes closed getting into a more incandescent mood. To her delight the first tang of desire announced itself about half-way down the bed and she hugged herself.

She heard Artus dry off, stamp about a bit, open the door, creep over. She felt his soft kiss on her brow and a finger, perhaps two, brushing her cheek. There was no need to open her eyes yet and she simply smiled.

'Don't get up, *chérie*,' he said. 'Sleep well, thanks for everything, I'll give you a ring tomorrow.'

Her eyes popped open and simultaneously she leaped out of the bed to find Balestra fully dressed and on his way out.

'Bye bye,' he said with a cheery wave.

The door closed and her torrid mood changed instantly to shocked dismay.

Frustrated and angry she dressed again, telling herself that if he'd actually seen her in bed again, all was not lost.

When she strode into her office soon afterwards, she found Armand dozing on the couch.

She yelled: 'The whole place is on fire, and all you can do is snore your head off!'

'How nice,' he murmured. 'I can always be sure of a welcome in an emergency.'

'We're in deep trouble,' his sister said.

'Let's hear about your trouble first,' he said. 'For a start whose brilliant idea was it to order those guards? You could hardly have picked a bigger bunch of crooks.'

'You're not going to . . '

'I certainly am. Fancy doing business with Schultz of all people, a complete thickhead with a criminal record as long as your arm. Surely you could tell just by looking at him!'

'I-I just thought they all looked like that.'

Armand glared at her: 'There's a lot more to this than thinking up headlines, you know.'

'So you think I'm incompetent, is that it?'

Armand adopted a kinder tone: 'Poor Flo, it can't be easy. In your position I'd have got rid of the whole caboodle ages ago. Where's the fun in it?' He ran his hand over her hair, kneaded it gently as he used to before.

'We used to be such friends,' she whispered.

'Now don't go all fragile, Flo. You're forty and tough, and that's why they're after you.'

'Whoever they are. If I only had a good clue. You won't let me fight this on my own?'

'We're both grown-ups now.'

Florence drew away from him just as Edelman knocked and poked his head in.

'Come right in,' she ordered.

He did and produced the dummy from *L'Eveil* reading LA DEPECHE SPATTERED. There was a sub-head which said: The Chickens Come Home to Roost.

'That *must* be Boulard. But how did you get hold of the dummy?'

456

'Trade secret, *Madame,*' Edelman said. He took his leave.

Florence stared at the sheet of paper for a long while, then realized that Armand was not reacting.

'It doesn't seem to worry you,' she said sharply.

'*L'Eveil* is only doing its job.'

'Boulard can't do a thing!'

'As you wish. But he knows you have money problems, family problems . . .'

'Keep off that subject please.'

Scornfully he wondered: 'Is it the family that's spattered?'

'Oh clear out!' she snarled.

Armand took a step or two in the direction of the door and stated: 'I have news of your love life.'

'What does that mean?'

'Your scientist. What's so interesting about him—the Nobel Prize or the pansy boy.'

Florence stiffened: 'Oh no!!!' She became a statue.

'You didn't know?' Florence made no reply. 'He won't get the Nobel, Flo, and it's because he's a homosexual.'

At last she spoke: 'This must be the end. There can't be any more surprises left. Armand, my sweet, you've simply got to have dinner with me, a late one, there's still time.'

'Sorry Flo, I'll be in touch.'

Sleeping at the studio was out of the question now, and on her way to La Commanderie she went past *L'Eveil*. They were undoubtedly chortling over their front-page story and already working on the follow-up. Florence jabbed her foot on the accelerator.

Inside *L'Eveil* were only Bernard and Maryse, idly chatting about the big story, but discussing others too. Jean-Jacques had gone off hours ago, saying he would need some sleeping pills that night.

The phone went, Maryse took it, listened and finally thrust it at Bernard, saying 'Boulard!'

'That you Kovalic? The telephoto's come over of your front page. Have you gone raving mad? What's all this about *La Dépêche* spattered?'

457

Bernard coughed: 'Seems clear enough, in view of what's been going on . . .'

'Tell me, Kovalic, who are you working for?'

'I'm sorry I don't . . .'

'They told me you'd got at least one brain in your head. Here's this unfortunate woman with a major challenge on her hands, and you choose to make things worse for her. You're in the wrong business, Kovalic. Never engage a frontal attack, or if you do you have the guts to sign your piece. I'm certainly not signing that. I never used the word spattered in my life, especially about a woman I admire and respect. Because I do, Monsieur Kovalic!'

Bernard protested: 'Even so you certainly intended . . .'

Boulard cut him off again: 'What do you know about my intentions. We aren't bedfellows, you and I!'

There was a pause and Bernard said: 'Well, what should I do now?'

'Don't make me say it, I don't want to be vulgar.'

But he said it all the same, as only Boulard could.

Bernard told Maryse fifteen seconds later: 'He wants the entire issue destroyed.'

Together they went to the printers after a quick call. It was a jobbing firm that bore no comparison with *La Dépêche* and its big print shop. The foreman, called the clicker, said he had a call from Paris, too, and that the shredder was already disposing of 13,000 copies, the print run for that night.

'Gives me the the shivers to see that,' Maryse said quietly as they watched.

'We've certainly dropped a clanger this time,' Bernard said placing an arm round her. 'It's not the end of the world.'

That morning the readers learned from the newsagents that *L'Eveil* would not be coming out, due to a machine breaking down.

Travers was one of the first to be told, and he instinctively thought to phone Florence at once. But he left it as a thought. He was feeling somewhat less devoted to Madame Berg of late.

458

Chapter Eight

It was a spectacular funeral, as Albertas had intended, and he was well pleased. The Kovalic driver had a send-off worthy of the family.

The clan chief had the most luxurious of the town's hearses. It was loaded high with bouquets and wreaths, blood red being the dominant colour. The cars that followed in its wake were no less luxurious, headed by the Mercedes which Teddy drove.

Cousins attended from Italy and elsewhere, and the family turned up in strength. There were many others from the town, who came out of respect or curiosity. An Orthodox pope stood by the waiting grave with a choir, which chanted to the accompaniment of a pair of guitar players. A delegation of drivers bade their colleague farewell, led by the fleet manager at *La Dépêche*, Charles. Melchior represented the paper. Mayor Adrien Jerome headed the party from the town hall.

Travers and Edelman were at a discreet distance, covering the story for the paper. Commissaire Nicolo and Inspector Germain stood by, the latter with a small but efficient camera.

The hearse and following cars came to a halt inside the massive wrought iron gate of the cemetery, and the shining coffin with silver handles was taken by Kovalic men—Albertas, Bernard, Teddy and three others—while old Gregor looking feeble and waxen-faced walked behind, aided by one of the youngsters. After him came Marfa and Zoë each with a hand under the elbows of Marishka, the deceased's mother. With them was Catherine, whose face gave nothing away. Finally some thirty assorted Kovalics including those from Trieste waddled along in their expensive suits and dresses, not all of them black and many in alpaca.

Amid chanting the coffin was lowered onto trestles, and the family formed a ring. Alexandra Wilson came up behind Teddy and slipped a hand into his.

The pope waited for complete silence and declared: 'A man of this town has died by fire, the fire that burns in the entrails of the earth. There is fire, too, in the hand of God, and this he uses to warm the bodies and hearts of mankind, not to kill. Those who use the fire to kill shall in turn know the flames of hell. God will punish them, but it is not for us to excercise vengeance. Let us offer up our bitterness and suffering to Almighty God as a sign of our obedience and our love . . .'

Albertas, standing in the most prominent position in the family circle, coughed in irritation. He at least found reasons to disagree with the papal stance on these matters.

The officiating minister went on: 'For him who prays from the heart the whole world is his church. Let us pray now for Nestor Kovalic, the victim of this occasion. Our thoughts and our prayers unite to send his soul to its creator.'

Nestor's mother Marishka made no attempt to hide her tear-soaked face. Still aiding her, Marfa and Zoë were crying too. Catherine's eyes were closed; she remembered the funeral of her darling Paul Bossis in this same cemetery. Paul and Nestor had both perished in the service of *La Dépêche*.

The pope blessed the coffin, as the choristers wrenched the last ounce of emotion from the congregation. Albertas, however, had had enough and signed for the celebrant and the choir to cut the ceremony short.

Travers and Edelman noted this along with the other details for possible use. Nicolo's eyes flashed back and forth over the sea of faces, while Germain snapped away with his Minox.

Now everyone was singing, or at least moving their lips, and like the others Albertas made the sign of the cross each time the word God was pronounced.

460

But when the pope said he would now read from the sacred works, Albertas moved forward and said: 'Thank you Father. Nestor is now in heaven. You told us we should not seek vengeance.' (His voice grew distinctly louder, so that his thanks turned into a speech for all to hear.) 'We shall not avenge Nestor, because God is against it, but nobody can prevent me saying what comes from my heart. The Kovalics have been in this town for thirty years now, thirty years in which we have been rejected, laughed at, humiliated and ignored. Even though we have done much of our work at night, in the muck for Chateauvallon. Our reward is the killing of Nestor.' (He glared at Jerome.) 'When's the next one to be, *Monsieur Le Maire*? When's the next reward for thirty years of good and loyal service?'

The mayor attempted a gesture to say that this was unfair, but Albertas, his eyes blacker than Jerome's coat buttons, pushed his arm out of the way.

At this, Edelman deftly pulled out an aerial and spoke into a walkie-talkie: 'Kovalic's being historic, listen to this.'

Albertas said grandly: 'We shall not avenge ourselves, but as this town doesn't care for the Kovalics, *Monsieur Le Maire*, the Kovalics will leave. Yes, we shall leave Chateauvallon, all together with our sorrow. We shall leave our dead in your cemetery, including this innocent victim. That way, there will be no second innocent victim. Where shall we go? That I don't know, but we are used to moving on, we are not afraid to set out again. On the other hand I shall leave you 300 more people out of work, and there's no point in denying it. There is always a price to be paid. The killers should have thought of that first, *Monsieur le Maire*. I feel for the unemployed, but we have had enough. That's what I wish to tell you, in the boy's name and in my own. I'd like also to thank everyone for coming here to express their last farewell.' (The speech was over now, and he turned back to the priest.) 'Go on Father, just one more prayer.'

Edelman spoke into his microphone again: 'That seems to be it.'

'Super!' said Florence at the other end. 'What did Jerome look like?'

461

'Didn't seem too pleased with himself, *patronne*.'

'Wish I'd seen it all.'

Within minutes everyone was saying goodbye at the gate. The two newsmen went past Nicolo and he told them: 'You can say I've got the killer, but I'm no further forward for all that.'

Travers said: 'Reckon there's something here?'

Nicolo shrugged: 'Germain's taken some pictures. You never know. Anyway they've certainly got the family spirit. Takes some doing to come all the way from Trieste to bury a van driver.'

Florence had listened in to Albertas's back-handed pane-gyric from Les Glycines Clinic, which Armand still owned. She had been anxious about attending the ceremony and decided not to. Armand had advised her to stay away and she was still wondering precisely why. Goodness knows she did not want to go, but was now regretting that she had fallen in with his view.

Her brother was decidedly strange these days: in a panic, offhand, worried sick and derisive in turn. She was puzzled, for example, as to why he should want her to be present when he received one of the two ladies whose valuables had been stolen. During the interview he was excessively courteous and yet his mind was elsewhere. The woman in question was in her sixties, stinking rich, perfectly turned out and very amiable. She was one of the traditional top-drawer women who never questioned her rightful place in the world and her supremacy.

When she left Armand's office, he laughed and Florence copied him.

'What an idiot-woman,' he cackled. 'Insignificance allied to insufficiency. A ghastly combination.'

There was a wickedness in his voice that made Florence stop laughing and draw away. He was definitely peculiar, and she said: 'Don't talk in that way.'

Armand merely buzzed through and asked the head nurse, Fernandez, to bring in some whisky. He sat on the arm of the settee and told Florence: 'I've got problems in

462

Paris. Friends are letting me down and enemies are giving me the glad eye.'

'That's a change. Are you switching over?'

'Oh, it hasn't come to that yet.'

'But you're sort of leaning?'

Armand released a sigh of exasperation: 'Why the hell do you have to keep on asking questions? Father used to say never answer Flo's questions, she's a tell-tale-tit. Anyhow you get on my wick.'

She demanded: 'And what tittle-tattle have you got for me now?'

Fernandez entered, and the ball was suspended in mid-air. She placed the drinks tray on the table and went out having uttered no word; she was possessive about Armand, and Florence was intruding. Armand drank alone, a large whisky which he downed in two closely adjacent gulps.

Florence said truculently: 'I asked you what there was to tell, and if you don't answer I will.'

'I won't and you'd better keep your trap shut!'

Her brother then did something that left her totally nonplussed. He took his jacket off, poured everything from the pockets into his trouser pockets, had another whisky and asked her to throw the jacket out onto the lawn.

Having done so, she said: 'Why?'

'So that I can go out and join it, duckie.'

Was he actually deranged? Florence pretended that the joke was a good one, although it seemed pointless to her.

'Have you got turncoat problems?' she asked in a further effort to achieve normality between them.

He looked wildly at her, and went out slamming the door.

When Paul Bossis was alive he used to run a red Alfa-Romeo, and his father Gilbert Bossis gave it to Catherine after he was killed. She made little use of it: an occasional trip to a shady spot with baby Paul and Gilbert, or a run out with a friend she had made at the secretarial course.

On this particular day she decided to fill up her larder, loading up the Alfa during her lunch break. She put the car in the underground car park at *La Dépêche* and eventually returned to it carrying two bulky stiff paper bags with the foodstuffs and such. It was a sinister place, dusty, ill-lit with lots of shadows, but she had never really worried about it; after all, it was private property.

Having lowered her two parcels onto the ground next to the car boot, she opened the boot and went round to the driver's door, opened it and flung her handbag onto the seat. Then she went back to the boot to complete the job.

The routine dulled her mind, and she was weary in any case from the physical effort. Which was why Catherine failed to hear or see two men creep up to the Alfa in tennis shoes and stocking masks. It was only when she heard the click of the handbrake being released that she became alert. One of the men was already at the wheel, and the other one was making as if to push the car backwards. He did more than that; to her horror he actually gave it a mighty shove so that the rear bumper hit her shins. She retreated a few centimetres but the car kept moving and she was imprisoned between the bumper and the concrete wall.

Catherine shrieked with terror. She was too close to fainting to notice the man at the wheel applying the brake again at the last moment. The next thing she knew was that the two men were jumping about with Red Indian whoops and shouting: 'Kovalic, Kovalic, Kovalic!' Then one of them found a hosepipe and sprayed water over the young woman. Finally the pair ran off, leaping up to smash some of the fluorescent lamps in the roof.

She was found, heaving and shivering, a few minutes later by a page-layout man called Aldebert who came in with his Renault 5.

Upstairs, some while later, Travers walked in from an outside assignment to hear screams and the noise of crashing objects from Florence's office. He quickened his pace and found Melchior and Edelman apparently mounting guard outside the room.

'What the hell's going on?'

'Catherine, she's having hysterics. Someone attacked her in the car park, as far as we can gather, but she's babbling a lot of nonsense. She's soaking wet too,' Edelman said.

Melchior added: 'Some of the girls are trying to calm her down.'

Travers barked: 'I'd better go in, she's capable of anything, nearly scratched my eyes out when I told her Paul Bossis had been killed. She jabbed me with some scissors instead.'

He charged in to find a scene of utter confusion with Madame Frochot the accountant and the trainee Beatrice Bonnenfant endeavouring simultaneously to calm her down, undress her and wipe her all over. Catherine wanted none of this and fought like a tigress. Florence's superb desk lamp lay crumpled on the floor.

In answer to Travers's wordless enquiry, Madame Frochot said: 'Aldebert and the doorman brought her up, but we can't find out what happened. She wants to get to her boy Paul, says he's in danger. At least I think that's what she's saying.'

Travers got her in his arms and she sobbed herself still. He then laid her on Florence's couch and said: 'Don't worry about Paul, I'll look after him. Now Catherine, you've got to tell us exactly what happened.'

The wild look came back into her eyes and she yelled: 'Huh, what happened? You should know, it's your fault, everyone's fault!' She struck out at him with new frenzy and her ring gouged a tiny furrow in Travers's forehead. Madame Frochot handed him a towel, which he ignored, more concerned to reassure Catherine that her boy would come to no harm.

When the doctor arrived, she was lying in his arms, herself like a baby.

The doctor treated the bruises on her shins, examined her elsewhere but found no other injuries.

'She'll be all right now, the initial state of shock is receding,' he pronounced.

Florence sat quietly in her studio answering a few personal letters and catching up on some accounts.

She blessed the silence, and not for the first time glanced down at a leather skirt she had just bought. It was straight and had a cheeky slit at the left thigh, which lay on the chair half exposed. With her khaki shirt sporting breast pockets to go with it, she thought she looked peachy. Like one of those girls in the Israeli army!

Florence had almost finished when there was a knock at the door. It was Artus Balestra, once more looking sorry for himself. She gave a little giggle as he hesitated before entering, seeming to apologize mutely for his behaviour on his last visit.

'I've had a bath, so I won't bother you this time,' he said quietly.

'How interesting,' she said with sarcasm. 'Let's sit down and run over some of your other fascinating activities!'

They did as she said, facing each other. Then he knelt down before her and removed one of her sandals, stuffing it in a pocket.

'I can't wait to see what's coming next,' she mocked.

'It's like in the crime films; the hired killer gets half the money first, and the other when the contract's completed.'

'And who've I got to kill?'

'Not love, dear Florence, not love.' She gave him a look of puzzlement. 'I feel this is one of my lucky years, and I want to get the most out of it.'

He held out his arms to her, and she handed him her other sandal.

'Contract completed?' she said.

He threw the sandal back: 'You know it's not. I must have that Nobel Prize, Flo!'

She was spared replying. The phone rang, and she had time only to say 'yes' when the doorbell went too. She signed to Artus and he opened the door, letting in Travers whose forehead was caked with blood. Artus gaped as Travers went through to the bathroom.

Artus informed Florence: 'There's a bloodstained man in your bathroom.'

466

'I'll see to him. Here, the call's for you.'

While she was fixing up Travers, he filled her in with the Catherine incident: 'When she was back to normal, she described the details. Apparently what frightened her most was that cry of "Kovalic, Kovalic" echoing through the garage.'

'What's it signify?'

'It was intentional, but why try to scare Catherine?'

'You look pretty furious about it,' she said.

'Naturally.'

'Of course. Poor Travers, what do we do about it?'

The voice of Artus, suddenly louder, reached them and as one they stopped to eavesdrop.

'That's enough,' the biologist was yelling. 'I forbid it, I detest bearded men. That's why I broke it off with Jean-Luc!'

Travers gaped at Florence, but she turned her head away. Artus went on: 'Anyhow you can find someone else for dinner tonight, I'm busy. It happens sometimes. Well you can boil your head!'

Travers thereupon decided to take a bath. Florence half-closed the door behind her, wondering why everyone was behaving so freakishly: Armand, Artus, Travers, even herself. Artus spat a final retort into the receiver and slammed it down.

He then shouted at Florence: 'Listening at keyholes now?'

'I never realized you had a son,' she said cunningly.

'I haven't got a son!'

'Oh sorry.'

Florence regarded him indulgently: 'According to my keyhole, you're busy tonight.'

'Not at all!' He was still fuming.

'Nor am I.'

'And you want to have an evening out?'

'I do, provided I get my other sandal back.'

Artus produced it and growled: 'Who's the man of blood? If he's coming out with us, I hope he doesn't start bleeding again.'

467

Balestra had evidently found quiet waters once more, and Florence said she had a phone call to make. While she was doing this, Artus Balestra rose and positioned himself so that he could see Travers through the bathroom door. He studied his athletic body, its muscles, its haunches, its tousled hair and (when he turned round) its private parts.

Behind Balestra, Florence was asking Melchior if the police had been informed about the Catherine incident, adding that she wished to lodge an action for assault on the premises of *La Dépêche* against one of its employees. Melchior said Nicolo wasn't keen, and she said he had better be and that Melchior should call him back. She wanted the culprits, she rapped.

Balestra was waiting for her to end. He had a satisfied smile on his shiny countenance.

Florence told him: 'They're picking another quarrel.'

Artus took her shoulders: 'Play it like a game of chess. Everyone quarrels, everyone except the dead.' He spoke much as he had when they first met at La Jouterie, and in memory of that she laid her head against his. He ran his hand up and down her spine. She couldn't let on that she knew about him, not now.

'Let's go out and eat,' she said gaily.

'All right, but what about the injured man? He's in your bed stark naked.'

'Asleep I hope.'

'Like a baby.'

'He has busy days sometimes.'

'Have you any other babies like him?'

'No, just him.'

'If he hasn't got a home, I could take him in.' He became serious. 'Florence, I feel I ought to explain . . .'

She cut him short: 'Tell me while we eat.' She went into the small bedroom to collect her bag and a light jacket. Travers was indeed asleep, and she planted a soft kiss on his forehead next to the sticking plaster.

Thérèse and Aldo became lovers, and the affair was beginning to last.

468

She was delighted and astonished at this turn of events, and could not get him out of her mind; he was a pop tune repeated over and over again in her brain. He was common in his manners, and to match this she told herself she was behaving wantonly, especially for a Berg. He was also very handsome, and between meetings the mere thought of him would cause heat to spread through her body. On the other hand she knew there was no love element, especially on his side, for he was clearly using her for his pleasure—or else as some kind of a screen. He was keeping plenty back, while at the same time she was cheating on Julien and the children, lying to them constantly. But when she was grappling with Aldo, breathing in his ruttish fragrance, holding on to him for dear life as they reached orgasm—then she ceased thinking. Yes, her trips to Switzerland were unforgivable, and that made them even more exciting. It was enough for Aldo to fix a date for her to wrestle with her conscience for days, until the moment when they arrived and he said cheekily: 'How about a little siesta?' Then she yielded with alacrity to the call of the male.

One of their flights to Lausanne in the Cherokee co-incided approximately with the big Kovalic funeral.

They lugged their things into the terminal building. She had a black taffeta-covered hold-all and Aldo carried two more of his long bags like golf clubs. Aldo told her to get their drinks ready at the bar while he dealt with Customs. They let her through with a wave and then he filled in some forms, which he signed. The Customs man rubber-stamped them and added them to a pile behind him without a glance.

At this juncture, Aldo went straight out to the car park, placed the two bags next to the boot of a Mercedes and walked on. Immediately another man put the bags into the boot, then drove off.

Joining Thérèse at the bar he remarked: 'They're very easy here. I could get through with ten kilos of heroin.'

'I hope you didn't,' she said anxiously, and took another sip at her Americano.

'Nobody'd take me for a drug runner.'

She twitched her nose and said: 'One day you'll tell me what's in the bags.'

'Another day, *chérie*, but let's have fun first, we can talk afterwards. How about a little siesta when we get to the hotel?'

She flashed her eyes at him: 'I can only tremble before your onslaught, tough guy.'

The man in the Mercedes knew Lausanne's every back street and took only ten minutes to reach the basement car park at the Banque Croquelet. He took Aldo's two bags to the lift, inserted a key, put the bags in, and turned the key again to shut the door. On the ground floor another man got the bags out using a similar key, and carried them into a white room that was bare except for a large table and some safes. Two others, a man and a woman in white gloves, unlocked the bags and extracted wads of banknotes. Expertly they counted the notes and stacked them, regularly entering figures in a book.

Suddenly the woman said: 'Something's up. I've got forty sets numbered in order.'

The man compared the notes with his own pile: 'My God, the whole lot is in a straight series.'

The woman used the phone on the table: '*Monsieur Le Président*, this is Greta. We are checking the Kovalic bags. There's a problem.'

'They're forged notes?'

'No, but we've got eighty series in a straight run. And the others are one figure out.'

She heard the banker say: 'Put it all on ice, I'll make enquiries.'

It was little short of a banquet at noon on the day after the funeral. Albertas was playing host to the cousins from Trieste, who were about to set out on the long journey home.

Overnight they had shown off Paris to their women, superb creatures with black hair and dark eyes, too much

470

make-up, flashy scarves and gold about their necks, wrists and ears. Solid gold, all of it, Albertas was informed. Gold too were the chains, rings, cufflinks and cigarette lighters sported by the two men Djilas and Marko. The last of the drinks were on the table when a BMW swung into the yard.

'Ah, the American,' said Djilas with more than a hint of contempt. 'Hey Bernard, you should have been here; your mother makes a better *lonac* than mine does, God forgive me for saying it.'

'I couldn't get away,' Bernard said crisply.

'You should have forced yourself,' one of the women crooned in a deep serenade. 'Why don't you come down and see us, we'll treat you like a prince? Don't like the sun, eh?'

'I'd love the women too much,' Bernard said pleasantly. His eyes scoured the premises, looking for Albertas, and caught sight of him in his office on the phone.

Marko, who had an arm round Teddy's neck, said: 'I hope you're looking after your cousin Teddy.'

'He can look after himself,' Bernard threw back, giving a wink to show he bore no hard feelings.

'Too easy,' Marko cried. 'Not much solidarity on your part, I'd say.'

The woman intervened: 'Leave him alone.' She took the two cousins by the hand and placed them in position for a photo. 'Don't they look handsome, almost like real men, my French cousins.'

There was general laughter at this, and Albertas appeared in the doorway: 'I'm sorry you're leaving. I do like to see you all friendly and cracking jokes. But I ought to remind you that Nestor left two orphans in the care of their grandmother; their mother cleared off about three years ago. So . . '

Marko declared with the ease of a potentate: 'Don't worry about them, they won't starve in our family. Well, we'd better be off.'

He pulled himself up and strutted out to the cars, where Zoë and Marfa were loading up the luggage. The two women of Trieste took their places. Before taking the wheel Marko called Teddy over.

'I've taken a great liking to you, cousin. If you're ever in need of help, you only have to give me a call.' He then peeled off two fifty-dollar notes from a wad and shoved them into the boy's hand: Teddy smiled his thanks, and gave a quick glance at Bernard as if seeking his approval. Bernard shrugged and said nothing, for his attention was riveted on Albertas who was in animated conversation with Djilas. But he had no time to reflect on it, as a joyous Marko pulled a gun from his jacket and fired two shots in the air.

'Hey Albertas,' he shouted. 'Let Djilas go, there's thousands of kilometres in front of us.'

'*Qui va piano vo sano!*' Albertas counselled, bringing Djilas over.

When the cars had gone, Zoë told her sister-in-law: 'That Marko, he could have hooted like anybody else. The neighbours will think we're playing cowboys.'

In accordance with established practice, Teddy took the two fifty-dollar notes to *L'Eveil* and asked Bernard to change them into francs.

He found him at his desk with the phone handset clamped between his shoulder and his ear looking very busy. In front of him were several photos and he had evidently picked out one of Catherine.

He said: 'The story's ready and I've a good black-and-white photo. I'm sending Maryse with it.'

Teddy asked him if anything had happened to Catherine.

'Attacked in the garage at *La Dépêche*. They tried to cut her legs off, by the look of things, and *La Dépêche* will be running the story, so we've got to cover it too. Getting lively is our Chateauvallon!'

Teddy nodded in agreement, and produced the dollars.

'Huh, you don't waste any time,' his cousin said. 'Lucky you, money for jam and no need to play that whistle of yours to earn it. Does he often give you dollars?'

Teddy tossed his head: 'First time, but I hope it's not the last.'

They were both smiling a little. Bernard put the photos back in his wallet and pulled out seven hundred francs, taking the dollars in exchange.

'That makes three,' he said, placing the two fifty-dollar notes next to a hundred-dollar note already in the wallet. 'Recognize it? That's the one you handed over the other day. Where did you get it?'

'Well, I already told you.'

Bernard became stern: 'And you reckon I should believe you? You think I was born yesterday?' He jumped up and gave the boy a mighty clout on one cheek. 'This time you're going to tell it like it was. I want the truth, and I've got a trouser belt too!'

The lad stared at him like a frightened rabbit. He fell into a chair, rubbing his cheek: 'I stole it from Albertas,' he whispered.

'When? How?' Bernard kept his eyes level and he did not blink. Teddy visibly surrendered, his shoulders hunching forward. He told Bernard about being kept in the barn, everything he saw and heard, how he got the dollar bill out of the big leather bag.

'Afterwards?'

'When you got me out of there, I went back and the bag was gone. It still ain't there, so he must have found another hide-out for it.'

Bernard allowed himself a smile: 'Good boy Teddy. We'll keep this to ourselves, you can trust me. But you might keep looking out for bags like that. And when you find any, I'd like to know. Is it a deal?'

Teddy nodded: 'I wouldn't want to see uncle in trouble, Bernard. He's got his funny ways but we owe everything to him, especially you.'

'I'm the one to judge that. Just you do what I tell you and we'll get along fine.'

Teddy took his leave, crestfallen but feeling the seven hundred francs rolled up in his pocket. He relished the weight and walked a little taller.

Returning to La Commanderie that night, Florence learned from Mathilde that Teddy had not shown up. She had a yen to visit the blue room, where she found Alexandra lying on her back smoking a cigarette with a glass of whisky in easy reach.

'That way the smoke won't get in your eyes,' she said lightly, at the same time detecting a sheaf of paper under the bed. So she had been reading her father's manuscript again.

Florence strolled casually over to the window and looked out: 'What page have you got to now?'

'I don't need to read it, I know it by heart.'

'Don't you think I could look after it? It's about me in parts, you say, and he was my husband after all.'

The girl got up and climbed on to the bed, sitting there cross-legged: 'I don't know. You ought to explain first.'

'Explain what exactly?' her mother said with heroic patience.

'Why you gave evidence against him. Why you claim he drank to pluck up the courage to kill you.'

'We've already been over that, surely.'

Alexandra stubbed out her cigarette: 'Why did he want to kill you, what did you do to him?'

'Come now, what can a girl of twenty-three do to a man of forty, when there is a five-year-old daughter and you don't know if you'll wake up alive.'

'You see, you're twisting it again.'

Florence sat close to the girl: 'He wanted to kill me because I was a Berg, part of a family with children, uncles and aunts and cousins. We were linked together in a bond and he couldn't understand us. He envied us perhaps.'

'People don't kill for that.'

'He tried, he tried to kill *you*.'

'That's not true.'

Florence explained: 'Some men have a need to destroy, it's a kind of passion with them, but it's tough living with them. You have to leave sooner or later.'

'And that's how you're still alive?' Alexandra said icily.

'Exactly, and so are you.'

'But he's dead.'

'And so was the Hartfield girl.'

During this exchange they had got on their feet and were now nose-to-nose.

At length Alexandra drew back and said: 'How did he try to kill me?'

'He gave you a glass of neat whisky when you were four.'

'I took only one sip,' the girl said, tossing off her glass. 'Is that all you have to say?'

'No. To change the subject, I'd prefer that your bloke slept elsewhere but here.'

'Afraid he'll steal off with the family treasure?'

'No. I'm afraid he'll steal you.'

'Too much dirt on him perhaps? And your homo, d'you think that's nice for me?'

'At least he hasn't a drink problem,' Florence declared firmly.

Alexandra's lips puckered up, and her mother stroked her cheek. Then she left the room.

It was a bad night for Florence, but she dropped off to sleep at last, to be wakened by a rustling sound at her door. The nightmarish scenes slipped from her mind, and she struggled onto an elbow. There was a sheet of paper on the floor inside the door.

She read: 'November 19, 1964. Again this evening Florence went out without saying where. But I know and she knows I do. It's the same bunch of homosexuals she gives money to and she knows I know that too. That's her way of not sleeping together, with them and with me. But there's no cash for me, because I'm supposed to be big enough to earn it myself. Now it's 10.00 p.m. and the bed's empty, I don't feel like doing any writing and the girl's asleep. I feel as if the house is going to slide into the sea, and that nobody will notice it's gone. Her bastard of a brother won't have anything, and that's something. But they don't need the phone, he'll find her wherever she is, and they don't need to look for each other. They always know where the other is, and they'll know even if there's nobody left on the earth. Only he doesn't have a daughter asleep.'

Florence laid the sheet of paper on the coverlet, crossed her hands behind her neck and looked at the ceiling.

No wonder Alexandra was upset with passages like that! But why the hell couldn't she just hand the whole thing over, and let her justify it or admit her fault openly?

Chapter Nine

Bernard was digging. As a journalist or as a private eye, it did not matter, he was digging.

After the encounter with Teddy, he had gone to see Caprioli the accountant and learned nothing, except that, according to Caprioli, Albertas had pledged him to silence.

Apart from that, there were the regular visits from the Trieste man, who came with news of Djilas and Marko and of the old chap with cancer.

When Teddy found another bag containing dollars, he would be getting somewhere. But Teddy had found none.

In Bernard's mind there was no doubt that Albertas was in some kind of currency racket, possibly other shady businesses too. But he was unsure what his own attitude ought to be. The word solidarity was not one he tended to use, preferring to think in terms of the percentage coming to him. But it was hard to look after number one if you didn't know where to look!

His stomach gave a little jolt when Nicolo phoned saying he would like to see him. The commissaire seemed convivial enough when he shook hands, and the leather bags went out of his mind completely when he was told there had 'been a complaint concerning noise at the farm'.

Nicolo smiled as he said: 'The fact is I'd be grateful if you would try and put a bit of a damper on your uncle's lust for life. I've had an anonymous complaint, which I don't go for anyway and I propose to ignore it as no one's been booked into the hospital. So be a sport and stop him firing off guns.'

Bernard smiled back, but his expression changed as Nicolo went on: 'However, this morning he went and threw a brick through Schultz's window. He's the one who supplied those guards for Madame Berg. What's more he left a pile of money on the pavement. In that incident, witnesses came forward and I have to do something. You're uncle's a bit touched, it seems to me; that speech of his about the three hundred jobless at the cemetery was completely daft. Well, let him leave the town, we'll work something out for the three hundred.'

As Nicolo proceeded, his listener's face depicted a variety of emotions, ending with indifference: 'You should be telling all this to my uncle, not me.'

'Oh, I don't want him here. He arrives on time but you never know when he'll leave. Ah yes, and there's another thing; the man who bumped off your cousin Nestor, well it's not clear at all. He denies he set fire to the van.'

'I know that.'

'Sure you do, but we found out he did some work on a farm forty kilometres from here a year ago.'

'So what?'

'The barn burned down with all the harvest for the winter. Hay it was.'

'Must have been a fine sight.'

'Yeah. Better than what we found the next day. The farmer strung up on a beam. We could never make a charge on that fire, but . . '

'What's this have to do with me?'

'Just tell your uncle, that's all. Can't you see, he has to realize it was not some kind of plot, but the guy's a nutcase, a pyromaniac. Tell your uncle that, and maybe he'll get out of our hair.'

Having said that, Nicolo sat back and busied himself with his pipe. There was a silence between them, then Bernard said: 'And suppose it was a plot that *made use* of a pyromaniac?'

The commissaire stopped pumping out smoke: 'Oh no, Kovalic, don't *you* start!'

'You said not five minutes ago that it wasn't clear.'

'That was simply to introduce the subject. I just want you to quieten your uncle down, that's all.'

Bernard had a sneer on his lips: 'And what should I tell

478

him about Catherine? She's a cousin of mine too, and she got wet in case you've forgotten.'

Nicolo aimed a puff of smoke at a passing gnat: 'Suggest he sends her a bunch of flowers. Might do them both good.'

Chantal, the Paris correspondent on *La Dépêche*, spent two days every month in Chateauvallon.

She knew she could count every time on the Three Musketeers—Travers, Favrot and Edelman—fighting for the honour of taking her out to dinner. They would work hard at it, forcing the jokes, making awful puns and generally behaving queerly. But the fact was that she laughed a lot, and that was better than a dull meal alone and early bed in the hotel. To be more precise, the three men played craps for her, with Colette, the woman at the Bijou-Bar, ready with the board as soon as they entered the premises.

On that night it was Edelman who won the lady, but he explained: 'I know a marvellous restaurant on the other side of the town, but I'm on my motorbike and I don't know . . .'

Favrot cried: 'Give her your crash helmet, I bet she loves bikes, all sexy girls do.'

Chantal laughed again: 'I can hardly reply to that. But I had my hair done this morning, and I get claustrophobia in those things.'

The bike was leaning against a concrete pillar outside the door of the Bijou-Bar. He put the helmet on himself, got astride the machine, watched Chantal cock her leg over, and felt her arms round his middle. Edelman kick-started the bike and roared off.

'Stop!!!' Travers yelled.

Too late, the machine stopped dead and the two riders skimmed over the handlebars and landed in the road.

'Colette! Ambulance quick!!!' Travers shouted, bursting into the bar. Then he went out and joined Favrot. Edelman was only groggy, thanks to his crash helmet, but Chantal was sprawled on her stomach unconscious, with a tiny trickle of blood coming from her nose. Travers patted her cheek and her eyelids moved.

'That wasn't funny,' she said, and fainted.

Travers cracked: 'She's dead right, look at this.' He pointed to a strong nylon cord going from the back wheel hub to a ring on the concrete pillar. 'No, it wasn't a joke, someone did this deliberately. I'm going to call Nicolo, he ought to see this right away. Nobody touch a thing.'

Chantal was taken off to hospital, and when Nicolo and Pradal had finished their examination and got the facts down, all five men went up to Florence's office.

Pradal said: 'The cord is actually fishing line. For big fish like tunny or swordfish. Whoever did it tied three lengths, which would probably have stopped a small tank.'

'Incredible,' Favrot murmured.

'I saw it too late,' Travers added.

'Not surprising, it was coated over with sand,' Pradal said. 'This sort of line can be bought anywhere no doubt. But I find it hard to imagine there's much of it sold in Chateauvallon. Not many swordfish in the Loire!'

Nobody added anything further and they all turned towards Florence, in a natural movement. She gave the impression it was nothing to do with her, that there was no reason why she should speak any more than another person. Then she decided to react.

'I've had two vans burnt out, a driver and a guard murdered, a girl in a state of nervous collapse and another in hospital now with a twisted backbone. *Monsieur Le Commissaire*, when are you going to take your hands out of your pockets, to put it politely?'

Nicolo mumbled: 'You have enemies, like the prosecutor told you, Madame.'

'And I suppose nothing short of a bomb going off when I take the wheel of my car will actually get you moving. Damn it, Nicolo, I pay my taxes—and how!!!'

Nicolo adopted an amenable pose: 'You see, *Madame*, the problem is too big for a local SRPJ. I do what I can but the strings are pulled elsewhere, as you well know. If the Boulard Group is after you, there's nothing a few provincial cops can do about it. I might be able to track down the small boys doing the dirty work, but you won't be better off for all that.'

Travers suggested: 'You could resign on the grounds that you are not receiving any backing, and you could make it known.'

Nicolo wagged his head: 'You must be dreaming, old boy. When a cop resigns, there's only one thing left for the rest of his life: selling cheap ties on the pavement from a tray. That's the Ministry of the Interior for you.'

They all looked glum, but Travers added: 'All right, I'll believe you. But where do the Kovalics come into this?'

'It's my belief they're not involved. The Kovalics have pulled themselves up out of the gutter, and made a fortune here out of dustbins and such. They wouldn't mess their own doorstep.'

'And yet, Bernard is under orders from Boulard.'

'True,' Nicolo consented. 'But he also has shares in *La Dépêche*, not a lot, but still they're shares. Besides, things aren't too sweet between him and Albertas, though I don't rightly know why at present. It's my guess they are as confused as you are. Well, Madame Berg, I must say I'm very glad to have met you again, this is the first time I've been in here. None the less, I can give you no comfort as things are, and I'm extremely sorry about it. *Mes hommages, Madame.*'

He gave a little bow and so did Pradal, they shook a couple of hands and trotted out.

Florence wailed: 'Back to Boulard. He can't imagine he'll beat me by sending people who work for me to the morgue and the hospital!'

Melchior smiled weakly: 'Florence, there are eight hundred of us in all. He might possibly be feeling his way, seeing what can and can't be done.'

Travers thumped a hand on the desk: 'Stop beating about the bush, Melchior. If nobody else will say it, I will. Boulard feels strong because he's got an ally in the Berg family.'

Florence banged down a fist in turn: 'Travers! I'm pre-pred to take a great deal from you, but watch it! If you start

481

denigrating my brother, you're out. You understand?'

He moved slowly towards her: 'Perfectly, and I don't say it lightly. I haven't stuck with you this far to hear it. I'm telling you something you can't deny too: I usually know what I'm talking about, Madame Berg.'

He always tended to lope rather, and this time he showed it, walking loosely out of the office without a word more. Florence felt herself go pale under her make-up.

'Do you want to run something on the accident, Madame?' Melchior requested.

'Er-yes. But phone through first to find out how Chantal is.'

Those dollars kept Bernard awake at night, and as he had no wife or children he decided to confront his uncle, eyeball to eyeball.

He found him cleaning his guns in the main room at the farmhouse. He loved his guns, having brought some with him to France along with four items of furniture, some kitchen utensils and the clothes they had on their backs. He had bought more guns since, and nobody else had the right to touch them. Albertas cleaned his guns regularly, lovingly and well. Perhaps because he didn't use them so much these days.

Bernard looked on interestedly as his uncle oiled and rubbed a pair of old guns piece by piece like a professional in a gunsmith's shop. After about five minutes he asked the old man if he had sent some flowers to his daughter as he had suggested.

'I bought a bunch and delivered them myself,' Albertas grunted.

'That's great.'

'Never asked to see me, the bitch. That'll teach me. Yeah, that'll teach me. Even so, if they'd killed her I'd have set this whole rotten town alight. That's no idle threat either.'

'All right, I believe you,' Bernard said, slipping in a question quickly: 'By the way, why's Caprioli so scared of you?'

482

'Everybody is, and that's how it should be.'

'I'm not.'

'You could be some time in the future, boy.' He clicked some gun parts in. 'Caprioli, I'll tell you about him. He used to be Copriolic by name, had a bit of trouble one time, and I got him out of it and he's working for me.'

'And he refuses you nothing.'

'He's part of the family,' Albertas croaked, laughing to himself.

'He was at Nestor's funeral, I noticed, like Djilas and Marko. That's something, coming all the way from Trieste to bury someone they'd never seen.'

Albertas stopped polishing a gun: 'You wouldn't understand, you yankees have no sense of family.'

'They haven't lost it in Italy. They even send you someone regularly with news of their side. You must be very thick.'

Bernard was choosing his words carefully, working into his subject. But Albertas pretended to make nothing of it. He put the guns in a rack, and came back with a couple of carbines, one of which he deftly dismantled.

He said: 'You can mock, lad, but affection's a rare thing and you have to cultivate it, especially if people spit on you at the drop of a hat. In our family we have to stick together.'

'Tell me another one,' Bernard jeered.

In a flash Albertas had a clip on the gun and flipped a round in the breech: 'Wash your mouth out before you speak to me in future. You ask too many questions.'

Bernard stood his ground: 'If you don't answer them I'll have to ask elsewhere.' He was pale-faced and his knuckles were bloodless on the edge of the table. He felt his brow scorching hot but he did not lower his gaze.

Albertas said quietly: 'I could scare the balls off you too, my lad, if I wanted to, even put a shot into you. Could have done it any time in the past ten minutes.'

'That would be most unwise,' Bernard said. 'Better to start talking. I want to know everything: those bags, the cousins, the dollar bills. Afterwards you can do the killing, go to jail for the rest of your life. But first I mean to find out.' He was on his feet, his words spitting out.

Albertas chuckled: 'At last, I've seen you angry. But tell me, where did you get those funny ideas?'

'That's my little secret. I want yours first, and stop messing about with those toys of yours. And be careful, I can move fast.'

To show it he whipped his arm sideways in a massive sweep across the table, sending the guns to the edge, so that some parts fell on a chair. Albertas got up slowly and put them back on the table. He took the edges of the white cloth he had laid on the table to protect it, and folded the cloth over the guns. Finally he sat down again and placed his arms along the edge of the table on his side.

'Right,' he said. 'I'm going to treat you as a friend. I may regret it, but I owe it to you.'

Bernard sat down again too.

Albertas continued: 'It's like this. When I brought you back here, it was because I needed you for one or two little jobs. I had money, a lot of money, and I wanted my own back. You know that as well as I do.'

'Tell me about the cousins.'

'I didn't know them originally. You know how it is, we've got relations as far as the North Pole. They came for a visit, nice-looking boys, they kind of moved in on me. I wasn't any too clear what they were after, but I didn't have the heart to refuse them, you understand.'

'So you agreed.'

'It was tempting, especially when you arrived and I saw what you were aiming at with your big projects and everything. With Aqua Viva and the rest I wasn't sure I'd have enough. Shit, I just had to agree.'

'What did you agree?'

'Why, to launder some money.'

'Dirty money?'

'Naturally, as it had to be laundered,' Albertas cried with a cackle.

'I don't like your jokes, Albertas. Where does it come from, the cousins' money?'

'Where they find it.'

'Kidnaps? Robberies?'

Albertas spread his gnarled hands: 'How should I know, I don't deal with the technicalities. I know the family, and the family's sacred.'

Bernard said nothing for a moment, then: 'What happens when we're all behind bars?'

'We'll be all Kovalics together. They let you play cards till lights out.'

Bernard rose: 'You can count me out, uncle, you won't be playing with me.'

'Oh yes we will, young Bernard. You're part of the family and you stay with us. Otherwise we'll show you something you've never seen in your life.'

'And what would that be?'

Albertas came round and tapped his cheek affectionately. Then he gently took hold of his nephew's neck.

'The skin off your throat, Bernard,' he said.

Bernard was shaking as he drove away from the farm.

It was obvious that his uncle had told the simple facts, hard as it was to accept them. Albertas had produced vast sums of money for Aqua Viva and other ventures, he walked around with a small fortune in his pockets, and besides there was Teddy's story too. Yes, it was true, his uncle laundered dirty money. He had said nothing of how it was done, the technicalities, but it was on a huge scale, that was certain.

The boy from Harvard snorted in disgust, although he felt incapable of deciding whether he should simply go along with his uncle or fight him. He thought about it constantly for days, unable to decide what his next move should be, if any.

He felt lonely, wanted to talk to someone, and one evening he rang Catherine's bell and said he thought he'd like to take a peek at little Paul.

The boy was eighteen months old now and had curly hair, the picture of innocence and Bernard was affected. But Catherine did not care to wake him up.

'Want a drink?' she said.

He asked for a whisky and sat on her settee, loosening his tie and undoing his top shirt button. He swallowed the drink in one gulp and asked for another.

'There sits a man with a problem,' she said softly. 'Is it Boulard?'

'Boulard!' he snorted. He knocked off the second whisky and it all came out, the whole story much as his uncle, her father, had told it.

Catherine seemed unimpressed and this surprised him: 'You mean to tell me you knew all the time?'

'Of course not,' she said abstractedly. 'I've seen my father twice in as many years, at Paul's christening and Nestor's funeral. Besides, making money from nothing is a Kovalic speciality, and nothing that he does would ever surprise me. What does intrigue me is why you bothered to tell me all this. Why me?'

Bernard shrugged: 'Who else is there? I don't know anyone in this town, and you're my cousin.'

'That's no reason at all. You know perfectly well that I made a deliberate decision not to see my father. Huh, I might even put the cops onto you the moment you walk out of here.'

'But you won't, of course.'

Catherine stood over him as he fiddled with his tie. He looked miserable enough, and she said: 'No, I won't. To tell you the truth I'm thinking of leaving Chateauvallon altogether.'

'And leave me in this mess?' Bernard said, suddenly nervous.

'My father's just a gangster now, that's it, a gangster.'

'Listen, he said he'd finished with it all now, that it's over.'

'And you believe that?'

'I don't know,' Bernard sighed.

'In any case, even if he stops, he's done it and it's too late. What am I expected to tell my son—that his grandad is a crook?'

'He might find it romantic!'

'That's nothing to make jokes about. I'm leaving this town anyway.' Catherine paced the room seemingly tugged between anger and tears. She waved both fists: 'I could feel there was something, all that money in no time at all, it wasn't natural. The ring for my mother, the Mercedes, his completely new standard of living after years of pinching and scraping. He made a point of looking poorer than he was.'

Bernard interjected: 'Listen, Catherine, you have to understand him . . .'

She spun round on him: 'Oh no, not you too! You're not going to sing that old dirge about the immigrants having to do anything they can because nobody'll give them a helping hand. That's why I got out, and I'm prepared to go even further. I want no part of crime.'

Bernard seized her wrists: 'D'you think I ought to go back to the States?'

She snatched back her wrists: 'Don't make me laugh! When you've got used to the idea, you'll want to stay and sort it out. To your own advantage of course, seeing as how you're an up-and-coming big-shot!'

'You're being very hard.'

'You're right,' she admitted. 'I'm fond of you Bernard, and I wouldn't want us to start another feud. Obviously, I haven't got many people I can confide in either.'

Bernard got up and made for the door. He stood there for a moment and then suggested: 'It would be best if you kept quiet about this money business for the present.'

Catherine gave him her first smile since he arrived: 'Of course I will and you know it. Come back and see me when you want another chat. We used to get on fine years ago.'

'That's true enough. Thanks for listening, it did me good,' said her cousin, embracing her on each cheek in turn.

'I'm not surprised,' she quipped. 'Now there are two of us wondering what the hell to do! Go on, off with you.'

She waited a good ten seconds before closing the door. To show that she meant well towards him.

Jacky of the corn-coloured hair was charged with murder, still denying that he deliberately set fire to the van and killed the two men. His version was that Nestor killed the other guard and that the gun went off and killed Nestor while they were subsequently struggling.

La Dépêche carried the news straight. Meanwhile Chantal came out of hospital wearing a neck-brace which she had to keep for three weeks. The person or persons responsible for the fishing line trick remained at large. As did Catherine's attackers and the person who set fire to the first paper van.

Florence was bubbling with frustration. She hated this baffling guerrilla warfare and told one of the editorial conferences that the next incident involving *La Dépêche* personnel or property would be the signal for an all-out attack against Boulard. He would sue the newspaper, but that was too bad, she said levelly.

Travers tried to calm her down: 'Boulard loves court battles, Florence. He's got about forty going at the present time. Besides, he would carry on harassing us. One more case wouldn't lose him a minute's sleep, believe me.'

'He must have a weak spot like everyone else, and I'll find it,' Florence retorted, then changed the subject. 'While we're waiting I'd like to come to terms with Albertas Kovalic. Melchior, be a nice chap and fix up a meeting with him at the farm.'

She left the room, and Travers and Catherine strolled out together.

'Funny idea wanting to see your dad,' Travers said.

'She knows what's she's up to, or she thinks she does. It's her worry. I'm off to Paris tomorrow looking for another job.'

It was Travers who had found her this one. He said: 'Well I'll be blowed.'

'If you want my opinion, you'd do the same,' Catherine returned.

'Full of ideas, aren't we today? I suppose you just thought that up.'

'No, as a matter of fact. Anyhow while you're meditating on it could I ask you a favour? There's no one to look after Paul at night.'

'And you want me to baby-sit.'

'He's very easy, and you don't have to change him, the woman does that. He's clean now in the day time of course.'

Travers repeated: 'Of course.'

She added: 'Here's a key. I'll stay with Chantal and I'll be back at 9.45 tomorrow evening—I mean the day after.'

From the moment her mother asked her not to, Alexandra went out of her way to bring Teddy Kovalic back to the house. Mathilde had given up making remarks to all and sundry, while Albertas Kovalic had other things on his mind.

The upshot was that young Teddy had many a breakfast in bed at the blue room, a fair number of bubble baths and an elegant sufficiency of magic moments in the arms of Florence's daughter. Her defiance of the Berg family gave zest to her love life and she toyed with the idea of Teddy settling in for good. She wanted to see the shocked faces of her mother, Mathilde and Gilbert Bossis when they saw his suitcases in the front hall.

Her father's diary became something of an obsession with her meanwhile. She read it over and over, finding hidden meanings in the prose, at the same time yearning to bridge the gulf between her parents. She saw herself taking one of her father's dead hands and placing it in that of her mother, so they were reconciled eternally.

Early one evening she was sitting cross-legged and nude on the unmade bed reading the now dog-eared manuscript. Teddy was sorting out her cassettes and had put one on, raising the volume.

'Not so loud,' she said dreamily as she read, then repeated it: 'Not so loud, I said!'

Teddy put up the volume some more, grabbed his saxophone and began adding his contribution.

Exasperated, Alexandra yelled: 'It's terrific Teddy, but for God's sake stop!!!'

'It's the music of the poor folk,' he rapped out between phrases.

She made as if to explode, but then suddenly remembered: 'That's strange. Father used that expression too several times.'

The boy ceased playing: 'Can't you stop nattering about your father for once?'

She ignored the remark and found what she was looking for.

'Listen to this: "March 30, 1967. Dined yesterday with Kassowitz the pianist. He told me in his Russian accent you could hardly cut with a knife that he would have liked to be a jazz player in Brooklyn, a Jewish one with a couple of negro players wearing big check jackets. They would have played Tea for Two for the tourists and ended up with a jam session for 20 lousy dollars. True, Kassowitz is out of this world playing Liszt in Carnegie Hall to an audience of 6,000 but it's true too that he would have been sensational in a flaked-out bar with a piano."'

Alexandra put the sheets back in order, and looked lovingly at Teddy, convinced he knew what she was getting at.

But instead of falling in with her dream, he snarled: 'What am I supposed to do, cry my eyes out?'

'Why are you so stupid?' she said woefully.

'Because I am. I've never said anything else since I first saw you. I'm stupid. And you know what you can do with all that gubbins of your dad's. Look at you nursing all that stuff like it was a little baby. You must be daft.' And with that, he snatched the manuscript from her and threw the sheets into the air. They flew about everywhere.

'You're mad!!!'

'That'll give you something to occupy your mind for a change,' Teddy taunted.

Alexandra tried to hit him, but he seized her wrists and pushed her back.

'You'll pay for that,' she hollered.

'I'd like to see it!'

'Clear out, clear out!!!'

'As you wish, princess!'

With a determined expression Teddy quickly put on his T-shirt, socks and boots, then scooped up his jacket and sax: 'Cheers. I'm writing a diary too, but it's in chalk on the ground and when it rains the words all disappear.'

'Write my name then, and I hope it rains tomorrow!!!'

Alexandra listened to the noise of his boots on the marble floor, and then there was no sound.

She was sad, exhausted and sorry for Teddy, for herself and all the little things that made them close and divided them. She felt out of her depth and longed to see her mother and nestle into her arms and seek repose there without talking, simply communing with her. On an impulse she went off to find Mathilde and was crestfallen to learn that her mother was not at La Commanderie, or at the office or at her studio. Mathilde told her she had got Jeannou to drive her in the Rolls.

'The Rolls!' Alexandra exclaimed. 'She never uses that!'

Mathilde screwed up her nose: 'She went off sitting in the back. Obviously had an appointment with someone important.'

The someone was of course Albertas Kovalic, and the appointment was for 6.30. Florence Berg was exactly on time, and the Rolls swung into the yard, scattering the fowls.

Albertas, dressed in his best, came half-way to the Rolls and they shook hands: 'This is a great event, Madame Berg.'

'Ah, you don't change a bit, Kovalic,' she said with condescension. 'Nice to see chickens in a farmyard still. All we've got at La Commanderie are dogs.'

'You used to have peacocks and Australian turkeys when your mother was alive. I supplied them.'

'I'd like to know what you haven't supplied to someone over the years!'

Albertas smiled politely: 'It would be hard to think of anything, Madame Berg.'

They went inside and sat down at the table where Albertas had cleaned his guns. Florence admired the lace edging on the embroidered cloth.

'The women did that of an evening while they watched the television. Shall we go into the sitting room?'

Florence glanced towards it and saw the Napoleon III armchairs, the ornate sideboards, the icons: 'If you don't mind I'd prefer it in here. We can be more frank.'

'I'm sure you're right, Madame Berg.'

'At least we agree on that,' she said gaily.

On his best behaviour, Albertas smiled cautiously and said: 'Perhaps you would like some water, or I can get Zoë to make you some coffee.'

'What do you have normally, Kovalic?'

'A plum liqueur normally, at this time of day. When a man's done an honest day's work, it's his right, don't you think?'

'And an honest woman?'

'An honest woman? Well I wouldn't know, but you certainly make an honest man, if you don't mind me saying so!'

'I'll take the plum liqueur then.'

They had launched off on what appeared to be friendly terms, on neutral ground as it were. Albertas went into the sitting room and brought back two glasses and a bottle of slivovitz on a tray covered with a lace napkin.

'I warn you this is pretty strong, and if you don't care for it I shan't be offended. Zoë and Marfa make blackcurrant liqueur too, and that's very good too but not as sharp.'

Florence signed for him to pour out the slivovitz.

'Do we clink?' Albertas said, his eyes narrowing, but with a smile.

Florence smiled too and shook her head. She then took a fair-sized sip and gave an almost imperceptible jerk.

'Too strong for you? I'll fetch . . .'

'Oh please don't. It's strong but superb. Besides I did not come here to compare the merits of slivovitz and blackcurrant.'

'Of course. I must apologize, I should have made the first move. I swear I was getting round to phoning.'

'You should have. Kovalic, what's happening to us? One of your men working for me has been murdered, you hit my daughter, somebody mugged your daughter. She works for me too, her boy is my mother's grandson, my nephew in a sense. What's more your nephew sleeps at my place and you know why. Meanwhile Bernard has declared war on my paper, even though he has acquired some shares in it. So I repeat, what's happening, where have we got to? And we don't even have anything to do with each other.'

Albertas filled the glasses again and put the bottle delicately back on the tray: 'If we keep apart, it's not my fault. You remember the mess-up over Paul's christening. The ill-feeling's not on our side, I assure you. Personally I wish you no harm. The Bergs have been hard on us in the past, but the past is the past. I respect you as a woman and in my opinion your paper is excellent.'

Florence responded: 'Thank you. I value your compliments.' She put her glass down and Albertas topped it up again. From the kitchen came the sound of the women preparing dinner and talking quietly.

Albertas resumed: 'Mind you, I wasn't too pleased about that article you did on the Kovalics. I was hurt by it, but no doubt you had your reasons.'

'It was not written against you.'

'I came round to that way of thinking afterwards. You had to strike out, and it hit us as it happens. At least, it helped the paper I suppose.'

'Your lawyers were too quick off the mark. But that doesn't explain all the rest.' She knocked back her drink.

'It's really quite simple, it seems to me,' Albertas said as he refilled the glasses, his voice growing husky. 'There are people trying to get at your paper, at your family, and it suits them for us to quarrel, you and me.'

'Ah but we aren't going to fall in with their plans.'

'That's certainly my feeling, I swear by my forebears!'

'And would Bernard be prepared to swear that?'

'It's not me who pays him in that business.'

'I know that.'

'He has no morals, and I have no control over him.'

'But we might bring pressure to bear together perhaps?'

'Who can tell?' Albertas growled, sinking another slivovitz. Florence did likewise, and they remained like that for a while, a little smile on their lips. The television began booming out in the kitchen; a baby gurgled and a madonna-like voice-over extolled the merits of a new leak-proof nappy.

Albertas said: 'Zoë and Marfa like to watch the regional news. It's coming on now.' He poured out another drink for them both.

Florence's smile was permanent by now, and she was even prepared to accept that Kovalic was being sincere.

Zoë appeared suddenly and said: 'Albert, the mayor's coming on.'

'Can we watch?' Florence said quickly.

'We must watch,' Albertas declared royally.

They went in and he arranged chairs for them side by side. Marfa lowered the gas under a big saucepan of soup, and joined Zoë a short distance apart.

The anchor woman said: 'What's happening at Chateauvallon these days, *Monsieur Le Maire*? Murders, intimidation. That's unusual. Is it connected with the November election?'

The camera switch showed Adrien Jerome filling the screen. He seemed a litle stilted, but his amiable smile was there: 'There may be something in that, *Madame*, people always get a little worked up before an election and the climate is rather more tense than usual. Chateauvallon is normally a quiet town, with people going about their business. But in less than two years a journalist has been killed, my predecessor committed suicide, and now we have guards murdering one another and paper vans burnt out. Yes, Chateauvallon has changed. However I'd like to make two points. A certain type of press, said to be on the Left, is keeping up an atmosphere of racism that is most uncalled for. Worthy hardworking immigrant families are being outrageously persecuted, and this is of course completely unacceptable!'

494

Zoë and Marfa exchanged a glance and leaned forward in unison to see the effect on Florence and Albertas. Florence gave nothing away, but Albertas semed shocked.

Jerome continued: 'And the second point is that an honourable family, rightly respected in the past, apparently fails to understand the gravity of the situation and is doing its best to aggravate it.'

Marfa chipped in quickly: 'Who's he mean?'

Albertas waved her down and the mayor got into his stride: 'It must be clearly understood that a town hall is not a castle to be stormed by hussars! There are voters and people elected properly. This is universal suffrage. Unfortunately the town hall on its own cannot prevent the chicanery, intrigue and intimidation you mentioned. I would prefer to leave it at that.'

The anchor woman came back: 'That was Adrien Jerome, mayor of Chateauvallon. I ought to explain that the family the mayor was referring to is the Berg family, which owns *La Dépêche Republicaine*, the oldest son being the member of parliament for Chateauvallon. Thank you, *Monsieur Le Maire*. At Orleans a bank robbery . . .'

Albertas switched the set off: 'It's unbelievable!' He took Florence's arm and they went back to the table, where he handed her one of the full glasses and took the other for himself. 'He didn't have the guts to pronounce your name, and the girl had to say it for him. Ought to be ashamed of himself. Is he going to stand for election, d'you think?'

'I have no facts yet, but I should imagine so.' She looked a long time at Albertas and said: 'What do you think?'

'He's quite capable of it,' he said darkly. 'Myself, I would—but it's none of my business—all the same, I'm going to say it. Your brother Armand ought to stand. He's a good member of parliament and he'd make a good mayor. Mind you there's a lot of work to it, too much perhaps.'

His visitor scratched her head: 'You are incorrigible, Kovalic.' She had some trouble getting the word out.

'We can clink now?' he said with a grin.

'We can,' she said with some emphasis.'

Albertas filled the glasses once more, and they both observed that the bottle was empty.

'What do we drink to, Kovalic. People in our town?'

'And to *La Dépêche*!'

They clinked the glasses and threw the last of the slivovitz down their throats.

Madame La Directrice sat back and breathed out heavily: 'I really don't know if I am capable of driving . . .'

'You have your chauffeur!'

'Of course I have, I quite forgot. Now where's my bag?' She rose and walked stiffly in the general direction of the front door. Albertas switched the yard lights on and put his arm in hers. She looked round at him and giggled.

'I can hardly see you, Madame Berg,' he said, in a gallant bid to assure her they were equal in their dissipated condition. 'It was you who made me drink more than was wise. Never mind, we shall see clearer when the moon goes down.'

This was too much for Florence and she laughed unreservedly: 'You must have got it wrong.' Jeannou opened the rear door to its fullest extent, but diplomatically refrained from aiding her.

'Not at all, Madame Berg, it's an old poacher's saying.' She sank back in her seat: 'Ah, that explains everything!'

Jeannou lost no time manoeuvring through the yard gate, and Florence gave Kovalic a regal wave. She then slumped into her corner and was asleep before the Rolls had gone fifty metres.

Paul Bossis was a good as gold, and Travers had a perfect night's sleep. Around 8.30 a.m. the woman came in, bathed the infant and fed him before taking him off to her own flat. Travers watched the proceedings, made bubbly noises in response to Paul's. He wasn't too sure but he thought the child said *'papa'* at one point, and he was strangely moved.

He was still thinking about it when Catherine came through the exit, looking lively but a little pale from fatigue. She embraced Travers and asked him to take her home so that she could change for the office.

'I saw Lorieux,' she told him.

'And what did he have to say, the dirty rat?'

'At least one thing that shows he's not such a rat as you think. He said you ought to quit Chateauvallon, that you've been out of things long enough, that the past is the past and Paris awaits you with open arms.'

'That's a new angle.'

They were silent for the rest of the short journey. Travers found it hard to believe that Lorieux was offering him a job out of kindness. More likely his idea was to snatch him from *La Dépêche*, knowing that he was after all a valuable prop for Florence. There was a third possibility, that Boulard's right hand man was being misreported by Catherine for personal reasons, that she was making it sound more attractive. But that would assume she had plans for him, Travers, which was a presumptuous thought. So he put it out of his mind.

At her flat he made himself some instant coffee while she took a shower. He returned to the living room and found her, wearing only scanty briefs, fussing in a chest of drawers. Her breasts trembled as she leaned over and Travers lost interest in his cup of coffee.

Suavely he asked: 'About Lorieux, did he have a job for you, or for me if it comes to that?'

'Not right away,' she said with equal aplomb.

'Ah,' he said, taking a sip none the less.

She straightened up waving a bra, and Travers sat a little straighter too.

He said: 'Say, I've never seen you stripped.'

'Yes you have, hundreds of times; you never noticed?'

'Sure I have. You've a superb body, I must have told you.'

'Sure you haven't, as you never noticed.' She put the bra on.

'I will not let it happen again. But about Lorieux, your news isn't worth much if there's no job dangling on the end.'

'Suppose so,' she mumbled. 'I saw Chantal anyway and . . .'

'How is she?'

'Completely recovered.' She donned some jeans and a jumper, then went past Travers.

'You know whose daughter she is, I take it?' she said.

'No idea.'

'Chénin-Bernard's, but she doesn't want to use his name to get on, uses a different name. But she'd be glad to put a word in with her dad to help me. Help you too. In fact she wants us both to have dinner with him.'

'Aha!'

'I'd like that,' Catherine murmured with a casual air. Too casual to be true, Travers thought. He also thought that if she was putting ideas into his head he had better do something about it.

Catherine had fine features, cheeks a wee bit hollow, a clear skin, hungry eyes and mouth. He watched the mouth quivering as she got a cigarette from her bag, lit it and pulled on it.

'So I conclude,' he declared, 'that you want to clear out and I have to come with you?'

She took in a hugh quantity of smoke, then released it with a soft whistle. They were now face to face.

Her eyes were even larger when she said: 'One day soon you'll have to take it or leave it. Next month Paul will have been dead two years.'

'I know.'

'You don't sound like it,' she retorted, rising quickly.

Travers threw back in a thick voice: 'You're building up to a scene?'

'I've no choice,' she replied, a quake in her voice.

'Catherine, come here.'

She needed no second bidding, and knelt down, placing her head on his shoulder—which *ipso facto* placed her crotch against his knees. He pushed his nose into her hair and kissed her, ending with a big intake of breath.

'Exquisite,' he pronounced. 'I-er-saw Bernard the other day, we were both jogging along the Loire. He looked seedy, it surprised me.'

'He's got problems,' she murmured. 'Unanswered questions.'

Travers was alert of a sudden but gave no sign of it: 'What sort?'

'Oh, questions. Who hasn't got problems!'

'You seem to be hiding something.'

Catherine kept her head nestling into him: 'Don't mix things, Travers. Why bring him up just now?'

'He seems to regret you are his first cousin. Wanted to know if we slept together.'

'And you said?'

'You know my lips are sealed tight when a girl's reputation is involved.'

With a hint of bitterness, Catherine said: 'My reputation will stand the truth.'

Travers took her head between his palms: 'That's nice.'

She leaned on him and her arms were round his neck. They breathed in together as their lips met. The kiss spread and they sought the pleasure of it greedily. Travers's hands applied pressure to her breasts, then slipped under the jumper. She let out a moan as he ministered to her need, responding with short excited kisses around his mouth. He slid the bra up, fondling her nipples, and she gave a whimper of relief.

Then she pulled away and shook her hair straight: 'Oh how I wanted that, wanted it for so many months.' She compressed her lips and her eyes were wet. She sniffed: 'I work for *La Dépêche* until further notice. I'd better go.'

'What a coincidence, so do I. And I'd rather not lose sight of you at this point.'

In the absence of Florence it was Melchior that morning who was staking out the day's events like butterflies on a board. The job sheet for the day lay before him at the editorial conference.

'All that's left is Balestra,' he said, wiping his brow. He glanced up to scan Edelman, Favrot, Béatrice Bonnenfant, Travers and Catherine. Physically Melchior looked in good shape but the burden of activity since Antonin

Berg's death was slowly getting the better of him. Neither *La Dépêche* nor Chateauvallon would ever be the same again, and he saw no cause to rejoice over it.

'What's Balestra up to?' Travers enquired.

'He's the new boss at those labs in Rouen,' Edelman said. 'All the latest gadgets. They're inaugurating it today, with ministers and the upper crust from Paris and Normandy.'

'We don't have to cover Rouen,' Travers rapped.

'Balestra, my friend, comes under the heading of people in our town, as our esteemed *patronne* puts it. He had a house near Chateauvallon, and I expect you remember that whole page thing we ran on him,' Favrot said.

Edelman put in: 'And she says he's going to be even more famous. Nobel Prize three months from now.'

'Oh yes?' Travers said.

'It's all in the foreign press, dear chap. I can read in all sorts of languages. Science mags too, and I even understand what I'm reading.'

Melchior raised his voice: 'Come on, we're wasting time. Edelman, you cover it, take Béa with you, she might pick up a scoop.'

Favrot mumbled something incomprehensible and Travers tossed his head in disdain. Catherine sat there still enjoying the taste of the kiss.

The phone rang and Melchior snatched it in irritation: 'Yes Florence, I've just this moment assigned it to Edelman and Béa. Ah, you mean . . .? Right I'll tell them.' He turned to them: 'That was Florence, forgot to tell me she'll be handling the lab thing herself.'

Edelman opened his mouth wide: 'Oh goodie, if she's going to do my job, I'm going to sit in her office and show you people how a paper ought to be run. Naturally my salary will leap overnight!'

A mixture of groans and snorts greeted this contribution. Travers was crouched on his chair, a Napoleon whose Josephine had expressed a preference for the Duke of Wellington.

Catherine, who thought it was her fault, whispered in

his ear: 'Don't forget to phone Chantal right away.'

He smiled wanly at her, and squeezed the hand she extended to him, as if his life depended on it.

Alexandra quoted from the manuscript: 'I can never tell what she is going to say, or do; she is as inscrutable as a cat. I don't know whether she hears me or whether she even sees me. But she is there. She is like some secret that is hidden in the house, and I know that I must not try to find it.'

The girl looked across to her mother who was making-up with particular care at her dressing table.

'Are you listening, *maman*?'

Florence indicated to her that she was, and observed her daughter via the mirror, reading the now-scruffy manuscript on the floor.

Alexandra went on: 'I did not marry her because she is beautiful or young, but because she is magical. Which means that one day, instead of disappearing, she will appear. Then like everyone else she will start speaking, yelling, ruminating and noticing me. The spell will have been broken and one of us will need to take a big decision.' At this point Florence stopped brushing her mascara on, and cupped her face. 'As to myself, I know what I shall have to do. The fear of losing her is so compelling that in my heart I am already rehearsing my departure. I hope that the child will resemble her and they will therefore be two people walking the earth.'

Florence interrupted with a loud cry: 'Stop! Stop it now!!!'

Her daughter put the manuscript down, and changed to a squatting position on her heels: 'You can't say he didn't love you!'

Florence told her through tears, her cheeks running with black: 'He put it in writing but he never said it, never!'

Alexandra went to her, pulled out a paper handkerchief and cleaned her mother up. She then kissed her brow, gathered up the manuscript and put it on the dressing table.

'I'll leave it with you, read it if you want to, but be careful because it's the only copy.'

She rubbed Florence's spine and neck. Then from the doorway blew her a kiss.

In the grounds Alexandra met her uncle Julien, haggard and wild-looking. He was striding back and forth behind the garages with his hands over his ears, even though there was complete silence with not even a bird intruding.

Seeing her, he demanded testily: 'What are you doing here?'

'Nothing special, just walking about like you.'

'That's what you say,' he replied. She was taken aback, and sorry too because she had always liked Julien and would have loved to confide in him. For example, that she did not know what to do about Teddy, that the way her parents had behaved to each other had thrown her into complete disarray and torment. She simply took his arm and they went along several paces together until it dawned upon her that he was actually crying. True, he was not much older than she was, but all the same!

'What are you up to apart from walking about?' she enquired diplomatically.

After a pause he admitted: 'I dare not go indoors, I don't want to see Thérèse. I shouldn't be bothering you with my troubles; you're so young, and I hope you are still full of illusions!'

She still would not believe that this chirpy man, her favourite uncle, was letting himself go like this. He needed her aid, and at once.

'Let's sit down,' she murmured. 'I've got all the time in the world. Why are you afraid of Thérèse?'

'Not of her, but of her look. If she looks guilty, I couldn't bear it. If she is innocent, it would be even worse!'

Frowning, Alexandra sought to draw him out: 'Tell me all about it.'

He seized her shoulder: 'She's going with another man, and she's been lying to me for weeks. Those trips to Switzerland aren't for skiing, but to see him. I imagine them actually in the same bed . . . oh, oh.'

The girl comforted him, brushing a curl off his brow in an already-adult gesture: 'Julien, you know I'm terribly fond of you, and I feel awful about this. I feel it with you. But are you so very sure about it? Is it so very serious? Thérèse wanted to get away from it all, like they say. All women have this feeling today; women's lib and all that.'

Her calculated blend of tenderness, conviction and banter failed to penetrate, and he said: 'All right for women's lib. But I can't accept lies and tricks while she brazens it out with an angel face. And the chldren are sad and anxious, they know there's something dreadful in the air . . . Anyhow I've said too much, but I was with Gilbert over there just now talking about which trees to fell, which breaks my heart because I've always known the trees, every one of them, and Jean-Jacques and I used to build huts like Tarzan—anyhow there we were when the plane landed.'

'Plane?'

'Yes, a red thing. I'd never seen it before, but the kids said they had. I remember too that Thérèse had spoken about some pilot. Then I met Matton, our friend where she was supposed to be staying, and he said he hoped we'd accept their invitation one of these days.'

Desperately trying to understand, Alexandra said: 'I don't see the connection.'

Julien gabbled on: 'The plane went over La Commanderie, and landed in one of the meadows over there without switching off. Thérèse got out and ran towards the house. We both saw it, Gilbert and I, although Gilbert pretended not to and found some excuse to go indoors.'

Alexandra said: 'Huh, he's pretty self-centred since his son was murdered and Antonin died; it's understandable, I suppose.'

'So that's why I'm here, not daring to go in. She doesn't know I saw the plane and everything, she'll play-act like a little girl, not realizing I know everything. Oh God, what a situation!'

The girl, knowing she was the stronger at that moment, scolded him: 'Pull yourself together, you're overdramatizing things. What counts are the children, Julie and Jean-Claude. Their parents must work it out, they have to make up. Believe me, Julien, I know how important . . .'

She could get no further, and it was his turn to comfort her. A great warmth of human kindness flowed between them and they smiled.

'Be a man, Julien, please. I want that. And if it helps, think of me,' she said.

Manuscript or no manuscript, Florence's mood was in stark contrast with theirs, as she drove through Rouen. She felt heady, so much so that she omitted to study the little map on the back of the invitation and ended up in the city centre in a traffic snarl when she ought to have followed the Seine round.

It was of no consequence. Nothing could make her downhearted today, she was seeing Artus again, the exotic impenetrable Artus who had so decently taken her in at La Jouterie and painstakingly and intelligently given her back her will to live. When all was said and done, homo or no homo, he was a trusty friend and a gentleman. There weren't too many of those about these days.

She was awaited by a young man of twenty-seven or twenty-eight, specially earmarked by Balestra to look out for her. He was good-looking, pleasant and had a neat silky beard.

Sylvain, which was the only name he gave, provided her with the regulation white overall and a name badge. He explained: 'For pity's sake don't take it off. Balestra's a maniac about dust. Even wanted me to shave my beard off.'

Florence made her eyes go big, in surprise and amusement: 'How about your hair?'

'Not the same sort of hair, I'll explain it later. And in addition the women here have to wear tights.'

'I never wear tights,' she said in mock shame.

'Never mind, we're not in a vacuum in this part.'

'God be praised for that!'

Sylvain took her through the crowd and they reached a

couple of seats that were reserved for them. Almost at once, the new boss Balestra charged onto a plinth looking every ounce the part in his white overall. He looked confident, efficient and handsome. She would have liked to work for him, she reflected, thinking for an instant of Pierre and Marie Curie and laughing to herself about it.

'Thank you all for coming,' Balestra said in a firm voice, leaning on a microphone-laden table. 'The Government has thought fit to reward the work of this team by giving it the space it deserves. Otherwise we should have had to give up.' She liked this unpretentious style. 'But as we all know this work is not for the Government as such, but for the advancement of the whole human race; on the other hand the human race needs Government money and the Government needs votes. With the result that nobody knows what the devil he's up to, and that's a very good thing. I personally am a champion of complexity, and so far in my work I have proved highly successful in that regard.'

The audience lapped it up, aside from those people who couldn't follow his quick mind and double meanings. Florence was in genuine admiration of the magnetism surrounding him, his gift of making everyone feel good.

Continuing his technical badinage, he said: 'Our chaps working here have an artistic vocation, which can't be said of the Americans and Japanese who are great performers on computer keyboards but can't boil a litre of water correctly!' More laughs. 'Those people are still trying to pick up rice with two bits of wood, and the others are beating up folks who never did them any harm. Meanwhile we here are inventing the human body, and the job's not finished yet!'

Sylvain whispered to Florence: 'He's tipsy.'

'You think so? I think he's marvellous.'

Flashes went off all round as Balestra shot his arms into the air: 'That's why we've got these luxury huts here with three billion francs of equipment and nobody to work it. Which is lucky for them because we couldn't pay them any wages anyway!'

A Ministry woman sniffed: 'He's making fools of us.'

Her colleague said: 'Not at all, I think he's spot on!'

Amid further chuckles, Balestra ended: 'Well, that's about all for now. Oh by the way, about those rumours, I have to confess I don't really like Stockholm especially when it's night-time round the clock. I prefer the sun. So there!'

He jumped down like a two year old. A crowd gathered round him, while others stayed distant, frowning and arguing.

One young man took off his white overall with a deliberate gesture and said: 'I could tell him what to do with his Nobel Prize!' He marched out past the buffet.

Sylvain invited Florence to have a drink, and they were heading for the buffet table when Artus came up waving a champagne bottle. He grabbed three glasses.

'Delighted you've met. You must get along together, please, because you are the two most precious people in the world to me, though for diametrically opposed reasons!'

He released the champagne which squirted into Sylvain's beard.

'So sorry,' Artus said. He then took Florence by the elbow. 'I've something I want you to see.'

He guided her to a door marked NO ENTRY, muttering 'We'll see about that!' and led her along immaculate corridors smelling of fresh paint.

'What do you want to show me?' Florence cried.

'This,' he stated, taking her into a room, 'will be my office. The couch arrives tomorrow, but we don't need that now.'

He flung off his overall, then unbuttoned Florence's, then started on her dress buttons down the front.

'I know you're crazy, Artus, but . . .' she wailed.

He hoisted her up onto the desk, laid her flat so that her legs dangled over the end, and began caressing her knees.

'But Artus, I thought . . .'

'What?' he growled, undoing his belt.

'That you, that you—er—didn't have a predilection for women.'

'You thought wrong, and if you want proof of it . . .' He pulled her towards him, whipped off her panties and gently eased her thighs apart. He was slowing down now, the jokes were over, and Florence gave herself up to his advances, concentrating as he was now.

'Oh Artus, darling, if you make fun of me, I'll never speak to you again.'

'Shut up then,' he said. 'I've never been more serious in my life!'

Chapter Ten

For a while, the enemy left *La Dépêche* and its *patronne* alone
subsequent to the laboratory opening. No more vans were
burnt out, nobody was mugged, nobody murdered. The
paper came out regularly and continued thriving. Florence
was in full vigour, quietly confident and above all cheerful.

Then the run of luck, as she secretly termed it, came to
an end. It was Melchior who took Nicolo's call in his office
one Sunday as he was reading some proofs for the Monday issue.

As he listened, the blood drained from his face, he asked
urgent questions, noted the details on a pad, slammed the
phone down and tore the paper off the pad. He rushed
along to Florence's office in case she happened to be there,
found no one and hurtled down the stairs into his car.

Chateauvallon was its usual Sunday night self with the
streets empty except for a few people window-shopping,
the cake shops doing a busy trade, lines of people patiently
waiting outside the cinemas. As a journalist on a daily,
Melchior had long ago treated Sunday as just another day,
and today he never gave a glance at the town. The vision of
what Nicolo had described to him blotted out everything.

Driving fast he reached the road along the River Loire
and perceived the disaster some 500 metres before he got
to the scene. A big articulated lorry occupied half the road,
its rear facing the river, the back axle in the mud. Further
on in the water were eight rolls of newsprint, half submer-
ged. Near the lorry were four cars: Nicolo's and three
owned by people who happened to be taking a drive along
the river.

Marching up to Nicolo, Melchior said: 'They're ours all
right.'

508

'I've examined the marks on the road. No question of an accident, they're after you again.' Melchior stood shaking his head. 'How much would they be worth?'

Melchior brushed the question away with a hand: 'It's not the value, the trouble is we don't carry stock.'

'What!'

'It's in the nature of the business. Too much expense. We get the paper twice a week, and on Sunday it's the start of the new cycle.'

'You mean that's tonight's paper? Can't you get any more straight away?'

'You're joking.'

They reached the lorry cab, where Pradal was inspecting the floor, seats and under the dashboard. He said: 'A packet of Gitanes, lighter, glasses. Must have been in a hurry to leave them.'

'How were you notified?' Melchior asked the commissaire.

'Anonymous call half an hour ago.'

Nicolo showed Melchior the retaining cables cut through on the half-trailer.

'No question it was planned. Took some cutting through, I'd say,' Nicolo commented.

They went back to the police car and phoned Florence: 'The whole damn lot in the river, *ma petite Flo*. A total loss.'

'Get everyone in my office. This time we'll give 'em the works!' she shouted, and immediately rang off.

Melchior was about to open his car door when he saw Inspector Germain arriving with a man and a woman. They all merged into a huddle of five.

'This is the driver,' Germain announced.

The woman said at breakneck speed: 'I found him. I stopped my car to do a wee-wee behind a tree, and there were quite a lot of trees, and as I was doing it I heard this moaning noise behind me. Scared me stiff, I can tell you. Anyway when I looked round there was this gentleman tied up to a tree with a scarf in his mouth. Good job I turned up, eh? So I adjusted my clothing, as they say, and took the scarf out and undid the rope. I hope I did the right thing.' She ended breathlessly, delighted to be mixed up in a cops and robbers adventure.

'You did, *Madame*,' Nicolo stated. 'Where exactly is your car?'

'Over there.'

'My assistant will accompany you and jot down a few details if you don't mind. Thank you for your help.'

He mumbled a few words to Germain who went off with the woman. Melchior watched them and was surprised to see them laughing. He was about to question the driver, when the man's eyes veered sideways and he crumpled to the ground. Nicolo tapped his cheeks while Pradal examined his head.

'Big bump on the back, chief,' Pradal said.

The driver was still conscious and informed them: 'They whacked me in the neck and then dragged me out of the driving seat. Otherwise I'd have fought 'em off, but I was all of a daze.'

'How many were they?'

'Two, at least I think there was two of 'em. They had motorbike goggles and scarves over their faces. Hit me with wood slats, they did. I couldn't identify either of them, but they had a BMW car with a Hauts-de-Seine numberplate. That's what they cut in on me with, so I had to stop the lorry.'

Melchior had heard enough. When he arrived everyone seemed in a flat spin, and Florence was clearly more flustered than she had been on the phone. In her office were the fleet manager Charles and the foreman Velpeau.

'You've got paper for how many copies?' she demanded.

'About 24,000.'

'A fat lot of good that is!'

'We've always worked hand-to-mouth like that, *Madame*.'

'Not even a day's reserve—ever?'

'Oh yes, but not Sundays,' Velpeau stressed.

Florence blew out her cheeks in disgust: 'You're in charge of the paper, Velpeau, aren't you?'

'I load it on the machine, I don't do the ordering.'

'Then who the devil does?'

'I can't say, *Madame*. I don't think anyone does, the paper just comes, has been coming for years. Marchetti knows what's needed, and we've never had any trouble, except one time when the drivers were on strike. We got some paper from another supplier when that happened.'

Florence was hissing through her teeth: 'Anyone know Marchetti to speak to?'

Charles said: 'We just know the drivers.'

Dismissing the two men, Florence moved into the main editorial room, where Béatrice Bonnenfant was handling two phone calls. The girl put both receivers down at roughly the same moment, and turned to Florence.

'No Marchetti,' she lamented. 'He's not at home or at his country house. It's Sunday. Just guards, that's all.'

'Keep trying, you might strike lucky.'

Florence took Melchior's arm, and hurried him into her office: 'He's completely off his rocker, Boulard! Literally, it's highway robbery, it's out of the Middle Ages. I've made him so jumpy he's resorting to the morals of the playground! But he can just wait, he'll finish up shooting himself in the—in the—'

'Foot?'

'The head, I hope!'

Melchior said firmly: 'And you make sure you keep yours. Where's your proof?'

'Who cares about proof! I want a formal complaint against Boulard, not against persons unknown, it has to be against Boulard.'

In the editorial room, just about everyone was on the phone. Catherine Kovalic was an exception, but she was deep in thought.

Melchior asked Madame Frochot: 'Where's the Holy Trinity?'

'Travers and Edelman are on their way to the Marchetti plant, Favrot's trying to get a lorry.'

'Can't we salvage the other one?'

'Nicolo refuses to have it moved.'

Melchior raised his eyes skyward: 'If you'll pardon the expression Madame Frochot, they have us by the short and curlies. We need paper in six hours; we'll never make it!'

'Make that seven hours, and we still won't manage it.'

They failed to notice Catherine now talking quietly into a phone handset with her fingers cupped round so that nobody could hear.

The people at *L'Eveil* learned of the paper incident from a technician who called to fix one of the teleprinters. He thought it a huge joke.

'It's nothing to laugh about,' Jean-Jacques Berg said.

The technician pulled a face and went on with his work. He had imagined the loss of the paper for the rival publication would have suited them. But while he fiddled about with pliers and screwdriver he also thought it strange that Bernard Kovalic and Maryse looked pretty chuffed with themselves. Still, it was none of his business.

A phone rang and after the usual preliminaries, Bernard took the call in the next office.

'Good evening, Monsieur Boulard,' he said bowing to the wall.

'What's happened to *La Dépêche*?' the press baron roared.

'Ah, you know already.'

'If I knew I wouldn't be asking you, Kovalic. I know nothing, get that in your head. I trust you have nothing to do with this business. To be more accurate, I am *convinced* you are a stranger to it. Understand?'

Bernard adopted a man-to-man attitude: 'What's on your mind, Monsieur Boulard?'

'I would find it extremely awkward if *L'Eveil* was believed to be behind it.'

'The management here is not involved in any way, and of course you know that, Monsieur.'

'It's all very difficult, you understand.'

'Understand what?' Bernard gasped.

'You will know how to get the most out of this.'

512

'But I'm a stranger to it!'

'Quite. But you can still offer to help them, those poor people without a single reel of newsprint. Offer your help, it's the least you can do.'

Bernard screwed up his features, attempting to follow the man: 'They print 300,000, and you don't imagine we have that much paper in stock.'

'I never said you should give them any paper, Kovalic! Just offer them the hand of friendship. You get me?'

'It's crystal clear, Monsieur, I walk into *La Dépêche* in my best suit with a rope dangling round my neck.'

Boulard gave a little giggle and Bernard heard him ring off. He banged the receiver down, and muttered: 'That guy has a mind like a sewer system.'

He pulled his tie straight, walked back to the others and told Berg: 'I'm going to offer some newsprint to your sister.'

The sister in question was at that moment pouring glass after glass from a whisky bottle on one side of her desk. Travers phoned in, Melchior took the call, passed it to Florence.

'Well?' she screamed.

'The place is locked everywhere, just one guard with the sole job of keeping people out.'

'Put him on!'

'Won't do any good, he's got his orders, and . . .'

'Put him on!' A pause. 'I'm so sorry to annoy you, Monsieur. I fully understand your position, but I wonder if you could possibly let me know where I can get hold of Monsieur Marchetti. It's very urgent.'

The guard said: 'Very sorry, Madame, you're out of luck. It's the France–England match tonight at the Parc des Princes. No hope of getting in touch.'

'Oh, I see. Well, I hope France wins anyhow. Could I have my chap back on the phone please?' When Travers came back she said: 'Can we bribe him?'

'Er-not the type.'

'Couldn't you and Edelman knock him out?'

'Come off it, Florence!'

'It's not asking much. We've been knocked out.'

'I said come off it, Florence.'

'Well it was worth asking. What about Favrot?'

'He's a hundred metres away from us with a lorry that is banned from the roads on Sundays. But it's of no consequence, because there's nothing to load it with.'

'So we're beaten?'

"Fraid so, Flo. Don't take it too bad, it's only one issue.'

'Come back, Trav, I need you,' she said, and the phone went dead.

She poured out another nip, and Bernard Kovalic walked in: 'What's *he* doing here?' She put the question to Melchior.

'Maybe he's offering us some paper.'

'Hah!' she said. 'And Boulard's in the yard with the lorry!' She rose menacingly. 'Listen here Kovalic. I believe I once said I imagined you as a son-in-law. Well, I've got a different daughter, but this is the same newspaper. You understand me?'

'Er?' said Bernard, now seriously questioning his own mental faculties. 'In any case the message is striking. A short cut in reasoning.'

'I have another for you,' Florence said, baring her teeth. 'In one minute from now I'll have you thrown out of the window. It's the shortest way out.'

The visitor rapped back: 'I came to find out if I could help, but if not, then I wish you good evening and good luck, *Madame*.'

He scurried out and clip-clopped down the stairs as fast as his legs would carry him.

Bernard would have been interested in Catherine's phone call. She was saying: 'Oh papa, we really are in a mess this time.'

She had got Zoë to start with, and she had gone to fetch Albertas from the pigsties. When he spoke it was to say: 'Catherine? Catherine who? Kovalic, like me? I don't know any Catherine Kovalic. I used to have a daughter by that name, but she left me years ago . . .' Eventually, from the noises she made, he realized that Catherine was upset and he said: 'Come on girl, I can tease you a bit, can't I? I'm your old dad after all.'

It was then that she explained things.

He answered: 'So you're in a mess, eh? What's it this time, newsprint?'

Catherine said quickly: 'How do you know it's newsprint?'

'A little bird told me. So what?'

'I know you can fix anything. Can't you work something out for us?'

Her father became businesslike: 'How many tons?'

'I don't know, tons and tons.'

'Does your boss know you're phoning me?'

'No.'

'Good. That shark in Paris is after her again. I'll get her out of it, don't you worry your little head. Call me back in one hour. That suit you?'

Catherine felt woozy. She had taken it upon herself to negotiate and she suddenly lost confidence, especially as there seemed to be no one about much now. She got up and took the lift to the ground floor, and went across to the Bijou-Bar. There she drank two Ricards in quick succession.

Colette went back to wiping glasses, glancing at her from time to time.

Albertas was beside himself. His daughter had phoned him, and asked him for something. It must be seven years since she said she wanted nothing more to do with him.

'Albert,' Zoë scolded him, 'you'll have an attack, working yourself up like that.'

'They want some newsprint,' he said swiftly. 'I've got to find it, otherwise it'll be another ten years before she phones again!'

'Try Pavel,' Zoë advised, taking off her apron.

'Pavel? He makes coffins. What does he want paper for?'

'He knows everyone. He'll find a way.'

He cocked his head in a mock threat: 'Be careful what

515

you're saying, Zoë my gal. *I'm* the one who knows everyone.'

She had no time to answer back, for Teddy walked in carrying a rolled up poster, which he put on the sideboard, and said hullo to them.

'Know what, Teddy?' his uncle said. 'Catherine telephoned.'

'Reversed the charges I expect!'

'Oh don't be like that.'

'Wasn't looking for some rolls of paper, I suppose?'

'How do you know?'

'The whole town knows, and they're crying because they'll have nothing to read at breakfast.'

The boy disappeared, and Albertas called Pavel.

By now Catherine was on her fourth Ricard, the bar was filling up and she felt even woozier. Everyone seemed to be drowning their sorrows, for her cousin Bernard was at the other end of the counter with a brandy.

Travers appeared at this juncture, shouldering his way towards her. 'Kiss me,' she ordered.

'What, here? What are we celebrating?' She leaned slightly towards him and toppled onto him.

Looking up she moaned: 'The newsprint. I phoned my dad.'

Keeping a firm hand under her arm he said: 'Really? How's he getting on?'

'Haven't spoken to him for seven years. He's clever. Knows everything about paper.'

'Has he got some?'

'He will have.'

'I'll raise my hat to him, because we've come up against a brick wall.'

Catherine whispered loudly: 'You can't fiddle things. He can because he—because he . . .'

She broke off, realizing she was going too far. Travers now caught sight of Bernard, and was none to pleased to see a Boulard man among the people from *La Dépêche*.

'Because he?' Travers said, coaxing her.

To no avail. She stammered: 'Take me out of here,

André, I'm utterly tiddly, don't know what I'm saying.'
She slipped off her stool, walking slowly. 'Don't look at me
so nastily. One day I'll talk to you like I want to talk to you.
Can't today, but I promise I will.'

'Fine, fine. But about the paper?'

'Take me out, take me out and hurry up about it.'

Bernard watched them negotiate the door. The brandy
was putting him in a foul temper, but he ordered another.

Zoë kept squinting through the door, wondering when
she should get the meal up. Each time Albertas, in shirt-
sleeves and chain-smoking small cigars, waved her away
as he battled with the phone. This was the kind of challenge he loved, and even as he fought his way through the
web he was thinking it took him back years.

At last, around 8.00 p.m. he called Pavel: 'Hullo there
Pav, I got to thank you. I've been on to your bloke, and he
fixed me up. You know we've got the local election coming
up? Well, Jerome's going to get his posters done. The
paper's a bit glossy, and it's one metre sixty wide, but the
newspaper wants two metres. They can do it small for
once, what do you think? Ah, you reckon it'll work.
There's only one thing, we need a lorry now and there's
only three hours left. You can find one? Good old Pavel, I
knew I could count on you. I'll pray for you every night for
a month, thanks for everything, you're a real mate Pavel,
you'll go straight to heaven.'

A whiff of cabbage and bacon reached his nostrils, and
he called Teddy in: 'Get on your bike, boy, and go over to
Pavel. He'll have a lorry. Take it with him to a bloke called
Bourguignon about fifteen kilometres away and load up
the newsprint and deliver it to *La Dépêche*.'

Teddy said: 'What's that lorry? I've got a licence for three
tons.'

'Don't let that worry you, there's a good lad. I'll arrange
everything.'

'All right then, but if you promise you won't kick my sax
any more.'

'I'll kick it to pieces if you pull this off. Tomorrow you'll tell me what I've got to buy you, anu you'll have a brand new one, exactly what you want.'

Teddy scampered out and his uncle saw him off, even granting him a cheery wave.

Then he went back inside, pinched Zoë's bottom and parked his own in the best chair for the evening meal.

Travers forced Catherine to drink three full cups of black coffee, so that she was capable of following up her initiative.

He watched her make the call and listen. Her eyes were wet when she said: 'Super! You did it! Just a moment.'

She told Travers: '*Papa's* got some, it's only one metre sixty and it's a bit glossy.'

'Should be all right, but how much?'

'Ten tons.'

'Wonderful. Tell him we're in a hurry.'

She went back to her father: 'That's fine, *papa*. You're really someone. I send you a million kisses.'

Catherine flung herself at Travers, and they did a little dance.

'It's mayor Jerome's paper.'

Travers wagged his head: 'You're so right, your dad's really someone.'

An hour later Teddy pulled the lorry onto the wrong side of the road, heaved the wheel back the other way and drove round to the rear of *La Dépêche*. Albertas followed in his Mercedes.

At the loading bank, Florence was waiting with virtually the entire staff. The men had the first reel on the travelling crane within sixty seconds, and the foreman slit the thick brown paper covering with a knife to see what the paper was like. Albertas joined Florence and they stood awaiting the verdict, two bosses anxious for their project to succeed.

'The shmidt'll dig offset?' the foreman asked a man.

'Yeah, but we'll have to densify.'

Florence murmured to Melchior: 'What's shmidt?'

'Ink.'

The other man said: 'We'll need bibs, 'cos offset . . .'

Florence looked at Albertas, suddenly humble. He was lost, too, in the technicalities.

'No good?' he asked meekly. She nodded encouragingly.

At last the foreman officially reported back to her: 'Well, *Madame*. It's paper, that's the main thing. But we've got three problems: first it's web offset, thicker, and we'll have to run in slow, then we'll have to mess about with the ink which'll take time too, and then there's the size and we'll have to do three recto/three verso instead of four. Either you give us another make-up or we dump two pages.'

Florence said: 'What do you think, Melchior?'

'We dump the two, otherwise it's eight o'clock before we're out.'

'Whereas?'

'Whereas this way we'll be ready at four,' the foreman said.

'Right, forget the two pages.'

The reels trundled on the crane towards the press.

With a huge smile Florence shook Albertas by the hand: 'You're a genius, Monsieur Kovalic. I must settle up with you at once.'

Albertas beckoned Catherine over: 'I've been paid already, *Madame*. You owe me nothing, and I'm very glad to have been of use. A pleasure, I assure you.'

The rotary began rolling and Melchior explained: 'Testing the tension, to see if the paper holds at full speed.'

Florence said: 'Keep me informed, I really must go now, I'm only just standing up. I'll call you in an hour.' Turning to Kovalic, she added: 'Many thanks indeed, Albert.' Florence left the loading bank with the editorial people.

Catherine was nestling into her father's arms: 'Thank you *papa*, I'm proud of you.'

Albertas grinned: 'You heard what she said? She called me Albert!'

The print workers were yelling at one another, and Catherine left the bank too. Albertas stood alone, and

Teddy unwound himself from a squatting position against an iron pillar.

'Here son,' Kovalic said, 'I've had enough too. Be a good lad and drive us home.'

He threw the car keys at Teddy, and the two of them made for the Mercedes, as the rotary reached full speed.

It was no easy task getting Catherine home. Florence produced champagne, took a sip herself and left. The others celebrated their victory, but the effect on Catherine was disastrous by all normal standards.

Once in her flat, she proceeded to peel off her clothes with magnificent gestures. They fell about her feet and when she was completely naked, she made to sit among them. Travers forced her to remain upright, led her giggling into the bathroom, put her in the bath and gave her a tepid shower all over.

'That's not nice,' she drawled, 'you're trying to drown me.'

These were her first words since leaving the office. Her Good Samaritan lifted her bodily out of the bath and enveloped her in a large towel, rubbing her down. She accepted this like a little girl. Finally she slid down onto the floor and sat with her back against the side of the bath, her legs straight out in front of her.

She recovered a little: 'I feel as if I've gone through the rotary. I've hardly slept for a week too.'

'You work too hard,' he smiled.

'It's an escape.'

Travers said: 'I know. I'll rustle up some strong coffee.'

As he moved into the kitchen she cried out uncertainly: 'What do you mean, you know? You don't know anything at all, big head! Ha ha ha. Big head!'

'Oh yes I do,' he shouted back conversationally. 'You've had a mite too much to drink, you've patched it up with your dad, and you're fed up with Chateauvallon.'

'Ho! Aren't you clever! Big head!'

'You're joking.'

She appeared at the kitchen door draped in the bathtowel.

He told her: 'Don't you think I'm fed up here too?'

'Ah,' she said. 'Tell me more.'

'We'll have a little flat in the 15th arrondissement, you'll make sure I have a clean shirt, darn my socks, fill in the Social Security forms. When I'm hungry you'll put a frozen pizza in the oven. Saturdays we'll go for a stroll in the Bois de Boulogne, but otherwise we'll hardly see each other, just leave notes for each other on the kitchen table. After a year you'll write a book about it, and it'll be a best seller!'

He took two cups of coffee into the main room, and she followed him like a lamb: 'What on earth are you talking about?'

'Sit down and drink this, it's got salt in it.'

She obeyed, and then spluttered, putting her cup on the table: 'It's disgusting!'

'Keep drinking.'

She shook her head, grinned at him and with shining eyes wriggled onto his lap, letting the bathtowel do what it wanted.

Perking up, she ordered: 'André, dear André, you've got to get me out of all this. You've got to leave as well. We're both lost on the sea-bed and we only have to give a big kick and we'll come up to the surface again. We'll do it together.'

Catherine kissed him again and again all around his neck, rubbing her hands over his chest, pressing his muscle pads.

'We'll swim to the shore together, is that it?' he said with a smile.

'You mustn't laugh, Travers. Kiss me, Travers, kiss me and make love to me. I've been alone for two years, lived like a nun, I've forgotten what it's like. Oh Travers I want you now so much. Love me.'

Without her realizing it he had already begun to, tenderly, reverently. He moved awkwardly, she uncoiled and they found themselves on the floor using her cast-off garments as a bed.

Artus penetrated Florence's office while she was phoning

521

late one evening. She blew him a kiss, and opened her eyes to mark her appreciation. He looked like a million dollars, and his mischievous smile sent a shock wave through her loins. He took a seat.

'Yes I know he's in the Assemblée,' she was saying with fire in her throat. 'It's tricky for you, but for me it's a matter of survival, d'you hear! Calm down? Certainly I will not!'

She twisted the amplifier control and signed for Balestra to listen. Armand boomed out: 'I told you I don't want any ripples. It's the wrong moment for me, and in any case it will serve no purpose. He will deny it outright.'

She retorted: 'So I just do nothing?'

'That'll be a change for you.'

'In other words you're leaving me high and dry.'

'Flo, you're a lawyer, you know as well as I do that he's covered by parliamentary privilege. With the present government there's no chance of getting him out of the Assemblée.'

'Damn Boulard! You're pretty cynical, I must say. Where are your principles?'

'Look,' her brother exclaimed, 'you can't make a fuss about a bit of paper in the Loire. You're being ridiculous.'

'Really? A little matter of 900,000 francs if we hadn't found replacement supplies.'

'Well you found it, so what are you worried about?'

'And the next jape will be what? A pack of dynamite in the rotary?'

'Calm down Flo, for goodness sake. I'll see if I can have a word with him.'

'Is he that hard to get at?'

'He's a busy man.'

'Don't I know it!'

'I can't alter his character.'

'That's very obvious. I thought at least I could count on my own brother. Goodnight!'

Balestra was lighting a cigar when she finished. He told her: 'I think he's right, you know. He's squirmy, though. How do you really get on together?'

'He thinks of himself all the time.'

'Nothing wrong in that, but he can still spare a thought for others.'

'He can't. You can see for yourself.'

Artus raised a philosophical arm: 'Thus you have at last understood. I always knew it, but I said nothing, left you to work it out for yourself. He's changing sides, your little brother. I suspect he wants the town hall here, and he's prepared to pay the price.'

Florence stared at him: 'D'you honestly think he's going over to them?'

'A matter of cause and effect. When your back's to the wall, you have to jump over it, or face the music.'

She wrinkled up her nose: 'What do you advise me to do?'

'I suggest you turn the key in the door and close the curtains.' In point of fact he immediately did it himself, and she sank into his arms, hungry for his kisses. It seemed to her, even so, that their relationship was not one of mindless passion, it was much deeper.

They spent the night together in her hide-away apartment, but when Artus left she went to La Commanderie. To change clothes but more importantly to try and understand her so-distant daughter, to request her comprehension in so many words. How she longed for a natural ease between them, between mother and daughter. Would it ever happen? Of course, she told herself, she should have got down to reading her ex-husband's diary. That might have helped.

Thankfully, their meeting led to no row or tears this time. Alexandra evidently heard her arrive and came to her room. She glanced at the manuscript still lying on the dressing table, exactly where she put it days before.

She picked it up: 'I think I'll send this back to New York, Barnes is pulling his hair out over it. No, don't say anything, I don't want to know. I'm not angry, *maman*.'

'You mustn't be. I love you, you know that.'

'I'll try to remember it.'

Florence found it hard to be angry. Alexandra was nasty sometimes but she was also attractive, enchanting, vulnerable, tough, courageous. Exactly like herself.

Her daughter added: 'I'd like to read you one more passage, it's about you and your brother Armand: "He can do roughly anything with her, but she's ready for it and seems to experience a kind of jubilation about it. Last evening he refused to lend her the money for that car. Today he stood up to her, then said on the phone he had given the money to someone who did not really need it. The someone was a woman we all know who eats three times a day or more. Flo told her brother he was absolutely right, she adopts his view, justifies what he did, comforts him and then she started offering money. And he did not refuse it. A moment ago when she dropped off to sleep she told me we must know how to love traitors, they need it more than others".'

Alexandra put the sheets in order again. Florence had listened without a word, seated stiffly in a small armchair, watching her daughter with an expression of astonishment.

'Why do you read that to me today? Why specially today?'

'I don't know. I didn't know it would affect you specially today. There are stacks of other bits like that.'

'That one's enough, *ma chérie*.'

Florence went into the bathroom and ran the taps. When she came back, Alexandra had gone.

Maryse and Jean-Jacques were ruminating the business of the newsprint in the Loire. Bernard Kovalic was absent, called to Paris by Boulard.

'Wouldn't surprise me if he got rid of him,' Jean-Jacques said at one point. 'He calls people in to give them a job or to fire them. There's trouble brewing, Maryse, you'll find yourself out of a job again, and it'll be my fault for dragging you into this place.'

He had spoken in short bursts, his hands clenching and unclenching on his belly. Suddenly he fell out of the chair and uttered a desperate cry.

'What's the matter?' Maryse said, squatting down to him.

'I let my sister down for no reason at all. I'll get the blame for it all. Oh God!'

She knelt cradling his head. Jean-Jacques looked dreadful and was staring vacantly.

'I'll call an ambulance, you need attention.'

'Not the hospital, I won't go there,' he mumbled. 'Les Glycines, at least it's in the fam . . .'

He could manage nothing more. Maryse called an ambulance and then Marie-Lou. Then she realized that Berg had actually passed out.

She took his shoes off, loosened his tie and put his overcoat on him.

He had always been weak, she reflected.

Nobody would have denied that, but this time it was genuinely physical. He had hepatitis B.

Armand informed him: 'It doesn't look good in your case, you've always been short of red corpuscles. If we don't take you in hand, it's curtains for you, J-J Berg. Absurd at your age.'

'Can't you do anything?'

'Don't worry, it's already in hand, old chap. But I need your help.'

Jean-Jacques released a heavy sigh: 'Armand, I lack the will to live, I've never done anything but mess things up.' Then changing his mood. 'It'll be awful not seeing Flo again, not seeing you. I need her, and you too.'

Armand disregarded his depressed state. He said: 'Marie-Lou's here, perhaps you'd like to see her.'

Jean-Jacques gripped his brother's hand: 'Not now. Tell me, d'you think people can genuinely make a new start in life?'

'That's a big question. But I swear I'll get you through this.'

'This? What do you mean?'

'Don't talk so much. You've got to rest.'

Outside in the corridor, he instructed Fernandez to keep a close watch on the sedimentation rate. The patient's condition was serious, though there was a big mental factor. Fernandez noted this, and told him his sister-in-law

525

was in his office.

'D'you want to see him?' Armand asked. She was waiting patiently on the couch, looking smart.

'Not now.'

Armand frowned. Why ever did they get married, he wondered.

'He's got hepatitis B,' he told her.

She said disdainfully: 'Boulard called Kovalic to Paris, and he thinks it's the beginning of the end. He believes he'll have to take the rap. So he gets ill, that's his way out.'

'Yes, I suppose. But it's serious, you know. We'll be lucky if we pull him through, frankly. You're very fond of him?'

'He's my husband. I'll be sad if he dies.'

'So will I. He's my brother.'

'We'll be sad,' she added, crossing her legs the other way, and glancing at Armand.

'How about a quickie?' he said.

'Is there time?'

'We'll find it.'

He pulled her up, and her face was transformed. She ran her tongue over her lips and a gleam entered her eyes. Armand deftly undid her blouse and she unclipped her bra. He played with the hem of her skirt for a moment, caressed her knees and thighs, finally unbuttoning her skirt band and undoing the zip. The skirt fell to the floor and she parted her legs.

Marie-Lou had nothing on beneath the skirt. This did not surprise Armand, and certainly did not deter him.

Bernard Kovalic was a changed man. Boulard treated him like a dog when he was shown into his grandiose Paris office suite.

In taking over as Boulard's man at *L'Eveil*, the Harvard graduate had supposed that he was a member of the Boulard 'gang', and that he would acquire power in one of the swiftest ways open to young men in France. He meant real power. But he had come to realize that, by sapping his strength and humiliating him, the press baron had taken away the very character that had impressed even Albertas and given him his look of steel.

Contemptuous and crude, Boulard charged him with failing to bed Alexandra Wilson, failing to be a drinker or a smoker, failing to smile and look successful. In a word he was a beaten man before he started, Boulard told him.

In a last-ditch bid to acquire some stature, Bernard started to tell Boulard about the dollars and his uncle's goings on, but Boulard waved all that away: 'Small stuff, Kovalic. You should write a crime story about it. Now get the hell out of here. You're a creep, a youngster of no substance, and you give me the willies. Go on, off with you, I don't want to see you!'

Outside, as he walked aimlessly down Boulevard Malesherbes, not seeing the fashionable shops and the symbols of elegance in perhaps the world's most fascinating capital, Kovalic wondered whatever had gone wrong. His great plans had run into the sand, and he was still puzzled as to how it had come about. He comprehended neither Boulard nor his uncle Albertas, and at the same time they certainly failed to understand him. They seemed to fear him as well as laughing at him, as if they too were unsure of themselves. The whole business was a mystery.

Back in Chateauvallon he went straight to the farm. He drove into the yard with immense reluctance, but the place drew him.

Albertas was on his own, reading a newspaper and smoking one of his small cigars. On the table to one side were a bottle of slivovitz and a jug of water. The old man seemed to welcome company, for he laid down the paper and studied Bernard as he entered the room, looking the picture of misery.

'Hullo then, boy,' he said. 'You don't look too pleased with yourself. Some days you're bound to feel under the weather. I'm a bit like that myself; I was just thinking that dying must be like going to the market and suddenly you find there ain't no *basilic* any more. And you're dead. You look for tomatoes, leeks, melons, but what you're really after is *basilic*. And you're too late.' Albertas ended with a little chuckle.

The younger man ignored his ramblings. He said: 'I'm going back to America.'

'They've thrown you out of that paper?'

'Good as.'

'Will they pay you any severance money?'

'Don't know, couldn't care less.'

Bernard went to the window and looked out on the yard. Whereas the farmhouse had something of a petty bourgeois air about it after all these years, the yard was still a dirty mixture of chicken crap, mud and embedded stones, with straw and fowls and the pigs for ever grunting and squealing. In the States he had acquired big ideas, but perhaps it had been a mistake. He should have stayed here. At one stage that morning Boulard had said: 'Funny idea of your uncle to send you to Harvard, funny for a rag and bone man. Like the Prince of Wales walking about in a jellaba.' The shaft had struck home, and as he thought about it again, he hated Boulard. Especially as he was probably right; Harvard had simply turned him into a stateless person!

His uncle was prattling on: 'I got a great pleasure out of them there letters you wrote us. Told myself I didn't throw money down the drain sending you over there. Then you came back, you came back to us . . .'

'Well, I'm going back now.'

'Don't forget to say goodbye then.'

Bernard again ignored him: 'That fellow sleeping with Catherine, the journalist, I'm sure he knows everything.'

'What's the matter?'

'It means you'll look pretty silly sooner or later. He works for the Berg woman.'

Albertas beamed: 'She won't hurt me, especially if you keep your trap shut. Trouble is you can't stop shooting your mouth off.'

'That difficulty's settled, since I'm going back.'

His uncle's face twisted and he shook his head: 'For two pins I'd pull you back by your braces. You're a traitor, a traitor in the family. Never thought I'd see that when I got to sixty-four. Be off with you! Clear out before I feed you to the pigs—if they want you!'

'You make me sick, Albertas. I'm off!'

Bernard realized his uncle was simply laying it on thick, playing a part. But the thought failed to solve his own problem. Perhaps for the first time in his life, he experienced real solitude with no one to turn to. He was opening his car door when Teddy breezed up.

'My mother's brought out the earthenware pot. Yours has bought three kinds of meat, some pigs' feet, a big ham . . .'

Bernard snapped: 'You know what you can do with it.'

'She's going to make some *lonac*, that means. Cousin Djilas says she makes the best in the world, so that means . . .'

'That crook's on his way? Be careful Teddy. Be on your guard, and watch out.'

Bernard slid behind the wheel, and Teddy waved as the BMW slewed out through the gate.

Chapter Eleven

Of old Gregor's three grandchildren, Catherine was undeniably the bravest, the one with most spiritual muscle, and the one with her feet on the ground.

Catherine had had the guts to break away from the Kovalic clan at a moment of her own choosing. She had lived her own life ever since, and more especially had resurfaced eventually some time after the murder of the man she loved, Paul Bossis.

Not only that. Over two years, she had lucidly observed the tumult of events involving *La Dépêche* and the town hall. Her overall conclusion was that the bonds with her family were closer than her behaviour led everyone to believe; she would not betray her father, but she was scared for him. As to herself, she resolved to quit Chateauvallon to avoid being drawn into the rumpus ahead, and she wanted Travers with her. Travers knew what he was doing.

The other two grandchildren, Teddy and Bernard, were as confused as Catherine was clear-sighted. Teddy was distraught with unrequited love for Alexandra, and Bernard was like a one-legged man trying to climb a ladder. Doubtless because they knew she was the most level-headed of the three, the two young men clung to Catherine. Finally Alexandra, another lost soul, felt the need of her counsel.

So it was that on the day Bernard fell out with both Boulard and Albertas, she rang Catherine's bell and invited herself in for a chat. Confiding in Catherine, she ended up weeping in her arms, ultimately curling up asleep on her settee.

Shortly afterwards Teddy phoned, and asked if he could

pop in. Catherine explained that she had a visitor and he would have to come another day.

Then Bernard stomped up the stairs, banged on the door and shouted. She told him to come back when he had less of a sore head. The total silence that followed this injunction so preyed on her mind that she gingerly unlocked the door, took the chain off and glanced out, to see Bernard sitting on the stairs like a man who had lost his keys and was waiting for the locksmith.

'Go away,' she said in a loud whisper, 'I can't see you tonight.'

'Aren't we friends any more?'

'I've got another friend in.'

'Your father?'

'No. Now clear off!' To tell the truth she had had enough of Bernard; he worked for Boulard, had a jumpy mind, and had forced upon her the news of her father's misdoings whether she wanted it or not. 'Get out, I say!'

At this, Bernard got to his feet and rushed for the door, but she managed to close it in time. She stood behind it trembling for a while, expecting him to try battering it down, and then heard him clatter down the stairs. Seconds after that, Teddy phoned again, and on hearing his voice she replaced the receiver without a word. Then she called the Bijou-Bar and told Travers to come quickly.

She watched for him from the window and opened the door before he had a chance to ring the bell. Catherine put a finger to her lips and pulled him into the bedroom.

'What's going on?' he rasped.

'Bernard came, but I didn't let him in. I was afraid he'd break the door down. Have you seen him?'

'No.'

'He didn't look normal to me. Sort of wild.'

Travers said: 'I thought you were buddies.'

She shrugged: 'He's got something going, but Lord knows what.'

The journalist found a chair, lit a cigarette and said: 'He's concealing something, that's a certainty. Any ideas?'

Catherine lay back on the bed, and Travers went and

squatted next to it, drawing little circles with his fingertip round her nipples. He said: 'And what are you concealing?'

'I've nothing to hide, André,' she lied, rubbing her face in his sweater.

'Why are we keeping our voices down?'

'Alexandra's asleep in there. Down in the dumps. Wanted a natter.'

Travers said: 'Huh, I saw a youngster hiding up behind a car outside. Could be Teddy.'

'He phoned twice. Now you see why I needed you. I think they reckon I'm the Salvation Army.'

Travers crept into the room, looked at Alexandra a moment and slunk back: 'You must be a lovely person, Kate, everyone likes you.'

She led him into the kitchen, got a whisky bottle and ice cubes and glasses: 'Pour them out, I'm fed up with being an emergency service. It's got to stop.'

'Are you going to come clean?'

'Me? I'm clearing out,' she said, not answering the question.

'I know, with me. But not before you tell me what I ought to know.'

Irritated at being found out, but still brazen, she said: 'You don't believe anyone, it's a sickness with you.'

'No one would ever think you've slept with at least two journalists!'

Catherine's eyes shone with anger at this reference to Paul, but she had no time to speak. Teddy came on the line again.

'No, Teddy,' she said quietly but firmly. 'I can't see you and Alexandra's not here.'

Before she could put the receiver back, Travers grabbed it and said: 'This is Travers, come up Teddy. I'll open up for you.'

Catherine was beside herself. As he rang off she spat out: 'That's clever of you!'

'Better he comes up than rings every ten minutes.' She sighed, and he took her hands in his. 'Let me deal with him, but before he gets here tell me what's going on and why Bernard is in such a stew. I can keep it quiet, you know me.' She shook her head. 'As you wish.'

When Teddy arrived, Travers opened up and told him: 'Come in, don't make a noise, sit down and don't move.'

The boy did all this, and then saw Alexandra. He shot a severe look at his cousin. Travers asked if he'd like a drink.

'Yes, something to make me sleep. Fix it so I don't wake up!'

'Keep your voice down.'

'It doesn't matter as she's not here.' He glowered at Catherine.

'Listen . . .' Travers began.

Teddy sneered: 'That's all I've been doing for twenty-two years. What patience! What was he doing here just now, ugly mug? He only stayed three minutes. What can he do in three minutes?'

'Get himself thrown out!'

'Ah, that's not nice between cousins, and it's an awkward moment too. D'you know that, Travers? It's awkward.'

Travers realized that Teddy was the worse for drink: 'Take it easy Teddy.'

But Teddy stood up and grabbed them both by their clothes: 'I got news for you, ol' friend. We're a united family, it don't always look like it, but we're solid as concrete, ain't that so Catherine? Your dad's a treat, he is, a real father.' He brayed like a calf. 'I'm Teddy, you're the whore, and Travers is the customer!'

Catherine's hand flashed to her cousin's cheek. While Teddy had been mouthing his words, Alexandra had woken up and now stood looking at the three of them with her chin down. Teddy bowed low to the others.

'Roll up, roll up,' he cried, forcing the tone. 'It's a free show. He'll eat his hat if you asked him. But he's a new clown and you gotta help him.' He seized Catherine's glass and polished it off. 'Gotta help him, gotta help him!' Teddy then sank to the floor like an injured ballet dancer.

'Pull yourself together,' Travers said, holding his arm in an iron grip.

'I would do, but I know you don't like the show, so I'm carrying on with it.'

Travers hauled him towards the door: 'Not much longer, you won't!'

Alexandra shrieked: 'No, Travers!'

Everyone froze, and Teddy at last fell at her feet.

She ordered: 'You stop too. Stand up for yourself, but stop making an exhibition, stop squawking. I only came here to get some rest, not to move in. I haven't slept properly since I was born, and it was you who told me, remember. Look at me Teddy. You're a fine chap, and I'm a lousy intellectual, you said that too. Give me time to catch you up, just give me time. Then who knows, we'll get together again, Teddy, you believe that, don't you?'

It was no good. Teddy, his cheeks bright with tears, looked at her for a long while, and then said thickly: 'Goodbye!'

He let himself out and bundled down the stairs.

'Teddy!' cried Travers from the doorway. 'Teddy!'

The main iron door to the street clanged to and it was too late to get him back.

The next day Bernard left his apartment. He drove to within 500 metres of the Kovalic farm and turned off into a dirt road that led to a spinney. He parked the car under some trees and went along a tiny track across a field lying fallow to the farm.

Behind the house was a wall, long and with no way in except for some small windows and a door to a cellar. He tried the handle to the door and was relieved to find that it opened. Here, many years ago he had played scary and fabulous games with Catherine and Teddy. He knew every inch of the walls, the floor and the roof. He knew also that Albertas had had an electric light fixed up, but he had no need of this to find the stairs going up to the kitchen.

He was scared now. Bernard did not have a plan, he had

534

simply got the idea of going into the farm by the back. The kitchen was void of life except for the earthenware pot with the *lonac* bubbling away, giving off a good odour of hot wine and herbs. The table was full and there was a big pile of plates and knives and forks in a basket. The dining room was empty too, and he went over to the glazed double doors and, without moving the curtains, looked through the crochetwork into the yard.

Everyone was there, although as usual Gregor had not gone out it seemed. By the pigsties was a BMW car with a Trieste numberplate. Albertas, Djilas and Marko were bending over, looking into the open boot, while Zoë, Marfa and Teddy were a few paces behind them. Albertas shouted something and the two women joined the others, taking out two leather bags like the ones Teddy had seen and described to Bernard. Then Albertas went towards the pigs. Teddy still had not moved; he sat down on a crate and began putting a magnificent new saxophone back into its case.

Bernard could hardly believe his eyes; it was a scene from television, he thought. Then he became alert and strode over to the gun rack, choosing a double-barrelled Remington that would have felled an ox. He knew where the rounds were kept, in one of the sideboard drawers. He slid two rounds in, and went back to the double doors, flinging them open.

'Nobody move!!!' he yelled, bringing up the gun. 'Put the bags back in the car, and drive off. I won't have that here, nor will Albertas! Jump to it!!!'

Teddy put the saxophone down and stood up. Djilas, Marko and the two women froze but held on to the bags. Bernard advanced towards them.

Albertas emerged from the pigsties: 'Stop that, you dunderhead. Give me that gun!!!' He moved deliberately towards Bernard. 'Give me the gun!'

Teddy also took a step or two towards Bernard.

'You gone mad, yankee?' Djilas said, and he produced a fat revolver from inside his jacket.

Bernard aimed and fired over his head. Albertas and

Teddy kept coming on, and the boy veered off, evidently intending to approach Bernard from the side. Djilas parted his legs, held his gun with two hands, aiming at Bernard's head.

'No!!!' Zoë shrieked.

'No!!!' Albertas barked, spinning round.

'You're crackers!' Marko shouted at his brother. He jogged Djilas's arm as the shot went off, the bullet missed Bernard and struck Teddy who spun round on himself and fell on his back.

'Holy Mother!!!' Djilas roared.

Marfa sank to her knees and covered her face, unable to look at her son. Albertas and Zoë ran to the boy, and Marko rushed at Bernard, who let fall the Remington.

Marko punched Bernard repeatedly, shouting: 'It's your fault, you bloody idiot, look what you've done!!!'

'Leave it,' Albertas ordered. 'You'll settle that later. Teddy's losing blood.'

Zoë peeled open Teddy's shirt. The bullet had gone right through his chest, and blood was pouring from both holes.

Marfa was praying: 'Don't take him, merciful God! Or take me with him!'

Marko kicked Bernard in the groin, sending him in agony to the ground.

'Call an ambulance,' Albertas told Marko. 'It's marked SAMU next to the phone. Don't give any details, just say it's a serious accident.'

Zoë began tearing her apron into strips and covering the wound on the boy's front. He squirmed and managed to say: 'Don't throw out the sax, don't give it away. Let Alex . . .'

His eyes rolled and locked.

'He's dead!' Zoë said.

'Dead!' Marfa cried, running to him. 'Oh God, you've taken my only son!' She smothered his hand with kisses.

Djilas had remained motionless, but when the truth sank in he threw himself on the ground. He said thickly: 'I've killed Teddy, the boy I loved!'

536

Albertas took full command at this point: 'Git up Djilas. Give me your revolver, and find the bullet. You never killed him, you understand. He killed himself.'

Marko came out of the house: 'No, say it was an accident. He was cleaning the revolver.'

'That's better,' Albertas agreed. 'We've got to find the round from the rifle, and clean the rifle. I'll do that. You people, get away as fast as you can. Disappear!'

'The bags!' Djilas remembered.

'I'll see to them. Clear off quick and drive as fast as you can. I'll be in touch. Don't phone me, whatever you do!'

Marko was already on his way to the car and he grabbed Djilas. He then slammed the car boot shut, ignoring the bag still inside. Within sixty seconds the car was away.

Albertas searched for and found the bullet from the revolver, then he ran back. He had the bullet in his handkerchief, and carefully placed it one metre from Teddy's body. Djilas's revolver he now cleaned thoroughly and placed in Teddy's right hand. He found the rifle round and put it in his pocket.

'Nobody touch anything,' he said quietly to the others. Gregor appeared and started praying with the two women. Albertas said: 'Father, take Marfa indoors. Remember, it was an accident. He was cleaning the revolver and it went off.'

Albertas had not finished yet: 'Zoë, you come with me. Get a move on, the SAMU will be here in five minutes.'

Together they collected the bags and took them in with the pigs. Albertas pushed some straw aside and found a lid. This he took off and threw the bags down in the hole. He pushed the straw back into place.

While all this was going on, Bernard was sitting on the ground.

His uncle strode over to him and said: 'I don't know how you got in, but I want you out of here. It's all over between us now. Just get out of my sight. But remember this, get it into your stupid noddle: you never came here today, you saw nothing, you know nothing. We'll struggle along without you, but don't forget you never came here. Go on, clear out, clear out!!'

Albertas went indoors and saw the Remington starkly on the table.

Zoë came in from the kitchen: 'No time to clean it now, give it me.' She took the weapon and went.

Albertas walked into his office, and pulled the phone towards him. As he waited with the receiver to his ear, he could detect Marfa and Gregor mumbling together.

'Hullo, SRPJ,' he heard.

'Albertas Kovalic, give me Nicolo.' A pause. 'Hullo Commissaire. Something dreadful's happened here. One of my people killed himself like a fool cleaning a gun. You'd better get out here quick.

'Must be Teddy,' Pradal told Nicolo and Germain.

Inspector Germain said: 'Very likely. And he wasn't cleaning anything, he just shot him.elf. Albertas was too much for the poor little beggar.'

Nicolo's eyebrows went up: 'Possible. All right, we'd better go out there. But I want to call the deputy prosecutor first.'

This he did, summarizing what he knew so far. He added: 'I'd like Albertas's phone tapped, I don't believe a word he says, and I want to know what's going on the same moment that he does.'

'But Nicolo, you know we have to get clearance from Paris.'

'Yes, but you could forget that for five or six hours. We'll go through the formalities afterwards.'

'Just like that. And the telecoms people?'

'I'll fix them. Well, is it yes or no?'

'No, of course. But I'm still thinking about it.'

Nicolo screwed up his face and flung the receiver back. He hauled a drawer open, took out a gun and waved Pradal and Germain out to the car with him.

They reached the farm ten minutes later. As they expected, the ambulance was there and a doctor was still leaning over Teddy.

The doctor told Nicolo: 'Aorta severed by the projectile, leading to a full-scale haemorrhage. Not a hope anyway.'

'Time of death?'

'Twenty to forty minutes. He's pliable and warm, he still had a peridural reflex when we arrived. Besides he's still urinating.'

Nicolo observed this fact without emotion: 'Take your blood waggon off, we'll attend to the body.'

'Yes,' the doctor said, signing to his assistants. 'I'll do you a report for the record. There's a peculiar hardening of the top lip.'

'He played the saxophone. Very well too, they say. Doc, I'd be grateful if you'd keep this one quiet for a wee bit.'

'I'll keep quiet, and I'll tell the others but I can't exactly gag them. Oh, by the way, the gun was in the right hand, Commissaire. He was probably left-handed though.'

When the ambulance had gone, Nicolo asked Pradal: 'How does he know Teddy was left-handed?'

'I believe you can tell by the eyes, the pupils.'

'Suffering snakes, another left-hander, like Quentin, Let's hope this one's a bit easier for us. Come on, let's have a look at Albertas.'

The head of the clan was waiting for them in the doorway, dignified, upset and cautious. Nicolo and Pradal went in with him, Germain stayed outside 'to look around'.

Commissaire Nicolo began: 'Well, Monsieur Kovalic, so the boy was cleaning a Magnum 357. Not the kind of toy for a boy his age!'

Albertas looked like a bloodhound: 'In our family, guns are part of our very existence. We are born with a gun in our hands.'

'Well if you say so. How could he be so clumsy? There are six bullets in the cylinder, and he leaves them all in. Then he takes his little bit of rag and his oilcan—oh, by the by, where are they?—and he sits down in the sunshine . . .'

'Teddy loved the sunshine.'

Nicolo said quickly: 'I'd like to see the licence please.'

'Must be upstairs. Of course, we're doing some redecorating and everything's mixed up. I expect it's there. Can't remember how long we've had the old Magnum. I remember my old dad firing off at empty bottles when I was . . .'

'You must have been a big baby, Kovalic. Because that model came out only in 1965.'

Albertas stiffened for a split second, he glanced heavenwards, his nose twitched and he said blandly: 'Yus, well in '65 I must have been about thirty I suppose.'

Nicolo leaned forward, and said softly: 'If you hadn't acquired a vast fortune, Monsieur Kovalic, I would have sworn you were illiterate. In 1965 you were fifty years of age. It must have been you who shot at the bottles.'

'Fancy that now. I'm getting a bit past it these days, you know. The old nut ain't what it used to be. We've always done a lot of shooting, a great sport Monsieur Nicolo. We've got five rifles alone, apart from the rest.'

'I see only four.'

'Well, there ought to be five. But why are you asking all these questions? I'm really not in a fit state to . . .' Albertas pulled out his handkerchief, wiped his eyes and blew his nose like a trumpet. Pradal got up and prowled around the kitchen, while his superior stuffed some tobacco in his pipe.

'When did you call the SAMU?'

'Why, just after it happened of course. How should I know what time it was?'

'Who heard the shot?'

'We all did. Made a lot of noise.'

'Who do you mean by "we"? Who was here?'

'Like as usual, my old father, my two sisters-in-law, Teddy.'

'And you?'

'Of course.'

'Five people, then. With a big appetite, judging by what's on the hob there,' Pradal said coming back. 'Smells nice, Commissaire, and there's enough for a regiment.'

Albertas wiped his eyes again and whimpered: 'It's *Ionac*, one of our dishes. With five sorts of meat, plenty of

540

vegetables. We make a lot at a time, and it does for several meals.'

Pradal asked: 'The plates too, you get those ready in advance? I can see twenty-four up on the table.'

Albertas gave a casual wave: 'You'll have to ask the women about that. I don't meddle with their work.'

There was a short silence while Nicolo sniffed the *lonac*, wondering how much of the old chap's story was true.

Germain came in from the yard, and it was he who put the next question: 'What do you usually smoke, Monsieur Kovalic?'

Gaining time, Albertas said: 'I try to keep it down, you know. Got to think of my health.'

'Right, but what do you smoke. Cigars, cigarettes or what?'

'Both. It depends.'

'What brand of cigarette?'

'No special brand. I try to cut it down, as I say.'

Germain tilted his head, and observed: 'There are exactly eleven fag-ends in the yard. The brand is Nazionali. Don't see them much in the shops here.'

'My cousins bring me a few sometimes. When they came for Nestor's funeral, they left a couple of cartons. I still got one.' Albertas rose with an effort and went over to the sideboard, the same sideboard where Bernard had loaded the Remington. From a different drawer, he produced a carton of cigarettes and placed it in front of Nicolo.

Germain extracted a plastic bag from his pocket and put the cigarettes in it. He sealed it meticulously. Next to this he put a small bag containing the eleven fag-ends, and another with the bullet.

The commissaire instructed him: 'Remove the body now, and take a sample of the soil from underneath.'

The two subordinates went out, and the main protagonists faced each other.

Nicolo said at length: 'Was Teddy left-handed?'

'Don't you think you've got enough? I'm very weary.'

'The revolver was in his right hand.'

Kovalic stiffened again, and then said as cool as a

cucumber: 'Naturally, if he was left-handed he held the gun in his right hand and cleaned it with his left.'

The commissaire let out a long sigh. He said as he rose to go: 'I'll see you again tomorrow, Kovalic. None of you may leave the town until further notice.'

Later Nicolo had an envelope sent round to *La Dépêche* with his official summary of the tragedy.

Florence was away in Paris and Melchior read the sheet of paper twice, wondering why the commissaire had taken the trouble to inform the local press in this way. It had to be a pack of lies. His view was confirmed in a chat with a junior reporter who had teamed up with Teddy some years ago. The young man said Teddy was not interested in guns in the slightest. His ruling passion was the saxophone, he said.

And Alexandra, Melchior reflected. He decided to run the story in the late news section, straight but in the conditional.

Bernard's troubles were far from over. He returned to the spinney and drove off in his car, going a long way round back into town.

In some instinctive way, though he could not analyse it, he thought it wise to be seen in Chateauvallon, and went to La Grande Librairie bookshop. That was where he had first run into Alexandra. He planned to pick up some Paris newspapers and the *International Herald Tribune*.

By a disastrous coincidence, Alexandra was in there. It was impossible to avoid her as she bore down on him, smiling winningly, fiddling coquettishly, and breathing out oodles of sex appeal. She seemed not to notice Bernard's subdued air and twittered on about how she had broken off with Teddy.

He smiled back heroically and said: 'I'm sorry to hear it. I thought you got on so well. The same age and everything.'

'Age doesn't count,' she pronounced. 'Sometimes I think Teddy was already in his grave before I was born. I'll explain it some time.'

'Ah yes, I'd be interested,' he stammered, and escaped,

pretending he was in a hurry.

At *L'Eveil* it was even worse. With infinite tact, Maryse informed him that Albertas had phoned in, telling them that Teddy had died in a gun accident. Bernard had to act his astonishment and dismay as she unfolded the tale. He was amazed more than anything at his uncle's cheek and sang-froid. He excused himself and went to the toilet, where he vomited. He emerged with sweat on his brow, and Maryse nursed him, making some herbal tea.

But eventually she said: 'Boulard ought to be told.' She put the call through and negotiated the distant switchboard and a couple of secretaries. When Maryse handed him the receiver he took it as in a dream.

'Good evening,' he said. 'Kovalic here.'

'Yes? What's the matter, you sound peculiar.'

'My cousin shot himself cleaning a gun this morning.'

'That's some news!' the other barked. 'Does *La Dépêche* know?'

'That's something I can't say. I don't suppose so.'

'I hope you're right. Anyhow, whatever you've got on the front page, scrap it and you . . .'

'Yes?'

'Do you really think it was an accident?'

'What else?'

'Suicide of course. How old was he?'

'Twenty-two.'

'Just the age,' Boulard cried triumphantly.

'Monsieur Boulard!'

'What's up? Feeling sorry about it?'

'Of course, does it surprise you?'

'Sorry, old fellow. But you'll stick it on the front page. Your cousin killed himself, and you'll put the whole blame on Florence Berg. The line is that she's been persecuting your family for months and so on and so on.'

'But it wasn't suicide, Monsieur!'

'They look alike. Here's your chance to get back at Madame Berg, it's handed to you on a plate!'

'But . . .'

'There's no but, old fellow. It's an order. Have you

forgotten why I took you on? You've produced enough mess already, and it's time you did something right!'

'It's scandalous what you're suggesting!'

'Scandalous or not, that's how it's got to be. Goodnight!'

Maryse, who had listened in on an extension, said: 'That's all Jean-Jacques needs in the state he's in.'

'In his state he'll know nothing about it,' Bernard said with force. 'As to my state . . . anyway, take this down: Teddy Kovalic's last words were: "Thank you, Monsieur Boulard!"'

'You can't put that,' she protested.

Bernard slumped: 'Of course not. But I've got no choice. Write A KOVALIC SUICIDE. Four columns in the boldest you've got. Begin: As the result of racist persecution against an immigrant family by a large regional newspaper . . .'

Maryse objected again: 'Oh no! If Boulard wanted to sink us he couldn't do better than that.'

'Maybe he does want to sink us. Or he's nuts. Anyway he's the boss.'

When they had finished Maryse said: 'You know I'm rather glad Jean-Jacques is in hospital. At least he is escaping this lot.'

Bernard scowled at her: 'Add another bit: You cannot play with fire and get away with it. Today's tragedy is cruel proof of this basic fact, and . . .'

Travers and Florence were awake early the next morning. At 7.00 a.m. they had *L'Eveil* spread out on a desk.

Travers had taken it upon himself to tell Alexandra the news on the previous evening. He had searched for her at La Commanderie, at Julien's house, at Catherine's place. Finally he ran her to earth at La Grange disco, dancing with people he did not know. With infinite precaution he had broken it to her step by step, but the girl had wailed horrifically outside before crumpling onto the car park mud in drenching rain. He had taken her home and Mathilde had looked after her, giving her sleeping pills.

As far as he knew she was still asleep as he and Florence

contemplated Bernard's moral strictures.

'I would not care to be in Bernard Kovalic's shoes,' Travers murmured, casting his eye down the columns once more.

'When Jean-Jacques reads that . . .'

'He has the excuse that he is gravely ill, but for Bernard to accept an order like that he must be as much of a bastard as Boulard. I don't get it. With all the Kovalic wealth behind him, surely he doesn't need to lick Boulard's boots to that extent.'

Florence scratched her ear: 'I'm certain now that Boulard is off his rocker. This proves it for me. The man's mad.'

'What's Albertas going to say when he sees this?'

'And Alexandra!'

'I wish we could keep it from her. Last night she kept saying it was all her fault, she was in a shocking state, cried her heart out. But I know he didn't kill himself because of her.'

'Is that your honest opinion?'

'He wouldn't have done it. I saw them the other night at Catherine's place. They had words, but she constantly told him there was a future for them. There's something else behind this, the whole thing stinks.'

'What does Nicolo say?'

'His lips are clamped tight. He's working on it as I've never seen him work before. He's on to something big, Flo.'

'He informed us officially.'

'Might suit him. Doesn't want us to start nosing around, so he gives us a statement. I honestly couldn't say. I have a feeling he rather likes us after all.'

'Possibly. Be an angel and pour me a whisky. I didn't sleep a wink last night after Mathilde told me. Perhaps I'll have a brandy instead. I feel sick.'

'*L'Eveil?*'

'No, Teddy himself. He was only twenty-two, he used my house as if he owned it and I wasn't too keen on him, but . . .'

'Of course.' He had two brandies ready and they drank

545

them together as if it were medicine. He felt groggy too, not least because he still had to break the news to Catherine. Another blow for her, that would be.

The switchboard put the public prosecutor through. It was to tell Florence that a large percentage of the copies of *L'Eveil* had been seized as she had requested. He told her roughly 3,000 to 4,000 had got through.

'Huh,' Travers snorted. 'Doesn't happen often; one paper getting another seized.'

He glanced up at Florence and there was no mistaking the gleam in her eyes.

Inspector Pradal called on Albertas Kovalic, who heard his car and stood at the door to welcome him. Albertas looked as if he had lost some sleep, but he held himself well.

He demanded of Pradal: 'When are we going to have Teddy back? We have a vigil for the dead, it's our custom. We give them a good funeral. His mother's out of her mind. How much longer is this autopsy thing going to last?'

'Couldn't say,' Pradal answered. 'It's not just the autopsy, there's the inquiry.'

'Yes, of course. I'll have to explain that to poor Marfa.'

'You see, Monsieur Kovalic, there's a hitch. The Magnum 357 is a fearsome weapon. If someone fires it at himself at point blank range, there ought to be a huge deposit of powder all around the wound and on the clothing.'

'Ah.'

'On your boy there was absolutely no trace.'

'Perhaps there wasn't much powder, they were old bullets.'

'Interesting. How do you know they were old?'

'Well, I don't,' the older man rumbled. 'I'm just trying to find an explanation, like you are.'

Pradal continued: 'Those cigarettes too, the Italian ones. The tobacco was manufactured a year after the tobacco in your carton of cigarettes.'

For some moments Kovalic had been pulling at an

imaginary beard on his chin. Now his hand moved to his neck, which he scratched. Pradal was smiling in a kindly way but the old man knew he was in trouble this time. 'You move very fast,' he said noncommittally. 'Got to think of everything. Splitting hairs, it's our job. It's all part of the routine.'

Kovalic's attention was elsewhere, some yards away in the pigsties where Zoë was feeding the grunters. It was his business, but the two women sometimes did it, if he was away, for example. Zoë was on her own today, and she suddenly let out a piercing cry, and the pigs were squealing now.

'Excuse me a moment,' Albertas said, going over to the sties. Pradal followed him, and saw that one of the pigs had got out and was charging about in the yard. Zoë held the gate closed to stop any more escaping. Pradal moved like lightning and grabbed the loose pig by the ears, hanging on for dear life. He got it back in the pen, and the noise died down.

Recovering his breath Pradal jested: 'You ought to put that one in for the one thousand metres.'

The owner of the pig quipped back: 'You'd beat him every time. Ha ha ha!'

They were standing in with the pigs, and Pradal chivvied the straw about a bit. Then he said: 'Sounds hollow there.'

'The manure pit,' Albertas said quickly. 'Got a pump and everything, cost a fortune but I'd do anything for my pigs.'

'Like to see it some day,' Pradal responded.

'Bring your gas mask,' Albertas shouted after him as he made for his car. 'See *L'Eveil* this morning?'

'How could I? It was seized!'

'Imagine my own nephew doing that to me!'

'He's not his own master,' Pradal said. 'It's another generation, they've got no morals.'

Albertas made sure he really had gone before leaving the main gate. 'Zoë,' he told his sister-in-law, 'we got trouble again. Make sure you have a good nap this afternoon, I'm going to need you tonight.'

Zoë asked no questions. Since her husband's death she merely took orders from Albertas. She was a good worker too: splitting logs, hoeing the garden, feeding the pigs and almost anything else a man could do. But on Sundays and public holidays she dressed up as a lady, complete with the ring Albertas had given her.

Even so, she never imagined she would have to do what she did that night. Just after 1.00 a.m. they drove together in the Mercedes to one of the dumps on the town's edge. Both of them wore gumboots and Zoë had a big scarf over her head, while her brother-in-law had an old trilby jammed well down over his head. From the car boot they pulled out the two leather bags the Trieste brothers had left, and dragged them to a point several metres into the rubbish. Albertas got a spade from the car and dug out a hole in the compacted garbage. That is where he placed the bags' contents, spilling out thousand of marks, guilders, lire and dollars—more dollars than the rest. He got them into a kind of nest, making sure there was plenty of air circulating around the banknotes. While he was attending to this, Zoë took the bags back to the car and returned with a jerrican of petrol. Albertas poured the canful onto the notes and set fire to the nest egg.

The pair stared at the flames, mesmerized by the fortune disappearing under their eyes. Albertas had the satisfaction of thinking that it was less than the money he had made over the years handling the town's rubbish.

'It's like magic,' he breathed.

'Yes, but I never thought I'd live to see it,' his accomplice murmured. 'It's getting cold, feels like rain, and Marfa's on her own with the old chap. Let's be off.'

Albertas took her arm affectionately, and helped her as they staggered back over the uneven waste. They took their boots off and got in the car, not speaking until they reached the farm.

The flames were less bright at the dump by now. Most of the banknotes were only half burned, and many fluttered up and fell back in a wide circle like dying butterflies.

Then, as Zoë had said, it began raining. Gradually the fire hissed until it went out. Burned, wet or both, the notes were all unrecognizable by the dawn. Or almost.

Alexandra was more deeply forlorn over Teddy's death than most people realized, saying as they did that she was young and would soon get over it. But she found a valued friend in Artus Balestra.

Florence's instinct from the moment she had met him now proved sounder than ever. He refused to take life too seriously, it was true, but for those in sorrow he had the gift of bringing consolation with the precisely appropriate blend of sympathy and encouragement. Her mother cursed Bernard for his despicable handling of the tragedy, which engraved the scene on Alexandra's mind for ever. Florence beseeched Artus to come to La Commanderie one evening and have a talk with the girl.

As may be imagined, Alexandra was mute at first, refusing to discuss Teddy or how she felt. Artus paid several visits, perceiving from the few words she uttered that her dismay and confusion dated from well before Teddy's 'suicide'. It went back to her childhood and the appalling rows between her parents, to the years she spent with her mother living in fear and horror of grandpa Antonin and his autocratic ways. At length, little by little, Artus won her confidence and he learned an important thing: that, despite her decision to stay with her father in the United States, she had been no happier with him. In the early months she had been heady with the freedom he allowed her, and then increasingly she had grown afraid of his easygoing morality, confused over his whims and those of his many friends and associates. They were all brilliant people like her father but they shared his taste for folly, nihilism and mental perversion. That was her word, perversion, and when the truth dawned on her she 'wanted out'. Alexandra had tried to kill herself in God's own country.

Her revelations and feelings began tumbling out and Artus merely had to listen in the end. Finally she began blaming herself, wishing she had done this or that, and then sobbed once or twice in his arms saying there was nobody she could trust any more.

Artus knew at that point that she was well on the road to recovery. And he told Florence so.

Inspector Pradal, who was not all that much older than Teddy, had once heard him play the saxophone and had been impressed. It was a stormy evening when he had to make some enquiries at the disco. Perhaps it was because of this, because the boy was at least trying to get something out of life and better himself, that Pradal had a soft spot for him. Thus, he conducted his investigation with special care. Nicolo was being extra thorough too, but for other reasons.

Their concern brought them together in spirit within a day or two of the shooting, when they received a telex message via Interpol.

It told them that the Magnum 357 that killed Teddy had also killed a *carabiniere* a month previously in Turin during an abortive robbery, the authors of which were still on the run. The message was clear: the weapon had a slight defect that had transmitted itself to the two bullets.

'God Almighty!' Nicolo exclaimed. 'Get me those photos from the Nestor funeral, the pictures Germain took. I'm getting on to Italy. This is much bigger than we thought, Pradal, a hell of a sight bigger!'

Chapter Twelve

Like everyone else in the Bijou-Bar that day, Travers was eyeing the tramp with a mixture of amusement, tolerance and annoyance as he jabbered on about nothing and everything while downing an unusually large number of Picon-citrons.

He was thinking too that you could hardly call him a tramp; he was a youngish man, one of the New Poor, you might say. The fellow had merely taken over from the old generation of winos and there was nothing altogether surprising in that. Except that he suddenly produced from a dirty, well-stuffed wallet a fifty-dollar banknote.

For a couple of minutes now the man had been pressing Travers to have a drink on him. Travers naturally refused each time, and the man eventually declared: 'I've got enough, sure I have, take a look at this!'

Travers did exactly that, edging up to the man and telling him that, in that case, he'd be glad to join him and would like a Scotch if he didn't mind. The man was far from paralytically drunk and seemed proud of his fifty-dollar note, which was proof that he had not stolen it.

The explanation came within seconds: 'Talk about a piece of luck. You'd never believe where I found this.'

'If there are any more where that came from, you'd best keep it to yourself,' Travers cracked, meaning to come back at him a minute or two later.

But the new owner of the note pulled himself up, assumed the posture of a gentleman who was not to be trifled with, and added: 'Well, I'll tell you just the same. A dump, that's where I found it. The very idea of it— throwing good money away when there's so many like me out of work!'

'Yeah,' said Travers confidentially, 'funny idea now you mention it.'

The man proffered the note and the barmaid Colette said: 'Sorry, I can't take that. Don't know where it came from.'

'But I just told you!'

'Never mind about that, dear, no foreign money. Guvnor's orders.'

The customer roared: 'Well he's wrong. The dollar's going up, you know!'

Travers jumped in, producing a note of his own: 'I'll settle it. Keep the change Colette, it's your lucky day.' To the man he whispered. 'I'll change it for you. Let's move over to that table.'

Which they did, with their drinks. It was in both their interests.

At about that moment, Nicolo and Pradal swooped into the yard and found Albertas with his pigs.

They conducted him into the house and all three of them sat down.

'Tell me. You say your Teddy was cleaning the 357?'

'That's what I said. What are you on about?'

'Putting a 357 into the hands of a youngster not weighing even sixty kilos is like putting an elephant on my Renault 5,'' Nicolo suggested.

Pradal cut in: 'Did you find the licence for it?'

'Still looking. All them papers up there, it's like looking for a . . .'

'You won't find it,' Nicolo rapped.

'Oh yes?'

'Because if you do I wouldn't want to be in your shoes.'

Albertas said nothing for a moment, and then: 'If you wouldn't mind explaining it a bit . . .'

'With pleasure. That gun killed a cop in Turin three weeks ago.'

'Turin, Turin? I've never been to Turin in my life!'

Nicolo rose and put his chair back in its place. Pradal copied him. Albertas glared at the table.

'Either you find that permit or you don't. It's up to you

now,' the commissaire told him.

This time Kovalic did not watch the police car leave. He sat with his elbows on the table, nursing his head.

'Florence!' Travers bellowed, causing her to jump and mess up the cheque she was writing out.

'Travers!' she yelled back. 'Please don't do that! My goodness, what's happened to you? You're filthy, I can smell you from here.'

'It's not me, it's the trousers. I'm putting a new pair on expenses. But you'll love me for it. This time we've really hit the jackpot!'

He lifted up a plastic shopping bag and plumped it onto her desk. He dipped into it and pulled out a handful of banknotes.

'Where did you get those?'

'Promise I get my expenses and I'll tell you.'

She laughed gaily, and he said: 'I met this *clochard* in the Bijou and he produced a fifty-dollar note.'

'And?'

'And I got him in the car, telling him I'd give him four hundred francs for it if he showed me where he got it.'

'Daylight robbery.'

'He showed me all right. The main dump. I searched it with him and we found a burnt-out bonfire. I dug around a bit and came up with this little lot. Mainly dollars but other notes too, all foreign money.'

Still plunging into the plastic bag, he showed her a wad with the edges burned, some notes sopping wet, others good.

'Why didn't he take all that lot, your *clochard*?'

'Didn't want to get his hands dirty. He found half a dozen some distance away. A lazy tyke, so all he got from me was his four hundred francs.'

'Put that on expenses too, along with your shoes.'

Gingerly she spread many of the notes out on her desk, and observed: 'Some of these are in numerical order.'

'I noticed that.'

'What's the total? All that was dumped, I mean?'

553

'Lord knows. Thousands by the look of the mess out there.'

Florence borrowed Travers's trousers to wipe her fingers: 'Let's get this straight. There's someone in Chateauvallon who took the trouble to stock up dollars and other currencies, and then had fun setting them alight. Who?'

'Must have been in a hurry,' Travers said.

'They could be counterfeit.'

'They don't look like it, but who am I to say? It's obvious tht someone, presumably from Chateauvallon, was caught napping and had to lose this money quickly. Any guesses?'

Florence nodded several times: 'The Kovalics. After Teddy was shot.'

'Certainly not before, I'd say.'

Florence left her desk and opened her safe. Travers put the plastic bag with the notes inside.

'What do we do now?' she said, shutting the door and twiddling some knobs on the electronic lock.

'With your permission I'm going to think about that in my bath. I'll be back later with a fragrance that enhances my real personality, unquote.'

However Travers decided to call on Catherine before returning. He found her rummaging through some old photos of herself and Teddy as children. Rejected photos lay all around and her eyes were glazed.

'Give me those,' he said gently. He threw all the photos on the settee and knelt down with her, taking her head and rocking her, stroking her curls.

'Have you been to the farm?'

'Yes. Marfa's still in a state, and Zoë's not much better. Grandad says his prayers all the time.'

'And your father?'

'Like a brick wall. He's getting things ready for the funeral. He's mad because the police won't give him back the body. That's all he goes on about. He's a hard man, Travers.'

'Bernard there?'

'He stopped by. Why?'

'Read *L'Eveil*?'

'No. Should I have read it?'

'They say Teddy killed himself because of *La Dépêche*. He was upset because of the revelations about the Kovalic family. So he killed himself.'

'They said that? But that's preposterous!'

Travers looked at her levelly: 'Do you think Bernard believes that?'

'I don't know.'

He put a finger under her chin and gently forced her to look at him: 'Did you talk to him?'

'No,' she said, flicking her head aside.

The phone rang and she signed for him to take it. Florence was on the line and told him to get back to the office at once. She needed him urgently.

'Damn,' he told Catherine. 'The *patronne* wants me at once.'

'How will you retaliate against Bernard's story?'

'We won't take it up, I suppose. Until further notice, it was an accident.'

'Why do you say until further notice?'

'Because,' he replied, and gave her a kiss.

'I can make you a quick coffee,' Catherine said.

'It's urgent, the boss told me.'

Her hand on his shoulder, she went with him to the door: 'I've got some news for you, but it'll wait.'

'Anything to do with Teddy?'

'Nothing at all.'

'I'll be right back, then.'

At the law courts, Nicolo was trying to extract a favour from the deputy public prosecutor. He informed him of the Interpol message about the revolver.

The official told him: 'You realize what this means?'

'Perfectly. But if we give it to the magistrate right away, I'm finished. The revolver's all very well, but what's left is much better.'

'Go on.'

The commissaire began lifting his pipe from his pocket, and then put it back: 'Murder or accident, that's not the problem. I'm interested in Kovalic.'

'So you want a time delay.'

'Three days at least.'

'I'll have to ask the prosecutor.'

'He'll refuse!' Nicolo cried. 'If you mention Italians he'll apply at once to the magistrate, tomorrow morning!'

'Let me handle it, Nicolo,' said the official with a smile.

The commissaire tossed his head: 'I'm not saying it's the crime of the century, but there's going to be some fireworks, believe me!'

'I neither believe nor disbelieve, *mon cher*. Three days then, not a minute longer.'

Nicolo shook his hand: 'I won't forget this, believe me!'

Florence must have come up with something on the banknotes, or else about the Kovalics.

He strode out of the lift and along to her office.

'Read that!' she ordered.

He did as he was told, letting his tongue loll out over his lower lip: 'Armand sent you that? Whatever for?'

'No reason given, as you can see.'

'Can you see a reason?'

'No. I thought, as far as that was concerned, that I was in for a respite.'

Travers reread the sheet of paper, persuading himself that he hadn't misunderstood. There was no doubt about it: Armand Berg had formally summoned his sister to a board meeting of *La Dépêche* within ten clear days, invoking the emergency provisions under Articles 9 and 9b of the statutes. He gave no reason.

Reaching the end of the text, he said: 'It's daft, completely ridiculous.'

'I'm not so sure,' Florence said. 'Obviously there's something behind it. I tried to get him at his Paris flat, at the Assemblée, at Les Glycines. Nobody knows where he is.'

'Well you'll be seeing him in a week when Rue Antonin Berg is inaugurated.'

'Exactly, in a week, two days before the board meeting. Very convenient!' She got up and began wringing her hands.

'What's the panic?' he asked. 'What's hanging over you?'

She hissed through her teeth: 'My newspaper, *mon cher*. I'm not too sure where I stand, but I have the impression I have a smaller and smaller stake and the family is increasing theirs.'

'You're talking nonsense, Flo.'

She laughed derisively: 'I hope you're right, André. God, I need you Trav. I don't know whom to turn to.'

'Well, there's me.' He took her by the shoulders and smiled fondly. True, their love story hadn't lasted long, and she had treated him pretty rotten at times, but they were allies. In the fight for the paper, journalistically. They had been through much together and were firm friends. He gave her a short kiss on the forehead.

'See you tomorrow,' he said.

Catherine looked more perky when he got back to her. She had prettied herself up, done her make-up again and got a meal ready. Young Paul was in bed.

She told him she'd done some shopping and got *Le Monde*. He kissed her on the neck, and she told him to take things easy while she finished off her *tarte Tatin*.

'D'you like *tarte Tatin*?' she asked, adding honey to her voice.

'Been dreaming of it all day.'

Travers, who felt he must have walked forty kilometres since breakfast, stripped off his shirt and tie and sat on the settee watching Catherine playing with the pastry. He wanted silence for a moment, and had no desire to talk seriously with Catherine of all people. The reason in a nutshell was that he had called in at the Bijou-Bar on the way, found Nicolo waiting for him, compared notes and concluded that the storm clouds were gathering for Albertas Kovalic. Which was not something he could break to Catherine in a shouting match between the room and the kitchen. He picked up *Le Monde* and started reading the headlines—which normally took about twenty minutes on their own.

'Travers?' she said after all of ninety seconds.

'Huh?'

'I told you I had news for you, remember? And it wasn't the right moment?'

'Uhuh.'

'Well the news is I'm pregnant,' she said, appearing in the doorway with her ball of pastry.

'By whom?' he enquired, lowering the newspaper a fraction.

Which was unwise, for the delectable vision of Catherine was blotted out instantly by the ball of pastry skimming the top of the paper. It caught him between the eyes.

Leaping up he spluttered in protest.

'Say that again!' she yelled.

'Say what again?'

'Who's the father, you said.'

'I said that?'

'Let's start again. I'm going to have a baby.'

'You're joking.'

'*Non, Monsieur.*'

'You mean you're not on the pill?'

'The doctor forbids it.'

'But Catherine, there are other ways.'

'Well it's too late now.'

Throughout this exchange Travers had spoken like a man, the classic phallocrat in Catherine's view. She had remained calm. Travers got out a cigarette and lit it with trembling hands.

'You're not going to keep it!'

'Don't turn away, Travers. You see this rolling pin. Where would you like it, on your Adam's apple or on your male chauvinist sweetmeats?'

He rose and said pleadingly: 'But Catherine, I'm not the fatherly type.'

'Not yet. I simply wanted to inform you, I expect nothing more from you. I can cope with the rest. You don't even have to give him your name.'

Travers pulled himself together: 'You're out of your mind.'

'How so?'

'You are going to bring a kid into the world when half his family is in jail. There, I've said it!' She chuckled, forcing the laugh. 'Is that all the effect it has on you?'

Catherine replied coolly: 'You poor sap, I know everything. Bernard let it all out. Told me everything.'

'Is he involved?'

'No.'

'Are you sure?'

She nodded, put the rolling pin down on the kitchen table and came and sat next to him. She was sad and picked off some bits of the pastry from his forehead.

'My father is laundering the dirty money his cousins bring from Italy,' she said. 'He uses a plane that does the trip to Switzerland regularly.'

'Something must have gone wrong, because I found a whole pile of banknotes on the main town dump.'

'Have you told anyone?'

'Florence, nobody else.'

Catherine snatched her hand away: 'You did that!'

'She'll keep it to herself, so will I. We don't intend to use it as a story. Florence is fond of your dad, strange as it may seem. But tell me, who killed Teddy?'

'It was an accident!'

'Was Bernard there?'

'What difference does that make?'

'Calm down, sweetie, I'm not a cop! Actually I don't suppose it matters. Come on Catherine.' He put an arm round her. 'Now you look at me. Do you want me to marry you?'

She avoided looking at him: 'You're not obliged to, but I'd like it for the baby. I don't want him to be called Kovalic. Oh dear, I'm saying it so badly.' She buried her face in her hands.

'But I got the message.'

Her mouth opened and closed twice. She said: 'I-I-don't know what to do, André. I admit it, I'm counting on you.'

559

'You didn't say that too badly,' he whispered with a big grin.

A caged lion, Albertas Kovalic went round and round the waiting room at the SRPJ. He had been there an hour now, and knew they were talking about him in the commissaire's office. Knew they would trap him.

Nicolo and Pradal were ninety-nine per cent sure it was no accident that killed Teddy, at least not an accidental shot while he was cleaning the gun. The lack of any powder on his clothing and around the wound indicated that the bullet was fired from a distance of at least three metres. The boy was left-handed, as shown in a photo taken at the disco in which he had his left hand at the top of the saxophone instead of the usual right hand, which meant he did not kill himself. There was no doubt in their minds: Albertas was covering up a murder.

The two men were preparing to put this to Kovalic, when a junior man came in with another message from Turin. They each read the telex twice, then got out Germain's photos from the funeral. Then they told a man to bring Albertas in.

Kovalic immediately complained of the long wait, and Nicolo told him to sit down. He did so and took off his hat. The commissaire clenched and unclenched his hands several times, then put this two thumbs against his top teeth.

'*Sono belle le colle giro de Torino,*' he said.

'Torino?' Kovalic grunted.

'Torino. *Il mio padre è nato a Torino, e me dice siempre que sono belle le colle . . .*'

'Why are you talking Italian, Commissaire?'

Nicolo rose and walked round his desk, to put his hands on Kovalic's shoulders: 'Djilas and Marko were killed this morning in the hills. At 5.30. They tried to rush a road-block and it went badly for them.'

He took his hands off and went back to his seat.

'Block?' Albertas whispered. 'What are you saying?'

Nicolo smiled wryly: 'Poor Albertas, it's tough for you.

It's a lot to take in a few days. Wasn't Marko the lad who used to play for Juventus about twelve years back?'

'Played in the centre.'

'He was driving, and took a bullet in the nape of his neck. Djilas didn't have his seat belt on and the sliding roof handle split his skull open. They both died outright.'

Albertas looked grey, but he recovered valiantly: 'What's all that to do with now?'

'Because of the car, Kovalic. A BMW 728 registered in Trieste. As well as the two men the car was carrying . . .'

'Hold on Commissaire, what are you driving at?'

'Thirty thousand dollars in a golf bag,' Nicolo stated coldly.

'Oh yes? Is that all you've kept me waiting an hour for?'

'I sympathize with you Kovalic. Three boys in a few days.'

'I don't understand.'

'The number of the BMW is the same as that on a BMW at Nestor's funeral. It is the same car.'

Nicolo slowly pushed the photos across to him.

'What does that prove?' Kovalic said.

'Nothing.'

Albertas leaned back: 'I'd like to go now.'

Nicolo gave him a chance to add to that, but the old man kept quiet, and the commissaire told him: 'Leave if you like. You're free.'

Albertas rose, hesitated and said: 'I had a great affection for my cousins. I'll have to see about things now.'

'Obviously. The bagful of dollars is with the *carabinieri*. I can give you their number.'

'I don't need it. If you want me you know where to find me.'

'I won't. It's up to the magistrate from now on. But you must not leave Chateauvallon.'

'Magistrate?'

'He won't call you for a couple of days. I'm sorry, Kovalic, really sorry.'

Albertas gave a curt nod, fixed his hat and left.

After a silence Pradal said: 'Think he'll throw himself in the Loire?'

561

'Not him!' Pradal's superior still had something on his mind. He said: 'I'm going for a stroll.'

It was to the Bijou-Bar that he went once more. He shook hands with Travers and the two men went over to a table. They chatted a long moment, after which Travers hurried out, heading for Florence.

He rang the doorbell at her private apartment and when she opened up he took her swiftly into the lounge and made her sit on the settee with him.

When he had finished she said: 'He told you all that of his own accord?'

'Absolutely,' Travers said. 'I think we like each other. And besides he may have another reason. I must admit I'm dumbfounded. He got the picture in less than twenty-four hours, imagine that!'

'What picture?'

'Well, that the two brothers who caught it at the Turin road-block paid trips here. Amazing intuition on Nicolo's part!'

Florence thought an instant and asked: 'D'you think they were in Chateauvallon when Teddy . . .?'

'More than likely. What's more the Italian police found a bag of dollars in their BMW.'

'Dollars! Again?'

'Precisely. Can we prove any connection with the ones I found?'

'Oh no, that'd be too easy.'

Travers went on to explain that he wanted to fly to Turin and see the dollars. If they tallied, then it would be curtains for Albertas.

'Is that what you want?' she asked.

'Not at all. But it's my professional nose. I've got to know the facts. Just the facts, that's all.'

Florence looked none too pleased and warned him: 'Don't forget that Albertas has a grandson and I am the boy's auntie.'

He met her point: 'And that little boy's going to have a brother and his name will be Travers!'

They grinned at each other and she said at length: 'You can't be sure it's a boy.'

'Sure I'm sure.'

She sighed: 'What a family!'

'Soon we'll be setting up a joint-stock company. We can't be sure who's who, but I don't suppose it matters. What does count is that as few of us as possible finish up in jail.'

Florence laughed: 'Wow, you *have* been working it all out!'

He squeezed her hand: 'You know you agree with me.'

Travers pulled himself up from the settee precisely as Artus Balestra swanned out of the bathroom in a peignoir. His bare feet padded towards the settee.

He said: 'Hullo Travers. You've undoubtedly noticed how showers are always at the wrong temperature whatever you do with them. So you're off to Italy. Lucky you.'

'So you've been eavesdropping.'

'It's a sport with an honourable past.'

Travers shrugged: 'Well you're part of the family.'

'Charming!!!' Artus said, genuinely delighted. 'Isn't that nice, Flo.'

Travers left, promising to phone her from Italy, and giving her a quick peck on the cheek.

When he had gone Artus sighed: 'I'd love a Scotch if there's one going.' He seemed subdued and with the drink in his hand he said: 'I like Travers, but he's starting to nettle me rather.'

'That's unkind.'

'You're right, I'll take it back. Not the right moment, of course.' He gulped back his drink and poured himself another which he also swallowed. 'Er-Florence. Oh, I have to say it. Florence, I am deeply in love with you. I mean it, you'll have to marry me.'

Her eyebrows shot up: 'Really?'

'Really. I mulled it over and there's no way out for either of us. If you won't be my wife, I don't want the Nobel. Life will have lost all meaning, so will whisky, baths— everything.'

She did not smile. She sat down again and crossed her legs above the knee, looking at Artus.

'But do you think I want to get married? Me?'

He was startled, or appeared to be: 'What! You and me, I mean it's as if we were . . .'

'As if, exactly. I'm very sorry Artus, I don't feel I'm up to darning your socks.'

'Good grief!' he cried. 'People don't darn socks any more! Oh this is awful, I knew it was a bad day. But at least I tried.'

He turned away and Florence ran into his arms: 'Artus, you're a wonderful guy.'

'Though not sufficiently nubile, or whatever the word is for us men!'

'Do come and have a bath from time to time. When you rise up from the deep you look like Neptune.'

'And twice as old?'

'Silly! You can't ask me to do the impossible. I feel dreadfully ashamed refusing you, but I can't, I can't.' Her eyes filled and the tears soaked into the peignoir.

'If I've made you cry, I haven't entirely wasted my day,' he said with feeling.

'Oh shut up,' she said weakly, thumping him and crying some more. 'You don't think it's easy for me, do you?'

Artus lifted her hair, fondled it all over: 'Nothing's easy, Flo.' He watched her go limp on the settee, thinking that he had never seen anyone cry such hot tears.

Balestra got dressed and she made no attempt to keep him. Just as well, he thought, it was deeply embarrassing. He hoped he had hidden his utter dejection. Balestra had experienced and felt much in his life, and he knew that he had never loved any woman as he loved Florence. He had responded to her from the very first second, was seized with an overwhelming urge to please her, to win her. When he had taken her in the world stopped, and he would never forget that first meeting. By the time she was ready to leave his house he was convinced that Florence was the only woman in the world he could possibly live

564

with. That was a supreme surprise and a shock for him, realizing his secret weaknesses. Since childhood he had fought to reconcile his ebullience and his fragile nature, his sloth and his urge to affirm his intelligence, his desire to become brilliant and those fearsome arid periods when he gave in and lowered his guard. He had a keen taste for provoking people and this had taken his inner struggle into the arena where all could watch it, for it took the form of a penchant for intellectual paradoxes. He had displayed his admiration for fine young men as if throwing out a challenge to the world.

Although she did not realize it, Florence had made him clean. She had in turn responded to his charm, had seen what was best in him, had allowed herself to trust in him and believe he would get her out of the web of intrigue that threatened to ruin her. Then slowly he had come around to the notion that he might even marry her. Entwined with her as lovers, he discovered that he truly loved Florence. This love had sustained him throughout the investigation by the Swedish authorities, had shown them that he was engaged and about to wed. Foolishly as he now told himself, he had never doubted that she would accept him, that she would actually be at his side when the Nobel Prize was formally presented.

Now she had refused and the let-down was unbearable. Not only did he feel he had committed perjury with the Swedish officials, his heart was bleeding.

The phantoms of the past escorted him as he drove to La Jouterie. He was trembling when he applied the handbrake and was oddly incapable of going indoors. He walked for a long time in the grounds before entering the empty house at last. A primitive fear, made worse by his sensitivity and rapid keen intelligence, took hold of him as he groped his way into the library.

How utterly sad it looked as he switched the lights on one by one. Fully illuminated it seemed worse. An awful minute went by.

'It's her fault,' he said out loud. 'It's her bloody fault!!!' Everything was too stark for him to feel sorry for himself.

He made his decision, and with renewed confidence he strode over to the phone on the small desk near the door.

'Hullo, is that you Inge? I wondered if I'd get you. But of course it's feeding time for my cat, how is he? And you? Have you managed to get through all those notes? Oh good, I'm so glad, a thousand thanks. What ever would I do without you?'

By now he was squatting on the edge of the desk, a familiar pose. As the conversation progressed he caught sight of Florence's photo in an expensive frame, grabbed it and flung it with all his might to the far end of the library.

Thankfully Inge was rattling on about this and that, but finally he interrupted her: 'Inge, do stop nattering. Darling Inge, I want to ask you one more favour, and if you say yes I shall be happy for the rest of my life.'

He took a deep breath and said: 'Inge, will you marry me?'

The magistrate's name was Bourgoin. A stout man in his late forties, Bourgoin summoned Albertas Kovalic the day after Nicolo had told him he could not leave Chateauvallon.

Albertas thought it strange that the magistrate asked no questions about Teddy. All he seemed interested in was a small red aeroplane, the Cherokee.

Bourgoin referred to some details on a sheet of paper: 'Monsieur Kovalic, I understand this aircraft, Alpha Tango 646, belongs to you. It appears you bought it as a used item eighteen months ago from a Belgian firm for the sum of 240,000 French francs.' Bourgoin shot him a quick glance. 'Quite a big sum that, Monsieur Kovalic.'

Albertas countered: 'It was a bargain. Would cost twice that these days.'

'May I ask why you needed an aeroplane?'

'I was thinking of the children, trips around Chateauvallon and all that kind of thing.' The magistrate gave a curt nod, inviting him to go on. 'Well I made a mistake. Costs too much with that plane, and I'm putting it up for sale.'

Bourgoin resembled a sphinx as he put the next question: 'I see also that you employ a pilot, a certain Aldo Baggio. Does he work for you full time?'

'Oh, course not, in view of what I said. He does little jobs for the travel agencies.'

'And he hands you some of the takings?'

'We have an arrangement, but I don't check up on him and I suppose he hides some of it from me.'

The magistrate studied other sheets of paper and declared: 'That's strange.'

'What is, *Monsieur Le Juge*?'

'Where is this plane? Generally speaking, and more specially at this moment?'

Albertas heaved his massive head to one side: 'How should I know? Better ask Villacoublay. Like I said, Aldo doesn't tell me all his business, especially who he's working for each day. I've got plenty more to think about anyway.'

'Very well,' Bourgoin said, cleaning his spectacles with the end of his tie. 'In that case, I must ask you to obtain from your pilot all his flight plans for the past six months. And, Monsieur Kovalic, I want them within forty-eight hours.'

Albertas exploded in mock horror: 'But that's not possible! Forty-eight hours!'

'Yes it is, Monsieur Kovalic. They have an excellent computer at Villacoublay, and they'll give you a print-out in thirty minutes. Nice to have met you, Monsieur Kovalic. Good day to you.'

'Good day, *Monsieur Le Juge*,' Albertas muttered. It was the magistrate who opened the door for him.

Bernard Kovalic had an even more immediate problem at *L'Eveil*. There was not a sou in the bank to pay the personnel and the printer. He and Maryse had been working on the figures, and she had gone off to the accounts office.

Returning she told him: 'The town hall's phoned. They want you at once.'

'Jerome?'

'A secretary. Bernard, try not to get the worst of it, for once!'

Bernard snorted. He might have snorted much louder had he known who was waiting for him there. Boulard! And it did not require more than half a second for Bernard to realize he had not come down from Paris to pat him on the back. Even so, Bernard, who was growing more exasperated day by day, decided to get his shot in first.

'Glad you've come down,' he said. 'We need the month's cheque. At once.'

'Money,' Boulard growled. 'There's money every-where, old chap. I believe you're not short of it at the moment.'

Boulard strode back and forth as if he owned the town hall and its entire contents. Bernard stood there much like a schoolboy being ticked off by the headmaster, and he wondered for an instant whether he might throw down the gauntlet, precipitate the coming row by deliberately taking a seat—since neither Boulard nor Jerome had invited him to do so. Jerome looked haughty in an impeccable dark blue suit, with one haunch perched on his desk; it was not the same Jerome as had sucked up to him and called him his dear friend not so long ago. Bernard recalled Maryse's advice and fired a broadside.

'Our agreement, Monsieur Boulard,' he stated firmly, 'provides for you to transfer on the twentieth day of each month whatever sum is necessary to meet the bills at the close of the month. I need this month's money.'

Swapping a quick glance with Jerome, the press mag-nate replied with an air of sweet reason: 'Kovalic, I have the distinct impression that I have backed the wrong horse. In forty years, I have never done that.'

'You are changing the subject, Monsieur.'

Boulard again looked at Jerome in assumed mis-apprehension: 'What did he say? What did he just say?'

It was a favourite ploy of his, designed to show his adversary up as an oaf. He had found it always worked.

Jerome said: 'Come now, Kovalic. Monsieur Boulard

has taken the trouble to come down and see you. Let's be reasonable, please.'

Boulard thanked the mayor with a curt nod, and stroked his brow, resorting this time to pathos: 'You are irascible, far too irascible. How do you expect me to go along with such behaviour? I feel I have a liability on my hands, and I'm sure you will understand my position, Jerome.'

'Only too well, my friend. I myself . . .'

Boulard cut him off and took a step towards Bernard: 'So it's a matter of a cheque that worries you. Money, that's all that concerns you. Money is how we keep the score, eh? That must be distressing to you, old chap, and I don't envy you.' He placed a paternal hand on Bernard's shoulder. But Bernard took a quick pace backwards.

'That's enough, Monsieur,' he said, raising his voice. 'Kindly tell me where you stand!'

Another surprised glance at Jerome: 'Where I stand? He wants to know where I stand? Incredible!'

Jerome suggested with deference: 'He must have made some mistake.'

Boulard emitted a nasty cackle: 'A mistake, that's it, a mistake! Now see here, Kovalic. Hand over your stake in *La Dépêche* and your accountant will have the cheque in fifteen minutes!'

Bernard burst out: 'My uncle will never agree!'

'That's as may be. Alas it is true, but you will negotiate the transfer, won't you? I know you can do that. Now let's get that down on paper, shall we?'

Nobody spoke for a moment, then Jerome guided Bernard to his chair. The mayor placed a clean sheet of paper before him and offered him a ballpoint pen. He then dictated the Act of Sale, which Bernard wrote out and signed while Boulard observed the ceremony from a chair some ten paces away, recapitulating in his mind how he would proceed with the next phase of his campaign.

Nicolo and Pradal had been outdone. Aldo Biaggi had flown, to Australia according to their information, and not to Mexico where he was a fully-fledged national.

569

'It was to be expected,' the senior man observed. 'But he's not that important. The point is that we have his flight plans. You'll notice he did a lot of winter sports work: Paris-Courchevel, Paris-Mégève. And some trips into Switzerland.'

'Nothing unusual about that,' Pradal said.

'True, but each time he went to Switzerland he took off from Villacoublay and landed at Gstaad, Zurich, Lausanne or elsewhere. We have noted also that on several flights he went off the radar screens just about half-way.

'How did we find that out? I've forgotten.'

'Our glorious French Air Force. They follow every plane day and night that uses our air space. The whole lot is stored in computers.'

Pradal suggested: 'This Aldo bloke, maybe he liked hedge-hopping. Maybe it was thunderstorms affecting the screens.'

'That's what I want to find out. Now Pradal, how about a peep at those little Swiss misses? While you're there you will chat up the Swiss Customs, anyone who had any contact with this Aldo Baggio. Keep on to it until you have a complete picture.'

'I certainly will,' Pradal enthused, seeing his career entering a higher sphere.

'Do a good job, Pradal. I'm certain you'll come up with something, I'll put my shirt on that!'

Florence was more interested in Teddy's death.

She asked Albertas to drop in and see her, choosing a time when they were unlikely to be disturbed. Kovalic looked weary but he seemed to be prouder than ever, which annoyed Florence as she herself was exhausted. Her head was swimming from an almost sleepless night thinking about Alexandra and Teddy, more especially about Alexandra's views on Teddy's death.

Albertas sat in her office facing her, his voluminous hat stuck on one knee: 'I'm sorry about your nightmares, *Madame*, really I am. But I have troubles too; they forced me to bury Teddy like a pauper, and the police are after me.'

Florence realized that their conversation might well be confused, and she asked point-blank: 'Who killed Teddy, Kovalic?'

'It was an accident, you know that, you put it in your own paper.'

'And your two cousins, was that an accident? That'll be in my paper tomorrow.'

She stood over him, forcing him to look up: 'These are bad times, Madame Berg.'

She persisted: 'Who killed the boy? Which cousin?'

After a long wait, Albertas rumbled: 'I don't find your question at all interesting.'

She tried another approach, thrusting some of the dumped banknotes under his nose: 'These are more interesting perhaps. You may be aware that the banknotes found in your cousins' car were in the same series as some of these.'

Placidly he replied: 'There are a lot of dollars in circulation round the world at the moment, you should read your own reports!'

Florence raised her eyes to the ceiling, Albertas fiddled with his hat. He kept turning it by inching his fingers along the brim, and every so often he gave a little snap to his fingers. This told Florence he was more agitated than he appeared. She kept up the pressure, brandishing some notes in front of him.

'What do I do with these? Take them to Nicolo?'

'That would hardly be decent.'

'Decent!' she laughed.

'When your newsprint was in the Loire, I didn't just stand around laughing about it.'

'Point taken. That was decent, what you did for us.'

'Then what else do you want?'

Struggling to keep the conversation in some semblance of order, she said: 'Another gesture on your part, Kovalic.'

'That's asking a lot, Madame Berg.'

'It'll be our secret, I promise you. But I need to know, for Alexandra's sake. For example, tell me about the fight in your yard.'

571

'What fight?'

'Stop messing about. My girl believes Teddy killed himself, and it's tearing her to pieces. That's what I mean!'

Albertas took a deep breath: 'I don't know how you found out, but it's true there was an argument. A family tiff, nothing serious.'

'Except that Teddy died in it. You were four men: you, Teddy and the two cousins.'

'Five. Bernard was there.'

'Bernard! Did he fire the shot?'

Albertas put his hat on the desk and mopped his brow: 'Bernard wanted to shoot Djilas. Djilas fired in self-defence. His brother jogged his arm, and the bullet hit Teddy instead.'

Florence sat down again, put her hands together in an attitude of prayer with her elbows on the desk edge: 'Why not tell that to the magistrate?'

'Because it's none of his business! If I give him an inch he'll build a whole case on it. That's his job. Mine is to defend the interests of my family, the living and the dead.'

Not for the first time, Florence marvelled at the two worlds which failed to meet. His was a hardy view of morality, and it was impossible to shake.

'So that's it,' she resumed. 'Bernard wanted to kill Djilas.'

'He doesn't understand us, that Bernard. I sent him off to America to give him some culture, and he's come back more wild than we are!'

'I've always considered him well brought up and civilized.'

'Too civilized. He doesn't look on money as we do, doesn't have any sense of family loyalty. I do. If there's too much money it must go to Switzerland. By mule if necessary.'

Florence stopped praying and clenched her fists once or twice. He was impossible to fathom. As she continued scrutinizing his features, she noticed that his lips gave a tiny tremor, the small quiver of a man about to play a good card.

Albertas went on: 'I needed a mule, and I had a great idea when I went to the airfield and saw the pilot there. I said to myself, Albertas you got yourself a mule, it's standing right there and you're unlikely to see another one as perfect as that for the rest of your life.'

Florence interrupted: 'That's enough, Kovalic. Your mule stories don't interest me.'

'I think they do, Madame Berg. I thought when I saw her there at the airfield with her two kids that she must be bored, that her husband couldn't give her enough of it. Your brother Julien is a bit of a dreamer, not attentive enough. So I thought to myself . . . Anyway, it was a good idea and it worked like clockwork.'

'You mean my sister-in-law Thérèse?'

'She was my mule. Weekends in the snow, trips into Switzerland with the pilot, the baggage in her name, her name on the labels and everything.'

'I don't see the significance.'

'Then I'll spell it out. If anything went wrong, I told myself, it wouldn't matter that the plane was in my name if the money was on the way to the laundry with the name Berg on it. Even if the mule knew nothing, if you get my point, it would be all the same to the nosy-parkers.'

'The Bergs have gone through worse. I suppose there's no trace of the contents of the bags.'

'True. But with the police, those Swiss bankers can be co-operative and they let things out, little details, provided it costs them nothing. Makes 'em look more honest.'

The two looked at each other and neither of them blinked for twenty seconds.

It was Florence who spoke first: 'What happens now?'

'One goal to each of us,' Albertas said, and then roared with laughter.

Florence could not avoid smiling. She played with a dollar bill burned at one end: 'Quite a system you had, Kovalic. You must have lost a great deal of sleep.'

'It's like a boil when it bursts, you're chuckling afterwards. Now it's my opinion it would be embarrassing to have these half-burned notes hanging around. They ought to be properly burnt. That was the original idea anyway.'

'And I'll have nothing left.'

Albertas leaned forward amicably: 'You have my word. What Thérèse gets up to is none of my business. I've already forgotten it.'

Florence got up and threatened: 'Just wait till I get to that little hussy!'

Albertas smiled and shook his head: 'Forget it, if I was you. She's the type that gives herself up, and Chateauvallon's got enough martyrs to be going on with.'

Nodding agreement, Florence paced the office thoughtfully. Then she returned to her desk, took the whole pile of banknotes, stuffed them in the grate and set fire to them with her gold lighter.

'My father would turn in his grave,' she said quietly.

Albertas squatted down with her and they watched the paper money consume itself.

'He would agree with you,' Kovalic said. 'He held the family to be sacred, like I do. We didn't go to the same church, but we had the same God. The family.'

Chapter Thirteen

Pradal's enquiries among the Swiss Customs officials produced nothing of any importance. But they turned up a huge surprise.

He told Nicolo on his return that the documents relating to Alpha Tango 646's freight mentioned *Personal baggage of Mme Berg, Chateauvallon, France*.

'My God, whatever next!' Nicolo cried. 'Which one? There are three of them.'

'Precisely, *Monsieur Le Commissaire*, there are three Berg ladies at Chateauvallon.' Pradal spread out some photos on the boss's desk. 'These come from a photographer who does the restaurants and night clubs. They were taken in the dining room at the Charleston in Zurich. It was Aldo Baggio's birthday two months ago.'

Nicolo studied the three prints, one showing a couple kissing, the second gazing at each other as if they couldn't wait for the meal to end and get back up to their room, the third depicting them facing the camera. From the last photo Nicolo had no difficulty recognizing Thérèse Berg. There was no doubt either that it was the same couple in all three pictures.

Pradal commented: 'I don't think she knew the pictures were being taken. For her, it must have been just a love affair because they really do look gone on each other. It was genuine for her, at any rate.'

'The Customs?'

'They couldn't care less what was in the baggage. Must have been something hot inside, I'd say.'

'So would I. Suppose Alpha Tango 646 took off from Chateauvallon but not from the airfield? Stands to reason it is Kovalic's plane. Pradal, take what men you need and scour the likely fields, look for oil traces. A Cherokee should leave some drips when it takes off. I'm not much on aero engines but there must be some mess left behind.'

Pradal growled: 'A needle in a haystack job.'

'You find it, that's all. Off with you, and thanks for the Swiss material.'

Travers's work in Italy was completed when he phoned Florence to say that the dollars in the cousins' car tallied with those found at the dump outside Chateauvallon.

Returning to base, he headed for Catherine and found her sorting out a cupboard.

He quipped: 'I've been dreaming of this moment since I went away, and all you can do is sort out cupboards! What's more you're so glad to see me you can't wait to finish the job.'

Catherine, who had climbed up on her stool again, said: 'I'm thrilled to see you, but I went to Paris yesterday.'

'Ah.' As there was no explanation he continued: 'Where's Paul?'

'In Paris with Chantal.'

'Ah. So it's decided.'

'Yep,' she said, turning round.

'And what do you propose to do in Paris?'

She jumped down, her skirt forming a parachute: 'Bring Paul up and wait for number two. I'm a lady in waiting, remember?'

He continued the interrogation: 'What exactly will you eat? Where will you live?'

'Don't worry about that.' She sat down, took out a cigarette and lit it calmly.

'You ought to stop smoking.'

'Does it inconvenience you?'

'Right now, yes,' he said, kneeling down and taking her in his arms. 'Where do I fit in with these plans?'

'I really don't know, you're a grown man now.'

He scanned her features: 'Something's happened while I've been away. Have you learned anything?'

'Oh stop working for a minute. I'm just fed up with

576

living here, fed up with being a Kovalic.'

Travers gave her a peck on the cheek, and she added: 'You don't tell me everything you get up to.'

'Ah,' he said again.

'I'm just worked up, that's all. And two days without you is too long. So there!'

Travers smiled at last and they both stood up. He kissed her tenderly, and they went into the kitchen hand in hand, both glad that nothing had changed between them.

About two hours later Travers went to *La Dépêche* and found Florence pushing papers about on her desk. Visibly, it was routine work. She looked pale and drawn, and he saw dark half-moons under her eyes behind the make-up. He told her she looked under the weather.

'Nobody else can sleep for me,' she said with a shrug. 'I feel all in. Alexandra worries me, she spends all the time in her room with the curtains drawn, won't eat and won't touch the cakes and things I bring her.'

'Have you told her about the banknotes and the cousins?'

'No. She knows I know something, senses that I've seen Albertas. She keeps on provoking me, telling me one thing so that I'll deny it and tell her the truth. All day she keeps to herself and then at night when I need sleep she constantly bursts into my room.'

Travers thought for a moment: 'Why don't you move into your town apartment for good?'

'That's precisely what she wants. I've been through all that and I won't give in a second time. Her father played the same game and I stuck it for ten years.'

Taking a seat, he smiled fondly on her. Ten years of hell, no doubt, he reflected. He sincerely wished he could help.

'So your husband couldn't beat you down, and nor will she. What's going to happen?'

'I dread to imagine. It's like the sword of Damocles. She is capable of anything.'

'Like what?'

'Like going to see Nicolo, telling him I know something he doesn't.'

'That's nothing.'

'Listen,' Florence said, scratching her head and smoothing her hair. 'I think she's trying to convince herself that Bernard killed Teddy. Yesterday I took her a bunch of flowers, and she threw it across the room and shouted: "All I want from you is the copy of your paper when you've the courage to say who killed Teddy".'

'She wants Bernard on the front page. She's clever, your daughter.'

'What does that mean?'

'I'll explain one day.' Florence merely looked sharply at him, and he changed the subject.

'Meanwhile the world goes on,' he said. 'Chantal wants to give up being our Paris correspondent, she told Catherine. Do you know of a replacement?'

'No, and in any case it's not urgent. Why, do you want the job?'

'Not likely, that's how I started out twenty years ago!'

'Which means you'll go onto another paper for the money. A nice moment to leave the sinking ship.'

Travers showed concern: 'It's not a case of sinking ships at all, and you know that Florence. It's nothing to do with you. It so happens I'm in my forties, and not getting any younger, especially at Chateauvallon. I was lucky to land up in this town when I was pushed out from the Paris job.'

'Nice to know it,' she said with a wafer-thin smile.

He endeavoured to sweep the whole conversation under the mat: 'Oh come on, Flo, nothing's decided about Paris. I promise you I won't budge from here until the Kovalic business is cleared up. It's exciting and . . .'

He broke off. Florence did not seem interested, he could tell from the way she was holding her pen, waiting to get on with her paperwork.

Thérèse had no idea the Renault 5 was following her at a snail's pace as she did her shopping in Chateauvallon.

She came to a halt outside a leather goods shop and inspected the window display. The Renault stopped ten paces behind her and Commissaire Nicolo jumped out. He touched her arm as she entered the shop and flipped his police card at her discreetly.

'Sorry to upset your plans, Madame Berg, but I'd like a word with you. In the car.'

'Where will you take me?' she exclaimed in frightened tones.

'Into the country.'

'The children! Something's happened to them!'

'Not at all, nothing to worry about. But you'll have to come with me.'

'And if I refuse?' She began looking about her as if trapped.

'Then I should have to send a police van to your house with uniformed officers and the siren going. With a warrant.'

Thérèse seemed to slump and her jaw dropped. Then she recovered and stalked off to the car with her nose in the air.

'This won't take long,' Nicolo said quietly. 'On the way perhaps you'd take a look at these.'

Thérèse did no such thing, she was far too concerned whether anyone had noticed her getting in the car with Nicolo, and gave little birdlike twitches to see if any people had stopped to stare as they drove off.

'You don't seem very interested,' Nicolo said. 'Don't you realize what they are?'

She looked down at the photos at last and flushed scarlet. She snapped: 'I gave him two hundred Swiss francs to destroy the negatives!'

'Who?'

'That bastard of a photographer!'

Nicolo said gently: 'Somebody may have given him more to keep them. For example, the gentleman who filled in your papers at the Customs for you.'

Thérèse now saw there were some documents with the photos. They concerned Cherokee Alpha Tango 646 and included the words *Personal baggage of Mme Berg, Chateauvallon, France.*

She came to life and looked at Nicolo. How did he come

to have these documents? Why did he want them? Where was Aldo? Where had he been all this time anyhow? The questions hurtled through her brain. It was true that he had given no sign of life for weeks, and she was thankful in the end, glad to feel honest again with her children, and with Julien who had retrieved his smile. Some days she had told herself she would soon forget about him, Aldo Baggio whose sole merit in the end was that he knew how to make love to perfection. On other days she regretted the whole episode and was jumpy, but at the same time weary of living. Now the police had picked her up in the street, in the street in her home town of Chateauvallon!

As Nicolo drove, the explanation dawned on her. She recognized the route which she had driven over several times herself. Her brain released the memory of the excitement the first time as she approached the field lying fallow and hid the car in the hut on the edge.

'Is this it?' Nicolo said suddenly, applying the handbrake.

She held her tongue, and another series of questions flooded into her mind. How did the commissaire know this was the field? Did he know about the bags they took with them? He knew all right, and knew there was something screwy about the bags, just as she had done. The entry on the document stared up at her and she understood.

'Good flying to take off in this little field!' Nicolo said as they got out. She made no comment and Nicolo repeated the remark, taking her gently by the arm.

'I knew it was touch and go.'

'Did he tell you it was?'

'No, but once we hit a tree, just a branch, over there.'

'You must have been terrified.'

'I was, but the plane kept going.'

'So you agree it was here?'

'Yes.'

'You play golf, Madame Berg?'

'I have done.'

'What's your handicap?'

'My what?'

'I see,' Nicolo said, evidently satisfied. 'You carried your things in golf bags?'

'I didn't. Aldo did.'

'Did you know what was inside?'

'No, I didn't want to know.'

'Can you prove that?'

She sensed she was no match for the commissaire and said nothing. Then she volunteered: 'He was good-looking, he made me laugh, I liked his company.'

Nicolo still held her arm: 'And in bed?'

She jumped aside and started running, her face bright red. Nicolo wagged his head, got back in the car and drove after her, catching her up next to the trees she had pointed to. He leaped out and grabbed her. Thérèse Berg fought to get free and in the struggle she scratched him on the cheek with her ring.

'Calm down,' he said, 'forget what I said.'

Nicolo wiped the blood away with the back of his hand, and guided her, still with infinite caution, back into the car. Her eyes were closed and she offered no resistance.

'Listen to me, Madame Berg,' he said in a fatherly tone when they were no longer quite so out of breath. 'Naturally your personal matters are of no concern to me, but in this case you have been as unwise as I was just now with my question. We all make mistakes. The difficulty here is that there are offences involved against the law.' He explained it slowly so that it sank in. 'I might be obliged to give your name.'

At length she moaned: 'I don't care. I did sometimes wonder about it all, it seemed suspicious, but to be honest he swept me off my feet—swept me off with his damned aeroplane. Now I don't feel anything any more.'

Which was more than Nicolo could have said; he wouldn't have minded sweeping her off her feet there and then. A dishy little lady was Madame Thérèse Berg.

She sobbed most of the way back to La Commanderie, and Nicolo made no attempt to speak, until he said quietly: 'We'll be there in a couple of minutes.'

It was just enough time for her to do something about her make-up.

All Antonin Berg's children were assembled together under his roof, a rare event these days, so that they could set out as a family for the inauguration of Rue Antonin Berg.

In view of their personalities and pasts, the atmosphere was strained. Jean-Jacques was yet to recover fully from his hepatitis and looked yellow and glum, wearing a sober suit as if heading for a funeral. Gilbert Bossis and Mathilde the housekeeper were deeply moved and frowned at Armand engaged in a slanging match with Marie-Lou. Julien was silent, for Thérèse should have been back from shopping ages ago, even if it was to buy a handbag. Alexandra was ostentatiously garbed in casual wear consisting of a creased-up T-shirt and fringed jeans, thinking it silly to show respect for an old bear who had made all their lives hell while he was alive. Florence, who had joined the group last, told them with thinly disguised satisfaction that her daughter would not be attending the ceremony, adding that they had agreed on this together.

It was still a little too soon to move off, and they hung about glancing at Jeannou outside giving the Rolls a dust off. It was Jeannou who announced Nicolo and Thérèse, creating an instant silence. Julien's heart missed a beat and Florence paled. Alexandra, who had gone to put a dress on having decided she would attend and annoy her mother despite their deal, now bumped down the stairs, buttoning up the front and darting her eyes from one to the other, a habit she had formed since Teddy's death.

Nicolo entered with his hand under Thérèse's elbow. His cheek was not bleeding now, but the scratch was obvious.

'I'm so sorry,' he said, 'I've evidently chosen a family reunion to burst into. I ought not to have come inside. Madame Berg will explain.' He prepared to go.

'One second, Commissaire!' Florence said loudly. 'What does this mean?'

'It's of no importance. It is no longer in my hands.'

'What the devil d'you mean?' Julien barked with unusual ferocity. 'Why is my wife in that state? Have you been hitting her?'

Marie-Lou cracked: 'He's been banging his head against her nails!' Nobody thought it funny.

Nicolo persisted: 'It's nothing, Madame, I assure you. I hope the ceremony goes off well.'

As he drove off, the entire company looked at Thérèse. She was indeed in a state, her blouse open and showing her bra, hair all over the shop, eyes swollen with a gleam of defiance in them.

Florence ordered: 'Julien, take her upstairs so that she can lie down.'

Armand said testily: 'But whatever's going on? I want to know.'

His sister replied sharply: 'There's nothing to know, otherwise the commissaire would not have brought her back. It's time we were going. Mathilde, phone the town hall and say we'll be there in fifteen minutes.'

Upstairs in the apartment Alexandra refused when she first arrived, Julien helped his wife onto the bed. He was being deliberately kind in his gestures, and said simply 'Tell me' as he slipped her shoes off.

'Don't worry, he got nothing out of me.'

'About what?'

She rolled her head about on the pillow, like she often did when they made love, and at the sight of Julien's boyish innocence she suddenly let out a giggle: 'My poor Julien, you certainly picked a bad number. You'll find me a good lawyer, won't you?'

'B-but why? What were the police doing with you?' He was completely mystified, and it evidently irritated her.

She spoke like some harpy: 'Because Nicolo's smart, he's on to everything, but he can't prove a thing.'

'Come on,' he urged, 'explain it.'

'Oh I can't now. I need sleep, I'm worn out.'

Florence's voice broke in from the doorway: 'She's right. Leave her now, and hurry up.' He arranged the eiderdown over her and they crept out.

'I gather she's done something awfully stupid. And I have an idea what it might be.'

'I know,' Florence said, kicking out her skirts as they went down the stairs. 'But don't worry, Julien, I'll look after you.'

The rest of the family were huddled round the bottom of the staircase. Armand said: 'Don't worry, Julien, I'm here to help.'

The Rolls and the other cars reached the spot where Rue Antonin Berg was about to come into existence. The traffic had been stopped and they saw an imposing delegation from *La Dépêche* headed by Melchior and including Madame Frochot, Travers and others. They joined the delegation and Antonin Berg seemed to be present among them through the family, his friends and the staff he had formed. Adrien Jerome mounted a platform and gave a speech, merely banalities, but impressive none the less, moving by the very fact that a departed soul was the subject. Florence was half attending and half wandering off into her own thoughts, wiping the beginnings of a tear from her lower lid, when she realized that the mayor had entered unexpected territory.

Her eyes popped as he declared: 'Your newspaper, Antonin, has been through some difficult times, but it has indeed come through and is no longer in danger. With a firm hand and new measures, it will recover the influence it ought never to have lost. Rest in peace, Antonin. Through your newspaper with its fresh life and this street which will now bear your name, you will always . . .'

Moments later, Gilbert Bossis, Antonin's close friend for so many years, pulled a cord to let fall a dark blue cotton curtain and reveal the street nameplate. Loud applause drowned the end of Jerome's speech, and he came across to shake hands solemnly with the family. Then he went off, and nobody kept him.

Alexandra was contemptuous of the masquerade. At one point she settled into a mood of genuine nostalgia, but the end of the speech had shaken her out of it. She signed to Gilbert, indicating that she would go back home in the Rolls with him, Mathilde and Julien. Jean-Jacques and Marie-Lou departed forthwith.

As to Florence, she tugged at Armand's jacket and asked him to spare her a few moments in her office. He consented to this, and they were alone facing each other within minutes. Both of them recalled that they had been together like this, brother and sister, thousands of times for better or worse, either in total complicity of mind or hating each other uncontrollably.

It was Armand who spoke first: 'Florence, I must tell you something. I have a dull mind but I have managed to conclude that being a member of the Assemblée is a waste of time. People won't take you seriously in the ministries except when you represent something local, for example when you are the mayor of a big town.'

Florence got the whisky and some ice cubes. 'I can see you arriving in your hobnail boots, Armand,' she said in a singsong voice. 'You are interested in the town hall and to achieve what you want you are prepared to do anything. Is that it? Even to the extent of changing sides.' An ironic smile played about her lips, and she displayed neither anger nor irritation. With the whiskies poured out, she pushed one over to Armand.

'I'm not a turncoat, I'm merely going with the current.'

'It makes you no less dull—your word. You have failed to understand that Jerome counts for less than a rabbit's squeak. In the eyes of the people here he is sullied with the mysterious death of Quentin, by the halt to the Aqua Viva project, by a thousand and one little things that one can see only when one breathes Chateauvallon day and night as I do.'

Armand objected: 'He'll get more votes than you think, and with my votes, we shall storm the town hall together. And I shall be the mayor. Jerome is a born deputy mayor, and he will get no further in practice.'

'How nice for him to have a partner like that. Does he know?' Her brother smirked nastily, and she was taken aback. 'I, on the other hand, believe that if you stood for election against him we could squash him like a beetle.'

'Will *La Dépêche* back me?'

'You've come out of it fairly well so far, I should say.'

'Agreed, and thanks. But I am analysing things differently now. In view of the way you are handling the paper, my victory is anything but a certainty.'

'Really! Even with the new firm hand your crony Jerome mentioned? Who is the firm hand, you?'

'Oh no, don't worry about that,' Armand said, taking hold of his drink. 'I shall have better things to do.'

'And the new measures will come from Boulard, I take it.'

'Boulard, Boulard! You see Boulard under your bed, for pity's sake. Boulard is a product of the age, a necessary product who exactly matches the restructuring phase in the written press.'

'Is he paying you cash or by cheque?'

'Very funny,' Armand said, putting his glass down. 'But I'll put it to you another way. I possess thirty-five per cent and Boulard has seven per cent.'

'Seven! Jean-Jacques sold four per cent, where did he get the other three? Bernard Kovalic?'

'I don't know. I know only that forty-two per cent means you, Sissy, do as you're told.'

'Ah!' Florence cried, making a long note of it.

'Yell as much as you like, my beauty, but I intend to save *La Dépêche* from you! And you will come running to lick my boots!'

'So that's it,' she said, grabbing her glass so that Armand shied away. Her eyes blazed but she was motionless, holding his gaze until he capitulated. 'Just now when our friend Jerome was going on, how did you feel? At peace with father?'

'I'm sorry, I don't drink with the dead,' he retorted, his eyes shining.

'In that case clear out!' his sister shouted, rising brusquely. She came round and stood glaring at him.

'Flo,' he said, 'do you realize what you are doing at this moment?'

586

'Clear out!' she shouted much louder. 'Go out of the door and go down. That's your natural gradient—down. Isn't it?'

Armand looked around him, giving little jerks to his head as if he were seeking some means of rescue, a way to salvage the irreparable. Florence added nothing, turned her back on him and emptied the glasses into her waste paper basket.

Armand shrugged and left.

The public prosecutor called in Nicolo and the examining magistrate Bourgoin. They were trying to gauge the best tactic.

Bourgoin said: 'The snag is the motive: if we charge Kovalic, is it to be homicide or currency trafficking?'

'Both, of course,' Nicolo said firmly, evidently thirsting for blood.

'Have you enough proof?' the prosecutor said.

'Monsieur, there's the plane, the secret landing ground, the ballistics report, the weapon, the photos and documents brought back by Pradal. I should say all that was circumstantial evidence enough!'

'I grant you that, but there's our little Berg lady right there in the middle. That's a problem and a half.'

The magistrate said: 'Does that really worry us?'

The prosecutor nodded his head two or three times: 'Of course, she could have been a bit more careful with what she was up to, but . . .'

'And how!' Nicolo and Bourgoin said in unison.

The prosecutor sat with his elbows on his desk, rubbing his palms up and down against each other: 'All right Nicolo, you can have your warrant. Tomorrow morning, if that suits you.'

'Have I your word on that?'

'You have. But don't let me regret it. Or you will!'

Nicolo smiled his assurance, and then turned to the magistrate: 'Do we call him in, or do I charge him at his place?'

'At his place,' the magistrate said. 'That'll take the fire out of his belly.'

Bernard Kovalic was back in Harvard with his girlfriend Phyllis Bianchetti. He hadn't written to her for months but at last they were together again, kissing and laughing and moving into the preliminaries of something more eventful. He moved his arm to envelop her more completely and his hand touched the rough surface of the wall.

He stirred and woke, his eyes half closed. There was no such wall that he knew of at Harvard, and there was no Phyllis Bianchetti in his arms. Nobody at all, in fact. Bernard shook himself into full consciousness, sensing that somebody was watching him. He jerked his eyes open and found that he was in his office at *L'Eveil* on the camp bed he had brought in aeons ago. There really was someone watching him, Travers from *La Dépêche*, his cousin Catherine's man of the moment. Travers was smoking a cigarette.

'You been there long?' Bernard mumbled, running his tongue round his mouth. Both objects felt leathery.

'Less than half an hour,' Travers said. 'Do you always grin in your sleep?'

'What's your business here?'

Travers hauled himself up from the office chair he had commandeered and began pacing up and down. There was not a lot of room to do it in, but he had to none the less. All that morning he had been thinking, ever since the inauguration ceremony; thinking about himself, Catherine, their baby on the way, Paul, Alexandra. He had taken a long time to reach his decision, but now he was here with Bernard. And Bernard was still half asleep, combing his thick hair with his fingers and blinking fast, squinting at the light.

'Kovalic,' Travers said, 'your family's in the shit up to its nostrils.' Travers used the familiar *tu* form, and Bernard said since when had they been using *tu*, and Travers said he wouldn't if Bernard didn't like it, and Bernard said he couldn't care less.

Then Travers asked: 'Why didn't you stay in America?' He kept to the *tu*.

'They told me they needed me back here, and every day

I'm asking the same question you are.'

'With your studies, you could have got on well over there.'

'Yup. I could have been a fast rider from the word go.'

'But you came back. And now your cousin's dead, the cops know and will prove it sooner or later.'

'I tried to stop it.'

Travers said: 'I know you tried. But your uncle . . .' He took hold of the chair again and sat on it close to Bernard. 'Your uncle, it's not really the money he was after. He wanted to become respectable too, honourable.'

'Don't I know it! I don't see why he dabbled in that ridiculous money business.' Bernard was a man who had lost all will to fight, Travers judged.

'He was in a hurry perhaps. Wanted to impress you possibly.'

'Impress *me*?'

Bernard got up, went over to a refrigerator and fetched a small bottle of beer which he opened and then offered to Travers who shook his head. Bernard sat down again and took several gulps straight from the bottle.

'You planning to live with my cousin?' he asked conversationally.

'It's likely. There's a bun in the oven, and besides I reckon I love her, love her, that's true. Yes, it's likely.'

'Fine.' He realized that he was using *tu* also.

Travers said: 'Catherine's deeply upset about Teddy. She's afraid for her father too.'

'You getting at me?'

'Not at all. I believe you are the one man in the family with your head screwed on straight. Just wanted you to know how I feel, that's all.'

'So what do I do with this wonderful head?'

'I don't know, Kovalic. Or rather I know what you ought to do, but it's none of my business. Anyway if you want to sell that BMW of yours, give me a call.'

'Huh, so it's developed that far?'

'Got to think of all the possibilities.'

'OK, OK. Don't forget to bring me a bunch of grapes

when I'm behind bars.'

Travers smiled: 'I don't think so, you're too fast for me. Cheers now, I'm glad to have got acquainted. See you.'

A final smile and Travers left. Bernard found it was past midnight, and he listened to Travers's steps on the pavement, then heard him get in his car and drive off. To Catherine and the bun in the oven. Bernard snorted at the thought, feeling sad. He thought about his head that was screwed on straight, and went and poured water over it from the washbasin tap. An attempt to comb his hair, and then he emptied his desk drawers, taking his personal things which he put into a plastic bag. He was still smiling wanly when he approached the BMW, sad at the idea of getting rid of it. In a sense, he told himself, he was relieved and happy. Maybe he was a man at last, seeing the world as it was. He didn't care for it much.

He found his uncle still up at the farm, smoking one of his small cigars in the dark outside in the yard. The old man displayed no astonishment at seeing Bernard.

'I've decided to go and see the police,' his nephew announced when they went inside. 'I'll take the blame, that'd be best for everyone, don't you reckon?'

'Have you thought it out well?'

'Yes.'

'Good. But you'll say it was an accident, understand. There was just you and me here.'

Bernard took a long look into his uncle's eyes: 'You and me, you and me!'

Albertas went on: 'You'll have the best lawyer money can buy. They'll give you two or three years and you'll serve only the half of it. When you come out there'll be a hundred smackers waiting for you. So off you go, lad. They'll bring us together, but don't forget, I'll stick to the story. It was an accident.'

'OK.' Then when he was at the door: 'The hundred smackers, not when I come out, tomorrow in Catherine's account. Otherwise I might decide it wasn't an accident. And there's not just you and me. Don't forget.'

He did not wait for a reply.

Early the next day he went jogging along the Loire. He had kept it up all this time, seeing it as a symbol, although he found it hard to discern what it represented. Perhaps it meant he was being true to himself in spite of the mud that had been thrown at him in Chateauvallon.

Bernard took his usual route and on his return to the BMW changed into a clean T-shirt after rubbing himself down with eau de cologne. Then he put on a dark suit from the car boot, and a tie.

Applying the handbrake outside the law courts, he waited until Bourgoin the magistrate mounted the steps. The man seemed in less of a hurry than he himself was.

Bernard unlocked the boot, took out a travel bag containing his things, locked the boot and walked up the steps. Giving his name to an official, he said he wanted to see Monsieur Bourgoin.

Within an hour he was charged with manslaughter.

An hour after that the news was all round the town.

Alexandra walked taller from the moment Bernard gave himself up. The effect was immediate and startled everyone at La Commanderie. A great weight had slid from her mind, she was friendly, more natural, and in more than one person's mind—unrecognizable.

Even so, she had decided to return to the United States and let Florence know that she hadn't changed her mind. Her mother saw it coming and was prepared for it, but was none the less mortified.

'Are you sure you want to go to New York now?' she asked with a glimmer of hope.

'Oh yes, at least for a while.'

'I don't like seeing you go so quickly. You still look rather pale.'

The exchange took place as they were viewing one of Gabrielle's old films, seated in a pair of armchairs they had used when Antonin and Gilbert ran the movies. Afterwards Alexandra opened the curtains, and suddenly remembered that it was here that they had chatted about Teddy's future when she first brought him back to La

591

Commanderie. All Teddy had now was a past, but the girl was less pained now that she knew it hadn't been suicide.

She came back to her mother and stroked her cheek: 'I must go, *Maman*. I need a change, and of course I have to take back the manuscript which is now urgent.'

'You can have some photocopies run off and then send it by mail. You realize that.'

'I do,' Alexandra said brightly. 'But there are other things, and I have to see Barnes.'

'About the cuts?'

'There won't be any, *maman*. Does that worry you?'

Florence took her daughter by the waist: 'No. You're right, it ought to be published as it is. Your father is still a great writer although he's passed away. The reader should have it without cuts, it's only fair. One day other people will be writing books about him, and they will need the full text.'

'Let people draw their own conclusions. It's true he talks a lot about you, but his own character comes through. With what I know from my own experience, I can see how difficult he must have been for you. It's taken a while for me to comprehend that and allow for it.'

'So?' Florence said with renewed interest. After all it was her they were discussing.

'So nothing. We'll go into it later when the book comes out and has produced a few shockwaves.'

'As you like, *ma chérie*.'

Alexandre continued chattily: 'When I get back I'll move out of the New York apartment. It'll take time, I suppose. The Maine house too, I want to sell it. I have to sort out my things, go through the boxes, say goodbye to some friends . . .'

Florence stared glumly at the carpet: 'What happens after that?'

'Well I'll come back here of course! Unless you don't want me to.'

'Don't want you! B-but I gathered . . .'

'That I couldn't stomach you? At first that was true, and I admit I was wrong. We were both wrong. It's astonishing how hard it is to see people as less than perfect.'

But Florence did not hear the end of the sentence, her eyes were blurred and her mouth trembled. Without a word she drew her daughter to her, breathing out in tiny quivers.

Alexandra had glazed eyes too, and her smile had a tinge of gold to it. She said excitedly: 'When I come back you'll find me a job on *La Dépêche*, won't you *maman*? I shall want a job of work to grapple with. And if it's OK with you, I'll have a swimming pool put in here. It's amazing nobody thought of it before!'

'Your grandfather hated swimming pools. You won't be too long in New York?'

Florence sat down again, getting used to the idea that their separation was not for ever. Alexandra extended her arms and swiftly came over and sat on her mother's lap, putting her arms round her neck. Florence hugged her, enjoying the warmth of the young body, rubbing her cheek against Alexandra's hair so that their strands mingled.

'You know *maman*,' Alexandra said. 'It's lovely just having you.'

Florence was still beaming two hours later when she strode into her office. Her emotion surprised her. It was like falling in love, she told herself. It was the same kind of happy feeling.

And it made everything else seem so petty: the future of the paper, her dreadful clash with Armand that looked so final. It was true after all that love made the world go round, love in all its forms, the love you give as well as receive. She giggled to herself, realizing she felt like singing. Singing, for heaven's sake!

The intercom buzzed and she coughed herself sober. André Travers and Catherine Kovalic wondered if she had a moment to spare. Of course she had! She loved them too, she loved everyone!

Florence knew what they wanted to tell her. They were off to Paris.

'I'm not entirely unprepared. 'I'm sincerely glad if that's where your future lies. Sad too, of course, very. So tell me, what are your plans?'

'I've got the chief editorship at *Paris-Journal* on a colour supplement they're starting up in a big way,' Travers answered.

'With Chénin-Bénard's daily, then?'

'The same. He's got stars in his eyes, sees a big future for supplements, wants fresh ideas.'

Florence grinned: 'It'll certainly be fresh ground for you, after the purgatory here. How many years is it, Trav?'

'Lost count. Eight perhaps.'

'My father leaned heavily on you, and so have I. It's awful losing you both.'

'Come now, if there's the slightest thing you want doing . . .'

'I know,' Florence said, getting up. She slid between them and held both by the waist as they moved to the door. Catherine remained silent, thinking of the ghosts hovering over the three of them, the underlying feud between the Bergs and the Kovalics. Her boy Paul was Florence's nephew and the next would be Travers's son. She felt it was all rather momentous.

Florence said: 'We'll be together, Paris isn't that far!'

'Sure we will,' they both said, and Catherine gave her a warm kiss.

Florence was left contemplating a large photo of her father on the wall. Travers's departure marked the end of an epoch, she supposed, and that always made you stop and think. But within months, perhaps weeks, Alexandra would be back and she would join her in the venerable walls, bringing new earnestness and, she hoped, devotion to *La Dépêche*. The next generation! Meanwhile there was Armand pulling the rug from under her, but she would beat him. She didn't know how, but she was not finished yet. Ah no, not by a long chalk!

The restaurant at the Hotel des Messageries had come through the economic crisis so far without a scratch. And for a very good reason: quality had again triumphed. The cuisine was superb, the atmosphere relaxing and the customers loyal. It was a venue for families seeking an evening out, a quiet place in which to flirt, an ideal spot in which to clinch a business deal. There was never any trouble.

Until that evening. The clientele included Edmond Boulard, plus a hulk of a man he used as a bodyguard, Adrien Jerome the mayor, and Armand Berg. By the main course they were already into their third bottle of wine, and Boulard seemed unusually agitated, less in control of himself than he normally was. He had removed his jacket, and Jerome and Berg had done likewise.

At a nearby table, not far from the passage leading to the rooms and a side door to the hotel, Edelman and Favrot were sipping an aperitif in the company of a photographer. The three were on form and got to teasing Solange whenever she went by. But they were also hoping to pick up something from Boulard's party.

As luck would have it, Florence Berg and Albertas Kovalic walked in, without malice aforethought but simply because Florence had run out of petrol and all the filling stations were shut at that time of night. Albertas had walked by exactly at that moment and offered to drive her home to La Commanderie. His Mercedes was parked outside the hotel and, as neither of them had eaten, they resolved to do so there and then.

Entering the restaurant, Florence waved discreetly to the journalists, and Favrot as discreetly switched his eyes to Boulard's table, giving her a quick tip-off. Solange came up and led the newcomers past the Boulard table and nobody made a remark. Solange placed Florence with her back to Boulard, so that Albertas faced the table with the four men.

In a loud voice Boulard declared: 'Suddenly smells like old grouse in here!'

Kovalic's eyes gleamed with mischief, and he asked Solange: 'Have you got grouse tonight?'

'No, Monsieur, it's not the season.'

'No matter, what do you suggest we start with?'

'How about some fillet of snake-mackerel, Monsieur, the chef's own recipe. Delicious!'

'Snake-mackerel! Ho ho ho, we've got some snake in town! Came in from Paris, I suppose!'

Solange said deadpan: 'Might have. Two mackerel, then.'

Florence had her fingers over her mouth, stifling a laugh, and nodded her consent.

'Afterwards?'

'Crab!' Boulard shouted across. His companions turned away in shame.

The photographer was quietly readying his Nikon as Albertas remarked: 'I have a feeling I'd like to snap that fellow's claws.'

Florence was shaking with amusement: 'Don't take any notice.'

This was easier said than done, as Boulard yelled at Solange: 'And give them a bottle of gut-rot! Book it to me!'

Albertas went rigid, and Florence rasped: 'Don't you move Albertas. Whatever happens keep your seat.'

She herself got up and went over to a trolley containing things for doing flambé dishes. She dipped a napkin in some alcohol, set the corner alight and threw it onto the Boulard table. There was a chorus of outrage and the four men began hitting the fiery missile with their own napkins. Solange rushed up with a jug of water and the crisis was over, leaving an acrid smell over the table.

Florence addressed her brother: 'I see you like burning your fingers in such company! What's going on?'

It was Boulard who replied, standing: 'Nothing special, Madame. We know you are wearing the trousers, but they don't fit very well. We were discussing the problem.'

Albertas was on his feet by now. Edelman was alert.

Florence retorted: 'And *you* are wearing a silly grin. If you removed it I'm sure the mirrors round the walls would feel better.'

Boulard growled: 'You will have to take your hand off the helm, Madame, whether you like it or . . .'

The flash from the camera went off precisely as Florence's hand thwacked Boulard on his left ear. Jerome and Armand jumped up, as did the bodyguard whose hand was half-way inside his jacket.

Boulard cried: 'You slut!' His fist drew back and flew towards Florence just as Albertas intervened and took it on one shoulder. Armand meanwhile grabbed Boulard by his collar and pulled him backwards. Jerome tried to separate Boulard and Berg, failed, and gathered up the jackets, pushing his companions towards the door.

'Careful, there's a photographer,' he warned.

'What do I care!' Boulard roared. 'I'll smash the camera!'

The camera, however, was on its way to *La Dépêche*.

While this was going on, the bodyguard was roughing up Albertas, but stopped abruptly on realizing that his boss had left.

Florence and Albertas resumed their seats. Kovalic called Solange over.

'Now, where were we?' he said, handing the menu to Madame Berg.

Two pictures leaped out of the front page of *La Dépêche* the next morning. One showed Boulard hurling his fist at Florence. The other depicted Armand Berg and Adrien Jerome struggling with Boulard. The caption read simply: *A hooligan is taught manners at Chateauvallon.*

At *L'Eveil*, Maryse and Jean-Jacques Berg looked at the page for minutes on end.

'That's what I call real journalism,' J-J said with a laugh.

'Exactly,' Maryse said. 'And I for one don't care to work for this dead-beat rag any longer. I won't take his money, I tell you. I'm worth more than this, and there's my pride too.'

Jean-Jacques said earnestly: 'Maryse, you look terrific when you're angry.'

He moved towards her, taking her in his arms. Maryse had been his mistress for years, but nothing had occurred between them since they joined *L'Eveil*. Now he wanted her, badly, right there on the desk!

597

Alas, J-J Berg had to absorb yet another failure as she snapped: 'Please! This is hardly the moment!'

He disagreed, but could do nothing about it. Two men from Electricité de France surged into the office asking where the meter was. The men extracted the fuses and sealed the meter. One of them presented J-J Berg with a document, showing him where to sign.

Left to themselves, Maryse and Berg gaped at each other in the gloom.

'Well,' said Berg, 'it looks like we've had our last pay cheques.'

'Oh Christ,' she moaned, 'what happens now?'

Jean-Jacques could not face the board meeting at *La Dépêche* and asked Marie-Lou to deputize for him. She found Julien there already, on his own. Favrot and Madame Frochot represented the joint works council, and Madame Frochot had been instructed to take the minutes of the meeting.

While they waited, Marie-Lou scolded him about Thérèse with a sweet smile on her lips and told him he should keep her in order.

Julien eventually reacted: 'If you don't want to spend the next few weeks having dental treatment, you'd better get out of here fast.'

She was about to reply when Armand walked in. He immediately remarked that there were few persons present, and Madame Frochot told him the small shareholders had sent in proxy forms.

Armand took the seat next to Julien. Nobody knew why Armand had called the meeting.

Florence arrived a minute later and the proceedings began, after she suggested that Armand might like to wait for Boulard, although his presence was not necessary under the statutes. Armand said Boulard need not attend.

After that, a silence. Florence was unwilling to break it, determined as she was that her brother should declare himself.

At length, Armand pulled a sheet of paper from his

inside pocket, and told Madame Frochot it was to be recorded verbatim in the minutes. He read: 'Armand Berg informed the Board that he transfers all his shares in the publication to his sister Florence along with all rights relating thereto. As from this day she will employ them as she considers appropriate without need to inform the avowant subsequently.'

After a decent pause Madame Frochot said: 'In law, a formal assignment will be necessary.'

'You will receive it,' he answered.

Florence said: 'What the devil are you up to now?'

'Take it or leave it. It's your decision.'

Marie-Lou cried: 'Have you gone mad, Armand?'

'Shut your trap, sweetie.'

Favrot raised a finger and said: 'The works council has its rights, Monsieur Berg. A concentration has occurred. We shall seek guarantees.'

'You'll have them, Favrot.'

Favrot said: 'Make a note of that, Madame Frochot.'

Florence gave a huge sigh: 'Armand, you realize what this means?'

'Perfectly.'

'But the town hall?'

'What town hall?'

Having wriggled impatiently on her chair for some moments, Marie-Lou intervened: 'I am opposed to this statement, I demand . . .'

Armand cut her down: 'You are in no position to demand anything.' He told Florence: 'With seventy per cent of the share capital, you might perhaps feel inclined to back an outsider.'

'You're joking. Boulard . . .'

'Boulard has a horrible looking thing, a swelling, under his left arm. I am not keen to operate.'

He laughed hideously and it became kinder.

Florence flung her arms round his neck: 'You're completely idiotic.'

He turned to Julien: 'Idiotic because I don't like hoodlums ploughing into my own sister?'

'Perhaps not an idiot, but a late conversion,' Julien said. 'I never did care for it, and I'm delighted it's ended up this way. I don't like underhand dealing. I'm talking nonsense but I know what I'm trying to say.'

'You're up in the clouds, Julien, but you've got a harp in your lap. I'm sure you're the holiest of us all! Come on, Marie-Lou, where's that champagne!'

Madame Frochot told him Marie-Lou had left.

'That's another reason for celebrating,' Armand said. 'But I know where the champagne is kept.'

'That's another reason I employ you!' Florence put in. She took her brothers by the hand and led them into her office.

Immediately the two-line flash came over from Agence France-Presse, Florence phoned La Jouterie.

'I wish to speak to the Nobel Prizewinner for Physiology and Medicine, if I can pronounce it all,' she said with a gay laugh.

'Oh Florence, I'm exhausted.'

'It's just come over the wires. Heartiest congratulations, and a big, big kiss from your greatest admirer. I expect you here for a drink at six.'

He was late, and the aperitif had been waiting an hour.

They did a little dance and she said: 'You are the first Nobel Prizewinner I have allowed in my office! Tell me, Artus, you must be swimming about like a molecule or something.'

'I'm honoured to be invited to your office,' he said. 'But to be quite honest, it's like having your first sports car. At twenty-five you dream of it, but at fifty it doesn't seem all that great.'

'Oh don't be a sour-puss. You can still drive a sports car.'

'Unfortunately I'll have to go by plane, and I hate flying.'

She put up a hand: 'No problem. I'll fix you up by train.' She buzzed through to Madame Frochot and told her to reserve a double plus a single.

Then she came bounding over to him: 'This I have to see. I want to hear your speech.'

'Ah, but only the literature chaps give a speech.' He took her face between his soft hands and added: 'I must tell you . . '

'Never mind the speech, I just want to be there, holding your hand and sharing your tears of joy!'

He was still holding her radiant face: 'It's not possible Florence, I have someone to do that, I'm getting married tomorrow!'

Artus Balestra went on to explain that his fiancée was one of his former students, that he met her fifteen years or so ago at Heidelberg, that she had done work for him like compiling dossiers and watering his plants and feeding his cat.

Florence backed away and told him: 'And you get married right on schedule! That's a high price to pay for sorting out a pile of papers. And where am I in all this? Do I go and boil my head?'

'B-but the other day you didn't seem . . .'

She yelled at him: 'So we have to seem right as well! Does your German woman seem right? Artus Balestra, you are the biggest cretin that ever won the Nobel Prize, because you play for low stakes. You spoil everything!!!'

Balestra scuttled out and jumped when she slammed the door behind him.

Behind the door she swallowed her whisky in one gulp, then Balestra's. She screwed up her eyes at the bitter-sweet taste and then recovered quickly, seizing the hand-set from the telephone cradle.

Less than two hours later Albertas Kovalic drove Antonin Berg's old Rolls out of Chateauvallon. By his side was Florence in a black skirt and white blouse.

'Life's strange,' she said, her lips parted eagerly.

'Certainly is,' old Kovalic said. 'I understand your brother Armand has linked arms with you again. I'm glad of that. Mind you, it doesn't surprise me after the punch-up the other night.'

She laid an arm on his: 'Thank goodness you were there,

Albert. Something else I have to pay you back for.'

He waved a hand vaguely: 'Delighted to be of service. Now where are we supposed to be going?'

'It's a secret. You'll never be bored if you stick with me!'

'I learnt that a long time ago.'

'Turn right here. After that it's straight for twenty kilometres. Then I'll tell you.'

Florence squirmed in her seat, purring voluptuously, as was the engine. Albertas glanced fondly at her and pushed the speedometer needle round two more centimetres. He was feeling pretty voluptuous too, behind the wheel of the world's finest car.

Some twenty minutes later, she told him to pull up alongside a wall just ahead of a pair of iron gates. A short distance before the entry was a small wooden gate, which Florence pointed at.

'In a moment I'll give a whistle like this.' She imitated a bird call. 'Then you'll come through the door too. I shall be next to a window and I'll tell you what to do.'

'The things I do for love,' old Kovalic sighed.

Florence grinned at him and slipped out of the Rolls. Once through the little gate she headed for the manor house, which she recalled exactly. Thirty seconds later she eased open a tradesman's entrance, went by the kitchens and crept up the stairs to the bedrooms and the library. As she neared the big library she caught the sound of a woman talking shrilly in anger. She found the linen room and picked out a maid's apron and pleated cap. She got hold of a pile of damask cloths and strode off to the library. There she saw a tall, good-looking woman talking in French with a heavy accent at a dummy wearing a wedding dress. Two dressmakers and a chambermaid were listening to her tirade. And then she saw Artus, and realized that the woman was in fact attacking him. As far as she could gather he had brought the wedding dress from Paris but it wasn't the one she had chosen and the trimmings were ridiculous.

'And Artus, why get red shoes? You can't wear red shoes with a wedding dress!'

Balestra's mouth curled puckishly: 'But Ingrid, *chérie*, red shoes are more amusing. I thought they'd have such an effect . . .'

'It's grotesque,' the bride shrieked. 'Nobody will imagine my stupid husband is to blame. It will reflect on me and me only! Get me some white shoes this minute!'

'Yes Inge,' he replied meekly.

'And another thing Artus. Don't forget I want no photographers and no journalists. Neither here, nor at the town hall nor at the airport—nowhere!'

'Airport? You promised we'd go by train.'

'I loathe trains,' she declared.

'And I loathe planes!'

'At your age, that's absurd. Now leave us, I must try this awful dress on, which these ladies are trying to make presentable.'

In her maid's outfit Florence waited in the doorway and nobody noticed her. As Artus, poor Artus, started to move she turned round and hurried down the passage ahead of him. Then suddenly she stopped and faced him, dragging him deftly into the linen room. She closed the door and put the cloths back.

'Florence! What ever are you doing here?'

'I'm beginning to wonder,' she said. 'I had hoped to see my hero in command of the situation and found your wife-to-be wiping the floor with you. She'll destroy you, Artus, destroy you completely!'

'She had immense qualities,' he protested. 'She was soft and yielding and everything before, and then . . .'

Florence demanded: 'And me, what qualities have I got?'

'My darling Florence, I asked you to marry me and . . '

'Don't call me darling. You must realize you are about to make the worst blunder in your entire life. She is doing you a service by marrying you, and you will pay for it for the rest of your existence. You'll die of that woman, Artus, and so will I.'

Balestra's face looked desolate: 'But you refused me, *chérie*.'

'You should have *kept on at me*! I expected a man like you to woo me, I thought you had real character, and now I see that I was mistaken and . . . Oh dear, I shall never have any confidence in myself again, Artus. I am devastated at what you are about to do, devastated for both of us!' She sank into his arms.

'But it's too late, *chérie*, the whole thing's going like clockwork now and there's no stopping it.'

'You must stop it! Stop it now, at once, and come with me.'

Terror widened his eyes: 'I can't do that. I could never ask her . . . she'd tear me to pieces!'

Florence stood back and considered him: 'I understand, you're flaked out. We must use other weapons.'

She signed for him not to move, then opened the window and started whistling. Artus gaped as she flung her arms about. 'I've summoned up help, from your best friend.'

He squawked: 'I haven't got a best . . .'

'Of course you have.' She opened the door. 'In here Albertas. You know Monsieur Balestra, don't you?'

'Why yes,' Kovalic cried, squeezing into the linen room. 'It was at *La Dépêche*, you got control of me and . . .'

Florence interrupted: 'Exactly, he stopped you making a huge mistake. Now is the time for you to pay him back.'

Albertas let his mouth hang open, as Florence hopped up on the table and let her legs swing back and forth. She said: 'Now see here, Kovalic. There's a lady here wants to get married if it's the last thing she does. I don't want to force you to marry her, but just to explain to her that she cannot marry Artus.' Florence hitched her skirt up, showing her knees and rocking this way and that, a large grin on her face. She was even more delighted with herself when she saw that Artus was leering at her knees.

'How do I go about it?' Kovalic said. 'I can't just say that's how it is and no messing.'

'Well . . .' she said, hesitating.

'I'll think of something. I'll twist her arm, and she'll see it my way. Come on, Balestra, it'd be best if you spoke first.'

Florence blew them a kiss as they stole out of the linen room: 'Artus, I'll be waiting in the Rolls. And don't take too long!'

It took only ten minutes for Balestra to reach the car.

As he slid in beside her, she said: 'Well how did it go?'

'Kovalic was simply . . '

'And the bride?'

'Pretty damned furious when I told her I had to call it off.'

'Did she go for you?'

'My God yes. But Albertas gently explained that I was subject to fits, that I'd attempted suicide several times and had been convicted of assaulting women.'

'And then?'

'He said I was nevertheless highly courageous, as I loved her, but was giving her her freedom before it was too late.'

'Then what?'

'I crept out on tiptoe and I don't know what happened then. She seemed enchanted with Albertas, almost swooning under the effect of his charm. Amazing fellow, Kovalic.'

Florence started the car: 'Albertas can do anything once he puts his mind to it. I know. Is there a phonebox here? You will have to tell the town hall that the wedding's off. It's the least you can do.'

Artus scowled at her: 'But there's a phone here in the car.'

'That's for me. I want to confirm the train reservation.'

His face lit up: 'The train! D'you mean it, Florence?'

'I do mean it. I've got you back, by the skin of my teeth.'

They stopped at the phonebox, put in their calls and prepared to move off. A toot-toot behind them revealed Kovalic at the wheel of Balestra's car and Inge beside him. They were chatting away as they went by. Inge gave Florence a complicated wave which she imagined signified good luck. Then, with the car slowing down, Inge chucked a metal object out of the window and it bounced on the road. Balestra's car disappeared from view.

'Lord, what's that?' Balestra said. 'Perhaps it's a time bomb.'

Florence put the Rolls into gear and they went slowly up to the object. She ordered him: 'Open the door and pick it up, *chéri*. I think I know what it is.'

He picked it up, a ring with two wondrously big sapphires. He said wide-eyed: 'Her engagement ring. Kovalic persuaded her.'

Florence said nothing, she simply placed her left hand on his right thigh, the finger next to the little finger curiously prominent. Artus looked at the finger, then at her face, willing her to return his gaze, but she stared at the finger.

Until he took her hand. Only then did she consent to look into his eyes.

Balestra began sliding the ring over her nail, then stopped. He looked intently at her and she nodded, after which he pushed the ring beyond the knuckle.

'It's my Nobel Prize,' Florence said. 'I won it, I deserve it, and you're stuck with me now.'

'Stop the engine,' Artus ordered. She did so and silence engulfed them.

He went on: 'This is a moving moment. Wouldn't it be terrific if we lived happy ever after!'

'Together if possible,' she added. 'I'll tell you this, Artus, you'll never find another woman like me. And if you do I'll scratch her eyes out!'